知識工場
nowledge.
Knowledge is everything！

別瞎忙，看過就記住！

4000 英單 早該這樣背

拋開繁複冗長的學習枷鎖，重拾你對背單字的熱忱！

獨家揭密 ▷ 100%的關鍵英單都藏在文章裡！

加贈傳授 ▷ 用閱讀取代死背，單字才能記得快、用得對！

名師 **張翔** ／編著

大廈 **mansion**

挺直 **straighten**

爬行 **crawl**

洞穴 **cavity**

booth 電話亭

鐵路 **railway**

使用說明

1

層層推進，對症下藥

本書共分為6個Level，依序為高中7000單字初階和進階、全民英檢中級和中高級、新多益單字藍色和金色證書。依照這六個層級往上邁進，金色證書保證讓你拿到手。

2

熟悉原文，戰勝閱讀

英文文章是外國人天天都在接觸的，要想學好英文就和老外一樣，熟悉原文文章的脈絡，增進英文語感，讓你看英文就和看中文報紙一樣快！

3

道地俚語，一次搞懂

文章除了單字需要注意之外，作者也經常引用英文俚語或慣用語，書中也會針對這些特殊用法做詳細解說，讓讀者更瞭解文章含意。

4

外師發音，無懈可擊

收錄美籍外師最道地且最活潑的文章及單字朗誦，讓你在一片落落長的英文朗讀聲中不會昏昏欲睡，反而能在外師引領下，激發更多對英文的興趣。

Find your level of English.

Now

Level1　Level2　Level3　Level4　Level5　Level6

🎧 MP3 059　短文 059　字彙 060

Essay 030

Living a life full of lies is like being a lily-livered[0349] wimp[0350] who always tries to escape from danger and never faces problems. It won't take long before the lies are exposed[0351], and it's likely to happen anytime. No matter how perfectly the lies are covered, the truth will come to light one day. When that time comes, no one will listen to the liar ever again. There's a fine line between weakness and bravery, and it depends on whether the person admits his own fault and strives[0352] to compensate[0353] for it. To err[0354] is human, but to lie is a shame.

A little child cheated[0355] on a test and got caught. His lips trembled[0356] nervously, but he didn't lie and faced this problem like a brave lion when confronted[0357] with his cheating. Because of his honesty, his mind progressed[0358] to a higher level. Making the right choice also lifted[0359] his spirit. When the child grew up, he became an A-list celebrity[0360].

ℹ️ come to light 水落石出、真相大白
ℹ️ there's a fine line between A and B A 和 B 之間只有一線之隔
ℹ️ A-list 最好的、最優秀的

中譯 Translation

過著充滿謊言的人生就像一個總想逃離危險的膽小鬼，從來不肯正視問題。謊言很快就會被揭穿，而且任何時候都有可能發生。不管謊言隱藏得多好，總會有真相大白的一天。等到那個時候，就再也沒有人會聽信一個騙子的話了。軟弱和勇敢之間只有一線之隔，端看這個人是否承認自己的錯誤，並且努力做出補償。犯錯是人之常情，但撒謊卻是恥辱。

有個小孩在考試時作弊被抓到。他的嘴唇不安地顫抖著，但他沒有說謊，像隻勇敢的獅子般面對自己作弊的行為。因為他的誠實，他的心靈進展到一個更高的層次。做出正確的選擇提升了他的靈魂。當這個孩子長大後，他成為了社會上一流的成功人士。

5

破解單字,懂了再背

收錄文章中的重要單字,讓讀者更了解該單字在文章中或句子中的使用時機。另外也補充了該單字其他詞性的釋義、同反義字、片語用法、衍生字等補充。音標後的星號 ★ 表示該單字在老外生活圈中的使用頻率。

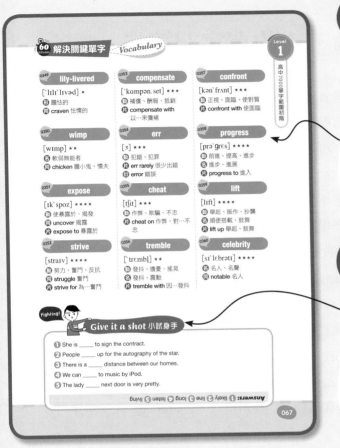

6

小試身手,實戰考場

精心編寫的單字填空除考驗讀者在本單元學過的單字外,也有可能是從前面單元累積的單字,或是文法相關的填空,讓讀者在親上考場時不至於亂了陣腳。

7

附錄索引,查找迅速

附錄單字從 A-Z 排列,補充了該單字最常使用的詞性及中文釋義,以及老外使用頻率。若想找出某單字所對應的文章,只要對照一下頁碼就能找到,非常方便。

時間偷不走的單字記憶法

　　一般說來，英語初學者在走入書店時購買的第一本學習書一定非單字書莫屬，業者深知其市場廣大，陸續推出許多1000、2000、3000甚至是20000字（目前看過最多的）的英文單字書，而令我感到疑惑的是，絕大多數的結構都是一個單字、一個音標、一個字義搭配一個例句，這樣的編排真的有可能幫助讀者增進英文能力嗎？更遑論其中有非常多的例句都是魚目混珠，完全沒有顯示出使用該單字的「精準度」。舉例來說，orange大家都知道是柳丁的意思，我看過經常出現在市面上卻最不負責任的例句就是：I bought a tangerine yesterday.，這裡的orange若換成tomato、tangerine、magazine等風馬牛不相及的單字都可以，但如此一來，讀者又該如何從這個無法聯想情境的句子來記憶單字呢？相較之下，若是從文章中擷取的：I bought a bag of oranges last evening, because I want to make orange juice. Moreover, oranges are rich in vitamin C. 這個句子提供了較為完整的上下文脈絡，及內容較為豐富的使用情境，也讓orange 這個單字有存在感多了！

　　此種記憶方式的優勢在於，即使你不怎麼清楚某個單字的中文含意，但經由一而再、再而三的閱讀，讀者也能藉由文中的前後脈絡揣摩出單字的使用時機、意義、甚至是文法上的使用！換句話說，讀者並不是在不了解單字的情況下死背單字，而是在熟悉該單字之後，再補充清楚的中文釋義增加讀者對單字的記憶，相較之下，單字也較不會隨著時間的流逝消失於無形，而是安安穩穩的儲存在讀者的長期記憶中！所以各位，跟著我一起從現在開始改變老舊的祖母級學習方式，讓英文單字變身為人生前進的籌碼！

張翔

CONTENTS

名 名詞

動 動詞

形 形容詞

副 副詞

介 介係詞

同 同義字補充

反 反義字補充

片 片語補充

俚 俚語補充

衍 衍生字補充

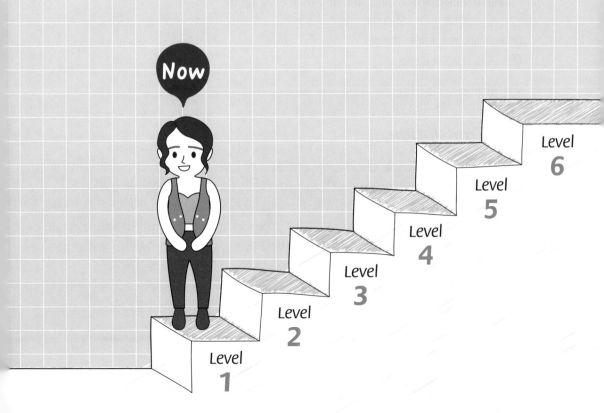

001

Essay

Rebecca was a beautiful and popular actress. She was able[0001] to date three different actors in one afternoon. She considered[0002] dating many people at the same time a commonplace[0003] in today's world, so she was not afraid[0004] of men being jealous[0005] or angry.

One day, Rebecca drove her car very fast and lost control of it. She <u>crashed into</u> the median[0006] and was severely[0007] injured[0008], so she was <u>rushed</u> by an ambulance[0009] <u>to</u> hospital. All of her lovers ran straight to the hospital after they heard about it. After the operation[0010], she slept for many hours due to the anesthesia[0011]. When she woke up and looked around, she could only see a nurse, who was adding water to her glass. She asked whether her boyfriend had come or not.

"You mean your 'boyfriends'? They had a quarrel[0012] when they found out you were dating all of them. Then they left you alone out of anger." Rebecca felt deep regret and decided not to date so many men ever again.

> ⓘ crash into 衝入、闖進
> ⓘ rush to 趕緊、倉促行動

中譯 *Translation*

瑞貝卡是個美麗又受歡迎的女演員。光是一個下午她就能和三個不同的男演員約會。她認為這在現代社會早已是司空見慣，所以她也不擔心男人為她爭風吃醋。

有一天，瑞貝卡因為車速過快，車子一時之間失去了控制。她一頭撞上中央分隔島，身受重傷，因而被救護車緊急送往醫院急救。她所有的情人一得知這個消息，都立即衝往醫院。手術過後，麻醉藥的作用讓她昏睡了好幾個小時。當她醒來後，看了看四周，卻只看見護士正在替她的玻璃杯加水。她問她的男朋友是否有來過。

「妳是指『男朋友們』嗎？他們一發現妳跟他們所有人交往後吵了起來，然後就氣得把妳一個人丟下離開了。」瑞貝卡很後悔，決定不再跟這麼多男人約會了。

0001 able

[`ebl̩] ★★★★★

形 能夠、有能力的
同 capable 有能力的
片 be able to 能夠

0002 consider

[kən`sɪdɚ] ★★★★★

動 考慮、細想、認為
反 ignore 忽略
片 consider + ving 考慮

0003 commonplace

[`kɑmənples] ★★★★

名 司空見慣、老生常談、陳腔濫調
形 普通的

0004 afraid

[ə`fred] ★★★★★

形 害怕的、擔心的
反 brave 勇敢的
片 be afraid of 害怕

0005 jealous

[`dʒɛləs] ★★★★

形 妒忌的、小心守護的
同 envious 妒忌的
片 jealous of 妒忌…

0006 median

[`midɪən] ★★★

名 中央分隔島
形 中間的

0007 severely

[sə`vɪrlɪ] ★★★★

副 嚴重地、嚴格地、嚴肅地
同 rigorously 嚴厲地

0008 injured

[`ɪndʒɚd] ★★★

形 受傷的
片 an injured look 委屈的表情

0009 ambulance

[`æmbjələns] ★★

名 救護車、傷患運輸機

0010 operation

[ɑpə`reʃən] ★★★★

名 手術、操作、經營
片 come into operation 生效、起作用

0011 anesthesia

[ænəs`θiʒə] ★★

名 麻醉、麻木
片 general anesthesia 全身麻醉

0012 quarrel

[`kwɔrəl] ★★★★

名 爭吵、不和
動 爭吵、埋怨
同 argument 爭執

Fighting!

Give it a shot 小試身手

1. There is a mirror _____ the washbasin.

2. Sixty people voted _____ the new project.

3. This film is suitable for both _____ and children.

4. The professor gave a speech _____ global warming.

5. Arnold was _____ the best actor in America.

002

Essay

Almost all teenagers[0013] agree that it's embarrassing to admit[0014] to being alone when they are above a specific[0015] age. If one has already had several relationships, it seems easy for him/her to get involved in a new one; otherwise[0016], he/she might always remain single. The story of a young man named Jimmy illustrates[0017] that point very well.

Three years ago, Jimmy worked at the airport and met a nice girl named Lisa, who was a flight attendant. Every time the airplane she went aboard[0018] took off, Jimmy would run along and wave her goodbye. Lisa knew very well that Jimmy had a big crush on her. One day, Lisa sent him an email and said she was married, and she told him to forget about her. As soon as he finished reading the letter, he dashed[0019] to the airport. Lisa never showed up, even though he waited all day for her. Her coldness[0020] seemed quite cruel[0021] to Jimmy, which made him lose the courage[0022] to chase[0023] any girl again since that time many years ago. Now, Jimmy is thirty years old. He doesn't dare admit that he's still a bachelor[0024] and doesn't even have a girlfriend.

(!) take off 在此文中表示飛機起飛，另也有休假、突然大受歡迎等意

(!) have a crush on sb. 喜歡、煞到某人

中譯 *Translation*

　　幾乎所有的年輕人都認同，當到了一定年紀時，承認自己單身是很難為情的。如果一個人已經有過幾次戀愛經驗，要找到新對象似乎是很容易的事；要不然，或許就會一直這樣單身下去。一名叫做吉米的年輕男子，他的故事成功說明了這項論點。

　　吉米三年前在機場工作時，邂逅了一位叫麗莎的可愛女孩，她是名空服員。每次她搭乘的飛機起飛時，傑米就會跟著向前奔跑，一邊向她揮手道別。麗莎很清楚傑米深深迷戀著她。某天，麗莎寄了一封電子郵件向他表明自己已婚了，並且要吉米忘了她。吉姆一看完郵件，隨即火速衝往機場。即使吉姆在機場等了整整一天，麗莎卻不曾再出現了。她的冷淡對吉米來說似乎很殘忍，從幾年前的那時候開始，吉米就失去了追求其他女孩的勇氣。現在，吉米已經三十歲了。他不敢承認自己仍是個單身漢，甚至連個女朋友都沒有。

0013 teenager

[ˋtinedʒɚ] ★★★

名 十幾歲青少年

衍 teenage 十幾歲的、青少年時期

0014 admit

[ədˋmɪt] ★★★★

動 承認、准許進入、可容納

片 admit (to) + ving 承認

0015 specific

[spɪˋsɪfɪk] ★★★★★

形 特定的、明確的

名 特性、特效藥

同 particular 特定的

0016 otherwise

[ˋʌðɚˏwaɪz] ★★★★

副 不同地、否則、除此之外

同 or else 否則、要不然

0017 illustrate

[ˋɪləstret] ★★★★

動 說明、插圖於、圖解

片 illustrate with 以(圖、實例)闡明

0018 aboard

[əˋbord] ★★★

副 在(船、飛機、火車)上

介 在(船、飛機、火車)上

反 ashore 上岸

0019 dash

[dæʃ] ★★★★

動 急奔、擊碎、潑灑

名 急衝、短跑、打擊

0020 coldness

[ˋkoldnɪs] ★★

名 寒冷、冷酷、冷靜

同 chill 寒冷

反 hotness 炎熱、熱烈

0021 cruel

[ˋkruəl] ★★★★

形 殘忍的、慘痛的

同 brutal 殘忍的

衍 cruelty 殘酷的行為

0022 courage

[kɝɪdʒ] ★★★

名 膽量、勇氣

理 Dutch courage 酒後之勇

0023 chase

[tʃes] ★★★★

動 追逐、追求、追捕

名 追捕、追趕

片 chase sb. away 趕走

0024 bachelor

[ˋbætʃələ] ★★★

名 單身漢、(B)學士

片 eligible bachelor 條件佳的未婚男子

Fighting!

Give it a shot 小試身手

1 My dad drives a car _____ the river.

2 For years Mary lived _____ in New York.

3 Our grandmother's home is located on the hills _____.

4 John sent a letter by _____ last night.

5 Since you've accepted the invitation, I'll _____ accept it.

Answers: 1 along 2 alone 3 ahead 4 airmail 5 also

003

Essay

In the army, Alex was the smallest among his comrades[0025]. He looked like an ant in front of the tallest person, who seemed like an ape. As a result, he avoided making any of them angry and did his best to be very obedient[0026], just like a tame[0027] animal people bred in the cage.

In April, a test of physical[0028] fitness[0029] was going to be held. Alex was very anxious about that. He knew he was too weak to stand the physical training and that if he fainted[0030] or got hurt people would laugh at him. He imagined an even worse situation in which people would bully[0031] him more impudently[0032] than before. He didn't want that nightmare to come true, but the solutions he thought of were not feasible[0033]. Finally, he found another possibility.

On the day of the test, the commander[0034] went to wake him up.

"My right arm is injured. The doctor said it needs three days to recover," Alex lied, pretending that his arm hurt greatly. "OK. Then you have to patrol[0035] at night around the area." Alex stared at him in anger but had no choice but to comply[0036].

中譯 *Translation*

在軍隊裡，艾力克斯是同儕之中最矮的。當他站在最高的人面前時，看起來就像螞蟻對上猩猩一樣。因此，他避免惹怒任何人，盡可能表現得很順從，像隻被人類豢養在籠子裡的溫馴動物。

四月時，有一場體能競賽。艾力克斯為此感到非常焦慮。他知道自己體力太差，無法承受體能訓練，萬一昏倒或是受傷，一定會遭人嘲笑。他甚至設想了一個更糟的情況，就是大家會比之前更變本加厲地欺負他。他不希望惡夢成真，但他想到的解決方案都行不通。最後，他找到了另一個可能的方法。

競賽那一天，中校前去叫醒他。

「我的右臂受傷了，醫生說要三天才能康復。」艾力克斯撒謊，假裝他的手臂痛得很厲害。「沒關係。那你晚上就得在這一區附近巡邏。」艾力克斯只能忿忿地瞪著他，乖乖服從。

0025 comrade

[`kɑmræd] ★★
名 同事、共患難的夥伴
片 comrade in arms 戰友

0029 fitness

[`fɪtnɪs] ★★★★
名 健康、恰當
反 unfitness 不適當

0033 feasible

[`fizəbḷ] ★★★
形 可行的、合適的
同 practical 可實施的

0026 obedient

[ə`bidjənt] ★★
形 服從的、順從的
反 disobedient 違抗的

0030 faint

[fent] ★★★★
動 昏厥、變得微弱
形 頭暈的、暗淡的
同 blackout 昏厥

0034 commander

[kə`mændə] ★★★★
名 指揮官、領導人
片 commander in chief 總司令

0027 tame

[tem] ★★
形 溫順的、易駕馭的
動 馴養、使順從
反 unruly 難駕馭的

0031 bully

[`bulɪ] ★★★
動 威嚇、欺侮人
名 惡霸
衍 bullying 霸凌

0035 patrol

[pə`trol] ★★★
動 巡邏、偵查
名 巡邏、巡邏隊
片 on patrol 巡邏中

0028 physical

[`fɪzɪkḷ] ★★★★★
形 身體的、物質的
名 身體檢查
同 corporal 身體的

0032 impudently

[`ɪmpjədəntlɪ] ★★
副 無禮地、放肆地
同 pertly 無禮地

0036 comply

[kəm`plaɪ] ★★★★
動 依從、遵守
同 conform 遵守
片 comply with sth. 遵從

Fighting!

Give it a shot 小試身手

1 Flies buzzed _____ the dead cow.

2 I don't like this one. Please show me _____.

3 The defendant failed to _____ in court.

4 Tom has always been popular _____ his classmates.

5 There were over two inches of rain in coastal _____.

Answers: 1 around 2 another 3 appear 4 among 5 areas

MP3

短文 007

字彙 008

Essay 004

Three of my single aunts formed[0037] a rock band and named it "Naughty Bananas" because they like that fruit. Although I call them "auntie", they are not <u>middle-aged</u> women but young ladies whose average[0038] age is 25. They all work in banks, so they get off work very early. Without husbands and babies, they are also freer than many other women of the same age, so there is plenty of time for them to practice in their band. One of them plays bass, another is a guitarist and the other is a vocalist[0039]. The vocalist sometimes plays keyboard as well. They compose[0040] most of the songs they perform, and they write various[0041] styles of music.

As the bad economy has resulted in a high unemployment[0042] rate, art seems to be an inspiration[0043] for people. The band was asked to play at a concert in August, but it was a pity that one member was away and wouldn't get back until autumn[0044]. I prepared balloons[0045] and colorful balls to <u>root for</u> them. My aunts were like two superstars on the stage, and their encore[0046] was the climax[0047] of the concert. That was indeed[0048] a fun experience!

> ⚠ middle-aged 中年的
> ⚠ root for 聲援、為⋯加油

中譯 *Translation*

　　我有三個單身的阿姨組了一個搖滾樂團，叫做「淘氣香蕉」，因為她們喜歡香蕉。雖然我稱她們為「阿姨」，但她們並非中年婦女，而是平均年齡二十五歲的年輕小姐。她們都在銀行工作，所以她們都很早就下班了。因為沒有家累，她們也比同齡的女性來得自由，因而有充裕的時間練團。樂團中有一位彈奏貝斯，其餘兩人分別是吉他手和主唱，主唱有時候也兼彈奏鍵盤樂器。她們表演的歌曲大多都是自創曲，曲風多變。

　　由於經濟衰敗導致高失業率，對人們來說，藝術似乎是能夠激勵人心的。這個樂團在八月時受邀開演唱會，但很可惜的是其中一個成員不在，要到秋天才能歸隊。我準備了汽球和彩球為她們加油。我的阿姨們在舞台上就像兩個超級巨星，她們的安可曲更讓演唱會達到高潮。那實在是個有趣的經驗！

0037 **form**

[fɔrm] ★★★★★
動 形成、組織、養成
名 外形、表格、做法
片 in form 表現如常

0038 **average**

[`ævərɪdʒ] ★★★★★
形 平均的、普通的、中等的
名 平均、一般

0039 **vocalist**

[`vokəlɪst] ★★
名 歌手、聲樂家
同 songster 歌手

0040 **compose**

[kəm`poz] ★★★
動 作曲、構圖、使鎮靜、組成
同 constitute 構成、組成

0041 **various**

[`vɛrɪəs] ★★★★★
形 形形色色的、許多的
反 uniform 相同的、一致的

0042 **unemployment**

[ˌʌnɪm`plɔɪmənt] ★★★
名 失業、失業人數
片 high unemployment 高失業率

0043 **inspiration**

[ˌɪnspə`reʃən] ★★★
名 靈感、鼓舞、啟示
同 stimulation 激勵

0044 **autumn**

[`ɔtəm] ★★★★★
名 秋天、凋落期
同 fall 秋天

0045 **balloon**

[bə`lun] ★★★
名 氣球、球狀物
動 激增、像氣球般鼓起
形 像氣球般鼓起的

0046 **encore**

[`aŋkor] ★★
名 要求加演、加演曲目
動 要求…加演

0047 **climax**

[`klaɪmæks] ★★★
名 頂點、高潮
動 達到頂點或高潮

0048 **indeed**

[ɪn`did] ★★★★★
副 確實、當然、甚至
同 certainly 確實、無疑地

fighting!

Give it a shot 小試身手

1. Tony just came _____ from Japan yesterday.
2. An apple a day keeps the doctor _____.
3. The girl was startled when the _____ exploded.
4. Philip was called _____ in August last year.
5. I like spring better than _____.

Answers: 1 back 2 away 3 balloon 4 up 5 autumn

005

Essay

According to the police, the deceiver[0049] was a beautiful girl who always targeted[0050] baseball and basketball players. She had two basic tricks[0051]. One was pretending to be a barber[0052]. She asked the men to take a hot bath in her newly[0053] built bathroom, charging them a lot for the experience. The victims then had to pay more money to get their clothes back from a locker[0054] to which she had the only key; otherwise, they had to go home naked[0055]. Even if one <u>had the cheek to</u> walk out of the bathroom without any clothes on, she would scream loudly and accuse him of exhibitionism[0056] until he paid. Since those baseball and basketball players were all notables[0057], their reputation[0058] was much more important to them than money.

Another trick she used was inviting victims[0059] to a bar or beach. She would wear little clothing, and some men would lose all control in the company of such a sexy woman and <u>spend a fortune on</u> her. Eventually, though, the police discovered her deceit[0060] and <u>put her in jail</u>.

- 🔊 have the cheek to do sth. 厚著臉皮做某事
- 🔊 spend a fortune on 花一大筆錢在…上
- 🔊 put sb. in jail 將某人送進監獄

中譯 *Translation*

　　根據警察的說法，這名騙子是個美女，目標大多是棒球或籃球選手。她有兩個基本詐術。一種是偽裝成理髮師。她會請他們在她新建好的浴室裡洗熱水澡，並藉此向他們索取高價。然後，受害者必須再付更多的錢把鎖在置物櫃裡的衣服贖回，因為唯一的鑰匙在她手裡，不然他們就得光著身子回家。即使有人敢厚著臉皮走出浴室，她也會大聲尖叫，指控對方是暴露狂，直到他付錢了事。因為這些棒球和籃球選手都是名人，他們的名譽要比錢來得重要多了。

　　另一種手法則是邀請他們去酒吧或海灘。她會穿得很少，有些男人會因為這麼一位性感尤物的陪伴而控制不了自己，在她身上花一大筆錢。儘管如此，最後警方還是找到關於她詐欺的證據，將她送進監獄。

0049 deceiver

[dɪ`sivə] ★★★

名 騙子、詐欺者
衍 deceive 欺騙、蒙蔽

0050 target

[`tɑrgɪt] ★★★★

動 把…作為目標
名 目標、靶子
片 meet targets 達到指標

0051 trick

[trɪk] ★★★★

名 詭計、癖好、竅門
動 哄騙、戲弄、打扮
片 trick out 打扮、裝飾

0052 barber

[`bɑrbə] ★★★

名 理髮師
動 給人理髮、修整(草木)

0053 newly

[`njulɪ] ★★★

副 以新的方式、重新
衍 newlyweds 新婚夫婦

0054 locker

[`lɑkə] ★★★

名 寄物櫃、冷藏室、上鎖的人
片 locker room 衣帽間

0055 naked

[`nekɪd] ★★★★

形 裸體的、無覆蓋的、無證據的
片 the naked eyes 肉眼

0056 exhibitionism

[ˌɛksə`bɪʃənˌɪzəm] ★★

名 裸露癖、表現狂

0057 notables

[`notəbl̩z] ★★★

名 著名人士、顯耀人士
形 notable 顯著的

0058 reputation

[ˌrɛpjə`teʃən] ★★★

名 名聲、信譽
同 name 名聲、名譽
反 discredit 喪失名譽

0059 victim

[`vɪktɪm] ★★★★

名 犧牲者、受害者、祭品
片 fall victim to 成為…的受害者

0060 deceit

[dɪ`sit] ★★★

名 欺騙、騙局
同 fraud 欺騙
衍 self-deceit 自欺

fighting!

Give it a shot 小試身手

❶ These poor people lack the _____ necessities of life.

❷ Sally put on her clothes after taking a _____ in a bathtub.

❸ He could not _____ that his friends should laugh at him.

❹ Little children like to _____ drums.

❺ The view from the top of the mountain is _____.

Answers: ❶ basic ❷ bath ❸ bear ❹ beat ❺ beautiful

Essay

The once happy couple[0061] had decided to divorce[0062]. They thought it would be best because they no longer trusted each other. Shortly after their marital[0063] life began, they began to sleep in different beds. The husband became <u>as busy as a bee</u>, so he thought sleeping apart was better for his wife. That way, he thought, he would no longer wake her up when he got into bed at midnight. However, the wife became suspicious[0064] for he was never beside[0065] her, and she began to think that his heart didn't belong to her anymore. To <u>keep an eye on</u> him, she often followed him in her car without his knowledge[0066]. Also, she limited the money he could spend to below $2,000 per month so he could not afford to date another woman. He couldn't even afford to treat[0067] a big client to dinner on his limited budget. When the husband complained about this, his wife said she was just being an economical[0068] housewife. On the weekends, she rode a bicycle and tracked[0069] him wherever he went. In the end, suspicion ruined[0070] their marriage.

ⓘ as busy as a bee 忙得不可開交
ⓘ keep an eye on 照看、注意、監視

中譯 *Translation*

　　這對曾經非常幸福的夫妻決定離婚了。他們覺得這是最好的方法，因為他們已不再相信彼此。在他們展開婚姻生活後不久，就開始分房睡。丈夫變得很忙，所以他認為分開睡對太太比較好。他覺得那樣一來，他就再也不會因半夜跳上床而吵醒她。然而，太太對丈夫起了疑心，因為他總是不在身邊。她認為他的心已不再屬於她。為了監視他，她經常在丈夫不知情的情況下開車跟蹤他。另外，她還限制他的開銷每個月要低於兩千元，這樣他就無法負擔和其他女人的約會。甚至連和客戶吃頓大餐他都負擔不起。當丈夫抱怨妻子的限制，她就說她只是為了做好一個節儉的家庭主婦而已。週末的時候，她會騎著腳踏車四處跟蹤他。最終，懷疑摧毀了他們的婚姻。

0061 couple

[`kʌpḷ] ★★★
名 (未婚)夫妻、一對
動 結合、聯想、使成夫妻
片 a couple of 幾個

0062 divorce

[də`vors] ★★★★
動 離婚、使分離
名 離婚、分離
片 divorce from 與…離婚

0063 marital

[`mærətḷ] ★★
形 婚姻的、夫妻的
慣 marital status (正式)婚姻狀況

0064 suspicious

[sə`spɪʃəs] ★★★
形 懷疑的、有蹊蹺的
用 be suspicious of + sb./ sth. 對某人或某事起疑

0065 beside

[bɪ`saɪd] ★★★★
介 在旁邊、和…無關
同 next to 在…旁邊
片 beside the point 離題

0066 knowledge

[`nɑlɪdʒ] ★★★★★
名 知識、學問、了解
片 without sb's knowledge 某人不知情

0067 treat

[trit] ★★★★
動 請客、對待、處理
名 款待、樂趣

0068 economical

[ikə`nɑmɪkḷ] ★★
形 節約的、精打細算的
同 frugal 節約的

0069 track

[træk] ★★★★
動 跟蹤、留下足跡、走過
名 行蹤、軌道、思路
片 track down 追查出

0070 ruin

[`ruɪn] ★★★
動 毀壞、使成廢墟
名 毀滅、斷垣殘壁

0071 independent

[ˌɪndɪ`pɛndənt] ★★★
形 獨立的、自主的
名 無黨派者

0072 threat

[θrɛt] ★★★★
名 威脅、恐嚇、凶兆
片 pose a threat 構成威脅

Fighting!

Give it a shot 小試身手

① My sister has moved away from home and ＿＿＿ independent[0071].
② There's a small garden ＿＿＿ the villa.
③ They planted a lot of trees ＿＿＿ the two buildings.
④ I ＿＿＿ to the Department of Engineering.
⑤ Don't ＿＿＿ their threats[0072] for real.

Answers: ① becomes ② beside ③ between ④ belong ⑤ believe

007

MP3

短文 013　字彙 014

Essay

Someone born into a wealthy[0073] family receives[0074] all the advantages[0075] of birth. But not everyone has <u>blue blood</u> and the ability to blow[0076] money on fancy cars, tailor[0077]-made clothes and private[0078] boats. Most of us <u>work our fingers to the bone</u> to get a better life and struggle against financial[0079] difficulties. When someone's career <u>bites the dust</u>, a person has barely[0080] enough to <u>keep body and soul together</u>. An unemployed man's job, and likely his girlfriend, are both lost, and life is all in a black despair; it is then time to take a look at the problems. Is it lack of knowledge? If it is, buy some books to read. Are there any obstacles[0081] in the way? Examine them and get rid of them. Are you suffering from poor health?? Eat a bowl of oatmeal[0082] every morning. Are you late all the time? Get up early in the morning like an early bird. Facing the facts brings you one step closer to making big money. As an average person, you haven't gotten a fortune from your parents, but you can make a fortune on your own. It might be a long and difficult period[0083], but you will be extremely excited to see the fruits of your labor[0084].

(!) blue blood 出身高貴的人

(!) work one's fingers to the bone 拼命工作、做牛做馬

(!) bite the dust 大敗、死亡

(!) keep body and soul together 維持生計

中譯 *Translation*

　　生於富有家庭的人一出生就享盡各種優勢。但並非每個人都出身名門，有能力把錢揮霍在名車、訂製服和私人帆船上。我們大多數的人都拼命工作，以求更好的生活，並和經濟困境搏鬥。當事業失敗時，薪水僅能勉強餬口而已。一名失業男子的工作和女友都沒了，生活陷入一片黑暗與絕望，於是，正視問題的時候到了。是因為學識不足嗎？如果是的話，就買些書來看。是因為遇到障礙嗎？檢視它並除掉它。身體不好嗎？那就每天早上吃碗麥片。老是遲到嗎？像早起的鳥兒一樣早起吧。面對現實就會讓你朝賺大錢更近一步。身為普通人，你未能從父母那裡繼承一大筆財產，但你可以靠自己賺錢。或許這是一個漫長又辛苦的階段，但在你見到成果時會欣喜若狂。

0073 wealthy

[`wɛlθɪ] ★★★★
形 富裕的、豐富的
同 rich 富有的

0074 receive

[rɪ`siv] ★★★★★
動 接收、容納
片 receive from 從…獲得

0075 advantage

[əd`væntɪdʒ] ★★★
名 優勢、利益
動 使處於優勢
片 to advantage 有效果地

0076 blow

[blo] ★★★★★
動 吹、隨風飄動、使爆炸
名 吹動、吹氣、吹牛
片 blow on 吹涼

0077 tailor

[`telɚ] ★★★
名 裁縫師、(男裝)服裝店
動 裁製、修改
片 tailor-made 訂製的

0078 private

[`praɪvɪt] ★★★★★
形 私人的、喜歡獨處的
同 personal 私人的
片 in private 私下地

0079 financial

[faɪ`nænʃəl] ★★★★
形 金融的、財政的
片 financial backing 財務
支援

0080 barely

[`bɛrlɪ] ★★★
副 僅僅、幾乎沒、公開地
片 barely enough to 勉強
夠

0081 obstacle

[`ɑbstəkl̩] ★★★
名 妨礙、障礙物
片 put obstacles in the
way of 設法阻撓

0082 oatmeal

[`ot͵mil] ★★★
名 燕麥片、燕麥粉、淺棕
色
同 burgoo 牛奶燕麥粥

0083 period

[`pɪrɪəd] ★★★★★
名 時期、週期、月經
片 come to a period 結束

0084 labor

[`lebɚ] ★★★
名 工作、勞工、陣痛
動 努力、勞動
片 labor on 繼續工作

Fighting!

Give it a shot 小試身手

1 My mother gave _____ to me and brought me up on her own.

2 This film is suitable for _____ adults and children.

3 The police _____ off the street after the accident.

4 A breeze _____ over the garden.

5 Rabbits do not usually _____ humans.

Answers: 1 birth 2 both 3 blocked 4 blew 5 bite

008

They are all around us. They usually have breakfast at expensive coffee shops and never take the bus or subway[0085]; a taxi is the first choice of transportation[0086] for them. These kinds of girls are of slim[0087] figure[0088] with short, brown hair, beautiful and bright. After sitting in a nice office building all day, these "gold diggers[0089]" start their other "job" at fancy[0090] restaurants and nightclubs.

"Gold diggers" are busy dating rich guys in the city. Dating rich and famous men is the bread and butter for a "gold digger." At parties, there are always guys trying to please[0091] them, and, because they are so attractive, even fathers and brothers are obsessed[0092] with them. Especially for wealthy engineers[0093], who deal with computers all day, the beauty and passion[0094] of "gold diggers" are irresistible[0095]. Any man who tries to form a relationship with one of them had better bring enough cash; otherwise, "gold diggers" will break up with them in a flash[0096].

> (!) gold digger 淘金者，目前普遍指以美色騙取男人錢財的女子
>
> (!) be busy + ving 忙著做某事
>
> (!) bread and butter 生計、主要收入來源
>
> (!) break up with sb. 與某人分手

中譯 *Translation*

　　她們隨處可見。她們通常會在昂貴的咖啡店享用早餐，從不搭公車或地鐵，計程車才是她們首選的交通工具。這類女孩體型纖細，有著一頭棕色短髮，看起來明豔照人。在體面的辦公大廈坐了一整天之後，這些「拜金女」就會在高級餐廳和夜店開始她們的另一份「工作」。

　　「拜金女」忙著和城內的富家子弟約會。與有錢人或名人約會是這些「拜金女」的主要收入來源。在派對中，總是有許多男人試圖討好她們，然而因為她們實在是太迷人了，甚至是父親們和兄長們都難逃誘惑。尤其是有錢的工程師，由於整天都在電腦前工作，「拜金女」的美麗與熱情對他們來說更是難以抵擋。任何想和她們談戀愛的男性們最好帶著足夠的現金，否則，「拜金女」可是會立馬把你給甩了。

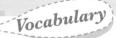

0085 subway

[`sʌb,we] ★★★

名 (美)地下鐵、(英)地道

補 英國倫敦地鐵為 Underground

0086 transportation

[,trænspɚ`teʃən] ★★★

名 運輸工具、交通費

同 conveyance 運輸

0087 slim

[slɪm] ★★★

形 苗條的、微薄的

動 減輕體重、縮減

同 slender 苗條的

0088 figure

[`fɪgjɚ] ★★★★★

名 體態、人物、數字

動 計算、描述、出現

片 figure out 想出、算出

0089 digger

[`dɪgɚ] ★★

名 挖掘者、挖掘機

同 excavator 開鑿者

0090 fancy

[`fænsɪ] ★★★★

形 別緻的、昂貴的

名 愛好、幻想

動 設想、喜愛

0091 please

[pliz] ★★★★★

動 討好、使滿意、請

同 satisfy 使滿意

反 displease 得罪

0092 obsess

[əb`sɛs] ★★

動 使著迷、纏住、使煩擾

片 be obsessed with 沉迷於⋯

0093 engineer

[,ɛndʒə`nɪr] ★★★★★

名 工程師、技師、專家

動 策劃、建造、設計

0094 passion

[`pæʃən] ★★★

名 熱情、情慾、盛怒

片 fly into a passion 大發雷霆

0095 irresistible

[,ɪrɪ`zɪstəbl̩] ★★

形 無法抗拒的、不可避免的

反 resistant 抵抗的

0096 flash

[flæʃ] ★★★

名 閃光、新聞快報、閃現

動 使閃光、反射、掠過

片 in a flash 瞬間、片刻

Fighting!

Give it a shot 小試身手

1. If you _____ that vase you'll have to pay for it.

2. Mother _____ home a box of chocolates.

3. The new hospital is a big _____.

4. The _____ is full, so we have to wait for the next one.

5. We honored the _____ solider who killed the enemy.

Answers: 1 break 2 brought 3 building 4 bus 5 brave

009

Essay

MP3　短文 017　字彙 018

　　How can you date a supermodel without going bankrupt[0097]? Playboys[0098] have some tricks. Dating a model is a piece of cake for them. A playboy doesn't need to be a billionaire[0099] or a movie star, but he should at least spend some money on buying a nice car and stylish[0100] outfits[0101]. At a party, they are social butterflies. They know what they want and prowl[0102] around like an animal on a hunt[0103]. Playboys aren't afraid of wearing flashy[0104] jewelry and clothes to a party. To make a big impression and be flamboyant[0105] is their goal. A cool cap and a camel overcoat are both popular choices for them. They never act before careful consideration and observation[0106]. While picking up girls, they often show funny photos to them on their smartphones, which usually works. Most importantly, they phone and butter girls up once they get their phone numbers. They also send cards and flowers to girls, especially on special occasions[0107], to show they care. No girl can resist such gentlemanly[0108] behavior. It is so easy for playboys- like <u>taking candy from a baby</u>.

> ⓘ to take candy from a baby 形容辦事容易

中譯 *Translation*

　　要怎麼和一個名模約會而不破產呢？花花公子們自有一些招數。邀約模特兒對他們來說易如反掌。一個花花公子不必是個億萬富翁或電影明星，但至少能花點錢買輛不錯的車和時髦的服裝。在宴會中，他們是交際老手，很清楚自己要的是什麼，然後就像狩獵中的動物般四處覓食。花花公子並不怕穿戴華麗的珠寶和服裝赴宴，讓人印象深刻和耀眼才是他們的目的。一頂帥氣的帽子和駝色大衣對他們來說都是受歡迎的選擇。他們總在仔細考量和觀察之後才行動。在搭訕女孩的時候，亮出智慧型手機中有趣的照片通常很有用。最重要的是，他們一旦得知女孩們的電話號碼，就會打電話用甜言蜜語討她們歡心。尤其是在特別的場合，他們也會寄卡片和送花給女孩們，表示關心。沒有女孩能抵抗這種溫柔的舉動。這對花花公子來說很容易，就像從娃娃手裡搶糖吃一樣簡單。

0097 bankrupt

[`bæŋkrʌpt] ★★★
形 破產的、喪失…的
動 使破產、使赤貧
名 破產者、完全喪失…者

0098 playboy

[`ple͵bɔɪ] ★
名 尋歡作樂的有錢男子
同 womanizer 玩弄女性者

0099 billionaire

[͵bɪljə`nɛr] ★★
名 億萬富翁
衍 billion 十億

0100 stylish

[`staɪlɪʃ] ★★
形 時髦的、流行的
同 fashionable 流行的

0101 outfit

[`aut͵fɪt] ★★★
名 全套服裝、裝備、全套用品、團體
動 配備、供給

0102 prowl

[praul] ★★★
動 四處覓食、徘徊、潛行
名 四處覓食、徘徊
片 on the prowl 徘徊

0103 hunt

[hʌnt] ★★★★
名 打獵、搜尋、搜索
動 獵食、尋找、追捕
片 hunt for 尋找獵物

0104 flashy

[`flæʃɪ] ★★
形 俗艷的、閃爍的、一瞬間的
同 gaudy 華麗俗氣的

0105 flamboyant

[flæm`bɔɪənt] ★★
形 艷麗的、炫耀的、火紅色的
同 ornate 華麗的

0106 observation

[͵ɑbzɝ`veʃən] ★★★
名 觀察、注意、言論
片 be under observation 受嚴密監視

0107 occasion

[ə`keʒən] ★★★★
名 場合、時機、理由
動 引起、惹起
片 on occasion 偶而

0108 gentlemanly

[`dʒɛntḷmənlɪ] ★★
形 紳士的、有禮貌的
衍 gentleman 紳士、有教養的男子

fighting!

Give it a shot 小試身手

1. Digital _____ doesn't need a film but a memory card.
2. The only thing he seems to _____ about is money.
3. My mother _____ me a box of paints.
4. Mary came up to me, _____ a basket of apples.
5. The canary is singing sweetly in a _____.

Answers: 1 camera 2 care 3 bought 4 carrying 5 cage

Essay

Having fair[0109] skin and a skinny body is the dream of most Taiwanese girls. They do whatever they can to achieve[0110] this goal. However, a good case can be made against doing this. The odds[0111] of making skin significantly whiter is less than five percent. In addition, skin is certain to become tanned[0112] under sunshine, and sunscreen can only help so much. When men chase a chick[0113], they are attracted by not only appearance[0114] but also something else. The chief reason for focusing on appearance is lack of confidence[0115]. Beyonce and Jennifer Lopez, with the most hit songs on the charts[0116], are not fair-skinned or skinny, but they are still attractive. Therefore, forget about buying bleaching[0117] agents[0118] and similar cosmetics[0119]. Be active and have some fun outdoors. Eating some turkey on Christmas will not kill you, either. Every girl should eat well and play like a child!

⚠ be certain to 的確、一定會

⚠ hit songs 暢銷歌曲

⚠ fair-skinned 皮膚白皙的

中譯 *Translation*

　　擁有白晰的皮膚和骨感的身材是大部分台灣女孩的夢想。她們竭盡所能達成這個目標。然而，這裡有個很好的實例可以讓你停止這麼做。要從黑肉底明顯變成雪白肌的機率低於百分之五。此外，不管你塗了多少防曬油，在陽光下曬黑是必然的。當男人在追女孩的時候，他們並不只會受外表吸引，還會有其他的因素。注重外表的主要理由是因為缺乏自信。排行榜上有著最多暢銷金曲的碧昂斯和珍妮佛羅貝茲，她們既不白皙也不骨感，卻依然如此迷人。所以，別再買美白產品或類似的化妝品了。讓自己變得活潑，並到戶外玩耍。聖誕節時吃點火雞肉也不會要了你的命。每個女孩都應該像個孩子般快樂地吃喝玩樂才對！

0109 fair

[fɛr] ★★★★★

形 白皙的、公正的、晴朗的

名 (定期)集市、展覽會

0110 achieve

[əˋtʃiv] ★★★★

動 實現、贏得

片 achieve one's goal 達到目標

0111 odds

[ɑds] ★★★

名 機會、區別、不和

片 at odds with 與…不和

0112 tanned

[tænd] ★★★

形 被曬成棕褐色的

反 untanned 未曬黑的

0113 chick

[tʃɪk] ★★★

名 (俚)小妞、小雞

片 chick magnet 吸引女生注意的男性

0114 appearance

[əˋpɪrəns] ★★★

名 外貌、出現

片 keep up appearances 裝闊氣

0115 confidence

[ˋkɑnfədəns] ★★★

名 自信、信賴

片 in confidence 祕密地

0116 chart

[tʃɑrt] ★★★★

名 進排行榜、圖表

動 繪製…圖表、詳細計畫

同 graph 圖表

0117 bleaching

[ˋblitʃɪŋ] ★★

形 漂白的

名 漂白

0118 agent

[ˋedʒənt] ★★★★★

名 (化)劑、仲介、代理人

片 travel agent 旅行社

0119 cosmetics

[kɑzˋmɛtɪks] ★★

名 化妝品

同 makeup 化妝品

0120 robber

[ˋrɑbɚ] ★★

名 強盜、搶劫者

同 bandit 強盜

Fighting!

Give it a shot 小試身手

1. The doctor was _____ that the young man had gone mad.

2. What was the _____ of the accident?

3. I have _____ your answers and none of them are correct.

4. The strong coach _____ the robber⁰¹²⁰.

5. The _____ reason for going to school is to learn.

Answers: 1 certain 2 cause 3 checked 4 caught 5 chief

011

Essay

　　Is it smart to buy a house in Taipei City, especially at such a high price? For average middle-age citizens[0121], it is like a dream that never comes true. Most people spend their whole life savings[0122] on an old apartment with stairs to climb and moldy[0123] walls that need <u>a coat of</u> paint[0124]. Some people need to borrow so much money that they struggle[0125] to make their mortgage[0126] payments and <u>end up</u> asking help from God in the church. However, buying a home is only one option[0127]. Renting[0128] a nice and clean apartment close to downtown[0129] costs much less than buying one. Instead of going deep into debt[0130], it's so much better to have enough money to take a trip. Life is a race against the clock, and taking a vacation by the coast, enjoying a cup of coffee or a glass of whiskey with coke, is better than working as a slave[0131] in order to buy a home, and it adds[0132] more color to life.

(!) a coat of 一層…

(!) end up + ving 以…作為結束

中譯 *Translation*

　　在台北買房子，尤其是以這麼高的價位買進，是個明智之舉嗎？對一般中年市民來說，這就像個永遠不會實現的夢。大多數人將畢生積蓄花在購置一間老舊的公寓，有樓梯要爬，還有一層斑駁的牆壁要漆。有些人需要借這麼多錢，以至於他們得努力付清貸款，還落得要到教堂求助上帝的下場。然而，買房子只不過是一項選擇罷了。在靠近市中心的地方租一間又好又乾淨的公寓，比買房子便宜多了。與其身陷債務泥沼，不如用足夠的錢來趟旅行要好上許多。人生就是和時間賽跑，在海岸邊享用一杯咖啡或威士忌可樂度假，比像個奴隸般為了買房而工作，更能讓生命豐富多彩。

0121　citizen

[ˋsɪtəzn̩] ★★★
名 公民、老百姓
片 senior citizen 老年人

0122　savings

[ˋsevɪŋz] ★★★★
名 存款、積蓄
片 savings bond 儲蓄債券

0123　moldy

[ˋmoldɪ] ★★
形 發霉的、乏味的
同 musty 發霉的

0124　paint

[pent] ★★★★
名 油漆、塗料
動 塗以顏色、繪畫

0125　struggle

[ˋstrʌgl̩] ★★★★
動 奮鬥、掙扎、對抗
片 struggle against 為反對…而鬥爭

0126　mortgage

[ˋmɔrgɪdʒ] ★★★
名 抵押
動 以…做擔保
同 pledge 抵押

0127　option

[ˋɑpʃən] ★★★★
名 選擇、選擇自由
片 keep one's options open 暫不表態

0128　rent

[rɛnt] ★★★★
動 租用、出租
名 租金
片 rent out 租出

0129　downtown

[ˏdaʊnˋtaʊn] ★★★
名 城市商業區
副 在市中心
形 市中心的

0130　debt

[dɛt] ★★★★
名 債務、人情債
片 in debt 負債

0131　slave

[slev] ★★★
名 苦工、奴隸
動 苦幹、販賣奴隸

0132　add

[æd] ★★★★★
動 增加、加起來、補充説
片 add sb./sth. in 把…計算在內

Fighting!

Give it a shot 小試身手

❶ Smith is a very _____ last name in England.

❷ _____ your eyes and count up to 10.

❸ They pray for God in the _____.

❹ I heard your shout and _____ back as quickly as I could.

❺ How did you _____ to the top of that building?

Answers: ❶ common ❷ Close ❸ church ❹ came ❺ climb

There was an extraordinary[0133] cook who worked so hard and tried to bake the best cookies in the world. He was planning to go to Paris to study at the best cookery[0134] school in France. However, his parents wanted him to stay in the country to be a farmer, taking care of cows and corn they had planted. He couldn't go to Paris without his parents' permission[0135], because the tuition[0136] fee[0137] of the school was so costly[0138] that he couldn't afford it. Despite[0139] this, he still continued making great cookies. He tried different ingredients[0140] and various shapes in order to make his cookies unique[0141].

On a cool afternoon of September, after having a cup of coffee alone, he decided to leave town. Even though this would make his mother cry, he was sure that what he was going to do was correct. After being an apprentice[0142] for years in Paris, he had made thousands of cookies, too many to count in fact. He had become famous for his special way of cutting, and he was even featured[0143] on the cover of a prestigious[0144] magazine.

中譯 *Translation*

　　有一名出色的廚師，他努力工作，想烤出全世界最好吃的餅乾。他計劃前往巴黎，攻讀法國最棒的廚藝學校。然而，他的父母希望他留在國內當一名農夫，照顧牛群和他們栽種的玉米。沒有父母的許可他根本去不了巴黎，因為學費很昂貴，是他所負擔不起的。無論如何，他仍持續製作餅乾。他嘗試不同的材料和各種形狀，為了讓他的餅乾獨一無二。

　　九月某個涼爽的午後，他獨自喝完一杯咖啡之後，就決定離開城鎮。即使這麼做會使母親哭泣，他仍確定他所做的是對的。在巴黎當了幾年的學徒之後，他已經做出數以千計的餅乾，實際上根本就多到數不清了。他以獨特的切片方式出名，甚至登上一本知名雜誌的封面。

0133 extraordinary

[ɪk`strɔrdṇ͵ɛrɪ] ★★★★

形 異常的、非凡的、破例的、特派的

反 commonplace 普通的

0134 cookery

[`kʊkərɪ] ★

名 烹調、烹飪術

同 cooking 烹調

0135 permission

[pə`mɪʃən] ★★★

名 許可、同意

片 give sb. permission to 准許某人…

0136 tuition

[tu`ɪʃən] ★★★

名 學費、講授

同 instruction 講授

片 tuition fees 學費

0137 fee

[fi] ★★★★

名 服務費、入場費

動 付費給

片 charge a fee 收費

0138 costly

[`kɔstlɪ] ★★★

形 貴重的、代價高的

同 high-priced 高價的

0139 despite

[dɪ`spaɪt] ★★★★★

介 儘管、任憑

名 惡意、侮辱

0140 ingredient

[ɪn`gridɪənt] ★★★

名 原料、構成要素

同 component 構成要素

0141 unique

[ju`nik] ★★★★

形 獨特的、無可匹敵的

名 獨一無二的人或事物

同 matchless 無敵的

0142 apprentice

[ə`prɛntɪs] ★★★

名 學徒、初學者

動 當學徒

反 master 師傅、能手

0143 feature

[`fitʃə] ★★★★★

動 特載、以…為特色

名 特徵、特別報導

慣 feature sb. as 某人主演

0144 prestigious

[prɛs`tɪdʒɪəs] ★★★

形 有名的

同 celebrated 著名的

衍 prestige 名望

Fighting!

Give it a shot 小試身手

1 After a small break, the teacher _____ his lecture.

2 It _____ a lot of money to stay in a five star hotel for one night.

3 The little girl is able to _____ from 1 to 100.

4 People can take open _____ through Internet.

5 There are various races in the _____.

Answers: 1 continued 2 costs 3 count 4 courses 5 country

013

MP3
短文 025　字彙 026

Essay

Lady Gaga, the eldest daughter of her Italian-American daddy, is the most controversial[0145] artist since Madonna. Young people have a deep affection[0146] for her music and creative performances[0147]. Gaga and her dancers dress in amazing styles, which add a lot to her shows. You can even sometimes see cute panda eyes on her face or deer horns[0148] on her head. Gaga's taste in fashion never dates[0149]; she has her own creative production team that creates many of her stage designs and hairdos.

She had initially[0150] signed with Def Jam Recordings in December 2005. Three months later, she decided to join producer RedOne. At the beginning of her career, she was once in danger of being addicted[0151] to drugs, and had no idea how to deal with it. She said her dear ones ignored[0152] her for several months. That was the darkest period of her life. Her creativity[0153] and vitality[0154] was dead then. However, Lady Gaga overcame[0155] all that and proved herself to be extremely[0156] talented.

!　be in danger of + n./ving 有…的危險

!　I have no idea. = I don't know. = I have no clue.，表示什麼都不知道

中譯 *Translation*

　　女神卡卡，義裔美籍父親的長女，是繼瑪丹娜之後最具爭議性的藝人。年輕人熱愛她的音樂和創意十足的表演。卡卡和她的舞群以驚人的造型出現，為她的演出增添更多的可看性。你甚至可以看到她臉上畫著可愛的熊貓眼，或是頭上戴著鹿角。卡卡的時尚品味從不過時，她有自己的創意團隊，創作出許多的舞臺設計和髮型。

　　2005年12月，她率先和 Def Jam Recordings 唱片公司簽約。三個月後，她決定加入 RedOne 唱片。在她演藝生涯之初，曾經陷入染毒的危機，也不知道如何處理。她說她的親人好幾個月都對她視若無睹。那是她一生最黑暗的時期，她的創意和活力在那時一度停擺。儘管如此，女神卡卡克服了這一切，並且證明了自己極具天賦的表演才華。

0145 controversial

[ˌkɑntrəˈvɝʃəl] ★★★
- 形 有爭議的
- 同 arguable 有疑義的
- 衍 controversy 爭議

0146 affection

[əˈfɛkʃən] ★★★
- 名 鍾愛、感情、影響
- 片 win sb's affection 贏得某人的愛

0147 performance

[pɚˈfɔrməns] ★★★★
- 名 演出、履行
- 片 What a performance! 真沒教養！

0148 horn

[hɔrn] ★★★
- 名 角、喇叭、警笛
- 動 強行參加、闖入

0149 date

[det] ★★★★★
- 動 過時、約會
- 名 日期、約會
- 片 date back to 追溯至

0150 initially

[ɪˈnɪʃəlɪ] ★★★
- 副 最初、開頭
- 同 at first 最初
- 衍 initiative 初步的

0151 addict

[əˈdɪkt] ★★★
- 動 沉溺、成癮
- 名 入迷的人
- 片 be addicted to 沉溺於

0152 ignore

[ɪgˈnɔr] ★★★★
- 動 忽視、不顧
- 同 disregard 不理會
- 衍 ignorance 無知

0153 creativity

[ˌkrieˈtɪvɪtɪ] ★★★★
- 名 創造力
- 同 ingenuity 獨創性

0154 vitality

[vaɪˈtælətɪ] ★★★
- 名 活力、生命力
- 同 animation 活潑

0155 overcome

[ˌovɚˈkʌm] ★★★★★
- 動 克服、戰勝
- 同 conquer 克服
- 反 surrender 投降

0156 extremely

[ɪkˈstrimlɪ] ★★★
- 副 極端地、非常
- 同 exceptionally 例外地、非常

fighting!

Give it a shot 小試身手

1. The boat is in _____ of sinking.
2. Tom doesn't know how to _____ with the difficult problem.
3. He already _____ to quit his job.
4. Don't cry over the _____ pet. Cheer up!
5. _____ is the last month of the year.

Answers: 1 danger 2 deal 3 decided 4 dead 5 December

014

Essay

Lil Wayne is considered the best rapper[0157] alive. His talent was discovered in his early childhood. Wayne wrote his first rap song while he was washing dishes after dinner at the age of eight years old. In 1997, Lil Wayne joined the entertainment[0158] industry and earned more than one million dollars a year. His first wife was his high-school sweetheart[0159] who lived next door. And his first child, Reginae, who loves dolls, was born when he was just 15. Because of Wayne's success, many teenagers hope for shortcuts[0160] and do not want to do desk jobs like everybody else. To help guide children in the right direction, the US President mentioned[0161] Lil Wayne in a public speech by, stating[0162], "Different from Lil Wayne, it's difficult to have a meteoric[0163] rise to fame. You can aspire[0164] to be a scientist, engineer or doctor, not just a rapper. Doing bad things is digging your own grave. You might die on the dirty streets like a dog one day." Although there has been criticism[0165] of Lil Wayne, his influence[0166] is beyond doubt.

(!) dig one's own grave 自掘墳墓

(!) beyond doubt 無庸置疑

中譯 *Translation*

　　李爾·韋恩被認為是現今最棒的饒舌樂手。他的才華早在幼年時期就被發掘了。年僅八歲的小韋恩在晚餐後洗盤子時，寫下了人生中的第一首饒舌歌。1997年，李爾·韋恩加入演藝圈，一年收入超過百萬。他的第一任妻子是他高中時期住在隔壁的甜姐兒。而他的第一個孩子，熱愛洋娃娃的雷吉娜，在他還只有十五歲那年出生。由於韋恩的成功，許多年輕人寄望著成功的捷徑，不想像大家一樣從事辦公室工作。為了引導孩童們走向正途，美國總統在一場公眾演講中提及李爾·韋恩，說道：「和李爾·韋恩不同，要一夕成名很難。你可以嚮往成為科學家、工程師或醫生，而不只是饒舌歌手。做壞事就是自掘墳墓，某天你可能會像條狗一樣，死在骯髒的街道上。」雖然一直有針對李爾·韋恩的批評，但他的影響卻是無庸置疑的。

0157 rapper

[ˋræpɚ] ★★
- 名 饒舌歌手、敲門者
- 同 knocker 敲擊者

0158 entertainment

[ˌɛntɚˋtenmənt] ★★★
- 名 娛樂、演藝、款待
- 同 amusement 消遣

0159 sweetheart

[ˋswitˌhɑrt] ★★
- 名 心上人、甜心
- 動 與…戀愛
- 同 darling 心愛的人

0160 shortcut

[ˋʃɔrtˌkʌt] ★★
- 名 捷徑
- 形 提供捷徑的

0161 mention

[ˋmɛnʃən] ★★★★
- 動 提到、說起
- 名 提及、提名表揚
- 片 at mention of 一提到

0162 state

[stet] ★★★★★
- 動 說明、聲明
- 名 狀態、國家、身分
- 片 state visit 國事訪問

0163 meteoric

[ˌmitɪˋɔrɪk] ★★
- 形 疾速的、流星的
- 片 a meteoric rise to fame 迅速成名

0164 aspire

[əˋspaɪr] ★★★
- 動 嚮往、懷有大志
- 同 desire 渴望
- 片 aspire to 渴求

0165 criticism

[ˋkrɪtəˌsɪzəm] ★★★★
- 名 批評、評論、指責
- 同 judgment 批評
- 反 praise 讚揚

0166 influence

[ˋɪnfluəns] ★★★★
- 名 影響力、權勢
- 動 影響、感化

0167 scoop

[skup] ★★★
- 名 一勺、獨家新聞
- 動 挖出、搶在…之前
- 片 scoop out 舀出

0168 symbol

[ˋsɪmbl] ★★★★
- 名 象徵、記號
- 動 象徵
- 衍 symbolize 象徵

Fighting!

Give it a shot 小試身手

1. It's getting more and more _____ to find a job.
2. _____ are considered as men's royal friends.
3. I just _____ a terrible secret about Mini.
4. My shirt got _____ as I was eating a scoop[0167] of ice cream.
5. A _____ is a symbol[0168] of peace.

Answers: 1 difficult 2 Dogs 3 discovered 4 dirty 5 dove

015

Essay

Summer season is the most exciting time. The weather is warm and dry during summer time. Taking a breath[0169] of summer air in the early morning gives people vitality and energy and life can seem just like a dream.

As the day started, I went downstairs[0170] to <u>answer a call</u> from my friend. Beautiful beaches are the best places on earth, and I especially like driving there with dozens[0171] of friends. We talked and laughed with each other excitedly on the way. Lying[0172] down on the surfboard[0173] and drifting[0174] on the surface[0175] of the water like a duck can ease[0176] the pressures[0177] of life. Watching birds and eagles hovering[0178] in the sky was a nice experience. My friends and I held a party and drank a lot in the evening. At the party, a DJ played ear-piercing[0179] music, and our eyes were drawn[0180] to the girls in bikinis. Tomorrow we will do that again. That's how we enjoy the summer time!

> ⚠ answer a call 接電話

中譯 *Translation*

夏季是最令人興奮的時節。夏季的天氣溫暖又乾燥，吸一口夏日早晨的空氣，會使人們活力充沛，讓人生看起來就像場夢一般。

這一天從我下樓接起朋友的電話開始。美麗的沙灘是世界上最美的地方，我特別喜歡和一群朋友一起在此開車兜風。我們一路上興奮地說說笑笑。躺在衝浪板上，然後像鴨子般漂在水面上，能夠紓解生活中的壓力。望著天空中的鷹鳥盤旋是個美好的體驗。我和朋友們在傍晚舉辦一場派對，大口暢飲。派對上，DJ 播著震耳欲聾的音樂，我們的視線則被比基尼女孩吸住了。明天我們還要再來一次。這就是我們享受夏日時光的方式。

0169 breath

[brɛθ] ★★★★

名 呼吸、微風

片 save your breath 別白費唇舌

0170 downstairs

[ˏdaʊnˋstɛrz] ★★★

副 往樓下
形 樓下的
名 樓下

0171 dozen

[ˋdʌzn̩] ★★★

名 一打、許多

片 baker's dozen 十三

0172 lie

[laɪ] ★★★★

動 躺臥、置於、撒謊
名 位置、狀態、謊言
片 lie about 無所事事

0173 surfboard

[ˋsɝfˏbord] ★★

名 衝浪板
動 衝浪

0174 drift

[drɪft] ★★★★

動 漂流、漂泊
名 漂移、傾向
片 drift out 漂走、散開

0175 surface

[ˋsɝfɪs] ★★★★★

名 表面、水面、外觀
動 浮出水面、顯露
片 on the surface 表面上

0176 ease

[iz] ★★★★

動 減輕、緩和
名 容易、不拘束
片 at ease 自在

0177 pressure

[ˋprɛʃə] ★★★★

名 壓力、困擾、催促
動 對⋯施加壓力

0178 hover

[ˋhʌvə] ★★

動 盤旋、徬徨、停留
名 盤旋、徘徊、猶豫
片 hover over 盤旋於

0179 piercing

[ˋpɪrsɪŋ] ★★★

形 刺耳的、有洞察力的、刺骨的
同 cutting 刺骨的

0180 draw

[drɔ] ★★★★★

動 吸引、拉長、描寫
名 平手、精彩節目
片 draw up 草擬

---

fighting!

Give it a shot 小試身手

① Do you _____ a cup of coffee every day?

② I _____ to work every day.

③ We had an _____ dinner today because I felt hungry.

④ Some babies cry _____ the night.

⑤ An expensive vase fell _____ to the ground.

Answers: ① drink ② drive ③ early ④ during ⑤ down

016

 MP3　短文 031　字彙 032

Essay

Owning[0181] a car seems to give guys an edge[0182] in attracting girls. It is fabulous[0183] to drive a fancy car in the east district of Taipei and enter the parking lots[0184] of clubs. When men reach a certain age and have enough money, they think about buying either a car or an apartment first. Is it easier for men to <u>hook up with</u> girls with a car? It often is, but it's no guarantee[0185] of success. Indeed, a rich man can afford to live in an eighteen-storey[0186] luxury[0187] apartment or eat lobster on a date. He is also able to drive his girlfriend to work at eight o'clock in the morning and <u>pick her up</u> later in the evening. He can even spend eighty thousand dollars on car modifications[0188]. Nevertheless[0189], a girl might not fall in love with his expensive car, and it's possible that she ends up dating someone else. Then, buying a fancy car is somewhat[0190] like spending money on a <u>white elephant</u>. A luxurious car does not automatically[0191] give a man charm.

> (!) hook up with 和某人勾搭上
> (!) pick sb. up 用汽車搭載或接某人
> (!) white elephant 浪費錢又無用的東西、累贅

中譯 *Translation*

擁有一輛車似乎就擁有吸引女孩目光的優勢。在台北東區開著一輛時髦的跑車，接著駛進俱樂部停車場，實在是件很棒的事。當男人到了一定的年紀，並擁有足夠的財富後，他們就會考慮要先買車還是買房。有車的男人把妹是否更容易呢？通常是這樣沒錯，但這並不保證會成功。一個有錢的男人，確實有能力住在十八層樓的豪華公寓，或是在約會時大啖龍蝦。他也能在早上八點載女友去上班，然後晚上晚一點接她下班。他也可以砸下八萬元來改裝車子。然而，女孩並不會和他的豪華車談戀愛，最後也可能會轉而和別人約會。所以，買一輛昂貴的車子有點像是將錢花在一個浪費錢又沒用的事物上。一輛豪華車並不會自動讓一個男人變得迷人。

0181 own

[on] ★★★★★
動 擁有、承認
形 自己的
片 own to + ving 承認

0182 edge

[ɛdʒ] ★★★★★
名 優勢、邊緣、激烈
動 使鋒利、徐徐移動
片 on edge 緊張不安

0183 fabulous

[`fæbjələs] ★★★
形 驚人的、極好的、巨額
的、傳說中的
同 amazing 驚人的

0184 lot

[lɑt] ★★★★★
名 一塊地、很多
動 劃分、抽籤
片 parking lot 停車場

0185 guarantee

[,gærən`ti] ★★★★
名 保證、擔保品
動 保證、擔保
同 promise 允諾

0186 storey

[`storɪ] ★★
名 樓層
用 –storey 有…層樓的

0187 luxury

[`lʌkʃərɪ] ★★★
名 奢華、奢侈、享受
片 in the lap of luxury 在
優裕的環境中

0188 modification

[,mɑdəfə`keʃən] ★★
名 修改、緩和、修飾
同 adjustment 調整

0189 nevertheless

[,nɛvəðə`lɛs] ★★★
副 儘管如此、不過
同 notwithstanding 儘管

0190 somewhat

[`sʌm,hwɑt] ★★★
副 有點、稍微
代 某物、重要人物
片 somewhat of 有點

0191 automatically

[,ɔtə`mætɪkḷɪ] ★★★
副 自動地、無意識地
同 mechanically 機械地

0192 define

[dɪ`faɪn] ★★★
動 給…下定義、限定
片 define as 解釋為
衍 definition 定義

Fighting!

Give it a shot 小試身手

1. People under _____ are defined[0192] as teenagers.
2. All men are born _____.
3. China faces the Pacific on the _____.
4. _____ of us is willing to help you.
5. Don't _____ without knocking, please.

Answers: 1 eighteen 2 equal 3 east 4 Either 5 enter

017

MP3　短文 033　字彙 034

Essay

Have you ever been pressured into smoking marijuana[0193]? Never touch it. Marijuana may lead a person to try <u>harder drugs</u>. In fact, it is far more harmful[0194] than people think. There are many symptoms[0195] after smoking a lot of marijuana: hollow[0196] eyes, thin face, and difficulty in falling asleep in the evening. Addicts are not interested in anything except smoking, and usually have problems with their families.

Researchers have examined the effects of marijuana on <u>long-term memory</u>. After years of medical[0197] examination on a factory worker who smokes marijuana constantly[0198], they have found that the worker's memory weakened[0199] due to smoking marijuana. There are other examples suggesting daily[0200] cannabis[0201] smokers have a 5.7 times higher risk of lung cancer than non-users. It even increases the risk of leukemia[0202] for babies if pregnant[0203] mothers smoke marijuana.

Why not choose another way to relax? Remember, health is priceless[0204].

ⓘ harder drugs 毒性更強的毒品
ⓘ long-term memory 長期記憶

中譯 *Translation*

你是否曾因壓力而吸食大麻？千萬別碰它。大麻會導致人們嘗試毒性更猛烈的毒品。事實上，大麻比人們所想的還要有害。大量吸食大麻之後會產生許多症狀：眼神空洞、臉頰消瘦、晚上睡不著。上癮者除了吸大麻之外對任何事都興趣缺缺，而且通常會產生家庭問題。

研究員調查大麻對長期記憶的影響。他們針對一名經常吸大麻的工廠勞工進行數年的醫療檢查，發現這名勞工因為吸大麻造成記憶力衰退。還有其他的實例顯示每日吸食印度大麻者，罹患肺癌的風險比非吸食者高出5.7倍。如果有孕在身的母親吸食大麻，甚至會增加胎兒罹患血癌的風險。

為什麼不選擇其他方式放鬆呢？切記，健康是無價的。

0193 marijuana

[ˌmarɪˋhwanə] ★

名 大麻、大麻煙

片 marijuana abuse 濫用大麻

0194 harmful

[ˋharmfəl] ★★★

形 有害的

片 be harmful to 對⋯有害

0195 symptom

[ˋsɪmptəm] ★★★

名 症狀、徵兆

同 indication 徵兆

0196 hollow

[ˋhalo] ★★★

形 空洞的、凹陷的

名 窪地、山谷

動 挖空、凹陷

0197 medical

[ˋmɛdɪkl] ★★★★★

形 醫學的、醫療的

片 medical history 病史

0198 constantly

[ˋkanstəntlɪ] ★★★

副 不斷地、時常地

同 perpetually 不斷地、永恆地

0199 weaken

[ˋwikən] ★★★

動 削弱、減少、動搖

反 strengthen 增強

0200 daily

[ˋdelɪ] ★★★★

形 每日的、日常的

副 每日

名 日報

0201 cannabis

[ˋkænəbɪs] ★

名 印度大麻、大麻煙

同 marijuana 大麻

0202 leukemia

[luˋkimɪə] ★

名 白血病

片 chronic leukemia 慢性白血病

0203 pregnant

[ˋprɛɡnənt] ★★★

形 懷孕的、多產的

片 get sb. pregnant 使某人懷孕

0204 priceless

[ˋpraɪslɪs] ★★

形 貴重的、無價的

同 invaluable 無價的

Fighting!

Give it a shot 小試身手

1 We will have an ＿＿＿ in mathematics tomorrow.

2 The museum is open every day ＿＿＿ Mondays.

3 I can't understand. Can you give me an ＿＿＿?

4 Leaves ＿＿＿ from the trees in the autumn.

5 We should feed the baby ＿＿＿ hour.

Answers: 1 exam 2 except 3 example 4 fall 5 every

018

Essay

 MP3   短文 035   字彙 036

Unlike students from farming[0205] families, less than fifteen percent of urban[0206] students feel happy. In a typical[0207] Taiwanese family, the mother feeds[0208] and educates[0209] the child, and the father works fifty hours a week to pay for his children's education. Most parents find it hard to raise a child. Stress[0210] fills[0211] in their daily lives. They fear their children will lag[0212] behind others and send them to cram schools. Cram schools are fast-growing businesses in Taiwan and have made a fat profit[0213] over the last two decades[0214], especially in February and September, when a new semester[0215] starts.

It's sad to see that parents only focus on school performance. What they only seem to care about is whether their children do well on final exams, not whether they fight or do something bad at school. Few parents care about what their kids do in their leisure[0216] time. Although some parents take their children to the farm on the weekends, for example, others do little or nothing with them. <u>From my point of view</u>, making kids happy is much more important than making them perfect students.

> ⓘ from one's point of view 從某人的立場看來，特別指由於身處不同的身分立場，所以和其他人的看法可能不同

中譯 *Translation*

    和農家家庭的學生不同，都市學生感到快樂的比例低於百分之十五。在傳統的台灣家庭中，母親負責撫養與教育孩子，而父親為了孩子的教育費，一週工作五十個小時。多數的家長都覺得養小孩很不容易。他們的生活每天充斥著壓力。他們害怕孩子會輸人一截而送他們去補習班。補習班在台灣是個快速成長的行業，過去二十年來更是獲利豐厚，尤其在新學期開始的二月和九月。

    看到父母只注重學校課業是很可悲的。他們關心的似乎只有孩子期末考考得好不好，而不在乎他們在校時有沒有打架或做什麼壞事。只有少數家長關心孩子閒暇時做些什麼。舉例來說，雖然有些家長會在假日時帶孩子們去農場走走，但其他家長卻是很少或是完全不會這麼做。就我看來，讓孩子快樂比起當模範生來得重要多了。

0205 farming

[`farmɪŋ] ★★
名 農業、農場經營
同 agriculture 農業

0206 urban

[`ɝbən] ★★★★
形 城市的、住在都市的
片 urban sprawl 城市擴張

0207 typical

[`tɪpɪkl] ★★★★
形 典型的、獨特的
同 representative 典型的

0208 feed

[fid] ★★★★
動 餵養、撫養、滿足
名 一餐、飼料
片 feed on 以…為食

0209 educate

[`ɛdʒə,ket] ★★★
動 教育、培養、訓練
同 instruct 訓練

0210 stress

[strɛs] ★★★★★
名 壓力、緊張、著重
動 強調、使緊張
片 lay stress on 著重於

0211 fill

[fɪl] ★★★★★
動 使充滿、滿足、填滿
名 足夠、填充物
片 fill up 裝滿

0212 lag

[læg] ★★★
動 落後於、衰退
名 落後程度
片 lag behind 落後於

0213 profit

[`prɑfɪt] ★★★★
名 利潤、收益
動 有利、獲益
片 profit from 得益於

0214 decade

[`dɛked] ★
名 十、十年
衍 decennary 十年間的

0215 semester

[sə`mɛstə] ★★★
名 (美)一學期、半學年
同 term (英)學期

0216 leisure

[`liʒə] ★★★★
形 空閒的、業餘的
名 閒暇、安逸
片 at leisure 閒暇時

Fighting!

Give it a shot 小試身手

1. My father owns a _____ in the countryside.
2. Don't eat too much unless you want to get _____.
3. I have a great _____ of dark.
4. John had a big _____ with his brother.
5. The swimming pool is _____ with water.

Answers: 1 farm 2 fat 3 fear 4 fight 5 filled

019

🎧 MP3　短文 037　字彙 038

When you start to get angry, the first thing you should do is to stop and think. In the office, if your subordinates[0217] can't finish the work on time and <u>mess up</u> the schedule[0218], you might want to yell at them and fire[0219] them all. You can choose to either scream at them or calm down and relax. Try to understand what's wrong. If you get mad easily, taking a break and having some fun will help. It's fine to have delicious food, follow[0220] the latest[0221] fashions, join flower-arranging[0222] classes, or get a foot massage. If it is affordable[0223], you can go fishing, or go traveling abroad, flying to beaches in Thailand or elsewhere[0224] to refresh[0225] your mind and body. You will feel like a new person after a trip. Clear the fog[0226] from your mind and try to be nicer to those who work for you. Also, don't forget to give your staff[0227] a high five when they do a good job!

⓵ to mess up sth 把⋯弄壞、搞砸了

中譯 *Translation*

　　當你開始發怒時，第一件事就是要靜下來並思考。在辦公室裡，如果你的下屬無法準時完成工作而搞砸了進度，你或許會想對他們大吼並把他們全都開除。你可以選擇大罵他們，或是冷靜下來放鬆一下，試著瞭解哪裡出了差錯。如果你很容易抓狂，休息一下來點娛樂活動會有幫助。吃美食、追隨最新流行、參加插花課程，或來個腳底按摩都很棒。如果負擔得起的話，去釣魚、或是出國旅行，飛到泰國的沙灘或其他地方消除身心疲勞。在一趟旅行過後，你會覺得自己變成一個全新的人。清除籠罩你內心的濃霧，也試著用更和善的態度對待為你工作的人。同樣地，別忘了當你的下屬有好的表現時和他們來個擊掌歡呼。

0217 subordinate

[səˋbɔrdṇɪt] ★★★
名 部屬、部下
形 下級的、隸屬的
動 使居次要地位

0218 schedule

[ˋskɛdʒʊl] ★★★★
名 計畫表、清單
動 將…列表、安排
片 on schedule 準時

0219 fire

[faɪr] ★★★★★
動 開除、激起、開槍
名 火、熱情、磨難
同 dismiss 開除

0220 follow

[ˋfɑlo] ★★★★★
動 跟隨、密切注意
片 follow through 堅持完成

0221 latest

[ˋletɪst] ★★★★
形 最新的、最遲的
副 最近地
片 at the latest 最晚

0222 arrange

[əˋrendʒ] ★★★★
動 整理、布置、安排、改編、商妥
片 arrange for 為…安排

0223 affordable

[əˋfɔrdəbḷ] ★★★
形 負擔得起的
同 inexpensive 花費不多的

0224 elsewhere

[ˋɛls͵hwɛr] ★★★★
副 在(往)別處
同 anywhere else 其他地方

0225 refresh

[rɪˋfrɛʃ] ★★★★
動 恢復精神、重新振作
片 refresh one's memory 使某人想起

0226 fog

[fɑg] ★★★★
名 霧氣、困惑
動 以霧籠罩、使困惑
片 fog up 蒙上霧氣

0227 staff

[stæf] ★★★★
名 (全體)工作人員、幕僚、支撐
同 personnel 員工

0228 yucky

[ˋjʌkɪ] ★★
形 討人厭的、噁心的
同 revolting 討厭的

Fighting!

Give it a shot 小試身手

1 He had ＿＿＿ the work by ten o'clock this morning.

2 Sunday is the ＿＿＿ day of the week.

3 All the employees ＿＿＿ his lead.

4 I usually go to school on ＿＿＿ instead of by bus.

5 I cannot put up with the yucky⁰²²⁸ ＿＿＿ in this restaurant.

Answers: 1 finished 2 first 3 followed 4 foot 5 food

020

Essay

Mahjong is a game for four players that originated[0229] in China. I have been addicted to mahjong since I was fourteen. It's fun to play mahjong with a few friends on Friday night. After forty rounds, I feel less stress and feel so free; it's like being in a forest[0230] that is full of fresh[0231] air. I forget all about any depressing[0232] things in my life, at least temporarily[0233].

There is a way to bring good luck to yourself when playing mahjong: place a fake[0234] frog in front of the mahjong board[0235]. It can help a player win more money during the game. It's also believed that placing a fork on a mahjong table will make players lose all they have. I've played mahjong for many years and have obeyed[0236] all these traditional customs[0237]. I have won a lot of money from my friends. My Gucci handbag is the fruit of my years of practice.

中譯 Translation

　　麻將是源自於中國的一種四人遊戲。我從十四歲開始就沉迷於麻將。和一群朋友在週五晚上打麻將是很有趣的事。在摸了四十圈之後，我的壓力盡釋，感覺十分暢快，就像置身於滿是新鮮空氣的森林中。我幾乎忘卻了生活中所有令人沮喪的事，至少在那短暫的當下。

　　打麻將時有個方法可以帶來好運：那就是在麻將桌前放一隻假青蛙。這種方法可以幫助玩家贏得更多錢。在麻將桌上放叉子也被認為會讓玩家輸個精光。我玩麻將已經好幾年了，也遵從所有這些傳統習俗。我從朋友那裡贏了許多錢。我的古馳手提包就是我這幾年來練習的成果。

0229 originate

[əˈrɪdʒəˌnet] ★★★
動 發源、引起、產生
片 originate in 源自

0230 forest

[ˈfɔrɪst] ★★★★
名 森林、林區
動 植林於
同 timberland 森林

0231 fresh

[frɛʃ] ★★★★★
形 新鮮的、清新的、無經驗的
片 fresh blood 新成員

0232 depressing

[dɪˈprɛsɪŋ] ★★★
形 令人沮喪的、憂愁的
片 discouraging 令人沮喪的

0233 temporarily

[ˈtɛmpəˌrɛrəlɪ] ★★★
副 暫時地、臨時地
反 permanently 永久地

0234 fake

[fek] ★★★★
形 假的、冒充的
動 偽造、假裝、迷惑
名 冒牌貨、騙子

0235 board

[bord] ★★★★★
名 板、委員會、布告牌
動 上(船、飛機、車)
片 bulletin board 布告欄

0236 obey

[əˈbe] ★★★★
動 聽從、遵守、執行
片 obey an order 服從命令

0237 custom

[ˈkʌstəm] ★★★★
名 習俗、慣例
形 訂製的
衍 Customs 海關

0238 shrub

[ʃrʌb] ★★★
名 灌木、果汁甜酒
片 shrub forest 灌木林

0239 emit

[ɪˈmɪt] ★★★
動 散發、發表、發行
同 give off 發出
反 absorb 吸收

0240 chimney

[ˈtʃɪmnɪ] ★★★
名 煙囪、岩石裂縫
片 smoke like a chimney 抽菸抽得很厲害

Give it a shot 小試身手

1. My father _____ to put salt in the soup.
2. He enjoys _____ coffee every morning.
3. Plant these shrubs[0238] in _____ sun.
4. The smoke is emitting[0239] _____ the chimney[0240].
5. We're going to _____ a friend in hospital.

Answers: 1 forgot 2 free 3 full 4 from 5 visit

021

Essay

Tomorrow we will hold a garden party in our community center, and everyone is thinking about what games we can bring to entertain people. I thought of a good idea to surprise people. <u>In general</u>, <u>when it comes to</u> parties, people normally[0241] think of food and drink vendors[0242], games with prizes[0243], ice cream or popcorn sellers, etc. I am particularly[0244] fond[0245] of scary things; therefore, a ghost house is what I am planning to create, and I will give the ghost house a really scary atmosphere[0246] complete with different themes[0247]. One of my themes is pirates[0248], so I am going to decorate the walls with fake gold, jewelry and glass treasure chests[0249]. I will wear a pair of odd[0250] glasses to scare the girls. I cannot wait to see the scared expressions[0251] on people's faces as they scream, "Oh my God!"

I am happy to arrange such a wonderful party because having fun with my friends is a gas[0252].

ⓘ in general 一般說來、通常
ⓘ when it comes to + ving/sb./sth. 每當提到…

中譯 *Translation*

明天我們將在社區中心舉辦一場花園派對，每個人都在思考要用什麼遊戲來娛樂大家。我有個好主意能帶給大家一個驚喜。通常，每當提到派對時，大家一般都會想到小吃攤、飲料攤、贈獎遊戲、冰淇淋或爆米花攤販等等。我特別喜歡驚悚的主題，所以我打算設計一個鬼屋，也會藉由不同主題讓鬼屋充滿詭譎氣氛。我的其中一項主題是海盜，所以我會用假黃金、珠寶和玻璃寶箱來裝飾牆壁。我還會戴一副古怪的眼鏡來嚇唬女孩們。我迫不及待想看到人們尖叫著：「老天啊！」的驚嚇臉孔。

我很高興能安排這麼一場精彩的派對，因為和朋友同樂是件很愉快的事。

0241 normally

[`nɔrmḷɪ] ★★★★★
副 通常、正常地
同 ordinarily 通常
反 abnormally 反常地

0245 fond

[fɑnd] ★★★★
形 喜歡的、溺愛的
片 be fond of 喜歡、愛好
衍 fondness 鍾愛

0249 chest

[tʃɛst] ★★★★
名 箱子、胸腔、金庫
片 get sth. off one's chest
傾吐心裡的煩惱

0242 vendor

[`vɛndɚ] ★★★
名 小販、自動售貨機
同 seller 賣方

0246 atmosphere

[`ætməs͵fɪr] ★★★★
名 氣氛、大氣、魅力
同 ambience 氣氛、情調

0250 odd

[ɑd] ★★★★
形 奇特的、奇數的
片 odd fish 古怪、舉止反
常的人

0243 prize

[praɪz] ★★★★
名 獎品、獎金
形 得獎的、第一流的
動 重視、評價

0247 theme

[θim] ★★★★
名 主題、話題、文章
同 subject 主題、題目

0251 expression

[ɪk`sprɛʃən] ★★★
名 臉色、表達、措辭
片 find expression in
在…中表現出來

0244 particularly

[pɚ`tɪkjələlɪ] ★★★★
副 特別、詳細地
同 especially 特別

0248 pirate

[`paɪrət] ★★★
名 海盜、剽竊者
動 剽竊、非法翻印
衍 plagiarist 剽竊者

0252 gas

[gæs] ★★★★★
名 快樂的事、氣體、胃
(腸)氣
動 用毒氣殺人、閒聊

Fighting!

Give it a shot 小試身手

1 Our volleyball team won the _____ with ease.

2 This watch was a _____ from my mother.

3 She _____ her sister a lollipop.

4 The steam fogged my _____.

5 Aging of population is a _____ problem nowadays.

Answers: 1 game 2 gift 3 gave 4 glasses 5 general

MP3
短文 043　字彙 044

Essay 022

The Chinese New Year used to be interesting, but it has become less so as we have become older. When we were small children, the Lunar New Year was a grand[0253] event for us. Our grandfathers and grandmothers were generous[0254], giving every grandchild a big red envelope[0255]. However, when we turned thirty, the Lunar[0256] New Year became kind of a gray holiday. Now, every year, we give away a great amount[0257] of money to a group of children and even guests who are not really familiar[0258] to us. When we are past childhood, Chinese New Year holds little charm for us, somewhat like a once lush[0259] grassland that has turned barren[0260] after a drought[0261]. Guess what we plan to do next Chinese New Year? We thought of a good idea and booked[0262] a plane ticket to take a trip overseas. That saved us a lot of money. My husband and I have been dreaming of taking a great vacation for a long time. While traveling, we must remember to bring back some souvenirs[0263], which will make our relatives[0264] and friends happy.

中譯 *Translation*

中國新年向來是很有趣的，但隨著我們年紀漸增後，就再也不是這麼回事了。當我們還是小孩子的時候，農曆新年對我們來說是件盛事。爺爺和奶奶對每個孫子都很慷慨，紅包都給得很大方。然而，當我們到了三十歲，新年就變成一個有點陰鬱的假期。如今每一年，我們發送大量錢財給孩子們，甚至是不太熟的客人。當我們揮別孩提時代，農曆新年對我們來說不再具有吸引力，反而有點像是一塊曾經綠草如茵的草原在乾旱後變成了不毛之地那樣。猜猜我們下個中國新年打算做什麼？我們認為訂張機票到海外旅行是個好主意。那幫我們省下許多錢。我丈夫和我一直夢想著要來趟精彩的假期。旅行時，我們必須得記得帶些紀念品回來，這可以讓我們的親戚朋友們開心一點。

0253 grand

[grænd] ★★★★

形 重要的、雄偉的、全部的

片 grand total 總和

0254 generous

[`dʒɛnərəs] ★★★★

形 慷慨的、豐富的

片 be generous with 在…方面很大方

0255 envelope

[`ɛnvə,lop] ★★★

名 信封、封套、外殼

片 pay envelope 工資袋

0256 lunar

[`lunə] ★★★

形 陰曆的、月球上的、蒼白的

片 lunar eclipse 月蝕

0257 amount

[ə`maunt] ★★★★★

名 總額、數量

動 合計、相當於

同 sum 總數

0258 familiar

[fə`mɪljə] ★★★★

形 熟悉的、親近的

片 be familiar to 某事或某物為某人所熟悉

0259 lush

[lʌʃ] ★★★

形 蒼翠繁茂的、豐富的

名 酒鬼、醉漢

同 drunkard 醉漢

0260 barren

[`bærən] ★★★

形 貧瘠的、不生育的、缺乏的

名 荒漠、貧瘠之地

0261 drought

[draut] ★★★

名 乾旱、(長期)缺乏

同 aridity 乾旱

0262 book

[buk] ★★★★★

動 預訂、登記

名 書籍、著作、帳冊

0263 souvenir

[`suvə,nir] ★★★

名 紀念品

同 remembrance 紀念品

0264 relative

[`rɛlətɪv] ★★★★

名 親戚、親屬

形 相對的、相關的

反 absolute 絕對的

Fighting!

Give it a shot 小試身手

1 Beethoven was a _____ musician.

2 She is the most active member in our _____.

3 That little girl has _____ up into a pretty woman.

4 A constant _____ is never welcome.

5 I am my grandfather's _____.

Answers: 1 great 2 group 3 grown 4 guest 5 grandchild

MP3

短文 045

字彙 046

Essay

023

"Get away, you ugly guy!" Have you ever faced this kind of rejection[0265]? If you are fat and ugly, it's not your fault[0266]. What you need is not a gun to shoot[0267] the mirror, but a guide[0268] to change yourself.

In order to lose weight[0269] successfully, it's necessary[0270] to work out in a gym at least three times a week. Half of the people who try that can only stand it for about the first month. It's hard at the beginning, but once you get through it, you will be used to it. Remember to eat food that is good for your health, like salads, instead of ham and junk food, to reduce[0271] the number of calories[0272] you consume[0273]. Regarding your appearance, don't scare people away with dirty fingernails; manicure[0274] them regularly. Make sure your body is clean from head to toe. Get a stylish haircut at a salon. Changing your hairstyle can dramatically[0275] change the way you look. If you are bald[0276], you can wear a cool hat. Stop hating yourself; create a happy life for yourself. The next time your friend meets you, he or she will say, "You look so wonderful!"

中譯 *Translation*

「滾開，醜八怪！」你是否曾遭到這類的回絕？如果你又胖又難看，這並不是你的錯。你需要的不是一把可以射穿鏡子的槍，而是一個自我改變的嚮導。

為了成功減肥，每週至少必須上健身房三次。半數的人通常撐不過第一個月。起頭的時候很難，但只要你熬過了就會習慣。記得吃對你健康有益的食物，像是沙拉，而非火腿和垃圾食物，以減少熱量的攝取。注重你的外貌，別用骯髒的指甲把人嚇跑，要經常修剪。確定自己從頭到腳都很乾淨。去髮廊剪個時尚的髮型。改變髮型就可以明顯地改變外觀。如果你是個禿頭，你可以戴頂很酷的帽子。不要自怨自艾，為自己創造一個快樂的人生。下回遇到朋友時，他(她)就會說：「你看起來真是棒極了！」

0265 **rejection**

[rɪ`dʒɛkʃən] ★★★
- 名 拒絕、退回、廢棄
- 同 turndown 拒絕

0266 **fault**

[fɔlt] ★★★★
- 名 缺點、錯誤、故障
- 動 挑剔、找毛病
- 片 to a fault 過度地

0267 **shoot**

[ʃut] ★★★★
- 動 發射、拍攝、投射
- 片 shoot sb. on sight
  一看到某人就開槍

0268 **guide**

[gaɪd] ★★★★★
- 名 嚮導、指導、簡介
- 動 指導、管理
- 片 tour guide 導遊

0269 **weight**

[wet] ★★★★★
- 名 體重、負擔
- 動 使變重、壓迫
- 片 carry weight 有影響力

0270 **necessary**

[`nɛsə‚sɛrɪ] ★★★★
- 形 必要的、必然的
- 名 必需品
- 片 if necessary 如果必要

0271 **reduce**

[rɪ`djus] ★★★★
- 動 減少、把…歸納
- 片 reduce to 使降低到

0272 **calorie**

[`kælərɪ] ★★
- 名 卡路里、大卡
- 片 low calorie 低熱量

0273 **consume**

[kən`sjum] ★★★★
- 動 花費、吃光、耗盡
- 片 be consumed with
  為…不斷受折磨

0274 **manicure**

[`mænɪ‚kjur] ★★
- 動 修指甲、修剪
- 名 修指甲、美甲
- 同 trim 修剪

0275 **dramatically**

[drə`mætɪkḷɪ] ★★
- 副 戲劇性地、引人注目地
- 同 theatrically 戲劇化地

0276 **bald**

[bɔld] ★★★
- 形 禿頭的、赤裸裸的、單調的
- 同 hairless 無毛髮的

 Fighting!

Give it a shot 小試身手

1 I got home _____ about half past six.

2 People were in great panic when the earthquake _____.

3 He works _____ in order to earn more money.

4 More and more people now _____ their own houses.

5 My uncle is the _____ of an international corporation.

Answers: 1 at 2 happened 3 hard 4 have 5 head

Essay

024

When the man saw the lady he secretly loved, everything around him seemed to become silent[0277], and he felt like he was on an isolated[0278] hill. He could hear his heart beating[0279]. His body was hot. His steps[0280] became much heavier.

The girl noticed his odd behavior[0281], and she said "Hello." Her smile was as sweet as an angel's. The man felt like he was hit by a stick on his head, and he couldn't help falling into a bottomless[0282] hole. He couldn't hold himself straight or even move any part of his body. He didn't know anything at all about the woman; he just knew she came to the market <u>from time to time</u>. He was too shy to say anything to her, so he just nodded[0283] to her every time they bumped[0284] into each other on the street.

One day, the man realized that it had been a long time since he had seen the woman. He hunted <u>high and low</u> for her, but in vain[0285]. Not finding her, all he could do was regret[0286] his cowardice[0287] very much.

> ⓘ from time to time 有時
> ⓘ high and low 到處

中譯 *Translation*

每當這名男人一看到暗戀的女性時，他身邊的一切似乎都變得悄然無聲，他覺得自己就像置身於一座孤丘上。他可以聽到自己的心跳，身體發燙，腳步變得沉重許多。

女孩注意到他奇怪的舉動，便說了聲：「哈囉！」她的笑容甜美如天使。這個男人就像受到當頭棒喝般，控制不住地向下墜落到一個無底洞裡。他無法挺直身子，全身甚至動彈不得。他對這位小姐一無所知，只知道她有時會到這裡的市場來。他害羞到無法和她攀談，只有在兩人於街頭偶遇的時候對她點點頭。

某天，男子意識到自己已經有好長一段時間未曾見到那名女子。他到處尋找卻徒勞無功。因為找不到她，他只能為自己的膽小後悔不已。

0277 silent

[`saɪlənt] ★★★★

形 沉默的、靜止的

片 be silent about 對⋯隻字不提

0278 isolated

[`aɪsḷˌetɪd] ★★★

形 孤立的、隔離的、偏僻的

同 detached 分離的

0279 beat

[bit] ★★★★★

動 跳動、擊、打敗

俚 beat around the bush 拐彎抹角

0280 step

[stɛp] ★★★★★

名 步伐、足跡、步驟

動 步行、踏進

片 out of step 跟不上

0281 behavior

[bɪ`hevjə] ★★★★

名 行為、(事物的)反應

片 be on one's best behavior 守規矩

0282 bottomless

[`batəmlɪs] ★★

形 深不可測的、無限的

同 abysmal 深不可測的

0283 nod

[nad] ★★★★

動 點頭表示、搖曳

名 點頭、打盹、擺動

片 nod at 向⋯點頭

0284 bump

[bʌmp] ★★★

動 碰撞、猛擊

名 重擊、腫塊

片 bump into 無意中遇到

0285 vain

[ven] ★★★

形 徒勞的、愛虛榮的

同 futile 無益的

片 in vain 徒然地

0286 regret

[rɪ`grɛt] ★★★★

動 懊悔、痛惜、遺憾

名 遺憾、悔恨、悲歎

片 to one's regret 很抱歉

0287 cowardice

[`kauədɪs] ★★

名 膽小、懦弱

同 timidity 膽怯

反 valor 英勇

0288 skyscraper

[`skaɪˌskrepə] ★★

名 摩天大樓、特別高的東西

同 building 建築物

Fighting!

Give it a shot 小試身手

1 I _____ an odd sound from next door.

2 Skyscraper0288 is a very _____ building.

3 Jack lost _____ of the rope and fell to the ground.

4 They have lived _____ over twenty years.

5 I will come here whenever you need my _____.

025

MP3   短文 049   字彙 050

When I was fifteen, during the last summer vacation of junior[0289] high school, I had a huge amount of homework to do and studied ten hours a day to prepare[0290] for exams. It was the most important set of exams for every junior high school student. I spent my whole holiday doing homework and reading hundreds of textbooks[0291] at home. It was in the middle of summer, and the house was hot like a sauna[0292]. Even though I sweated[0293] like a pig, I still kept studying. My parents hoped I would become successful one day. They also believed that I could become a great husband and father in the future, a man who would never let my family go hungry or get hurt. I spared[0294] no effort to live up to their expectations[0295] and my expectations, too. It's human nature to want to have a comfortable life. I knew that how much effort I put in would have a big impact[0296] on how much I could achieve. Because of my efforts, I did very well at school. My parents were very proud[0297] of me.

(!) spare no effort 不遺餘力

(!) live up to 實踐、不辜負

中譯 *Translation*

　　在我十五歲那年，正值國中最後一個暑假，我的課業繁重，每天得唸十小時的書來準備考試。那是對每個國中生而言最重要的考試。我用整個假日的時間在家做功課，苦讀許多參考書。那時正值仲夏，屋內熱得像間蒸氣室。即使我滿身大汗，我還是堅持唸下去。我的父母希望我有朝一日能夠出人頭地。他們也相信我將來可以成為一個好丈夫和好爸爸，不會讓家人挨餓或受傷。我不遺餘力地努力達成他們的期望，同時也是我自己的期望。想擁有舒適的生活是人之常情。我知道我付出的努力，對我的成就高低會有很大的影響。因為我的努力，我得到了很好的成績。父母也都為我感到非常驕傲。

0289 junior

[`dʒunjə] ★★★★
形 資淺的、年紀較輕的
名 晚輩、大三生
反 senior 資深的

0290 prepare

[prɪ`pɛr] ★★★★★
動 準備、籌劃、編纂
片 prepare for 為…作準備

0291 textbook

[`tɛkst,buk] ★★
名 教科書、課本
片 walking textbook 活教材

0292 sauna

[`saunə] ★★
名 蒸汽浴、桑拿浴
片 have a sauna 洗桑拿浴

0293 sweat

[swɛt] ★★★★
動 出汗、焦慮、剝削
名 汗水、水珠、苦差事
片 no sweat 輕而易舉

0294 spare

[spɛr] ★★★★
動 騰出、免去、剩下
形 剩下的、備用的
片 to spare 多餘的

0295 expectation

[,ɛkspɛk`teʃən] ★★★
名 期待、預期、前程
片 fall short of one's expectations 未達期望

0296 impact

[`ɪmpækt] ★★★★
名 衝擊、影響
動 對…產生影響
同 effect 影響

0297 proud

[praud] ★★★★
形 驕傲的、輝煌的
片 be proud of 為…而驕傲

0298 champion

[`tʃæmpɪən] ★★★★
名 冠軍、鬥士
動 擁護、為…而戰
形 優勝的、第一流的

0299 inadvertently

[,ɪnəd`vɝtn̩tlɪ] ★★★
副 不慎地、非故意地
同 absently 心不在焉地

0300 avoid

[ə`vɔɪd] ★★★★★
動 避免、防止、撤銷
用 avoid + ving 避免

---

fighting!

Give it a shot 小試身手

1 We work eight _____ every day.

2 I _____ to see my brother win the champion⁰²⁹⁸.

3 His cruel words inadvertently⁰²⁹⁹ _____ her feelings.

4 We should avoid⁰³⁰⁰ _____ error.

5 Our manager have been on _____ for three days.

Answers: 1 hours 2 hope 3 hurt 4 human 5 holiday

026

 MP3 短文 051 字彙 052

Essay

Bangkok is notorious[0301] for its traffic[0302] jams[0303]. It is not a good idea to drive on the streets in rush hours in Bangkok. If you find yourself driving in that crowded[0304] city, you will most likely be stuck[0305] in a traffic jam for hours and move only one inch every five minutes. The Thai people are also well known for being late, even for job interviews[0306]. This bad habit[0307] is the result of the terrible traffic conditions[0308] in the city. But there's another option: tuk-tuks. A tuk-tuk is a special kind of taxi in Thailand. It has been modified[0309] from a type of Japanese transportation, with more iron bars. It's an important form of transportation in Thailand. Its high mobility[0310] makes it possible to transport passengers[0311] everywhere, even in very small lanes[0312]. Taking a tuk-tuk is worth experiencing for tourists before or after a cup of Thai iced milk tea.

中譯 *Translation*

　　曼谷因交通擁塞而惡名昭彰。尖峰時間在曼谷的街道開車並不是個好主意。如果你發現自己正駛進擁擠的市區，你很有可能會被困在塞車潮中好幾個小時，每五分鐘只前進一點點。泰國人也以遲到聞名，甚至包括工作面試。這種壞習慣是因為市區糟糕的交通狀況所造成的。然而也有另一種選擇：那就是「嘟嘟車」。嘟嘟車是泰國一種特殊形式的計程車。由日本運輸車改裝而成，加上了更多的鐵條，是泰國重要的一種大眾運輸工具。其高度的機動性能將遊客載往任何地方，甚至是非常狹小的巷弄。在搭乘嘟嘟車前或下車後來一杯冰涼的泰式奶茶，對遊客來說非常值得一試。

你不可不知！

　　嘟嘟車是泰國特殊的交通工具之一，和計程車不一樣的是，他不以跳表而是喊價的方式來計算車資。另一項比較煎熬的特色就是沒有空調，所以在炎炎夏日裡還是建議搭計程車，至少有冷氣可以吹，也比較安全。

0301 notorious

[noˋtɔrɪəs] ★★★
形 惡名昭彰的
同 infamous 聲名狼藉的

0302 traffic

[ˋtræfɪk] ★★★★
名 交通、買賣、交流
動 作非法買賣
衍 trafficker 非法買賣者

0303 jam

[dʒæm] ★★★
名 擁擠、堵塞、窘境
動 塞住、使卡住
片 jam in 塞進…

0304 crowded

[ˋkraʊdɪd] ★★★
形 擁擠的、閱歷豐富的
片 be crowded with 擠滿、滿是

0305 stuck

[stʌk] ★★★
形 困住的、無法擺脫的
片 be stuck with 無法擺脫

0306 interview

[ˋɪntɚˌvju] ★★★★
名 面試、接見、採訪
動 訪問、面試、會見
同 meeting 會面

0307 habit

[ˋhæbɪt] ★★★★★
名 習慣、習性、氣質
片 in the habit of 有…的習慣

0308 condition

[kənˋdɪʃən] ★★★
名 情況、環境、條件
動 為…的條件、決定
片 in condition 身體健康

0309 modify

[ˋmadəˌfaɪ] ★★★
動 修改、緩和、修飾
同 alter 修改

0310 mobility

[moˋbɪlətɪ] ★★★
名 流動性、機動性
同 flexibility 靈活性
反 immobility 靜止

0311 passenger

[ˋpæsn̩dʒɚ] ★★★★
名 乘客、旅客
同 rider 搭乘的人

0312 lane

[len] ★★★★
名 巷弄、車道、泳道
片 the fast lane 快車道

Give it a shot 小試身手

Fighting!

1 Health is more _____ than money.

2 My _____ are going cycling and fishing.

3 What caused John to quit his _____?

4 The first day of _____ is a holiday.

5 He _____ his car inside the gate.

Answers: 1 important 2 interests 3 job 4 January 5 parked

027

 MP3　 短文 053　 字彙 054

June and July are the best times to attend[0313] dorm[0314] parties because students are on summer vacation then. In order to keep bringing laughs and joy to the party, there are several kinds of games that are usually played at dorm parties. The Game of King is the most exciting and popular one. The interesting part of the game involves joking about someone's secrets or seeing somebody doing something stupid, like kicking[0315] another person's bottom[0316], running and jumping in an odd way, drinking disgusting[0317] juice mixed[0318] with a variety of odd ingredients, and so on. Food and drinks are key elements[0319] of a wonderful party. If there's not enough time to prepare food, that's fine - just prepare enough alcohol[0320] to make everyone drunk. By the way, make sure that the noise is not too loud. If you wake up the dorm supervisor[0321], he or she will come <u>to put a stop to</u> the fun of the party.

⊘ to put a stop to 使…停止、制止

中譯 *Translation*

　　六月和七月是參加宿舍派對的最佳時機，因為這時學生們正在放暑假。為了讓派對隨時保持笑聲和歡樂，有許多種經常在宿舍派對中玩的遊戲。國王遊戲是最刺激且受歡迎的一種。這種遊戲有趣的地方在於取笑某人不為人知的祕密，或看別人做蠢事，像是踢另一個人的屁股、用怪異的方式跑跑跳跳、喝下混雜多種怪異成分的噁心果汁等等。食物和飲料是一場精彩派對的關鍵要素。如果沒有時間準備食物，沒關係，只要準備足夠的酒精飲料把每個人灌醉。順帶一提，要確認噪音不會太大聲。如果把舍監吵醒，他或她就會來破壞派對的樂趣了。

0313 attend

[əˋtɛnd] ★★★★
動 出席、照料、注意
反 ignore 忽視
片 attend to 關心、注意

0314 dorm

[dɔrm] ★★★
名 宿舍、寢室
同 dormitory 集體宿舍
衍 dormancy 休眠

0315 kick

[kɪk] ★★★★
動 踢、踢進得分
名 踢、反衝、刺激
片 kick off 踢開

0316 bottom

[ˋbɑtəm] ★★★★
名 臀部、底層、盡頭
動 對…追根究柢
片 bottom up 乾杯

0317 disgusting

[dɪsˋgʌstɪŋ] ★★★
形 令人作嘔的
同 nauseous 使人厭惡的

0318 mix

[mɪks] ★★★★
動 使混和、發生牽連
名 混合、結合
片 mix in 摻入、參與

0319 element

[ˋɛləmənt] ★★★★
名 元素、要素、適宜環境
片 in one's element 如魚得水

0320 alcohol

[ˋælkəˌhɔl] ★★★★
名 酒精、含酒精飲料
同 liquor 含酒精飲料

0321 supervisor

[ˌsupəˋvaɪzə] ★★★
名 監督人、指導者
同 conductor 管理人

0322 branch

[bræntʃ] ★★★★
名 樹枝、分公司、分支
動 分支、分岔
片 branch off 偏離

0323 court

[kort] ★★★★★
動 向…獻殷勤、追求
名 法院、場地、庭院
片 go to court 起訴

0324 evidence

[ˋɛvədəns] ★★★★
名 證據、跡象、清楚
動 證明、顯示
片 in evidence 明顯的

Fighting!

Give it a shot 小試身手

1 He never _____ the usual sports of the boys.

2 I _____ up to reach the branch0322.

3 He _____ courting0323 her until she turned him down firmly.

4 The shop sells all _____ of juice.

5 We found the _____evidence0324 to prove his crime.

Answers: 1 joined 2 jump 3 kept 4 kinds 5 key

061

Wulai is a large and mountainous[0325] area with few people and which is known for its beautiful landscape[0326]. It is romantic[0327] to go there with your loved one and spend the weekend at a cottage[0328]. In the morning, you can fly a kite[0329] and walk leisurely on a country road, go fishing by the lake, and watch lambs[0330] running on the grassland. In the evening, you can cook dinner in the kitchen of a cottage and have a candlelight dinner with your lover. Candlelight is better than electric[0331] light because it provides a more romantic atmosphere. It is sure to be an unforgettable[0332] and enjoyable[0333] experience for the both of you. Finally, don't forget to take a bath in the hot spring to relax your knees[0334], ankles[0335] and legs that you have used all day for walking. It's never too late for you to enjoy the beautiful scenery[0336]!

中譯 *Translation*

　　烏來是一個人煙稀少的大型山區，以美景聞名。帶著你心愛的女人在烏來的度假小屋裡度過週末，是非常浪漫的。早晨的時候，你可以放風箏、在鄉間小路悠閒散步、在湖邊釣魚、觀賞在草地上奔跑的羊群。傍晚的時候，你可以在小屋的廚房裡做飯，然後和情人享用一頓燭光晚餐。燭光比日光燈更有情調，因為它賦予了一個更加浪漫的氛圍。對你們倆來說，這的確會是一個難以忘懷又快樂的體驗。最後，別忘了在溫泉裡泡個澡來放鬆膝蓋、腳踝和你用來行走一整天的雙腿。享受大自然之美永遠不嫌晚！

你不可不知！

　　烏來除了老街和泰雅族原住民之外，小編還推薦一個美麗清幽的景點—內洞森林遊樂區。其舊稱為娃娃谷，相傳是該谷多有青蛙叫聲，因此而得名。園內的林相及生態豐富且多變化，烏紗溪瀑布也是園內相當知名的景點。

0325 mountainous

[`mauntənəs] ★★
形 多山的、巨大的
同 hilly 多山丘的

0326 landscape

[`lænd͵skep] ★★★★
名 風景、風景畫
動 美化景觀
同 outlook 景色、風光

0327 romantic

[ro`mæntɪk] ★★★
形 浪漫的、幻想的
名 富浪漫氣息的人
反 realistic 現實的

0328 cottage

[`katɪdʒ] ★★★
名 農舍、小屋、別墅
片 cottage industry 家庭
手工業

0329 kite

[kaɪt] ★★★★
名 風箏、空頭支票
片 fly a kite 放風箏、試探
輿論

0330 lamb

[læm] ★★★★
名 小羊、易上當受騙的人
片 like a lamb 順從地

0331 electric

[ɪ`lɛktrɪk] ★★★★
形 發電的、電動的、令人
震驚的
片 electric shock 電擊

0332 unforgettable

[͵ʌnfɚ`gɛtəbḷ] ★★
形 難以忘懷的
同 memorable 難忘的
反 forgettable 易被忘記的

0333 enjoyable

[ɪn`dʒɔɪəbḷ] ★★★
形 快樂的、有樂趣的
同 delightful 令人愉快的

0334 knee

[ni] ★★★★
名 膝蓋
片 bring to one's knees
迫使某人屈服

0335 ankle

[`æŋkḷ] ★★★
名 腳踝、踝關節
片 sprain one's ankle 扭
傷腳踝

0336 scenery

[`sinərɪ] ★★★
名 景色、舞台布景
片 chew the scenery 演出
過度誇張

Fighting!

Give it a shot 小試身手

❶ I dare not let my father _____ the truth.

❷ Elephants are the hugest animal on the _____.

❸ The manager was _____ for the meeting.

❹ A _____ number of people crowded to see the star.

❺ My father is busy cooking in the _____.

Answers: ❶ know ❷ land ❸ late ❹ large ❺ kitchen

MP3   短文 057   字彙 058

Essay

029

Universities in Western countries are different from those in Taiwan. In Australian⁰³³⁷ universities, for example, there are fewer lectures⁰³³⁸, and teachers let students spend more time thinking and discussing. Teachers lead students to think rather than tell them what to do. It's not necessary to memorize⁰³³⁹ every line of textbooks. Instead, researching and absorbing⁰³⁴⁰ knowledge comprehensively⁰³⁴¹ are more important. Take lessons in law for example: students are encouraged⁰³⁴² to also learn the spirit⁰³⁴³ rather than just the letter of the law. There is a lot more freedom⁰³⁴⁴ at Western universities, and students are encouraged to debate⁰³⁴⁵ issues⁰³⁴⁶, form their own opinions and follow their interests, wherever that may take them. However, students should at least respect⁰³⁴⁷ teachers. In order to become a leader in education, universities in Taiwan should place emphasis on students' independent thinking and the ability to problem solve. Otherwise, our next generation⁰³⁴⁸ will be left behind within the next two decades.

> place/put emphasis on 重視、著重

中譯 *Translation*

　　西方國家的大學和台灣不一樣。舉例來說，澳洲的大學比較少講課，老師會讓學生花更多時間思考和討論。老師引導學生思考，而非告訴他們要做什麼。沒有必要把參考書的內容逐行背起來。相反地，廣泛地研究和吸收知識比較重要。以法律課程為例，老師鼓勵學生去學習法律的精神而非法律的字面條文。在西方大學的課堂上要做什麼都很自由，學生也被鼓勵針對議題來辯論、組織自己的意見、追求自己的興趣，無論那會帶領他們到什麼樣的地方。不過，學生至少應該要尊重老師。為了成為教育的龍頭，台灣的大學應該著重學生獨立思考和解決問題的能力。否則，我們的下一代將會在未來的二十年內落於人後。

0337 Australian

[ɔ`streljən] ★★★

形 澳大利亞(人)的

名 澳大利亞人

0341 comprehensively

[kɑmprɪ`hɛnsɪvlɪ] ★★

副 廣泛地、全面地

衍 comprehend 了解、領會、包含

0345 debate

[dɪ`bet] ★★★

動 辯論、討論、思考

名 爭論、辯論會

同 dispute 爭論、爭執

0338 lecture

[`lɛktʃə] ★★★★

名 授課、演講、教訓

動 講課、教訓

片 lecture at sb. 教訓某人

0342 encourage

[ɪn`kɝɪdʒ] ★★★★

動 鼓勵、激發、支持

片 encourage sb. with sth. 用…方式鼓勵人

0346 issue

[`ɪʃjʊ] ★★★★★

名 問題、爭議、發行物

動 發行、核發

片 at issue 討論中的

0339 memorize

[`mɛmə,raɪz] ★★

動 記住、背熟

片 memorize the lines 記住台詞

0343 spirit

[`spɪrɪt] ★★★★

名 精神、心靈、氣魄

動 鼓勵、拐走

片 in spirit 精神上

0347 respect

[rɪ`spɛkt] ★★★★★

動 尊重、重視、顧及

名 敬重、重視、關係

片 respect for 因…欽佩

0340 absorb

[əb`sɔrb] ★★★

動 吸收、理解、承受

同 assimilate 吸收

片 be absorbed in 專心於

0344 freedom

[`fridəm] ★★★★★

名 自由、解脫、大膽

片 use freedoms with sb. 對某人放肆

0348 generation

[,dʒɛnə`reʃən] ★★★★

名 世代、產生

片 generation gap 代溝

Fighting!

Give it a shot 小試身手

❶ They _____ at my new hairstyle.

❷ The _____ encourage the morale of her members.

❸ You are never too old to_____ .

❹ Please _____ me know if you cannot come.

❹ My left hand has _____ strength than my right hand.

Answers: ❶ laughed ❷ leader ❸ learn ❹ let ❺ less

065

030

Living a life full of lies is like being a lily-livered[0349] wimp[0350] who always tries to escape from danger and never faces problems. It won't take long before the lies are exposed[0351], and it's likely to happen anytime. No matter how perfectly the lies are covered, the truth will <u>come to light</u> one day. When that time comes, no one will listen to the liar ever again. <u>There's a fine line between</u> weakness and bravery, and it depends on whether the person admits his own fault and strives[0352] to compensate[0353] for it. To err[0354] is human, but to lie is a shame.

A little child cheated[0355] on a test and got caught. His lips trembled[0356] nervously, but he didn't lie and faced this problem like a brave lion when confronted[0357] with his cheating. Because of his honesty, his mind progressed[0358] to a higher level. Making the right choice also lifted[0359] his spirit. When the child grew up, he became an <u>A-list</u> celebrity[0360].

(!) come to light 水落石出、真相大白

(!) there's a fine line between A and B A 和 B 之間只有一線之隔

(!) A-list 最好的、最優秀的

中譯 *Translation*

　　過著充滿謊言的人生就像一個總想逃離危險的膽小鬼，從來不肯正視問題。謊言很快就會被揭穿，而且任何時候都有可能發生。不管謊言隱藏得多好，總會有真相大白的一天。等到那個時候，就再也沒有人會聽信一個騙子的話了。軟弱和勇敢之間只有一線之隔，端看這個人是否承認自己的錯誤，並且努力做出補償。犯錯是人之常情，但撒謊卻是恥辱。

　　有個小孩在考試時作弊被抓到。他的嘴唇不安地顫抖著，但他沒有說謊，像隻勇敢的獅子般面對自己作弊的行為。因為他的誠實，他的心靈進展到一個更高的層次。做出正確的選擇同時也提升了他的靈魂。當這個孩子長大後，他成為了社會上一流的成功人士。

0349 lily-livered

[`lɪlɪ`lɪvəd] ★
形 膽怯的
同 craven 怯懦的

0350 wimp

[wɪmp] ★★
名 軟弱無能者
同 chicken 膽小鬼、懦夫

0351 expose

[ɪk`spoz] ★★★★
動 使暴露於、揭發
同 uncover 揭露
片 expose to 暴露於

0352 strive

[straɪv] ★★★★
動 努力、奮鬥、反抗
同 struggle 奮鬥
片 strive for 為…奮鬥

0353 compensate

[`kɑmpən͵set] ★★★
動 補償、酬報、抵銷
片 compensate with 以…來彌補

0354 err

[ɝ] ★★★
動 犯錯、犯罪
片 err rarely 很少出錯
衍 error 錯誤

0355 cheat

[tʃit] ★★★
動 作弊、欺騙、不忠
片 cheat on 作弊、對…不忠

0356 tremble

[`trɛmbl] ★★
動 發抖、擔憂、搖晃
名 發抖、震動
片 tremble with 因…發抖

0357 confront

[kən`frʌnt] ★★★
動 正視、面臨、使對質
片 confront with 使面臨

0358 progress

[prə`grɛs] ★★★★
動 前進、提高、進步
名 進步、進展
片 progress to 進入

0359 lift

[lɪft] ★★★★
動 舉起、振作、抄襲
名 順便搭載、鼓舞
片 lift up 舉起、鼓舞

0360 celebrity

[sɪ`lɛbrətɪ] ★★★★
名 名人、名聲
同 notable 名人

Fighting!

Give it a shot 小試身手

❶ She is _____ to sign the contract.

❷ People _____ up for the autography of the star.

❸ There is a _____ distance between our homes.

❹ We can _____ to music by iPod.

❺ The lady _____ next door is very pretty.

Answers: ❶ likely ❷ line ❸ long ❹ listen ❺ living

031

🎧 MP3   短文 061   字彙 062

Essay

I love to visit Thailand. I can find my way around there without a map[0361]. The best time to visit Thailand is from October to March, when the weather is not too hot. There are a lot of places to visit in Bangkok. The floating[0362] market is the most interesting place where many food and drink vendors are on boats. I <u>am mad about</u> spicy[0363] food, and chili is indispensable[0364] for my breakfast, lunch and dinner. I'm always looking for something special and cheap in the market; sometimes I'm lucky enough to find a treasure[0365].

Thai girls have beautiful eyes and skinny figures, but some of them were originally[0366] men. I used to meet a pretty "girl," who impressed[0367] me very much, beside a vending[0368] machine. I plucked[0369] up my courage to ask for her email address, and she answered in a very deep and loud voice. I was shocked but quickly collected[0370] myself. I think making friends with a Thai is not bad. It doesn't matter[0371] if you make friends with a man or a woman. Going to Thailand is indeed a cool experience.

❗ be mad about 對⋯著迷、對⋯狂熱

中譯 *Translation*

　　我喜歡到泰國旅行。在那裡我可以不需要地圖。探訪泰國最好的時間是十月到三月，那時天氣不會太熱。曼谷有很多地方可以參觀。水上市場是最有趣的一項，許多小吃攤和飲料攤都在船上。我熱愛辣食，辣椒是我三餐必備的東西。我總是在市集裡尋找一些特別又便宜的東西，有時候我可以很幸運地發現奇珍異寶。

　　泰國女孩有著漂亮的眼睛和骨感的身材，但其中有些本來是男人。我曾經在販賣機旁遇過一個讓我印象非常深刻的漂亮「女孩」。我鼓起勇氣向她要電子信箱，她卻用非常低沉又響亮的聲音回答我。我當時很震驚，但很快就恢復理智。我覺得和泰國人交朋友並不壞，不管是男人或女人都無所謂了。到泰國旅遊的確是個很酷的體驗。

0361 map

[mæp] ★★★★★
名 地圖
動 繪製地圖、勘測
片 map out 擬定、安排

0362 floating

[`flotɪŋ] ★★
形 漂浮的、流動的
同 afloat 飄浮著的
反 fixed 固定的

0363 spicy

[`spaɪsɪ] ★★★
形 辛辣的、有香料味的、下流的
同 piquant 辛辣的

0364 indispensable

[ˌɪndɪs`pɛnsəbḷ] ★★★
形 不可或缺的
同 essential 必要的
反 dispensible 可有可無

0365 treasure

[`trɛʒɚ] ★★★★
名 珍寶、財富
動 珍視、銘記
片 treasure hunt 尋寶遊戲

0366 originally

[ə`rɪdʒənlɪ] ★★
副 起初、原先、獨創地、新穎地
同 initially 最初、開頭

0367 impress

[ɪm`prɛs] ★★★★
動 給…極深印象
名 印記、印象
片 impress on 印壓於

0368 vend

[vɛnd] ★
動 出售、販賣
片 vending machine 自動販賣機

0369 pluck

[plʌk] ★★★
動 摘、拔、拉、扯
名 撥、拉、勇氣
片 pluck up 鼓起、振作

0370 collect

[kə`lɛkt] ★★★★
動 使鎮定、收集、聚積
片 collect sb's wit 恢復理智

0371 matter

[`mætɚ] ★★★★★
動 要緊、有關係
名 事情、問題、素材
片 a matter of 大約

0372 postcard

[`post͵kɑrd] ★★★
名 明信片
片 send/drop a postcard 寄明信片

fighting!

Give it a shot 小試身手

❶ He ＿＿＿ handsome in that blue shirt.

❷ The desk is too ＿＿＿ for me to use.

❸ There were ＿＿＿ fights between the two countries.

❹ You can buy some fresh fish in the ＿＿＿.

❺ He ＿＿＿ a postcard0372 to his friend.

Answers: ❶ looks ❷ low ❸ many ❹ market ❺ mailed

MP3
短文 063
字彙 064

Essay

032

I will join a dance audition[0373] in May. It matters to my future very much. I may become famous and meet many professional[0374] dancers around the world. On the other hand, if I fail, it might be the last time I ever dance. Dancing is my passion and also my career, but I haven't made a lot of money from it. I am thirty years old and about to marry soon. If I miss this shot[0375], it means I'll lose my job.

My expertise[0376] is hip-hop[0377] dance; my movements[0378] match[0379] the beat perfectly. In order to have a perfect shape, I only eat chicken breast[0380], drink two glasses of milk every morning, and run ten miles a day. I do yoga for fifteen minutes in the middle of a rehearsal[0381] to release[0382] my stress. I have a strong passion for what I'm doing, and I will do my best to excel[0383] during the coming[0384] challenge.

中譯 *Translation*

　　我五月要參加一場舞蹈甄選。這對我的未來意義重大，我或許會成名，也會遇見許多來自世界各地的職業舞者。另一方面，如果我失敗了，這或許會是我最後一次跳舞。我熱愛舞蹈，這同時也是我的職業，但我還沒有因為跳舞而賺大錢。我已經三十歲，而且即將結婚。一旦我錯失良機，就意味著我將失去工作。

　　我是一個專業的嘻哈舞者，我的動作和節拍搭配得天衣無縫。為了擁有完美的體態，我只吃雞胸肉，每天早上喝兩杯牛奶，一天跑步十英里。我會在彩排過程中做十五分鐘的瑜伽，以消除自己的壓力。我對我所做的事充滿熱情，並且會在即將來臨的挑戰中傾盡全力獲勝。

你不可不知！

　　最初的街舞主要是為配合嘻哈音樂而做出的有節奏感的動作，起源於1970年代美國貧民區的街頭。但現今因為其他音樂類型興起，導致新舞蹈形式的出現，演變為一系列舞蹈形式的總稱。

0373 audition

[ɔ`dɪʃən] ★★
- 名 試鏡、試聽、聽力
- 動 進行試演、試唱
- 片 audition for …的試鏡

0374 professional

[prə`fɛʃənl] ★★★★
- 形 職業性的、內行的
- 名 職業選手、行家
- 片 amateur 業餘的

0375 shot

[ʃat] ★★★★★
- 名 嘗試、射擊、注射
- 形 (口)破舊的、用壞的
- 片 big shot 大人物

0376 expertise

[,ɛkspə`tiz] ★★★★
- 名 專門知識、專門技術
- 同 skill 專門技術
- 片 expertise in …的知識

0377 hip-hop

[`hiphap] ★★
- 名 說唱的嘻哈文化
- 片 hip-hop music 嘻哈音樂

0378 movement

[`muvmənt] ★★★★
- 名 動作、傾向、行動
- 同 motion 運動、移動

0379 match

[mætʃ] ★★★★
- 動 和…相稱、比得上
- 名 競賽、對手
- 片 match up to 與…一致

0380 breast

[brɛst] ★★★★
- 名 胸部、乳房、心情
- 動 挺胸面對、抵抗
- 同 bosom 胸、乳房

0381 rehearsal

[rɪ`hɝsl] ★★★
- 名 排練、彩排、詳述
- 同 practice 練習
- 片 in rehearsal 排演中

0382 release

[rɪ`lis] ★★★★
- 動 釋放、豁免、發行
- 名 解放、發表、流露
- 片 release from 從…釋放

0383 excel

[ɪk`sɛl] ★★★★
- 動 勝過、優於、擅長
- 同 surpass 勝過、優於
- 片 excel at 擅長

0384 coming

[`kʌmɪŋ] ★★★★
- 形 即將到來的、接著的
- 名 到來、來臨
- 片 have it coming 活該

---

fighting!

Give it a shot 小試身手

1. My sister is going to _____ next month.

2. Your blouse _____ the skirt very much.

3. It took ten _____ to the station.

4. Susan is the best professor in my _____.

5. Put the sofa in the _____ of the living room.

Answers: ① marry ② matches ③ minutes ④ mind ⑤ middle

Essay 033

Miss Chiu wanted to be a successful singer and songwriter. Unfortunately, her mother did not support[0385] her. Without financial support from her family, she was out of money. She lived alone in a small apartment. She practiced the keyboard and guitar in her bedroom in the morning, every single day of the week. The more music she created, the more passion she gained[0386]. After working hard for one month, she had improved a lot and written the most beautiful melody[0387]. After that, she realized she had <u>a mountain of</u> dirty clothes to wash, and her bedroom was full of garbage[0388] that occasionally[0389] attracted mice. She had not taken a shower for a week, and she smelled[0390] bad; even her mouth stank[0391]. However, she was <u>over the moon</u> with her new song and jumped joyfully[0392] like a monkey. She released her first album[0393], and it reached a high position[0394] on Billboard. No one should miss any chance to pursue[0395] his or her dreams.

ⓘ a mountain of 堆積如山、大量的

ⓘ over the moon 欣喜若狂

中譯 Translation

邱小姐想要成為一位成功的歌手和詞曲創作人。不幸的是，她媽媽並不支持她。沒有家庭的經濟支援，她窮得身無分文。她目前獨自居住在一間小公寓裡。從週一到週日的每個早晨，她都在房間練習彈奏鍵盤樂器和吉他。她創作出越多音樂，就會產生更多熱情。努力工作一個月之後，她進步了更多，寫出了最美麗的旋律。而在這之後她才發現，她有堆積如山的髒衣服要洗，她的臥室積滿了垃圾，還有老鼠不時會來光顧一下。她已經一個禮拜沒洗澡了，身體實在臭得要命，連口氣也很差。但她為她新歌的誕生欣喜若狂，並像猴子般開心地跳來跳去。她發行了第一張專輯，成為榜上前幾名的暢銷歌手。每個人都不該錯過任何追夢的機會。

0385 support

[sə`port] ★★★★★
動 支持、擁護、扶養
名 支撐、維持生計
片 in support of 支持

0386 gain

[gen] ★★★★
動 得到、增添、獲利
名 獲得、收益
片 gain ground 取得進步

0387 melody

[`mɛlədɪ] ★★★
名 歌曲、旋律、美妙的音樂
同 tune 曲調、旋律

0388 garbage

[`gɑrbɪdʒ] ★★★
名 垃圾、剩菜、廢話、無聊作品
同 rubbish 垃圾

0389 occasionally

[ə`keʒənlɪ] ★★
副 偶而、間或
同 now and then 有時
片 very occasionally 難得

0390 smell

[smɛl] ★★★★
動 發出…氣味、嗅到
名 氣味、臭味、跡象
片 smell out 嗅出、發現

0391 stink

[stɪŋk] ★★★
動 發惡臭、名聲臭
名 臭氣、大吵大鬧
片 stink out 充滿臭氣

0392 joyfully

[`dʒɔɪfəlɪ] ★★
副 喜悦地、高興地
同 gleefully 歡欣地
反 joyless 沉悶無趣的

0393 album

[`ælbəm] ★★★
名 唱片集、相簿、(美)來賓簽到簿
片 stamp album 集郵簿

0394 position

[pə`zɪʃən] ★★★★
名 位置、身分、立場
動 安置、定位
片 in position 在適當位置

0395 pursue

[pɚ`su] ★★★★
動 追求、追捕、進行
反 flee 逃避
片 pursue after 追趕

0396 resume

[͵rɛzju`me] ★★★★
名 (美)履歷、摘要
動 重新開始、繼續
片 resume + ving 繼續

Fighting!

Give it a shot 小試身手

❶ _____ makes mare go.

❷ Do not blame others for small _____.

❸ I went jogging this _____.

❹ What she cares _____ is her test score.

❺ He _____ off his resume⁰³⁹⁶ a month ago.

Answers: ❶ Money ❷ mistakes ❸ morning ❹ most ❺ sent

073

034

Essay

My name is David Brown. My grandparents, Mr. and Mrs. Brown, are friendly⁰³⁹⁷ and gracious⁰³⁹⁸ old people, living in a small town near Dallas, Texas. They moved there in 1986. My grandparents love nature⁰³⁹⁹, so there is a great view at the back of their house. They don't spend much money on the house, but their simple⁰⁴⁰⁰ home is comfortable. Grandpa is a retired⁰⁴⁰¹ army⁰⁴⁰² solider, contributing⁰⁴⁰³ his whole life to the nation. He is a heavy⁰⁴⁰⁴ smoker; he must smoke two packs of cigarette and drink two mugs⁰⁴⁰⁵ of coffee every day. Grandpa is also an artist. He loves war movies and jazz music. My girlfriend, Amanda, and I made the long trip by car to visit my grandparents last weekend. After eight hours driving along country roads, the car was covered⁰⁴⁰⁶ in mud, and my neck was sore⁰⁴⁰⁷. But we had a great time there with the beautiful scenery and delicious food. I wished I could have stayed there for the rest of my life.

中譯 *Translation*

　　我的名字是大衛·布朗。我的祖父母，布朗先生和布朗太太都是友善且慈祥的老人家，住在一個靠近德州達拉斯的小城鎮。他們於1986年搬到那裡。我的祖父母喜愛大自然，因此他們的家後面有著一片美景。他們並沒有砸很多錢在房子上，卻是簡單舒適。祖父是一名退休的軍人，畢生都奉獻給國家。他是個老菸槍，每天都要抽兩包煙、喝兩杯咖啡。祖父也是個藝術家。他喜歡戰爭片和爵士樂。我女朋友亞曼達和我上個週末開長途車到我祖父母的家拜訪。沿著鄉間小路開了八小時後，我的車泥濘不堪，我的脖子也痠痛得很。但我們有美景和美食相伴，度過了愉快的時光。我希望我的餘生都可以在那裡度過。

0397 friendly

[ˋfrɛndlɪ] ★★★★
形 友好的、贊成的
同 genial 親切的
片 be friendly to 對…友善

0398 gracious

[ˋgreʃəs] ★★★
形 親切的、慈祥的
慣 Good gracious!/
Gracious me! 天啊！

0399 nature

[ˋnetʃə] ★★★★★
名 大自然、簡樸、天性
片 in one's nature 是某人
的本性

0400 simple

[ˋsɪmpl] ★★★★★
形 簡單的、樸實的、笨的
慣 (置於所指名詞後) pure
and simple 純粹的

0401 retired

[rɪˋtaɪrd] ★★★★
形 退休的
同 emeritus 榮譽退職的
動 retire 退休、退隱

0402 army

[ˋɑrmɪ] ★★★★
名 陸軍、大批、團體
反 navy 海軍
片 be in the army 當兵

0403 contribute

[kənˋtrɪbjut] ★★★
動 貢獻、捐助、投稿
同 donate 捐獻
片 contribute to 捐獻

0404 heavy

[ˋhɛvɪ] ★★★★★
形 大量的、重的、劇烈的
反 slight 輕微的
片 heavy hand 高壓手段

0405 mug

[mʌg] ★★★★
名 一杯的量、惡棍
動 扮鬼臉、拼命用功
片 mug up 死記硬背

0406 cover

[ˋkʌvə] ★★★
動 覆蓋、適用於、報導
名 (書)封面、保險
片 cover for 代替、頂替

0407 sore

[sor] ★★★★
形 痛的、痠痛的、身心的
名 (身、心)痛處、傷口
片 sore throat 喉嚨痛

0408 colony

[ˋkɑlənɪ] ★★★★
名 殖民地、僑居地、群體
片 develop a colony 開發
殖民地

Fighting!

Give it a shot 小試身手

1 I was _____ to receive such a welcome here.
2 The mother loves her baby very _____.
3 My apartment is _____ the school.
4 You _____ clean up your room right now.
5 The colony⁰⁴⁰⁸ became an independent _____ a decade ago.

Answers: 1 moved 2 much 3 near 4 must 5 nation

MP3 短文 069 字彙 070

035

Essay

We may never need to buy a newspaper or watch news on TV in the future. The Internet has revolutionized[0409] our lives, and this technology will get better and better in the next ten years. There are about 1.9 billion Internet users in the world. Ninety percent of these users are under forty, and the number of users under 19 is surging[0410]. Neither time nor space will be limited[0411]. We can have a business meeting at night via webcams[0412] and e-whiteboards, or have a cocktail[0413] party at noon and broadcast[0414] it live to branches around the world. Twenty years ago, personal computers were notorious for their loud noise and heavy weight. The computers we have now are smaller and faster, more powerful and attractive, and quieter. The potential[0415] for development of computers and the Internet is infinite[0416]. Have you ever heard of "cloud computing"? That is another improvement. We can do everything online wherever we are with numerous[0417] devices rather than be restricted[0418] to processing the data[0419] at home. However, no matter how incredible technology becomes, there is no substitute[0420] for the human brain.

中譯 *Translation*

　　未來我們也許再也不需要買報紙或在電視上看新聞。網際網路徹底改變了我們的生活，這項科技在未來十年之內，還會變得越來越好。全世界有將近十九億的網路用戶。超過百分之九十的使用者都在四十歲以下，而且十九歲以下的使用者數量一直不斷攀升。無論是時間或空間都不會再受到限制。我們可以在夜裡透過視訊和電子白板開企業會議，或在中午時開雞尾酒派對，並實況轉播給世界各地的分公司看。二十年前，個人電腦因噪音和笨重而為人詬病。我們現在所用的電腦不僅小得多也快得多、功效更強大且更吸引人、也更安靜了。電腦和網路的發展潛能無窮盡。你有聽過「雲端運算」嗎？那又是另一項進展。無論我們身處何方，我們都可以利用許多裝置上網做任何事情，而不用受限在家裡處理資料。然而，不管科技多麼令人難以置信，還是無法取代人腦。

0409 revolutionize

[ˌrɛvəˈluʃənˌaɪz] ★★
- 動 徹底改革
- 同 overturn 推翻
- 衍 revolution 革命

0410 surge

[sɝdʒ] ★★★
- 動 激增、洶湧、澎湃
- 名 大浪、洶湧、澎湃
- 同 soar 猛增

0411 limit

[ˈlɪmɪt] ★★★★
- 動 限制、限定
- 名 界線、極限、範圍
- 片 limit...to 把…限制在

0412 webcam

[ˈwɛbkæm] ★
- 名 網路攝影機，亦作 web camera

0413 cocktail

[ˈkɑkˌtel] ★★★
- 名 雞尾酒、(西餐)開胃品
- 片 seafood cocktail 涼拌海鮮

0414 broadcast

[ˈbrɔdˌkæst] ★★★★
- 動 廣播、播放
- 名 廣播、廣播節目
- 同 circulate 流傳

0415 potential

[pəˈtɛnʃəl] ★★★★★
- 名 可能性、潛力
- 形 潛在的、可能的

0416 infinite

[ˈɪnfənɪt] ★★★
- 形 無限的、極大的
- 名 無限、無窮
- 同 limitless 無限的

0417 numerous

[ˈnjumərəs] ★★★★
- 形 許多的、為數眾多的
- 同 abundant 大量的
- 反 few 幾乎沒有的

0418 restrict

[rɪˈstrɪkt] ★★★
- 動 限制、約束
- 同 confine 限制
- 片 restric...to 把…限制在

0419 data

[ˈdetə] ★★★★★
- 名 數據、資料
- 同 information 資訊
- 片 data on …的數據

0420 substitute

[ˈsʌbstəˌtjut] ★★★
- 名 代替品、代用品
- 動 代替、代理
- 片 substitute for 代替

Fighting!

Give it a shot 小試身手

1. She _____ practices what she has said.
2. There is neither river _____ stream nearby.
3. He did not sleep well last _____.
4. The nurse called the _____ patient.
5. No _____ is good _____.

Answers: 1 never 2 nor 3 night 4 next 5 news

036

MP3　短文 071　字彙 072

Polar bears live in the ocean near the North Pole. The number of polar bears, however, is declining[0421]. The warning from the International Union for the Conservation[0422] of Nature (IUCN) notes[0423] that global warming is now the most significant threat to the polar bears. A polar bear has a sensitive[0424] nose that can detect[0425] food from a long distance. Polar bears spend most of their lives off the land for hunting, breeding and nursing their young.

However, as their prey[0426] diminishes[0427], it is very likely they will kill each other for food. What a tragedy that humans have brought about! Meanwhile, October is a great time to visit the North Pole. Cubs[0428] are born between November and February, but it's not O.K. to feed them. Polar bears look adorable, but that cuteness hides their real nature. Polar bears are stealthy[0429] hunters, and the victim is often unaware of the bears' presence[0430] until the attack is underway[0431]. You can even be attacked at four o'clock in the morning when you are asleep. They are carnivores[0432], after all.

中譯 *Translation*

北極熊住在靠近北極的海域。然而北極熊的數量卻正在減少中。世界自然保護聯盟發出警告，指出全球暖化是目前對北極熊最主要的威脅。北極熊有著靈敏的嗅覺，所以牠們可以從很遠的地方就察覺到食物的存在。北極熊大半輩子都在陸地上狩獵、繁殖和餵養下一代。

然而，隨著牠們的獵物減少，牠們非常有可能會自相殘殺。這正是人類帶來的悲劇啊！與此同時，十月是造訪北極的好時節。幼熊是在十一月到二月之間出生，但是不能餵食。北極熊看起來很可愛，但可愛的外型隱藏了牠們的天性。北極熊是鬼鬼祟祟的獵人，受害者往往察覺不到牠們的存在，直到攻擊的那一刻。你甚至可能在清晨四點的睡夢中遭到襲擊。畢竟牠們是肉食性動物啊！

0421 decline

[dɪ`klaɪn] ★★★★
- 動 下降、衰退、婉拒
- 名 下降、衰退、晚年
- 片 on the decline 在衰退

0422 conservation

[ˌkɑnsə`veʃən] ★★★
- 名 保存、保護、守恆
- 同 preservation 保護
- 反 decay 腐朽

0423 note

[not] ★★★★
- 動 提到、注意到、記下
- 名 筆記、紙幣、口氣
- 片 take note of 留意

0424 sensitive

[`sɛnsətɪv] ★★★★
- 形 靈敏的、敏感的
- 同 susceptible 敏感的
- 衍 sensible 意識到的

0425 detect

[dɪ`tɛkt] ★★★★
- 動 察覺、看穿
- 同 spy 察覺、發現
- 片 detect in 在…中察覺到

0426 prey

[pre] ★★★
- 名 獵物、犧牲者、捕食
- 動 掠食、折磨
- 片 prey on 捕食

0427 diminish

[də`mɪnɪʃ] ★★★
- 動 減少、縮減、失勢
- 同 curtail 縮減
- 片 diminish by 因…減少

0428 cub

[kʌb] ★★
- 名 幼獸、毛頭小子、新手
- 同 greenhorn 新手
- 片 cub scout 幼童軍

0429 stealthy

[`stɛlθɪ] ★★
- 形 鬼鬼祟祟的、悄悄的
- 同 sneaky 鬼鬼祟祟的

0430 presence

[`prɛzn̩s] ★★★★
- 名 存在、出席、風度
- 同 attendance 出席
- 片 presence of mind 鎮定

0431 underway

[ˌʌndə`we] ★★
- 形 進行中的、不斷發展的
- 同 ongoing 進行的
- 片 get underway 啟動

0432 carnivore

[`kɑrnəˌvɔr] ★★
- 名 肉食動物
- 關 omnivore 雜食動物
- 反 herbivore 食草動物

fighting!

Give it a shot 小試身手

1 A ＿＿＿ of people protested against the policy.

2 A cold wind ＿＿＿ from the north.

3 She looked at the blue ＿＿＿ and the boats on the surface.

4 ＿＿＿ can change the facts.

5 Did you ＿＿＿ the stranger in our classroom?

Answers: 1 number 2 blew 3 ocean 4 Nothing 5 notice

037

Essay

 MP3 短文 073 字彙 074

Taiwan's government workers <u>are known for</u> their bureaucracy[0433]. They often have higher salaries[0434] but may do less work than employees in private companies. That type of lazy behavior will get you fired in the private sector[0435].

In contrast[0436], people who work at non-governmental jobs often need to work long hours. Moreover, due to downturns[0437] in the economy, they sometimes need to worry about being laid off, which is quite stressful[0438]. The best strategy[0439] for the average worker is to constantly upgrade[0440] his or her knowledge and skills to be able to find work in the event they are laid off. Although it's possible for government employees to also be laid off, working for the government typically provides more job security[0441] and benefits[0442]. That's why so many people want to get a job with the government. Good job security, excellent benefits and pensions[0443], and less stress are things that appeal[0444] to many people.

> ⓘ be known for 以…而眾所周知

中譯 *Translation*

　　台灣的政府官員以官僚主義聞名。他們通常擁有較高的薪水，但工作量卻比私人企業的員工來得少。那種怠惰的行為會讓你在私人企業中遭解雇。

　　相較之下，在非政府機關工作的人通常需要工作較長時間。此外，由於經濟衰退，他們有時還必須擔心自己是否會被裁員，壓力相當大。對一般工作者來說，最好的對策就是不斷提升自己的學識和能力，讓自己在遭到裁員時還有辦法找到工作。雖然政府機關的員工也有可能遭裁員，但為政府工作基本上提供了更多的就業保障及福利。這就是為什麼有那麼多人想進入政府機關工作。好的工作保障、優厚的福利及退休金，以及更少的壓力是吸引許多人的原因。

0433 bureaucracy

[bjuˋrɑkrəsɪ] ★★★
名 官僚政治、繁文縟節
同 officialdom 官場、官僚主義

0434 salary

[ˋsælərɪ] ★★★
名 薪資
動 給…薪水
片 on a salary of 薪水為

0435 sector

[ˋsɛktə] ★★★★
名 部門、部分、扇形
動 把…分成部分

0436 contrast

[ˋkɑn͵træst] ★★★★
名 對比、對照、反差
動 使成對比
片 in contrast 相較之下

0437 downturn

[ˋdaʊntɜn] ★★
名 衰退、下降、低迷
同 recession 衰退
反 upturn 情況好轉

0438 stressful

[ˋstrɛsfəl] ★★★
形 充滿壓力的、緊張的
同 tense 緊張的

0439 strategy

[ˋstrætədʒɪ] ★★★★
名 對策、戰略、計謀
同 tactics 策略、手段
片 strategy for …的策略

0440 upgrade

[ʌpˋgred] ★★★
動 使升級、提高
名 升級、提高標準
反 downgrade 使降級

0441 security

[sɪˋkjʊrətɪ] ★★★★
名 保障、安全、債券
同 safety 安全
片 high security 嚴密保護

0442 benefit

[ˋbɛnəfɪt] ★★★★
名 津貼、利益、優勢
動 對…有益、受惠
片 benefit from 因…獲益

0443 pension

[ˋpɛnʃən] ★★★
名 退休金、撫恤金
片 draw a pension 領退休金

0444 appeal

[əˋpil] ★★★★
動 有吸引力、訴諸、上訴
名 呼籲、吸引力
片 appeal to 向…呼籲

Fighting!

Give it a shot 小試身手

1. _____ you give up, our efforts are all in vain.
2. Tom _____ wears a pair of brown shoes.
3. He took the TOEIC test in _____ to get promotion.
4. Work and play do not contradict each _____.
5. He took _____ a bill from the right pocket.

Answers: ❶ Once ❷ often ❸ order ❹ other ❺ out

038

MP3　短文 075　字彙 076

Essay

Last Friday night, I went to a party with my friends at a famous club in the city. My parents don't know about it, and they would probably kill me if they ever found out, because I'm only fourteen. Obviously[0445], I don't have my own car, so I sneaked[0446] out of the house at night with my papa's car. At the parking lot outside the club, my friends made fun of my outfit for I wore a pair of my grandpa's pants. I paid more money to the guy at the club entrance[0447] so I could get in with a fake ID. The club looked fancy and stylish; it was painted all pink. That night, I talked to an attractive[0448] girl, but when my friend passed[0449] me a drink, I accidentally[0450] spilt[0451] my drink all over the girl's T-shirt, soaking[0452] not only the shirt but her jeans[0453] as well. She was so mad, and I ran to the restroom[0454] to get some toilet[0455] paper for her. My friend wrote this embarrassing[0456] story in his blog so we could remember our crazy night.

(!) make fun of 取笑、嘲笑
(!) flying colors 非常出色

中譯 *Translation*

　　上禮拜五晚上，我和朋友去城裡一間知名的俱樂部狂歡。我的父母並不知情，如果他們知道一定會殺了我，因為我才十四歲而已。顯然地，我沒有自己的車，所以我在夜裡開著爸爸的車偷偷溜出家裡。在俱樂部外的停車場，朋友嘲笑我的打扮，因為我把爺爺的長褲穿來了。我多付了些錢給守在俱樂部入口的傢伙，如此一來我就能拿到假證件入場。俱樂部看起來很奢華時尚，牆壁全漆成了粉紅色。那晚我和一個迷人的女孩聊天。但當我朋友遞飲料給我時，我不小心把它全打翻在女孩的T恤上，不僅是衣服連她的牛仔褲也都濕透了。她幾乎要抓狂了，我就跑去廁所拿些衛生紙給她。我朋友把這樁糗事寫在他的部落格上，紀念我們這瘋狂的一晚。

0445 obviously

[`ɑbvɪəslɪ] ★★★★

副 明顯地、顯然地

同 evidently 顯然

0446 sneak

[snik] ★★★

動 偷溜、偷偷地做

名 鬼鬼祟祟的人、溜走

片 sneak out 偷溜出

0447 entrance

[`ɛntrəns] ★★★★

名 入口、登場、入學許可

動 使陶醉、使狂喜

片 entrance to …的入口

0448 attractive

[ə`træktɪv] ★★★

形 吸引人的、有魅力的

同 charming 迷人的

反 repulsive 令人厭惡的

0449 pass

[pæs] ★★★★★

動 傳遞、通過、消失

名 經過、通行證、及格

片 pass out 分發、分配

0450 accidentally

[͵æksə`dɛntḷɪ] ★★

副 意外地、偶然地

片 accidentally on purpose 故意卻裝無心

0451 spill

[spɪl] ★★★

動 濺出、溢出、洩密

名 濺出、湧出、暴跌

片 spill out 溢出

0452 soak

[sok] ★★★

動 濕透、浸漬、吸收

名 浸泡、爛醉

片 soak through 滲透

0453 jeans

[dʒinz] ★★★★

名 牛仔褲、工裝褲

同 overalls (寬大)工作褲

片 wear jeans 穿牛仔褲

0454 restroom

[rɛstrum] ★★

名 公共廁所、洗手間、休息室

同 toilet 廁所

0455 toilet

[`tɔɪlɪt] ★★★★

名 廁所、盥洗室、沖洗式馬桶

片 flush the toilet 沖馬桶

0456 embarrassing

[ɪm`bærəsɪŋ] ★★★

形 尷尬的、令人為難的

同 awkward 尷尬的

動 embarrass 使尷尬

fighting!

Give it a shot 小試身手

1 I didn't want to share my _____ room with others.

2 We had a lot of fun at the _____ last night.

3 I _____ the test in English with <u>flying colors</u>.

4 He forgot to _____ the tuition fee.

5 When he was a child, his _____ divorced.

Answers: **1** own **2** party **3** passed **4** pay **5** parents

039

Essay

I live in a lavish[0457] villa[0458]. People envy[0459] its luxury very much because living in one is really <u>a pie in the sky</u> dream for them. As you can see, I am a successful person, especially for someone so young.

I have a special pet in my house, a mini-pig. I keep it in my beautiful backyard[0460] with blooming[0461] plants all around. I have spent five hundred thousand dollars on gardening[0462]. In my leisure time, I play piano in my own studio[0463] at home and regularly invite[0464] all of the professional piano and guitar players I know to my house. I drew a picture of my mini-pig with a pencil last week, and I plan to place[0465] it in the living room beside my collection[0466] of Montblanc pens. I had a lavish party last night. We drank <u>first growth</u> French red wine and smoked[0467] Cuban cigars[0468]. Next week, I'll do that again. I love my life. I'm young and rich!

ⓘ a pie in the sky 指事情非常不切實際，也就是希望很渺茫的意思

ⓘ first growth 第一級別，通常用來指稱紅酒的等級

中譯 *Translation*

我住在一棟華麗的別墅裡。人們都非常羨慕它的豪華，因為要能住在這樣的房子裡對他們來說是遙不可及的夢想。如你所見，我是一個事業有成的人，尤其是我還這麼年輕。

我在家中養了隻特別的寵物，一隻迷你豬。我把牠養在我美麗的後院，四周都是花開茂密的植物。我在園藝上花了五十萬元。在我閒暇之餘，我會在家中的個人錄音室彈琴，也會定期邀請我所認識的專業鋼琴家和吉他手到家裡來。上禮拜我用鉛筆為我的迷你豬畫了張畫，打算放在客廳，我收藏的萬寶龍筆旁邊。我昨晚開了一場奢華的派對，我們喝了法國頂級紅酒、抽古巴菸。下禮拜我還要再來一次。我熱愛我的生活，我年輕又富裕！

0457 lavish

[`lævɪʃ] ★★★
- 形 過分鋪張的、大量的
- 動 揮霍、浪費
- 片 lavish on 慷慨施予

0458 villa

[`vɪlə] ★★
- 名 別墅、莊園
- 同 estate 莊園
- 片 holiday villa 度假別墅

0459 envy

[`ɛnvɪ] ★★★★
- 動 妒忌、羨慕
- 名 妒忌、羨慕
- 片 envy at 在…方面羨慕

0460 backyard

[`bækjɑrd] ★★
- 名 後院、後花園
- 形 本地的、私人的
- 同 base-court 後院

0461 blooming

[`blumɪŋ] ★★★
- 形 開著花的、繁盛的
- 同 flowering 開花的
- 衍 bloom 開花

0462 gardening

[`gɑrdŋɪŋ] ★★★
- 名 園藝
- 同 horticulture 園藝
- 衍 garden 從事園藝

0463 studio

[`stjudɪˏo] ★★★★
- 名 錄音室、畫室、攝影棚
- 同 atelier 畫室
- 片 movie studio 製片場

0464 invite

[ɪn`vaɪt] ★★★★
- 動 邀請、招待、徵求
- 同 ask 邀請、要求
- 片 invite sb. to 邀…參加

0465 place

[ples] ★★★★★
- 動 放置、安置、想起
- 名 位置、場所、職務
- 片 place sth. on 重視

0466 collection

[kə`lɛkʃən] ★★★★
- 名 收藏品、募捐、大量
- 片 take up a collection 募款

0467 smoke

[smok] ★★★★★
- 動 抽煙、燻製、冒煙
- 名 煙、煙霧、混亂
- 片 smoke out 查出

0468 cigar

[sɪ`gɑr] ★★★
- 名 雪茄煙
- 同 cigarette 香煙
- 片 light a cigar 點雪茄煙

fighting!

Give it a shot 小試身手

1 Eric drew a _____ of his father.

2 These _____ are hardly seen in the mountains.

3 The children are _____ basketball.

4 The _____ standing on my right is my best friend.

5 The wedding will take _____ in September.

040

The city is my playground[0469]. I have a lot of money in my pocket and a mansion[0470] on the beach, with a pond[0471] and a swimming pool in the backyard. I know a lot of people in the city, such as the mayor, the owners[0472] of the cinema, and the police. I have VIP status[0473] and get free popcorn when I go to a movie. I have the power to fluctuate[0474] the stock[0475] market through my large investments[0476]. My friends are pleased to be around me because I understand the poetry[0477] of life. I have a high position in society now. However, in the past, I was poor and unemployed, and my life was a disaster. One time, I stole cigarettes and chocolate bars from the supermarket and was caught by a policeman. I realized that living like this was pointless[0478]. I began to prepare for the qualification[0479] exam to be a securities broker[0480], studying hard and practicing my English skills. I got a job, and my life got better. Anything is possible, <u>as long as</u> you try hard to achieve your goal!

ⓘ as long as 只要

中譯 *Translation*

　　這座城市是我的遊樂場。我很有錢，還有一棟建在海灘上的豪宅，豪宅後院有池塘和游泳池。我認識城裡的很多人，像是市長、電影院老闆和警界人士。我去看電影時有貴賓身分和免費的爆米花。由於我的大量投資，我有能力操控股市的波動。我朋友都很喜歡和我在一起，因為我懂得生活的詩意。現在的我擁有崇高的社會地位。然而，以前的我不僅窮還失業，我當時的生活就像一場災難。有一次我從超市偷了香菸和巧克力棒，接著就被警察逮捕了。我瞭解到過著這樣的人生毫無意義。我開始準備證券交易員的資格考，努力唸書並練習英文能力。我得到了工作，人生也漸入佳境。任何事都是有可能的，只要你努力，就能達成目標。

0469 playground

[`ple͵graʊnd] ★★★

名 操場、遊樂場、運動場

片 the playground of 某特定群體的享樂之地

0470 mansion

[`mænʃən] ★★★

名 大廈、宅第、公館

片 Mansion House 倫敦市長官邸

0471 pond

[pɑnd] ★★★★

名 池塘、大西洋別稱

片 across the pond 大西洋對岸，即美國或英國

0472 owner

[`onɚ] ★★★★

名 物主、所有人

同 proprietor 所有人

片 owner of …的所有人

0473 status

[`stetəs] ★★★★★

名 身分、地位、狀態

同 position 身分

片 status quo 現狀

0474 fluctuate

[`flʌktʃʊ͵et] ★★★

動 動搖、波動、變動

同 vacillate 動搖

衍 fluctuation 波動

0475 stock

[stɑk] ★★★★★

名 股票、存貨、蓄積

動 進貨、庫存

片 out of stock 沒庫存

0476 investment

[ɪn`vɛstmənt] ★★★★

名 投資、投入、花費

片 undertake investment 承擔投資

0477 poetry

[`poɪtrɪ] ★★★★

名 詩、作詩技巧、詩意

反 prose 散文

片 epic poetry 史詩

0478 pointless

[`pɔɪntlɪs] ★★★

形 無意義的、不得要領的

慣 it is pointless + to v/ ving …是沒用的

0479 qualification

[͵kwɑləfə`keʃən] ★★

名 取得資格、能力、執照

同 competence 能力

片 qualification for …資格

0480 broker

[`brokɚ] ★★★

名 經紀人、掮客、代理人

動 作為中間人協調、安排

---

fighting!

Give it a shot 小試身手

1 I _____ the baby with a lollipop.

2 I totally agree with your _____.

3 Although I am _____, I am rich in spirit.

4 She _____ him a meal before he got home.

5 He owns the most _____ in the company.

Answers: 1 pleased 2 points 3 poor 4 prepared 5 power

041

Essay

MP3   短文 081   字彙 082

It's quite hard to be a successful writer. Nowadays, there is a quick way to push your articles to the public. A lot of writers choose to write blogs at first. It takes a lot of time and effort to gain popularity[0481]. Writing is a quiet and lonely job, and it requires[0482] a lot of sacrifice[0483] before one's work gets published[0484]. In order to attract more Internet users, writers need to answer all the questions from readers, including ones about their personal lives or relationship problems. Writers need a clear purpose[0485] and interesting subjects[0486] for their articles. Putting some photos on the blog, or decorating[0487] the blog with bright colors, like purple or red, will help attract readers. The number of questions and comments[0488] from readers of the blog indicates[0489] the popularity of a writer. A famous blog writer, Queen, spent five years writing her blog before her first book was printed[0490]. Everything has a purpose, doesn't it?

中譯 *Translation*

　　要成為一名成功的作家很不容易。如今，有一個快速將你的文章推廣給大眾的方式。許多作家選擇先在部落格上寫作。增加人氣需要花費大量的時間和努力。寫作是一個安靜又寂寞的工作，而且在作品付梓之前必須做出很多犧牲。為了吸引更多網民的關注，作家必須回答讀者的所有問題，包括他們的私生活及感情狀況等問題。作者創作的文章其目的必須清楚明瞭，主題也要能令人感興趣。在部落格上放些照片，或用亮色系裝飾部落格，例如紫色或紅色，都有助於引起讀者的興趣。部落格中讀者發問和評論的數量在在顯示了作者受歡迎的程度。知名部落客，女王，在她第一本書發行之前，花了五年的時間寫部落格。每件事都有其目標，對吧？

0481 popularity

[ˌpɑpjəˈlærətɪ] ★★★
名 聲望、流行、受歡迎
片 gain in popularity 開始流行

0482 require

[rɪˈkwaɪr] ★★★★
動 需要、要求、命令
反 refuse 拒絕
片 require + ving 需要

0483 sacrifice

[ˈsækrəˌfaɪs] ★★★
名 犧牲的行為、虧本出售
動 犧牲、獻出、虧本出售
片 sacrifice for 為…犧牲

0484 publish

[ˈpʌblɪʃ] ★★★★
動 出版、發行、刊登
片 publish in two parts 分上下冊出版

0485 purpose

[ˈpɜpəs] ★★★★★
名 意圖、用途、決心
動 意圖、決意、打算
片 on purpose 故意

0486 subject

[ˈsʌbdʒɪkt] ★★★★★
名 主題、科目、實驗對象
形 易受…的、受支配的
動 使服從、提供

0487 decorate

[ˈdɛkəˌret] ★★★
動 裝飾、修飾、布置
同 adorn 裝飾
衍 decorative 裝飾性的

0488 comment

[ˈkɑmɛnt] ★★★★
名 評論、意見、閒話
動 發表意見、做註解
片 comment on 評論…

0489 indicate

[ˈɪndəˌket] ★★★★
動 表明、象徵、指出
片 indicate one's intention 表明意圖

0490 print

[prɪnt] ★★★★
動 出版、印刷、銘記
名 印刷字體、印記、指紋
片 out of print 已絕版

0491 reasonable

[ˈriznəbl] ★★★★
形 合理的、有理智的
片 be reasonable in price 價格公道

0492 decayed

[dɪˈked] ★★
形 爛了的、腐敗的
同 rotten 腐爛的
衍 decay 腐爛、蛀蝕

fighting!

Give it a shot 小試身手

1. The _____ is reasonable⁰⁴⁹¹ because the quality is super.
2. The dentist _____ out my decayed⁰⁴⁹² tooth.
3. There is no solution to the _____ so far.
4. I _____ my mobile phone in the drawer.
5. No one knows his real _____ to do this.

Answers: ① price ② pulled ③ problem ④ put ⑤ purpose

MP3   短文 083   字彙 084

Essay 042

It was an ordinary[0493] afternoon for my grandfather. I remember that it was a rainy day. Grandpa read the newspaper and listened to a report[0494] of a horse race on the radio. His house is situated[0495] near railway[0496] tracks and, whenever the train passed, he <u>reached over</u> to the radio to turn up the volume[0497] to maximum[0498]. After my grandfather finished reading the newspaper, the rain finally stopped. It was almost nightfall[0499] by then, and there was a rainbow in the red sky. Rats <u>came out</u> after the heavy rain, and I guess the reason was that the rats' holes were all wet. Then dinner was ready. Before we started to eat, the doorbell rang. Grandpa received a package[0500] from a store delivery[0501] person. It was a birthday gift that I had bought from the store. I felt sorry to grandpa, because I had always forgot his birthday in the past. But this time, I remembered. I wished him a happy birthday and we had a wonderful dinner.

⚠ reach over sth. 伸手拿某物

⚠ come out 在本文中表示「出現」，另外也有出版、發表、開花、解決等意思

中譯 *Translation*

　　對我祖父來說這是一個普通的午後，我記得那是個雨天。祖父讀著報紙，聽著收音機裡的賽馬報導。他的房子位在鐵道附近，每回火車經過時，他都會伸手去把收音機的音量調到最大聲。在祖父讀完報紙之後，雨終於停了。那時將近傍晚，紅色的天空裡出現一道彩虹。大雨過後，老鼠隨之竄出，我猜這是因為老鼠洞全都溼了的緣故。接著，晚餐上桌了。在我們開動之前，門鈴響了。祖父收到郵差送來的一個包裹。那是我先前在一家店裡買的生日禮物。我對祖父感到很不好意思，因為我過去總是忘記他的生日。但這次我記得了。我祝福他有個快樂的生日，我們享用了一頓美好的晚餐。

0493 ordinary

[`ɔrdṇ, ɛrɪ] ★★★★★
形 普通的、不精緻的
名 尋常、平凡
反 exceptional 特殊的

0494 report

[rɪ`port] ★★★★
名 報告、報導、成績單
動 報告、記述、揭發
片 report on 針對…報告

0495 situate

[`sɪtʃʊ, et] ★★★
動 使位於、使處於
同 locate 把…設置在
衍 situation 處境

0496 railway

[`rel, we] ★★★
名 鐵路、鐵道、鐵路系統
同 railroad 鐵路
片 light railway 輕軌鐵路

0497 volume

[`vɑljəm] ★★★
名 音量、卷冊、容積
片 turn the volume up 調高音量

0498 maximum

[`mæksəməm] ★★★
名 最大限度、最大量
形 最大的、頂點的
反 minimum 最低限度

0499 nightfall

[`naɪt, fɔl] ★★
名 黃昏、傍晚、日暮
同 sunset 日落

0500 package

[`pækɪdʒ] ★★★★
名 包裹、包裝、一套
動 把…打包、包裝
片 package up 打包

0501 delivery

[dɪ`lɪvərɪ] ★★★
名 傳送、交貨、分娩
片 cash on delivery 貨到付款

0502 anthem

[`ænθəm] ★★★
名 國歌、頌歌、讚美詩
同 hymn 讚美詩
片 national athem 國歌

0503 athlete

[`æθlit] ★★★★
名 運動員、身強力壯的人
同 sportsman 運動員
片 athlete's foot 香港腳

0504 delay

[dɪ`le] ★★★★
名 延遲、耽擱
動 延誤、耽擱
片 delay + ving 延遲做

Fighting!

Give it a shot 小試身手

1 I practice my English by listening to the _____.
2 He _____ the flag and sang the anthem[0502].
3 The athlete[0503] finally _____ his goal.
4 I wonder the _____ for his delay[0504].
5 Would you mind if I _____ out the essay?

Answers: 1 radio 2 raised 3 reached 4 reason 5 read

Level
2

高中7000單字
範圍進階

Essay 043~Essay 084

名 名詞 　　　同 同義字補充

動 動詞 　　　反 反義字補充

形 形容詞 　　片 片語補充

副 副詞 　　　俚 俚語補充

介 介係詞 　　衍 衍生字補充

MP3　短文 085　字彙 086

043

Essay

Linkin Park is a rock-and-roll band from America, originally consisting[0505] of three high school friends, Mike Shinoda, Brad Delson and Rob Bourdon. The band began recording[0506] songs in Shinoda's studio in 1996. In 2000, Linkin Park released the album, Hybrid[0507] Theory, which was a massive[0508] success. Linkin Park's popularity made the price of their memorabilia[0509] go through the roof. The rise of this rock band made every member rich and famous. After their enormous[0510] success, they didn't take a break. They returned to work right after their concert tour. Fatigue[0511] brought dark rings under Shinoda's eyes, and, as a result, he began to eat healthy Asian food, like rice and noodles[0512], instead of McDonald's or Red Rooster[0513]. Not only did he ride his bike home every day, he also drank rivers of green tea. A live DVD, "Road to Revolution: Live at Milton Keynes," which used robot[0514] animation[0515] in the music video, was released in 2008 and brought Linkin Park to the next level.

> ⚠ go through the roof 字面意思為衝破屋頂，表示超過最高極限，用來形容一種「飛漲」、「直線上升」的狀態

中譯 *Translation*

聯合公園是一個來自美國的搖滾樂團，原先由三位高中好友組成，分別是麥克信田、布萊德達爾森、羅伯博登。1996年，這個樂團開始在信田的錄音室裡錄歌，並於2000年發行《混合理論》這張專輯，獲得了巨大的成功。聯合公園的人氣，使得成員們所佩帶的配件價格跟著水漲船高。這個樂團的發跡，更讓每位團員都名利雙收。在巨大的成功之後，他們無暇休息。他們巡迴演唱一結束，就要返回工作崗位。疲勞讓信田長出了黑眼圈，也因此他開始吃健康的亞洲食品，像是飯和麵，不再吃麥當勞或紅公雞速食店。他不僅天天騎腳踏車回家，也喝大量的綠茶。2008年，《革命之路終結.進化》的現場版光碟發行，音樂錄影帶中使用機器人製做動畫，帶領聯合公園進入另一個層級。

0505 consist

[kən`sɪst] ★★★
動 組成、存在於、符合
同 comprise 由…組成
片 consist of 由…組成

0506 record

[rɪ`kɔrd] ★★★★
動 錄音、記錄
名 記錄、最高紀錄
片 record on 錄製…

0507 hybrid

[`haɪbrɪd] ★★★
形 混合的
名 混合物、雜交種
同 mongrel 雜交動植物

0508 massive

[`mæsɪv] ★★★
形 大規模的、厚實的、大量的
同 immense 巨大的

0509 memorabilia

[`mɛmərə`bɪlɪə] ★★
名 重要記事、紀念品

0510 enormous

[ɪ`nɔrməs] ★★★
形 巨大的、龐大的
同 vast 巨大的
反 diminutive 小的

0511 fatigue

[fə`tig] ★★★
名 疲勞、勞累
動 使疲勞
同 exhaust 使精疲力盡

0512 noodle

[`nudl̩] ★★
名 麵條、傻瓜
片 instant noodles 泡麵

0513 rooster

[`rustɚ] ★★
名 公雞、狂妄自負的人
同 cock 公雞
反 hen 母雞

0514 robot

[`robət] ★★★
名 機器人、自動控制裝置、行動呆板的人
同 android 機器人

0515 animation

[ˌænə`meʃən] ★★★
名 動畫片、活潑、熱烈
同 liveliness 充滿活力
反 inanimation 不活潑

0516 beggar

[`bɛgɚ] ★★
名 乞丐、窮光蛋
動 使貧窮、使不能
同 cadger 乞討者

Fighting!

Give it a shot 小試身手

1 He will _____ home after one week.

2 The _____ man looked down on the beggars0516.

3 The _____ of unemployment rate is continuing.

4 He booked a _____ in the hotel.

5 We should help him _____ now.

Answers: 1 return 2 rich 3 rise 4 room 5 right

MP3　短文 087　字彙 088

Essay

044

I used to love my girlfriend. When we were seeing each other, she received roses from me every week. It went like that for half a year. Recently, I argued with my girlfriend over a mere[0517] trifle[0518]. For example, she always put salt and pepper in the wrong place, forgot to tie[0519] her long hair with a rubber[0520] band when cooking, made an ink stain[0521] on my Gucci shirt that could never be removed[0522]. She could also be violent[0523] sometimes. It wasn't safe to live with her. Also, there were too many rules in her house. Last week, she sold a necklace of pearls[0524] that I had given her. I was sad and angry. I thought she didn't love me anymore, and that was the root[0525] of all our problems. I decided to run away from this and to take Star Cruise's Super Star Virgo to travel round the world. The ship will sail[0526] tomorrow for Singapore. Next week, I will be lying on the sand of Sentosa Beach. I wish I could forget about her.

ⓘ see sb. 和某人約會、交往

中譯 *Translation*

　　我以前很愛我的女朋友。當我們交往時，她每個禮拜都會收到我送的花，半年以來依舊如故。最近我和女友因為一點瑣事起了口角。例如，她總是把鹽和胡椒放錯位置、煮菜時忘了用橡皮筋將她的長髮紮起來、讓我的古馳襯衫沾到墨汁，永遠都擦不掉。她有時候也很暴力。和她住在一起很不安全。況且，她家裡還有許多規定。上個禮拜她賣掉我送她的一串珍珠項鍊，我又難過又生氣，認為她再也不愛我了，而那就是一切問題的根源。我決定逃離這一切，搭乘麗星郵輪的處女星號去環遊世界。這艘船明天會航向新加坡。下禮拜我就會躺在聖淘沙的沙灘上。我希望我能夠忘記她。

0517 mere

[mɪr] ★★★★
形 僅僅的、極小的
名 淺湖
反 considerable 重要的

0518 trifle

[`traɪfl] ★★
名 瑣事、小玩意兒、少量
動 戲弄、輕視、浪費
片 trifle with 玩弄、輕視

0519 tie

[taɪ] ★★★★
動 繫上、打結、約束
名 帶子、聯繫、平手
片 tie down 捆住、束縛

0520 rubber

[`rʌbə] ★★★
名 橡膠、橡膠鞋、本壘板
形 橡膠製成的
片 rubber band 橡皮筋

0521 stain

[sten] ★★★
名 汙點、瑕疵、色斑
動 變髒、玷汙、染色
片 stain with 被…弄髒

0522 remove

[rɪ`muv] ★★★★
動 消除、移動、把…免職
名 間隔、搬家
片 remove from 從…移開

0523 violent

[`vaɪələnt] ★★★
形 暴力的、激烈的
同 mighty 強大的
片 turn violent 變得暴躁

0524 pearl

[pɝl] ★★★
名 珍珠、珠狀物、珍品
動 成珍珠狀
同 gem 珍品、寶物

0525 root

[rut] ★★★★
名 根源、根部、本質
動 使紮根、根除
片 root out 徹底根除

0526 sail

[sel] ★★★★★
動 航行、駕駛、飄過
名 乘船遊覽、帆、篷
片 sail through 順利通過

0527 forbid

[fə`bɪd] ★★★
動 禁止、妨礙
片 forbid sb. to do sth. 禁止某人做某事

0528 minor

[`maɪnə] ★★★★
名 未成年人、副修科目
形 較少的、次要的
動 副修、兼修

fighting!

Give it a shot 小試身手

1 The earth is _____.
2 He does everything by _____.
3 The dog is _____ after the postman.
4 The law forbids0527 the _____ of alcohol to minors0528.
5 We _____ down the river.

Answers: 1 round **2** rules **3** running **4** sales **5** sailed

045

Essay

Last Saturday, I went to the elementary[0529] school I had studied at before. It seemed that there hadn't been too much change; almost everything looked the same as before. The only thing I didn't see from the past was the big tree in front of the seesaw[0530]. It had been sawn[0531] off a few years ago, but they had planted[0532] another.

I went to my old classroom and sat down on the seat[0533] I used to sit in, which transported[0534] me back to the past in an instant[0535]. I lacked[0536] self-confidence and was scared to interact[0537] with people when I was young. Everyone in the class always made fun of me and said rude[0538] things to me. But there was one person who always came to help me. He was my best friend. He was like a person who saved me from drowning[0539] in the sea, giving me a cup of hot tea in the winter and planting the seeds of friendship. I still appreciate[0540] him, and I hope I can meet him again one day.

中譯 *Translation*

上星期六我回到以前就讀的小學。看起來似乎沒有太大的改變,幾乎都和以前一樣。我唯一沒看過的就是蹺蹺板前的一棵大樹。原本的那棵幾年前被鋸掉了,然而他們又種了一棵新的。

我來到以前的教室,坐在我以前的位子上,這樣的情景讓我頃刻間回到了過去。我小時候很沒自信,害怕與人們互動。班上每個人都喜歡嘲笑我,或用粗魯的言詞罵我。但有一個人總是會來幫助我。他是我最好的朋友。他就像是把溺水的我從大海裡救出的人,在寒冷的冬天遞給我一杯熱茶,種下我們之間的友誼種子。我依然感激他,也希望某天可以再次遇見他。

0529 elementary

[,ɛləˋmɛntərɪ] ★★★
形 初級的、基本的
同 basic 基本的
反 advanced 高級的

0530 seesaw

[ˋsi,sɔ] ★★
名 蹺蹺板、上下動
動 玩蹺蹺板、上下搖動
同 teeter-totter 蹺蹺板

0531 saw

[sɔ] ★★★★★
動 鋸開、拉鋸般來回移動
名 鋸子、格言
片 saw off 鋸掉

0532 plant

[plænt] ★★★★
動 栽種、設置、插入
名 植物、工廠
片 plant onself 站立不動

0533 seat

[sit] ★★★★★
名 座位、席位、所在地
動 使就坐、容納…人
片 take a seat 就坐

0534 transport

[ˋtræns,pɔrt] ★★★
動 運送、使激動、流放
名 運輸、交通工具、狂喜
片 transport to 運送到

0535 instant

[ˋɪnstənt] ★★★
名 頃刻、一剎那
形 立即的、迫切的
片 in an instant 立刻

0536 lack

[læk] ★★★★
動 缺少、不足
名 欠缺、需要的東西
片 for lack of 因缺乏…

0537 interact

[,ɪntəˋrækt] ★★★
動 互動、互相影響、交流
片 interact with 與…互動

0538 rude

[rud] ★★★★
形 粗魯的、無禮的、天然
的、未開化的
片 be rude to 對…無禮

0539 drown

[draʊn] ★★★
動 溺死、淹沒、蓋過
同 submerge 淹沒
片 drown sth. in 把…浸在

0540 appreciate

[əˋpriʃɪ,et] ★★★★
動 感激、欣賞、領會
片 appreciate sb's help
感謝某人的幫助

Fighting!

Give it a shot 小試身手

1 He left without _____ good-bye.

2 I saw a bloody _____ of car accident.

3 The boss _____ satisfied with his plan.

4 Mother's Day is on the _____ Sunday of May.

5 The ship sank deep into the _____.

Answers: 1 saying **2** scene **3** seemed **4** second **5** sea

046

MP3

短文 091　字彙 092

Essay

Chen Shui-bian, the former president of Taiwan, was good at selling himself. Chen won a seat on Taipei City Council in 1981 and served until 1985. He established a good bus service during his term[0541]. Chen was reportedly[0542] shot in the stomach while campaigning[0543] in 2004, the day before the presidential election. The following day, Chen narrowly won the election with a margin[0544] of seventeen thousand votes. The opposition thought the incident was staged[0545] by Chen. On September 11, 2009, Chen received a life sentence[0546] on several charges[0547]. The Supreme[0548] Prosecutor[0549]'s Office arranged a seven-member investigative[0550] unit to take charge of his case, and Chen's approval[0551] rating fell from seventy-nine percent to just twenty-one percent. He was sent to Tucheng Penitentiary[0552] and shall spend a long time in jail. But all these didn't shake Chen's supporters' faith in him.

Chen's <u>fall from grace</u> was really a blow to our country!

> ! fall from grace 原意為失寵於上帝，但現今已不侷限於宗教，也可用來比喻失去上司或他人的信任、恩寵；或團體、政黨的「失勢」、「失利」；另也有「墮落」、「誤入歧途」、「丟臉」等意

中譯 *Translation*

　　台灣前總統陳水扁，非常懂得自我宣傳。他在1981年當選台北市議員，並服務至1985年。他於任期內建立了良好的公車服務。根據報導，陳水扁在2004年總統大選前一天的競選活動中遭槍擊射中腹部。隔天，陳水扁以一萬七千票的極小差距獲選。反對黨認為那是陳水扁自導自演。2009年9月11日，陳水扁因諸多罪名被判無期徒刑。最高法院檢察署籌組七人調查小組負責此案，陳水扁的支持率也從百分之七十九掉到只剩百分之二十一。他被送往土城看守所，勢必是要長期吃牢飯了。但這並沒有動搖陳水扁支持者的信心。

　　陳水扁的墮落對國家實在是一個重大的打擊！

0541 term

[t3m] ★★★★★
- 名 任期、條款、術語
- 動 把…稱為
- 片 in terms of 就…而言

0542 reportedly

[rɪ`portɪdlɪ] ★★
- 副 據傳聞、據報導
- 同 allegedly 據傳説

0543 campaign

[kæm`pen] ★★★★
- 動 參加競選、從事運動
- 名 競選活動、運動
- 同 movement 活動

0544 margin

[`mardʒɪn] ★★★
- 名 差數、邊緣、頁邊空白、利潤
- 片 by a margin 以…之差

0545 stage

[stedʒ] ★★★★★
- 動 上演、籌畫、發動
- 名 舞台、戲劇、階段
- 衍 onstage 台上演出的

0546 sentence

[`sɛntəns] ★★★
- 名 判決、宣判、句子
- 動 宣判、使遭受
- 片 life sentence 無期徒刑

0547 charge

[tʃardʒ] ★★★★
- 名 指控、索價、責任
- 動 收費、指控、譴責
- 片 charge for 要價、收費

0548 supreme

[su`prim] ★★★
- 形 最高的、最大的
- 同 utmost 最大的
- 片 Supreme Being 上帝

0549 prosecutor

[`prasɪ,kjutə] ★★
- 名 檢察官、公訴人、原告
- 片 chief prosecutor 檢察長

0550 investigative

[ɪn`vɛstə,getɪv] ★★
- 形 調查的、研究性的
- 同 exploratory 探究的
- 動 investigate 研究

0551 approval

[ə`pruvl] ★★★★
- 名 認可、贊同、批准
- 反 disapproval 不贊成
- 片 on approval 供試用的

0552 penitentiary

[,pɛnə`tɛnʃərɪ] ★★
- 名 監獄、宗教裁判所
- 形 監獄的、悔過的
- 同 prison 監獄

Fighting!

Give it a shot 小試身手

1. I tipped the waiter for his good _____.
2. She has written _____ books on the subject.
3. The cake was made in the _____ of heart.
4. A rainbow has _____ colors.
5. I _____ the clock at nine a.m..

Answers: 1 service 2 several 3 shape 4 seven 5 set

047

Essay

 MP3 短文 093 字彙 094

Mrs. Shi is an editor[0553] of a women's fashion magazine. She is a busy woman with a heavy workload[0554]. She shines[0555] at her work and thinks herself an elegant[0556] and tasteful[0557] woman. However, she has a <u>sharp tongue</u> sometimes. She will shout at her secretary[0558] all day if she doesn't feel good.

Boutique[0559] shops are the only places for her to go shopping, and she will buy at least three pairs of Gucci shoes, five D&G shirts, and a few pairs of shorts every month. Only furniture[0560] and accessories[0561] of high quality are acceptable[0562] in her house, such as the Cashmere sheep wool sheets in her bedroom. She likes to <u>take shots</u> of her Persian cat. It's not surprising that she eats the best shark fin[0563] soup. She lives on the shore of St. Kilda beach, and cruises[0564] on her own boat on weekends. She works hard and enjoys life.

> ⓘ sharp tongue 形容說話尖酸刻薄
> ⓘ take a shot 拍照，也可以說 take a picture

中譯 *Translation*

施小姐是一家女性時尚雜誌的編輯。她工作量繁重，非常忙碌。她的工作表現非常出色，而且自認為是個優雅且有品味的女人。然而，她有時說話很刻薄。如果她心情不好，就會對著祕書咆哮一整天。

她只到精品店購物，而且她每個月至少會買三雙 Gucci 鞋，五件 D&G 襯衫和一些短褲。她家裡只用高質感的家具，像是臥室裡的喀什米爾羊毛床單。她喜歡幫她的波斯貓拍照。想當然爾，她也吃最頂級的魚翅。她住在聖基爾達的海岸邊，週末時乘著自己的小船旅行。她努力工作，同時也享受生活。

0553 editor

[`ɛdɪtə] ★★★★★
名 編輯、主筆、校訂者
同 reviser 校訂者
片 editor in chief 總編輯

0554 workload

[`wɝk,lod] ★★
名 工作量、工作負荷
片 increase sb's workload 增加工作量

0555 shine

[ʃaɪn] ★★★★
動 出眾、照耀、顯露
名 光亮、擦亮、陽光
片 shine at sth. 擅長…

0556 elegant

[`ɛləgənt] ★★★
形 優美的、講究的、巧妙的、簡練確切的
同 refined 精緻的

0557 tasteful

[`testfəl] ★★
形 有鑑賞力的、高雅的
同 elegant 優美的
反 tasteless 庸俗的

0558 secretary

[`sɛkrə,tɛrɪ] ★★★★
名 秘書、書記官、部長

0559 boutique

[bu`tik] ★★★
名 精品店、流行女裝店
片 boutique hotel 精品酒店

0560 furniture

[`fɝnɪtʃə] ★★★★
名 家具、設備
同 furnishings 家具、室內陳設

0561 accessory

[æk`sɛsərɪ] ★★
名 配件、房間陳設、同謀
動 附加的、同謀的
同 addition 附加

0562 acceptable

[ək`sɛptəbl] ★★★
形 合意的、可接受的
片 acceptable to do sth. 做某事是可接受的

0563 fin

[fɪn] ★★★
名 鰭、鰭狀物、散熱片
同 flipper 鰭狀肢
片 tail fin 尾鰭

0564 cruise

[kruz] ★★★★
動 航行、航遊、漫遊
名 巡航、巡邏
片 cruise along 沿…航行

Fighting!

Give it a shot 小試身手

1 Mother usually irons her _____.

2 Those _____ do not fit my feet.

3 We should tell her that her skirt is too _____.

4 The sun is _____ in the sky.

5 Did you know why that client _____ at him?

Answers: 1 shirt 2 shoes 3 short 4 shining 5 shouted

103

048

🎧 MP3   短文 095   字彙 096

Essay

Kelly and her sister, Jenny, are both singers. They have done hundreds of shows since they were young. Even so, at the beginning of their performing career, they didn't sing well and were shy. They once sat on the bench[0565] and waited for an audition for six hours, but the judges[0566] still shut[0567] the door and asked them to leave. Although they seemed silly, the boss of a record company appreciated them and signed[0568] them to a contract[0569].

One day, Kelly was very sick. Her eyes were infected[0570], and she almost lost her sight[0571]. Her sister asked their boss, "Sir, can we postpone[0572] the show to another day?" The boss replied[0573], "No way, don't be stupid. You've got a big show to do tonight." Therefore, Kelly had to sit on the side of the stage with an intravenous[0574] drip[0575] and performed as usual. They are popular now, and a Hollywood filmmaker has come to talk to them. It won't be long before Kelly and Jenny make it on the silver screen.

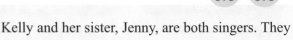

中譯 *Translation*

　　凱莉和姊姊珍妮都是歌手。她們從年輕時就開始表演，已經做過上百場演出了。然而，在她們表演生涯的一開始，她們唱得並不好，而且很害羞。她們曾經坐在長凳上等待甄選，等了整整六個小時，但評審們還是把門關上，並要求她們離開。雖然她們這樣似乎很蠢，唱片公司的老闆卻很賞識她們，並和她們簽了合約。

　　某天，凱莉生了重病。她的眼睛遭到感染，而且幾乎失明。她姊姊請求老闆：「先生，我們可以把表演延到改天嗎？」老闆回答：「不可能，別傻了。你們今晚有一場重要的表演必須演出。」因此凱莉得吊著點滴坐在舞台邊，一如往常地進行表演。她們現在非常火紅，好萊塢製片也找上了她們。凱莉和珍妮躍上大螢幕的日子不遠了！

0565 bench
[bɛntʃ] ★★★★
名 長凳、法官、替補球員席、工作台
片 on the bench 當法官

0566 judge
[dʒʌdʒ] ★★★★
名 裁判員、鑑定人、法官
動 審判、判斷、認為
片 judge by 根據…判斷

0567 shut
[ʃʌt] ★★★★
動 關上、停止營業、夾住
名 關閉
片 shut down 完全關閉

0568 sign
[saɪn] ★★★★★
動 簽約雇用、簽名、示意
名 記號、手勢、前兆
片 sign with 簽約受雇用

0569 contract
[`kɑntrækt] ★★★★
名 契約、合同、婚約
動 訂契約、承辦、收縮
片 sign a contract 簽合約

0570 infect
[ɪn`fɛkt] ★★★
動 傳染、感染、汙染
同 contaminate 汙染
片 infect with 染上…

0571 sight
[saɪt] ★★★★
名 視力、見解、目睹
動 看見、發現、瞄準
片 on sight 一看見就…

0572 postpone
[post`pon] ★★★★
動 使延期、延緩
反 advance 將…提前
片 postpone + ving 延遲

0573 reply
[rɪ`plaɪ] ★★★★★
動 回答、回應
名 回答、答覆
片 reply to 回覆

0574 intravenous
[ˌɪntrə`vinəs] ★
形 靜脈內的
片 intravenous injection 靜脈注射

0575 drip
[drɪp] ★★
名 點滴、滴下、滴水聲
動 滴水、充滿、溢出
同 drop 使滴下

0576 license
[`laɪsn̩s] ★★★★
名 執照、許可、放縱
動 許可、准許
片 be licensed to 獲准

Fighting!

Give it a shot 小試身手

1 She felt a little _____ and took some medicine.
2 Anna and her _____ look like each other.
3 He has become a doctor _____ he graduated.
4 He _____ in the back seat of the car.
5 I _____ the driver's license0576 to the policeman.

Answers: 1 sick 2 sister 3 since 4 sat 5 show

049

Essay

Heavy smokers usually start smoking <u>at the age of</u> about sixteen. At first, they start with a small amount, but the addiction begins to grow in the smokers' bodies. The slow growth of the addiction poisons[0577] their health enormously <u>in the long run</u>. When smokers turn sixty and have snow-white hair, any kind of disease[0578] may come to them. It's not smart to <u>keep up</u> the habit. Tar[0579] causes yellow, dark teeth, and ugly smiles. Bad breath harms[0580] the social[0581] life of smokers. Smokers often have sleeping problems and unhealthy[0582] skin. Smoking also causes impotence[0583]. For men, size may not matter, but smoking turns a dragon into a snake. Don't let impotence worsen[0584] your relationship[0585] with your partner. Quit[0586] smoking as soon as possible and have a good life. Let the sun shine again in your sky!

> (!) at the age of 在幾歲的時候
> (!) in the long run 從長遠來看、最後、終究
> (!) keep up 在本文中表示「保持」、「繼續」，另外也有「精神或價格不下跌」的意思

中譯 *Translation*

　　癮君子通常都在十六歲時開始抽菸。一開始他們少量地抽，但身體卻會慢慢上癮。這種慢性成癮終究會嚴重危害健康。當吸菸者到了六十歲，頭髮雪白之時，任何疾病都有可能找上他們。持續這種習慣是不明智的。焦油會造成牙齒暗黃，笑容醜陋。臭味會使吸煙者的社交生活遭到排擠。吸煙者通常有睡眠問題，皮膚也不健康。吸菸還會造成陽萎。雖然對男人而言，大小並不重要，但吸菸會把一條巨龍變得像條小蛇一般，別讓陽萎破壞你與伴侶的關係。儘早戒菸，才能擁有好生活。讓陽光在你的天空中再度閃耀吧！

0577 poison

[`pɔɪzn̩] ★★★
- 動 毒害、破壞、汙染
- 名 毒藥、毒害、酒
- 片 poison with 用…毒害

0578 disease

[dɪ`ziz] ★★★★★
- 名 疾病、不健全、弊病
- 動 使生病
- 片 catch a disease 染病

0579 tar

[tɑr] ★★★
- 名 焦油、柏油、瀝青
- 動 塗焦油於、玷汙
- 同 asphalt 瀝青、柏油

0580 harm

[hɑrm] ★★★★
- 動 危害、傷害
- 名 危害、傷害
- 片 come to harm 遭不幸

0581 social

[`soʃəl] ★★★★
- 形 社交的、喜歡交際的
- 名 聯誼會、聯歡會

0582 unhealthy

[ʌn`hɛlθɪ] ★★
- 形 不健康的、有病的、不良的、反常的
- 同 infirm 衰弱的

0583 impotence

[`ɪmpətəns] ★★
- 名 陽萎、無能
- 同 inability 無能

0584 worsen

[`wɝsn̩] ★★
- 動 使惡化、使變差
- 同 deteriorate 惡化
- 反 amend 改進、改善

0585 relationship

[rɪ`leʃən`ʃɪp] ★★★
- 名 關係、關聯、戀愛關係
- 片 relationship with/between 與…的關係

0586 quit

[kwɪt] ★★★★★
- 動 放棄、退出、辭職
- 反 remain 保持
- 片 quit + ving 戒除…

0587 fit

[fɪt] ★★★★★
- 動 適合、合身、與…相稱
- 名 適合、合身
- 片 fit in 使適應

0588 comfort

[`kʌmfət] ★★★★
- 動 安慰、慰問
- 名 安慰、舒適
- 同 console 安慰

Fighting!

Give it a shot 小試身手

1. The _____ of the clothes does not fit0587 me.
2. Reading and writing are different _____.
3. Einstein was a _____ learner in his boyhood.
4. I lost the keys, _____ I could not enter my house.
5. The nurse's sweet _____ comforted0588 me.

050

Essay

I had pumpkin[0589] soup and sweet potato[0590] for dinner with my family last night. My son was really naughty[0591]. He ran around and accidentally <u>turned over</u> my plate[0592] while we were having dinner. My shirt was stained, and he felt really sorry about it. I didn't scold[0593] him. If someone does something wrong and admits it, sometimes it's not good to criticize[0594] him or her.

After dinner, we watched a soap opera[0595] together. My son had some homework to do, and therefore he went back to his room soon after the TV show was over. My wife and I laid on our soft sofa, listening to a soulful[0596] song from the 80s. I had a glass of <u>whisky and soda</u>[0597]. My wife was singing along with the music, and her voice sounded[0598] very beautiful. That is an example of my sweet family life.

> ① turn over 打翻、使翻倒；若將兩字連在一起，turnover 則為名詞用法，有翻轉、翻倒、營業額等意思

> ① whisky and soda 是以威士忌為基酒然後加入蘇打水的調酒，這類烈酒+冰塊+碳酸飲料的喝法，一般稱作 highball，而當中最著名的即為 whisky soda

中譯 *Translation*

昨晚我和家人吃了南瓜湯和地瓜當晚餐。我兒子非常調皮，在我們用餐時四處跑來跑去，還不小心把我的盤子打翻了。我的襯衫被弄髒，他也感到非常抱歉。但我沒有責備他。如果有人做錯事勇於承認，有時就不適合責罵他。

晚餐過後，我們一起看肥皂劇。我兒子有些功課要做，所以電視節目一結束他就回房了。妻子與我躺在柔軟的沙發上，聽著 80 年代的靈魂音樂。我喝了一杯威士忌蘇打，妻子則跟著音樂哼唱，她的聲音聽起來很美。那就是我甜蜜家庭生活的寫照。

0589 pumpkin

[ˋpʌmpkɪn] ★★
名 南瓜、稱呼所愛之人
片 pumpkin pies 南瓜派

0590 potato

[pəˋteto] ★★★★
名 馬鈴薯、洋芋
片 hot potato 棘手問題

0591 naughty

[ˋnɔtɪ] ★★★
形 頑皮的、不守規矩的
同 disorderly 無秩序的
反 well-mannered 有禮的

0592 plate

[plet] ★★★★
名 盤子、碟、薄板
動 電鍍、用金屬板固定
同 platter 淺盤

0593 scold

[skold] ★★
動 責罵、訓斥
名 責罵
片 scold for 為…而責罵

0594 criticize

[ˋkrɪtɪˏsaɪz] ★★★
動 批評、評論、苛求
反 praise 稱讚
片 criticize for 因…指責

0595 opera

[ˋɑpərə] ★★★★
名 歌劇、歌劇院
片 go to the opera 聽歌劇

0596 soulful

[ˋsolfəl] ★★
形 深情的、充滿感情的
同 affecting 令人感動的
衍 soulfulness 充滿感情

0597 soda

[ˋsodə] ★★★
名 蘇打、碳酸氫鈉、汽水
同 soda pop 汽水
片 soda biscuit 蘇打餅乾

0598 sound

[saund] ★★★★
動 聽起來、發聲、響起
名 聲音、喧鬧聲
形 健全的、紮實的

0599 imprison

[ɪmˋprɪzn̩] ★★★
動 監禁、束縛、禁錮
同 jail 監禁
反 liberate 使自由

0600 annoying

[əˋnɔɪɪŋ] ★★
形 惱人的、討厭的
同 irritating 煩人的
衍 annoy 惹惱、使生氣

---

fighting!

Give it a shot 小試身手

1 I used a _____ to wash my hands.

2 You can imprison⁰⁵⁹⁹ my body but not my _____.

3 The _____ of the clock is quite annoying⁰⁶⁰⁰.

4 I'm _____ to show up late.

5 I had a bowl of chicken _____.

051

Essay

MP3　短文 101　字彙 102

It is scary to stand in front of people and make a public speech[0601]. To make an interesting speech, you need to practice in advance[0602]. As with sports competitions[0603], we should spend a lot of time and effort to be the best we can be. To start with, find a comfortable space at home and look at yourself in the mirror when you are talking. Spell[0604] every word you use, and then pronounce[0605] it loudly and clearly. Following that, talk as much as possible, anywhere, anytime. Seize[0606] every opportunity[0607] to talk to strangers, when you are taking a bus, climbing the stairs, or requesting[0608] a fork and spoon from a waiter, for example. If you have an annoying accent[0609], find a pronunciation teacher. <u>Take advantage of</u> any chance possible to speak in public and don't be afraid that your audience[06010] may give you a critical[0611] look. Any temporary failure[0612] is part of the process to become a good speaker. You will finally become a star on the stage, and your public speaking ability will come naturally and easily to you.

ⓘ take advantage of 利用、善用、佔便宜

中譯 *Translation*

　　站在人群面前公開演說是件可怕的事。想要發表一場有趣的演講，需要一些事前的練習。就像運動比賽一樣，我們應該要付出大量的時間和精力盡自己所能成為最優秀的選手。一開始，在家中找出一個舒適的空間，然後邊講話邊看著鏡中的自己。拼出每個你會用到的字，並且大聲清楚地唸出來。接著，讓你隨時隨地處於健談的狀態。利用每一個和陌生人說話的機會，像是搭公車時、爬樓梯時、跟服務生索取叉子和湯匙時。如果你有惱人的腔調，就找一個正音老師。善用任何可能在眾人面前說話的機會，並且不要畏懼聽眾臉上批判性的表情。任何一時的失敗，都是成為一名傑出講者過程中的一部分。最後，你將成為舞台上的一顆星，而你的公開演說能力將會變得自然且輕而易舉。

0601 speech

[spitʃ] ★★★★
名 演說、言論、說話方式
同 address 演說
片 make a speech 演說

0602 advance

[əd`væns] ★★★★
名 前進、發展、預付
動 將⋯提前、前進、進展
形 先行的、預先的

0603 competition

[ˌkɑmpə`tɪʃən] ★★★
名 競爭、比賽、競爭者
同 contest 競爭
片 in competition 競爭中

0604 spell

[spɛl] ★★★
動 拼字、招致、暫時代替
名 咒語、一段時間、輪班
片 spell out 拼寫

0605 pronounce

[prə`nauns] ★★★★
動 發音、宣稱、表示
片 pronounce on 對⋯發
表意見

0606 seize

[siz] ★★★★
動 抓住、掌握、利用
同 clutch 抓住
片 seize on 利用、把握

0607 opportunity

[ˌɑpə`tjunətɪ] ★★★
名 機會、良機
片 at every opportunity
利用一切機會

0608 request

[rɪ`kwɛst] ★★★★
動 要求、請求給予
名 要求、需求
片 request from 向⋯請求

0609 accent

[`æksɛnt] ★★★★
名 腔調、重音、著重
動 強調、極力主張
片 strong accent 口音重

0610 audience

[`ɔdɪəns] ★★★★
名 觀眾、聽眾、謁見
同 spectators 觀眾

0611 critical

[`krɪtɪkl̩] ★★★★
形 批判的、愛挑剔的、關
鍵性的
片 critical of 對⋯挑剔的

0612 failure

[`feljə] ★★★★
名 失敗、不足、故障、不
及格
片 failure to 沒能做到

Fighting!

Give it a shot 小試身手

❶ There is no _____ for more people.

❷ _____ still when hearing the national anthem.

❸ Mexico is in the _____ of North America.

❹ I _____ to do my homework in the evening.

❺ It's not convenient for the elders to climb _____.

MP3　短文 103　字彙 104

Essay
052

I once tried to <u>pick up</u> a girl on the street, and it <u>turned out to be</u> an embarrassing experience for me. At that time, I was a student, studying at Great University. I saw a girl in the comic[0613] book store near the train station, and her beauty astonished[0614] me. When I first saw her, I was frozen[0615] like a stone. After standing still there for a few minutes, I stepped toward[0616] her. I stated to her that she was a very beautiful woman who was really attractive to me. I told her my personal story, about my hobbies, job, friends, and my strong passion for the arts. The girl thought I was really strange, so she screamed[0617] and told me to stay away from her or she might call the police. I was dumbfounded[0618] and felt stupid. However, I did learn a lesson from that experience. Afterwards[0619], I looked in the mirror and noticed[0620] that I had forgotten to trim[0621] my nasal[0622] hair that day. I'm sure that was the reason she rejected me so strongly!

(!) pick up sb. 與某人搭訕

(!) turn out to be 結果是…

中譯 *Translation*

　　我曾經在路上搭訕一個女孩，結果卻變成一個很尷尬的經驗。當時我還是學生，在優等大學唸書。我在靠近火車站的漫畫店看到一名女孩，她的美貌令我為之驚艷。當我第一眼見到她時，我像石頭一像僵在原地。呆立了幾分鐘之後，我朝她走過去。我告訴她，她是個很漂亮的女生，非常吸引我。我向她述說我個人的故事，我的嗜好、工作、朋友和對藝術的熱情。女孩覺得我是個怪人，大聲尖叫要我離她遠一點，不然她就要報警。我嚇呆了，覺得自己真的是有夠愚蠢。後來我照了鏡子，發現我那天忘了剪鼻毛了。我確定這就是她如此激烈拒絕我的原因。

0613 comic

[`kɑmɪk] ★★★
形 連環漫畫的、喜劇的
名 連環漫畫、喜劇演員
反 tragic 悲劇的

0614 astonish

[ə`stɑnɪʃ] ★★★
動 使吃驚、使驚訝
同 surprise 使吃驚
反 ease 使安心

0615 frozen

[`frozn̩] ★★
形 嚇呆的、冰凍的、極冷
的、無情的
片 frozen good 冷凍食品

0616 toward

[tə`wɔrd] ★★★
副 朝、接近、關於
形 即將來到的
片 lean toward 傾向於

0617 scream

[skrim] ★★★
動 尖叫、放聲大哭
名 尖叫、呼嘯聲
片 scream at 大聲叫嚷

0618 dumbfounded

[ˌdʌm`faʊndɪd] ★★
形 驚得目瞪口呆的
同 astonished 驚訝的

0619 afterwards

[`æftəwədz] ★★★
副 隨後、後來
反 beforehand 預先

0620 notice

[`notɪs] ★★★★
動 注意到、通知、提到
名 公告、通知、察覺
片 notice sb. + ving 注意

0621 trim

[trɪm] ★★★★
動 修剪、削減、使平穩
名 修剪、整齊、平衡
片 trim down 修剪、削減

0622 nasal

[`nezl̩] ★★
形 鼻子的、鼻音的
名 鼻音
片 nasal mucus 鼻涕

0623 asleep

[ə`slip] ★★★
副 進入睡眠狀態
形 睡著的、麻木的
片 sound asleep 熟睡

0624 earthquake

[`ɝθˌkwek] ★★★
名 地震、社會大動盪
同 quake 地震、震動

---

fighting!

Give it a shot 小試身手

❶ Mother always tells me a bed time _____ before I fall asleep⁰⁶²³.

❷ I like to go shopping in the department _____.

❸ The teacher told us to _____ calm when the earthquake⁰⁶²⁴ happened.

❹ Don't make _____ decisions or you might regret it.

❺ We will meet each other at the bus _____.

Answers: ❶ story ❷ store ❸ stay ❹ stupid ❺ station

053

Essay

Last Sunday afternoon, I had tea with my friend, Eric. He told me some fascinating[0625] tales[0626] about his life in China. Last summer, he had relationships with four different girls at the same time in Shanghai. He took different girls back to his hotel every day. They swam in the hotel swimming pool and sunbathed[0627] on the deck[0628], and they had supper[0629] at a super Italian restaurant, ordering[0630] a lot of expensive food. That story surprised me, but I wasn't really sure if it was true or not. Eric is not tall and handsome, but rather[0631] short, fat, and homely[0632]. But one thing was for sure - Eric's really good at sweet-talk. Still, I couldn't believe he was a sugar daddy in China. If he really was, though, I guess that explains[0633] why every Taiwanese guy in China seems to be so popular. However, my interest in Chinese girls tailed[0634] off after listening to Eric's story.

> ! sweet talk 花言巧語、甜言蜜語
> ! sugar daddy 贈送貴重禮物來博取年輕女人歡心的老頭

中譯 *Translation*

上禮拜天下午，我和朋友艾瑞克一起享用下午茶。他告訴我他在中國生活的一些迷人趣事。去年夏天，他在上海同時與四名女孩交往。他每天都帶不同的女孩回旅館。他們在旅館的游泳池游泳、在露天平台上做日光浴，他們還在超級豪華的義大利餐廳用晚餐，點了滿桌的昂貴食物。這故事讓我非常驚訝，但我不確定是不是真的。艾瑞克不高也不帥，反而又矮又胖且其貌不揚。但有件事是真的，艾瑞克很懂得花言巧語。儘管如此，我仍是無法相信他在中國居然成了送錢討好年輕女孩的老色鬼。然而若真是如此，我想這就解釋了為什麼每個台灣男人在中國似乎都非常受歡迎。不過，在聽完艾瑞克的故事後，我對中國女孩也變得興趣缺缺了。

0625 fascinating

[`fæsn̩etɪŋ] ★★★
形 迷人的、極好的
同 absorbing 引人入勝的
反 boring 令人生厭的

0626 tale

[tel] ★★★★
名 故事、敘述、閒話
同 narrative 講述
片 fairy tale 童話故事

0627 sunbathe

[`sʌn,beθ] ★★
動 做日光浴
名 sunbath 日光浴

0628 deck

[dɛk] ★★★★
名 露天平台、甲板、底板
動 裝飾、打扮
片 upper deck 船艙上層

0629 supper

[`sʌpə] ★★★★
名 晚飯、晚餐時間
同 dinner 晚餐
片 at supper 吃晚飯時

0630 order

[`ɔrdə] ★★★★★
動 點菜、命令、訂購
名 順序、規律、命令
片 in order 合乎程序的

0631 rather

[`ræðə] ★★★★
副 相當、寧願、倒不如
同 pretty 相當
片 would rather 較喜歡

0632 homely

[`homlɪ] ★★
形 不好看的、家常的、家
　 庭的、不做作的
同 plain 平常的

0633 explain

[ɪk`splen] ★★★★
動 解釋、說明、闡明
片 explain away 透過解釋
　 消除

0634 tail

[tel] ★★★★
動 變少、尾隨、跟蹤
名 尾巴、跟蹤者
片 tail off 變小、減弱

0635 information

[ɪnfə`meʃən] ★★★★★
名 消息、報導、資訊
片 mine of information 知
　 識寶庫

0636 teapot

[`tipɑt] ★★
名 茶壺
片 a tempest in a teapot
　 小題大作、大驚小怪

fighting!

Give it a shot 小試身手

❶ We love to eat ice cream in _____.

❷ Are you _____ the information0635 is correct?

❸ The grandfather _____ his grandson to the zoo.

❹ Put the teapot0636 on the _____, please.

❺ The ducks are _____ around the pond.

Answers: ❶ summer ❷ sure ❸ took ❹ table ❺ swimming

短文 107　字彙 108

Essay 054

Mr. Lin is a college[0637] professor[0638], and he teaches a wine tasting[0639] course[0640]. Mr. Lin has good taste in tea, coffee, and alcoholic beverages[0641], and his taste in red wine is better than any other professor at the school. But he has a serious problem. His fondness[0642] for drinking has caused him to be late more than ten times this term. Because of his hangovers[0643], he always wakes up late and then has to take a taxi to school. Students tell him to stop drinking like this. They sometimes have to wait for Mr. Lin for more than half an hour before the class begins, but they still like Mr. Lin's class. Their support has allowed[0644] Mr. Lin to keep teaching at the school, and he is grateful[0645] to them. At the end of the course, Mr. Lin will bring several bottles[0646] of AOC wine to school for his students. This is his favorite collection of French red wine worth[0647] twenty thousand dollars. Mr. Lin loves his students and red wine, and he will keep drinking as he pleases.

中譯 *Translation*

　　林先生是名大學老師，教授品酒課程。林老師對茶、咖啡和酒精飲料都很有鑑賞力，對紅酒的品味更是勝過學校的其他老師。但是他有一個嚴重的問題。他對喝酒的熱愛導致他這學期遲到超過十次。因為宿醉，他總是晚起，必須搭計程車去學校。學生們告訴他不要再這樣喝下去了。有時候他們得等超過半個小時才能開始上課，但他們還是喜歡林老師的課。他們的支持使得林老師能夠繼續任教，他也很感謝他們。待課程結束後，林老師會帶幾瓶 AOC 紅酒到學校給學生喝。這是他最愛的法國紅酒收藏，價值兩萬元。林老師愛他的學生也愛他的紅酒，而且只要他願意他還是會一直喝下去。

0637 college

[`kɑlɪdʒ] ★★★★
名 大學、學院、學會
同 university 大學
片 at college 念大學

0638 professor

[prə`fɛsə] ★★★★
名 教授、老師、專家
同 educator 教師

0639 tasting

[`testɪŋ] ★★
名 品酒集會、嚐味
同 degustation 品嘗
片 wine tasting 品酒

0640 course

[kors] ★★★★★
名 課程、路線、方針
動 流動、追逐
片 course on/in …課程

0641 beverage

[`bɛvərɪdʒ] ★★
名 飲料
同 drinks 飲料

0642 fondness

[`fɑndnɪs] ★★
名 喜愛、鍾愛
片 a fondness for 對…的
喜愛、鍾愛

0643 hangover

[`hæŋ,ovə] ★★★
名 宿醉、殘留物、遺物
片 a hangover form 從以
前留下來的習慣

0644 allow

[ə`lau] ★★★★★
動 允許、給與、認可
反 prohibit 禁止
片 allow for 考慮到

0645 grateful

[`gretfəl] ★★★★
形 感激的、表示感謝的
同 thankful 感激的
片 grateful for 對…感激的

0646 bottle

[`bɑtl] ★★★★
名 瓶子、酒、一瓶的量
動 把…裝入瓶中、約束
片 hit the bottle 喝醉酒

0647 worth

[wɜθ] ★★★★★
形 值…、有…價值的
名 價值、財富
片 worth nothing 不值錢

0648 firefighter

[`faɪr,faɪtə] ★★
名 消防隊員
同 fireman 消防隊員

Fighting!

Give it a shot 小試身手

1. The teacher _____ us to make a cake.
2. I have a bigger room _____ my brother's.
3. Do you notice the girl standing _____?
4. How the firefighters[0648] saved _____?
5. Never _____ a lie to your lover.

Answers: 1 taught 2 than 3 there 4 them 5 tell

MP3　短文 109　字彙 110

Essay

055

Wednesdays and Thursdays are ladies' nights at most nightclubs, which means free entry[0649] to the clubs[0650] for females[0651]. But it is different for guys, and the tickets for them may cost almost one thousand dollars. Thus[0652], throwing[0653] a party at a club is costly. This is why I don't go to clubs, but I do love drinking. I go to the bar three times a week. I prefer to go to quiet locations[0654], like lounge[0655] bars and those kinds of places. I don't think I'm good at dancing, so it's not something I like to do. My friends say I am like a thirty-year-old man for I like to go to jazz clubs. My friends consider jazz to be boring[0656]. I started to listen to jazz when I was thirteen, and I love Latin jazz most. I've been to almost one third of the jazz clubs in the city, and I will keep searching to find the best jazz club in the city.

中譯 *Translation*

大多數的夜店，淑女之夜都在星期三或星期四，也就是女性免費入場。但男人就不一樣了，他們的票價幾乎高達一千元。因此在夜店辦派對是非常昂貴的，這就是我不去夜店的原因。但是我喜歡喝酒。我一個禮拜去酒吧三次。我比較喜歡去某些安靜的地方，像是沙發酒吧那類的場所。我認為我不擅長跳舞，所以這並不是我喜歡做的事。我的朋友都認為我就像是個三十歲的男人，因為我老愛去爵士酒吧。我的朋友都認為爵士樂很無趣。我十三歲時就開始聽爵士，最喜歡的是拉丁爵士。我去過城裡大約三分之一的爵士酒吧，並且會持續尋找最棒的爵士酒吧。

0649 entry

[`ɛntrɪ] ★★★★

名 入場、參加、通道

同 entrance 入口

片 entry intio 進入、參加

0650 club

[klʌb] ★★★★★

名 俱樂部、社團、會所

動 用棍棒打、捐獻、集資

片 club for …的社團

0651 female

[`fimel] ★★★★

名 女人、雌性動物

形 女性的、雌性的

同 feminine 女性的

0652 thus

[ðʌs] ★★★★★

副 因此、以此方式

同 therefore 因此

片 thus far 到此為止

0653 throw

[θro] ★★★★★

動 舉行(宴會)、投擲

名 投擲、冒險

片 throw at 投向、擲向

0654 location

[lo`keʃən] ★★★★

名 場所、位置、外景地點

同 spot 場所、地點

片 on location 外景拍攝

0655 lounge

[laʊndʒ] ★★★★

名 休息室、候機室

動 倚靠、躺、閒蕩

片 lounge around 閒逛

0656 boring

[`borɪŋ] ★★★

形 令人生厭的、乏味的

同 monotonous 單調的

反 interesting 有趣的

0657 umbrella

[ʌm`brɛlə] ★★★★

名 雨傘、保護傘、庇護

同 sunshade 遮陽傘

0658 dump

[dʌmp] ★★★★

名 垃圾場、沮喪

動 傾倒、拋棄、倒垃圾

片 dump on sb. 詆毀某人

0659 concert

[`kɑnsət] ★★★★

名 音樂會、一致、和諧

動 協調、商議

片 in concert 一致

0660 admirer

[əd`maɪrə] ★★

名 讚賞者、欽佩者

同 devotee 愛好者

片 a secret admirer 暗戀者

---

fighting!

Give it a shot 小試身手

1. I _____ this umbrella0657 is yours, right?

2. Please _____ the garbage in the dump0658.

3. The _____ for Lady Gaga's concert0659 is expensive.

4. She is fed up with _____ admirers0660.

5. It is the third time I _____ you today.

056

Essay

Tiger Woods is a top American professional golfer and the most successful golfer of all time. Few golfers can touch him in golf. Woods became a professional golfer in 1996 and signed endorsement[0661] deals worth $40 million with Nike, Inc. The payment[0662] was the highest in golf history and gave him both money and fame. In 1997, Woods won his first major, The Masters. He has set a total of 20 Masters records and tied six others. He was quoted[0663] as saying[0664], "Today America, tomorrow the world." In 2009, he became one of the most notorious athletes in the world because his infidelity[0665] was revealed[0666] by the media. It seems that many famous athletes who are in good shape become involved in sex scandals[0667]. As a result of the scandal, Woods held a press[0668] conference[0669] and spoke in a sorrowful[0670] tone, "Tonight, I'll apologize to my fans for what I've done. I've made too many mistakes. Please give me another chance," he said. His speech was instrumental[0671] in rebuilding[0672] his image. Despite his affairs, Tiger Woods is, unquestionably, the greatest golfer ever.

中譯 *Translation*

　　老虎伍茲是一個頂尖的美國高爾夫球職業選手,也是史上最成功的高爾夫球員。很少有球員的高爾夫球技能與他相比。伍茲在1996年成為一位職業高爾夫選手,並和 Nike 公司簽下價值四千萬的代言交易。這個簽約金創下高爾夫球史上最高,使他名利雙收。1997年,伍茲贏得他的第一個四大錦標賽冠軍—名人公開賽。他在名人公開賽創下總數二十次的紀錄,並與其他六人打成平手。引述老虎伍茲的話:「今天是美國,明天就是全世界。」到了2009年,他因被媒體爆料出軌,而成為全世界最聲名狼藉的運動員之一。許多體態健美的知名運動員似乎都會捲入性醜聞中。由於這次的醜聞,伍茲召開一場記者會,以充滿歉意的語氣說:「今晚,我要為我的行為向球迷道歉。我犯下太多錯了。請給我另一個改過的機會。」他的演講有助於他重建形象。即使如此,老虎伍茲無疑仍是最棒的高爾夫球手。

0661 endorsement

[ɪn`dɔrsmənt] ★★
名 背書、支持、簽署
同 signature 簽署
動 endorse 背書、簽署

0662 payment

[`pemənt] ★★
名 支付、付款、報償
反 default 拖欠
片 in payment of 支付…

0663 quote

[kwot] ★★★★
動 引述、引用、報價
名 引號、報價
片 quote from 引述

0664 saying

[`seɪŋ] ★★★★
名 格言、常言道、言論
片 go without saying 不言
而喻、不用說

0665 infidelity

[ˌɪnfə`dɛlətɪ] ★
名 不信神、不貞行為
同 disloyalty 不忠
反 fidelity 忠誠、忠貞

0666 reveal

[rɪ`vil] ★★★★
動 揭露、展現、洩漏
名 揭示、洩露
片 reveal to 向…透露

0667 scandal

[`skændḷ] ★★
名 醜聞、恥辱、流言蜚語
片 a scandal breaks 醜聞
廣為流傳

0668 press

[prɛs] ★★★★★
名 新聞界、報刊、壓平
動 壓、熨平、催促
片 go to press 付印

0669 conference

[`kɑnfərəns] ★★★
名 會議、協商會、會談
同 meeting 會議
片 in conference 在開會

0670 sorrowful

[`sɑrəfəl] ★★
形 悲傷的、令人傷心的
同 melancholy 憂鬱的
反 joyful 高興的

0671 instrumental

[ɪnstrə`mɛntḷ] ★★
形 有幫助的、樂器演奏的
片 be instrumental in ving
對…有幫助的

0672 rebuild

[ri`bɪld] ★★
動 重建、改建、恢復原貌
同 reconstruct 重建

Fighting!

Give it a shot 小試身手

❶ _____ and tide wait for no man.

❷ The _____ pages of this book are 364.

❸ Birds of a feather flock _____.

❹ The man behind me _____ my thigh.

❺ Don't eat _____ much butter.

Now

057

MP3　短文 113　字彙 114

Essay

My brother turned twelve last Tuesday, and my parents took a trip to Beijing with him by train. They planned[0673] to buy some birthday presents[0674] for my brother. It took twenty hours to get there. On the way as the train moved toward the city, it <u>passed through a</u> vast[0675] mountainous area. My brother saw lots of trees. After they got there, my parents bought a toy robot for him. Afterwards, he tried on some T-shirts in a sports shop and had a big meal, eating ice cream and hot dogs at the same time. Later that day, my brother felt a great pain in his stomach, and he feared he was suffering[0676] from a serious stomach problem. Unfortunately, his fears turned out to be true and, the next day, he had serious diarrhea[0677]. My parents took him to a clinic[0678] twice, but it didn't help. Tummy[0679] aches[0680] still troubled[0681] him on the way back home. My brother had a horrible[0682] trip for his birthday, and he swore[0683] that he would never go to Beijing again.

ⓘ pass through 通過、穿過、經歷

中譯 *Translation*

　　我弟弟上禮拜二滿十二歲了，我爸媽帶著他搭火車到北京旅行。他們計劃買一些生日禮物給我弟弟。抵達北京要花二十個小時。在火車駛向城市的途中，會穿過一片遼闊的山區，弟弟也因此看到許多的樹。他們到了那裡之後，我爸媽買了一個玩具機器人給他。後來，弟弟在體育用品店試穿了幾件T恤，還吃了一頓大餐，同時也吃了冰淇淋和熱狗。稍晚，弟弟覺得肚子一陣劇痛，他很擔心自己得了什麼嚴重的胃病。不幸的是，隔天惡夢就成真了，他腹瀉得很厲害。我爸媽一天帶他去兩次診所，但是卻沒有用。直到回程，肚子痛依舊折磨著他。弟弟的生日之旅實在是糟透了，他發誓再也不要去北京了。

0673 plan

[plæn] ★★★★★
動 計畫、打算
名 計畫、方案、辦法
片 plan to 打算

0674 present

[`prɛznt] ★★★★
名 禮物、贈品、目前
形 出席的、當前的
片 at present 目前

0675 vast

[væst] ★★★★
形 遼闊的、龐大的
片 the vast majority of
　…的絕大多數

0676 suffer

[`sʌfə] ★★★★
動 患病、遭受、經歷
同 undergo 經歷
片 suffer from 受…之苦

0677 diarrhea

[͵daɪə`riə] ★★
名 腹瀉

0678 clinic

[`klɪnɪk] ★★★
名 診所、會診、臨床實習
　課、醫務室
同 polyclinic 聯合診所

0679 tummy

[`tʌmɪ] ★★
名 肚子、胃
片 tummy bug/upset 肚
　子痛

0680 ache

[ek] ★★★★
動 疼痛、渴望、極為想念
名 (持續)疼痛
片 ache for 同情、渴望

0681 trouble

[`trʌbl̩] ★★★★
動 使憂慮、費心、折磨
名 煩惱、困難、故障
片 make trouble 製造麻煩

0682 horrible

[`hɔrəbl̩] ★★★
形 糟透的、可怕的
同 terrible 極差的
片 horrible to 對…不友善

0683 swear

[swɛr] ★★★★
動 發誓、詛咒、宣示
同 vow 發誓要
片 swear by 以…起誓

0684 platform

[`plætfɔrm] ★★★
名 平台、月台、講台、黨
　綱、政綱
片 platform for …的平台

Fighting!

Give it a shot 小試身手

1 I saw her walking _____ the bank.

2 His request is really a big _____ for her.

3 Is it _____ that they are getting married?

4 He heard her voice and _____ back.

5 He got off the _____ and stepped on the platform⁰⁶⁸⁴.

Answers: 1 toward 2 trouble 3 true 4 turned 5 train

058

Essay

MP3　短文 115　字彙 116

I have two uncles, and they are both colonels[0685] in the army. They understand how to promote[0686] themselves and earn more money in the army. When I served[0687] in the military[0688], my uncle sent me to a unit[0689] that was under his control and therefore provided me a more comfortable environment[0690]. My uncle's power was very useful, and he used it for everything. For example, I had better meals with more vegetables and slices[0691] of meat. My bedroom was upstairs and had the best view in the base[0692]. My family and friends could visit me anytime I wanted. This all continued until the day some other soldiers voiced their indignation[0693] about the special treatment[0694] I got, and I started to feel a lot of pressure from my peers[0695]. I no longer went up to my room but stayed with them in the dorms. I thought it was the best for all of us to do that.

> (!) serve in the military 在軍中服役、當兵
> (!) voice one's indignation 某人表示憤慨

中譯 *Translation*

　　我有兩個叔叔，他們都是軍中的陸軍上校。他們洞悉在軍中獲得升遷的方法，也懂得如何賺更多的錢。當我在服兵役時，我叔叔就把我送到他掌管的單位，因此也提供我一個更舒適的環境。我叔叔的權力非常有用，他也四處行使他的權力。舉例來說，我的餐點比一般人好，有更多的蔬菜和肉片。我的房間在樓上，是全軍營中視野最好的。只要我願意，我的家人和朋友隨時都可以來探訪我。直到有天其他軍人因為我所受到的特殊待遇而表示憤慨，我開始感覺到相當大的同儕壓力。我不再上樓去我的房間，而是和他們一起待在宿舍裡。我想這麼做對我們大家而言是最好的吧！

0685 colonel

[ˋkɝnḷ] ★★★★
名 陸軍上校
片 lieutenant colonel 陸軍中校

0686 promote

[prəˋmot] ★★★★
動 晉升、促進、宣傳
反 degrade 使降級
片 promote to 提升為

0687 serve

[sɝv] ★★★★★
動 為…服務、供應、任職、對…有用
片 serve in 在…任職

0688 military

[ˋmɪlətɛrɪ] ★★★
名 軍隊、軍方、陸軍
形 軍事的、軍用的
片 in the military 服役

0689 unit

[ˋjunɪt] ★★★★
名 單位、一員、組件
片 monetary unit 貨幣單位

0690 environment

[ɪnˋvaɪrənmənt] ★★★
名 環境、四周狀況
同 surroundings 環境

0691 slice

[slaɪs] ★★★★
名 切片、部分、曲球
動 切成薄片、割去
片 a slice of 一片…

0692 base

[bes] ★★★★★
名 基地、總部、基礎
動 以…為基礎
片 military base 軍事基地

0693 indignation

[ɪndɪgˋneʃən] ★★
名 憤怒、憤慨
同 outrage 憤慨
衍 indignant 憤怒的

0694 treatment

[ˋtritmənt] ★★★
名 對待、待遇、治療
片 special treatment 特殊待遇

0695 peer

[pɪr] ★★★
名 同儕、同輩
動 凝視、隱約出現
片 peer at 凝視

0696 theory

[ˋθiərɪ] ★★★★
名 理論、學說、意見
片 in theory 理論上

Fighting!

Give it a shot 小試身手

1 My _____ is my father's brother.

2 This theory⁰⁶⁹⁶ is hard to _____.

3 She did not sleep _____ midnight.

4 Do not _____ others without informing them.

5 You should _____ red pen to correct the answers.

Answers: 1 uncle 2 understand 3 until 4 visit 5 use

059

Essay

MP3　短文 117　字彙 118

I am <u>a man of weak character</u>[0697], and I work in a restaurant. I work in the kitchen and wash hundreds of plates every night, but I earn very little money. However, I waste[0698] all my salary on fancy clothes and luxuries. Whenever my friends buy a new pair of Gucci sunglasses or DKNY jeans, I feel like a hillbilly[0699]. I want to dress like them, like wearing a Rolex watch or owning an LV wallet[0700]. With those things, I can walk on the street confidently. One night, the weather was cold, and the rain was heavy. I was on the way home after work, and the water on the ground soaked my feet. I suddenly thought of my girlfriend and felt a feeling of warmth[0701] in my heart. We are getting married soon, but I still have no money for our wedding[0702]. I can't let her wait any longer. Every time she mentions money, it means war. I think I had better pawn[0703] my luxury items[0704] to win back her love.

(!) a person of + adj. + character …性格的人

中譯 *Translation*

　　我是一個性格懦弱的男人，在一間餐廳上班。我在廚房工作，每晚都要洗上百個盤子，但錢卻賺得不多。然而，我把所有的薪水揮霍在昂貴的服飾和奢侈品上。每當我朋友買了一副新的 Gucci 太陽眼鏡或 DKNY 的牛仔褲時，我就覺得自己像個鄉巴佬。我想穿得和他們一樣，像是戴著勞力士錶，或擁有一個 LV 皮夾。有了這些東西，我就可以自信地走在街上。某個天氣很冷的晚上，下著傾盆大雨。我走在下班回家的路上，路上的積水浸濕了我的雙腳。我突然想起女友，心裡覺得很溫暖。我們很快就要結婚了，但我還是沒錢辦婚禮。我不能再讓她等太久了。每次只要她提起錢，就會有爭吵戰。我想我最好把我那些奢侈品當掉，這樣才能贏回她的愛。

0697 character

[ˋkærɪktɚ] ★★★★
名 性格、特性、名聲、角色、字體
同 nature 天性

0698 waste

[west] ★★★★
動 浪費、濫用、使荒廢
名 廢棄物、消耗
片 waste on 浪費在

0699 hillbilly

[ˋhɪlbɪlɪ] ★
名 (帶侮辱性字眼)鄉巴佬、(美國南方)山區居民

0700 wallet

[ˋwɑlɪt] ★★★
名 錢包、皮夾、皮製公事包
同 billfold 皮夾

0701 warmth

[wɔrmθ] ★★★
名 溫暖、親切、熱情
同 cordiality 熱誠
片 with warmth 熱情地

0702 wedding

[ˋwɛdɪŋ] ★★★★
名 婚禮、結婚紀念日
衍 wed 結婚

0703 pawn

[pɔn] ★★★
動 典當、抵押
名 抵押品、人質
片 in pawn 典當

0704 item

[ˋaɪtəm] ★★★★
名 品目、細目、條款
同 detail 細部
片 an item of 一件、一項

0705 check

[tʃɛk] ★★★★★
動 核對、檢查、開支票
名 檢查、支票、格子布
片 check on 檢查

0706 changeable

[ˋtʃendʒəbl] ★★
形 易變的、不定的
同 capricious 善變的
反 stable 穩重的

0707 patient

[ˋpeʃənt] ★★★★
名 病人
形 有耐心的、能忍受的
片 be patient with 有耐心

0708 correct

[kəˋrɛkt] ★★★★
形 正確的、恰當的
動 改正、校準、懲治
片 correct to 把…改成

 Fighting!

Give it a shot 小試身手

① Please _____ a minute. I'll check[0705] it for you.

② Remember to _____ your hands after going to the toilet.

③ _____ in April is changeable[0706].

④ Doctor, why the patient[0707] looked so _____?

⑤ His _____ didn't tell the correct[0708] time.

Answers: ① wait ② wash ③ Weather ④ weak ⑤ watch

060

Essay

Fat people are sometimes <u>looked down upon</u>. My cousin[0709], who weighs[0710] 120 kilograms[0711], has a plan to lose weight. He calculates[0712] the amount of calories in the food he eats, no matter what he eats. No matter where he goes, he walks. He <u>works out</u> in the park every weekend, whether the weather is good or not. But he broke[0713] his rules[0714] last week. He had spicy hot pot last Wednesday, and I couldn't believe how much food he ate. When we finished the delicious spicy hot pot, he weighed himself on the scales[0715]. When he stood on the scales, he found that he had gained another two kilograms, which surprised me so much. In order to lose the weight that he had just gained, we decided to ride our bikes home. That was tough[0716], but we all tried to do it well. After three hours of riding, my face turned pale[0717], and I was exhausted[0718]. Losing weight is hard, but perseverance[0719] helps you achieve that goal.

(!) be looked down upon 受人鄙視、遭人看不起

(!) work out 做大量運動的鍛鍊

中譯 *Translation*

　　胖子到哪都不受歡迎。我的表哥，體重一百二十公斤，正計劃著要減肥。不管吃什麼，他都會計算食物的熱量。不管去哪裡他都走路。他無論天氣好壞，每個週末都到公園運動。但是上禮拜他破戒了。他上禮拜三吃了麻辣鍋，我實在是不敢相信他居然吃了這麼多食物。當我們吃完美味的麻辣鍋，他就用體重計稱重。他一站上去，就發現自己又增胖了兩公斤，這真是太令我驚訝了。為了讓他減掉剛增加的體重，我們決定騎腳踏車回家。那很辛苦，但我們都試著努力達成。騎了三個小時之後，我的臉色發白且精疲力盡。減重很困難，但堅持不懈會幫助你達成目標。

0709 cousin

[`kʌzn̩] ★★★★

名 堂(表)兄弟姊妹、同性
質的人或物

0710 weigh

[we] ★★★★

動 有…重量、權衡
片 weigh down 壓垮
衍 weight 重量

0711 kilogram

[`kɪləgræm] ★★

名 公斤

0712 calculate

[`kælkjəlet] ★★★

動 計算、估計、打算
同 count 計算
片 calculate on 指望

0713 break

[brek] ★★★★★

動 打破、毀壞、闖入
名 破裂、休息、決裂
片 break into 強行闖入

0714 rule

[rul] ★★★★

名 常規、規定、支配
動 控制、支配、管轄
片 as a rule 通常

0715 scale

[skel] ★★★★

名 磅秤、規模、刻度
動 攀登、到達…頂點
片 scale dowm 縮減

0716 tough

[tʌf] ★★★★★

形 棘手的、堅韌的、結實
的、固執的
片 be tough on 嚴格對待

0717 pale

[pel] ★★★★

形 蒼白的、淡的、微弱的
動 變蒼白、顯得遜色
同 dim 暗淡的

0718 exhausted

[ɪg`zɔstɪd] ★★★

形 精疲力竭的、耗盡的、
用完的
同 fatigued 疲乏的

0719 perseverance

[pɜsə`vɪrəns] ★★

名 堅持不懈、毅力
同 persistence 堅持

0720 twice

[twaɪs] ★★★★

副 兩次、兩倍
同 double 雙倍地
片 twice a day 一天兩次

Fighting!

Give it a shot 小試身手

❶ I go to the gym twice⁰⁷²⁰ a _____.

❷ He _____ the eggs and told me the price.

❸ _____ one do you like, purple or pink?

❹ That's the boy _____ won the champion yesterday.

❺ What do you usually do on the _____?

Answers: ❶ week ❷ weighed ❸ Which ❹ who ❺ weekends

061

Essay

I wish[0721] relationships were never about winning or losing, but it often seems that way. Love should be mutual[0722]. But sometimes, your partner[0723] may love you more, or you may care about him/her more than he/she does about you. It can happen to any man or woman, even to husbands and wives. Why is it so complicated[0724]? When your partner is the only thing you care[0725] about in the whole world, it can be very sweet but dangerous. You worry about whom he/she goes out with, whose perfume or cologne[0726] smell is left in the car, and what he/she does when you are away. In that event, love becomes a burden[0727]. If you think about it philosophically[0728], you'll find that you are happier if you love yourself. There are still a lot of things worth experiencing, even if you have relationship problems. Have you ever tasted red wine in the woods in New Zealand? Have you ever watched the polar[0729] lights in the winter at the North Pole[0730]? Open the window and let the wind blow on your face. Life is full of beautiful things!

> ! in that event 如果那種情況發生、那樣一來

中譯 *Translation*

　　我希望在一段感情裡不要有輸贏，但一般似乎都是這樣的情況。愛應該是雙向的，但有時候，你的伴侶可能會愛你多一點，或是你對他的關心比較多。這種情況在任何男女身上都會發生，即使是夫妻亦然。為什麼會這麼複雜呢？當你的伴侶成為你全世界唯一關心的人，這會是非常甜蜜但卻也危險的一件事。你會擔心他和誰一起出門？車子裡是誰的香水味？你不在的時候他會做些什麼？那樣一來，愛就變成了負擔。如果你冷靜地思考一下，你會發現多愛自己一點會使你更快樂。雖然你的感情出了問題，還是有很多事值得體驗。你曾經在紐西蘭的樹林裡品嘗過紅酒嗎？你看過北極冬季的極光嗎？打開窗讓微風拂過你的臉龐。生命中滿是美好的事物！

0721 wish

[wɪʃ] ★★★★
動 希望、但願、渴望
名 希望、願望
片 wish to do sth. 想要

0722 mutual

[`mjutʃuəl] ★★★★
形 相互的、共同的
同 joint 共有的
反 disparate 不同的

0723 partner

[`partnɚ] ★★★★
名 搭檔、合夥人、配偶
動 同…合作、合夥
片 partner off 配成對

0724 complicated

[`kampləketɪd] ★★★
形 複雜的、難懂的
同 comlex 複雜的
動 complicate 使複雜化

0725 care

[kɛr] ★★★★★
動 關心、擔心、想要
名 關懷、看護、謹慎
片 care for 喜歡、牽掛

0726 cologne

[kə`lon] ★★
名 古龍香水
同 perfume 香水

0727 burden

[`bɝdṇ] ★★★★
名 重擔、負擔
動 加負擔於、煩擾
片 burden with 揹負著

0728 philosophically

[ˌfɪlə`safɪkḷɪ] ★★
副 冷靜地、哲學上
名 philosophy 哲學、哲理、人生觀

0729 polar

[`polɚ] ★★★
形 極地的、電極的、截然對立的
片 polar circle 極圈

0730 pole

[pol] ★★★★
名 極地、柱、竿
片 be poles apart 南轅北轍

0731 raise

[rez] ★★★★★
動 提出、舉起、增加
名 加薪、提高
同 elevate 舉起

0732 literature

[`lɪtərətʃɚ] ★★
名 文學、文獻資料
片 literature on 關於…的文獻

fighting!

Give it a shot 小試身手

① That is ＿＿＿ he raised[0731] the question.

② ＿＿＿ bag was left on the chair?

③ He looked at me ＿＿＿ anger.

④ The ＿＿＿ in middle age was her mother.

⑤ Hemingway once ＿＿＿ the Nobel Prize for literature[0732].

Answers: ① why ② Whose ③ with ④ woman ⑤ won

062

Essay

🎧 MP3 短文 123 字彙 124

I <u>deal with</u> words and sentences every day. The lights are always on in my room at four o'clock in the morning. It's quiet at night, and, therefore, I can write the most beautiful essays in the world at that time. However, I don't have a very comfortable life. I am a worker on a farm in the daytime, and my job is to spray[0733] pesticide[0734] on yams[0735] to kill worms. At night, I work as a writer, expressing[0736] myself through my writing. My readers can feel my deep passion whenever they read my work, as I am always optimistic[0737] about the future. Although I have made mistakes in the past, I don't worry about anything. I've experienced the worst[0738] types of situations[0739], so I can handle[0740] anything. Even though I do not earn[0741] much and just <u>make ends meet</u>, it doesn't mean that things will be this way all my life. Because I know that I'm really special, one day I will shine.

> (!) deal with 處理、對待、關於
>
> (!) to make ends meet 使收支平衡，也可以說 make both ends meet

中譯 *Translation*

　　我每天都在寫作。我房間的燈到了凌晨四點都還是亮著的。夜裡很安靜，因此我可以在那當下寫出世上最優美的文章。然而，我的生活並不寬裕。我白天在田裡工作，我的工作是在蕃薯上噴殺蟲劑除蟲。到了晚上，我是一名作家，透過寫作來表達自己的想法。我的讀者隨時都能從我的作品中感受到我的深切熱忱，因為我總是樂觀面對未來的一切。儘管我過去犯了許多錯誤，我卻一點也不擔心。我曾經歷過最糟的情況，所以有辦法應付任何事。雖然我的收入不多，只能剛好維持收支平衡，但不代表我的人生都將如此。因為我知道我很特別，總有一天我會大放異彩。

0733 spray

[spre] ★★★
動 噴灑、濺散
名 噴霧、浪花、噴灑器
片 sprary with 用…噴灑

0734 pesticide

[`pɛstɪ͵saɪd] ★★★
名 殺蟲劑、農藥
片 organic pesticide 有機農藥

0735 yam

[jæm] ★★
名 蕃薯、山藥、馬鈴薯、山芋類植物

0736 express

[ɪk`sprɛs] ★★★★
動 表達、快遞、擠壓出
名 快遞、快車
形 直達的、明確的

0737 optimistic

[͵ɑptə`mɪstɪk] ★★
形 樂觀的
片 be optimistic about 對…抱持樂觀態度

0738 worst

[wɜst] ★★★★★
形 最壞的、最差的
副 最壞地、最不利地
片 at the worst 起碼

0739 situation

[͵sɪtʃʊ`eʃən] ★★★★
名 處境、情況、位置
同 position 境況
片 no-win situation 輸定

0740 handle

[`hændl̩] ★★★★
動 處理、操作、經營
名 把手、把柄
同 deal 處理

0741 earn

[ɜn] ★★★★
動 賺得、贏得、博得
反 consume 花費
片 earn a living 謀生

0742 viewpoint

[`vju͵pɔɪnt] ★★
名 觀點、視角、見解
同 standpoint 觀點

0743 vote

[vot] ★★★★★
動 投票決定、選舉、提議
名 選舉、選票、得票數
片 vote sth. down 否決

0744 protest

[prə`tɛst] ★★★
動 抗議、反對、聲明
名 異議、反對、聲明
片 protest against 反對

Fighting!

Give it a shot 小試身手

❶ Although his answer was _____, he provided a new viewpoint0742.

❷ How cruel were you to hurt her by saying those _____!

❸ She _____ about the interview tomorrow.

❹ He was voted0743 the _____ dressed celebrity.

❺ The _____ protested0744 for the low pay.

MP3 短文 125 字彙 126

Essay

063

When I was young, about seventeen years old, I took my girlfriend to the zoo on a date. That was a very exciting place! However, it was not exciting enough for my girlfriend, so afterward we chose to go to an amusement[0745] park for a date. I loved the roller[0746] coaster[0747], but I was also afraid to ride on it. One day, I went to an amusement park with my girlfriend as usual. While we were riding on the roller coaster, I knew there was something wrong with my stomach. Maybe the yummy[0748] but spicy food I had eaten yesterday caused it. Even before the roller coaster had started moving, I was sweating all over my body. I was suffering from both fear and a stomachache[0749]. "Three, two, one, zero, yes!" my girlfriend shouted[0750] excitedly. As the roller coaster went forward, I <u>couldn't help but</u> have the trots[0751]. When we got off the roller coaster, my girlfriend saw brownish[0752] stains on my pants. She said, "Oh, you yucky guy! What did you do in your pants?" After that date, I called her several[0753] times, but she has never returned any of my voice messages.

ⓘ couldn't help but 忍不住、不得不，couldn't 也可替換成 can't

中譯 *Translation*

　　在我還年輕、大約十七歲的時候，我帶著女朋友到動物園約會。那真是個刺激的地方！但對我女朋友而言卻不夠刺激，所以後來我們都去遊樂園約會。我喜歡雲霄飛車，但也很害怕乘坐。有一天，我和情人一如往常地前往遊樂園。當我們坐上雲霄飛車時，我就發覺我的胃有點不太對勁。可能是我昨天吃的那美味卻辛辣的食物造成的。甚至在雲霄飛車啟動之前，我就已經全身冒汗，恐懼和胃痛同時折磨著我。「三、二、一、零，耶！」女友興奮地大叫。當雲霄飛車一前進，我忍不住拉肚子了。我們一下雲霄飛車，女友就看到我的褲子有黃色的汙漬。她說：「噢，髒鬼！你在你的褲子上做了什麼？」那次約會之後，我打了好多通電話給她，但她卻未曾回覆我的任何一通留言。

0745 amusement

[əˋmjuzmənt] ★★
- 名 娛樂、消遣、樂趣
- 同 entertainment 娛樂
- 反 boredom 無聊

0746 roller

[ˋrolə] ★★★
- 名 滾動物、滾筒、捲軸、巨浪、壓路機
- 片 roller skate 輪式溜冰鞋

0747 coaster

[ˋkostə] ★★
- 名 沿岸貿易船、杯墊
- 片 roller coaster 雲霄飛車

0748 yummy

[ˋjʌmɪ] ★★
- 形 美味的、令人喜愛的
- 名 美味的東西
- 同 delicious 美味的

0749 stomachache

[ˋstʌmək͵ek] ★★
- 名 胃痛、腹痛
- 同 bellyache 腹痛
- 衍 stomach 胃、肚子

0750 shout

[ʃaut] ★★★★
- 動 喊叫、大聲說出
- 名 呼喊、喊叫聲
- 片 shout at 對…大喊

0751 trot

[trat] ★★★
- 名 拉肚子、慢跑、急行
- 動 小跑步、帶領
- 片 on the trot 接連

0752 brownish

[ˋbraunɪʃ] ★★
- 形 呈褐色的
- 同 brown 褐色的

0753 several

[ˋsɛvərəl] ★★★★
- 形 幾個的、數個的
- 代 幾個、數個
- 同 various 許多的

0754 complementary

[͵kɑmpləˋmɛntərɪ] ★
- 形 互補的、相配的
- 片 complimentary colors 互補色

0755 previous

[ˋpriviəs] ★★★★
- 形 以前的、先的
- 同 former 早前的
- 片 previous to 在…以前

0756 lovely

[ˋlʌvlɪ] ★★★★
- 形 可愛的、令人愉快的、(口)好極了
- 同 delightful 令人愉快的

fighting!

Give it a shot 小試身手

① _____ and blue are complementary⁰⁷⁵⁴ colors.

② The temperature has _____ to zero.

③ I haven't finished reading the book _____.

④ Their sales improved compared to the previous⁰⁷⁵⁵ _____.

⑤ I'm going to the _____ to see lovely⁰⁷⁵⁶ pandas.

064

Essay

A good environment can aid[0757] language learning. In Taiwan, the absence[0758] of the chance to use English makes it difficult to learn that language. My goal was to be an English teacher, so I studied abroad[0759] three years ago in order to advance my English ability. Now I am back in Taiwan. Whenever I look at the album with pictures from my time in Australia, it reminds[0760] me of my school, friends, and people I dated. I am an active[0761] person, and I'm quite tolerant[0762] and accepting of different cultures. I accepted every invitation[0763] I got to a party, so I made a lot of good friends in Melbourne. Last month, I went back to Australia. As soon as my China Airlines flight landed[0764] at the airport in Melbourne, I felt like I was back in the past. Everything looked the same, the streets, the coffee shops, and the people. I had a really great time and wished I could have stayed longer. But I had a lot of works to get back to in Taiwan. In addition[0765] to this, I still had to take care of my elderly[0766] parents. What a pity[0767] it was for me to have to say goodbye to Australia once again!

中譯 *Translation*

　　好的環境有利於學習語言。台灣缺乏使用英語的機會，使學習英文變得困難。我的目標是成為一名英文老師，因此我三年前出國讀書以增強英語能力。現在我回到了台灣。每當我看著在澳洲時的相簿，就會想起我的學校、朋友和交往的對象。我是個積極的人，很樂於接受不同的文化。我從未缺席任何的派對邀請，所以我在墨爾本交到了很多朋友。上個月我回到澳洲。當中華航空班機抵達墨爾本機場的時候，我彷彿回到了過去。街道、咖啡館和人群，一切看起來都還是一模一樣。我過得很愉快，也希望可以久留。然而我在台灣還有很多工作等著我。除此之外，我還得照顧年邁的雙親。很遺憾我還是要再次向澳洲說再見。

0757 aid

[ed] ★★★★★
- 動 幫助、支援、有助於
- 名 援助、助手、副官
- 片 aid sb. in + ving 幫助

0758 absence

[`æbsn̩s] ★★★★
- 名 缺乏、缺席
- 反 presence 出席、存在
- 片 absence of 缺乏

0759 abroad

[ə`brɔd] ★★★★
- 副 到(在)國外、傳開
- 名 異國、海外
- 片 go abroad 出國

0760 remind

[rɪ`maɪnd] ★★★
- 動 使想起、提醒
- 同 recall 使想起
- 片 remind of 使回想起

0761 active

[`æktɪv] ★★★★
- 形 活潑的、積極的
- 同 energetic 精力旺盛的
- 反 inactive 無生氣的

0762 tolerant

[`tɑlərənt] ★★
- 形 容忍的、有耐性的
- 同 liberal 心胸開闊的
- 片 tolerant of 對…忍耐

0763 invitation

[͵ɪnvə`teʃən] ★★★
- 名 邀請、引誘、鼓勵
- 同 invitation to do sth. 應邀做某事

0764 land

[lænd] ★★★★
- 動 登陸、卸貨、使陷於
- 名 陸地、田地、國土
- 片 land on/in 降落於

0765 addition

[ə`dɪʃən] ★★★
- 名 附加、加法、增建部分
- 反 subtraction 減少
- 片 in addition to 除…之外

0766 elderly

[`ɛldəlɪ] ★★★
- 形 年長的、老式的
- 同 aged 年老的
- 反 young 年輕的

0767 pity

[`pɪtɪ] ★★★★
- 名 憾事、憐憫、同情
- 動 憐憫、同情
- 片 take pity on 同情

0768 excellent

[`ɛksl̩ənt] ★★★★
- 形 出色的、傑出的
- 同 marvelous 非凡的
- 反 inferior 較差的

fighting!

Give it a shot 小試身手

1 Her _____ of marketing was excellent[0768].

2 Diana decided to study _____ after graduating from college.

3 The boss treats everyone _____.

4 We discussed about how to deal with the _____.

5 In _____ to sausages, I prepared hotdogs.

065

Essay

I used to be lonely all the time. My friends held parties every weekend, but I just stayed in my apartment and played on-line games. Anyway, being alone was better than being ignored during social occasions. My appearance was horrible. Once on a date, a girl told me that she had no appetite[0769] because of my ugly teeth. I cried aloud[0770] that night. I decided to change my life, and I swore that nobody would ever laugh at me again as long as I lived.

I started to spend a large amount of money on buying nice clothing and participated[0771] in every social activity[0772] I got invited to. I also worked out whenever I possibly could and even hurt my ankle because I exercised so much. Although I had a more attractive appearance, I was still very shy. Altogether[0773], I lacked social skills, but, anyhow, I kept trying to improve myself. It was surprising that recently a female classmate asked me some questions about the English alphabet[0774], and another one invited me to see an antique[0775] car exhibition[0776]. I think that shows I have successfully[0777] transformed[0778] myself into a more attractive person!

中譯 *Translation*

　　我過去一直都很寂寞。我的朋友們每個週末都會辦派對，但我都只待在我的公寓裡玩線上遊戲。無論如何，一個人總是比在社交場合被忽略來得好。我的長相很不討喜。有一次我和一名女孩約會，她說我難看的牙齒讓她毫無食慾。那一晚我放聲大哭。我決定改變我的人生，並且發誓只要我還活在這世上，就不會再被人嘲笑。

　　我開始花大錢添購好看的衣服，並且參與每一個受邀參加的社交活動。我也隨時隨地運動，甚至因為運動過度而傷到腳踝。雖然我有了更好看的外表，我還是很害羞。總而言之，我缺乏社交能力，但無論如何我都持續努力讓自己變得更好。出人意料的是，最近有個女同學在課堂上問我字母表的問題，還有另一個同學邀我去看古董車展。我想這表示我成功改造為一個更有魅力的人！

0769 appetite

[ˋæpə͵taɪt] ★★★

名 食慾、胃口、愛好

同 hunger 食慾

片 appetite for …的慾望

0770 aloud

[əˋlaud] ★★★

副 大聲地、出聲地

反 silently 沉默地

片 think aloud 自言自語

0771 participate

[parˋtɪsə͵pet] ★★★

動 參加、分擔、帶有

同 partake 參加

片 participate in 參加

0772 activity

[ækˋtɪvətɪ] ★★★

名 活動、活躍、消遣

同 action 活動

片 inactivity 不活潑

0773 altogether

[͵ɔltəˋgɛðɚ] ★★★

副 總之、完全、合計

同 partially 部分地

片 not altogether 不完全

0774 alphabet

[ˋælfə͵bɛt] ★★★

名 字母表、初步、入門

同 letters 字母

0775 antique

[ænˋtik] ★★★

形 古董的、古老的

名 古董、古玩、古風

同 ancient 古老的

0776 exhibition

[͵ɛksəˋbɪʃən] ★★★

名 展覽、顯示、陳列品

同 exposition 展覽會

片 on exhibition 展出中

0777 successfully

[səkˋsɛsfəlɪ] ★★

副 順利地、成功地

反 unsuccessfully 失敗地

0778 transform

[trænsˋfɔrm] ★★★

動 改變、改觀、變換

同 convert 變換

片 transform into 轉變為

0779 entire

[ɪnˋtaɪr] ★★★★

形 整個的、完全的

同 whole 整個的

反 partial 部分的

0780 abase

[əˋbes] ★★

動 貶低、使謙卑

反 exalt 使得意

片 abase oneself 自貶身分

Fighting!

Give it a shot 小試身手

1 Read the entire⁰⁷⁷⁹ text _____, please.

2 The bill _____ to one thousand dollars.

3 The ugly girl is self-abased⁰⁷⁸⁰ for her _____.

4 Call me _____ you need company.

5 Dragon is a symbol of Chinese _____ culture.

Answers: 1 aloud 2 amounts 3 appearance 4 anytime 5 ancient

066

Essay

When the city is asleep, a group of artists are busy on every corner in a city. Their pieces[0781] are everywhere, at train stations, on buses, on road signs, and on phone booths[0782]. They are graffiti[0783] artists, and they spray paint images on walls everywhere. Graffiti artists catch the public's attention by painting walls, and they are like other kinds of artists. Writers debate the various forms of writing, installation[0784] artists discuss the best way to organize displays in public buildings, and graffiti artists also talk about the various techniques[0785] they use. Graffiti culture arrived in Taiwan a few years ago, but city councils[0786] attacked graffiti artists for their activity was still illegal[0787] in most places. They could be arrested[0788] if they painted in the wrong places, unless they had applied[0789] for permission ahead of time. An assistant[0790] of a well-known graffiti artist, <u>armed with</u> various kinds of painter's paraphernalia[0791] and her apron[0792], sat on an armchair and said in an interview, "Graffiti is one kind of art. Art is not a type of crime!"

> ⓘ be armed with 在本文中表示「配備」，另也有「用…武裝」、「準備」等意思

中譯 *Translation*

　　當這個城市沉沉睡去的時候，有一群藝術家正忙著在城市的每個角落創作他們的藝術。他們的作品隨處可見，車站、公車、交通號誌及電話亭都有。他們是塗鴉藝術家，他們在牆上四處噴灑漆畫。塗鴉藝術家藉由在牆上作畫吸引大眾注意，就像其他類型的藝術家一樣。作家會爭論各種寫作的形式，裝置藝術家討論著在公共建築安排最佳的陳列方式，而塗鴉畫家也會討論他們所使用的各種創作技巧。塗鴉文化在數年前來到台灣。但市議會認為塗鴉在多數地區仍屬違法，因而抨擊塗鴉畫家。他們會因畫錯地方而遭到逮捕，除非他們事先申請。一位知名塗鴉畫家的助理，帶著各式各樣的畫具並穿著工作裙，坐在扶手椅上，於一場訪談中表示：「塗鴉是一種藝術。藝術不是一種罪！」

0781 piece

[pis] ★★★★★
名 作品、一片、一則消息
動 拼湊、修補
片 piece up 拼湊成

0782 booth

[buθ] ★★★
名 公共電話亭、貨攤、投票站
片 ticket booth 售票亭

0783 graffiti

[grə`fɪtɪ] ★★
名 塗鴉、亂塗亂抹
片 graffiti art 塗鴉藝術

0784 installation

[ˌɪnstə`leʃən] ★★★
名 裝置、設置、就職
片 installation art 裝置藝術

0785 technique

[tɛk`nik] ★★★★
名 技巧、技術、手段
同 skill 技術、技能
片 technique for …的技巧

0786 council

[`kaʊnsḷ] ★★★★
名 地方議會、會議、商討
同 assembly 議會
片 city council 市議會

0787 illegal

[ɪ`ligḷ] ★★★★
形 非法的、違反規則的
名 非法移民、間諜
反 legal 合法的

0788 arrest

[ə`rɛst] ★★★★
動 逮捕、阻止、吸引
名 逮捕、遏止、奪取
片 arrest for 因…逮捕

0789 apply

[ə`plaɪ] ★★★★
動 申請、塗、應用、使適用、致力於
片 apply for 申請…

0790 assistant

[ə`sɪstənt] ★★★★
名 助理、助手
形 助理的、有幫助的
同 aide 助手

0791 paraphernalia

[ˌpærəfə`nelɪə] ★★
名 隨身用具、設備、複雜程序
同 gear 設備、裝置

0792 apron

[`eprən] ★★★
名 工作裙、圍裙、停機坪
片 be tied to sb's apron strings 受某人控制

---

fighting!

Give it a shot 小試身手

❶ The worker kept _____ about the wages.

❷ The party was _____ well by the staff.

❸ He was already gone when I _____.

❹ Pay _____ to your teacher in the class, please.

❺ What I saw in his _____ was a brand new idea.

Answers: ❶ arguing ❷ arranged ❸ arrived ❹ attention ❺ article

067

Essay

Mr. Brown lived next to my house, and I couldn't bear[0793] the noise he made. He had barbecue parties every evening. He got drunk and shouted at night, and his dog barked[0794] all the time. I couldn't sleep, and, therefore, I moved my bedroom to the basement[0795] to avoid the noise. When I stood on my balcony[0796], I could see a lot of garbage piled[0797] up in his backyard. Mr. Brown didn't look friendly. He had a beard[0798] and tattoo[0799] on his chest. I heard that he was a retired soldier who had fought in the battlefields[0800] of Iraq. After he came back, he started working in a steak restaurant.

One day, while I was baking some bread at my bakery, and he suddenly came in with a bamboo stick. I moved backwards[0801] and threw a basket[0802] of beans at him. He said in a low voice, "I smell something burning. From my experience, that means I should do something to help <u>put out the fire</u>." We both burst[0803] out laughing. Since then, we have been very good neighbors.

ⓘ put out the fire 滅火

中譯 *Translation*

　　布朗先生住在我家隔壁，我實在無法忍受他製造的噪音。他每晚都會舉辦烤肉派對。晚上他會醉醺醺地大聲咆哮，他的狗也一直叫個不停。我無法入睡，所以我把臥室移去地下室以避開噪音。當我站在陽臺時，可以看到他的後院積了一大堆垃圾。布朗先生看起來很不友善，他蓄鬍，胸前又有刺青。我聽說他是曾上伊拉克戰場打仗的退休軍人。他回來之後，就在一間牛排館工作。

　　某天，我在我的烘焙店裡烤麵包，他突然帶著一根竹棒走進來。我往後退，把一籃豆子丟向他。他用低沉的聲音說道：「我聞到有東西燒焦了，根據經驗，那表示我必須做點什麼來幫忙滅火。」我們都大笑起來。從那之後，我們成了非常要好的鄰居。

0793 bear

[bɛr] ★★★★★
動 忍受、承擔、運送
名 熊、魯莽的人
片 bear in mind 記住

0794 bark

[bɑrk] ★★★
動 吠叫、咆哮、厲聲說出
名 狗叫聲
片 bark at 對著…吠叫

0795 basement

[`besmənt] ★★★★
名 地下室、地窖
同 cellar 地下室、地窖

0796 balcony

[`bælkənɪ] ★★★
名 陽台、劇場包廂
同 deck 露天平台

0797 pile

[paɪl] ★★★★
動 堆積、疊、累積
名 一堆、大量
片 pile up 堆積、增多

0798 beard

[bɪrd] ★★★
名 鬍鬚、山羊鬍
動 與…對抗、公然反對
片 grow a beard 留鬍子

0799 tattoo

[tæ`tu] ★★
名 紋身
動 刺花紋於

0800 battlefield

[`bætl̩ˌfild] ★★
名 戰場、戰地、爭論的問題
同 battleground 戰場

0801 backwards

[`bækwədz] ★★★
副 向後、逆、往回
片 know sth. backwards 對…瞭若指掌

0802 basket

[`bæskɪt] ★★★★
名 一籃的量、籃網
片 put all one's eggs in one basket 孤注一擲

0803 burst

[bɜst] ★★★
動 爆發、破裂、塞滿
名 爆炸、爆發、破裂
片 burst out 突然…起來

0804 brake

[brek] ★★★
動 煞車、抑制、約束
名 煞車、阻礙、揉麵機
片 brake sharply 緊急煞車

Fighting!

Give it a shot 小試身手

1 She braked[0804] suddenly and _____ an accident.
2 She bought some bread in the _____.
3 The girl locked herself in the _____.
4 Stressed is desserts spelled _____.
5 We knew the dog found something for it kept _____.

Answers: 1 avoided 2 bakery 3 bedroom 4 backwards 5 barking

MP3　短文 135　字彙 136

Essay

068

It's my belief[0805] that birthdays should be celebrated[0806]. At my 21st birthday party, I drank five bottles of bitter[0807] beer and half a bottle of vodka. It was unforgettable. My friends played a <u>drinking game</u> where people had to drink a shot if they lost, but I kept losing. Besides that, I was still new to drinking. After five shots of Bacardi, I went beyond my limit. I begged my friends to stop making me drink. I was too drunk to know what I was doing. I even forgot to <u>pay my bill</u> and <u>kicked down</u> the blackboard[0808] menu when I left the bar. I sat on a bench outside, and my pants felt too tight[0809] around my stomach. I took off my belt so I could breath. I bent[0810] down and started to vomit[0811]. At the same time, my vision[0812] went blank[0813], and I felt like a blind[0814] person. I had an awful[0815] hangover next morning. Was that a good way to celebrate my birthday?

ⓘ drinking game，行酒令，亦即朋友間喝酒時助興圖開心而玩的遊戲

ⓘ pay the bill 付帳

ⓘ kick down sth. 或 kick sth. down 把…踢倒

中譯 *Translation*

　　我認為生日就是要慶祝。在我二十一歲的生日派對上，我喝了五瓶苦啤酒，以及半瓶伏特加。那真是令人難以忘懷。我和朋友行酒令，凡是輸的就要喝一杯，而我卻輸個不停。況且，我還是一個喝酒新手。在喝完五杯百加得之後，我已經超出了我的酒量。我拜託朋友不要再灌我酒。我已經醉到對自己的行為毫無所覺。我甚至沒付帳就要離開酒吧，還踢倒黑板菜單。我坐在外面的長板凳上，褲子把我的胃勒得很緊，要把皮帶拿掉才能呼吸。我彎下身體開始嘔吐。同時，我的視線一片模糊，我覺得自己就像盲人一樣。我隔天早上宿醉得非常嚴重。這種慶生方式真的好嗎？

0805 belief

[bɪ`lif] ★★★★
- 名 看法、相信、信仰
- 反 doubt 懷疑
- 片 hold a belief 相信

0806 celebrate

[`sɛlə‚bret] ★★★★
- 動 慶祝、頌揚、舉行
- 同 commemorate 慶祝
- 衍 celebration 慶典

0807 bitter

[`bɪtə] ★★★★
- 形 苦的、尖刻的、慘痛的
- 片 bitter pill to swallow 不得不忍受的苦差事

0808 blackboard

[`blæk‚bord] ★★★
- 名 黑板
- 同 chalkboard 黑板

0809 tight

[taɪt] ★★★★
- 形 繃緊的、牢固的、排滿的、棘手的
- 副 緊緊地、牢牢地

0810 bend

[bɛnd] ★★★★
- 動 彎曲、屈從、致力於
- 名 彎腰、傾向
- 片 bend down 俯身

0811 vomit

[`vɑmɪt] ★★★
- 動 嘔吐、噴出、吐出
- 名 嘔吐、嘔吐物
- 同 retch 作嘔、反胃

0812 vision

[`vɪʒən] ★★★★
- 名 視力、所見事物、眼光、憧憬
- 片 field of vision 視野

0813 blank

[blæŋk] ★★★★
- 形 空白的、茫然的
- 名 空白格、空白處
- 動 變模糊、刪去、封鎖

0814 blind

[blaɪnd] ★★★★
- 形 盲的、未加思考的
- 名 百葉窗、掩飾、埋伏處
- 片 blind alley 絕境

0815 awful

[`ɔful] ★★★★
- 形 可怕的、極糟的
- 副 十分、極其
- 同 terrible 可怕的

0816 questionnaire

[‚kwɛstʃən`ɛr] ★★
- 名 問卷、調查表
- 片 fill in the questionnaire 填妥問卷

Fighting!

Give it a shot 小試身手

1 I'm responsible for teaching the _____.

2 He _____ down and kissed the child.

3 The drama has an ending _____ our expectation.

4 Do we have to separate the _____?

5 Please fill up the _____ in the questionnaire0816.

Answers: 1 beginner 2 bent 3 beyond 4 bill 5 blanks

MP3

短文 137 字彙 138

Essay 069

Al-Qaeda is a bloody Islamist group that has attacked civilians[0817] and the military in many countries. Their typical tactics[0818] include suicide[0819] attacks and simultaneous[0820] bombings[0821] in different areas. Osama Bin Laden, the late head of Al-Qaeda, set up branches that use the Al-Qaeda name and terrorize[0822] a lot of countries all over the world. They torture[0823] their prisoners, tread[0824] on their bowed heads, or drown them in a tank of water. They enjoy brick[0825] cheese and other food while watching their prisoners suffer. The things they have done make me boil with anger. The attack on September 11, 2001, in New York was their most notorious event. Terrorists[0826] are trained in camps for years in a broad[0827] range of areas, such as architectural[0828] engineering and bomb installation. Before the September 11, 2001 attacks, they gained knowledge from the Internet so they could board planes and take control of them until they could crash them. Terrorists may be anywhere. They might even be next to you when you are bowling or doing some other activity!

中譯 *Translation*

　　蓋達組織是一個嗜殺的伊斯蘭團體，曾經攻擊許多國家的軍隊與百姓。他們的典型戰術包括自殺攻擊，以及不同區域的同步爆炸。奧薩瑪·賓拉登，蓋達組織的已故首領，在全世界設立了以蓋達組織為名的分會，使許多國家感到威脅。他們凌虐戰俘，踩他們低著的頭，或把他們壓進水槽裡淹死。他們一邊享用磚形乳酪和其他食物，一邊看著戰俘受苦。他們的所作所為令我怒火沸騰。紐約911恐怖攻擊是最惡名昭彰的事件。恐怖分子在軍營接受各種領域的訓練長達數年，像是建築工程和炸彈裝置。在2001年的911恐怖攻擊發生之前，他們透過網路獲取知識，以至於能夠登上飛機並控制整架飛機直到墜毀。恐怖分子無所不在。甚至連你打保齡球或從事其他活動時，他都有可能在你身邊！

0817 civilian

[sɪ`vɪljən] ★★★

名 平民百姓
形 百姓的、民用的

0818 tactic

[`tæktɪk] ★★

名 戰術、策略、手法
同 maneuver 策略
片 delaying tactic 拖延術

0819 suicide

[`suə,saɪd] ★★★

名 自殺、自毀
形 自殺的
片 commit suicide 自殺

0820 simultaneous

[,saɪml`tenɪəs] ★★★

形 同步的、一齊的
同 concurrent 同時發生的

0821 bombing

[`bamɪŋ] ★★★★

名 轟炸、砲轟
片 wave of bombings
一連串爆炸

0822 terrorize

[`tɛrə,raɪz] ★★

動 使恐怖、恐嚇、脅迫
同 terrify 使害怕

0823 torture

[`tɔrtʃə] ★★★

動 拷打、折磨、扭曲
名 酷刑、折磨、歪曲
片 torture by 受…折磨

0824 tread

[trɛd] ★★★

動 踩、步行、踐踏
名 踩踏、踏板、腳步聲
片 tread on air 歡天喜地

0825 brick

[brɪk] ★★★★

名 磚塊、積木、可靠的人
動 用磚砌
形 磚砌的、似磚的

0826 terrorist

[`tɛrərɪst] ★★★★

名 恐怖分子
片 terrorist attack 恐怖攻擊

0827 broad

[brɔd] ★★★★

形 廣泛的、遼闊的、明顯的、概括的
同 roomy 廣闊的

0828 architectural

[,ɑrkə`tɛktʃərəl] ★

形 建築學的、有關建築的、符合建築法的

Fighting!

Give it a shot 小試身手

1 The magazine was _____ from my classmate.

2 We have to report everything to our _____.

3 She's quite tired; don't _____ her nap.

4 The road is not _____ enough for a truck.

5 Eating fish is beneficial to your _____.

Answers: 1 borrowed 2 boss 3 bother 4 broad 5 brain

070

MP3   短文 139   字彙 140

Essay

I had a health check last month, and my doctor told me that I had lung cancer. After I heard this shocking[0829] news, I rushed[0830] away and burst into tears in the cafeteria of the hospital. I didn't know what to do, because it was all so sudden[0831]. I canceled[0832] all the appointments[0833] on my calendar[0834] since I needed to calm down for a while. This morning, after I brushed my teeth, I went to a café and had brunch alone. I ordered a cabbage salad and watched a cable[0835] news broadcast. A business scandal was in today's headlines[0836]. However, I wasn't in the mood[0837] to <u>hear about</u> businesspeople fighting each other over nothing and was sick of that kind of news. I went outside and enjoyed the sunshine. The sun burned brightly in the sky, and I decided I would live my life <u>to the fullest</u> in the limited time I had left. It's possible there would be a bundle[0838] of opportunities waiting for me, right?

! hear about 知道

! to the fullest 達到最大的程度、充分地、完全地

中譯 *Translation*

　　我上個月做了健康檢查，醫生告訴我得了肺癌。聽到這個震驚的消息之後，我匆匆離開，然後在醫院的餐廳裡放聲大哭。我不知道該怎麼做，一切都來得太突然了。我取消了行事曆上的所有行程，因為我想要讓自己冷靜一下。今天早上我刷完牙之後，一個人到咖啡廳吃了早午餐。我點了高麗菜沙拉，看著有線電視播出的新聞。今天的頭條是一起企業醜聞。然而，我一點也不想知道商人們彼此無謂的鬥爭，也厭倦了那類的新聞。我走出戶外享受陽光。太陽在天空明亮地閃耀著，而我決定將在有限的時間裡盡情享受人生。也許還會有許多機會等著我，對吧？

0829 shocking

[`ʃɑkɪŋ] ★★★
形 令人震驚的、不正當的、糟糕的
同 stunning 令人震驚的

0830 rush

[rʌʃ] ★★★★
動 衝、匆忙地做、湧現
名 匆忙、緊急、激增
片 rush out 衝出

0831 sudden

[`sʌdn̩] ★★★★
形 迅速的、突然的
名 突然發生的事
片 all of a sudden 突然地

0832 cancel

[`kænsl̩] ★★★★
動 取消、刪去、互相抵消
名 取消、刪除
片 cancel out 抵銷

0833 appointment

[ə`pɔɪntmənt] ★★★
名 約會、委派、職位
片 an appointment with 與…有約

0834 calendar

[`kæləndɚ] ★★★
名 行事曆、日曆、曆法
動 把…排進日程表
片 lunar calendar 陰曆

0835 cable

[`kebl̩] ★★★★
名 有線電視、電纜、鋼索
動 發越洋電報
片 cable car 登山纜車

0836 headline

[`hɛd,laɪn] ★★★
名 頭條新聞、章節標題
動 給…加標題、大力宣傳、當主角

0837 mood

[mud] ★★★★
名 心情、生氣、喜怒無常、氣氛
片 be in a mood 心情不好

0838 bundle

[`bʌndl̩] ★★★★
名 捆、包裹、大量
動 捆、亂堆亂塞
片 a bundle of 一大堆

0839 encounter

[ɪn`kauntɚ] ★★★
動 遭遇(敵人)、偶然相遇
名 遭遇、衝突、偶然碰見
片 meet 遇見

0840 robbery

[`rɑbərɪ] ★★★
名 搶劫、盜取
片 highway robbery 漫天要價、獅子大開口

fighting!

Give it a shot 小試身手

1 Next month they'll go to China on _____.

2 The _____ shows 4th, September.

3 Helen died of stomach _____.

4 Keep _____ when you encounter⁰⁸³⁹ a robbery⁰⁸⁴⁰.

5 I feel warm with the fire _____.

Answers: 1 business 2 calendar 3 cancer 4 calm 5 burning

071

MP3   短文 141   字彙 142

Essay

John is the owner of a cartoon[0841] production company. He has a special way of living that he believes <u>allows him to</u> be more creative[0842] at work. He doesn't read magazines, but he reads Shakespeare. He lives in an 18th-century castle, and the carpet[0843] and ceiling decorations are in Gothic[0844] style. There's a cell[0845] in the cave at the back of the castle. He uses no electric lights but candles instead, no CDs but rather cassettes[0846], no highlighters[0847] but rather chalk[0848], and no credit cards but rather cash. He has never eaten cereal in the morning, because he grows his own potatoes and carrots in the garden in the central part of the castle. That's why we never see him pushing a shopping cart in a supermarket. In addition, he has no idea how to use the Internet, mobile[0849] phones, fax machines, etc. He's recently started to learn how to operate[0850] a cash register[0851]. He always <u>prefers to</u> imagine he lives in the 18th century.

(!) allow sb. to 讓某事對某人來說成為可能

(!) prefer to 寧願、更喜歡

中譯 *Translation*

　　約翰是一個卡通製作公司的老闆。為了在工作時擁有更多創意，他的生活方式十分特別。他不讀雜誌，卻讀莎士比亞。他住在一棟十八世紀的城堡中，以哥德式的地毯和天花板做裝飾。在城堡後方的洞穴中有一個小房間。他不用燈光，只用蠟燭；不用光碟，只聽卡帶；不用螢光筆而用粉筆；不用信用卡而用現金。他早晨不吃麥片，因為他在城堡中央的菜園種馬鈴薯和紅蘿蔔。那就是為什麼我們從來不曾看過他在超市裡推車購物的原因了。還有，他也不懂怎麼用網路、手機和傳真機等等。他最近正在學怎麼操作收銀機。他總是寧願想像自己活在十八世紀。

0841 cartoon

[kar`tun] ★★★★
- 名 卡通、諷刺畫
- 片 animated catoon 卡通影片

0842 creative

[krı`etıv] ★★★★
- 形 創造的、啟發想像力的
- 同 inventive 創造的
- 反 imitative 模仿的

0843 carpet

[`karpıt] ★★★
- 名 地毯
- 動 在…上鋪地毯
- 同 rug 小地毯

0844 Gothic

[`gaθık] ★★★
- 形 哥德式的、中古時代的、粗野的
- 名 哥德語、哥德式建築

0845 cell

[sɛl] ★★★★★
- 名 小囚房、細胞、電池、基層小組
- 同 cubicle 小隔間

0846 cassette

[kə`sɛt] ★★★
- 名 錄音帶、膠捲盒
- 同 tape (錄音、錄影)磁帶
- 片 cassette player 錄音機

0847 highlighter

[`haı,laıtə] ★★
- 名 螢光筆
- 衍 highlight 強調

0848 chalk

[tʃɔk] ★★★
- 名 粉筆、白堊岩
- 動 用粉筆寫、規劃
- 片 chalk up 記下

0849 mobile

[`mobıl] ★★★
- 形 移動式的、流動的、易變的、機動的
- 片 mobile phone 手機

0850 operate

[`apə,ret] ★★★★
- 動 操作、營運、起作用、開刀
- 片 operate on 為…動手術

0851 register

[`rɛdʒıstə] ★★★★
- 名 收銀機、註冊、登記簿
- 片 註冊、標示、正式提出
- 片 cash register 收銀機

0852 troop

[trup] ★★★★
- 名 軍隊、一群、許多
- 動 成群結隊地走、群集
- 片 troop into 列隊走進

Fighting!

Give it a shot 小試身手

1 She was _____ of the hockey team at school.

2 Can you _____ the check for me?

3 This _____ is said to be a _____ of geniuses.

4 The enemy troops[0852] attacked the _____.

5 Doraemon is a famous _____ in the world.

Answers: 1 captain 2 cash 3 century 4 castle 5 cartoon

072

MP3　短文 143　字彙 144

Essay

Many small restaurants are very dirty. There's too much bacteria[0853] on the chopsticks in 90 percent of them. Kids who put their chins[0854] on the table may get some kind of skin disease. Restaurants usually claim[0855] that they use natural[0856] ingredients. Don't be <u>so</u> naive[0857] <u>as to</u> believe them. There are too many chemical[0858] substances[0859] in beverages, such as those in hot chocolate. These kinds of restaurants or cafés are usually located[0860] in small streets and don't charge much. These cheap restaurants will cheat customers and harm their health. Customers don't have a choice[0861], because there are dirty places wherever they go. In order to eat healthily[0862], choose a restaurant that is owned by people of good character. It's also important to change your habits and those of your family. Don't let your kids eat food after playing chess or lying on the floor. Wash your hands frequently[0863]. Being careful is better than being sorry!

! so + adj. + as to 太過…以至於，另一句型為 so...that...

中譯 *Translation*

　　許多小型餐廳都很髒，其中百分之九十的筷子上都含有過量的細菌。小孩把下巴放在餐桌上可能會引發某種皮膚疾病。餐廳總是聲稱自己使用純天然的原料。別天真到相信他們。飲料中有太多化學物質了，像是熱巧克力。這種餐廳或咖啡廳通常座落在狹窄的街道上，而且不貴。這些便宜的餐廳會欺騙消費者，並且傷害他們的健康。消費者沒有選擇，因為不管他們去哪都一樣髒。為了要吃得健康，選擇一間性格可靠的人所經營的餐廳。改變自己和家人的習慣也非常重要。不要讓你的孩子在下完棋或是躺在地上後拿食物來吃。時常洗手。小心總比後悔好！

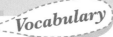

Level 2

 bacteria 0853

[bæk`tɪrɪə] ★★★★
名 細菌
同 germs 細菌

 chin 0854

[tʃɪn] ★★★★
名 下巴、頦、聊天
片 keep one's chin up 毫不氣餒

 claim 0855

[klem] ★★★★
動 聲稱、索取、要求
名 要求、權利、主張
片 claim on 提出要求

natural 0856

[`nætʃərəl] ★★★★
形 自然的、天然的、合乎常情的
反 artificial 人工的

 naive 0857

[nɑ`iv] ★★★
形 天真的、輕信的
同 artless 不諳世故的
反 sophisticated 世故的

 chemical 0858

[`kɛmɪkḷ] ★★★★
形 化學的、化學用的
名 化學製品、化學藥品
片 chemical industry 化工

 substance 0859

[`sʌbstəns] ★★★
名 物質、主旨、要義
片 the substance of …的主旨

locate 0860

[lo`ket] ★★★
動 座落於、設置在、找出
同 situate 使位於
片 locate in 定居於、設於

 choice 0861

[tʃɔɪs] ★★★★★
名 選擇、供選擇範圍
形 精選的、挑三揀四的
片 of choice 精選的

healthily 0862

[`hɛlθɪlɪ] ★★
副 健康地
衍 healthy 健康的

frequently 0863

[`frikwəntlɪ] ★★★
副 頻繁地、屢次地
同 often 時常
反 rarely 很少、難得

department 0864

[dɪ`pɑrtmənt] ★★★★
名 部門、系、局、某人的職責範圍
同 division 部門

---

 fighting!

Give it a shot 小試身手

1 He has a changeable _____.

2 I have no _____ but to break up with her.

3 Indians eat by hands instead of _____.

4 Nothing in a department 0864 store is _____.

5 You have _____ greatly since we met.

Answers: 1 character 2 choice 3 chopsticks 4 cheap 5 changed

073

Essay

MP3 短文 145 字彙 146

I can confidently claim that my taste in fashion is fabulous. I am a clever and hard-working clerk at a boutique. I have many classic clothes in my closet⁰⁸⁶⁵. I clothe myself according to the weather. I wear a leather⁰⁸⁶⁶ jacket and boots⁰⁸⁶⁷ on cloudy⁰⁸⁶⁸ days and wear my Gucci sunglasses on sunny days. LV scarves are my favorites. They are made of the finest cloth⁰⁸⁶⁹ and lightweight⁰⁸⁷⁰. They are suitable⁰⁸⁷¹ for the climate in Taiwan. I once had a fight with my boyfriend, and he tried to tear my scarf in anger. Because of my love for the scarf, I immediately⁰⁸⁷² stopped fighting with him and protected my scarf with both hands. I almost broke up with him because of this! I also use hair clay⁰⁸⁷³ to style my hair up. Whenever I go out, I make myself as attractive as I can. At work, I am proper⁰⁸⁷⁴ and formal⁰⁸⁷⁵. In clubs, I love to have fun and clown around with friends. Beautiful clothing is the most important thing in my life.

ⓘ have fun 讓自己開心、玩得開心
ⓘ clown around 做蠢事、胡鬧，也可用 clown about

中譯 Translation

　　我可以自豪地宣稱我的流行品味非常棒。我是一個機靈又認真的精品店店員。我衣櫥內有許多經典的服裝。我會依照天氣狀況來穿衣服。陰天時我會穿皮夾克和靴子，晴天時會戴上 Gucci 墨鏡。LV 圍巾是我的最愛，它是用最好的布料製成，而且很輕，很適合臺灣的天氣。我曾經和男友打架，他在盛怒之餘企圖扯破我的圍巾。因為我太愛這條圍巾了，我立刻停止打他，用雙手護住我的圍巾。我差點因此而和他分手！我還會用髮蠟來為頭髮塑形。不管我去哪裡，都盡可能讓自己維持漂亮的狀態。工作的時候，我穿得正式且得體。去俱樂部時，我喜歡好好享受愉快的時光，並和朋友到處去做蠢事。美麗的穿著是我一生中最重要的事！

0865 closet

[`klɑzɪt] ★★★
- 名 衣櫥、碗櫥、小房間
- 形 祕密的、空談的
- 動 把…引進密室會談

0866 leather

[`lɛðə·] ★★★★
- 形 皮的、皮革製的
- 名 皮革、皮革製品
- 俚 hell for leather 飛快地

0867 boot

[but] ★★★★
- 名 靴子、解雇、後車箱
- 動 穿靴、猛踢、逐出
- 片 boot out 開除

0868 cloudy

[`klaʊdɪ] ★★★
- 形 多雲的、不愉快的、模糊不清的
- 反 clear 晴朗的

0869 cloth

[klɔθ] ★★★★
- 名 布、衣料、桌巾
- 同 fabric 布料
- 片 man of the cloth 教士

0870 lightweight

[`laɪt`wet] ★★
- 形 較輕的、思想膚淺的
- 名 標準重量以下
- 同 trivial 不重要的

0871 suitable

[`sutəbl] ★★★★
- 形 適宜的、合適的
- 反 unsuitable 不合適的
- 片 suitable for 適合…的

0872 immediately

[ɪ`midɪətlɪ] ★★★★
- 副 立即、直接地、緊接地
- 連 一…就
- 同 instantly 立即

0873 clay

[kle] ★★★★
- 名 泥土、黏土、肉體
- 同 mud 泥
- 片 feet of clay 致命弱點

0874 proper

[`prɑpə·] ★★★★★
- 形 循規蹈矩的、適合的
- 同 fitting 合適的
- 反 improper 不合適的

0875 formal

[`fɔrml] ★★★★
- 形 正式的、拘泥形式的、表面的、官方的
- 同 official 官方的

0876 silk

[sɪlk] ★★★★
- 名 絲綢、蠶絲
- 形 絲織的、絲狀的
- 片 artificial silk 人造絲

fighting!

Give it a shot 小試身手

1 He wore a _____ suit to attend the wedding.

2 The northern _____ is dry and cold.

3 This gown is made of silk⁰⁸⁷⁶ _____.

4 I take an umbrella with me in such a _____day.

5 Cats attacked dogs with their sharp _____.

Answers: 1 classic 2 climate 3 cloth 4 cloudy 5 claws

155

074

Essay

MP3 147 短文 147 字彙 148

Next month, my basketball team will have a match with a team from another school. Our coach[0877] trains[0878] us a lot, making us complain[0879] and feel uncomfortable. One day, we finished training and had a shower in the <u>changing room</u>. One of my teammates[0880] tried to scare me by throwing a cockroach at me. I was so angry and threw a comb back at him, and we started fighting with each other. Our coach scolded us for our bad behavior and said we needed to practice more compared to other teams. Afterwards, I bought a drink for my teammate and we reconciled[0881]. I went home in the company of my teammates, and I invited them in. I showed them the colorful[0882] photos of trains I collected from the Internet. We had a wonderful evening. The next day, our coach told us the date of the match was confirmed[0883]. I believe we can play well together to beat our rival[0884] and that everybody will say "congratulations[0885]!" to us.

🛈 changing room 運動場內的更衣室

中譯 *Translation*

　　下個月我的籃球隊要和別校的隊伍比賽。教練不斷訓練我們，使我們對此抱怨，心裡也不舒坦。某天，我們結束訓練在更衣室裡沖澡。其中一名隊友想嚇我，朝我丟了一隻蟑螂。我很生氣地拿起梳子丟回去，然後我們兩個大吵一架。教練因為我們不良的行為把我們訓了一頓，還說比起其他隊伍，我們需要更多的練習。後來，我買了罐飲料給隊友，然後就和好了。隊友們陪我回家，我邀請他們到家裡坐坐。我向他們展示我從網路上蒐集的彩色火車照片，度過了一個很棒的夜晚。隔天，教練告訴我們比賽的日期已經確定了。我相信我們可以團結起來打敗敵隊，然後每個人都會向我們道賀。

0877 coach

[kotʃ] ★★★★
名 教練、普通車廂
動 訓練、乘馬車旅行
片 coach in 針對⋯指導

0878 train

[tren] ★★★★
動 訓練、培養、瞄準
名 火車、系列、隨從
片 train for 為⋯接受訓練

0879 complain

[kəm`plen] ★★★★
動 抱怨、發牢騷、控訴
同 grumble 抱怨
片 complain about 抱怨

0880 teammate

[`tim͵met] ★★
名 隊友、同隊隊員
同 mate 同伴、伙伴

0881 reconcile

[`rɛkənsaɪl] ★★★
動 和解、調停、使一致
同 conciliate 調解
片 reconcile with 使和解

0882 colorful

[`kʌləfəl] ★★★
形 鮮豔的、多采多姿的
同 multicolored 彩色的
反 colorless 無趣味的

0883 confirm

[kən`fɝm] ★★★
動 確定、證實、鞏固
反 deny 否認
片 confirm in 堅定

0884 rival

[`raɪvl̩] ★★★★
名 競爭者、對手
動 與⋯競爭
片 rival in love 情敵

0885 congratulations

[kən͵grætʃə`leʃənz] ★★
名 祝賀、恭喜
片 congratulations on 對⋯表示祝賀

0886 material

[mə`tɪrɪəl] ★★★★
名 材料、資料、工具
形 物質的、關鍵的
片 raw material 原物料

0887 indulge

[ɪn`dʌldʒ] ★★★
動 沉迷、放縱、遷就、讓自己享受一下
片 indulge in 沉迷於

0888 satisfy

[`sætɪs͵faɪ] ★★★★
動 使滿意、符合、履行
同 gratify 使滿意
片 satisfy sb. of 使確信

Fighting!

Give it a shot 小試身手

1. Enough materials[0886] should be _____ before writing.
2. He indulged[0887] himself in _____ games.
3. The contract has not been _____ by both sides.
4. I will double the pay if you _____ the work.
5. The team's performance didn't satisfy[0888] the _____.

Answers: 1 collected 2 computer 3 confirmed 4 complete 5 coach

Essay

There's a young couple in Taitung County living their lives bravely. They grew up and still live in the countryside[0889]. The husband has had a lung disease for years, but he still works at a chemical factory[0890]. Even though the fumes[0891] from the chemicals make him cough[0892], he still needs to keep working to pay for his children's education because it is costly.

As a social worker, I contact[0893] them sometimes to help them. After first talking with them, I found that they didn't have an easy life. They don't have enough money to buy a rice cooker[0894]. The only thing they have is a pot for their stove[0895] in the kitchen. They use a dirty container[0896] to keep water for showers. Since their cotton[0897] sheets were stolen, they cover their bodies with cardboard[0898] when they sleep. They control their expenses[0899] carefully, but they did spend money on a copy of a Harry Potter book for their children. Considering their problems, I think the government should take responsibility and give them some help.

中譯 *Translation*

　　台東有一對勇敢過生活的年輕夫妻，他們在農村長大與生活。丈夫罹患肺病多年，但仍舊在一間化學工廠上班。雖然化學製品產生的煙霧會使他咳嗽，他還是得繼續工作才能支付孩子們的學費，因為這實在是太花錢了。

　　身為一名社工，我有時會和他們聯繫給予一些幫助。第一次和他們聊過之後，我發現他們的生活很窮困。他們沒錢買電鍋，他們所僅有的是廚房裡一個烹煮用的鍋子。他們用骯髒的容器盛水洗澡。由於他們的棉製床單被偷了，睡覺時只能用紙箱蓋著身體。他們謹慎地控制開支，卻還花錢買一本哈利波特的影印本給孩子看。考量到他們的問題，我認為政府應該要負起責任，伸出援手才對。

0889 countryside

[`kʌntrɪ‚saɪd] ★★
- 名 農村、鄉間
- 同 province 鄉間

0890 factory

[`fæktərɪ] ★★★★
- 名 工廠、製造處
- 同 plant 工廠
- 片 textile factory 紡織廠

0891 fume

[fjum] ★★★
- 名 煙、憤怒、煩惱
- 動 冒煙、發怒
- 同 smoke 煙

0892 cough

[kɔf] ★★★★
- 動 咳嗽、咳出
- 名 咳嗽、咳嗽聲
- 片 cough up 咳出

0893 contact

[kən`tækt] ★★★★★
- 動 聯繫、接觸
- 名 交往、聯繫、門路
- 形 接觸傳染的

0894 cooker

[`kukə] ★★
- 名 炊具、烹調器具
- 片 pressure cooker 壓力鍋

0895 stove

[stov] ★★★
- 名 火爐、爐灶
- 片 spirit stove 酒精爐

0896 container

[kən`tenə] ★★★
- 名 容器、集裝箱、貨櫃
- 片 container ship 貨櫃船

0897 cotton

[`kɑtṇ] ★★★★
- 名 棉花、棉布
- 形 棉製的、棉的
- 動 一致、和諧、親近

0898 cardboard

[`kɑrd‚bord] ★★
- 名 硬紙板、卡紙板
- 形 硬紙板製的、虛構的、沒有深度的

0899 expense

[ɪk`spɛns] ★★★★
- 名 開支、費用、損失
- 反 income 所得
- 片 on expenses 能報銷

0900 certificate

[sə`tɪfəkɪt] ★★★
- 名 證明書、執照、憑證
- 動 發證書給、用證書證明
- 同 testimonial 證明書

Fighting!

Give it a shot 小試身手

1. I _____ every possible result.
2. On hearing the news, Tony could not _____ his tears.
3. Send me the _____ of your certificate[0900].
4. I hit my knee on the _____ of the table.
5. A _____ of days later, the rain finally stopped.

Answers: 1 consider 2 control 3 copy 4 corner 5 couple

076

My cousin, Derek, was a lovely kid and liked drawing pictures with crayons. After he got to know a crowd of bad people at high school, he became short-tempered[0901] and even crazy, creating a crisis[0902] in his life. He committed[0903] several crimes[0904] and refused to appear in court frequently. He even drove a car in farmers' fields[0905] to damage[0906] crops with his friends. My uncle and aunt were worried that he had <u>come down with</u> some type of mental[0907] disease that was difficult to cure[0908]. After he spent three years in prison, he was released. However, he found it difficult to find a job. Life can be cruel for everyone, <u>let alone</u> someone with a criminal[0909] record. Fortunately, the Municipal[0910] Cultural Center created some jobs for prisoners[0911]. Derek got a job at a café. When I paid a visit there, I could tell that he was not a bad person anymore. He asked me with a friendly smile, "Do you like cream in your coffee?"

> ⓘ come down with 罹患、感染
>
> ⓘ let alone 更不用說、更別提

中譯 *Translation*

　　我的表哥德瑞克，以前曾經是個可愛的小孩，喜歡用蠟筆畫畫。高中時，他在學校認識一群壞蛋之後，就變得易怒甚至瘋狂，人生也陷入危機。他犯下多種罪行，屢次拒絕出庭。他甚至和朋友把車開進農地裡破壞農作物。我的叔叔和嬸嬸都很擔心他是否罹患了某種難以醫治的心理疾病。他坐了三年牢之後獲釋。然而，他發現他很難找到工作。對每個人來說，人生有時很殘酷，更遑論他還留有犯罪記錄。所幸，市立文化中心替犯人創造了一些工作機會。德瑞克得到一份咖啡廳的工作。當我到那裡探望他時，我看得出來他已經不再是個壞人了。他用友善的笑容問我：「你的咖啡要加奶精嗎？」

0901　short-tempered

[`ʃɔrt`tɛmpəd] ★★
形 脾氣暴躁的、易怒的、急性子的
同 quick-tempered 易怒

0902　crisis

[`kraɪsɪs] ★★★★
名 危機、緊急關頭
片 at a crisis point 處於危機時刻

0903　commit

[kə`mɪt] ★★★★
動 犯罪、做承諾、交託給
同 entrust 委託
片 commit a crime 犯罪

0904　crime

[kraɪm] ★★★★
名 罪行、罪過
片 scene of the crime 犯罪現場

0905　field

[fild] ★★★★★
名 田地、原野、領域
動 派⋯上場比賽
片 in the field of ⋯的領域

0906　damage

[`dæmɪdʒ] ★★★★
動 損害、毀壞
名 損害、損失、賠償金

0907　mental

[`mɛntl̩] ★★★★
形 精神的、智力的、內心的、精神病的
片 mental block 思路中斷

0908　cure

[kjʊr] ★★★
動 治癒、消除、糾正
名 治療、對策、療程
片 cure of 治好

0909　criminal

[`krɪmənl̩] ★★★★
形 犯罪的、刑事上的
名 罪犯

0910　municipal

[mju`nɪsəpl̩] ★★★
形 市立的、市政的、地方自治的
同 civic 城市的

0911　prisoner

[`prɪznə] ★★★
名 犯人、失去自由的人、俘虜
同 convict 囚犯

0912　account

[ə`kaʊnt] ★★★★★
名 帳戶、描述、理由
動 報帳、說明、把⋯視為
片 account for 解釋

fighting!

Give it a shot 小試身手

1 It is a _____ to cheat others money.

2 I have to _____ a new account[0912] for I forgot the password.

3 He walked away and disappeared into a _____ of people.

4 It is still not possible to _____ AIDS.

5 Her earrings are in the shape of _____.

077

Essay

I own a curtain⁰⁹¹³ shop, and I always pay my employees on time. There are many regular⁰⁹¹⁴ customers to my shop. Some of them pay very late or not at all, putting me <u>in debt</u>.

One day, a couple wanted to buy curtains to decorate their room. They debated what color to use for a long time. They couldn't make a decision. The wife was mad⁰⁹¹⁵ and deaf⁰⁹¹⁶ to what her husband said. This couple always argued⁰⁹¹⁷; it was their custom. However, they actually started fighting physically⁰⁹¹⁸ this time. It was a dangerous situation. As they threw stuff at each other, my shop was damaged. I was so irritated⁰⁹¹⁹ that I <u>kicked them out</u>. "Nobody with a similar⁰⁹²⁰ background⁰⁹²¹ to you would be as rude as you two are. I will never again deliver⁰⁹²² my curtains to you with delicious snacks for free!" I shouted.

⓵ in debt 負債，put sb. deeply in debt 表示某人負債累累
⓵ kick sb. out 把某人踢出去、開除

中譯 *Translation*

　　我經營一家窗簾店，我總是準時發薪水給員工。我的店有許多常客，有些人會拖款或是根本不還，導致我身負債務。

　　某天，一對夫婦想要買窗簾裝飾他們的房間。對於要選用哪種顏色他們爭論了好久，卻無法做出決定。太太非常生氣，對丈夫說的充耳不聞。這對夫婦總是在吵架，這是他們的習慣。然而，這次他們竟然大打出手，情況非常危險。由於他們朝對方互扔東西，導致我的店整個毀了。我非常惱怒地把他們逐出去，對著他們大聲咆哮：「和你們背景相似的人，沒有一個會做出像你們兩個一樣這麼沒禮貌的事。我再也不會送窗簾還免費附贈點心給你們了！」

0913 curtain

[`kɝtṇ] ★★★★

名 窗簾、帷幔、舞台布幕

動 裝上簾子、隔開

片 drape 窗簾

0914 regular

[`rɛgjələ] ★★★★

形 經常的、有規律的、標準的、正規的

片 regular visitor 常客

0915 mad

[mæd] ★★★★

形 惱火的、發瘋的、魯莽的、狂熱的

片 mad at 對…生氣

0916 deaf

[dɛf] ★★★

形 聾的、不願聽的

片 deaf to 對…充耳不聞

0917 argue

[`ɑrgju] ★★★★

動 爭論、主張、說服

同 debate 爭論

片 argue with 與…爭論

0918 physically

[`fɪzɪkḷɪ] ★★

副 身體上、實際上、全然、按自然規律

反 mentally 精神上

0919 irritated

[`ɪrətetɪd] ★★★

形 惱火的、急躁的

同 annoyed 惱怒的

片 irritated by 為…煩惱

0920 similar

[`sɪmələ] ★★★★★

形 相仿的、類似的

同 alike 相像的

片 similar to 和…相似

0921 background

[`bæk,ɡraʊnd] ★★★★

名 背景、經歷、幕後

同 backdrop 背景

反 foreground 前景

0922 deliver

[dɪ`lɪvə] ★★★★

動 傳送、投遞、宣布、生、履行

片 deliver on 履行

0923 displease

[dɪs`pliz] ★★

動 使不高興、得罪、觸怒

反 delight 使高興

片 displease with 不滿…

0924 festival

[`fɛstəvḷ] ★★★★

名 節日、慶祝活動

形 節日的、喜慶的

反 weekday 工作日

fighting!

Give it a shot 小試身手

❶ The _____ seems displeased⁰⁹²³ with her service.

❷ Such festival⁰⁹²⁴ is a special _____ for them.

❸ Exercise _____ benefits your health.

❹ She made a final _____ about the case.

❺ Nancy got her Master's _____ in Japan.

Answers: ❶ customer ❷ custom ❸ daily ❹ decision ❺ Degree

MP3　短文 155　字彙 156

Essay

078

Jenny worked at a department store. She loved pumps[0925] designed by Frida Giannini. She desired[0926] a rich boyfriend. She met a very nice guy three months ago and started a relationship with him. She was attracted to his depth of knowledge and his Lamborghini. His name was Jason, and he was a dentist[0927]. On Jenny's birthday, Jason took her to the best Italian restaurant for dinner. After dessert, he took out a diamond ring that was worth NT$300,000 as her birthday gift. Jenny was so touched and decided to marry him. Shortly after that, Jenny detected something was wrong. He became too busy to return her phone calls. Jenny asked him if he was dating other women, but he denied[0928] it. Jenny then read his diary[0929], which was all in English, and spent two hours looking up words in the dictionary so she could translate[0930] it. She also found that Jason had dialed[0931] some numbers she wasn't familiar with. She asked Jason's best friend about it, and his friend told her that she shouldn't depend on Jason. He described Jason as a playboy. Knowing the truth, Jenny dumped Jason and resolutely[0932] vowed[0933] never to see him again.

中譯 *Translation*

　　珍妮在一間百貨公司工作。她喜歡 Frida Giannini 設計的淺口包頭高跟鞋。她渴望交到一個多金的男朋友。三個月前她遇到一個很棒的男人，和他發展出一段戀曲。她為他廣博的知識和藍寶基尼跑車所吸引。他叫傑森，是一名牙醫。在珍妮生日那天，傑森帶她去最棒的義大利餐廳共進晚餐。用完甜點後，他拿出一個價值三十萬元的鑽戒作為她的生日禮物。珍妮非常感動，決定要嫁給他。近來珍妮發現他有一點不對勁。他忙到無法回她電話。珍妮問他是否有和其他女人約會，他卻否認。珍妮於是就去讀他的英文日記，查了二個小時的英文字典以便翻譯。珍妮還發現傑森撥過幾通她沒看過的號碼。她去詢問傑森最好的朋友，然而他的朋友告訴她傑森不可靠，他形容傑森是個花花公子。知道真相後，珍妮把傑森甩了，並下定決心發誓永遠都不會再和他見面。

0925 pump

[pʌmp] ★★★★
名 淺口包頭高跟鞋、抽水機、打氣筒
動 打氣、傾注、盤問

0926 desire

[dɪˋzaɪr] ★★★★
動 渴望、要求
名 慾望、渴望的人或事物
片 desire to 渴望

0927 dentist

[ˋdɛntɪst] ★★★
名 牙醫
衍 dental 牙齒的、牙科的

0928 deny

[dɪˋnaɪ] ★★★★
動 否認、拒絕給予、戒絕
反 confirm 確定
片 deny + ving 否認做…

0929 diary

[ˋdaɪərɪ] ★★★★
名 日記、日誌
同 journal 日記
片 keep a diary 寫日記

0930 translate

[trænsˋlet] ★★★
動 翻譯、解釋、調動
同 interpret 口譯
片 translate into 翻譯成

0931 dial

[ˋdaɪəl] ★★★★
動 撥號、打電話、收聽
名 撥號盤、刻度盤
片 dial tone 電話撥號音

0932 resolutely

[ˋrɛzəlutlɪ] ★
副 堅決地、毅然地
同 decisively 決然地
衍 resolution 決心

0933 vow

[vaʊ] ★★
動 發誓、鄭重宣告
名 誓言、誓約
片 vow to 發誓要…

0934 minister

[ˋmɪnɪstə] ★★★★
名 部長、大臣、執行者
動 給予援助、照料
片 minister of/for …部長

0935 bribe

[braɪb] ★★
名 賄賂、誘餌
動 行賄、收買
片 take bribes 受賄

0936 anonymous

[əˋnɑnəməs] ★★★
形 匿名的、來源不明的、無特色的
同 nameless 匿名的

Fighting!

Give it a shot 小試身手

1 The minister⁰⁹³⁴ _____ any bribe⁰⁹³⁵ from others.

2 Her latest _____ was appreciated by a superstar.

3 I _____ an anonymous⁰⁹³⁶ letter in the mailbox.

4 The delicious _____ were provided by Maggie.

5 He proposed to me with a _____ ring.

Answers: 1 denied 2 design 3 detect 4 desserts 5 diamond

MP3   短文 157   字彙 158

079

Essay

As we have entered the digital[0937] era[0938], it's not surprising that vinyl[0939] has disappeared like the dinosaurs. The main difference between vinyl and digital music is the storage[0940] capacity[0941]. It's difficult to store thousands of vinyl records, but thousands of songs can easily be kept in a hard drive. One day I had a discussion about vinyl versus MP3 files with my friends. We discussed the advancements made in recording technology, and I disagreed that vinyl should have been replaced[0942] by digital music. MP3 files allow dishonest music pirates to illegally download[0943] music. As a director of a music publishing company, I love music, and I especially love vinyl. I invited my friends to my house to take a look at my vinyl collection. It took us a long time to drive to my home, because it is quite a distance from downtown. After a few miles, my friends were getting dizzy[0944] on the mountain road. Finally, we arrived. My friends were amazed by the enormous collection of vinyl I had. I had divided my records into different sections[0945]. That's my irreplaceable[0946] treasure.

中譯 *Translation*

　　隨著我們進入數位時代，黑膠唱片像恐龍一樣消失也不令人意外。黑膠唱片和數位音樂的差別主要在於儲存容量。要存入數千張黑膠唱片很困難，但卻能將數千首歌存進一塊硬碟中。某天，我和朋友談到黑膠唱片和MP3音檔。我們討論錄音科技的進展，而我不認為黑膠唱片應該被數位音樂取代。MP3 音檔讓不誠實的音樂盜版商能非法下載音樂。身為一家唱片公司的主管，我熱愛音樂，也特別喜歡黑膠唱片。我邀請朋友到家裡看看我收藏的黑膠唱片。因為我家離市中心很遠，開車回家需要很長一段時間。過了幾哩路程之後，朋友們開始在行經山路時暈車。最後終於抵達了。我的朋友都很訝異我收藏了這麼多的黑膠唱片。我將我的唱片分門別類。那是我無可取代的珍藏。

0937 digital

[`dɪdʒɪt!] ★★★★

形 數字的、指狀的

名 鍵、數字顯示電子錶

同 numerical 數字的

0938 era

[`ɪrə] ★★★★

名 時代、歷史時期、紀元

同 epoch 時代

片 transitional era 過渡期

0939 vinyl

[`vaɪnɪl] ★★

名 黑膠唱片、乙烯基

同 disc 唱片

0940 storage

[`storɪdʒ] ★★★★

名 存儲器、貯藏、保管

片 storage space/
capacity 儲存容量

0941 capacity

[kə`pæsətɪ] ★★★★

名 容量、生產力、能力

反 incapacity 無能

片 vital capacity 肺活量

0942 replace

[rɪ`ples] ★★★★

動 取代、把…放回、歸還

同 substitute 代替

片 replace with 以…取代

0943 download

[`daʊn͵lod] ★★★

動 (電腦)下載

名 下載

同 upload 上傳

0944 dizzy

[`dɪzɪ] ★★★

形 頭暈目眩的、弄糊塗的

動 使頭昏眼花、使茫然

同 giddy 暈眩的

0945 section

[`sɛkʃən] ★★★★

名 部分、區域、片、塊、
部門、剖面

動 把…分成段、切片

0946 irreplaceable

[͵ɪrɪ`plesəbl̩] ★★

形 不能調換的、獨一無二

同 unique 獨特的

反 replaceable 可替換的

0947 permit

[pɚ`mɪt] ★★★★

動 許可、准許、容許

名 許可證、執照

片 permit of 容許

0948 resignation

[͵rɛzɪg`neʃən] ★★

名 辭職、放棄、順從

片 hand in one's
resignation 遞辭呈

---

fighting!

Give it a shot 小試身手

1 I will do my best in spite of _____.

2 They had a _____ about whether to permit0947 her resignation0948.

3 The _____ of the handicrafts was very wonderful.

4 She felt too _____ to stand upright.

5 He instanced Ang Lee when it came to Taiwan _____.

Answers: 1 difficulty 2 discussion 3 display 4 dizzy 5 directors

MP3　 短文 159　 字彙 160

080

We are the most famous rock-and-roll band in town. Life is dull[0949], and everybody needs excitement. Everybody used to doubt[0950] us, but our latest record sales figures have doubled those of our first album. I play drums in the band, and dress in a punk[0951] style. I use strong hair gel[0592] to style my hair before I go on stage. There's something special about our new album. We sing along with recorded sounds of dolphins, and nobody has done that before. The dragon on the CD cover was drawn by the guitarist, Kevin. Kevin is not only a professional guitarist but also good at drawing. One afternoon, we ordered doughnuts and coffee to be delivered to our studio. We were shocked when Kevin took some heroine from his drawer and took the drug. We dragged[0953] him to the bathroom and locked him in to prevent him from doing anything too unpredictable[0954] and dangerous. Bizarre[0955]? Our life is like a drama, sometimes great but also sometimes scary. While I believe in doing fun and wild[0956] things, I really think Kevin is playing with fire and taking too much of a risk[0957] with his life.

ⓘ play with fire 自尋毀滅、冒險、玩火自焚

中譯 Translation

　　我們是鎮上最有名的搖滾樂團。人生苦悶，每個人都需要刺激。以前大家都不看好我們，但我們最近的唱片銷售量比第一張增加了兩倍。我在樂團中打鼓，打扮成龐克風。上台表演前我會用強力定型髮膠做造型。我們的新專輯很特別，我們跟著錄製好的海豚音一起唱，這是前所未有之舉。CD封面的龍是吉他手凱文畫的。凱文不只是一位專業的吉他手，也很擅長繪畫。某天下午我們點了甜甜圈和咖啡的外送到工作室。當凱文從他的抽屜拿出一些海洛因來吸時，我們簡直嚇呆了。我們把他拖進浴室鎖起來，以免他做出任何意料之外的危險事情。很怪異？我們的人生就像一齣戲，有時很好，有時卻得提心吊膽。雖然我認為人應該做些有趣及瘋狂的事，但我真的認為凱文是在玩火，而且他的人生實在是有太多風險了。

0949 dull

[dʌl] ★★★★
形 乏味的、晦暗的、笨的
動 使遲鈍、緩和、減輕
反 keen 敏銳的

0950 doubt

[daʊt] ★★★★
動 懷疑、不能肯定
名 懷疑、不確實、疑慮
同 suspect 懷疑

0951 punk

[pʌŋk] ★★
形 龐克的、無用的
名 龐克搖滾、小流氓

0952 gel

[dʒɛl] ★★★
名 凝膠、膠體
動 膠化、變得清晰、合作

0953 drag

[dræg] ★★★★
動 拖著前進、拉
名 拖曳、阻力、累贅
片 drag on 拖延

0954 unpredictable

[ˌʌnprɪˋdɪktəbl̩] ★
形 出乎意料的、捉摸不定的
同 variable 多變的

0955 bizarre

[bɪˋzɑr] ★★★
形 奇異的、古怪的
同 eccentric 古怪的
反 normal 正常的

0956 wild

[waɪld] ★★★★★
形 瘋狂的、野生的、難駕馭的、熱衷的
名 荒野、未開發之地

0957 risk

[rɪsk] ★★★★★
名 危險、風險
動 冒…風險、遭受危險
片 at risk 有危險

0958 income

[ˋɪnˌkʌm] ★★★★
名 收入、收益、所得
同 earnings 收入
片 income tax 所得稅

0959 miserable

[ˋmɪzərəbl̩] ★★★
形 不幸的、痛苦的、淒慘的、討厭的
片 miserable failure 慘敗

0960 staple

[ˋstepl̩] ★★★
名 訂書針、主要產品
形 主要的、大宗生產的
動 用訂書針釘

Fighting!

Give it a shot 小試身手

1 His income[0958] is the _____ of mine.

2 She pities the miserable[0959] actress in the _____.

3 Her _____ was spotted with ketchup.

4 Please take some staples[0960] from my _____.

5 I _____ some lemon juice on the fish.

Answers: 1 double 2 drama 3 dress 4 drawer 5 dropped

081

MP3　短文 161　字彙 162

I don't have a good education, so I often think I do stupid things. I am a cleaner at a hotel. My job is to clean the floor of the lobby[0961], elevators[0962], and rooms in the hotel, but I just earn a very low wage[0963]. I lost almost all of my family in an earthquake a few years ago. My eldest son is alive, but he is paralyzed[0964]. I do the best I can to <u>make a living</u>, devoting[0965] all my energy to work. Due to lack of knowledge, I don't have very many opportunities to improve my life. Recently, at the annual[0966] staff meeting, they had a vote to see who would be the union[0967] leader. I was amazed when I was elected[0968]! I was filled with strong emotions[0969] and burst into tears. They said earnestness[0970], kindness and honesty were the main reasons I was selected[0971]. My victory[0972] also had effect upon those cleaners who felt people looked down on them because of their jobs. They were encouraged to work harder to get a chance for promotion. The experience taught me that, no matter what your job is, you should try your best.

ⓘ make a living 謀生、糊口

中譯 *Translation*

　　我並沒有受過良好的教育,所以我總是覺得自己在做蠢事。我是一名飯店清潔工。我的職責是清理大廳地板、電梯和飯店房間,但薪水不多。在幾年前的一場地震中,我幾乎失去了所有的家人。我的大兒子還活著,但是癱瘓了。我盡可能努力維持生活,把全部的精力都奉獻給工作。因為學歷不高,我並沒有很多能改善我生活的機會。最近,在年度員工大會中,公司投票選出工會領袖。當我雀屏中選時真的感到非常驚訝。我內心非常激動且淚流不止。他們說認真、善良和誠實是我獲選的主要原因。我的勝利也影響了那些覺得自己因為工作而被人看扁的清潔工。他們受到鼓舞要更努力地工作,以獲得升遷的機會。我的經驗使我明白不管你的工作是什麼,你都應該盡力做到最好。

0961 lobby

[ˋlɑbɪ] ★★★

名 大廳、門廊、會客室

動 對…遊說

片 hotel lobby 旅館大廳

0962 elevator

[ˋɛləˏvetə] ★★★

名 電梯、升降機、飛機升降舵

同 escalator 電扶梯

0963 wage

[wedʒ] ★★★★

名 薪水、報酬、代價

動 進行、從事

片 wage freeze 薪資凍結

0964 paralyze

[ˋpærəˏlaɪz] ★★

動 癱瘓、麻痺、使驚呆

同 deaden 使麻木

衍 paralyzation 癱瘓

0965 devote

[dɪˋvot] ★★★

動 獻身、投入、專用於

同 dedicate 獻身

片 devote to 致力於

0966 annual

[ˋænjʊəl] ★★★★★

形 每年的、全年的

名 年刊、一年生植物

片 annual ring 年輪

0967 union

[ˋjunjən] ★★★★

名 工會、聯盟、結合

反 division 分派

片 union with 與…聯盟

0968 elect

[ɪˋlɛkt] ★★★

動 選舉、推選、決定

形 當選的、選定的

名 上帝的選民

0969 emotion

[ɪˋmoʃən] ★★★★

名 情緒、情感、激動

同 feeling 感情

0970 earnestness

[ˋɜnɪstnɪs] ★★

名 誠摯、認真、一本正經

片 in all earnestness 嚴肅地

0971 select

[səˋlɛkt] ★★★★

動 挑選、選拔

形 精選的、卓越的

片 select for 為…挑選

0972 victory

[ˋvɪktərɪ] ★★★★

名 勝利、成功

同 triumph 勝利

反 defeat 戰敗

fighting!

Give it a shot 小試身手

❶ He ＿＿＿ respect and admiration for his success.

❷ There are many ＿＿＿ above 7.0 on the Richter scale.

❸ He is not good at expressing ＿＿＿.

❹ The boss asked his employees to work with ＿＿＿.

❺ Learning English with a CD is more ＿＿＿.

082

Essay

There has been a problem between my girlfriend and me <u>for some time</u> now. One evening, I went out with my ex-girlfriend and gave my current[0973] girlfriend some fake excuses[0974] about where I went, but now she knows the truth and is extremely angry. Valentine[0975]'s Day is <u>around the corner</u>[0976], and it was always a big event[0977] for us in the past. I bought an expensive necklace[0978] and a card with a heart on the envelope for her. I made a lot of errors[0979] when I wrote the letter. I couldn't find the exact[0980] words to use, so I erased[0981] them with an eraser again and again. I spent the entire afternoon on it. When that day comes, I'll take her to a renowned[0982] Japanese restaurant after she finishes her yoga class. They serve excellent sashimi, and the environment is very romantic. After we enjoy delicious Japanese food, I'll give her the gift and card in the restaurant as we are having dessert. I don't expect that she will forgive me, but I still hope she will be excited.

ⓘ for some time 一段時間

ⓘ around the corner 在本文中表示「即將來臨」，另外也有「在轉角」、「在附近」等意思

中譯 *Translation*

　　有個問題在我和女友之間存在一段時間了。某個夜晚，我和前女友出門，並對現任女友編造關於我去哪的假藉口，但現在她知道真相而且氣炸了。情人節即將到來，這對過去的我們來說一直都是件大事。我買了一條昂貴的項鍊和一張信封上有愛心的卡片給她。我在寫卡片的時候頻頻出錯，找不到合適的字眼，所以用橡皮擦反覆地擦了又擦。我花了一整個下午寫這張卡片。等到那天來臨時，我會在她上完瑜伽課後，帶她去一間知名的日式餐廳。他們提供很高檔的生魚片，環境氛圍也很浪漫。享用完美味的日式料理後，我會在我們吃甜點時把禮物和卡片交給她。我不期待她會原諒我，但我仍然希望她會因此感到興奮。

0973 current

[`kɜənt] ★★★★★
形 當前的、通用的
名 水流、電流、趨勢
片 main current 主流

0974 excuse

[ɪk`skjuz] ★★★★
名 藉口、辯解、道歉
動 原諒、辯解、免除
片 excuse for 原諒…

0975 valentine

[`væləntaɪn] ★★
名 情人
片 Valentine's Day 情人節

0976 corner

[`kɔrnə] ★★★★★
名 街角、困境、壟斷
動 轉彎、陷入絕境、壟斷
片 tight corner 絕境

0977 event

[ɪ`vɛnt] ★★★★
名 事件、大事、項目
同 incident 事件
片 in any event 無論如何

0978 necklace

[`nɛklɪs] ★★
名 項鍊
同 necklet 短項鍊

0979 error

[`ɛrə] ★★★★
名 錯誤、過失、誤差
同 mistake 錯誤
片 in error 錯的

0980 exact

[ɪg`zækt] ★★★★
形 確切的、精確無誤的
動 勒索、急需
同 precise 準確的

0981 erase

[ɪ`res] ★★★
動 擦掉、抹去、消除
反 record 記錄
片 erase from 從…中抹去

0982 renowned

[rɪ`naʊnd] ★★★
形 著名的、有名望的
同 famous
衍 renown 名聲

0983 newlywed

[`njulɪ͵wɛd] ★★
名 新婚的夫或婦
衍 newlyweds 新婚夫婦

0984 honeymoon

[`hʌnɪ͵mun] ★★★
名 蜜月期、蜜月旅行
動 度蜜月

Fighting!

Give it a shot 小試身手

① The newlyweds0983 _____ their honeymoon0984 in Japan.

② I _____ that David will come to ask for money again.

③ _____ me, do you know what time it is?

④ We got red _____ in the Lunar New Year.

⑤ There are some _____ in the report.

Essay

083

Jenny has had many boyfriends in her life. After several failed relationships as well as many successful ones, she could rightly[0985] claim to be an expert[0986] on love. Whenever her female friends had any problems with their boyfriends, she was always able to help them. She taught her friends how to manage[0987] relationships and express their feelings in a good way to their boyfriends. She even explained the details[0988] step by step, and her friends found her advice very helpful. She decided to found a consulting[0989] office, charging a reasonable fee for her services. She soon became a famous love consultant[0990] and a favorite of many women with relationship problems, and she received hundreds of friend requests and thousands of questions to answer on Facebook. She got all kinds of questions, even ones about how to trim eyebrows. Now, she is a writer and a talk show host[0991]. She says that everyone has his or her own faults that bring about failure. Nothing is fair in love; most desire a partner with very few or no faults even though we aren't perfect ourselves. That's just human nature, isn't it?

中譯 *Translation*

　　珍妮交過很多男朋友。鑑於幾次失敗的戀情，以及許多成功的經驗，她理所當然可以宣稱自己是一位戀愛專家。無論何時，只要她的女性朋友和男友發生任何問題，她都有辦法幫忙。她教她的朋友們如何經營一段感情，以及如何有效的向男友表達她們的感受。她甚至一步一步仔細講解細節，她的朋友們都覺得她的建議很管用。她決定開一間諮商工作室，收取價格公道的諮商費。她很快就成為一位知名的諮商師，是感情上有問題的女性們的最愛，而她的臉書收到數百個交友邀請，還有數千個問題需要回覆。各式各樣的問題都有，甚至包括了如何修眉毛之類的問題。現在她成為一位作家和談話節目的主持人。她說，每個人都有會導致失敗的缺點。愛情裡沒有公平可言，大部分的人都渴望對方幾乎沒有或是根本沒有任何缺點，即使我們自己並不完美。那就是人的本性，不是嗎？

0985 rightly

[ˈraɪtlɪ] ★★
- 副 理所當然地、公正地、恰當地、確切地
- 同 exactly 確切地

0986 expert

[ˈɛkspɚt] ★★★★
- 名 專家、能手、熟練者
- 形 熟練的、內行的
- 片 expert in 對…內行

0987 manage

[ˈmænɪdʒ] ★★★★★
- 動 經營、控制、設法做到
- 同 conduct 經營
- 片 manage with 湊合

0988 detail

[ˈditel] ★★★★
- 名 細節、詳述、局部
- 動 詳細說明
- 片 in detail 詳細地

0989 consulting

[kənˈsʌltɪŋ] ★★
- 形 諮詢的、任專職顧問的
- 同 advisory 諮詢的
- 衍 consult 諮詢

0990 consultant

[kənˈsʌltənt] ★★★★
- 名 顧問、諮詢者
- 同 adviser 顧問

0991 host

[host] ★★★★
- 名 節目主持人、主人
- 動 主辦、主持、作東
- 片 play host to 招待

0992 analyze

[ˈænḷaɪz] ★★★
- 動 分析、分解
- 同 dissect 仔細分析
- 反 synthesize 合成

0993 landslide

[ˈlændslaɪd] ★★
- 名 山崩、壓倒性大勝利
- 片 by a landslide 大獲全勝

0994 quality

[ˈkwɑlətɪ] ★★★★★
- 名 品質、特性、地位
- 形 優良的、內容嚴肅的
- 片 of quality 素質好的

0995 dye

[daɪ] ★★★
- 動 染上顏色
- 名 染色、染料
- 反 bleach 將…漂白

0996 endorser

[ɪnˈdɔrsɚ] ★★
- 名 背書人、轉讓人
- 衍 endorse 背書、簽署

Give it a shot 小試身手

① The _____ analyzed[0992] the cause of the landslide[0993].

② Chanel is my _____ brand for its high quality[0994].

③ He dyed[0995] his _____ and hair brown.

④ The brand endorser[0996] is always _____, not male.

⑤ A team without a leader is on the edge of _____.

  Answers: ① expert ② favorite ③ eyebrows ④ female ⑤ failure

MP3
短文 167
字彙 168

Essay

084

Chinese kung fu has been a part of Hollywood filmmaking for quite a while now. It came to Hollywood largely through Bruce Lee, an incomparable⁰⁹⁹⁷ fighter. Lee was an iconic⁰⁹⁹⁸ figure known throughout⁰⁹⁹⁹ the world who really started the martial¹⁰⁰⁰ arts craze¹⁰⁰¹ in the Western world. Fans crazily flooded¹⁰⁰² around him, snapping¹⁰⁰³ photos and waving flags at film festivals whenever and wherever he showed up. For me, the most impressive scene in any of his movies was when Lee stood fixed on the fence¹⁰⁰⁴ for several minutes with his left leg only. What's more, he could break a table with the palm of his hands, sprinkling¹⁰⁰⁵ the flour from the table all over the ground. As a martial artist, he was always in the best shape. His place in the history of martial arts is firmly cemented¹⁰⁰⁶. People, including fishermen, farmers, and those who seldom watch TV, are still fascinated by this legendary¹⁰⁰⁷ figure.

中譯 *Translation*

中國功夫進入好萊塢電影製作的領域已經有段時間了。中國功夫會打進好萊塢，主要是透過李小龍，他可說是位無人能及的武打者。李小龍是位全球知名的偶像，他著實地讓武術在西方世界掀起一股熱潮。無論何時何地，只要他出席影展，就會有大批影迷瘋狂地圍繞在他身邊拍照並揮動旗幟。對我而言，對他電影中印象最深刻的一幕，就是李小龍只用一隻左腳，就可以在柵欄上站定達數分鐘之久。他還可以一掌把桌子打垮，讓桌上麵粉撒得滿地都是。身為一位武打明星，他的身材總是十分強健。他在武術界的地位根本無法動搖。今天人們依舊著迷於這位傳奇人物，包括漁夫、農夫，和那些很少看電視的人亦然。

0997 incomparable

[ɪn`kɑmpərəbḷ] ★★
- 形 無比的、舉世無雙的
- 同 matchless 無敵的
- 反 comparable 比得上的

0998 iconic

[aɪ`kɑnɪk] ★★
- 形 肖像的、標誌性的
- 衍 icon 偶像

0999 throughout

[θru`aʊt] ★★★★
- 介 遍及、從頭到尾
- 副 處處、始終
- 同 all over 到處

1000 martial

[`mɑrʃəl] ★★
- 形 尚武的、戰爭的
- 同 warlike 尚武的
- 片 martial arts 武術

1001 craze

[krez] ★★
- 名 一時狂熱、風尚、時尚
- 動 發狂、出現裂紋
- 片 craze for 對⋯狂熱

1002 flood

[flʌd] ★★★★
- 動 湧進、淹沒、充斥
- 名 水災、大量、漲潮
- 片 flood in 湧進

1003 snap

[snæp] ★★★★★
- 動 快照拍攝、猛咬、急射
- 名 快照、劈啪聲、精力
- 片 snap off 折斷

1004 fence

[fɛns] ★★★★
- 名 柵欄、籬笆、擊劍術
- 動 用柵欄圍起來、擊劍
- 片 sit on the fence 持中立

1005 sprinkle

[`sprɪŋkḷ] ★★★
- 動 撒、點綴、下稀疏小雨
- 名 撒、稀疏小雨、少量
- 片 sprinkle on 在⋯上灑

1006 cement

[sɪ`mɛnt] ★★★
- 動 鞏固、水泥接合、黏牢
- 名 水泥
- 同 solidify 變堅固

1007 legendary

[`lɛdʒəndˌɛrɪ] ★★
- 形 傳奇的、著名的
- 名 fabled 寓言中的
- 衍 legend 傳說

1008 estimate

[`ɛstəˌmet] ★★★★
- 動 估計、判斷、估價
- 名 估計、評價
- 片 estimate at 猜測⋯為

Fighting!

Give it a shot 小試身手

1. The annual film _____ will take place tonight.
2. The _____ they estimated[1008] was not correct.
3. Morakot Typhoon caused Taiwan's worst _____ in 50 years.
4. I do not _____ the miniskirt for my fleshy legs.
5. I had a slight _____ and headache.

名 名詞　　　同 同義字補充

動 動詞　　　反 反義字補充

形 形容詞　　片 片語補充

副 副詞　　　俚 俚語補充

介 介係詞　　衍 衍生字補充

Essay

085

MP3   短文 169   字彙 170

A musical performance is a form of art. As a professional musician, I know that it is a shame to make any foolish[1009] mistakes during a public performance. Unfortunately, I caught the flu last week, and I had a solo[1010] flute[1011] performance the following day. That was the worst performance in my entire life. My concert was an international[1012] event, so everybody dressed formally. Half of the audience were foreigners[1013]. As the audience flowed[1014] into the hall[1015], I felt many <u>butterflies in my stomach</u>. After the first performer had finished, I stepped onto the stage. When I began to play, I found I couldn't focus properly. Even stranger and more troubling, I could only remember parts of the songs I had chosen to perform. The only thing I could do was play the flute in <u>fits and starts,</u> like a fool. My tutor[1016], who was like an old fox, had intended[1017] to earn his reputation by me, and he would never forgive me after that.

> ⚠ butterflies in one's stomach 由於緊張、焦慮而產生的忐忑不安的心理狀態
>
> ⚠ fits and starts 斷斷續續、一陣一陣、間歇的

中譯 *Translation*

　　音樂表演是藝術的一種類型。身為一名職業音樂家，在公開表演時犯下任何荒謬的錯誤是很丟臉的。不幸的是，我上禮拜得了流行性感冒，隔天還有一個長笛獨奏表演。那真是我此生最糟糕的表演了。我的演奏會是一場國際性的演出，所以每個人的穿著都很正式。有一半的觀眾是外國人。隨著觀眾湧進廳內，我也跟著緊張起來。前一個表演者結束後，我走上舞台。當我開始演奏時，我發現我完全無法聚焦。儘管感覺更加陌生及不安，我也只記得我要演奏的曲目中的片斷部分。我只能斷斷續續的吹著長笛，像個傻瓜一樣。我那老狐狸似的指導老師，本來想藉著我增加名氣，現在他絕對不會原諒我了！

1009 foolish

[`fulɪʃ] ★★★
- 形 愚蠢的、荒謬的
- 片 penny wise and pound foolish 因小失大

1010 solo

[`solo] ★★★
- 形 獨奏的、單獨表演的
- 名 獨奏、單獨表演
- 副 單獨地

1011 flute

[flut] ★★★
- 名 長笛、橫笛
- 動 吹長笛
- 片 play the flute 吹長笛

1012 international

[ˌɪntɚ`næʃənl] ★★★★
- 形 國際性的
- 名 國際運動比賽
- 同 worldwide 遍及全球的

1013 foreigner

[`fɔrɪnɚ] ★★★
- 名 外國人
- 同 alien 外國人
- 衍 foreign 外國的

1014 flow

[flo] ★★★★★
- 動 泛濫、流動、源自
- 名 流動、流暢、漲潮
- 片 flow out 流出、湧出

1015 hall

[hɔl] ★★★★★
- 名 會堂、大廳、走廊
- 同 auditorium 會堂
- 片 assembly hall 禮堂

1016 tutor

[`tjutɚ] ★★★★
- 名 家教、輔導教師
- 動 指導、當家庭教師
- 同 coach (英)家庭教師

1017 intend

[ɪn`tɛnd] ★★★
- 動 想要、打算、為…準備
- 同 plan 打算
- 片 intend to/ving 想要

1018 confused

[kən`fjuzd] ★★★★
- 形 困惑的、混亂的
- 同 bewildered 困惑的

1019 suit

[sut] ★★★★★
- 名 套裝、訴訟、懇求
- 動 適合、相稱
- 片 suit to 與…相符

1020 frank

[fræŋk] ★★★★
- 形 坦白的、真誠的
- 同 candid 坦率的
- 片 be frank with 坦白說

fighting!

Give it a shot 小試身手

1. The nurse called the _____ patient.
2. The _____ was confused[1018] with the Chinese menu.
3. We are requested to wear _____ suits[1019] to the meeting.
4. She moved _____ to see the sign clearer.
5. I _____ you for your frank[1020] apology.

Answers: ❶ following ❷ foreigner ❸ formal ❹ forward ❺ forgive

086

I'll be frank. The furniture in my house was all gathered[1021] from the streets. In fact, I just brought a freezer[1022] home from next door last week. The family living next to me is wealthy, and they always put their used furniture and appliances[1023] that they no longer want at the gate[1024] in front of their garage[1025]. Their gardener is friendly and generous to me. Maybe that second-hand stuff is garbage in their eyes, but it still functions[1026] well. However, there are some things I refuse to take. I once took a Barbie doll last year for my brother's daughter, but it frightened[1027] the little girl because the arms and legs came off it. So, I vowed never to take old toys again. I've gotten a lot of good things from my neighbors. My friends tell me to stop picking things up from the street, but it's a free world. It's none of their business anyway; furthermore[1028], I've got a big screen LCD Panasonic TV in my living room that someone was going to just throw away. I will probably go to IKEA and purchase[1029] the dining[1030] table in the future, if I can't find one on the street, that is.

中譯 *Translation*

　　我要坦白。我家裡的家具都是街上收集而來的。事實上我上週才從隔壁拿了一個冰箱回家。住在我家隔壁的那家人很有錢，而且他們總把用過且不要的家具和家電放在車庫前的出入口。他們家的園丁對我很友善也很慷慨。這些二手家具在他們眼裡或許是垃圾，但它們還是很好用。然而，還是有我不想拿的東西。我去年曾經拿過一個芭比娃娃，我把他送給我哥哥的女兒，然而卻因為芭比娃娃的手和腳脫落而把這個小女孩嚇得半死。所以我發誓，從此不再拿舊玩具了。我從鄰居那裡得到很多好東西。我朋友告訴我不要再從街上撿東西了，但那是我的自由。無論如何，這都不關他們的事，更何況，我還把一個才剛要被丟掉的國際牌液晶螢幕放在客廳裡。若將來我在街上找不到飯桌的話，我或許會去宜家家居買一個吧。

1021 gather

[`gæðə`] ★★★★
- 動 收集、積聚、漸增
- 名 聚集、收穫量
- 片 gather round 圍攏

1022 freezer

[`frizə`] ★★
- 名 冰箱、冷藏室、冰櫃
- 同 fridge 電冰箱

1023 appliance

[ə`plaɪəns] ★★★
- 名 家用電器、裝置、設備
- 片 kitchen appliance 廚房用具

1024 gate

[get] ★★★★
- 名 大門、登機門、途徑
- 動 限制學生外出
- 片 the gate to …的途徑

1025 garage

[gə`rɑʒ] ★★★★
- 名 車庫、汽車修理廠
- 動 把汽車停在車庫
- 片 garage sale 車庫拍賣

1026 function

[`fʌŋkʃən] ★★★★★
- 動 工作、運行、起作用
- 名 功能、作用、職責
- 片 function as 作…用

1027 frighten

[`fraɪtn] ★★★★
- 動 使驚恐、使害怕
- 同 scare 使恐懼
- 片 frighten away 嚇跑

1028 furthermore

[`fɝðə`mor] ★★★
- 副 而且、此外、再者
- 同 also 並且

1029 purchase

[`pɝtʃəs] ★★★★
- 動 購買、努力取得
- 名 購買、緊抓
- 同 buy 購買

1030 dining

[`daɪnɪŋ] ★★★★
- 名 進餐
- 片 dining table 餐桌
- 衍 dine 用餐

1031 scrap

[skræp] ★★★★
- 名 碎片、片段、資料
- 動 廢棄、拆毀、吵架
- 片 scrap of …碎片

1032 beautician

[bju`tɪʃən] ★★
- 名 美容師
- 同 cosmetician 美容師

Fighting!

Give it a shot 小試身手

1. In _____ situation, we do not enter the room.
2. I have _____ some scraps[1031] from newspaper.
3. She took out the black tea from the _____.
4. Jane made up his mind to be a beautician[1032] in the _____.
5. She _____ three kilograms last month.

Answers: 1 general 2 gathered 3 freezer 4 future 5 gained

Essay

087

Mr. Lee is a professor at National Taiwan University. He's a wise[1033] gentleman who is quite erudite[1034], and he is especially knowledgeable about geography[1035] and zoology. He specializes[1036] in animals such as giraffes, goats, and giant pandas. He plays golf, which is he very fond of, three times a week. He stitches[1037] his gold-colored gloves back together every time they rip[1038]. The gloves are old and dirty, but they are his favorite. When he is not grading his students' papers, Mr. Lee spends his time <u>keeping track of</u> and discussing political[1039] developments. When he talks about politics, Mr. Lee becomes intense[1040] and very different from his usual gentle self. He thinks all governments are essentially[1041] corrupt[1042], and he <u>has had his fill of</u> politicians who are greedy[1043] for power. Mr. Lee says one day he might get into politics himself, but he's not sure if he really wants to get involved in such a bureaucratic mess[1044]. He's also worried that he might get corrupted himself by dirty politics.

> (!) keep track of 了解某人的情況或某事件的進展
> (!) have had one's fill of 某人能忍受某事的限度

中譯 *Translation*

　　李先生是台灣大學的一名教授。他是一個有智慧的紳士,特別對地理學和動物學的知識非常豐富。他專門研究像長頸鹿、山羊和大貓熊這類的動物。他每個禮拜打三次他非常喜歡的高爾夫球。每次他的黃金手套裂開了,他就會把它縫好。這雙手套又舊又髒,但卻是他的最愛。除了幫學生的考卷評分之外,李先生把剩下的時間花在了解和討論政治進展上。每當李先生談到政治,他就變得激進,不像平常溫文儒雅的他。他認為所有的政府基本上都很腐敗,而他也受夠了這些貪求權力的政客。李先生說有一天他也許會從政,但他不確定他是否真的想要踏入這種官僚主義的混亂中。他也非常擔心自己可能會被骯髒的政治所腐蝕。

1033 wise

[waɪz] ★★★★
形 有智慧的、有見識的
反 unwise 不明智的
片 wise guy 自作聰明者

1034 erudite

[ˋɛrʊˏdaɪt] ★★
形 博學的、學問精深的
同 learned 博學的

1035 geography

[ˋdʒɪˋɑgrəfɪ] ★★★
名 地理學、地形、佈局
片 geography of …的地形、佈局

1036 specialize

[ˋspɛʃəlaɪz] ★★★
動 專攻、詳細說明
反 generalize 泛論
片 specialize in 專門從事

1037 stitch

[stɪtʃ] ★★★
動 縫合、固定、連結
名 針線、一塊布、少量
片 stitch up 縫合

1038 rip

[rɪp] ★★★★
動 裂開、劃破、拆
名 裂縫、破洞、巨瀾
片 rip off 扯掉、偷竊

1039 political

[pəˋlɪtɪk!] ★★★★
形 政治上的、政黨的
反 nonpolitical 非政治的
片 political party 政黨

1040 intense

[ɪnˋtɛns] ★★★★
形 劇烈的、熱切的
同 drastic 猛烈的
反 mild 溫和的

1041 essentially

[əˋsɛnʃəlɪ] ★★
副 實質上、本來
同 practically 實際上
衍 essential 必要的

1042 corrupt

[kəˋrʌpt] ★★★
形 腐敗的、貪汙的
同 rotten 腐敗的
動 墮落、腐化、賄賂

1043 greedy

[ˋgridɪ] ★★★
形 貪婪的、渴望的
同 rapacious 貪婪的
片 greedy for 渴望

1044 mess

[mɛs] ★★★★
名 混亂、一團糟、食堂
動 弄髒、陷入混亂、玩弄
片 in a mess 亂七八糟

Fighting!

Give it a shot 小試身手

1 Did you reach the sales _____ this month?

2 My boss invited me to play _____ after work.

3 I am a third-_____ student in high school.

4 The victims asked for _____ compensation.

5 Wearing a _____ ring is old fashioned for youngsters.

Answers: 1 goal 2 golf 3 grade 4 government 5 golden

088

🎧 MP3　短文 175　字彙 176

After I greeted[1045] my fans with a smile, I started a three-hour performance at a concert hall. It was the craziest night that I'd ever had. The show climaxed when I threw my handkerchief[1046] into the audience. Everybody was pushing each other to try to get my handkerchief. They almost broke through the line the security guards[1047] had set up. We are now the hottest band in Taiwan, and I play guitar in the band. The vocalist is a guy named Allen, a handsome guy. After he joined[1048] our band, the number of fans grew rapidly[1049]. He was very good at handling our fans. After the show, we went back to the hotel. We brought some French fries, hamburgers, and beer. We hung[1050] the coats[1051] on the hangers[1052] and turned on the heater[1053], starting our private party. We have a habit of holding parties at night, so we hardly[1054] get any sleep at night and aren't healthy. Take our band as a model in music but not in life!

中譯 *Translation*

　　在我用微笑招呼完樂迷之後，我就在音樂廳開始了長達三個小時的演奏。那是我經歷過最瘋狂的夜晚。這場表演在我把手帕丟向觀眾席時達到高潮。每個人都互相推擠，試圖搶到我的手帕。他們幾乎衝破了保全設下的防線。我們現在是臺灣最火紅的樂團，我在團裡負責演奏吉他。主唱是一名叫艾倫的大帥哥。在他加入本團之後，樂迷人數迅速成長。他很懂得如何對待我們的歌迷。表演過後，我們回到飯店。我們買了些薯條、漢堡和啤酒。我們把大衣掛在衣架上，打開暖氣機，開始了我們的私人派對。我們有開夜間派對的習慣，所以我們晚上幾乎都沒睡覺，身體也不健康。要把我們的樂團當成音樂典範，但可不要當成人生典範喔！

1045 greet

[grit] ★★★
- 動 問候、迎接、接受
- 片 greet with 以…迎接
- 衍 greeting 問候

1046 handkerchief

[`hæŋkɚˌtʃɪf] ★★★
- 名 手帕、紙巾
- 同 hankie 手帕

1047 guard

[gɑrd] ★★★★
- 名 守衛、衛兵、防守
- 動 保衛、看守、防範
- 片 guard against 防範

1048 join

[dʒɔɪn] ★★★★★
- 動 加入、連接、會合
- 名 接合點、接連處
- 片 join in 參加

1049 rapidly

[`ræpɪdlɪ] ★★
- 副 迅速地、很快地、立即
- 同 speedily 迅速地
- 衍 rapid 迅速的

1050 hang

[hæŋ] ★★★★★
- 動 把…掛起、吊著、逗留
- 名 懸掛方式、訣竅
- 片 hang on 堅持

1051 coat

[kot] ★★★★
- 名 大衣、皮毛、塗層
- 動 塗在…上、覆蓋…表面
- 同 overcoat 大衣

1052 hanger

[`hæŋɚ] ★★
- 名 衣架、掛鉤、懸掛物
- 片 clothes hanger 衣架

1053 heater

[`hitɚ] ★★
- 名 暖氣機、加熱器、暖爐
- 片 electric heater 電暖器
- 反 cooler 冷卻器

1054 hardly

[`hɑrdlɪ] ★★★★
- 副 幾乎不、簡直不
- 同 barely 幾乎沒有
- 片 hardly ever 幾乎從未

1055 production

[prə`dʌkʃən] ★★★
- 名 生產、產量、製作
- 反 consumption 消耗
- 片 production line 生產線

1056 surround

[sə`raʊnd] ★★★
- 動 圍住、包圍、圍繞
- 名 環繞物、圍飾
- 同 enclose 圍住

Fighting!

Give it a shot 小試身手

❶ The _____ of the production[1055] was up.

❷ He wishes he could break the _____ of smoking.

❸ Do you know how to _____ the problem?

❹ He can _____ afford the rent.

❺ The actor was surrounded[1056] by reporters in the _____.

Answers: ❶ growth ❷ habit ❸ handle ❹ hardly ❺ hall

089

Essay

I studied high school in America, living in New York. In the first month, I lived in a hotel in Manhattan. I moved to a homestay[1057] afterwards. I stayed with a family, living in an old house, and it was humid[1058] inside. The host was very friendly to me, and she taught me English. It was very helpful[1059]. When I felt homesick[1060], I went to have Chinese food in Chinatown. I once had a fight with an American kid because he made fun of my height[1061] and race[1062]. I took out a hidden[1063] weapon[1064] to beat him, and he jumped and kicked my hip[1065]. Both of us were taken to the hospital. Later, my honey stayed with me for three weeks. She was humble[1066], honest and lovely. I started my hobby of being a DJ in a club. I also rented a second-hand turntable[1067] from a musical instruments store. However, I didn't spend too much time on this hobby because of my heavy homework. My life in New York was very colorful. I will never forget it.

中譯 *Translation*

　　我在美國唸高中，居住在紐約。第一個月，我住在曼哈頓的一間旅館，後來才搬到寄宿家庭。我和這家人住在一間老舊的房子裡，屋內很潮濕。主人對我很友善，也教我英語，這對我來說很有幫助。每當我想家時，就會去中國城吃中國菜。我曾經和一個美國小孩打架，因為他嘲笑我的身高和種族。我拿出預藏的武器打他，他則跳起來踢我的屁股。我們兩個都進了醫院。之後我的情人陪了我三個禮拜。她很謙虛、誠實且可愛。我在社團裡發展出當 DJ 的興趣。我還從樂器行租了二手轉盤。然而，因為課業繁重，我沒有花太多時間在這項興趣上。我在紐約的生活非常多采多姿，我永遠都不會忘記。

1057 homestay

[`homste] ★★
名 客居外國家庭

1058 humid

[`hjumɪd] ★★★
形 潮濕的
同 moist 潮濕的
反 dry 乾燥的

1059 helpful

[`hɛlpfəl] ★★★★
形 有幫助的、有益的、樂於助人的
片 help in + ving 利於…

1060 homesick

[`hom͵sɪk] ★★
形 想家的、思鄉的
同 nostalgic 鄉愁的
衍 homesickness 鄉愁

1061 height

[haɪt] ★★★★
名 身高、高度、海拔
同 altitude 高度
片 in height 在…高度上

1062 race

[res] ★★★★★
名 種族、血統、競賽
動 和…競賽、全速前進
片 the human race 人類

1063 hidden

[`hɪdn̩] ★★
形 隱藏的、隱秘的
同 secret 秘密的
衍 hide 隱藏

1064 weapon

[`wɛpən] ★★★★
名 武器、兵器、手段
同 arms 武器

1065 hip

[hɪp] ★★★★
名 臀部、屁股
形 熟悉內情的、通曉的、趕時髦的

1066 humble

[`hʌmbl̩] ★★★★
形 謙遜的、卑微的
動 使謙卑、使威信掃地
同 modest 謙虛的

1067 turntable

[`tɝn͵tebl̩] ★★
名 轉盤、轉車台、錄音轉播機、圓餐桌上的旋盤

1068 speedily

[`spidɪlɪ] ★★
副 迅速地、立即
同 rapidly 迅速地
衍 speedy 迅速的

fighting!

Give it a shot 小試身手

1 She is the same _____ as her sister.

2 Grace _____ an assistant to help her.

3 The injured rider was speedily[1068] sent to the _____.

4 _____ environment is not suitable for all creatures.

5 Linda _____ the phone bill under the table cloth.

Answers: 1 height 2 hired 3 hospital 4 Humid 5 hid

MP3　短文 179　字彙 180

Essay

090

In Taiwan, some people still live with their parents when they are thirty; even some married people do as well. This suggests[1069] that Taiwanese parents ignore the importance[1070] of their children's independence. I can't imagine a thirty-year-old man asking his mom for food when he feels hungry. When he's ill[1071], does he go to a clinic in the company of his parents? If he is jobless[1072], does his dad push him to hunt for a job on the Internet? If he is a house-hunter[1073], does he have to ask permission from his parents? The characteristics[1074] of being an independent adult[1075] include not only increased income but also being responsible for one's own life. Independent adults have a sense[1076] of humor, <u>get along with</u> others very well, and improve[1077] themselves all the time. Parents don't need to direct[1078] all aspects[1079] of their children's lives, but rather let the kids <u>find their own way</u>.

ⓘ get along with 和…相處融洽

ⓘ find one's way 找到出路、找到辦法

中譯 *Translation*

　　在台灣，有些人到了三十歲還是和父母住在一起，甚至一些已婚人士也是如此。這顯示出台灣的父母忽視了讓孩子獨立的重要性。我無法想像一個三十歲的大男人，肚子餓了還要向媽媽要食物。當他生病的時候，難道他需要父母陪他去看醫生嗎？如果他失業，難道他的父親還要督促他上網找工作？如果他要找房子，他難道還要商請父母同意？身為一個獨立的成年人，其特徵不僅包括收入的增加，還要對自己的人生負責。獨立的成人擁有幽默感，和他人和睦相處，也懂得不斷自我提升。父母不需要完全掌控孩子們生活的所有層面，而是要讓孩子們找到自己的路。

1069 suggest

[sə`dʒɛst] ★★★★★
動 顯示、建議、使人想起
片 suggest + ving 建議做某事

1070 importance

[ɪm`pɔrtn̩s] ★★★★
名 重要性、重大、自大
同 significance 重要性
反 triviality 瑣事

1071 ill

[ɪl] ★★★★★
形 生病的、壞的、邪惡的
名 問題、禍害
副 惡劣地、困難地

1072 jobless

[`dʒɑblɪs] ★★
形 失業的
同 unemployed 失業的

1073 hunter

[`hʌntɚ] ★★★
名 追求者、搜尋者、獵人
同 pursuer 追求者
片 job hunter 求職者

1074 characteristic

[ˌkærəktə`rɪstɪk] ★★★
名 特徵、特性、特色
形 特有的、典型的
同 typical 典型的

1075 adult

[ə`dʌlt] ★★★★
名 成年人
形 成年的、成熟的
反 immature 不成熟的

1076 sense

[sɛns] ★★★★★
名 感覺、知覺、效用
動 感覺到、檢測、領會
片 make sense 說得通

1077 improve

[ɪm`pruv] ★★★★★
動 增進、改善、提高
同 better 改善
片 imrove on 改進、超過

1078 direct

[də`rɛkt] ★★★★
動 指揮、命令、針對、導演、指點
形 直接的、筆直的

1079 aspect

[`æspɛkt] ★★★★
名 方面、觀點、外觀
同 view 觀點

1080 industry

[`ɪndəstrɪ] ★★★★★
名 企業、工業、勤勉
片 captain of industry 產業巨頭

Fighting!

Give it a shot 小試身手

1. Please save the children suffering from _____ in Africa.
2. Jessica went out in a _____ and forgot her purse.
3. My sister has become _____ since she was twenty.
4. The _____ of people in different industries[1080] is various.
5. The expert _____ that it was a human error.

Answers: 1 hunger 2 hurry 3 independent 4 income 5 indicated

091

Essay

MP3

短文
181

字彙
182

Animals are hard workers. For instance[1081], ants are diligent[1082] insects. One afternoon, I watched ants working and moving orderly[1083] on the ground. In an instant, I was deeply inspired[1084] and influenced by their patience. As an engineer, I know the importance of research and development. Afterwards, I worked for one month in my laboratory[1085] alone. After I locked[1086] myself in this lonely space for 30 days, I invented[1087] 12 surgical instruments. Everybody was amazed by my inventions, and I got an invitation to an international surgical[1088] instruments forum[1089]. They invited me to introduce[1090] my products to some companies in the industry and to do a television interview. One company wanted to buy the patents from me and offered me a considerable[1091] fee. I signed the contract two days ago. They started to advertise[1092] it while the ink was still wet on the contract. I made a lot of money, because I put a lot of effort into research and development.

中譯 *Translation*

　　動物們都很勤奮工作。例如，螞蟻就是很勤勞的昆蟲。某個下午，我看著螞蟻在地上工作且井然有序地移動。剎那間，我深受他們的耐力所激勵與影響。身為一名工程師，我了解到研究與發展的重要。後來，我獨自待在實驗室裡工作了一個月。在我把自己鎖在這個與世隔絕的空間長達三十天後，我發明了十二樣手術儀器。每個人都為我的發明而震驚，我也獲邀參加一個國際性的手術儀器論壇。他們邀請我向業界的幾家公司和在一場電視專訪中介紹我的產品。有家公司還砸下重金想跟我購買專利。我兩天前簽下了合約，連合約上的墨水都還沒乾他們就開始大肆宣傳。我賺了很多錢，因為我確實在研發上付出了很大的心力。

1081 instance

[`ɪnstəns] ★★★
名 實例、情況、請求
動 舉…為例、引證
片 for instance 例如

1082 diligent

[`dɪlədʒənt] ★★★
形 勤勉的、勤奮的
同 industrious 勤勉的
反 idle 懶惰的

1083 orderly

[`ɔrdəlɪ] ★★★
副 按順序地、有條理地
形 整齊的、守秩序的
反 chaotic 混亂的

1084 inspire

[ɪn`spaɪr] ★★★★
動 鼓舞、激勵、喚起、賦予靈感
片 inspire sb. to 鼓勵做…

1085 laboratory

[`læbrə,torɪ] ★★★
名 實驗室、研究室
同 lab 實驗室

1086 lock

[lɑk] ★★★★★
動 把…鎖起來、卡住
名 鎖、一綹頭髮、止動器
片 lock in 鎖在裡面

1087 invent

[ɪn`vɛnt] ★★★★
動 發明、創造、虛構
同 originate 發源
反 imitate 模仿

1088 surgical

[`sɝdʒɪkl̩] ★★
形 外科的、手術用的
片 surgical techniques 外科技術

1089 forum

[`fɔrəm] ★★★★
名 論壇、討論會
片 forum on …的論壇

1090 introduce

[,ɪntrə`djus] ★★★★
動 介紹、引進、提出
片 introduce to 介紹、引見

1091 considerable

[kən`sɪdərəbl̩] ★★★
形 相當多的、重要的
名 大量
反 inconsiderable 瑣碎的

1092 advertise

[`ædvɚ,taɪz] ★★★
動 做宣傳、廣告、通知
同 promote 推銷
片 advertise for 廣告徵求

---

fighting!

Give it a shot 小試身手

❶ Eileen Chang has a considerable _____ on me.

❷ She _____ on my going with her.

❸ Ms. Huang had a great performance in the _____.

❹ Smile is an _____ language.

❺ What kind of _____ can you play?

Answers: ❶ influence ❷ insisted ❸ interview ❹ international ❺ instrument

092

Essay

"Don't judge a person by his or her appearance."
Mark always says. Mark is a kindergarten[1093] teacher
in Australia. He's quiet and maybe a little bit shy. He eats jam sandwiches in the
mornings and jogs[1094] in the evenings on weekdays[1095], just like some people. After
work, he buys a newspaper and French-fried potatoes with ketchup on the way home.
On the weekends, he wears a leather jacket and jeans. He drives his jeep, playing
country music, to the countryside like a cowboy. He sees koalas[1096] and other
wildlife[1097] along the way. He meets other off-road[1098] racers[1099] at a club at night.
Talking about cars is the common[1100] language for men. They gather together to drink
beer and share their knowledge of cars and engines[1101]. This place is like Mark's
castle[1102] and he's like a king when he's there. He works had all week and looks
forward to the coming weekends.

> (!) look forward to 期待、盼望，若 to 後面接的是動詞則要改為動名詞

中譯 *Translation*

　　馬克常說：「不可以貌取人。」馬克是澳洲的一名幼稚園老師，他很安靜，也許
還有點靦腆。他平日早上吃果醬三明治，晚上慢跑，就像某些人一樣。下班之後，他
會在回家途中買份報紙和附蕃茄醬的炸薯條。一到週末，他會穿上皮夾克和牛仔褲，
開著他的吉普車，播放著搖滾爵士樂，一路開往鄉村，就像個牛仔一樣。他沿途中看
見了無尾熊和其他野生動物。晚上他會在俱樂部和其他越野車騎士碰頭。車是男人之
間的共同語言。他們聚在一起喝啤酒，分享車子和引擎的知識。這地方就像是馬克的
城堡，而他在這裡就像國王一樣。他努力工作了整個禮拜，就是在等著週末到來。

1093 kindergarten

[`kɪndə,gɑrtn̩] ★★★
名 幼稚園、學前班
同 nursery school 托兒所

1094 jog

[dʒɑg] ★★★★
動 慢跑、輕搖、顛簸
名 慢跑、輕搖、提醒
片 jog along 平穩地向前

1095 weekday

[`wik,de] ★★★
名 平日、工作日
反 holiday 假日
片 on weekday 在平日

1096 koala

[ko`ɑlə] ★★
名 無尾熊
同 koala bear 無尾熊

1097 wildlife

[`waɪld,laɪf] ★★★
名 野生動物
形 野生生物的

1098 off-road

[`ɔfrod] ★★
形 越野的
同 cross-country 越野的

1099 racer

[`resə] ★★
名 賽跑者、比賽用汽車
同 runner 賽跑者

1100 common

[`kɑmən] ★★★★★
形 共有的、常見的、一般的、公共的
片 common sense 常識

1101 engine

[`ɛndʒən] ★★★★
名 引擎、發動機
同 motor 發動機

1102 castle

[`kæsl̩] ★★★★
名 城堡、堡壘
動 築城堡防禦
同 chateau 城堡

1103 prison

[`prɪzn̩] ★★★★
名 監獄、監禁、拘留所
動 監禁
片 in prison 坐牢

1104 convey

[kən`ve] ★★★★
動 傳達、運送、傳播
同 transport 運送
片 convey to 運往、傳達

Fighting!

Give it a shot 小試身手

❶ Jeff was sentenced _____ ten years in prison[1103].

❷ Body _____ can convey[1104] a man's real feeling.

❸ Quiet. Someone is _____ on the door.

❹ I live in the tallest _____ in the neighborhood.

❺ Travel increases one's _____ of the world.

Answers: ❶ to ❷ language ❸ knocking ❹ building ❺ knowledge

093

Essay

I am a lawyer and a legal[1105] representative[1106] for several listed[1107] companies. My colleagues[1108] admire me for my leadership[1109]. My latest case deals with patents. No matter how busy I am, I still find time to spend time with my family. My kids really enjoy the salads I make. Also, I squeeze[1110] lemon and mix it with soda to make lemonade. It's healthy for children to eat and drink natural ingredients. I borrow[1111] books from the library[1112] for them. My friends lend me some story books as well. Before they go to sleep, they lie on my lap[1113], listening to my stories. They love the story about a leopard[1114] licking[1115] a cat. <u>In my company</u>, they aren't afraid, even if they hear thunder suddenly or see the quick flash of lightning[1116]. It doesn't take long at all for them to fall asleep. Less than ten minutes into a story, their eyelids will be half-closed. I decorate my kids' room with a cute lantern, and they like it so much. I love my job, but I love my family more.

ⓘ in sb's company 與某人在一起，也可以用 in the company of sb.

中譯 *Translation*

　　我是個律師，也是許多上市公司的法定代表。我的同事都很羨慕我的領導能力。我最近的案子是處理專利權的問題。不管我有多忙，我還是會花時間陪伴家人。我的孩子們很喜歡吃我做的沙拉。除此之外，我還會擠檸檬混合汽水做成檸檬汁。成分天然的食物和飲料對小孩來說是很健康的。我會從圖書館借書給他們看，我朋友也會借我一些故事書。在他們上床睡覺之前，他們會躺在我的大腿上聽我說故事。他們很喜歡一個「豹舔小貓」的故事。有了我的陪伴，他們就算突然聽到打雷聲或看到閃電也不會害怕。讓他們入睡不用花很久的時間。在我開始唸故事不到十分鐘，他們的眼皮就已經快睜不開了。我用燈籠替孩子們裝飾房間，他們非常喜歡。我愛我的工作，但我更愛我的家人。

1105 legal

[`ligl] ★★★★
形 法定的、合法的
反 illegal 非法的
片 legal advisor 法律顧問

1106 representative

[rɛprɪ`zɛntətɪv] ★★★
名 代表、代理人、典型
形 代表性的、代理的
片 representative of 代表

1107 listed

[`lɪstɪd] ★★
形 登記上市的、列在單子上的
反 unlisted 股票不上市的

1108 colleague

[`kɑlig] ★★★
名 同事、同僚
片 work as sb's colleague 和某人共事

1109 leadership

[`lidəʃɪp] ★★★★★
名 領導地位、領導才能
片 under sb's leadership 在某人領導下

1110 squeeze

[skwiz] ★★★
動 榨出、擠出、強取
名 壓榨、擁擠、困境
片 squeeze in 擠進

1111 borrow

[`bɑro] ★★★
動 借入、採用、抄襲
反 lend 借給
片 borrow from 從…借走

1112 library

[`laɪˌbrɛrɪ] ★★★★
名 圖書館、藏書、書庫
同 bibliotheca 圖書室
片 library card 借書證

1113 lap

[læp] ★★★★
名 膝部、重疊部分
動 舐食、部分重疊、摺疊

1114 leopard

[`lɛpəd] ★★
名 豹、美洲豹、獅像
片 a leopard can't change its spot 本性難移

1115 lick

[lɪk] ★★★★
動 舐、輕拍、克服
名 舐、少量、快速
片 lick the dust 被擊倒

1116 lightning

[`laɪtnɪŋ] ★★★
名 閃電、意外的幸運
形 閃電的、閃電似的
片 lightning rod 避雷針

fighting!

Give it a shot 小試身手

1. The _____ style of costume has been very popular.
2. Do not drive over the _____ speed limit.
3. You can consult the periodical in the _____.
4. The little cat _____ my fingers.
5. The ruler you sold me doesn't have enough _____.

Answers: ① latest ② legal ③ library ④ licked ⑤ length

094

MP3　短文 187　字彙 188

Essay

　　Bruce spent all his money and time on his girlfriend, Carol. Carol was a lovely girl, and Bruce was a good listener[1117] to her. Carol was the most important person in the world to him, but Bruce tried to always control her and everything she did <u>out of</u> a desire to possess[1118] her. Carol's girlfriends told her to break up with him, not to lock herself in a prison. They thought Bruce was a loser who lacked confidence. He worked at a local[1119] restaurant located in Taitung County and earned just a little. They couldn't have a date at a nice restaurant. Bruce usually just had a loaf[1120] of bread for dinner. Carol decided to leave him, and later she fell in love with another man. Bruce didn't want to lose her, but the link[1121] between them had already broken. He couldn't accept the loss[1122] of the relationship and to be lonely for the rest of his life. But he moved to the beachside, built a cabin[1123] out of logs[1124], and lived a lonely life there with no electricity or gas.

> ⓘ out of 在本文表示「因為」、「出自於」，另外也有「在…範圍之外」、「用…作材料」、「沒有」等意思

中譯 *Translation*

　　布魯斯將所有的金錢和時間都花在女友卡蘿身上。卡蘿是一個可愛的女孩，布魯斯是她最好的傾聽者。卡蘿對他來說是世上最重要的人，但出自於對她的佔有慾，布魯斯總是試圖要掌控所有關於卡蘿的一切。卡蘿的女性朋友都叫她和他分手，不要把自己鎖在牢籠裡。她們認為布魯斯是個缺乏自信的失敗者。他在台東縣一間當地的餐廳工作，錢賺得不多。他們不能在好的餐廳裡約會。布魯斯常常晚餐只吃一條麵包。卡蘿決定離開他，後來就和另一個男人墜入愛河。布魯斯不想失去她，但他們之間的連繫已經斷了。他不能接受失去這段感情和接下來的寂寞人生。然而他搬到海邊，蓋了一間木造小屋，過著沒有電和瓦斯的孤獨生活。

1117 listener

[ˋlɪsn̩ə] ★★★
名 傾聽者、收聽者
同 auditor 聽者

1118 possess

[pəˋzɛs] ★★★★
動 擁有、支配、迷住
同 hold 擁有
片 possess of 擁有

1119 local

[ˋlokl̩] ★★★★★
形 當地的、局部的
名 當地居民、當地新聞

1120 loaf

[lof] ★★★★★
名 一塊麵包
動 遊蕩、閒逛、虛度
片 loaf away 消磨時間

1121 link

[lɪŋk] ★★★★
名 連繫、關係、環節
動 連接、連繫、挽住
片 link with 與…相連

1122 loss

[lɔs] ★★★★
名 損失、失敗、減少
反 gain 獲得
片 at a loss 不知所措

1123 cabin

[ˋkæbɪn] ★★★
名 小屋、客艙、駕駛艙
動 住在小屋裡
同 hut 小屋

1124 log

[lɔg] ★★★★
名 原木、日誌
動 伐木、把…記入日誌
片 log on 電腦開機

1125 subtle

[ˋsʌtl̩] ★★★★
形 隱約的、微妙的、不知
　　不覺起作用的、敏銳的
同 delicate 微妙的

1126 solidify

[səˋlɪdə͵faɪ] ★★
動 凝固、變堅固、團結
同 coagulate 凝固
衍 solidification 凝固

1127 emporium

[ɛmˋpɔrɪəm] ★
名 商場、商業中心

1128 opposite

[ˋɑpəzɪt] ★★★★
副 在對面
名 對立面、對立物
片 opposite to 與…相反

fighting!

Give it a shot 小試身手

❶ There is a subtle[1125] _____ between twins.
❷ The _____ will solidify[1126] at zero degree.
❸ A new emporium[1127] will be _____ opposite[1128] to the park.
❹ I feel _____ in the unfamiliar environment.
❺ Laziness made him _____ the job.

Answers: ❶ link ❷ liquid ❸ located ❹ lonely ❺ lose

095

Essay

David is a magician, and he has performed hundreds of magic shows. He acts in a mysterious[1129] manner[1130], and he always wears a mask in the show to maintain[1131] a particular[1132] image[1133]. Nobody has ever seen his face. His appearance is still a question mark in everyone's mind. There is a rumor[1134] that he married a Chinese woman and that he can speak fluent[1135] Mandarin. Another one is that he was born in a lower-class family. He once had an interview with a magazine journalist[1136], and he said that he had become a famous magician not only because of luck. He said the main reason was that he had done a lot of practice. His most famous performance is to make a mango disappear from a mat[1137]. Sometimes he plays his tricks on the streets. His life is like his magic performance - totally[1138] mysterious, but it is charming and attractive to his fans.

中譯 *Translation*

　　大衛是一名魔術師，他已經演出過上百場的魔術秀。他的演出方式很神祕，表演時也經常戴著一張面具，來維持他獨特的形象。沒有人看過他的長相。他的相貌依舊是每個人心中的問號。謠傳說他和一個中國女人結婚，而且他還會講一口流利的國語。還有人聽說他出生於一個下層階級的家庭。他曾經接受一名雜誌記者的專訪，他說自己成為知名魔術師並不純粹是靠運氣，主要的原因是他做了非常大量的練習。他最有名的表演是讓一粒芒果從毯子上消失。有時他會在街上表演魔術。他的人生就像他的魔術表演一樣──全然的神祕，但這對他的粉絲來說是非常迷人且具吸引力的。

你不可不知！

　　隨著科技日趨進步，魔術師的花招更是推陳出新。不過談到魔術，就不得不提及一位舉世聞名的魔術師──大衛考柏菲。其空中飛翔、消失的自由女神、穿越萬里長城，可說是經典代表作，當然，都是花費驚人的曠世巨作。

1129 mysterious

[mɪsˋtɪrɪəs] ★★★★
- 形 神秘的、不可思議的
- 同 mystical 神秘的
- 衍 mystery 神秘、謎

1130 manner

[ˋmænɚ] ★★★★
- 名 手法、方法、態度、規矩、習慣

1131 maintain

[menˋten] ★★★★
- 動 維持、保養、堅持
- 反 abandon 拋棄
- 片 maintain with 保持

1132 particular

[pɚˋtɪkjəlɚ] ★★★★
- 形 獨特的、特定的、挑剔的、詳細的
- 片 in particular 尤其是

1133 image

[ˋɪmɪdʒ] ★★★★★
- 名 形象、肖像、化身
- 片 image of …的翻版

1134 rumor

[ˋrumɚ] ★★★
- 名 謠言、傳聞、咕噥
- 動 謠傳、傳說
- 同 gossip 流言蜚語

1135 fluent

[ˋfluənt] ★★★
- 形 流利的、流暢的
- 同 eloquent 有說服力的
- 片 fluent in …上流暢的

1136 journalist

[ˋdʒɝnəlɪst] ★★★★
- 名 新聞記者
- 同 reporter 記者
- 衍 journalism 新聞業

1137 mat

[mæt] ★★★★
- 名 墊子、草蓆、(畫或照片的)襯邊
- 形 無光澤的、暗淡的

1138 totally

[ˋtotl̩ɪ] ★★★★
- 副 完全、整個地
- 同 entirely 完全

1139 poke

[pok] ★★★
- 動 把…戳向、伸出、探聽
- 名 袋子、錢包
- 片 poke at 戳向、刺向

1140 sticker

[ˋstɪkɚ] ★★★
- 名 標籤、貼紙、難題
- 片 sticker price 標價

---

fighting!

Give it a shot 小試身手

1. We tend to buy things at a _____ price.
2. The male model was _____ to be a drug addict.
3. The _____ poked[1139] his finger into a glass table.
4. His bad _____ suggest that he got drunk.
5. He _____ the page he has read by a sticker[1140].

Answers: 1. lower 2. said 3. magician 4. manners 5. marked

🎧 MP3　短文 191　字彙 192

096

Essay

I had a meeting[1141] with some members of my family and my mates[1142] at a restaurant yesterday. There were so many different types of food on the menu, such as melon salad, corn soup, pasta, etc. The restaurant used the best ingredients. The sauce[1143] matched the steak perfectly. There was a band performing live, and they played some classic old songs. The songs all had beautiful melodies, and they brought back memories from my childhood. We had a really big meal, and we were all satisfied. Anyway, the price was quite reasonable. To me, that is the true meaning[1144] of life – enjoying delicious food. After dinner, I sent a text[1145] message to my mom. She has had high blood pressure for years. I reminded her to take her medicine[1146] and measure[1147] her blood pressure regularly. Doctors <u>have no means</u> to cure her illness[1148], just to control it. That was also why she didn't join us for dinner. She needed to stay home to take a rest. I hope her condition will improve soon; if it does, then she can join us next time.

ⓘ have no means 沒辦法，means 在此表示「手段」、「方法」的意思

中譯 *Translation*

　　昨天我和一些家人以及夥伴們在餐廳聚會。菜單上有很多不同種類的食物，像是甜瓜沙拉、玉米湯、義大利麵等等。這家餐廳使用最好的食材，醬汁和牛排搭配得非常完美。餐廳裡還有樂團現場表演，他們也演奏幾首經典老歌。這些歌曲的旋律都很優美，也讓我想起我的孩提時代。我們吃了一頓非常豐盛的大餐，大家都感到很滿足。然而價格卻也相當公道，我認為這就是生命的真義——享受美食。吃完晚餐我傳了一封簡訊給媽媽。她高血壓的毛病已經很多年了，我提醒她要按時吃藥和量血壓。醫生沒辦法治癒她的病，只能控制。那就是她沒有和我們一起吃晚餐的原因，她必須留在家休息。我希望她可以很快地康復，這樣下次她就可以加入我們了。

1141 meeting

[`mitɪŋ] ★★★★★
名 會議、會面、匯合點
片 meeting of the minds 意見一致

1142 mate

[met] ★★★★
名 同伴、配偶、助手
動 使配對、交配
片 soul mate 知己

1143 sauce

[sɔs] ★★★★
名 醬汁、樂趣、莽撞
動 加調味醬、添加趣味

1144 meaning

[`minɪŋ] ★★★★
名 意義、重要性、含義
形 意味深長的
反 unmeaning 無意義的

1145 text

[tɛkst] ★★★★★
名 文字、正文、文本、課本、版本、主題
動 發簡訊

1146 medicine

[`mɛdəsṇ] ★★★★
名 內服藥、醫學、良藥
動 用藥物治療
片 take medicine 服藥

1147 measure

[`mɛʒɚ] ★★★★★
動 測量、估量、權衡
名 尺寸、措施、度量單位
片 measure up 測量

1148 illness

[`ɪlnɪs] ★★★★
名 患病、身體不適
反 health 健康
片 minor illness 微恙

1149 recognize

[`rɛkəg͵naɪz] ★★★★★
動 辨認、認可、認清、表彰、理睬
片 recognize as 認為是

1150 dish

[dɪʃ] ★★★★
名 菜餚、盤子、美女
動 盛於盤中
片 dish up 上菜

1151 surgery

[`sɝdʒərɪ] ★★★★
名 手術、外科、開刀房、門診時間
同 operation 手術

1152 brief

[brif] ★★★★★
形 簡略的、短暫的
名 簡報、概要
動 簡報

Fighting!

Give it a shot 小試身手

1 He could recognize[1149] the _____ in this dish[1150].

2 This instrument is used to _____ the body fat.

3 Van lost part of his _____ after the brain surgery[1151].

4 Her secretary made a brief[1152] _____ in the meeting.

5 He left a _____ for you when you're away.

097

Essay

I have been fond of models of military airplanes since I was young. My friend collects models of motorcycles, and his collection is worth five hundred thousand NTD. Mine is worth more than one million[1153] NTD. My favorite one is a giant[1154] F-16 aircraft[1155] model, a monster. I always polish[1156] its surface and make it shine like a mirror. It is made of metal[1157], and there are cool instruments inside. There are different ways to make models, and the most difficult and expensive methods[1158] allow the models to resemble[1159] the real aircrafts very much. Another one of my favorite models is not in good condition. It is minus[1160] one wing. I don't take care of it well, and it has become a home for mosquitoes and moths[1161]. My collection is a mixture[1162] of modern and classic styles. My hobby developed out of my desire to be a pilot[1163], but now I am an engineer. The biggest mistake I ever made was to choose the wrong career.

中譯 *Translation*

　　我從年輕的時候就很喜歡軍機模型。我朋友收集的是機車模型,他的收藏總共價值五十萬台幣,而我的則價值超過一百萬台幣。我最喜歡的是一台巨型的F-16飛機模型,非常巨大。我總是把它的表面擦得像鏡子一樣亮晶晶。它是由金屬製成,裡面有許多酷炫的儀錶。製作模型有很多種方式,而讓模型與實體飛機相似度極高的製作方式是最難也最貴的一種。另一架我最愛的模型狀態並不好,它少了一邊機翼。我沒有好好照顧它,而讓模型成了蚊子和飛蛾的巢穴。我的收藏綜合了現代和經典的款式。我會有這項嗜好是因為我渴望當一名機師,但我現在卻成了工程師。選擇錯誤的職業,是我一生所犯下最大的錯誤。

1153 million

[ˋmɪljən] ★★★★
名 百萬、無數、大眾
形 百萬的、無數的

1154 giant

[ˋdʒaɪənt] ★★★★
形 巨大的、巨人般的
名 巨人、偉人、巨物
片 literary giants 文豪

1155 aircraft

[ˋɛr͵kræft] ★★★★
名 飛機、飛行器
片 aircraft carrier 航空母艦

1156 polish

[ˋpɑlɪʃ] ★★★★
動 磨光、擦亮、潤飾
名 磨光、光澤、優美
片 polish up 改善

1157 metal

[ˋmɛtl] ★★★★★
名 金屬、金屬製品、合金
動 用金屬裝配
片 heavy metal 重金屬

1158 method

[ˋmɛθəd] ★★★★★
名 方法、條理、秩序
片 method of/for + ving
…的方法

1159 resemble

[rɪˋzɛmbl] ★★★
動 像、類似
反 differ 相異
衍 resemblance 相似

1160 minus

[ˋmaɪnəs] ★★★
介 失去、減去
名 減號、負數、缺陷
形 減去的、負的、不利的

1161 moth

[mɔθ] ★★★
名 蠹、蛾、蛀蟲
片 moth-eaten 蟲蛀的

1162 mixture

[ˋmɪkstʃɚ] ★★★
名 混合、混雜、合劑
俚 the mixture as before
換湯不換藥

1163 pilot

[ˋpaɪlət] ★★★★
名 飛行員、舵手、嚮導
形 引導的、試驗性的
動 駕駛(飛機等)、帶領

1164 shortage

[ˋʃɔrtɪdʒ] ★★★
名 缺少、匱乏、不足額
同 deficiency 不足
片 shortage of …短缺

fighting!

Give it a shot 小試身手

❶ A shortage[1164] of _____ police made the area insecure.

❷ Eight _____ four leaves four.

❸ _____ dance derived from ballet.

❹ Tina hit the jackpot and won one _____.

❺ These _____ of studying are very useful to me.

Answers: ❶ military ❷ minus ❸ Modern ❹ million ❺ methods

098

I took my son to a Taipei museum[1165] for the National Natural Animal Exhibition last week. My son was very naughty. He ran around in the MRT station, and he nearly hit a kid on the platform. After we entered the museum, my son gazed[1166] at the fake, movable[1167] mule[1168] and the models of naked primitive[1169] people. Afterwards, we went to a concert hall nearby for a symphony[1170] concert. The musicians were from Germany, and we enjoyed the performance so much, but my son just kept biting[1171] his nails[1172] all the time. Later, we went to a Greek restaurant. I told my son not to make a mess on the table while eating, but he still played with his napkin[1173]. I told him if he didn't sit properly, I wouldn't take him out again. He was scared, so he sat nicely.

Artistic exhibitions and performances have multiplied[1174] in Taiwan recently, and they don't cost much to attend. It's good to spend some time experiencing art and culture with your friends and family on weekends.

中譯 *Translation*

　　上禮拜我帶著兒子參觀台北博物館的國家自然動物展。我兒子非常調皮，在捷運車站裡跑來跑去，還差點在月台上撞倒一個小孩。在我們進到博物館後，我兒子就一直盯著會動的假驢子和裸體的原始人模型看。展覽過後，我們去附近的音樂廳聽交響音樂會。音樂家來自德國，我們都很享受這場表演，但我兒子卻全程都在咬指甲。稍晚，我們去一家希臘餐廳。我告訴兒子吃飯時要保持餐桌整潔，但他還是一直玩餐巾。我告訴他如果他再不坐好，我就不會再帶他出門。他嚇到了，只好乖乖坐好。

　　最近台灣的文藝展覽和表演越來越多，而且不用花太多錢就能參加。週末時和家人朋友一起花點時間來體驗藝術文化是非常棒的。

1165 museum

[mju`zɪəm] ★★★★

名 博物館、展覽館
片 science museum 科博館

1166 gaze

[gez] ★★★★

動 凝視、注視、盯
名 凝視、注視
片 gaze at 注視

1167 movable

[`muvəbl] ★★★

形 可移動的、動產的
名 動產、可移動之物
反 immovable 固定的

1168 mule

[mjul] ★★★

名 騾、固執的人
片 as stubborn as a mule 非常頑固

1169 primitive

[`prɪmətɪv] ★★★

形 原始的、早期的、純樸的、簡單的
名 原始事物、純樸的人

1170 symphony

[`sɪmfənɪ] ★★★

名 交響樂、和聲、和諧
片 symphony orchestra 交響樂團

1171 bite

[baɪt] ★★★★★

動 咬、啃、上當、纏住
名 咬、叮、一口之量
片 bite off 咬斷

1172 nail

[nel] ★★★★

名 指甲、釘子、爪
動 使固定、集中於、釘
片 nail down 固定、確定

1173 napkin

[`næpkɪn] ★★★

名 餐巾、小毛巾、衛生棉
同 serviette 餐巾
片 paper napkin 餐巾紙

1174 multiply

[`mʌltəplaɪ] ★★★★

動 增加、使相乘、繁殖
片 multiply by 乘以
衍 multiplex 多樣的

1175 spam

[spæm] ★★

名 垃圾郵件、(S)豬肉罐頭(商標名)
同 junk mail 垃圾郵件

1176 picky

[`pɪkɪ] ★★

形 吹毛求疵的、挑剔的
同 choosy 愛挑剔的

Fighting!

Give it a shot 小試身手

1 Da Vinci's painting will be exhibited in the _____.

2 The taxi is too _____ to contain all of us.

3 Just park your car _____. It won't take too much time.

4 She felt annoyed by the pictures of the _____ girl in the spam[1175].

5 It is _____ for parents to be picky[1176] about their son (daughter) in law.

Answers: 1 museum 2 narrow 3 nearby 4 naked 5 natural

099

Essay

🎧 MP3   短文 197   字彙 198

My nephew and niece live in northern China. I visited them last month, and I ate noodles and steamed[1177] dumplings every day there. Nobody ate rice there, so none[1178] of the restaurants serve rice. I brought a necklace for my niece and a notebook for my nephew. They live in the countryside. Everyone knows how to fish with nets[1179] there. It is necessary for every person to learn this skill while he or she is young. Every morning, my nephew goes fishing with his neighbors[1180]. When I stayed at their house, I woke up at 5 o'clock every morning. That was too early for me, so I always <u>nodded off</u> in the afternoon. My nephew built[1181] a comfortable nest[1182] for himself and his wife. When my nephew went out to fish, his wife stayed home and sewed[1183] her own clothing[1184]. They are not wealthy at all, but <u>neither</u>[1185] my nephew <u>nor</u> his wife has a negative[1186] attitude[1187]. I think that is what I should learn from them.

ⓘ nod off 打盹
ⓘ neither A nor B 既不是 A 也不是 B

中譯 *Translation*

　　我的姪子和姪女都住在中國北方。上個月我去探視他們，每天都吃麵食和蒸餃。那裡沒有人吃米飯，所以也沒有餐廳在賣。我帶了一條項鍊送給姪女，一台筆記型電腦送給姪子。他們住在農村裡，那裡的每個人都知道如何用網捕魚。當地居民在他們還年輕的時候，一定要學會這項技能。每天早上姪子都會和他的鄰居去釣魚。當我住在他們家的時候，我每天早上都五點就起床。這對我來說實在太早了，所以我下午的時候總是會打瞌睡。姪子為他和太太打造了一間舒適的窩。當我的姪子出外捕魚時，他太太就會留在家裡用針線縫衣服。他們一點也不富裕，但不管是姪子還是姪媳，他們從不抱持負面的態度。我認為那正是我該向他們學習的地方。

1177 steam

[stim] ★★★★
- 動 蒸、冒熱氣、行駛
- 名 蒸汽、精力、輪船
- 片 steam up 蒙上水氣

1178 none

[nʌn] ★★★★★
- 代 一個也沒、無一人
- 副 毫不、決不
- 片 bar none 無例外

1179 net

[nɛt] ★★★★★
- 名 網、陷阱、網狀系統、淨利
- 動 用網捕、用網攔住

1180 neighbor

[ˋnebə] ★★
- 名 鄰居、鄰國、同胞
- 形 鄰近的
- 動 與…為鄰

1181 build

[bɪld] ★★★★★
- 動 建造、發展、擴大
- 名 體格、體型
- 片 build on 以…為基礎

1182 nest

[nɛst] ★★★★
- 名 巢、窩、溫床
- 動 築巢、巢居
- 片 a nest of …的溫床

1183 sew

[so] ★★
- 動 做針線活、縫補、縫合
- 同 stitch 縫
- 片 sew up 控制、決定

1184 clothing

[ˋkloðɪŋ] ★★★★
- 名 (總稱)衣服、覆蓋物
- 俚 wolf in sheep's clothing 披著羊皮的狼

1185 neither

[ˋniðə] ★★★★
- 連 既不…也不
- 代 (兩者中)無一個

1186 negative

[ˋnɛɡətɪv] ★★★★
- 形 反面的、消極的、否定的、陰極的
- 名 否定、拒絕

1187 attitude

[ˋætətjud] ★★★★
- 名 態度、意見、看法
- 片 attitude towards/to 對…的態度

1188 object

[ˋɑbdʒɪkt] ★★★★★
- 名 物體、對象、目標
- 動 反對
- 片 object to 反對

Give it a shot 小試身手

1. The answer to that question is _____.
2. He likes _____ romance movies nor animation movies.
3. _____ of us have been to Japan.
4. She used a _____ to sew the button onto the shirt.
4. Throw the objects[1188] away if they are not _____.

Essay 100

Mandy is a book freak[1189], and she reads ten novels a week. Her mom is annoyed by that, but Mandy doesn't obey her mom and does her own thing. Schoolteachers also object to her constant reading, for Mandy doesn't listen to teachers in class when she is reading novels. She is fond of writing as well, and she's good at organizing the structure[1190] of essays. Her writing skill is far above the ordinary.

One day, something surprising occurred[1191]. She got an official[1192] letter from the Organization[1193] of Writers, which was an organ[1194] of the government operating internationally, and they offered[1195] Mandy a job. They even waived[1196] the job interview. She was so delighted[1197] and asked her mom's opinion[1198] about taking the job. Her mom thought it was a great chance[1199] for Mandy and decided to do something special to celebrate it. Her mom baked Mandy's favorite steak and onion pie in the oven. They had a wonderful dinner that night. After that, her mom no longer tried to control what Mandy did anymore.

中譯 *Translation*

曼蒂是一個小說迷，她一個禮拜要看十本小說。她母親對她這樣的行為很感冒，但她並不聽母親的話，照樣我行我素。學校老師也反對她一直看小說，因為曼蒂在課堂上不聽老師講解，反而在看小說。她也很喜歡寫作，而且她很擅長組織文章結構。她的寫作天份比一般人都還優秀。

某天，一件令人驚喜的事發生了。她接到一封從作家協會寄來的官方書信，那是跨國運作的一個政府機構，他們要提供曼蒂一個工作機會。他們甚至還捨棄了面試流程。她相當高興地詢問母親的意見。她媽媽認為這是曼蒂的大好機會，並決定做點特別的事好好慶祝一番。媽媽用烤箱烤了曼蒂最愛的牛排和洋蔥派。當晚他們享用了一頓豐盛的晚餐。在那之後，她媽媽再也不會阻止曼蒂做想做的事了。

1189 freak

[frik] ★★★
- 名 狂熱愛好者、怪誕的行動、反常現象
- 形 反常的、怪異的

1190 structure

[`strʌktʃə] ★★★★
- 名 結構、組織、建築物
- 動 建造、組織
- 片 construction 建造

1191 occur

[ə`kɝ] ★★★★★
- 動 發生、出現、浮現
- 同 happen 發生
- 片 occur to 被想起

1192 official

[ə`fɪʃəl] ★★★★
- 形 官方的、正式的、講究形式的
- 名 官員、幹事

1193 organization

[ˌɔrgənə`zeʃən] ★★★
- 名 組織、機構、編制、系統、有機體
- 衍 organize 組織

1194 organ

[`ɔrgən] ★★★★
- 名 機構、器官、風琴
- 片 an organ transplant 器官移植

1195 offer

[`ɔfə] ★★★★★
- 動 提供、給予、出價
- 名 提供、提議、報價
- 片 on offer 供出售的

1196 waive

[wev] ★★★
- 動 放棄、撤回、推遲
- 同 relinquish 放棄
- 反 claim 要求

1197 delight

[dɪ`laɪt] ★★★★
- 動 高興、喜愛
- 名 欣喜、愉快、樂事
- 片 delight in 以…為樂

1198 opinion

[ə`pɪnjən] ★★★★
- 名 意見、主張、輿論
- 片 opinion on 關於…的意見

1199 chance

[tʃæns] ★★★★★
- 名 機會、可能性、運氣、僥倖、冒險
- 片 by chance 偶然

1200 ambition

[æm`bɪʃən] ★★★
- 名 雄心、抱負、追求目標
- 動 有…野心、追求
- 同 aspiration 抱負

fighting!

Give it a shot 小試身手

1. It _____ to me that my suitcase was left in the restroom.
2. He _____ me a part time job.
3. She has an ambition[1200] to be different from _____ people.
4. The tutor _____ the first paragraph of my article.
5. Naughty Johnny did not _____ his parents.

Answers: 1 occurred 2 offered 3 ordinary 4 omitted 5 obey

101

MP3　短文 201　字彙 202

Bill was a painter who most liked to paint pictures of animals. He especially liked painting owls, oxen, and pandas in his works. Unfortunately, he couldn't sell any of his paintings. He decided to travel abroad to see if people in other countries liked his artwork[1201] more, but he ran out of money after he had been overseas[1202] for just a few weeks. He was kicked out of the house he rented by the owner. He packed[1203] his clothes and toothbrush with him, and to get attention[1204] he wore pajamas[1205] and hung around on the streets with his bag of painting tools[1206] and related paraphernalia. He slept under overpasses[1207] when it rained and palm trees when it was dry. He got sick after he strayed[1208] on the streets for a few months. His stomach was always sore, so he ate some papayas to ease the pain. He also stole a pan[1209] from a house to cook food. Even though he lived a hard life, he still kept painting. He still went to the market to try to sell his paintings every day. He believed one day his works would appeal to many people and make him a lot of money.

中譯 *Translation*

　　比爾是一名畫家，他最喜歡畫的就是動物畫。他尤其喜歡在他的作品裡畫貓頭鷹、公牛和熊貓。可惜，他的畫一幅也賣不出去。他決定到國外旅遊，看看是否其他國家的人會比較欣賞他的畫作，但到國外才幾個禮拜之後，他就把錢都花光了。他被房東從他租的房子趕出來。他打包衣物和牙刷離開，為了引起注意，他穿著睡衣，帶著一袋畫具和相關的隨身用具在街上流浪。雨天時，他睡在天橋下，而天氣好的時候他就在棕櫚樹下睡覺。幾個月後，他因為在路上流浪好幾個月而生病了。他的胃一直犯疼，所以他吃了些木瓜想要止痛。他還從某間屋子偷了一個鍋子來煮食物。即使他過得很艱辛，但他依然堅持作畫。他還是每天都去市場賣畫。他相信總有一天，會有許多人受他的作品吸引，並且讓他賺進一大筆財富。

1201 artwork

[`ɑrt,wɝk] ★★

名 美術品、藝術品、插圖

1202 overseas

[`ovɚ`siz] ★★

形 在海外(國外)的

副 在(向)海外(國外)

同 abroad 在國外

1203 pack

[pæk] ★★★★★

動 整理行裝、包裝、捆紮

名 包裹、一包、一群

片 pack...in 使塞進

1204 attention

[ə`tɛnʃən] ★★★★★

名 注意、專心、照顧

片 keep sb's attention
一直吸引某人的興趣

1205 pajamas

[pə`dʒæməs] ★★★

名 寬大的睡衣褲

俚 cat's pajamas 不同凡
響的人或物

1206 tool

[tul] ★★★★★

名 工具、器具、手段

動 使用工具、用車載人

片 down tools 罷工

1207 overpass

[`ovɚ,pæs] ★★

名 天橋、高架公路

動 通過、優於、忽略

同 viaduct 高架道路

1208 stray

[stre] ★★★

動 流浪、走散、分心、入
歧途

形 迷路的、流浪的

1209 pan

[pæn] ★★★★

名 平底鍋、秤盤、盆地

動 嚴厲批評、淘金

片 frying pan 煎鍋

1210 corporation

[,kɔrpə`reʃən] ★★★

名 股份公司、社團法人

同 company 公司

1211 beam

[bim] ★★★★

動 發送、對準、照射、眉
開眼笑

名 光線、電波、樑

1212 subtropical

[sʌb`trɑpɪkl̩] ★★

形 亞熱帶的

反 tropical 熱帶的

Fighting!

Give it a shot 小試身手

❶ Corporations1210 beamed1211 their products to _____ market.

❷ _____ is a tropical and subtropical1212 fruit.

❸ The package _____ two pounds.

❹ He felt great _____ in his toes after a long walk.

❺ Only the _____ of this villa has the right to enter.

Answers: ❶ overseas ❷ Papaya ❸ weighs ❹ pain ❺ owner

102

Essay

MP3　短文 203　字彙 204

My little brother always cried whenever we took him out on the weekend. He was annoying, but I was still patient with him. In order to stop him from disturbing[1213] the peace at home, I often gave him a pat[1214] on the back and comforted him. After I gave him a peach[1215] and a pear to eat, he finally stopped crying. I had nothing in particular to do on the weekend, so I took my little brother to the zoo with my partner. There were so many passengers on the bus to the zoo, and he started crying again. I was getting really angry and yelled[1216] at him. I kept saying "pardon[1217] me" to other passengers. Afterwards, we walked along[1218] the path[1219] at the zoo. My brother loved the parrots[1220] and penguins most. The parrots copied what humans said. That was very funny, and we fed them some seeds. Penguins are peaceful[1221] animals, and they looked chubby[1222] and stupid. We took a lot of photos, and I pasted[1223] them on the refrigerator[1224]. I hoped my brother would grow up soon and stop annoying me.

中譯 *Translation*

　　每當週末我們要帶年幼的小弟出門時，他總愛哭鬧。他很煩人，但我還是耐心以對。為了不要讓他破壞家裡的安寧，我輕輕拍著他的背並安撫他。在我讓他吃了一顆桃子和一顆梨子之後，他終於停止哭鬧。週末我沒有什麼特別的事要做，所以我和男友會帶著小弟去動物園。前往動物園的公車上有很多乘客，所以他又開始大哭。我很生氣地對著他大吼。我一直對著其他乘客說對不起。後來，我們沿著動物園內的小徑步行。小弟最喜歡的是鸚鵡和企鵝。鸚鵡會學其他人說話，非常好笑，我們還餵牠們吃了些種子。企鵝是種愛好和平的動物，看起來肥肥笨笨的。我們拍了很多照片，我把它們貼在冰箱上。我希望小弟可以趕快長大，不要再煩我了。

1213 disturb

[dɪsˋtɝb] ★★★★
- 動 擾亂、妨礙、心神不寧
- 反 settle 平靜下來
- 衍 disturbance 擾亂

1214 pat

[pæt] ★★★★
- 名 輕拍、小塊
- 動 輕拍、撫拍
- 片 a pat on the back 鼓勵

1215 peach

[pitʃ] ★★★
- 名 桃子、桃紅色、特別惹人憐愛的人或物
- 動 告密、告發、出賣

1216 yell

[jɛl] ★★★
- 動 叫喊著說、大聲嚷道
- 名 叫喊、吼叫、歡呼
- 片 yell out 喊出

1217 pardon

[ˋpardn̩] ★★★★
- 動 原諒、饒恕、赦免
- 名 原諒、赦免
- 片 pardon for 原諒

1218 along

[əˋlɔŋ] ★★★★
- 副 向前、一起、來到
- 介 沿著、順著
- 片 along with 除…以外

1219 path

[pæθ] ★★★★★
- 名 小徑、途徑、軌道
- 片 beat a path to sb's door 門庭若市

1220 parrot

[ˋpærət] ★★★
- 名 鸚鵡、應聲蟲
- 俚 parrot fashion 重複而不解其義地

1221 peaceful

[ˋpisfəl] ★★★★
- 形 愛好和平的、平靜的
- 同 untroubled 平靜的
- 反 agitated 激動的

1222 chubby

[ˋtʃʌbɪ] ★★
- 形 圓胖的、豐滿的
- 同 plump 豐滿的

1223 paste

[pest] ★★★★
- 動 用漿糊黏貼
- 名 漿糊、麵糰、糊狀物
- 片 paste up 用漿糊張貼

1224 refrigerator

[rɪˋfrɪdʒəˌretə] ★★
- 名 冰箱、冷凍庫、冷藏室
- 同 fridge 電冰箱

Fighting!

Give it a shot 小試身手

1. My _____ and I cooperate to get the work done.
2. He _____ the scraps to the notebook.
3. Be _____ to talk to your mother, no matter how busy you are.
4. He gave me a _____ on the shoulder.
5. The color of _____ is pink.

Answers: 1 partner 2 pasted 3 patient 4 pat 5 peaches

215

103

Essay

Would you ever eat a grilled[1225] pigeon[1226]? Pigeon feathers[1227] are suitable for making pillows[1228], and the pigeon is also extremely delicious after it is grilled. I'll share my own personal recipe[1229] with you. To pick the best pigeon meat from the market, you need to keep an eye on the color. Dark is unacceptable. The first step after <u>picking out</u> the meat is to put it on the BBQ until it is grilled. Timing[1230] is very important. If you leave it on the barbecue[1231] too long, the meat will be tough like a ping-pong ball. If you have timed it perfectly, the meat will be tender[1232]. Don't forget to sprinkle some salt and pepper on it while it is cooking. After the meat has been grilled for a period of time, put sliced pineapples on top of it. This dish is good for a picnic[1233] or barbecue party. My photographer has taken photos and videos of me grilling pigeons, and you can watch them on our website and print them out to pin[1234] on to your noticeboard[1235]. I am not an expert chef, but I believe this is the most delicious meal I've ever made.

(!) pick out 挑選、辨認出

中譯 *Translation*

　　你吃過烤鴿子嗎？鴿子的羽毛很適合用來做枕頭，而且鴿子烤過之後也超級美味。我要把這道私人食譜分享給你。要從市場挑選最棒的鴿肉，你必須注意色澤，顏色太深是不行的。挑選完鴿肉的第一個步驟，就是把它放在烤肉架上直到烤熟為止。時間控制非常重要，如果你放得太久，肉就會老得像乒乓球一樣硬。如果時間控制的剛好，肉質就會很軟嫩。別忘了烹調時要在肉上撒些鹽和胡椒粉。鴿肉烤了一段時間之後，在上面加上切片鳳梨。這道菜很適合野餐或是烤肉派對。我的攝影師拍了許多烤鴿肉時的照片和影片，你可以在我們的網站上觀賞，並且印出來釘在布告欄上。我並不是名專業的廚師，但我相信這是我做過最棒的一道菜。

1225 grilled

[grɪld] ★★
- 形 烤的、炙過的、有格子的
- 衍 grill 炙烤

1226 pigeon

[`pɪdʒɪn] ★★★
- 名 鴿子、易受騙的人
- 動 詐騙
- 同 dove 鴿子

1227 feather

[`fɛðɚ] ★★★
- 名 羽毛、羽飾、種類
- 俚 birds of a feather 物以類聚

1228 pillow

[`pɪlo] ★★★
- 名 枕頭、枕狀物、靠墊
- 動 枕著頭、靠在
- 片 pillow fight 枕頭戰

1229 recipe

[`rɛsəpɪ] ★★★
- 名 食譜、處方、訣竅
- 同 formula 配方、處方
- 片 recipe for …的做法

1230 timing

[`taɪmɪŋ] ★★
- 名 時間的安排、時機的掌握、計時

1231 barbecue

[`barbɪ͵kju] ★★
- 名 烤肉架、烤肉野餐
- 動 在戶外烤、炙
- 同 grill 炙烤

1232 tender

[`tɛndɚ] ★★★★
- 形 嫩的、溫柔的、敏感的
- 動 變柔軟、變脆弱
- 同 gentle 輕柔的

1233 picnic

[`pɪknɪk] ★★★★
- 名 郊遊、野餐
- 動 參加野餐
- 片 have a picnic 去野餐

1234 pin

[pɪn] ★★★★
- 動 釘住、壓住、歸咎於
- 名 大頭針、別針、瑣碎物
- 片 pin on 釘在…上

1235 noticeboard

[`notɪsbɔrd] ★★★
- 名 布告欄、布告牌
- 同 bulletin board 布告欄

1236 reprocessed

[rɪ`prasɛst] ★★
- 形 經過再加工的
- 衍 reprocess 再加工

Give it a shot 小試身手

1. She left her current job for _____ reasons.
2. My family and I went on a _____ on Sunday.
3. It's the toughest _____ in his whole life.
4. We _____ up reprocessed[1236] paper here for copying.
5. We should _____ up the trash wherever we see it.

Answers: 1 personal 2 picnic 3 period 4 pile 5 pick

217

MP3　短文 207　字彙 208

Essay

104

We went camping last week, and that was a pleasant[1237] excursion[1238]. We took the train for six hours. When we arrived there, we smelled the fresh air on the platform of the train station as we got off the train. We pitched[1239] a tent[1240] by the river, surrounded by pink flowers. I was in a playful[1241] mood. I <u>threw</u> my friend <u>into</u> the river, and my friends did the same thing to me. We ate home-made pizzas for dinner. After we finished the food on the plates, we lay on the ground and watched the clear sky. The view there was much better than that in the city. There were stars in the sky, and we guessed which constellations[1242] we saw. I lit[1243] my pipe[1244], smoked tobacco and read a poem written by Percy Bysshe Shelley, who was a Romantic poet plus[1245] a politician. He was opposed to the policies[1246] of the government at that time, so his works were considered protests in the 18th century. It was a pleasure to spend the night with my friends in the mountains.

ℹ️ throw sb./sth. into 在本文中表示「把某人或某物扔進」，另外也有「投身於」、「積極從事」等意

ℹ️ get off 下車，另外也有出發、下班等意思

中譯 *Translation*

　　我們上禮拜去露營，那是一場非常愉快的短程旅行。我們搭了六個小時的火車。當我們抵達目的時，一下火車就在月台上聞到新鮮的空氣。我們在河邊搭了一座帳篷，四周圍繞著粉紅色的花朵。我玩心大起，把朋友們都丟進河裡，他們也對我如法炮製。我們晚餐吃手工披薩。在享用完盤裡的食物後，我們就躺在曠野上望著晴朗的天空。視野要比城裡好太多了。天空中佈滿星點，我們都在猜是什麼星座。我點起煙斗抽煙，讀了一首浪漫主義詩人兼政治家雪萊的詩作。雪萊反對當時政府的政策，所以他的作品在十八世紀被視為異端。能和朋友在山裡度過這晚，真是相當愉快。

1237 pleasant

[ˋplɛzənt] ★★★★
- 形 令人愉快的、舒適的
- 同 pleasing 令人愉快的
- 反 unpleasant 討厭的

1238 excursion

[ɪkˋskɝʒən] ★★★
- 名 遠足、短途旅行、離題

1239 pitch

[pɪtʃ] ★★★★
- 動 搭帳篷、紮營、帶著特定感情說
- 名 投球、音高、程度

1240 tent

[tɛnt] ★★★★
- 名 帳篷、寓所、帷幕
- 動 住帳篷、暫時居住
- 片 pitch a tent 搭帳篷

1241 playful

[ˋplefəl] ★★
- 形 愛玩耍的、開玩笑的、嬉戲的
- 反 solemn 嚴肅的

1242 constellation

[͵kɑnstəˋleʃən] ★
- 名 星座、薈萃、群集
- 片 a constellation of 一群…

1243 light

[laɪt] ★★★★★
- 動 點燃、照亮、容光煥發
- 名 燈火、日光、啟發
- 片 light up 照亮

1244 pipe

[paɪp] ★★★★
- 名 煙斗、導管、管樂器
- 動 用導管運輸、尖聲叫嚷
- 俚 pipe dream 白日夢

1245 plus

[plʌs] ★★★★
- 介 加上、另有
- 名 加號、附加物、好處
- 形 正的、外加的

1246 policy

[ˋpɑləsɪ] ★★★★★
- 名 政策、方針、保單
- 片 policy maker 決策者

1247 remedy

[ˋrɛmədɪ] ★★★
- 名 補救法、治療、補償
- 動 醫治、補救、糾正
- 片 remedy for …的療法

1248 roll

[rol] ★★★★★
- 名 名單、滾動、左右搖晃
- 動 滾動、搖晃、運轉
- 片 call the roll 點名

Fighting!

Give it a shot 小試身手

1. Our old house was _____ on the plain.
2. The waitress accidentally broke the _____.
3. There is no remedy[1247] for this kind of _____.
4. The teacher stood on the _____ and called the roll[1248].
5. One _____ one equals two.

Answers: ① situated ② plates ③ poison ④ platform ⑤ plus

Essay 105

It is a small town with a population[1249] of less than ten thousand people. There's a small port[1250]. Country rock is the most popular music there. People are polite, and they go to church to praise[1251] God every Sunday. They are quite religious[1252] and have a strong faith[1253], and they all have a positive[1254] attitude towards life. My grandma has lived there for a long time. Whenever she sends a postcard to me, it reminds me of the pork pie, mashed[1255] potatoes, and big pot of chicken soup she makes. I stayed at my grandma's house for one month last year, and I gained 10 pounds. Recently, a company announced[1256] that it wants to build a nuclear[1257] power station there. The possibility[1258] that it will actually be built is rather high, and it will pose[1259] <u>a threat</u> for the natural environment. I pray[1260] that a nuclear power station will never be built in that town so the town can always remain the same as it is now.

> (!) pose a threat 造成威脅

中譯 *Translation*

　　這是個人口不到一萬人的小鎮，鎮上有一個小港口。鄉村搖滾是這裡最流行的曲風。居民都很有禮貌，他們每週日都會去教堂讚美上帝。他們對於信仰非常虔誠也很堅定，他們也對生命抱持著正面的態度。我的祖母在那裡已經住了很長一段時間。每次只要她寄明信片給我，我都會想起她做的豬肉派、馬鈴薯泥和一大鍋雞湯。我去年在祖母家裡住了一個月，體重增加了十磅。近來，某家公司宣稱想在當地興建核電廠。實際上興建的可能性相當高，而且會對自然環境造成威脅。我祈禱核電廠絕對別蓋在那座鎮上，這樣一來小鎮就可以一直維持著現今的樣貌。

1249 population

[ˌpɑpjəˈleʃən] ★★★★★
名 人口、全部居民、族群
片 aging of population 人口老化

1250 port

[port] ★★★★
名 港口、避風港、接口、姿勢、姿態
片 come into port 進港

1251 praise

[prez] ★★★★
動 讚美、表揚、歌頌
名 讚揚、崇拜
片 in praise of 讚揚

1252 religious

[rɪˈlɪdʒəs] ★★★★
形 篤信宗教的、虔誠的
同 pious 虔誠的
反 irreligious 反宗教的

1253 faith

[feθ] ★★★★
名 信仰、信念、約定
同 belief 信仰
片 keep faith 守信

1254 positive

[ˈpɑzətɪv] ★★★★
形 積極的、真實的、確信的、陽性的
名 正面、陽極

1255 mash

[mæʃ] ★★
動 搗成糊狀、壓碎
片 mashed potatoes 馬鈴薯泥

1256 announce

[əˈnaʊns] ★★★★
動 宣布、聲稱、播報
同 proclaim 宣告
片 announce to 向…宣布

1257 nuclear

[ˈnjuklɪə] ★★★★★
形 原子核的、核心的、細胞核的
片 nuclear test 核試驗

1258 possibility

[ˌpɑsəˈbɪlətɪ] ★★★
名 可能性、潛在價值
同 chance 可能性

1259 pose

[poz] ★★★
動 造成、擺姿勢、假裝
名 姿勢、裝腔作勢
片 pose as 裝作…

1260 pray

[pre] ★★★★
動 祈禱、懇求
同 implore 懇求
片 pray for 為…祈禱

Essay

106

MP3　短文 211　字彙 212

Last week, the president[1261] was present at a press conference with the prince and princess. The conference was mainly[1262] about the news of the prince's graduation[1263]. He had just graduated from Harvard University, so the presence of his old high school principal[1264] surprised him very much. The principal took pride in the prince, especially because he had made an astonishing decision after graduating from Harvard. He decided that he preferred[1265] being a social worker to being a politician. He wanted to take care of prisoners in prison. Serving and helping people was his life's goal, and he had made a lot of contributions[1266] to charities[1267] in private. He thought the ability[1268] to help others was the best gift he owned. He didn't live a luxurious[1269] life, and didn't have the habit of smoking and drinking. He even took a part-time job as a printer in a factory, and the money he earned was all donated[1270] to poor families. The princess supported what her brother did and respected him very much.

中譯 *Translation*

　　上禮拜校長陪同王子和公主出席了記者會。這場記者會主要和王子大學畢業的新聞有關。他剛從哈佛大學畢業，所以從前高中校長的出現讓他十分驚訝。校長以王子為傲，尤其是因為他從哈佛畢業後做了一個驚人的決定。他下定決心自己寧願當一名社工，也不願成為政客。他想照顧監牢裡的囚犯。服務與幫助人民是他的人生目標，他私下也為慈善事業作出極大的貢獻。他認為幫助他人的能力，是他與生俱來最棒的天賦。他的生活並不奢華，而且也沒有抽菸喝酒的習慣。他甚至在工廠兼職印刷工，他所賺的錢都捐獻給貧窮家庭。公主也很支持她哥哥的行為，並且非常尊敬他。

1261 president

[`prɛzədənt] ★★★★★
名 校長、總統、主席、會長、總裁

1262 mainly

[`menlɪ] ★★★★
副 主要地、大部分地
同 chiefly 主要地

1263 graduation

[,grædʒʊ`eʃən] ★★
名 畢業、畢業典禮、刻度
片 graduation ceremony 畢業典禮

1264 principal

[`prɪnsəpl] ★★★★
名 校長、首長、資本
形 主要的、資本的
同 capital 資本

1265 prefer

[prɪ`fɝ] ★★★★★
動 更喜歡、寧可、控告
同 favor 偏愛
片 prefer + ving 更喜歡

1266 contribution

[kɑntrə`bjuʃən] ★★★
名 捐獻、貢獻、投稿
片 make contributions to 貢獻給…

1267 charity

[`tʃærətɪ] ★★★
名 慈善團體、善舉、慈悲
反 cruelty 殘酷
片 charity event 慈善活動

1268 ability

[ə`bɪlətɪ] ★★★★
名 能力、能耐、才能
片 of great ability 特別擅長…

1269 luxurious

[lʌg`ʒʊrɪəs] ★★
形 奢侈的、豪華的、精選的、舒適的
衍 luxury 奢侈、奢華

1270 donate

[`donet] ★★★
動 捐贈、捐獻
同 contribute 捐獻
片 donate to 捐給

1271 impeach

[ɪm`pitʃ] ★★
動 檢舉、彈劾、懷疑
名 檢舉、彈劾、懷疑
衍 impeachment 彈劾

1272 corruption

[kə`rʌpʃən] ★★
名 貪汙、賄賂、墮落
反 incorruption 清廉
衍 corrupt 貪汙的

fighting!

Give it a shot 小試身手

❶ The _____ was impeached[1271] of corruption[1272].

❷ Those _____ were sentenced to death.

❸ You have no rights to look my _____ letters.

❹ We should calm ourselves down in the _____ situation.

❺ Which do you _____, Oolong tea or milk tea?

Answers: ❶ president ❷ prisoners ❸ private ❹ present ❺ prefer

107

Essay

Recently, I proposed[1273] a project[1274] featuring a brand-new[1275] style of music. I am a music producer[1276], and I am proud of my music. My new album is progressing. I have promised[1277] all my friends that I'll bring Taiwanese pop music into a new era and provide a different style of music to audiences. Everyone thinks my music is odd, the way I dress is odd, and my personality is odd. I have been different from others since I was young. When I was in sixth grade, I fought with other pupils[1278] to protect a puppy. I couldn't stand seeing those kids maltreat[1279] a puppy. After I stopped those kids from doing that, I gave my pumpkin pudding to the puppy. But one of the kids attacked me from behind, which made my blood boil[1280], and I hit him hard. Of course I was punished, but I insisted[1281] that I was correct in stopping them from harming the puppy. I decided I wanted to be very different from other students. I held a press conference in the school cafeteria and invited reporters from the student newspaper, and I proclaimed[1282] that no one should mindlessly[1283] follow others, especially when they are doing something bad like hurting a small dog.

中譯 *Translation*

　　最近我提出了一個全新風格的音樂企劃。我是一名音樂製作人，我以自己的音樂為傲。我的新專輯正在進行中。我對我所有的朋友保證，我將會把台灣流行音樂引進一個新時代，並將一種完全不同的音樂風格呈現給聽眾。每個人都認為我的音樂、我的穿著和我的個性很怪。我從年輕時就和別人不一樣。當我六年級的時候，我為了保護小狗和其他小朋友打了一架。我無法忍受那些小孩虐待小狗。在我阻止他們之後，就把自己的南瓜布丁給小狗吃。然而其中一個小孩從背後攻擊我，這個舉動令我怒火中燒，而用力的打了他。當然我受罰了，但我堅持阻止他們傷害小狗是對的。我下定決心成為和其他學生不一樣的人。我在學生餐廳舉辦一場記者會，並邀請校刊記者，我在記者會中聲明每個人都不該盲目跟從他人，尤其是當他們正在做像是傷害小狗一類的壞事時。

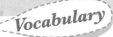

1273 propose

[prə`poz] ★★★
- 動 提議、計畫、求婚
- 同 present 提出
- 片 propose to 向…求婚

1274 project

[prə`dʒɛkt] ★★★★★
- 名 企劃、方案、工程
- 動 計畫、投射、突出
- 片 project on …的計畫

1275 brand-new

[`brænd`nu] ★★★★
- 形 嶄新的、新製的、未用過的

1276 producer

[prə`djusə] ★★★★
- 名 製作人、製造者
- 片 executive producer 執行製作

1277 promise

[`prɑmɪs] ★★★★
- 動 允諾、答應、有指望
- 名 承諾、希望、前途

1278 pupil

[`pjupl] ★★★★
- 名 小學生、弟子、瞳孔
- 同 schoolchild 學童

1279 maltreat

[mæl`trit] ★★
- 動 虐待、濫用
- 同 abuse 虐待
- 衍 maltreatment 虐待

1280 boil

[bɔɪl] ★★★★
- 動 沸騰、激動、起泡
- 名 沸騰、翻滾
- 片 boil away 燒乾

1281 insist

[ɪn`sɪst] ★★★
- 動 堅持、堅決主張
- 同 persist 堅持
- 片 insist on 堅持、強調

1282 proclaim

[prə`klem] ★★★
- 動 聲明、宣告、顯示
- 片 proclaim sb. sth. 宣布某人為

1283 mindlessly

[`maɪndlɪslɪ] ★★
- 副 不用腦子地、不費心思地
- 衍 mindless 不小心的

1284 sanatorium

[sænə`torɪəm] ★★
- 名 療養院、靜養地、避暑勝地

Fighting!

Give it a shot 小試身手

1. We have made great _____ in controlling cancer.
2. He decided to _____ to his girlfriend on Christmas Eve.
3. We _____ the sanatorium[1284] from being torn down.
4. They _____ the service of charging batteries.
5. I think death penalty is a necessary _____.

Answers: 1 progress 2 propose 3 protect 4 provide 5 punishment

225

108

 MP3　短文 215　字彙 216

Essay

It puzzled[1285] me why I always had the same problem. Whenever I met a girl, I tried so hard to make her happy, but things never seemed to <u>work out</u>. For example, I would spend a quarter[1286] of my salary on the best restaurant to please a girl. Then, I once stood in front of my ex-girlfriend's house on a rainy[1287] day for three hours, begging her to come back to me, but she had so many excuses to leave me. I was a rare[1288] kind of guy: a really good guy. Recently, I discovered what the main problem was. I decided that it would be much more beneficial[1289] for me to change my appearance rather than <u>burn a hole in my pocket</u> buying things for girls. I didn't go to expensive restaurants that were beyond my budget[1290] anymore. I met a beauty[1291] at a recent speech forum, and we exchanged[1292] telephone numbers. Then I started to date her. My friends were surprised by the sudden big change in me. They quizzed[1293] me about my pet rabbit's name to make sure it was really me. I told them that quality often mattered more than quantity[1294], so personality[1295] mattered more than money!

(!) work out 成功、解決，另外也可以表示運動的意思
(!) burn a hole in one's pocket 花錢如流水，形容一個人身上的錢怎麼樣都留不住

中譯 *Translation*

　　我很困惑為什麼我老是遇到同樣的問題。每當我遇見一個女孩，都會盡我所能去討她歡心，但這似乎未曾奏效。舉例來說，為了討好她，我會花四分之一的薪水帶她到最好的餐廳。此外，我曾經在雨天時，到我前女友的門前等了三小時，要求她回心轉意，但她有太多要和我分手的理由了。我真是稀有的好男人啊！直到不久前我才發現主要的問題所在。我下定決心，比起花大錢買東西給女孩們，倒不如改變我的外貌對我來說幫助更大。我不再去超出預算的昂貴餐廳。在最近的演講論壇上，我遇到一個美女，並且交換了電話號碼。然後，我們就開始交往了。朋友對我突如其來的大轉變感到驚訝。他們還考我我寵物兔子的名字，來確認我真的是同一個人。我告訴他們，質總是比量還重要，所以個性也比錢來得重要啊！

1285 puzzle

[ˋpʌzl̩] ★★★★
- 動 使困惑、苦思而得出
- 名 難題、困惑、拼圖
- 片 puzzle out 推測出

1286 quarter

[ˋkwɔrtə] ★★★★★
- 名 四分之一、一刻鐘
- 動 把…四等分
- 同 one fourth 四分之一

1287 rainy

[ˋrenɪ] ★★★★
- 動 下雨的、多雨的、被雨淋濕的
- 片 rainy day 艱難時刻

1288 rare

[rɛr] ★★★★
- 形 罕見的、珍貴的、稀疏的、半熟的
- 反 ordinary 平常的

1289 beneficial

[bɛnəˋfɪʃəl] ★★★
- 形 有利的、有幫助的
- 片 beneficial for/to 對…有利

1290 budget

[ˋbʌdʒɪt] ★★★★
- 名 預算、生活費、經費
- 片 budget airline 廉價航空

1291 beauty

[ˋbjutɪ] ★★★★
- 名 美人、美麗、優點
- 片 the beauty of 有意思的是…

1292 exchange

[ɪksˋtʃendʒ] ★★★★
- 動 交換、兌換
- 名 交換、交易、兌換
- 片 exchange for 用…換取

1293 quiz

[kwɪz] ★★★★
- 動 對…測驗、考問、嘲弄
- 名 測驗、提問、挖苦
- 片 quiz about 考問

1294 quantity

[ˋkwɑntətɪ] ★★★★
- 名 數量、大宗
- 反 quality 品質
- 片 in quantity 大量地

1295 personality

[pɜsṇˋælətɪ] ★★★★
- 名 個性、品格、名人
- 片 personality clash 性格衝突

1296 worse

[wɜs] ★★★★★
- 形 更差的、更惡化的
- 副 更壞、更猛烈地
- 片 get worse 越來越差

Fighting!

Give it a shot 小試身手

❶ Exercising is helpful for _____ smoking.

❷ I would _____ choose the bigger company than the small one.

❸ His dream to be a model has become a _____.

❹ The economic has become worse[1296] in _____ years.

❺ It is _____ to snow in April.

109

MP3 短文 217 字彙 218

My wife and I had been married for several years when one day I realized I couldn't stand[1297] her anymore. She nagged[1298] at me 24 hours a day. She talked as much as the reporters on TV. She repeated[1299] the same thing to me again and again. She kept a record of my daily expenses and complained that I spent money on tobacco instead of buying a new refrigerator for her. One day, I brought a rectangular[1300] table home. She didn't like the shape and loudly criticized my taste in furniture. Recently, she stopped sleeping with me. If I even tried to approach[1301] and talk to her, she refused[1302] to reply to me. I thought she didn't respect me at all. Our relationship nearly came to an end when I found out that she had had relations with another woman. After that, I regarded[1303] her as a lesbian[1304] who never loved me from the beginning. However, I know that both a husband and a wife must try hard in a marriage[1305]. We didn't realize that both of us required our own privacy[1306] and that we needed to understand each other's boundaries[1307]. Unfortunately, it was too late to save our marriage and we eventually[1308] got a divorce.

中譯 *Translation*

　　我太太和我結婚好幾年了，直到某天我發現自己再也受不了她了。她一天二十四小時都在我耳邊嘮叨。她話多得就像電視上的記者一樣，同樣的事情重複說了又說。她會記錄我每天的花費，還會抱怨我寧願花錢買菸，也不幫她買一台新的冰箱。有天我買了一張長方形的桌子回家。她不喜歡那張桌子的外型，大聲批評我對家具的品味。最近，她還拒絕和我同床。我甚至還試著接近她、跟她說話，她卻連回都不回。我覺得她一點也不尊重我。當我發現她和另一個女人有著不尋常的關係時，我們的婚姻差不多已經走到盡頭了。從那之後，我就認為她是個蕾絲邊，打從一開始就沒愛過我。然而，我知道丈夫和妻子都必須努力維持婚姻。我們沒有意識到我們兩人都需要擁有自己的隱私，同時也需要了解對方的界線到哪裡。很可惜，要挽救我們的婚姻只能說太遲了，最後我們離婚了。

1297 stand

[stænd] ★★★★★
動 忍受、站立、抵抗
名 站立、立場、看臺
片 stand by 準備行動

1298 nag

[næg] ★★★
動 不斷嘮叨、使煩惱
名 好嘮叨的人(女性)
片 nag at 對…嘮叨

1299 repeat

[rɪ`pit] ★★★★★
動 重複、背誦、重播
名 重複、重播、複製品
片 repeat to 對…重複說

1300 rectangular

[rɛk`tæŋgjələ] ★★
形 矩形的、長方形的、有直角的
衍 rectangle 長方形

1301 approach

[ə`protʃ] ★★★★★
動 靠近、接近、著手處理
名 接近、通道、方法
片 approach to 接近

1302 refuse

[rɪ`fjuz] ★★★★
動 拒絕、不准、不願
名 廢物、垃圾
片 refuse to 拒絕做…

1303 regard

[rɪ`gɑrd] ★★★★★
動 把…看做、注重、有關
名 注重、關心、關係
片 regard as 視…為

1304 lesbian

[`lɛzbɪən] ★★
名 女同性戀者
形 同性戀的

1305 marriage

[`mærɪdʒ] ★★★★★
名 婚姻、結婚儀式、緊密結合

1306 privacy

[`praɪvəsɪ] ★★★
名 隱私、私下、隱退
片 right of privacy 隱私權
衍 private 私人的

1307 boundary

[`baundrɪ] ★★★
名 限度、範圍、邊界
同 border 邊界
片 boundary line 邊界線

1308 eventually

[ɪ`vɛntʃuəlɪ] ★★★
副 最後、終於
同 finally 最後
衍 eventual 最後的

Fighting!

Give it a shot 小試身手

1 He is _____ as the best doctor in the municipal hospital.

2 My manager only gave me a brief _____.

3 The box office of the movie broke the _____.

4 The press is _____ for supervising the government.

5 It is said that the public security is poor in this _____.

Answers: 1 regarded 2 reply 3 record 4 responsible 5 region

229

110

Essay

My friend had been a sailor[1309] in the navy[1310]. After years of hard work, he became an important person in the military. He reviewed[1311] the troops when the president visited. The training was tough. When he was a new soldier, he needed to walk up a steep[1312], rocky[1313] road every day. He was in good shape and he was a good long-distance runner. He saved a large amount of money before he retired. I think soldiers have a very important role in defending[1314] the safety of our country, but some of them are rude. I think that has <u>resulted from</u> the fact that there are mostly men in the army. One day, we were treated to a royal[1315] feast[1316] at a restaurant at the five-star level. When we got there, a soldier rushed to the buffet and filled his plate with the best food. He shook his legs while eating, so the table rocked like during an earthquake. After he used the restroom, it was in a total mess. Other guests found it annoying, and I was embarrassed, but since soldiers protect our country, I tried to forget about it.

result from 起因於

中譯 *Translation*

　　我朋友以前是個海軍水手。經過幾年的努力,他在軍隊中位居要角。總統蒞臨時,他負責進行閱兵。軍隊裡的訓練非常嚴格,當他還是新兵的時候,他每天都要攀爬既陡峭又滿是岩石的石頭路。他的身體很好,也是名優秀的長跑跑者。他退休前存了一大筆錢。我認為軍人在保衛國家安全上扮演非常重要的角色,但有些軍人卻很粗蠻。我想那其實是因為軍隊裡多半都是男性。有天我們受邀參加一場在五星級飯店舉行的豪華宴席,我們一到那裡,有一位軍人就衝去自助用餐區,在盤中堆滿最高檔的食物。他吃東西的時候還會抖腳,所以餐桌就像地震一樣晃個不停。他上完洗手間後,也把廁所搞得一團亂。其他客人都覺得很反感,我也覺得很尷尬,但既然軍人會保衛國家,我也就試著不放在心上了。

1309 sailor

[ˋselə] ★★★

名 水手、船員

同 seaman 水手

片 sailor suit 水手服

1310 navy

[ˋnevɪ] ★★★★

名 海軍、海軍艦隊

反 army 陸軍

片 navy blue 深藍色

1311 review

[rɪˋvju] ★★★★★

動 檢閱、複習、回顧

名 閱兵、複習、評論

片 review for 為…寫評論

1312 steep

[stip] ★★★★

形 陡峭的、大起大落的

名 陡坡、懸崖峭壁

同 precipitous 陡峭的

1313 rocky

[ˋrɑkɪ] ★★

形 多岩石的、搖晃的、不穩定的

同 stony 多石的

1314 defend

[dɪˋfɛnd] ★★★★

動 保衛、防禦、為…辯護

片 defend from 保護…不受危險

1315 royal

[ˋrɔɪəl] ★★★★

形 盛大的、王室的、高貴的、極好的

同 noble 高貴的

1316 feast

[fist] ★★★

名 盛宴、宗教節日

動 盛宴款待、享受

片 feast on 盡情享受

1317 fatal

[ˋfet!] ★★★

形 致命的、無可挽回的、生死攸關的

同 deadly 致命的

1318 director

[dəˋrɛktə] ★★★★

名 導演、主管、指揮

片 board of directors 董事會

1319 thorough

[ˋθɝo] ★★★★

形 完善的、徹底的、十分仔細的

同 complete 徹底的

1320 democratic

[dɛməˋkrætɪk] ★★★★

形 民主的、民眾的、民主政體的

反 tyrannical 專制的

Fighting!

Give it a shot 小試身手

1. A careless mistake can lead to fatal[1317] _____.

2. The director[1318] taught the actor how to perform the _____.

3. I had a thorough[1319] _____ before the examination.

4. The _____ in a democratic[1320] country needs to be elected.

5. _____ spend most of their lives on the sea.

Answers: 1 results 2 role 3 review 4 president 5 Sailors

111

🎧 MP3　短文 221　字彙 222

Essay

My secretary knew where to buy the best sandwiches[1321] in the city. She had searched[1322] through every neighborhood[1323] of the city and selected the top three. Regarding her favorite coffee shops, the best one was on Collin Street. The food there really satisfied me. The owner has a secret sauce for sandwiches. It's neither too salty nor too sweet. The sauce matched the chicken perfectly and rated[1324] a <u>10 out of 10</u>. It's a small but comfortable place. They had air-conditioning, a big screen[1325] LCD TV, and stylish decoration[1326], so I loved to enjoy sandwiches there. The owner told me that making sandwiches was a science[1327]. He needed to experiment[1328] again and again, like a scientist[1329]. Then he used scissors[1330] to cut his new sandwiches, and gave some to me as samples[1331]. I was filled with joy since those were the best sandwiches I had ever eaten.

> ⓘ 10 out of 10 在滿分10分中得到了10分，用來形容某事物非常優秀、傑出

中譯 *Translation*

　　我的祕書知道城裡最好吃的三明治在哪裡。她一直都在城裡的各個街坊尋找，並且選出了前三名。關於她最愛的幾家咖啡店，最棒的莫過於柯林上那家。我非常滿意他們的食物。老闆有專為三明治特製的獨門醬汁。不會太鹹也不會太甜。醬汁和雞肉真是絕配，簡直是滿分之作。咖啡店地方雖小但很舒適。他們有空調、大型液晶螢幕和時髦的裝潢，所以我喜歡去那裡享用三明治。老闆跟我說做三明治是門學問。他必須像個科學家般不斷試驗。然後他用剪刀把他新發明的三明治剪開，做為試吃品給了我一些。我非常開心，因為那真是我吃過最好吃的三明治了。

1321 sandwich

[`sændwɪtʃ] ★★★
名 三明治
動 做成三明治、擠進

1322 search

[sɜtʃ] ★★★★★
動 搜尋、調查、穿過
名 搜查、搜尋、調查
片 search for 搜尋…

1323 neighborhood

[`nebəhud] ★★
名 鄰近地區、整個街坊
片 in the neighborhood of 在…附近

1324 rate

[ret] ★★★★★
動 對…評價、列為
名 比例、速率、等級
片 rate at 把…評價為

1325 screen

[skrin] ★★★★
名 螢幕、掩護、隔板
動 放映、選拔、掩蔽
片 on screen 電腦螢幕上

1326 decoration

[dɛkə`reʃən] ★★★
名 裝飾、裝潢、獎章
同 adornment 裝飾品
衍 decorate 裝飾

1327 science

[`saɪəns] ★★★★★
名 科學、學科、技術
片 blind sb. with science 用技術知識迷惑人

1328 experiment

[ɪk`spɛrəmənt] ★★★
動 進行實驗、試驗
名 實驗、試驗
片 experiment on …實驗

1329 scientist

[`saɪəntɪst] ★★★
名 科學家

1330 scissors

[`sɪzəz] ★★★
名 剪刀
片 a pair of scissors 一把剪刀

1331 sample

[`sæmpl] ★★★★
名 試用品、樣本、實例
動 抽樣檢驗、品嚐
形 樣品的

1332 diamond

[`daɪəmənd] ★★★
名 鑽石、菱形、內野
形 鑲鑽的、菱形的

Fighting!

Give it a shot 小試身手

1 The service in this restaurant didn't _____ me.

2 The _____ for the home team is 5.

3 She _____ a diamond[1332] from the collection.

4 Don't look at the _____ for all day long.

5 Those _____ are not for sale.

Answers: 1 satisfy 2 score 3 selected 4 screen 5 samples

233

MP3　短文 223　字彙 224

112

Essay

I took the books from off the shelf[1333]. It was the first day of the new semester, and I had been separated[1334] from my friends for two months. When I walked to school on the first morning back to school, it was a big shock for me to meet my friend, Mark. I was silent for a moment[1335] and then burst into laughter. Mark had become so fat! Mark's parents were public[1336] servants[1337], and they earned a lot of money. They took him to Thailand on vacation for two months, and he ate a lot and became fat. He was a shrimp, too, so he looked so funny in shorts. Mark was embarrassed and signaled[1338] me with a frown[1339] to stop laughing. I knew he was hurt, but I just couldn't help laughing. After I laughed for a few minutes, I settled[1340] down. Mark shared[1341] his interesting stories from Thailand with me. There were thundershowers in the afternoon every day in Thailand. He shot some beautiful pictures of shells[1342] on the beach. The trip was fun, but he really needed to diet[1343] to lose weight.

中譯 *Translation*

　　我從架子上把書取下。這是新學期的第一天，我已經和朋友們分別兩個月了。開學的第一個早晨，我在走路上學的途中遇到了我的朋友馬克，我大吃一驚。我先是沉默了幾分鐘，然後開始大笑。馬克變得超胖！馬克的父母都是公務員，賺了很多錢，他們帶馬克去泰國度假兩個月，他因為吃太多就變胖了。他還是個矮子，所以穿短褲看起來很好笑。馬克很尷尬，皺眉示意要我停止訕笑。我知道他受傷了，但我就是止不住笑。笑了好幾分鐘後，我終於平靜下來。馬克和我分享他在泰國發生的趣事。泰國每天下午都有大雷雨。他拍了很多沙灘上美麗貝殼的照片。這趟旅行很有趣，但他必須要節食減重才行。

1333 shelf

[ʃɛlf] ★★★★

名 架子、擱板

片 on the shelf 擱在一旁

1334 separate

[ˋsɛpəret] ★★★★

動 分開、區分、分居

形 個別的、分開的

片 separate from 使分離

1335 moment

[ˋmomənt] ★★★★★

名 片刻、時機、重要時刻

同 instant 頃刻

片 for the moment 暫時

1336 public

[ˋpʌblɪk] ★★★★

形 公務的、公眾的

名 民眾、大眾

片 in public 公開地

1337 servant

[ˋsɝvənt] ★★★

名 公僕、僕人、事務員

反 master 主人

片 public servant 公務員

1338 signal

[ˋsɪgnḷ] ★★★★

動 以動作向…示意、標誌

名 信號、暗號、導火線

形 作為信號的、顯著的

1339 frown

[fraʊn] ★★★

名 皺眉、不悅之色

動 皺眉、表示不滿

片 frown at 不贊成

1340 settle

[ˋsɛtḷ] ★★★★

動 鎮定下來、安頓、沉澱

反 unsettle 心神不寧

片 settle down 定居

1341 share

[ʃɛr] ★★★★★

動 分享、分擔、共有

名 分攤、一份、股份

片 share with 與…分享

1342 shell

[ʃɛl] ★★★★

名 貝殼、果殼、房子骨架

動 剝…的殼、剝落

片 shell out 付款

1343 diet

[ˋdaɪət] ★★★★

動 按規定進食、節食

名 飲食、特種飲食

片 go on a diet 節食

1344 row

[raʊ] ★★★★

名 一列、一排座位、口角

動 爭吵、吵鬧

片 in a row 成一行

Fighting!

Give it a shot 小試身手

1 He told me the bad news with a _____ expression.

2 The snail hid itself in the _____.

3 Many parents _____ their children in nursery schools.

4 Students walk on the _____ in a row[1344].

5 Thomas and I _____ a room. We're roommates.

113

MP3   短文 225   字彙 226

Essay

Christine is tall and skinny[1345], and she has a pair of long and slim legs. Her beautiful face and slender[1346] figure make her very popular, but she is still single[1347]. She's a skillful[1348] model on the runway[1349]. Her friends say that she is very similar to Lin Chi Ling in appearance. She once had an embarrassing experience, though. One day, she felt so sleepy[1350] during work. It was simply because she had a party last night and didn't have enough sleep. She was dressed in silk and a short skirt, and she was wearing slippers[1351]. Suddenly, she slipped[1352] while she was modeling[1353], and she fell down on the stage. But soon she got up and finished the show. The audience was silent for a moment and then applauded[1354] loudly. When she finished work, she washed her face at the sink to remove her makeup[1355], and she had a snack with a cup of coffee. The director came to her and praised her for her composure[1356]. She was such a professional model.

中譯 *Translation*

克麗斯汀很高又很骨感,還有一雙長又纖細的腿。她美麗的臉蛋和苗條的身材讓她非常受歡迎,但她依舊保持單身。她是個經驗豐富的伸展台模特兒,她的友人都說她長得很像林志玲。然而,她曾有過一次很糗的經驗。有天她工作時感到非常疲倦,純粹是因為她前一晚開了派對而睡眠不足。她穿著綢衣和短裙,腳上穿著拖鞋。當她在走秀時,突然跌了一跤,摔到台下去了。但她很迅速地爬起來,完成了走秀。觀眾本來沉默了一會,接著便掌聲雷動。她下工之後,到水槽旁洗臉卸妝,然後喝著咖啡配小點心吃。導演走到她身邊,讚美她的鎮靜。她就是這麼一名專業的模特兒。

1345 skinny

[`skɪnɪ] ★★
形 皮包骨的、極瘦的
名 小道消息
同 bony 骨瘦如柴的

1346 slender

[`slɛndə] ★★★
形 修長的、纖細的
片 slender figure 身材苗條

1347 single

[`sɪŋgl] ★★★★★
形 單身的、唯一的
名 單身者、單程票
動 挑出、選出

1348 skillful

[`skɪlfəl] ★★
形 熟練的、有技術的
同 expert 熟練的
反 awkward 笨拙的

1349 runway

[`rʌnwe] ★★
名 伸展台、跑道、車道
同 catwalk 伸展台

1350 sleepy

[`slipɪ] ★★★
形 想睡的、呆滯的、懶洋洋的
同 drowsy 昏昏欲睡

1351 slipper

[`slɪpə] ★★★
名 拖鞋
同 sandal 拖鞋、涼鞋

1352 slip

[slip] ★★★
動 滑一跤、滑落、下降
名 滑一跤、下降、疏忽
片 slip down 滑倒

1353 model

[`mɑdl] ★★★★★
動 當模特兒、做模型
名 模特兒、模型、模範
形 模範的、榜樣的

1354 applaud

[ə`plɔd] ★★★
動 鼓掌、喝采、稱讚
同 cheer 喝采

1355 make-up

[`mekʌp] ★★
名 化妝、構造、性格

1356 composure

[kəm`poʒə] ★★
名 鎮靜、沉著、平靜
同 calmness 平靜

fighting!

Give it a shot 小試身手

1 She just kept _____ during the discussion.

2 Jessica's voice is very _____ to her sister.

3 A smooth sea never makes a _____ mariner.

4 Eating too many _____ will make you become heavy.

5 The little girl _____ on the ice.

Answers: 1 silent 2 similar 3 skillful 4 snacks 5 slipped

114

Essay

MP3   短文 227   字彙 228

Patrick worked in a bank after graduating from school. He was a very slow[1357] worker, so he lost his job after a few months. He needed somebody to help him, and he needed somewhere to live. The high unemployment rate had caused a lot of social problems. There were thousands of people like Patrick in society. Patrick tried to find some job-hunting information and went to job expositions[1358]. He had no idea what sort of job was suitable for him, so he walked to an army recruitment[1359] booth. The speaker persuaded[1360] him to become a soldier. Patrick thought joining the army might solve[1361] his problems, so he signed up for military service[1362]. He served in a camp[1363] in southern Taiwan. He did the same thing every day: eat soybean and rice every morning, play soccer in the afternoon, and wash underwear[1364] and socks after taking a shower in the evening. He found that army life was boring and he started to worry about his future. "Will I still do the same thing when my hair is snowy-white? Is being a soldier really the solution for me?"

中譯 *Translation*

派翠克畢業後在一間銀行工作。他是個慢郎中,所以幾個月後就失業了。他需要有人來幫忙他,也需要住的地方。高失業率造成了很多社會問題。社會上像派翠克一樣的人比比皆是。派翠克試著尋找一些求職資訊,並去了就業博覽會。他不知道哪一類型的工作適合他,便走到軍隊招募的攤位。對方說服他從軍。派翠克認為入伍或許可以解決他的問題,所以就簽約服役。他在南台灣的一個營區服役。每天都做著一樣的事情:早上吃著摻入大豆的米飯,下午踢足球,晚上洗完澡後就洗內衣褲和襪子。他發覺軍隊生活非常無趣,開始擔心他的未來。「當我頭髮斑白之時,我是否還在做一樣的事?當軍人真的是我人生的解答嗎?」

1357 slow

[slo] ★★★★
形 遲緩的、慢的
動 變慢、變蕭條
片 slow down 慢下來

1358 exposition

[ˌɛkspəˈzɪʃən] ★★★
名 博覽會、闡述、說明
同 exhibition 展覽會
衍 expositor 講解者

1359 recruitment

[rɪˈkrutmənt] ★★
名 徵募新兵、補充
同 conscription 徵兵
衍 recruit 招募新兵

1360 persuade

[pəˈswed] ★★★
動 說服、使某人相信
同 convince 說服
衍 persuasion 說服

1361 solve

[sɑlv] ★★★★
動 解決、解答、清償
同 resolve 解決
衍 solvable 可以解決的

1362 service

[ˈsɝvɪs] ★★★★★
名 服役、服務、售後服務
動 為…服務
片 be of service 有用

1363 camp

[kæmp] ★★★★
名 兵營、營地
動 紮營、臨時安頓
片 camp out 露營

1364 underwear

[ˈʌndɚ‚wɛr] ★★★
名 (總稱)內衣、襯衣

1365 wonder

[ˈwʌndɚ] ★★★★
動 想知道、感到疑惑
名 驚奇、奇觀、奇才
形 奇妙的、非凡的

1366 ceaseless

[ˈsislɪs] ★★
形 不停的、不間斷的
同 endless 不斷的
衍 cease 停止

1367 mudslide

[ˈmʌdslaɪd] ★★
名 山崩、泥流、坍方
同 landslide 山崩

1368 reliable

[rɪˈlaɪəbl] ★★★★
形 可信賴的、可靠的
同 trustworthy 可靠的
反 unreliable 靠不住的

Give it a shot 小試身手

1 His behavior is a danger to the _____.

2 The shy girl doesn't like to join _____ occasions.

3 _____ the words in alphabetical order.

4 I wonder[1365] a _____ to the ceaseless[1366] mudslide[1367].

5 The news comes from a reliable[1368] _____.

MP3   短文 229   字彙 230

115

Essay

I have a high standard[1369] <u>when it comes to</u> food. I've opened branches of my restaurant up like mushrooms[1370] and spread[1371] them to every neighborhood of the city at a fast pace[1372]. Each restaurant has a distinct[1373] theme, such as Spider-Man, Superman, and Batman. The one downtown has a Spider-man theme, and it serves the best steamed fish, steak, spinach salad, and grilled squirrel. We use funny spellings[1374] to name[1375] the courses. There is a stage for live band performances. We even advertise our restaurant by distributing stamps[1376]. Other restaurants have stolen my idea and done the same thing as me, but mine are still the best. They are good at copying, but they don't have the same spirit in their restaurants. They have the appearance, but they don't capture[1377] the essence[1378]. The food and service of my restaurants are exclusive[1379]. That is why our customers come <u>time after time</u>.

⚠ when it comes to 每當提到
⚠ time after time 不斷地、一次又一次

中譯 *Translation*

我對食物的標準很高。我餐廳的分店如雨後春筍般迅速開張,並快速拓展至城裡的各個街坊。每間餐廳都有不同的主題,像是蜘蛛人、超人和蝙蝠俠。市中心那間分店的主題是蜘蛛人,店裡提供最棒的清蒸魚、牛排、菠菜沙拉和烤松鼠。我們用有趣的拼字替菜餚命名。那裡有一個供樂團現場演唱的舞台。我們甚至還發送郵票為餐廳宣傳。其他餐廳偷了我的點子,跟我做一樣的事情,但我的店始終還是最好的。他們很善於模仿,但他們的餐廳缺乏同樣的精神。他們只學到表面,卻沒有捕捉到精髓。我旗下餐廳的食物和服務都是獨一無二的。那就是為何顧客會如此絡繹不絕了。

1369 standard

[`stændəd] ★★★★

名 標準、規格、水準
形 標準的、一流的
片 to standard 合乎標準

1370 mushroom

[`mʌʃrum] ★★★

名 迅速增長的事物、蘑菇
動 雨後春筍般湧現

1371 spread

[sprɛd] ★★★★

動 蔓延、普及、伸展
名 伸展、蔓延
片 spread to 蔓延

1372 pace

[pes] ★★★★

名 速度、進度、步伐
動 踱步、調整…步調
片 keep pace 並駕齊驅

1373 distinct

[dɪ`stɪŋkt] ★★★★

形 不同的、有區別的、清楚的
片 distinct from 和…不同

1374 spelling

[`spɛlɪŋ] ★★★

名 拼字、拼寫、拼法
片 spelling bee 拼字比賽

1375 name

[nem] ★★★★★

動 命名、提名、列舉
名 名字、名聲
片 name after 以…起名

1376 stamp

[stæmp] ★★★

名 郵票、印花、特徵
動 貼郵票於、壓印於、標出

1377 capture

[`kæptʃə] ★★★★

動 獲得、俘虜、引起注意
名 捕獲、獲得、吸引
反 release 釋放

1378 essence

[`ɛsn̩s] ★★★★

名 精髓、本質、要素
片 in essence 本質上
衍 essential 必要的

1379 exclusive

[ɪk`sklusɪv] ★★★★

形 獨有的、排外的、獨家的、高級的
名 獨家新聞

1380 assembly

[ə`sɛmblɪ] ★★★★

名 集會、立法機關、組裝、裝備
同 gathering 集會

fighting!

Give it a shot 小試身手

❶ He plays piano with an amazing ＿＿＿.

❷ The ＿＿＿ of law is to protect human rights.

❸ Joanna walked on to the ＿＿＿ and started to sing.

❹ We had a weekly assembly[1380] on the ＿＿＿.

❺ Butterflies ＿＿＿ the pollen around.

Answers: ❶ speed ❷ spirit ❸ stage ❹ square ❺ spread

116

Essay

It was a summer afternoon during typhoon season, which is from June to September. The biggest storm in the past decade was raging[1381]. One steel[1382] rod[1383] fell directly on my stomach when I was sitting on the bridge[1384], striking[1385] my body heavily[1386], and I was hurt badly. It was too windy, so I lost my balance[1387] and fell off the bridge into the river. I struggled to swim in the river for two hours and finally got out of it on my own. After a string[1388] of accidents, I was totally in a panic. I knocked on the door of somebody's house. A guy opened the door, and he was shocked by a bloody stranger standing in front of him. He brought me in, kept me beside the stove and gave me strawberry cake and a glass of milk. When I drank the milk through a straw[1389], I found that I couldn't stretch[1390] my arms. I was sent to the hospital, and in a stern[1391] voice the doctor <u>laid</u> great <u>stress on</u> the importance of staying home during a typhoon. It was a lecture that I really deserved[1392].

⚠ lay stress on 強調、把重點放在…上

✎ 中譯 *Translation*

　　六到九月是颱風季，而那是一個夏日午後。一場十年來最大的暴風雨瘋狂肆虐。當時我坐在橋上，一根鋼棍直接砸向我的肚子，重重地擊中我的身體，讓我身負重傷。當時風非常大，以至於我失去平衡，從橋上掉進河裡。我在河裡奮力游了兩個小時，最後終於靠自己爬上岸。經過一連串的意外後，我徹底陷入恐慌。我敲著某戶人家的門，一個男人開了門，那名男子被他眼前這個渾身是血的陌生人嚇了一跳。他把我帶進屋裡，讓我坐在爐子旁享用草莓蛋糕和一杯牛奶。當我用吸管喝著牛奶時，我發現我無法伸展我的手臂。我被送到了醫院，醫生用嚴肅的嗓音強調颱風天留在家裡的重要性。我想我真是自作自受。

1381 rage

[redʒ] ★★★★
動 肆虐、發怒、流行
名 狂怒、肆虐、風靡一時的事物

1382 steel

[stil] ★★★★
形 鋼製的、堅強的
名 鋼鐵製品、冷酷、堅強
動 鋼化、使堅強、使冷酷

1383 rod

[rɑd] ★★★★
名 桿、棍棒、懲罰
同 stick 棍棒
片 kiss the rod 甘願受罰

1384 bridge

[brɪdʒ] ★★★★★
名 橋、鼻梁、橋梁
動 架橋於、把…連結起來

1385 strike

[straɪk] ★★★★
動 攻擊、簽訂、突然想到
名 打擊、罷工、意外成功
片 strike down 打倒

1386 heavily

[ˋhɛvɪlɪ] ★★★
副 猛烈地、沉重地、鬱悶地、濃密地
反 lightly 輕微地

1387 balance

[ˋbæləns] ★★★★
名 平衡、協調、鎮定
動 保持平衡、權衡
片 on balance 總的來看

1388 string

[strɪŋ] ★★★★
名 一串、細繩、弦
動 串起、拉直、使緊張
片 string along 追隨

1389 straw

[strɔ] ★★★
名 吸管、稻草、麥桿
片 the last straw 最後一擊

1390 stretch

[strɛtʃ] ★★★★
動 舒展肢體、拉直、展開
名 伸展、連綿
片 stretch out 伸出

1391 stern

[stɜn] ★★★
形 嚴厲的、堅定的
同 severe 嚴厲的
片 stern look 神色嚴厲

1392 deserve

[dɪˋzɜv] ★★★★
動 應受、值得
片 get what you deserve 罪有應得

fighting!

Give it a shot 小試身手

1 I felt great pain in my _____ after I ate something rotten.

2 He had a _____ after getting up.

3 Be careful when you cross the _____.

4 He drew a _____ line on the paper as X axis.

5 He was _____ by his mother for stealing money.

Answers: 1 stomach 2 stretch 3 stream 4 straight 5 struck

117

Essay

How could I be so stupid as to <u>make a mistake on</u> a question like subtracting[1393] ten from ninety? I failed two subjects, including mathematics, this semester. I walked to the subway station on a sunny day and thought about my future. My dad expected me to succeed, but I was kicked out of school. When I hung around the supermarket, I met a guy in a suit, who was as graceful[1394] as a swan. He said he was a successful sales representative for Amway. Amway is an international corporation supplying[1395] a wide range[1396] of consumer[1397] products. He told me that <u>in order to</u> survive[1398] in today's competitive[1399] society, a person has to swallow[1400] all of life's insults[1401] and keeps on working. He told me that success is supported by years of work and practice and that there's no such thing as instant success. On the surface, direct-selling doesn't seem like a good job for most people, but it's because most people don't really understand it. He urged[1402] me to join his sales team, and I accepted his offer. I hoped I would succeed in another way and live up to my dad's expectations somehow.

> ⓘ make a mistake on 在…上犯了錯誤
> ⓘ in order to 為了，使用時可以簡化為 to。

中譯 *Translation*

　　我怎麼會那麼蠢到犯下這種錯誤，連九十減十是多少都不會？我這學期有兩科不及格，其中一科是數學。這天天氣晴朗，我走路到地鐵站，一邊思索著自己的未來。我老爸期望我能成功，但我卻被退學。當我在超市閒晃的時候，遇到一個穿著西裝，像天鵝一般優雅的男人。他說他是安麗集團成功的業務代表。安麗是一間國際性的公司，供應多種產品。他告訴我為了在競爭激烈的社會存活，一個人必須把所有羞辱往肚裡吞，持續努力地工作。他也告訴我，成功是由多年的努力與練習所成就，沒有什麼是一蹴可幾的。就表面上來看，直銷對大多數人來說不是一份好工作，但那是因為大多數人不瞭解直銷。他遊說我加入他的業務團隊，而我也答應了，希望我可以用另一種方式成功，達到父親的期望。

1393 subtract

[səbˋtrækt] ★★★

動 減、去掉

同 deduct 扣除

片 subtract from 減去

1394 graceful

[ˋgresfəl] ★★★

形 優美的、典雅的、得體的

同 elegant 優美的

1395 supply

[səˋplaɪ] ★★★★

動 供應、補充、滿足

名 供給、供應量、補給品

片 supply for 為…提供

1396 range

[rendʒ] ★★★★★

名 一系列、範圍、類別

動 排列、把…分類

同 extent 範圍

1397 consumer

[kənˋsjumɚ] ★★★

名 消費者、消耗者

同 user 使用者

反 producer 生產者

1398 survive

[sɚˋvaɪv] ★★★★

動 倖存、比…活得長

片 survive sb. by 比某人多活…

1399 competitive

[kəmˋpɛtətɪv] ★★★

形 競爭的、好勝的

片 intensely competitive 競爭激烈的

1400 swallow

[ˋswɑlo] ★★★

動 吞下、吞併、耗盡、忍受、壓制、取消

片 swallow up 吞沒

1401 insult

[ɪnˋsʌlt] ★★★

名 辱罵、侮辱性言行

動 侮辱、辱罵

片 an insult to 對…的侮辱

1402 urge

[ɝdʒ] ★★★

動 慫恿、催促、驅策、強烈要求

名 衝動、推動力

1403 entrepreneur

[ˌɑntrəprəˋnɝ] ★★★

名 企業家、事業創辦者、承包商

同 enterpriser 企業家

1404 calligraphy

[kəˋlɪgrəfɪ] ★★

名 書法、筆跡

同 handwriting 筆跡、字跡、寫字風格

Fighting!

Give it a shot 小試身手

1 Sociology is the _____ I love the most.

2 The mechanic turned out to be a _____ entrepreneur[1403].

3 The _____ of the vase was Chinese calligraphy[1404].

4 He _____ the pill without water.

5 That purple sweater doesn't _____ me.

Answers: 1 subject 2 successful 3 surface 4 swallowed 5 suit

245

118

🎧 MP3　短文 235　字彙 236

I have a teenage nephew. He is talkative[1405], and he has a talent[1406] for music. His mom <u>passed away</u> when he was in his early teens. He shed[1407] a lot of tears with great grief[1408] then. Taking care of himself has been a difficult task. He stopped playing on the swings[1409] in the park with other kids and <u>threw away</u> his toy tanks[1410]. Every morning, he sweeps[1411] the house and goes to the market before school. After school, he looks after his little sister and makes dinner for her. He is adept[1412] at cooking. I've tried his chicken soup and it is very tasty[1413]. He even made a sweater for his sister by hand. He is a member of the school basketball team now, and his goal is to become a famous player. Every time I visit them, I bring some tangerines and videos for them. My nephew is the perfect example of a model student, and I sincerely[1414] wish him all the best for the future.

ⓘ pass away 過世，為 die (死亡)的委婉説法。

ⓘ throw away 丟棄、扔掉

中譯 *Translation*

　　我有一個正值青少年期的姪子，他很健談，而且很有音樂才華。他母親在他十幾歲時就過世了。他當時哭得傷心欲絕。要照顧自己是一件困難的任務，他不再和其他孩子在公園玩盪鞦韆，也把他的玩具坦克車都扔了。他現在每天早晨上學前，都會到市場買菜和打掃房子。放學後，他會照顧妹妹和做晚餐給她吃，他菜煮得很棒。我曾嚐過他的雞湯，非常美味。他甚至親手還打了一件毛衣給他妹妹。他現在是籃球校隊的成員，他的目標就是成為知名的選手。每次我去拜訪他們，我都會帶些橘子和錄影帶給他們。我姪子是模範生的理想楷模，我衷心希望他的未來能一路順遂。

1405 talkative
[`tɔkətɪv] ★★
形 健談的、多嘴的、喜歡說話的
反 taciturn 無言的

1406 talent
[`tælənt] ★★★★
名 才能、天資、藝人
片 talent for …的才能
衍 talented 有才幹的

1407 shed
[ʃɛd] ★★★
動 流下、散發、擺脫
名 分水嶺、小屋
片 shed light on 照亮

1408 grief
[grif] ★★★★
名 悲痛、不幸、失敗
反 glee 歡欣
衍 grieve 使悲傷

1409 swing
[swɪŋ] ★★★★
名 盪鞦韆、擺動、音律
動 搖擺、懸掛
同 sway 搖擺

1410 tank
[tæŋk] ★★★★
名 坦克車、大容器、槽
動 加滿油箱
片 tank up 灌滿一箱油

1411 sweep
[swip] ★★★
動 打掃、颳起、環視、掃蕩、掠過
片 sweep off 掃去

1412 adept
[ə`dɛpt] ★★★
形 熟練的、內行的
名 能手、內行
片 be adept at 擅長

1413 tasty
[`testɪ] ★★
形 美味的、高雅的、有吸引力的
同 delicious 美味的

1414 sincerely
[sɪn`sɪrlɪ] ★★★
副 由衷地、真誠地、敬上
同 heartily 衷心地
反 insincerely 無誠意地

1415 score
[skor] ★★★★
名 得分、成績、宿怨
動 得分、給…評分、贏得
片 keep the score 計分

1416 reluctant
[rɪ`lʌktənt] ★★★★
形 勉強的、不情願的、阻撓的、頑抗的
反 willing 樂意的

fighting!

Give it a shot 小試身手

1 The red circle on the map is a _____ of you.
2 The _____ of this game is to get the most scores[1415].
3 He was reluctant[1416] to _____ the restroom.
4 She was a beauty in her _____.
5 Please discuss the second question with your _____ member.

Answers: 1 symbol 2 target 3 sweep 4 teenage 5 team

247

119

MP3

短文 237　字彙 238

Essay

Most teenagers don't have a healthy life. They spend too much time watching TV and talking on the cellphone every day. <u>In addition to</u> a great amount of homework[1417], they need to read thick[1418] textbooks for tests at the end of every term. They don't get enough exercise[1419] and spend too much time on playing on-line games; therefore, they do not look thin but heavier and heavier. They should get involved in more outdoor[1420] activities. They can play basketball, soccer, or tennis and even go camping with their friends. Putting up a tent can provide[1421] them with some good exercise. What's more, they should not download movies but go to the theater to see movies because illegally downloading movies is not moral[1422]. As well, it's terrible[1423] to stay at home all weekend. My son is going to have a big exam next month and he stays awake[1424] all night studying. He is like a thief[1425], never sleeping at night. I plan to take him to the temple[1426] to worship[1427]. Maybe it will help him release the stress of studying.

> ⓘ in addition to 除…之外(還)，介系詞後接名詞。

中譯 *Translation*

　　許多年輕人都過著不健康的生活，他們每天花太多的時間在看電視和講手機，除了大量的功課，他們還必須閱讀厚重的參考書來準備每個學期末的考試。他們的運動量不足，花很多時間在玩線上遊戲，所以他們看起來非但不瘦，還越來越胖。他們應該要多參與戶外活動，可以打籃球、足球或網球，甚至和朋友出外露營，搭帳棚會帶給他們一些很不錯的鍛鍊。另外，他們不該下載電影，而應該要去電影院看電影，因為非法下載電影的行為很不道德，而且整個週末都待在家也很不好。我的兒子下個月要參加大考，每天晚上都在熬夜看書，他就像小偷一樣，晚上都不睡覺，我打算帶他去廟裡拜拜，這也許會幫助他舒解讀書的壓力。

1417 homework

[ˋhomwɝk] ★★★★
- 名 家庭作業、副業、準備工作
- 同 assignment 作業

1418 thick

[θɪk] ★★★
- 形 厚的、濃厚的、茂密的
- 反 thin 細的、薄的
- 片 thick skull 笨頭笨腦

1419 exercise

[ˋɛksəˏsaɪz] ★★★★★
- 名 運動、鍛鍊、行使
- 動 運動、練習、運用
- 片 exercise over 控制

1420 outdoor

[ˋautˏdor] ★★★
- 形 戶外的、露天的
- 片 outdoor activities 戶外活動

1421 provide

[prəˋvaɪd] ★★★★★
- 動 提供、供給、規定、撫養
- 片 provide with 供給

1422 moral

[ˋmɔrəl] ★★★
- 形 道德的、品行端正的、精神上的
- 名 道德、品行

1423 terrible

[ˋtɛrəbl̩] ★★★★
- 形 極差的、可怕的、嚴重的、令人敬畏的
- 同 horrible 可怕的

1424 awake

[əˋwek] ★★★
- 形 醒著的、意識到的
- 動 喚醒、使覺醒、激起
- 片 awake from 從…醒來

1425 thief

[θif] ★★★
- 名 小偷、賊

1426 temple

[ˋtɛmpl̩] ★★★
- 名 寺廟、聖殿、太陽穴、地方分會
- 同 church 教堂

1427 worship

[ˋwɝʃɪp] ★★★
- 動 信奉、做禮拜、崇拜
- 名 敬仰、敬神、禮拜儀式
- 反 contempt 蔑視

1428 insert

[ɪnˋsɝt] ★★★
- 動 插入、添寫、刊登
- 名 插入物、插頁、鑲嵌物
- 片 insert into 插入、加進

fighting!

Give it a shot 小試身手

1. She went to the _____ to worship.
2. He invited me to the _____ tonight.
3. It is a long- _____ trip from Taipei to Kaohsiung.
4. The bad weather made our picnic _____.
5. He inserted[1428] a coin into the pay _____ and dialed her number.

Answers: 1 temple 2 theater 3 term 4 terrible 5 telephone

120

I am a writer. I had my birthday party at a hot pot restaurant with my friends last week. After that, we went to a pub. My friends said I must have been really thirsty[1429] because I kept drinking. I drank all kinds of alcohol: lemon drop, tequila, cherry brandy, etc. After we toasted[1430] each other for several rounds[1431], I felt so sick. I felt like something was coming up through my throat[1432]. I ran to the restroom and vomited everything I had eaten, such as tomato and tofu, into the toilet. After that, though, I felt much better and came back to drink. My friend told me there was tofu on my teeth and my tongue[1433]. And I was too embarrassed to stay, forgetting to tip[1434] the beautiful waitress. I stood on the road and thumbed[1435] a ride, but I didn't see any cars passing by. Later came a thunderstorm. I wrote a book entitled[1436] "Alcoholic" afterwards, taking that night's activities as inspiration for the novel[1437].

中譯 *Translation*

　　我是個作家，我上禮拜和朋友在一間火鍋店舉辦我的生日派對，在那之後，我們就前往酒吧。朋友都說我肯定很渴，因為我一直喝個不停。我喝了各式各樣的酒，檸檬酒、龍舌蘭、櫻桃白蘭地等等。我們彼此敬酒數巡過後，我開始感到噁心，我覺得有東西要跑出喉嚨。我跑到廁所，把我那晚吃的東西都吐進馬桶，像是番茄、豆腐之類的東西。不過，在吐過之後我感覺好多了，所以就回去繼續喝。我朋友跟我說有豆腐黏在我的牙齒和舌頭上。我感到非常尷尬，實在無法再待下去，立刻起身走人，卻忘了給漂亮的女服務生小費。我站在街上豎起拇指要搭便車，但完全沒看到車子經過，後來還下起了大雷雨。那天之後，我寫了一本書名為《酒鬼》，小說的靈感來源就是我那日的事蹟。

1429 thirsty

[ˋθɝstɪ] ★★★
形 渴的、缺水的、渴望的
同 dry 乾的
片 thirsty for 渴求

1430 toast

[tost] ★★★
動 舉杯祝酒、烤麵包
名 敬酒、吐司
片 drink a toast 乾杯

1431 round

[raʊnd] ★★★★
名 一回合、巡迴、一連串
形 圓的、豐滿的、巨大的
動 發胖、兜圈子

1432 throat

[θrot] ★★★★
名 喉嚨、窄路、嗓門
片 stick in one's throat 難以接受、難以啟齒

1433 tongue

[tʌŋ] ★★★★
名 舌頭、口才、語言
片 Bite your tongue! 別再說了！

1434 tip

[tɪp] ★★★★
動 給小費、洩露、暗示
名 小費、提示、秘密消息
片 tip off 向…洩露消息

1435 thumb

[θʌm] ★★★★
動 請求搭便車、迅速翻閱
名 大拇指
片 thumb through 翻查

1436 entitle

[ɪnˋtaɪtḷ] ★★
動 給…命名、給予權利
同 name 給…命名
片 be entitled to 使有資格

1437 novel

[ˋnɑvḷ] ★★★★
名 (長篇)小說
形 新穎的、新奇的
同 new 新的

1438 dialogue

[ˋdaɪəˌlɔg] ★★★
名 交談、對白、意見交換
同 conversation 談話

1439 salty

[ˋsɔltɪ] ★★★
形 鹹的、含鹽的、下流的
同 saline 含鹽分的
衍 salt 鹽

1440 brush

[brʌʃ] ★★★★
動 刷牙、掠過、拂去
名 刷子、畫筆、小摩擦
片 brush off 刷掉、拂掉

fighting!

Give it a shot 小試身手

❶ We should understand each other _____ dialogues[1438].

❷ She washed her hands and left the _____.

❸ My dad showed his _____ to praise me.

❹ The salty[1439] cookies made me feel _____.

❺ Brush[1440] your _____ after every meal.

Answers: ❶ through ❷ toilet ❸ thumb ❹ thirsty ❺ teeth

121

Essay

I've done a lot of trading[1441] with my customers in Sri Lanka for years. Sri Lanka is a country full of opportunities and I've made a big fortune[1442] there. However, there are a lot of traps[1443] when I do business there. One customer once played a nasty[1444] trick on me, and it even got me involved in a complicated trial[1445]. It <u>is important to</u> respect the religious traditions[1446] of other cultures. I always try to remember that as I make my annual visit there. The largest city of the country, Colombo, is a modern but traditional place. There are skyscrapers and towers[1447], as well as dirt[1448] roads. Cows walk on the streets, which causes traffic jams. Remember to bargain[1449] when you buy anything. I once bought a pair of trousers[1450] for 1,000 rupees, but I saw the same ones at half that price somewhere else. Don't eat the food from street vendors; otherwise, you may have diarrhea for a week. Also, never use the towels[1451] in the hotel. However, if you have a chance to travel there, you'll find it interesting.

(!) be important to …很重要

中譯 *Translation*

　　我曾經和在斯里蘭卡的顧客進行了數年的貿易，斯里蘭卡是個充滿機會的國家，我也在那裡大賺了一筆。然而，和他們做生意有很多的陷阱，我的一名顧客曾對我耍惡意的把戲，讓我涉入一樁複雜的案件。尊重其他文化的宗教傳統是很重要的。我每年探訪當地的時候，都會謹記這一點。那裡最大的城市可倫坡，是一個既文明又傳統的地方，那裡有高樓大廈和高塔，也有滿布灰塵的街道景觀，牛會在街上行走，導致交通阻塞。記得買東西的時候要殺價，我曾經花了一千盧比買了一件褲子，卻在其他地方看到同樣一件褲子，而且只要半價就買得到。不要吃街上的小吃，否則可能會拉一個禮拜的肚子。另外，也不要使用飯店提供的毛巾。儘管說了那麼多，如果你有機會去那裡旅行，會覺得很有趣的。

1441 trading

[`tredɪŋ] ★★
- 名 貿易、交易
- 形 貿易的、交易的
- 衍 trade 貿易、交易

1442 fortune

[`fɔrtʃən] ★★★★
- 名 財產、巨款、好運
- 反 misfortune 不幸
- 片 make a fortune 發財

1443 trap

[træp] ★★★
- 名 陷阱、陰謀、困境
- 動 設圈套、堵塞
- 同 snare 陷阱、圈套

1444 nasty

[`næstɪ] ★★★★
- 形 惡意的、卑鄙的
- 片 be nasty to 對…不友善

1445 trial

[`traɪəl] ★★★
- 名 審判、試驗、嘗試
- 形 試驗的、審判的
- 片 on trial 受審

1446 tradition

[trə`dɪʃən] ★★★★
- 名 傳統、慣例、常規
- 同 custom 習俗、慣例
- 片 by tradition 根據傳統

1447 tower

[`tauə] ★★★★
- 名 高樓、塔、堡壘
- 動 高聳、屹立、勝過
- 片 tower over 遠遠超過

1448 dirt

[dɜt] ★★★★
- 名 泥、爛泥、灰塵、無價值物、閒話
- 片 dish the dirt 說壞話

1449 bargain

[`bɑrgɪn] ★★★
- 動 討價還價、達成協議
- 名 買賣、協議、便宜貨

1450 trousers

[`trauzəz] ★★
- 名 褲子、長褲
- 同 pants 褲子
- 片 short trousers 短褲

1451 towel

[`tauəl] ★★★★
- 名 毛巾、紙巾
- 片 throw in the towel 認輸

1452 inferior

[ɪn`fɪrɪə] ★★★
- 形 較差的、次於…的、下級的
- 名 屬下、部下

Fighting!

Give it a shot 小試身手

1. Our company does a lot of _____ with yours.
2. Women were inferior[1452] to men in _____ societies.
3. The criminal was brought to _____ last week.
4. He wants to play a _____ over his old pal.
5. The driver was fined for violating the _____ rules.

Answers: 1 trade 2 traditional 3 trial 4 trick 5 traffic

253

122

🎧 MP3　短文 243　字彙 244

My brother likes trumpeting[1453] his achievements, but nobody ever trusts him. From my point of view, he is a perfect idiot because of the stupid things he has done. That is the absolute[1454] truth. Once, for example, he forgot to wear his uniform[1455] to work, wearing only underwear. He has ugly, yellow teeth. He uses only one tube[1456] of toothpaste in an entire year because he seldom[1457] brushes his teeth. He has a scar[1458] on his upper[1459] lip that resulted[1460] from an accident few years ago. He drove my dad's truck to the mountains during a typhoon and he crashed[1461] into a wall of a tunnel[1462]. Two of his teeth were broken in that accident, so he can <u>no longer</u> eat his favorite turkey anymore. There's a Hello Kitty printed on his umbrella. He looks so annoyingly goofy[1463] every time he puts his umbrella up. He had a turtle as his pet, and he always slept with it. One day, he found the turtle dead under his body. My brother is the stupidest person in the world. I actually think he's from another planet[1464]!

⚠ no longer 再也不⋯

中譯 *Translation*

　　我哥哥很喜歡四處宣傳他的事蹟，但都沒有人相信他，在我看來，他是個笨蛋的絕佳典型，因為他做過很多蠢事，而這才是事實。有一次，他忘了穿制服去上班，只穿了內衣褲。他有一口又醜又黃的牙齒。他一年只用一條牙膏，因為他很少刷牙。他的上唇有一個傷口，是幾年前的一次意外造成的。他在颱風來襲時，開著我爸爸的卡車上山，結果一頭撞上隧道裡的牆。他有兩顆牙齒斷了，所以他再也不能吃他最愛的火雞。他的傘上印著凱蒂貓的圖案，每次他開傘的時候，看起來真的很蠢，很惹人厭。他曾經養過一隻寵物龜，他總是和牠睡在一起，某天卻發現烏龜被他的身體壓死了。我哥哥真是世界第一大笨蛋，我覺得他根本就是從另一個星球來的！

1453 trumpet

[ˋtrʌmpɪt] ★★★
- 動 大力宣傳、吹喇叭
- 名 喇叭、小號手
- 同 horn 小號

1454 absolute

[ˋæbsəˏlut] ★★★★
- 形 絕對的、專制的、完全的、確實的
- 反 relative 相對的

1455 uniform

[ˋjunəˏfɔrm] ★★★★
- 名 制服、軍服
- 形 一致的、不變的
- 動 使一律化、使穿制服

1456 tube

[tjub] ★★★★
- 名 軟管、管子、(英)地鐵
- 動 用管運輸
- 同 pipe 導管

1457 seldom

[ˋsɛldəm] ★★★★★
- 副 很少、難得
- 形 不常有的、難得的
- 同 rarely 很少

1458 scar

[skɑr] ★★★★
- 名 疤、傷痕、創傷
- 動 留下傷痕、結疤
- 同 blemish 傷疤

1459 upper

[ˋʌpɚ] ★★★
- 形 上面的、較高的、上層的、上流的
- 片 upper class 上層階級

1460 result

[rɪˋzʌlt] ★★★★★
- 動 導致、發生、結果
- 名 結果、效果、戰績
- 片 result from 起因於

1461 crash

[kræʃ] ★★★★
- 動 撞擊、墜毀、垮台
- 名 相撞、墜毀、垮台
- 片 crash into 撞上

1462 tunnel

[ˋtʌnḷ] ★★
- 名 隧道、地道、洞穴
- 動 挖掘隧道、打開通道
- 片 tunnel vision 目光狹窄

1463 goofy

[ˋgufɪ] ★★
- 形 愚笨的、傻的
- 同 foolish 愚蠢的
- 片 a goofy grin 傻笑

1464 planet

[ˋplænɪt] ★★★
- 名 行星
- 片 be on another planet 異想天開

Give it a shot 小試身手

fighting!

1. It became dark when the train entered the _____.
2. The plates on the _____ shelf were beyond my reach.
3. High school students look so youthful in _____.
4. He _____ a letter to his sister in Japan through his typewriter.
5. He plays the _____ in the orchestra.

Answers: 1 tunnel 2 upper 3 uniforms 4 typed 5 trumpet

123

Essay

MP3

短文 245

字彙 246

Jerry <u>was fond of</u> taking drugs and was a heavy drug user. It was normal for him to smoke marijuana all day. His dad tried to help him abstain[1465] from using drugs and <u>took a vacation</u> with him to Taitung. They visited an aboriginal[1466] village[1467] in a valley[1468]. The population was less than two hundred people. Before they came, the tribe[1469] had just voted for the new chief[1470]. Only males could vote. There weren't many visitors[1471] to the village, but they were welcomed[1472] by the villagers. They lived there for two months. Jerry went hunting with the male villagers every day and played volleyball with the kids. He learned many aboriginal words and phrases[1473] and got along with them pretty well. Jerry recorded a video of his daily life there. Before Jerry and his father left, Jerry gave his violin to the kids. It was of great value[1474] to him. After the vacation, his mind found peace. And he eventually stopped taking drugs completely. It was a mighty[1475] victory for Jerry!

⚠ be fond of 喜歡
⚠ take a vacation 度假

中譯 *Translation*

　　傑瑞過去沉迷於嗑藥，是一個重度藥癮者。整天吸大麻對他來說是一件稀鬆平常的事。他爸爸試著幫他戒除藥癮，帶著他去台東度假，他們拜訪了一個位於山谷的原住民村落，那裡的人口少於兩百人。在他們到這個村莊前，村民才剛選出了新村長，只有男性可以投票。那裡的訪客並不多，但是他們備受歡迎，他們在那裡住了兩個月，傑瑞每天都跟男村民們一起去打獵，並和小孩子玩排球，他學了很多原住民語彙，也和村民們相處得非常融洽，傑瑞錄下了在那裡生活的影片。在傑瑞與他的父親離開前，他把他的舊小提琴送給孩子們，那把小提琴對他來說價值非凡，假期過後，他的心靈恢復了平靜，也終於完全戒除了藥癮，這對傑瑞來說真是一大勝利！

1465 abstain

[əb`sten] ★★
- 動 戒、避開、棄權
- 同 refrain 戒除
- 片 abstain from 戒絕

1466 aboriginal

[,æbə`rɪdʒən!] ★★★
- 形 土著居民的、原始的
- 名 土著居民、土生動植物
- 衍 aborigine 土著居民

1467 village

[`vɪlɪdʒ] ★★★★
- 名 村莊、村民、聚居處
- 片 global village 地球村
- 衍 villager 村民

1468 valley

[`vælɪ] ★★★★
- 名 山谷、流域、低凹處
- 同 clough 狹窄的溪谷

1469 tribe

[traɪb] ★★★
- 名 部落、種族、一夥
- 同 group 群
- 片 a tribe of 一群…

1470 chief

[tʃif] ★★★★
- 名 酋長、首領、長官
- 形 為首的、最重要的
- 片 in chief 主要地

1471 visitor

[`vɪzɪtə] ★★★★★
- 名 觀光客、訪問者、探病者、視察者
- 衍 visit 參觀、拜訪

1472 welcome

[`wɛlkəm] ★★★★
- 動 歡迎、欣然接受
- 形 受歡迎的
- 名 歡迎、款待

1473 phrase

[frez] ★★★★
- 名 詞組、說法、片語
- 片 turn a phrase 能言善道

1474 value

[`vælju] ★★★★★
- 名 價值、重要性、價值觀
- 動 評價、重視
- 片 of value 值錢的

1475 mighty

[`maɪtɪ] ★★★
- 形 強大的、偉大的
- 同 powerful 強大的
- 衍 almighty 全能的

1476 overlook

[,ovə`luk] ★★★★
- 動 眺望、忽略、監督
- 片 overlook from 從…俯瞰

fighting!

Give it a shot 小試身手

1 I am planning a _____ for this summer break.

2 Memorize _____ is basic when you learn a language.

3 The house on the hill overlooks[1476] the _____.

4 He dressed as _____ to the international conference.

5 The _____ of one thing differs in everyone's eyes.

Answers: 1 vacation 2 vocabularies 3 valley 4 usual 5 value

Essay 124

MP3 247　短文 247　字彙 248

Jessica was a waitress at a café. She always woke up late and never arrived[1477] at work on time. She always forgot to tie an apron around her waist[1478], too. There were many customers on weekdays, but it took her a long time to take an order. All of these made her boss[1479] quite dissatisfied[1480]. One afternoon, Jessica spilled watermelon juice over a foreign[1481] customer's shirt. His shirt was wet[1482] and he demanded[1483] an apology[1484] from Jessica. However, she didn't speak English, so she couldn't understand what he said. A wave[1485] of anger[1486] swept over the customer. He took a weapon from his sports car and showed the whale tattoo he had on his right arm. Jessica was scared and her tears fell like a waterfall. Whatever she said, the customer didn't understand. She took out a pile of name cards from her wallet to desperately[1487] find someone she could turn to. Finally, she remembered a person who spoke English fluently: her fiancé, who was going to wed[1488] her soon. Whenever she got into trouble, her fiancé would show up and help her. However, when she called his number, she panicked because he didn't answer the phone. Fortunately, the Westerner finally gave up trying to talk to her and left without hurting her.

中譯 *Translation*

　　潔西卡是一間咖啡廳的女服務生，她總是很晚起床，從來沒有準時上班過，她也老是忘了在腰間繫圍裙。咖啡廳平日都有很多客人，但她點個餐就要花很長時間，這些都讓她的老闆很不滿。某天下午，潔西卡把西瓜汁打翻在一個外國客人的襯衫上。他的襯衫濕了，要求潔西卡道歉。然而，她不會說英語，所以聽不懂他在說什麼。那名顧客心裡一陣憤怒，從他的跑車拿出武器，並秀出他的鯨魚刺青。潔西卡非常害怕，眼淚像瀑布般落下，不管她說什麼，那個顧客都聽不懂。她從皮夾中拿出一疊名片，想找到可以求助的人。終於，她發現一個英文講得很流利的人，就是她的未婚夫，也是將要和她結婚的人。不管她在哪裡遇上麻煩，她的未婚夫都會出現幫她。但是，當她撥電話過去的時候，她感到很驚慌，因為她的未婚夫並沒有接電話。幸好，這名西方人最終放棄和她對話，沒有傷害她就離開了。

1477　arrive

[əˋraɪv] ★★★★★
動 到達、成功、達成
同 reach 抵達
片 arrive at 到達

1478　waist

[west] ★★★★
名 腰、腰部
片 from the waist up 上半身

1479　boss

[bɔs] ★★★★
名 老闆、有權勢者、上司
動 當…首領、指揮、掌管
反 worker 勞工

1480　dissatisfied

[dɪsˋsætɪsˏfaɪd] ★★
形 不滿的、流露不滿的
同 discontent 不滿的
衍 dissatisfy 感覺不滿

1481　foreign

[ˋfɔrɪn] ★★★★★
形 外國的、陌生的
同 alien 外國的
衍 foreigner 外國人

1482　wet

[wɛt] ★★★★
形 濕的、潮濕的、下雨的
名 濕氣、水分
動 把…淋濕、弄濕

1483　demand

[dɪˋmænd] ★★★★
動 要求、需要、查問
名 要求、需要
片 demand for 要求

1484　apology

[əˋpɑlədʒɪ] ★★★
名 道歉、賠罪、辯解
片 make an apology for 為…道歉

1485　wave

[wev] ★★★★
名 (情緒)高漲、波浪
動 揮手示意、起伏
片 in waves 一陣又一陣

1486　anger

[ˋæŋgɚ] ★★★★★
名 生氣、怒火
動 發怒
同 wrath 憤怒

1487　desperately

[ˋdɛspərɪtlɪ] ★★
副 拼命地、絕望地
反 mildly 溫和地、適度地
衍 desperate 鋌而走險的

1488　wed

[wɛd] ★★★★
動 與…結婚、使結合
同 marry 和…結婚
衍 wedding 婚禮

Give it a shot 小試身手

① The office is open from 9:00 a.m. to 5:00 p.m. on _____.

② My mother patted me to _____ me up.

③ I will come to your aid _____ you need me.

④ The _____ took our order and got back clean his table.

⑤ This toy car has four _____.

125

Essay

When winter comes, some wild animals will take a long sleep called hibernation[1489]. It's windy[1490] in that season, and the wind whispers[1491] everywhere. Wherever we go, there seems to be a lack of vitality. Bears don't look for food during that time, neither do squirrels. They take a rest and save their energy[1492] for spring. Plum trees are the winners in winter. The colder it becomes, the more beautifully they bloom. Whoever sees the blossom[1493] of plum trees will be amazed. Also, because of the ample[1494] rain, rivers swell. It is a miracle[1495] made by nature.

Since it's very chilly[1496] outside during winter, I make a wise decision to stay home whenever I can. During these lonely days and nights, I often phone[1497] my mother, but I sometimes find the line busy. Staying home with nothing to do is very boring, so I dial again and again. Even when I do get through on the phone, the housekeeper might say my mom isn't available[1498]. Then I have to idle my time away doing meaningless[1499] things.

中譯 *Translation*

　　當冬天來臨，部分野生動物就會冬眠。在這個季節風很大，颯颯作響地四處吹送。不管我們去哪裡，每個地方似乎都缺乏生機。熊不會在這個季節尋覓食物，松鼠也不會。牠們都在休息，為春天儲存能量。梅花樹是冬天的贏家，天氣越冷，花就開得越美，不管是誰看到梅花樹盛開的模樣，都會感到驚艷。另外，因為降雨帶來豐沛的水量，河流的水位會跟著上漲，這真是大自然的奇蹟。

　　因為冬天時外面冷颼颼的，因此，我做了個明智的決定，就是盡可能待在家裡面。在這段孤單的白天和夜裡我常常會打電話給我的母親，但有的時候，電話是忙線中。因為待在家裡無事可做真的很無聊，所以我會一撥再撥。但當電話終於接通時，管家也可能跟我說我媽媽不在家，這時候我可就真的要在家裡做些沒意義的事情了！

1489 hibernation

[ˌhaɪbəˈneʃən] ★★
- 名 冬眠、過冬
- 同 activity 活動力
- 衍 hibernate 冬眠

1490 windy

[ˈwɪndɪ] ★★★
- 形 風大的、颱風的、空話連篇的
- 同 blowy 風大的

1491 whisper

[ˈhwɪspə] ★★
- 動 颯颯地響、低語、耳語
- 片 whisper about 悄悄傳開

1492 energy

[ˈɛnədʒɪ] ★★★★★
- 名 能量、活力、精力
- 同 vigor 活力、精力
- 衍 energetic 精力旺盛的

1493 blossom

[ˈblɑsəm] ★★★
- 名 花、開花、生長期
- 動 開花、生長茂盛、興旺
- 片 in blossom 正在開花

1494 ample

[ˈæmpl] ★★★
- 形 豐富的、寬敞的
- 同 abundant 豐富的
- 反 scanty 不足的

1495 miracle

[ˈmɪrəkl] ★★★★
- 名 奇蹟、驚人的事例
- 同 wonder 驚奇
- 片 to a miracle 奇蹟般地

1496 chilly

[ˈtʃɪlɪ] ★★
- 形 冷颼颼的、冷淡的、使人沮喪的
- 衍 chill 寒氣

1497 phone

[fon] ★★★★★
- 動 打電話
- 名 電話、聽筒、耳機
- 片 phone in 打電話

1498 available

[əˈveləbl] ★★★
- 形 有空的、可利用的、可得到的
- 片 available to 可用的

1499 meaningless

[ˈminɪŋlɪs] ★★
- 形 無意義的、不重要的、無法解釋的
- 衍 meaningful 有意義的

1500 award

[əˈwɔrd] ★★★★
- 名 獎、獎狀、獎學金
- 動 授予、給予、判給
- 片 win an award 得獎

Fighting!

Give it a shot 小試身手

1. He insists on his points of view _____ he goes.
2. The _____ of the game refused to receive the award[1500].
3. He was _____ to donate his healthy organs after death.
4. Put on your jacket in such a _____ day.
5. This bird has a broken _____ and cannot fly.

Answers: 1 wherever 2 winner 3 willing 4 windy 5 wing

126

MP3　短文 251　字彙 252

Essay

　　There were goats and sheep on my family's farm[1501]. The sheep produced[1502] wool, which was worth a lot of money. Recently, I found wounds[1503] on the sheep and the wooden[1504] fence was broken. I wondered who had dared[1505] to <u>break into</u> my field and hurt my sheep. I had spent all of my youth in this place. After my parents passed away, I kept living and working at this farm. I was pretty[1506] sure that there are no other neighbors living within 15 miles of my cottage. I <u>stayed awake</u> at night to see who in the world broke into my yard[1507] without being noticed. I found that a wolf had done this. I set traps to catch the wolf, and the next day, the wolf was caught. I had no idea how to deal with it, so I just left it alone. Several days later, it had starved[1508] to death. Actually, I didn't mean to kill it; I just wanted to protect my livestock[1509]. However, without harm from their natural enemy[1510], my sheep had a wonderful night.

ⓘ break into 強行進入某處、闖空門

ⓘ stay awake 保持清醒

中譯 *Translation*

　　我家的後院有養山羊和綿羊，綿羊可以生產價值不菲的羊毛。最近，我發現羊隻身上有傷口，木製的柵欄也被破壞，我想知道誰敢闖進我的院子，傷害我的綿羊。我的青春歲月都在這裡度過，我父母過世之後，我就一直在這裡生活，在這塊田工作。我很確定我農舍的十五英里之內，沒有任何鄰居。我整夜沒睡，想看看到底是誰闖進我的庭院而沒有被發現。結果我發現原來是一匹野狼做的，便設下陷阱捉牠，隔天，野狼就被抓住了。我不知道要怎麼處置牠，就把牠丟在那裡，幾天之後，牠就餓死了。事實上，我並不想殺牠，我只想保護我的家畜而已。然而，少了天敵的危害，我的綿羊們度過了美好的一夜。

1501 farm

[fɑrm] ★★★★
名 農場、畜牧場、農家
動 耕作、務農
片 farm out 出租(土地)

1502 produce

[prə`djus] ★★★★★
動 生產、製造、創作、上映、引起
衍 stock 家畜、貯存

1503 wound

[wund] ★★★★
名 傷口、傷疤、創傷
動 受傷、傷害
片 flesh wound 皮肉傷

1504 wooden

[`wudn̩] ★★★
形 木製的、呆板的、僵硬的
同 stiff 僵硬的

1505 dare

[dɛr] ★★★★
動 膽敢、敢於面對
名 果敢行為、挑戰
片 I dare say 我敢説

1506 pretty

[`prɪtɪ] ★★★★★
副 相當、頗、非常
形 漂亮的、悦耳的
片 pretty well 幾乎

1507 yard

[jɑrd] ★★★★
名 庭院、天井、碼
同 court 庭院
衍 backyard 後院

1508 starve

[stɑrv] ★★★★
動 挨餓、餓死、渴望
同 hunger 挨餓
片 starve for 渴望得到

1509 livestock

[`laɪv,stɑk] ★★★
名 (總稱)家畜、牲畜
同 cattle 家畜
衍 production 生產

1510 enemy

[`ɛnəmɪ] ★★★★
名 敵人、敵軍、危害物
形 敵人的、敵方的
同 opponent 對手

1511 weed

[wid] ★★★
名 雜草、廢物
動 除雜草、清除、淘汰
片 weed out 清除

1512 strip

[strɪp] ★★★★
名 條、細長片、連環漫畫
動 剝去、掠奪、脱去衣服
片 strip down 拆開

Fighting!

Give it a shot 小試身手

1 The _____ was overgrown with weeds[1511].

2 The black and white strips[1512] on the _____ are very funny.

3 She tried to stop the flow of blood from the injured man's _____.

4 This interesting topic is _____ further discussion.

5 Our budget was limited _____ five thousand dollars.

Answers: 1 yard 2 zebras 3 wound 4 worth 5 within

MP3　短文 253　字彙 254

Essay

127

Peter was a man full of adventure[1513]. He also had advanced ideas regarding his job and life plans. His part-time job involved performing acrobatics[1514]. He tried his best to make every performance he did perfect. He believed that his perfectionism[1515] was the main reason that a lot of fans admired[1516] him so much. He was also very aware[1517] of the danger he might confront during the performances.

One day, he got an opportunity to do some performances on a ship. He carefully looked through the contract and saw that the terms were very favorable[1518] and that he would even be paid in advance. It was very attractive to him. However, there was a special condition that demanded that he perform no matter what aches he was experiencing or accidents[1519] happened during the performances. Peter thought it was acceptable and suggested that the boss remit[1520] the money to his account promptly[1521] before the performance started. The boss accepted his suggestion[1522] and promised he would do that. From that work and many other jobs, Peter really earned a fortune from his special skill.

中譯 *Translation*

彼得是一個充滿冒險精神的人。他也把這種精神發揮在他的工作及人生規劃上。雜技表演是他的兼職工作，他在表演上力求完美。他相信他的支持者會如此的仰慕他，是因為他能呈現完美的演出。他也明白表演過程中可能面臨的危險。

有一天，他獲得一個在船上演出的機會。他仔細地看了合約，發現合約內容對他十分有利，而且他能事先收到酬勞。這對他非常有吸引力。然而，附加條件是，表演過程中無論感到疼痛、不適或發生任何意外，都必須繼續演出。彼得覺得可以接受，並請老闆在表演開始之前，立即將款項匯至他的戶頭。老闆採納了他的的提議，也保證他會做到。彼得藉著優異的表演才能，從這次的演出機會及其他表演中賺得大筆財富。

1513 **adventure**

[əd`vɛntʃə] ★★★★

名 冒險、奇遇、投機活動

動 冒險去做、大膽說出

同 venture 冒險

1514 **acrobatics**

[ˌækrə`bætɪks] ★★

名 雜技表演、巧妙手法、特技飛行

1515 **perfectionism**

[pə`fɛkʃənɪzəm] ★★

名 完滿主義、圓滿論

衍 perfectionist 完美主義者

1516 **admire**

[əd`maɪr] ★★★★

動 欽佩、欣賞、稱讚

反 dishonor 侮辱

片 admire for 因…而稱讚

1517 **aware**

[ə`wɛr] ★★★★

形 知道的、察覺的、閱歷深的

片 aware of 明白

1518 **favorable**

[`fevərəbl̩] ★★★

形 有利的、贊同的、討人喜歡的

反 adverse 有害的

1519 **accident**

[`æksədənt] ★★★★

名 意外、事故、災禍

同 mishap 災難

片 by accident 偶然地

1520 **remit**

[rɪ`mɪt] ★★★

動 匯款、免除、移交、寬恕、緩和

片 remit to 提交、移交

1521 **promptly**

[`pramptlɪ] ★★

副 立即地、敏捷地、正好

同 directly 馬上

衍 prompt 迅速的

1522 **suggestion**

[sə`dʒɛstʃən] ★★★★

名 建議、聯想、暗示

片 open to suggestions 願意聽取意見

1523 **lest**

[lɛst] ★★★

連 唯恐、擔心、免得

同 for fear that 以免

1524 **orphan**

[`ɔrfən] ★★★

名 孤兒

形 無雙親的、孤兒的

衍 orphanage 孤兒院

Fighting!

Give it a shot 小試身手

1 We finally went _____ before it rained.

2 Do you know the _____ answer to the math question?

3 She likes indoor _____ lest[1523] she should get a suntan.

4 The couple _____ the poor orphan[1524].

5 Make the best use of your _____.

Answers: 1 aboard 2 accurate 3 activities 4 adopted 5 advantages

128

MP3   短文 255   字彙 256

Essay

A high school team tried to teach other students traditional agriculture[1525] in Taiwan. After much discussion, the school announced that they would make a short film as an advertisement to broadcast nationwide[1526]. The school also asked a consultant from an advertising agency[1527] to give them professional advice. He advised[1528] the school to start from an angle[1529] that showed Taiwan's agricultural development from the early stages to the present methods. However, the school's budget could not afford such a high expense. Therefore, the school representative tried to persuade the advertising agency to cut its price. The agency was so impressed by their ambition and agreed[1530] to the reduced price. The school representative was amazed and described[1531] the head of this agency as an angel who came from Heaven. "Agriculture is never really separate from our daily lives." The principal said, "Agriculture is everywhere, even down a narrow[1532] alley[1533] in your neighborhood. I will invite ambassadors[1534] from other countries to our school in the future."

中譯 *Translation*

　　一個高中團隊試圖教導台灣學生傳統農耕學。經過數次討論後，學校宣布他們將拍一部宣傳短片進行全國推廣。

　　學校還請來廣告公司的顧問提供專業建議。顧問提議從能呈現台灣早期農耕階段至近代發展歷程的視角開始。然而高額的開銷超出了學校的預算，因此學校代表試圖說服廣告公司降價。廣告公司被他們的理想抱負所感動，因此同意降價。學校代表感到非常吃驚，他把廣告公司領導人描述成天上下凡的天使。「農業與我們的生活一直以來都是密不可分。」校長說：「農業無所不在，甚至是在狹窄的街坊巷弄。未來，我將邀請來自其他國家的大使們參訪我們學校。」

1525 agriculture

[`ægrɪkʌltʃə] ★★★
- 名 農業、農耕、農學
- 同 cultivation 耕種
- 衍 agricultural 農業的

1526 nationwide

[`neʃənwaɪd] ★★★
- 副 在全國
- 形 全國性的、全國各地的
- 同 nationally 全國性地

1527 agency

[`edʒənsɪ] ★★★★
- 名 仲介、代辦處、作用
- 片 through the agency of 在…幹旋下

1528 advise

[əd`vaɪz] ★★★★
- 動 建議、勸告、通知
- 同 counsel 勸告、提議
- 片 advise with 和…商量

1529 angle

[`æŋgl̩] ★★★★
- 名 角度、立場、觀點
- 動 使帶某種傾向、歪曲
- 片 angle for 謀取

1530 agree

[ə`gri] ★★★★★
- 動 意見一致、贊同、相符
- 反 disagree 不符
- 片 agree to 同意…

1531 describe

[dɪ`skraɪb] ★★★★
- 動 形容、描述、描繪
- 片 describe as 把…說成
- 衍 description 描寫

1532 narrow

[`næro] ★★★★
- 形 狹窄的、心胸狹窄的、勉強的
- 動 變窄、減少

1533 alley

[`ælɪ] ★★
- 名 小巷、胡同
- 片 blind alley 沒前途的職業

1534 ambassador

[æm`bæsədə] ★★★
- 名 大使、使節
- 片 ambassador to 駐…的使節

1535 emphasize

[`ɛmfəsaɪz] ★★★★
- 動 強調、著重、加強語氣
- 同 stress 強調
- 衍 emphasis 強調

1536 embassy

[`ɛmbəsɪ] ★★★
- 名 大使館、全體外交官
- 同 consulate 領事館

Fighting!

Give it a shot 小試身手

1. The government emphasized[1535] on the development of _____.
2. You can apply for the position and hand in your resume _____.
3. It has always been his _____ to become an engineer.
4. An _____ lives and works in an embassy[1536].
5. My brother _____ me to quit the current job.

129

Essay

An athlete should possess a firm[1537] goal in life and diligent attitude toward his or her career[1538]. That is, he or she needs to know how to perform best to <u>appeal to</u> the audiences who pay money to sit in stadiums[1539] to watch him or her play. If athletes do this, fans will appreciate and support them fully. It's common to hear coaches joke with players, "You don't need to be good at arithmetic[1540]. However, you have to learn how to win over the fans when you are in a stadium." In addition to having the support of fans, athletes also need to improve themselves by attempting[1541] to overcome challenges[1542]. For most audiences, an athlete with great ambition is someone they admire a lot. If athletes <u>keep these things in mind</u>, they will become very popular and successful. On the other hand, lazy[1543] athletes who don't have passion for their sport will be hated[1544] by fans[1545].

(!) apeal to 有吸引力、呼籲、訴諸

(!) keep something in mind/ keep in mind that 記住

中譯 *Translation*

　　一個運動員應該擁有堅決的人生目標，並且以勤奮的態度去面對他(她)的職業生涯。換言之，他(她)必須知道如何呈現最好的一面來吸引坐在運動場邊的觀眾。如果運動員熟知此道，觀眾將報以充分賞識與支持。教練常會和選手開玩笑說：「你不必擅長算術，但是，你必須學習如何在場上贏得大眾的目光。」除了獲得粉絲支持，運動員也要試圖克服挑戰，以求進步。對於大多數的觀眾來說，一個有強烈企圖心的運動員是非常令人景仰的。如果運動員能將這些事情謹記在心，他們將會變得非常受歡迎、非常成功。

　　反之，對運動沒有熱情的運動員則會招致觀眾的厭惡。

1537 firm

[fɝm] ★★★★
形 堅定的、穩固的
動 使穩固、變堅實
名 商號、公司

1538 career

[kə`rɪr] ★★★★★
名 職業、生涯、歷程
形 職業的、專業的
同 vocation 職業

1539 stadium

[`stedɪəm] ★★★★
名 體育場、球場、競技場
同 gym 體育館

1540 arithmetic

[ə`rɪθmətɪk] ★★★
名 算數、算術知識、估計
片 mental arithmetic 心算

1541 attempt

[ə`tɛmpt] ★★★★
動 企圖、試圖做
名 企圖、嘗試、攻擊
片 attempt to 試圖去

1542 challenge

[`tʃælɪndʒ] ★★★★
名 挑戰、艱鉅的事、盤問
動 向…挑戰、反對、激發
片 challenge to 挑戰…

1543 lazy

[`lezɪ] ★★★
形 懶散的、怠惰的
同 idle 懶惰的
反 diligent 勤奮的

1544 hate

[het] ★★★★
動 嫌惡、不喜歡、憎恨
名 憎恨、厭惡、反感
片 hate to 不喜歡、抱歉

1545 fan

[fæn] ★★★★
名 迷、風扇、螺旋槳
動 煽動、激起、吹拂
片 fan out 分散

1546 center

[`sɛntɚ] ★★★★★
名 中心、中樞
動 集中、居中
片 center on 集中在

1547 discover

[dɪs`kʌvɚ] ★★★★
動 發現、找到、發覺
同 detect 察覺
片 discover that 發現

1548 wink

[wɪŋk] ★★★
名 眨眼、閃爍、瞬間
動 眨眼、故意忽視、閃爍
片 wink at 使眼色

Fighting!

Give it a shot 小試身手

1 It was _____ that they fell in love with each other.

2 The customer service center[1546] held a good _____.

3 His speech attracted a large _____.

4 They _____ to discover[1547] the truth.

5 If anyone _____, please give me a wink[1548].

Essay 130

MP3 短文 259 字彙 260

There was a famous author[1549] who had a diverse[1550] and interesting background. He was awarded literature prizes five times per[1551] year on average. His books were available in most libraries. His favorite passion, <u>though</u>, was driving his car. He had a cool sports car with many great options.

One day, he was eating a bacon[1552] cheeseburger while driving on Fifth Avenue[1553]. For some reason, he had a strange[1554] feeling that something bad was going to happen that day. He turned out to be right. In the blink[1555] of an eye, a woman playing badminton rushed out onto the street and the writer couldn't help but hit her with his car despite slamming[1556] on the brakes.

The woman was rushed to hospital by ambulance and the writer also followed in his car. At the hospital, the woman's condition worsened due to an infection[1557]. The author wondered if he would have been able to stop if he hadn't been eating the bacon cheeseburger. A policeman came into the hospital room and said he wanted to ask the writer some questions. The author wondered if he should tell the officer[1558] he had been eating while driving. What would you do?

中譯 *Translation*

　　有一位背景多元又有趣的的名作家。他平均一年得到五次文學獎，他的書在大部份的圖書館都能找到。然而，他最大的興趣是開著他的愛車。他有一台功能多元的酷炫跑車。

　　有一天，他在第五大道上，邊開車邊吃著培根起司漢堡。他莫名的感到不祥之事即將發生。他的預感果然成真了。一眨眼間，一名正在打羽毛球的婦人突然衝到街上，儘管作家猛踩煞車，仍躲避不及撞上婦人。婦人被救護車緊急送醫，而作家也開車尾隨在後。到了醫院，婦人的情況因傷口感染而惡化。作家心想，如果他沒有邊開車邊吃培根起司漢堡，也許就能阻止悲劇發生。一名警察走進病房，並表示想問作家一些問題。作家想，是否應該告訴警察自己邊開車邊吃東西？如果是你，你會怎麼做？

1549 author

[ˋɔθɚ] ★★★★
名 作家、創辦者
動 創作、寫作
同 writer 作家

1550 diverse

[daɪˋvɝs] ★★★★
形 不同的、多變化的
同 various 不同的
衍 diversity 多樣性

1551 per

[pɚ] ★★★★★
介 每、按照、經
片 per head 每人

1552 bacon

[ˋbekən] ★★★
名 培根、鹹豬肉
片 bring home the bacon
養家糊口

1553 avenue

[ˋævənju] ★★★
名 大街、大道、方法
同 boulevard 林蔭大道
片 avenue to …的途徑

1554 strange

[strendʒ] ★★★★
形 奇怪的、不熟悉的、外行的
反 familiar 熟悉的

1555 blink

[blɪŋk] ★★★
名 一瞬間、眨眼睛
動 閃爍、眨眼睛、視而不見、躲避

1556 slam

[slæm] ★★★
動 猛撞、猛地關上、猛烈抨擊
名 砰然聲、猛烈的抨擊

1557 infection

[ɪnˋfɛkʃən] ★★★
名 感染、傳染、影響
同 contagion 感染
衍 infect 感染、影響

1558 officer

[ˋɔfəsɚ] ★★★★
名 警官、官員、高級職員
動 指揮、統率
片 police officer 警員

1559 bracelet

[ˋbreslɪt] ★★
名 手鐲
同 bangle 手鐲
片 jade bracelet 玉鐲

1560 masterpiece

[ˋmæstɚpis] ★★★
名 傑作、名作、代表作
同 masterwork 傑作
衍 master 大師、能手

Give it a shot 小試身手

fighting!

1 My grandmother gave me a bracelet[1559] as an _____.

2 The _____ score of the class is eighty.

3 She was _____ to the importance of social skill.

4 These kinds of suits are _____ in any store.

5 I wonder who the _____ is of this masterpiece[1560].

Answers: 1 award 2 average 3 awakened 4 available 5 author

MP3　短文 261　字彙 262

131

Essay

Peter was surprised to learn that he had been chosen to participate in a unique competition. He and several other contestants[1561] were transported to an isolated island where they learned that the island was occupied[1562] by a large variety[1563] of animals, but none of the creatures were dangerous. In this strange contest[1564], the winner would be the one who could kiss the most animals. The island had a barn for participants to eat in and sleep in. All the participants had the bare necessities[1565] of life. The contestants were all allowed to choose from different types of bait[1566] they could use to lure[1567] the animals close enough to them to be kissed. Peter soon spotted[1568] a horse near the entrance to a forest, and he carefully approached it, but the animal kicked him in the belly. Peter struggled to go back to the barn[1569] and then took out a bandage[1570] beneath[1571] his seat. He wrapped[1572] his wound and tried to stand up. Unfortunately, he lost his balance and fell. He had to quit the competition and go home for he could barely walk. It took a little while for Peter to recover fully, but he finally did. When the show appeared on TV, Peter was like a celebrity to his friends. A lot of people felt sorry for him because he had been hurt so badly. They all treated him nicely and bought things for him. So, in the end, Peter was a winner after all!

中譯 *Translation*

　　彼得得知自己被選上參加特殊競賽時非常驚訝。他和其他幾位參賽者被送至一座孤島，他們得知島上有各式各樣的生物，卻都不具危險性。在這個奇特競賽中，能親吻到最多動物的人就是贏家。島上有個大穀倉供參賽者吃飯及睡覺，每位參賽者所擁有的僅僅是生活必需品而已。參賽者能從各式各樣的誘餌中選擇他們所需，以引誘動物靠近並親吻他們。彼得很快便在森林入口處附近發現一匹馬，他小心翼翼地接近牠，卻被那匹馬踢中了肚子。彼得掙扎著走回穀倉，從他的座位下拿出繃帶。他包紮傷口並試圖站起。不幸的是，他失去平衡跌倒了。由於他幾乎無法行走，只好放棄比賽，打包回家。彼得花了一些時間才完全康復，但他終究還是痊癒了。當比賽在電視上播出，彼得的朋友都把他視為名人。很多人為他的嚴重傷勢感到遺憾，他們都對他很好，還帶了東西給他。最終，彼得也算是一名贏家了！

1561 contestant

[kən`tɛstənt] ★★
- 名 參加競賽者、角逐者
- 同 competitor 競爭者
- 衍 contest 競賽

1562 occupy

[`ɑkjəpaɪ] ★★★★
- 動 佔據、使忙碌、擔任
- 片 be occupied in 忙於
- 衍 occupation 工作

1563 variety

[və`raɪətɪ] ★★★★
- 名 種類、多樣化
- 反 monotony 單調
- 片 a variety of 各式各樣

1564 contest

[`kɑntɛst] ★★★★
- 名 競賽、爭奪、爭論
- 動 競爭、角逐、提出質疑
- 同 competition 競賽

1565 necessity

[nə`sɛsətɪ] ★★★
- 名 必需品、必要性、貧窮
- 片 of necessity 必然
- 衍 necessary 必要的

1566 bait

[bet] ★★★
- 名 誘餌、圈套
- 動 引誘、置餌於
- 片 take the bait 上鉤

1567 lure

[lʊr] ★★★
- 動 引誘、誘惑
- 名 誘惑力、吸引力、誘餌
- 片 lure to 引誘至

1568 spot

[spɑt] ★★★★
- 動 發現、認出、弄髒、玷污
- 名 斑點、汙漬、地點

1569 barn

[barn] ★★★★
- 名 穀倉、糧倉、大車庫

1570 bandage

[`bændɪdʒ] ★★★
- 名 繃帶
- 動 用繃帶包紮
- 同 dressing 包紮用品

1571 beneath

[bɪ`niθ] ★★★★
- 介 在…下面、低於
- 副 在下、向下、較低
- 同 below 在…下面

1572 wrap

[ræp] ★★★★
- 動 包起來、覆蓋、纏繞
- 名 覆蓋物、披肩
- 片 wrap up 包好

fighting!

Give it a shot 小試身手

1 The child couldn't keep his _____ on the bicycle.

2 The food at the hotel was _____ edible.

3 We _____ according to customs in our culture.

4 The _____ dance performance really attracts me.

5 They found a letter buried _____ a pile of leaves.

Answers: 1 balance 2 barely 3 behave 4 belly 5 beneath

132

Essay

MP3
短文 263　字彙 264

Tom was addicted to gambling[1573] and lost a lot of money. His wife criticized him so much and divorced him. He had to beg people for food to survive. Such a poor life bored[1574] him greatly.

One day, he heard news that a factory near the border[1575] produced a million tons of brass[1576] each year. Even though he was poor and hungry, he desperately wanted to gamble once again. Tom drove to the factory and tried to ram[1577] the gate, but it was too strong. The guard at the plant pointed a gun at Tom and told him to get out of his car. Tom shot him in the stomach. The guard then shot back at Tom, hitting[1578] him in the neck. Both Tom and the guard were bleeding[1579] badly. Soon, the guard died, and shortly afterwards, Tom was dead, too. The guard is remembered as a brave[1580] person who died tragically[1581]. A plaque[1582] was put up at the factory to honor[1583] and remember him. Tom, on the other hand, is remembered as a murderer[1584] who got what he deserved.

中譯 *Translation*

　　湯姆沉迷於賭博，而且輸了很多錢。他的妻子狠狠的責怪他，跟他離婚了。他得跟人們討食物吃才活得下去，如此貧困的生活讓他感到非常厭煩。

　　有一天，他聽說邊境的工廠每年生產百萬噸的黃銅。即使他又窮又餓，他仍不顧一切地再次回去賭博。湯姆開車到工廠，並且試圖衝撞大門，但門實在太過堅固了。工廠警衛把槍口對準湯姆，並叫他下車。湯姆朝警衛的肚子開槍。警衛也朝湯姆回開了一槍，射中他的頸部。湯姆和警衛兩人都失血過多。很快地，這名警衛死了，不久之後，湯姆也斷氣了。這名警衛以壯烈犧牲的英勇形象為世人所懷念。工廠立了匾額以示尊敬和紀念。另一方面，湯姆則是以罪有應得的殺人犯為後人所記。

1573 gambling

[`gæmblɪŋ] ★★

名 賭博
同 betting 賭博
衍 gambler 賭徒

1574 bore

[bor] ★★★

動 使厭煩、煩擾、鑽孔
名 令人討厭的人或事物
同 irk 使厭倦

1575 border

[`bɔrdɚ] ★★★★

名 邊境、國界、邊緣
動 與⋯接壤、毗鄰、近似
片 border on 與⋯接壤

1576 brass

[bræs] ★★★

名 黃銅、黃銅色、銅器、銅管樂器
形 黃銅製的、聲音嘹亮的

1577 ram

[ræm] ★★★★

動 猛撞、硬塞、迫使接受
名 公羊
片 ram sth. home 塞滿

1578 hit

[hɪt] ★★★★★

動 擊中、碰撞、達到、說中、抨擊
名 擊中、風靡一時的事物

1579 bleed

[blid] ★★★★

動 流血、犧牲、榨取
片 bleed profusely 血流如注

1580 brave

[brev] ★★★★

形 英勇的、壯觀的
動 勇敢面對
同 bold 英勇的

1581 tragically

[`trædʒɪklɪ] ★★

副 悲慘地、不幸地
同 sadly 不幸
衍 tragic 悲劇的

1582 plaque

[plæk] ★★

名 匾牌、徽章、牙斑
片 commemorative plaque 紀念牌匾

1583 honor

[`ɑnɚ] ★★★

動 尊敬、使增光、實踐
名 光榮、信用、敬意
片 word of honor 諾言

1584 murderer

[`mɝdərɚ] ★★

名 謀殺犯、兇手
同 criminal 罪犯
衍 murderous 兇殘的

fighting!

Give it a shot 小試身手

1. Sarah felt depressed after being _____ by the tutor.
2. The trees were planted along the _____.
3. We promised the mutual _____ for both sides.
4. Girls with long legs look pretty in _____.
5. He received an award for his _____.

Answers: 1 blamed 2 border 3 benefits 4 boots 5 bravery

MP3　短文 265　字彙 266

133

Essay

A bride[1585] was holding her wedding ceremony[1586] in the backyard of her house because of her limited budget. Her backyard had a brook[1587] nearby[1588], which provided a great atmosphere for a wedding. The guests saw beautiful bubbles[1589] when they cast[1590] stones into the brook. She also provided a buffet[1591] and several different types of <u>beverages</u>. The weather was fantastic[1592]. A gentle breeze carried the attractive scent[1593] of peach flowers that were blossoming.

Suddenly, a bull ran from my neighbor's farm and crashed through the bride's fence. Everyone was shocked. The brilliant[1594] bride took a gun from her house and shot the bull in the chest with a tranquilizer[1595] dart[1596]. The bull fell down and began breathing slowly. They <u>went on</u> with their happy banquet after that frightening incident.

(!) beverage 飲料

(!) go on 繼續

中譯 *Translation*

有位新娘因為預算有限，在家裡後院舉行婚禮。她的後院旁有條小溪，絕佳的氣氛非常適合婚禮。賓客們丟石頭到溪裡時，可以看到漂亮的泡泡。她還提供自助餐點和各式飲料。天氣非常怡人。從輕柔的微風中可以嗅出正盛開的桃花的誘人香氣。

突然間，有隻公牛從隔壁農場奔來，撞毀了新娘家的籬笆。每個人都嚇到了。這位聰穎的新娘從家裡拿了槍，然後朝公牛胸口射了一彈鎮定劑。公牛倒下了，呼吸開始變得緩慢。這個驚險插曲過後，他們開心地繼續著宴會。

1585 bride

[braɪd] ★★★
名 新娘
反 bridegroom 新郎
衍 bridesmaid 伴娘

1586 ceremony

[`sɛrəmonɪ] ★★★
名 典禮、禮儀、客套
片 without ceremony 不拘禮節地

1587 brook

[bruk] ★★★
名 小溪、小河
動 容忍、容許
同 endure 忍受

1588 nearby

[`nɪrbaɪ] ★★★★
形 附近的
副 在附近
反 faraway 遙遠的

1589 bubble

[`bʌbl] ★★★★
名 氣泡、泡影
動 沸騰、冒泡、情緒高漲
片 bubble gum 泡泡糖

1590 cast

[kæst] ★★★★
動 投擲、投射、丟棄
名 投擲、演員陣容、氣質
片 cast light on 弄清楚

1591 buffet

[bu`fe] ★★★
名 自助餐、快餐
動 連續衝擊、打擊
片 buffet car 火車內餐室

1592 fantastic

[fæn`tæstɪk] ★★★
形 極好的、驚人的、不現實的、古怪的
同 odd 古怪的

1593 scent

[sɛnt] ★★★
名 氣味、香味、線索、察覺能力
動 嗅出、察覺、散發氣味

1594 brilliant

[`brɪljənt] ★★★★
形 優秀的、技藝高超的、明亮的
反 gloomy 陰鬱的

1595 tranquilizer

[`træŋkwɪlaɪzə] ★
名 鎮定劑
衍 tranquilize 平靜、鎮定

1596 dart

[dɑrt] ★★★
名 飛鏢、標槍、飛奔
動 投擲、投射、狂奔
片 dart a glance 瞥一眼

Fighting!

Give it a shot 小試身手

1 The child blew _____ happily.

2 It is essential for a company to balance its _____.

3 Dinner will be a cold _____, not a sit-down meal.

4 I've talked for one hour; let me take a _____.

5 Vicky received a _____ of flowers from her admirer.

134

Now

🎧 MP3   短文 267   字彙 268

Essay

I remember being involved in a play at the university I attended. The main cast was formed by several of us students who were good at acting[1597]. At the beginning of the play, a group of reporters, wearing casual[1598] clothes, took an airplane to a mysterious village. The locals held[1599] a ceremony to celebrate the anniversary[1600] of the first village head's birth[1601]. They asked a carpenter to fix the broken carriage[1602] in order to transport sacrificial[1603] offerings[1604] to the first village head's monument[1605]. They carried sugar cane, rice wine, and drove cattle they had captured from the bush for worship. The village head's monument was at the top of the canyon[1606]. The locals took out sacrificial offerings and buried[1607] animals in front of the monument. They explained to the reporters that it was one of the important steps in the ceremony. The play was like a documentary[1608] film about traditional customs and was highly praised. The other students and I originally thought it was a heavy burden to perform it at first, but the excellent results showed it was worth it.

中譯 *Translation*

　　我記得大學時曾經參與一場戲劇演出。主要的演員陣容是由幾位富有表演天分的學生所組成。表演一開始，一群穿著休閒服裝的記者搭乘飛機，抵達一個神祕的村莊。村民們舉行儀式慶祝第一任村長的誕辰。村民們為了將供品運送到村長的紀念碑，請了木匠把壞掉的馬車修好。他們帶了甘蔗、米酒，還有從灌木叢裡捕獲的牲畜來祭祀。這位村長的紀念碑在峽谷的頂端。村民們拿出祭品，把牲畜埋在石碑前。他們告訴記者這是儀式當中一個重要的程序。這齣戲可說是一部關於傳統習俗的紀錄片，而且獲得高度肯定。學生們一開始覺得這是個沉重的負擔，但是結果證明一切都是值得的。

1597 act

[ækt] ★★★★★
- 動 演戲、行動、見效、裝出、舉止
- 名 行動、法案、裝腔作勢

1598 casual

[ˋkæʒʊəl] ★★★★
- 形 便裝的、漫不經心的、碰巧的
- 反 planned 有計畫的

1599 hold

[hold] ★★★★★
- 動 舉行、抓住、支撐、抑制、擁有
- 名 握住、支撐、耽擱

1600 anniversary

[ænəˋvɝsɪrɪ] ★★★
- 名 週年紀念日、結婚周年
- 形 週年紀念的

1601 birth

[bɝθ] ★★★
- 名 出生、血統、誕生
- 反 death 死亡
- 片 give birth to 生、產生

1602 carriage

[ˋkærɪdʒ] ★★★
- 名 四輪馬車、火車車廂、運費
- 片 baby carriage 嬰兒車

1603 sacrificial

[sækrəˋfɪʃəl] ★★
- 形 獻祭的、犧牲的
- 衍 sacrifice 犧牲、獻出

1604 offering

[ˋɔfərɪŋ] ★★
- 名 祭品、提供、貢獻
- 同 oblation 奉獻物
- 衍 offer 提供、貢獻

1605 monument

[ˋmɑnjumənt] ★★★
- 名 紀念碑、遺跡、不朽的作品
- 同 memorial 紀念碑

1606 canyon

[ˋkænjən] ★★
- 名 峽谷
- 片 the Grand Canyon 美國大峽谷

1607 bury

[ˋbɛrɪ] ★★★★
- 動 埋葬、掩藏、使沉浸
- 同 conceal 隱藏
- 片 bury in 把⋯埋入

1608 documentary

[dɑkjəˋmɛntərɪ] ★
- 形 記錄的、記實的、依據文件的
- 名 記錄影片

fighting!

Give it a shot 小試身手

1 You can ride a bike in our _____.

2 The _____ of Australia is Canberra.

3 We hired a _____ to fix our wooden bookshelf.

4 She can get a higher pay for she is _____ of translating.

5 My old parents are my sweet _____.

Answers: 1 campus 2 capital 3 carpenter 4 capable 5 burdens

MP3　短文 269　字彙 270

Essay

135

I recall[1609] several memories[1610] of good times we had together during our childhood. Do you still remember? One chilly day, we were watching TV together, huddled[1611] next to a heater. Later, we challenged each other to a debate. The winner could eat the fresh cherries our mother had bought. You won the contest and wore a cheerful[1612] smile. Sometimes, we stayed up all night just chatting[1613] with each other. You lay on my chest, talking about everything, from baseball games to gossip[1614] about friends. We cheered[1615] when the baseball team we supported won. We also liked to take a bottle of beer and cheesecake from the kitchen and share them with each other. We were worried about our parents finding out we had been drinking because of our red cheeks[1616]. I am charmed[1617] by those interesting memories whenever I think of them. Now, we have grown up. It is time for us to make future plans for our lives. Those childhood memories remind us of one of the most wonderful chapters[1618] in our lives.

中譯 *Translation*

　　我回想起童年時期我們共有的美好時光。你還記得嗎？那一天天氣很冷，我們一起窩在暖爐旁邊看電視。之後我們比賽辯論，優勝者可以吃到媽媽買回來的新鮮櫻桃。你贏了比賽，臉上掛著愉快的笑容。有時候，我們徹夜閒談。你躺在我的胸膛上，我們天南地北地聊著，從棒球比賽聊到朋友的八卦。每當我們支持的球隊贏了，我們都會興高采烈地歡呼。還有，我們會從廚房拿一瓶啤酒和起司蛋糕分著吃。我們很怕父母看到我們紅潤的臉頰後，會發現我們偷喝酒。每當我想起這些有趣的回憶都會陶醉其中。現在我們長大了，是認真思考人生規劃的時候了。那些兒時回憶將會成為我們人生中一個美好的章節。

1609 recall

[rɪ`kɔl] ★★★★
- 動 回想、召回、取消、使恢復
- 片 recall + ving 憶起

1610 memory

[`mɛmərɪ] ★★★★★
- 名 記憶、紀念、記憶體
- 片 in memory of 對…的紀念

1611 huddle

[`hʌdl̩] ★★
- 動 聚在一起、縮成一團、倉促完成
- 名 雜亂的一堆

1612 cheerful

[`tʃɪrfəl] ★★★
- 形 興高采烈的、令人愉快的、樂意的
- 同 cheery 興高采烈的

1613 chat

[tʃæt] ★★★★★
- 動 聊天、閒談
- 名 閒談、聊天
- 片 chat with/to 與…閒聊

1614 gossip

[`gasəp] ★★★★
- 動 說長道短、說閒話
- 名 流言蜚語、閒話
- 同 chat 閒聊

1615 cheer

[tʃɪr] ★★★
- 動 歡呼、喝采、感到振奮
- 名 歡呼、振奮、鼓勵
- 片 cheer up 振作起來

1616 cheek

[tʃik] ★★★★
- 名 臉頰、腮幫子、厚臉皮
- 片 turn the other cheek 不反抗

1617 charm

[tʃɑrm] ★★★★
- 動 使陶醉、吸引
- 名 魅力、小飾物
- 片 charm with 對…陶醉

1618 chapter

[`tʃæptɚ] ★★★★
- 名 重要時期、章、回
- 動 把(書)分章節

1619 omit

[o`mɪt] ★★
- 動 省略、刪去、忘記
- 同 leave out 省略
- 片 omit from 從…中刪去

1620 sweater

[`swɛtɚ] ★★★
- 名 毛線衣、針織衫、大量出汗的人

---

fighting!

Give it a shot 小試身手

1 The editor suggested me omit[1619] the last _____.

2 Don't mention the sores in her _____.

3 Jane always _____ with her colleagues in working time.

4 I wore a sweater[1620] for it was _____ outside.

5 The documentary film would be broadcast on _____ 5.

Answers: **1** chapter **2** childhood **3** chats **4** chilly **5** Channel

136

Essay

There is a curio[1621] shop in town. Most of the classic[1622] collections in the shop are from people who have interesting occupations[1623]. For instance, the shop has a client[1624] who is a clown[1625] in a circus. One day, the circus gave a performance at a college. The clown showed students how to swallow a chip[1626] without injury, light a cigarette without a lighter[1627] or match, drink a cocktail without a straw with your hands behind your back, play a tune on coconuts with your hands and slide[1628] down a chimney like Santa Claus. The clown's special and funny performance was the big reason that this circus was so popular. However, an accident happened during the performance at the college. The clown's collar[1629] got hooked[1630] when he tried to slide down the chimney. He got stuck and even started choking[1631] badly while he was stuck in the chimney. Luckily, a worker was watching the performance and chopped[1632] at the chimney to get him out. Then the clown was sent to a clinic nearby right away. The doctor asked the worker many questions in order to find more about what had happened. Unfortunately, the clown died of his injuries and his circus life was over forever.

中譯 *Translation*

　　鎮上有間古董店，店裡最經典的收藏品都來自那些從事特殊職業的人。舉例來說，這家店的其中一位客戶是馬戲團的小丑。有一天馬戲團到了校園表演。小丑示範演出如何在不受傷的情況下吞下碎片，不用打火機點菸，雙手放背後、不用吸管就能喝酒，空手在椰子上彈奏一曲，學聖誕老人滑下煙囪。這個馬戲團會那麼受歡迎，正是因為小丑特別又滑稽的表演。然而，在演出時發生了意外。當小丑試圖溜過煙囪時，衣領被勾住了。他卡在煙囪裡動彈不得，幾乎要窒息了。幸好，有位工作人員發現了他，便把煙囪砍斷，將他救了出來。小丑馬上被送到附近的診所。醫生為了了解事情經過，問了工作人員很多問題。小丑不幸傷重不治，結束了他在馬戲團的表演生涯。

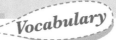
1621 curio

[`kjʊrɪo] ★
名 古董、珍品
衍 curiosity 好奇心、珍品、古玩

1622 classic

[`klæsɪk] ★★★
形 經典的、古典的、第一流的
名 經典著作、大文豪

1623 occupation

[akjə`peʃən] ★★★
名 職業、佔領時期、佔用
同 employment 工作、職業

1624 client

[`klaɪənt] ★★★★
名 客戶、委託人
同 customer 顧客

1625 clown

[klaun] ★★★★
名 小丑、丑角、無知的人
動 扮小丑、開玩笑、裝傻
同 buffoon 丑角

1626 chip

[tʃɪp] ★★★★
名 炸馬鈴薯片、碎片、瑕疵、瑣碎之物
動 削、剝落、插話

1627 lighter

[`laɪtə] ★★
名 打火機、點火器

1628 slide

[slaɪd] ★★★
動 滑落、滑行
名 滑行、下降、幻燈片
片 slide into 溜進

1629 collar

[`kɑlə] ★★★★
名 衣領、項圈
動 抓住、逮捕
片 in collar 在職

1630 hook

[huk] ★★★★
動 被鉤住、引人上鉤、欺騙
名 掛鉤、魚鉤、鐮刀

1631 choke

[tʃok] ★★★
動 窒息、堵塞、抑制
名 窒息、阻氣門
片 choke up 阻塞

1632 chop

[tʃɑp] ★★★★
動 砍、劈成、剁碎、削減
名 肋骨排、砍、切球
片 chop off 砍掉

---

fighting!

Give it a shot 小試身手

1 My father smokes five _____ a day.

2 The top _____ attracts most high school students.

3 We should try our best to persuade our _____.

4 I took my ill daughter to the _____.

5 The pipe is _____ up with rubbish.

137

Essay

MP3   短文 273   字彙 274

A number of professional pianists were ordered to carry out a command[1633] they received from the government. They needed to compete[1634] with other professional pianists from all over the world in a concert. They were under great pressure and therefore suffered from a lot of stress over this concert. They also couldn't understand why on Earth the government would possibly order them to do such a thing. They feared the competition was being held for some dastardly[1635] purpose. Because of their concerns[1636], they decided to ask for ridiculous[1637] conditions, hoping to make it too difficult for the concert to be held. For example, they asked the stage to be decorated with nine giant columns[1638] and to be decorated with every conceivable[1639] color. The government committee[1640] in charge of the concert heard of the pianists' demands and became very concerned. After communicating[1641] with those pianists, the committee comforted them and told them they didn't really have to perform in the concert if they didn't want to. Touched by this, the pianists decided to cooperate[1642] and all of them performed better than they ever had in the past. Thus, the concert was an outstanding[1643] success!

中譯 *Translation*

　　有一群專業的鋼琴家必須完成政府所下達的指令。他們要在一個演奏會跟來自世界各地的鋼琴高手一較高下。他們對此感到壓力很大,他們也無法理解為何政府會要求他們做這種事。他們害怕這場比賽是出於惡意而舉辦。出於擔憂,他們決定提出荒謬的要求,設法阻礙比賽的舉行。例如,他們要求以九根巨大的柱子、各式各樣的顏色裝飾舞台。負責此次競賽的政府委員會聽說了鋼琴家們的要求,非常擔憂。與鋼琴家們溝通之後,委員會安撫他們的情緒,並告訴他們,如果他們沒有意願表演,可以不用參加比賽。鋼琴家們被委員會所感動,決定配合演出,而他們這次的表演結果也比以往更精彩。因此,這次的演奏會可說是非常出色又成功!

1633 command

[kə`mænd] ★★★★
名 命令、指揮、掌握
動 命令、控制、博得
片 at command 自由使用

1634 compete

[kəm`pit] ★★★★
動 比賽、對抗、比得上
同 contend 競爭
片 compete with 競爭

1635 dastardly

[`dæstədlɪ] ★
形 殘酷的、懦弱的、卑鄙的、邪惡的
衍 dastard 懦夫

1636 concern

[kən`sɝn] ★★★★★
名 擔心、關係、關心的事
動 擔心、關心、涉及
片 of concern 重要的

1637 ridiculous

[rɪ`dɪkjələs] ★★★
形 可笑的、荒謬的
同 nonsensical 荒謬的
衍 ridicule 嘲笑

1638 column

[`kɑləm] ★★★★
名 圓柱、專欄、柱狀物、縱列、支柱
衍 columnist 專欄作家

1639 conceivable

[kən`sivəbl] ★★★
形 想得到的、可理解的
同 imaginable 能想像的
衍 conceive 想像

1640 committee

[kə`mɪtɪ] ★★★★
名 委員會、監護人
同 board 委員會

1641 communicate

[kə`mjunəket] ★★★★
動 溝通、表達、交流思想
同 convey 表達
片 communicate to 傳達

1642 cooperate

[ko`ɑpəret] ★★★
動 配合、合作
片 cooperate with 與…合作

1643 outstanding

[`aut`stændɪŋ] ★★★★
形 傑出的、凸出的、未完成的
同 eminent 卓越的

1644 zone

[zon] ★★★★
動 劃分為區、環繞
名 地區、氣候帶、範圍
片 zone off 與外界隔離

Fighting!

Give it a shot 小試身手

1. Anna decided to _____ the two departments together.
2. Diana's _____ was cancelled for the typhoon.
3. The downtown area is zoned[1644] for _____ use.
4. I will not follow his unreasonable _____.
5. They _____ with each other by cutting price.

Answers: 1 combine 2 concert 3 commercial 4 command 5 compete

138

Tom was a confident and resourceful[1645] businessman. No one knew that he had grown up in total poverty[1646]. He took long business trips every month because he had many international clients. However, after several years, he was tired of the frequent long-distance trips even though he made a considerable amount of money. One day, he got into a car crash on the way to the airport[1647]. He was injured and could not go on business trips[1648] for a couple of months. Upon[1649] arriving home after leaving the hospital, he lay on a couch and realized he didn't really like traveling on business at all anymore. He was confused and didn't know what to do. Suddenly, he saw a snail crawling[1650] on the floor, and it retreated[1651] into its shell when he touched it. He saw that as a sign that he should protect himself by quitting his job. Before he could resign[1652] from the job, though, he came to the conclusion[1653] that it would be foolish and cowardly[1654] to quit his job. Instead, he told his boss that he wanted to reduce the number of international clients he had and drastically[1655] cut back on his business traveling. Since Tom was such a great salesman, his boss agreed to his request.

中譯 *Translation*

　　湯姆是位充滿自信且足智多謀的生意人。但沒有人知道他其實是在貧困的環境中長大的。由於他有許多國外客戶，所以他每個月固定長途出差。然而，過了幾年，他對頻繁的長途出差感到厭倦，即使他因此賺了不少錢。有一天，他去機場途中發生車禍。因為受傷之故，他好幾個月都無法出差。出院後，他回到家，在沙發上躺下來。突然，他意識到自己不太喜歡因公事出差。

　　他對此感到困惑，而接下來要怎麼做他也毫無頭緒。突然間，他看到一隻在地上爬的蝸牛，他伸手一碰，蝸牛馬上縮回殼內。他把眼前的景象視為一種徵象，意味著他應辭職以保護自己。在付諸行動之前，他又覺得辭職是愚蠢、懦弱的行為。他告訴老闆，他想減少現有的國外客戶，以及大幅削減出差次數。由於湯姆是個出色的生意人，老闆便應准了他的請求。

1645 resourceful

[rɪ`sorsfəl] ★
- 形 機智的、資源豐富的
- 同 ingenious 足智多謀的
- 衍 resourceless 無機智的

1646 poverty

[`pɑvətɪ] ★★★★
- 名 貧困、貧乏、不毛
- 同 indigence 窮困
- 反 richness 富足

1647 airport

[`ɛrport] ★★★★
- 名 機場、航空站
- 衍 airline 航空公司、航線

1648 trip

[trɪp] ★★★★★
- 名 旅行、行程、失誤
- 動 旅行、絆倒、使失誤
- 片 take a trip 去旅行

1649 upon

[ə`pɑn] ★★★★★
- 介 在…後立即、在…上、根據、依靠
- 片 come upon 偶然遇到

1650 crawl

[krɔl] ★★
- 動 爬行、徐徐行進、充斥著、蔓生
- 片 crawl with 爬滿

1651 retreat

[rɪ`trit] ★★★
- 動 撤退、退縮、躲避
- 名 撤退、隱退處
- 片 retreat from 從…撤退

1652 resign

[rɪ`zaɪn] ★★★
- 動 辭去、放棄、順從
- 片 resign oneself to 順從
- 衍 resignation 辭呈

1653 conclusion

[kən`kluʒən] ★★★★
- 名 結論、結局、締結
- 片 jump to conclusions 草率下結論

1654 cowardly

[`kauədlɪ] ★
- 形 膽小的、懦弱的
- 同 craven 怯懦的
- 反 brave 英勇的

1655 drastically

[`dræstɪklɪ] ★
- 副 徹底地、激烈地
- 同 radically 徹底地
- 衍 drastic 激烈的

1656 network

[`nɛtwɝk] ★★★★★
- 名 網絡、網狀物、廣播網
- 動 用網覆蓋、通過…網絡播出

Fighting!

Give it a shot 小試身手

1. Please sign your name here after reading the _____.
2. The _____ of our networks[1656] was failed.
3. A girl was killed yesterday in a car _____.
4. Little babies need _____ attention.
5. Mozart was such a _____ musician.

Answers: 1 contract 2 connection 3 crash 4 constant 5 creative

139

MP3　短文 277　字彙 278

Essay

Ken Flannigan worked in a shop where all the employees came from the same cultural[1657] background, so they all got along very well with each other. They worked for a pet store that sold a large variety of animals. They loved their darling creatures so much, and that was the reason that they had worked there for such a long time. The store was located in a scenic[1658] area near a commercial[1659] port. One day, Ken and the other workers went out for lunch at a nice restaurant next to the sea. They spotted a group of very suspicious looking people on a ship docked[1660] in the harbor[1661]. They were talking loudly, and Ken and his fellow[1662] coworkers[1663] believed they were up to no good. So, they snuck on board to see what the suspicious people were doing. One of the sailors went to a cupboard[1664] on the deck and took some crickets[1665] out. For some reason, they were trying to put crickets into a dark bottle with some liquid[1666] inside. Ken and the other employees from the pet store dared not to move forward to stop what they were doing. They just left as soon as possible and went to the police to make a report. The policeman sighed and said the current slumping[1667] economy inevitably[1668] caused criminal behavior. The policeman said the men were probably using crickets as cheap ingredients so they could make more profit from selling the liquid to unsuspecting consumers.

中譯 *Translation*

　　Ken Flannigan 在一家店工作，而這間店的員工都來自相同的文化背景，所以彼此處得很好。他們在一間寵物店工作，這家店售有各類的動物。他們都熱愛動物，這也是為什麼他們會工作這麼久。這家店位在商港附近一個景色秀麗的地區。一天，肯和員工到海邊一家不錯的餐廳吃午餐。他們看到停靠在港口的一艘船上有一群看似可疑的人物。這些人講話很大聲，而肯和他的同事們認為他們圖謀不軌。因此，他們偷偷溜上船，要看這群可疑的傢伙在幹什麼勾當。其中一名水手到從甲板上的櫥櫃裡抓了幾隻蟋蟀出來。基於某些因素，他們試著將蟋蟀放在裝有些許液體的深色瓶子裡。肯和其他寵物店的員工不敢上前阻止他們。他們只是儘快地離開現場去報警。警察嘆了口氣說，由於經濟衰退，難免會有這種犯罪行為發生。他說這些人大概是想利用蟋蟀作為便宜的原料，藉由將這類液體賣給不疑有他的顧客，從中獲取更多利益。

1657 cultural

[`kʌltʃərəl] ★★★
形 文化的、修養的
片 cultural heritage 文化遺產

1658 scenic

[`sinɪk] ★★★
形 景色秀麗的、戲劇性的、描繪實景的
衍 scenery 風景

1659 commercial

[kə`mɝʃəl] ★★★★
形 商務的、商業的
片 commercial break 廣告時間

1660 dock

[dɑk] ★★★★
動 進港
名 碼頭、港區

1661 harbor

[`hɑrbɚ] ★★★★
名 海港、港灣、避風港
動 庇護、心懷、入港停泊
同 port 港口

1662 fellow

[`fɛlo] ★★★★
名 夥伴、同事、傢伙
形 同伴的、同事的
同 companion 同伴

1663 coworker

[`kowɝkɚ] ★★
名 同事、幫手
同 colleague 同事

1664 cupboard

[`kʌpbɚd] ★★★
名 櫥櫃、碗櫥
片 cupboard love 別有所圖的愛

1665 cricket

[`krɪkɪt] ★★★
名 蟋蟀、板球、光明正大
動 打板球
片 not cricket 不光明磊落

1666 liquid

[`lɪkwɪd] ★★★
名 液體
形 液態的、流動的、流暢的、不穩定的

1667 slump

[slʌmp] ★★★
動 下跌、衰弱、陷落
名 暴跌、不景氣、萎靡
片 slump to 跌落至

1668 inevitably

[ɪn`ɛvətəblɪ] ★★
副 必然地、不可避免地
同 unavoidably 不可避免地

Give it a shot 小試身手

fighting!

1 Whether the _____ should be put to death is undecided.

2 Your _____ limit is now 200 dollars.

3 The king wore the _____ at official ceremonies.

4 _____ difference caused their divorce.

5 The _____ headline was an air crash three hours ago.

Answers: 1 criminals 2 credit 3 crown 4 Cultural 5 current

140

MP3   短文 279   字彙 280

Essay

Tom lived in a democratic country. He was a diligent designer[1669] who worked very hard. Although he was on a diet in order to save money, he had a bad habit: excessive[1670] drinking. One day, he was drunk and sleeping soundly[1671] on the bed. He dreamed that a devil appeared in the dim[1672] light and told him, "You are trying to destroy[1673] your wonderful life because of excessive drinking. Drinking too much is not a noble[1674] deed[1675]. If you keep drinking like this, I will take all of the money out of your bank account." When he awakened, he had a purple bruise[1676] and a red scratch[1677] on his head. The next day, his coworker saw the marks and asked him what had happened to him. He gave a very detailed description of the dream he had the night before. His coworkers interpreted[1678] the dream as a hint[1679] that he should quit drinking. Even if he didn't believe them, he respected the fact that, in a democratic country, every one is free to speak his or her mind. After reflection[1680], he became determined to quit drinking. As a result, he would never again be late with the delivery of his work to his clients.

中譯 *Translation*

　　湯姆是個在民主國家勤奮工作的設計師。雖然他為了存錢而節食，但是他有個不良嗜好—酗酒。有一天，他喝得爛醉躺在床上呼呼大睡，夢到了魔鬼。魔鬼在昏暗的夢境中告訴他：「酗酒會把你美好的生活給毀了。做一名酒國英雄並不是什麼豐功偉業。如果你再繼續醉生夢死，我會把你戶頭裡的財產全部拿走。」他醒來後，發現頭上有紫色的瘀青和鮮紅的抓痕。隔天，他同事看到傷痕，便問他發生了什麼事。他詳細地敘述昨晚的夢境。同事們認為這在暗示他該戒酒了。雖然他不相信這些怪力亂神，不過，身在民主國家，他尊重他人的發言自由。經過深思熟慮，他下定決心要戒酒。戒酒成功後，他再也沒有遲交他的設計作品給客戶了。

1669 designer

[dɪˋzaɪnə] ★★★★
名 設計師、策劃者
片 interior designer 室內設計師

1670 excessive

[ɪkˋsɛsɪv] ★★★
形 過度的、過分的
同 extravagant 過度的
反 deficient 不足的

1671 soundly

[ˋsaundlɪ] ★★
副 酣然地、穩健地、堅實地、重重地
片 sleep soundly 熟睡

1672 dim

[dɪm] ★★★
形 暗淡的、模糊的
動 變暗淡、變模糊
片 dim out 使…變暗

1673 destroy

[dɪˋstrɔɪ] ★★★★
動 毀壞、消滅、打破、使失敗
同 demolish 破壞

1674 noble

[ˋnobḷ] ★★★
形 崇高的、高尚的、壯麗的、顯貴的
名 貴族

1675 deed

[did] ★★★
名 功業、功績、行為
動 立契出讓私人財產

1676 bruise

[bruz] ★★★
名 傷痕、青腫、擦傷
動 瘀傷、碰傷、挫傷
同 wound 傷疤

1677 scratch

[skrætʃ] ★★★
名 抓痕、亂塗
動 抓傷、劃破、潦草塗寫
片 scratch out 刮掉

1678 interpret

[ɪnˋtɝprɪt] ★★★
動 理解為、說明、口譯
同 translate 翻譯
片 interpret for 為…翻譯

1679 hint

[hɪnt] ★★★
名 暗示、微量、建議
動 暗示、示意
片 hint at 暗示某事

1680 reflection

[rɪˋflɛkʃən] ★★★★
名 深思、反省、反射、倒影、反映
片 on reflection 再經考慮

Fighting!

Give it a shot 小試身手

1 It is hard to _____ the symptoms of depression.

2 The typhoon _____ the houses over one night.

3 The heavy woman was on a _____ to lose weight.

4 Can you give me a _____ of the incident?

5 You must pay a _____ if you want to reserve the room.

MP3

短文 281 字彙 282

141

Essay

Recently, as reported by local news outlets[1681], a man lost all his money because of his addiction to gambling. For a long time, he always managed to keep his parents from discovering what he had done. Still, his parents found out about his gambling problem one day. They were disappointed[1682] in him and forced[1683] him to move out of their house. The man could not go to nightclubs anymore because he had no money. He sold all his CDs and DVDs and picked up coins people lost on streets and in ditches[1684] every day. He took the money to a restaurant to dine[1685]. Since he had not taken a shower for a long time and had dirt all over his clothes, the man was given a discount[1686] by the owner out of sympathy[1687]. He disliked[1688] being dirty and was scared that he might get some kind of serious disease. He discovered that he could take a free bath in a river. He passed by a dock and dove into the water so that he could get clean. People were shocked and thought he was an exhibitionist and called the police, who took him to jail[1689] where he could stay for a while, get free food and have a real shower.

中譯 Translation

　　最近國內新聞報導，有一名男子染上賭癮，輸得傾家蕩產。他想盡辦法不讓他父母知道，但最後還是被發現了。他父母對他感到非常失望，並把他逐出家門。這名男子沒錢花用再也無法去舞廳玩樂。他把自己的唱片和影片全都賣了，每天撿拾別人掉在路上或水溝的零錢。他帶著錢到餐廳用餐。他已經很久沒洗過澡了，衣服上都是髒污。餐廳老闆出於同情給他一些折扣。他不喜歡身上髒兮兮的，也怕自己會感染疾病。他發現在河裡洗澡不用錢。他經過一個碼頭便跳進水裡，把自己浸在水裡洗了個澡讓自己變乾淨。路人被他的行為嚇到，以為他是暴露狂，趕緊報警。警察把他關進牢裡，他能在牢裡待一陣子，享用免費食物，還能正常洗澡。

1681 outlet

[ˋaʊtlɛt] ★★★
名 出口、商店、銷路、排氣口、發洩途徑
反 inlet 入口

1682 disappointed

[dɪsəˋpɔɪntɪd] ★★★
形 失望的、沮喪的
片 be disappointed in 對…失望

1683 force

[ˋfɔrs] ★★★★★
動 強迫、強行攻佔、強作
名 威力、武力、影響
片 come into force 生效

1684 ditch

[dɪtʃ] ★★★
名 水溝、渠道
動 甩掉、拋棄、挖渠
同 trench 溝渠

1685 dine

[daɪn] ★★★★
動 用餐、宴請
片 dine at 在…用餐
衍 diner 用餐的人

1686 discount

[dɪsˋkaʊnt] ★★★
名 折扣、打折扣、不全信
動 打折、低估、不全相信
片 at a discount 減價

1687 sympathy

[ˋsɪmpəθɪ] ★★★★
名 同情、贊同、慰問
片 sympathy for 對…感到同情

1688 dislike

[dɪsˋlaɪk] ★★★
動 不喜歡、厭惡
名 不喜歡、厭惡
片 likes and dislikes 好惡

1689 jail

[dʒel] ★★★★
名 監獄、監禁、拘留所
動 監禁、拘留
同 prison 監獄

1690 toe

[to] ★★★★
名 腳趾、足尖
動 用腳尖踢或踩
片 from head to toe 全身

1691 temperature

[ˋtɛmprətʃə] ★★★★
名 溫度、氣溫、氣氛
片 take sb's temperature 量體溫

1692 merchandise

[ˋmɝtʃəndaɪz] ★★★
名 商品、貨物
動 買賣、經營、推銷
同 goods 商品、貨物

---

fighting!

Give it a shot 小試身手

1 Julie _____ her toe[1690] into the pool to test the temperature[1691].

2 That store _____ all its merchandise[1692].

3 _____ violence is an increasing social problem.

4 The manager's going to _____ with us tonight.

5 The old man died of severe _____.

Answers: 1 dipped 2 discounts 3 Domestic 4 dine 5 disease

142

MP3 短文 283 字彙 284

Essay

A well-educated editor was eager[1693] for success. She loved her job, which was to edit various kinds of books. The company she worked for had just published the sixth edition[1694] of a famous dictionary[1695]. She hoped the sixth edition could receive a lot of acclaim[1696] like the previous editions had. However, the company she worked for got into some financial problems last month and had trouble paying salaries on time. Eventually, the company couldn't afford to pay its employees anything. The editor was extremely frustrated[1697] and decided to use the little money she had to go to a bar. She got very drunk and then went home. She felt so drowsy[1698] and almost drowned herself accidentally in her bathtub. Meanwhile[1699], her mom came home and began dusting[1700] the living room. She heard her daughter screaming and ran into the bathroom. She drained[1701] the water from the bathtub and gave her daughter a cup of hot tea. In the morning, the editor woke up and wasn't sure if she had had a nightmare[1702] or actually nearly drowned in the bathtub.

中譯 *Translation*

　　一位受過良好教育的出版社編輯一直渴望著成功。她熱愛她的工作。她的工作是編輯各式各樣的書籍。她的公司剛出版了某知名字典的第六版。她希望第六版可以像之前幾版一樣引起熱烈的迴響。不過公司上個月陷入財務困難，無法如期支付員工薪水。最後，這間公司已無法再負荷任何支出了。這位編輯對此感到灰心喪氣，拿了僅剩的錢去酒吧喝酒。她醉醺醺地回家。洗澡時，她感到昏昏欲睡，半夢半醒間差點溺死在浴缸裡。同時間，她媽媽正好回到家，開始要打掃家裡。她聽到女兒的尖叫聲，馬上衝進浴室。她把浴缸的水排掉，然後幫她女兒泡了一杯熱茶。隔天早上起床時，編輯已無法分辨這只是一場惡夢，還是她真的差點溺死在浴缸裡。

1693 eager

[`igə] ★★★★
形 渴望的、熱切的
同 desirous 渴望的
片 be eager for 渴望

1694 edition

[ɪ`dɪʃən] ★★★★
名 版本、發行數、翻版
片 pocket edition 袖珍本
衍 editor 編輯

1695 dictionary

[`dɪkʃənɛrɪ] ★★★
名 字典
片 walking dictionary 學識淵博的人

1696 acclaim

[ə`klem] ★★
名 讚賞、歡呼
動 稱讚、喝采、擁立
同 applaud 稱讚

1697 frustrate

[`frʌstret] ★★
動 感到灰心、挫敗
形 受挫的、無益的
片 frustrate in 在…失敗

1698 drowsy

[`drauzɪ] ★★★
形 昏昏欲睡的、沉寂的
同 sleepy 昏昏欲睡的

1699 meanwhile

[`minhwaɪl] ★★★★
副 同時
名 期間
片 in the meanwhile 同時

1700 dust

[dʌst] ★★★★
動 打掃、灑農藥
名 灰塵、塵土
片 dust off 除去…灰塵

1701 drain

[dren] ★★★
動 排掉、使流出、耗盡
名 排水、流出、不斷外流
片 drain from 從…流出

1702 nightmare

[`naɪtmɛr] ★★★
名 惡夢、夢魘

1703 coupon

[`kupɑn] ★★
名 優惠券、贈貨券、聯票

1704 slightly

[`slaɪtlɪ] ★★★★★
副 稍微地、嬌弱地
片 slightly different 略為不同

---

fighting!

Give it a shot 小試身手

❶ Take a _____ once after dinner.

❷ Sam was _____ on only two cans of beer.

❸ The incident turned out to a _____ result.

❹ Remember the coupon[1703] is _____ tomorrow.

❺ The second _____ is slightly[1704] different from the first one.

143

Essay

An elderly employer used to be a mayor[1705] who was very popular with the public. After he retired from politics, he opened a shop that sold mainly electronic[0706] products.

He was very strict[1707]. His employees always described him as an emperor[1708] in the ancient[1709] palace. He arranged many training courses to enable[1710] his employees to be independent workers. Being able to work independently was an important qualification for him when he was recruiting[1711] new staff. Another important qualification he emphasized was that employees needed to be efficient[1712] at work. He thought employees should not slack[1713] off even when the shop was empty. One day, the shop suffered a blackout[1714]. None of the buildings in the area had any electricity. He took the chance to test his employees to see how they would <u>deal with</u> an emergency[1715]. A clerk went to check the main fuse[1716] box. Other employees helped customers to make sure they didn't fall down and get hurt in the complete darkness. For most of the employees, this test was tough but very educational.

! deal with 處理、涉及

中譯 *Translation*

　　有位年長的老闆曾經是頗受愛戴的市長，他從政壇退休後開了間電器行。

　　他非常嚴格，他的員工形容他就像個古代皇宮裡的皇帝。他安排非常多訓練課程讓員工可以獨立作業。獨立作業能力是他挑選員工一個很重要的門檻，另外，他也非常注重工作效率。他覺得就算店裡沒客人，員工也不能懈怠。有一天，店裡停電，這個地區沒有一棟大樓恢復電力。他正好趁著這個機會來考驗員工的危機處裡能力。一位店員去檢查總電源，其他員工則協助顧客確保他們在一片漆黑中沒有跌倒或受傷。對大部分員工來說，這是個艱辛卻非常具有教育意義的考驗。

1705 mayor

[`meɚ] ★★★
名 市長、鎮長
片 deputy mayor 副市長

1706 electronic

[ɪlɛk`trɑnɪk] ★★★★
形 電子的、電子操作的
衍 electronics 電子學

1707 strict

[strɪkt] ★★★★
形 嚴格的、嚴謹的、絕對的、周密的
片 be strict with 對…嚴格

1708 emperor

[`ɛmpɚɚ] ★★★
名 皇帝
反 empress 女皇
衍 empire 帝國

1709 ancient

[`enʃənt] ★★★
形 古代的、舊的
名 老人、古代人
反 modern 現代的

1710 enable

[ɪn`ebl] ★★★★
動 使能夠、賦予…能力
同 empower 使能夠
反 disable 使無資格

1711 recruit

[rɪ`krut] ★★★
動 聘用、徵募、恢復健康
名 新手、新兵、補給品
同 enlist 徵募

1712 efficient

[ɪ`fɪʃənt] ★★★★
形 效率高的、能勝任的
同 effective 有效的
片 efficient in 在…有成效

1713 slack

[slæk] ★★★
動 懈怠、放鬆、懶散
形 懈怠的、鬆弛的
片 slack off 鬆懈

1714 blackout

[`blækaut] ★★
名 停電、燈火管制、突然發昏、封鎖

1715 emergency

[ɪ`mɝdʒənsɪ] ★★★★
名 緊急情況、非常時刻
同 urgency 緊急
衍 emergent 緊急的

1716 fuse

[fjuz] ★★
名 保險絲、導火線
動 混合、結合
片 fuse with 與…接合

Fighting!

Give it a shot 小試身手

1 The minister _____ the importance of moral education.

2 This machine is more _____ than that one.

3 The reason for the _____ to be hired is his cordiality.

4 In case of _____, please press the alarm bell.

5 He signaled to me by patting my _____.

Answers: 1 emphasized 2 efficient 3 employee 4 emergency 5 elbow

144

MP3

短文 287   字彙 288

Essay

An engineer, Tom, was engaged[1717] in designing[1718] machines[1719] in a large firm. All of his friends envied him because of his beautiful and vivacious[1720] girlfriend. Tom was planning to propose to her. He came up with an idea to propose at an exhibition because his girlfriend was fond of arts. His friends thought it was an excellent idea because he could also share his joy with the people at the exhibition. They decorated the entry of the exhibition hall the day before he planned to propose. They believed that decorating the entrance beautifully would create[1721] a wonderful, romantic atmosphere. The next day, when his girlfriend entered the hall, all the people applauded, and he proposed to her at that same moment. His girlfriend was shocked and then escaped[1722] through the exit[1723]. She started her car and left in a hurry[1724]. She thought her boyfriend was so evil[1725] to propose in public, and it made her want to erase him from her memory. Meanwhile, back at the exhibition hall, Tom was extremely embarrassed and quickly got into his car and sped[1726] away, too.

中譯 *Translation*

　　湯姆是位工程師，他在一間大公司從事機械設計的工作，所有的朋友都很羨慕他，因為他的女朋友不但漂亮而且活力四射。湯姆正準備要向她求婚。他的女朋友熱愛藝術，所以他想到要在藝術展覽會上向她求婚。他的朋友認為這個計畫很棒，而且可以跟現場的民眾一起分享喜悅。他們覺得入口處美麗的裝飾能營造出美好、浪漫的氛圍。因此求婚前一天精心佈置了展覽會場的入口。第二天，當他的女朋友進入大廳，他便在眾人的鼓掌下當場求婚。他的女朋友驚嚇之餘，從出口逃離現場，發動汽車倉皇離去。她認為她的男朋友在大庭廣眾下跟她求婚很可惡，這樣的舉動令她很想將她的男朋友從記憶裡刪除。而同時，在展覽會大廳，湯姆覺得非常困窘，他也迅速地回到車上，並加速離開現場。

1717 engage

[ɪnˋgedʒ] ★★
- 動 從事、訂婚、佔用
- 片 engage in 參加、從事
- 衍 engagement 訂婚

1718 design

[dɪˋsaɪn] ★★★★★
- 動 設計、計畫
- 名 設計、圖案、圖謀
- 片 design for 為⋯設計

1719 machine

[məˋʃin] ★★★★
- 名 機器、機械、領導核心
- 動 用機器做
- 衍 mechanism 機械裝置

1720 vivacious

[vaɪˋveʃəs] ★
- 形 活潑的、快活的、有生氣的
- 同 lively 活潑的

1721 create

[krɪˋet] ★★★★★
- 動 產生、創造、創作
- 同 make 製造
- 衍 creation 創作品

1722 escape

[əˋskep] ★★★★
- 動 逃脫、逃跑、漏出
- 名 逃跑、逃避
- 片 escape from 從⋯逃脫

1723 exit

[ˋɛksɪt] ★★★★
- 名 出口、退場
- 動 離開、退出、退場
- 片 make one's exit 退出

1724 hurry

[ˋhɝɪ] ★★★★
- 名 急忙、倉促、急切
- 動 趕緊、催促
- 片 in a hurry 迅速地

1725 evil

[ˋivl̩] ★★★★
- 形 討厭的、邪惡的
- 名 邪惡、壞事、禍害
- 片 evil tongue 讒言

1726 speed

[spid] ★★★★★
- 動 加速、快行、快速傳送
- 名 速度、迅速
- 片 speed up 加速

1727 master

[ˋmæstɚ] ★★★★★
- 名 主人、能手、決定
- 動 做⋯主人、控制、精通
- 形 精通的、熟練的

1728 stub

[stʌb] ★★
- 名 票根、殘肢、殘根
- 動 連根拔起
- 片 stub out 踩熄

Fighting!

Give it a shot 小試身手

1. Housework _____ much of her time.
2. We went to the _____ of Miller's paintings.
3. The abused dog _____ from his master[1727].
4. We should persuade him out of the _____ idea.
5. You can _____ the ticket stub[1728] for a cup of coffee.

Answers: 1 engages 2 exhibition 3 escaped 4 evil 5 exchange

145

Essay

MP3   短文 289   字彙 290

Gary was a big fan of explosives[1729]. He was very familiar with the history and development of explosives such as dynamite[1730]. He always got extreme satisfaction from doing experiments on explosive materials. One time, he did an experiment without the instructor[1731]'s permission. He had great expectations for the results, but the bomb he was making exploded[1732] before he had finished. He fainted[1733] due to the heavy smoke and was sent to the hospital. The instructor came into his room and told him why his experiment had failed so miserably[1734]. It was due to the inferior material he had used. The instructor said, "You need faith in your experiment. Don't be opportunistic[1735] and <u>cut corners</u>, or your effort will turn out to be like the moral in a fable[1736], like faded[1737] flowers for want of water. You cannot earn people's trust and the bombs you make will never be exported worldwide if you don't do your very best. Your dreams will never come true, and you will never become a successful scientist." Gary was suddenly enlightened[1738] and gave his instructor an expressive[1739] nod.

> ! cut corners 走捷徑、投機取巧、偷工減料

中譯 *Translation*

　　蓋瑞是個熱愛研究炸彈的狂熱份子，他對炸彈的歷史及演進非常了解，他總是從做實驗中得到無比的樂趣。有一次，他沒經過教授的同意擅自做實驗，他對實驗的結果滿心期待，但是炸彈還沒完成就先爆炸了，他也因為吸入過多濃煙暈倒而被送到醫院。他的教授來到醫院，告訴他失敗的原因是因為他用了品質低劣的材料。教授說：「你必須對你的實驗充滿信心，不要投機取巧，不然你所付出的努力只會像寓言故事裡的教訓，像花兒那樣因缺水而凋零。你無法取得大眾的信任，所做的炸彈也無法銷到世界各地，你的夢想永遠無法實現，你也就永遠無法成為一名成功的科學家。」蓋瑞頓悟這一切道理，然後向教授意味深長地點了點頭。

1729 explosive

[ɪkˋsplosɪv] ★★★
- 名 炸藥、爆炸物
- 形 爆炸性的、暴躁的
- 衍 explosion 爆炸

1730 dynamite

[ˋdaɪnəmaɪt] ★★
- 名 炸藥、具爆炸性的事、具潛在危險的人
- 動 炸毀

1731 instructor

[ɪnˋstrʌktə] ★★★★
- 名 指導者、教練、大學講師
- 衍 instruct 指導訓練

1732 explode

[ɪkˋsplod] ★★★
- 動 爆炸、推翻、戳穿、迅速擴大
- 同 erupt 爆發

1733 faint

[fent] ★★★★
- 動 暈倒、昏厥
- 形 頭暈的、微弱的

1734 miserably

[ˋmɪzərəblɪ] ★
- 副 糟糕地、悲慘地、令人難受地
- 衍 miserable 不幸的

1735 opportunistic

[͵ɑpətjuˋnɪstɪk] ★
- 形 投機取巧的
- 衍 opportunism 投機主義

1736 fable

[ˋfebl] ★★★
- 名 寓言、無稽之談
- 動 虛構、撒謊
- 片 fable about 虛構

1737 fade

[fed] ★★★
- 動 凋謝、枯萎、褪色、變微弱
- 片 fade away 消失、死亡

1738 enlighten

[ɪnˋlaɪtn] ★★★
- 動 啟發、開導
- 片 enlighten sb. about sth. 使某人領悟某事

1739 expressive

[ɪkˋsprɛsɪv] ★★
- 形 意味深長的、表現的、表情豐富的
- 衍 expression 表情

1740 proposal

[prəˋpozl] ★★★
- 名 提案、計畫、求婚
- 同 scheme 方案
- 衍 propose 提議、求婚

Fighting!

Give it a shot 小試身手

1 It's very unhealthy for you to be under _____ pressure.

2 The tune of the song is _____ to me.

3 His father _____ when he heard his death.

4 Do you have _____ in their new proposal[1740]?

5 The ability of _____ is necessary in communication.

146

MP3　短文 291　字彙 292

Essay

Peter took a fancy to birds. He kept files[1741] on every kind of features of birds. He bred[1742] birds at home, and he thought it was a fashionable thing to do. He sold birds to make money as well. One day, a client faxed her order for ten birds and asked for them to be sent <u>cash on delivery</u>. She would pay the fare[1743]. When Peter arrived, the family were having a BBQ party. A woman was holding two plates with the flesh[1744] of birds on them. "Thank goodness you're here. We are almost out of meat." the woman said. She also said that she liked to flavor[1745] the bird meat with vinegar[1746], and then placed the bird meat on the grill, which was burning hot. Peter asked her why she had done it. She said she had eaten it in a flea market once and really liked it. Peter had to control himself to prevent[1747] himself from hitting her with his fists[1748] out of anger. He told the woman to keep her money and that she would never get his birds. He fastened[1749] his helmet strap[1750] under his chin and glanced[1751] at the birds in the cage attached[1752] to his scooter. "There's no way you're going to be somebody's barbecue dinner!" he told them.

> ⚠ cash on delivery(COD) 貨到付款

中譯 *Translation*

　　彼得很喜愛鳥類，他將鳥類的各種特性分門別類，他在家也飼養鳥兒並認為這是一種時尚。他同時也做鳥的買賣生意。有一天，有個客戶傳真了一張訂單給他，表示要買十隻鳥而且要求貨到付款，運費由她負擔。當彼得送貨到府時，他們正在辦家庭烤肉會，有位女士拿著兩個盤子，上面盛著鳥肉。「感謝老天，你終於來了！肉幾乎快被我們吃光了！」婦人說道。她還提到，她喜歡以醋調味，並放在烤肉架上用大火燒烤。彼得問她為何吃鳥肉，她說她在跳蚤市場吃過一次之後，就愛上吃鳥肉！彼得怒不可遏，他努力克制自己，以避免一時衝動朝她揮拳。他告訴婦人把錢留著，因為她不會拿到任何一隻鳥。他繫上安全帽，瞥了一眼固定在機車上的籠中鳥，對鳥兒說道：「我絕對不會讓你們變成別人的烤肉大餐。」

1741 file

[faɪl] ★★★★
名 檔案、文件夾、存檔
動 把…歸檔、提出訴訟
片 file for 起訴

1742 breed

[brid] ★★★
動 飼養、培育、引起
名 品種
同 raise 養育

1743 fare

[fɛr] ★★★
名 票價、車費、伙食
動 過活、吃、進展
片 fare forth 動身

1744 flesh

[flɛʃ] ★★★★
名 肉、果肉、肉體
動 長肉、發胖
片 in the flesh 親自

1745 flavor

[`flevɚ] ★★★★
動 給…調味、增添風趣
名 味道、風味、香料
片 flavor with 用…調味

1746 vinegar

[`vɪnɪgɚ] ★★★
名 醋

1747 prevent

[prɪ`vɛnt] ★★★★★
動 防止、阻擋、預防
同 prohibit 阻止
片 prevent from 防止

1748 fist

[fɪst] ★★★★
名 拳頭、掌握
動 緊握、握成拳頭
片 fist fight 鬥毆

1749 fasten

[`fæsn̩] ★★
動 扣緊、釘牢、全神貫注
反 loosen 鬆開
片 fasten up 扣上

1750 strap

[stræp] ★★★★
名 帶子、金屬帶、皮條、鞭打
動 被捆住、受束縛

1751 glance

[glæns] ★★★★
動 一瞥、掃視、簡略提及
名 一瞥、掠過、閃光
片 glance at 朝…看一眼

1752 attach

[ə`tætʃ] ★★★★★
動 固定、裝上、繫上、使附屬、歸於、附加
片 attach to 使…附在

---

fighting!

Give it a shot 小試身手

❶ Joey didn't _____ his belt and his pants loosened.

❷ There is an empty boat _____ on the river.

❸ I never believe my _____ has something to do with my name.

❹ The lady recognized the suspect by his _____.

❺ Her hair style is out of _____.

Answers: ❶ fasten ❷ floating ❸ fate ❹ feathers ❺ fashion

147

Essay

There was a foundation[1753] which was founded[1754] by folks[1755] who were fond of helping out charitable[1756] causes. The head of the foundation was a rich old man who had a scar on his forehead[1757]. He formed this foundation to help people who had been in accidents. The foundation's members came from different backgrounds; the only thing they had in common was they had large fortunes. Since they were all very charitable people, there were strong ties of friendship among them. They described charitable work as water flowing forth[1758] forever like the fountain in front of the foundation's headquarters[1759]. The foundation also held frequent activities during weekends. For example, they sponsored[1760] a speech for jobless people who felt frustrated by their lives, and served food, such as fried potatoes, roast[1761] chicken and desserts. Unfortunately, after a few years, this foundation folded[1762]. The reason was that many of the members had lost money in the stock market and because of the poor global[1763] economy.

ⓘ have in common 共同點、相似之處

中譯 *Translation*

　　熱衷於慈善事業的善心人士創立了慈善基金會，基金會會長是位富有的老先生，額頭上有道疤。他建立這個基金會，以幫助那些遭逢意外變故的人們。基金會是由一群來自不同背景的會員所組成的，但這些會員的共同點是他們都擁有龐大的財產。由於他們都是篤信助人為快樂之本的慈善事業家，他們彼此之間有著堅定的情感聯繫。他們形容慈善事業就像基金會門口前的噴泉那樣川流不息。基金會經常在週末舉辦活動，像是替那些為生活所苦的失業者舉辦講座，他們提供食物，像是炸馬鈴薯、烤雞，還有甜點給民眾。好景不常，幾年後，由於基金會成員在股市失利後損失了不少錢，再加上全球景氣低迷，基金會因此停止運作。

1753　foundation

[faunˋdeʃən] ★★★★

名 基金會、創辦、根據、地基、粉底霜

同 base 基底

1754　found

[faund] ★★★★★

動 創立、基於、鑄造

同 establish 建造

片 found on 建立在…上

1755　folk

[fok] ★★★

名 廣大成員、雙親

形 民俗的、通俗的

片 young folk 年輕人

1756　charitable

[ˋtʃærətəbl̩] ★★

形 慈善的、寬厚的、具有同情心的

反 uncharitable 苛刻的

1757　forehead

[ˋfɔrhɛd] ★★★

名 額頭、前額

1758　forth

[forθ] ★★★★

副 向前、向外

同 forward 向前

片 set forth 動身

1759　headquarters

[ˋhɛdˋkwɔrtəz] ★★

名 總公司、司令部、總署

衍 headquarter 將總部設在

1760　sponsor

[ˋspɑnsə] ★★★

動 發起、主辦、贊助

名 主辦者、贊助者

同 backer 贊助人

1761　roast

[rost] ★★★

形 烘烤的

動 烤、炙、烘暖、痛斥

名 烤肉、烘烤

1762　fold

[fold] ★★★

動 關閉、垮台、對摺、交疊、籠罩

名 摺疊、起伏、畜欄

1763　global

[ˋglobl̩] ★★★★★

形 全世界的、球狀的

同 universal 全世界的

衍 globe 地球

1764　settler

[ˋsɛtlə] ★★

名 開拓者、移居者、沉澱器、解決者

衍 settle 解決

---

fighting!

Give it a shot 小試身手

❶ A _____ of deer run through the meadow.

❷ His _____ were disappointed for the crime he had committed.

❸ Our friendship will last _____, right?

❹ Do not go _____, stay here.

❺ The town was _____ by English settlers[1764] in 1790.

Answers: ❶ flock ❷ folk ❸ forever ❹ folk ❺ forth ❺ founded

148

 MP3 短文 295 字彙 296

Essay

There was a gang[1765] of teenagers in town. They vandalized[1766] public facilities[1767], indulged in illegal gambling, smuggled[1768] weapons and fur from endangered[1769] animals, and imported furniture from other countries to fund[1770] their other illegal activities.

One day, the gang robbed[1771] a jewelry shop. After robbing the store, they burned it to the ground by lighting a gallon of gasoline on fire. They hid in the hills after the robbery. While the criminals remained at large, the police were under great pressure to find and arrest them, and people's confidence in public safety kept decreasing. However, one day the police got an extremely lucky break when one of the gang members went to town. A policeman glanced at him and recognized his identity[1772] instantly, and he gave a gesture[1773] to other policemen to help him arrest the suspect[1774]. They took the suspect back to the police station and questioned him for several hours. In the end, he told the police all about his criminal activities and gave the police the names of his fellow gang members, allowing the police to arrest them all and solve many crimes, including the high-profile robbery and arson[1775] of the jewelry store. The governor[1776] was very satisfied. He awarded the policeman a special medal. With such great glory, his face glowed all over with pride.

中譯 *Translation*

　　城裡有一幫不良少年，他們恣意破壞公物，沉溺於非法賭博，走私軍火和保育類動物的毛皮，並從其他國家進口家具來做非法生意謀財。

　　有一天，這幫人搶了珠寶店之後，用一加崙的汽油把店家燒了。他們犯案後藏身於山中。由於這群罪犯仍然逍遙法外，警方為了找出罪犯，並逮捕他們，承受相當大的壓力。人民對公共安全的信任度也不斷降低。然而，有一天，好運降臨了。一位犯罪成員進了城裡，警察一眼便認出他，他向其他警察做了個手勢，要他們協助他逮捕嫌犯。警察把嫌疑犯帶回警局，並審問他好幾個小時。最後，他從實招來，供出了所有罪行，及同夥的名冊。警察順利逮捕所有罪犯，並一併解決了好幾樁案件，包括備受關注的搶劫案以及珠寶店縱火案。州長對此次的圓滿結案非常滿意，他頒發了特別的獎章給立了功的警察。獲得這項殊榮，警察感到十分自豪，高興得容光煥發。

1765 gang

[gæŋ] ★★★★
名 一幫、一幫年輕人
動 成群結隊、結夥
片 gang up 聯合起來

1766 vandalize

[`vændḷaɪz] ★★
動 任意破壞
同 destroy 破壞

1767 facility

[fə`sɪlətɪ] ★★★★
名 設施、工具、能力、場所、熟練
片 with facility 容易

1768 smuggle

[`smʌgḷ] ★★
動 走私、偷運
衍 smuggler 走私犯

1769 endangered

[ɪn`dendʒəd] ★★★
形 瀕臨絕種的
片 endangered species 瀕臨絕種的動植物

1770 fund

[fʌnd] ★★★★★
動 積累、提供資金
名 資金、存款、積累
片 in funds 手頭寬裕

1771 rob

[rɑb] ★★★★
動 搶劫、盜取、使喪失
片 rob of 搶走、剝奪
衍 robber 搶匪

1772 identity

[aɪ`dɛntətɪ] ★★★★
名 身分、一致處、特性
片 mistaken identity 誤認
衍 identify 確認身分

1773 gesture

[`dʒɛstʃə] ★★★★
名 手勢、表示、姿態
動 做手勢、用動作示意
片 gesture to 向…做手勢

1774 suspect

[səs`pɛkt] ★★★
名 嫌疑犯
動 懷疑、察覺、猜想
片 suspect of 懷疑做某事

1775 arson

[`ɑrsṇ] ★★
名 縱火罪
片 commit arson 犯下縱火罪

1776 governor

[`gʌvənə] ★★★
名 州長、總督、調節器
同 administrator 管理人
衍 govern 管理

Give it a shot 小試身手

fighting!

1. Handshake is a _____ of friendship.
2. He indulged in _____ and lost his job.
3. Do not _____ about others' private affairs.
4. He _____ at the envelope and then tore it up.
5. The _____ on the pipe let the water leak out.

149

Essay

🎧 MP3 短文 297 字彙 298

After Paul graduated, he worked as a manager at a greenhouse[1777] on campus[1778]. His job was mainly to supervise[1779] everything in the greenhouse and the students who worked there. There were many grasshoppers[1780] there, but they didn't really <u>cause any harm</u> to the flowers, so Paul told the students not to bother[1781] them. One day, during break time, Paul wanted to buy some gum. He bought some gum and a few other items from a grocery[1782] store. Then he went to the barbershop where a female hairdresser[1783] he liked worked. He walked along the hallway[1784] and entered the barbershop, which was located next to a gym. Although Paul had a crush[1785] on her, she only knew him as a pleasant regular customer who always gave her a nice tip. So, she was surprised when Paul invited her to come to his greenhouse and see the beautiful flowers. Since she thought Paul was a nice guy, she accepted his invitation. However, once she got inside the greenhouse and saw all the grasshoppers, she ran quickly home because she had a strong fear of grasshoppers. That was a great disappointment for Paul! Ever since then, Paul has hated those insects[1786].

⚠ cause harm 造成危害

中譯 *Translation*

　　保羅畢業後，在學校的溫室裡擔任管理員，他的工作是管理溫室裡的一切事務，以及指導學生。溫室裡有許多蚱蜢，但牠們並不會對花卉造成任何危害。因此，保羅告訴學生不要去打擾那些蚱蜢。有一天，保羅想在休息時間去買些口香糖，他在雜貨店買了口香糖及其他物品，然後去理髮廳看看他心儀的女理髮師。他沿著走廊走到體育館旁的理髮廳。雖然保羅迷戀那位女理髮師，但保羅對她而言只是一位總是給她不少小費又親切的常客。因此，當保羅邀請她到溫室欣賞那些美麗的花，她感到很驚訝。然而，由於她認為保羅是一個和善的人，所以她接受了保羅的邀請。只是，當她來到溫室，看到那些蚱蜢，她立即飛奔回家，因為她對蚱蜢有很深的恐懼。保羅失望透頂，從此以後，保羅開始對昆蟲心生厭惡。

1777 greenhouse

[`grinhaus] ★★★
名 溫室
片 greenhouse effect 溫室效應

1778 campus

[`kæmpəs] ★★★★
名 大學、校園、大學生活
形 大學的、校園的
片 on campus 校園內

1779 supervise

[`supəˌvaɪz] ★★★
動 管理、指導、監督
同 oversee 監督
衍 supervision 監督

1780 grasshopper

[græshapə] ★
名 蚱蜢、蝗蟲
動 蚱蜢似地跳、見異思遷

1781 bother

[baðə] ★★★★
動 打擾、使惱怒、費心
名 麻煩、煩惱
片 bother about 擔心

1782 grocery

[`grosərɪ] ★★★★
名 食品雜貨店、食品雜貨業

1783 hairdresser

[`hɛrdrɛsə] ★
名 美髮師
同 hairstylist 髮型師
衍 hairdressing 理髮

1784 hallway

[`hɔlwe] ★★★★
名 走廊、玄關
同 corridor 走廊

1785 crush

[krʌʃ] ★★★
名 迷戀、極度擁擠、壓碎
動 壓碎、弄皺、壓垮
片 have a crush on 迷戀

1786 insect

[`ɪnsɛkt] ★★★
名 昆蟲
同 bug 蟲子、臭蟲

1787 guest

[gɛst] ★★★★
名 賓客、顧客、客座教授
動 款待、招待、當特別來賓

1788 passionately

[`pæʃənɪtlɪ] ★★
副 熱情地、激昂地
同 fervently 熱情地
衍 passionate 熱情的

fighting!

Give it a shot 小試身手

1 The host _____ the guest[1787]'s hands passionately[1788].

2 The change was so _____ that we hardly noticed it.

3 _____ the rope if you cannot keep your balance.

4 Mr. Lu _____ from high school three years ago.

5 I'm so mad that my hair was destroyed by the _____!

Answers: 1 grasped 2 gradual 3 Grab 4 graduated 5 hairdresser

150

MP3　短文 299　字彙 300

Essay

One of the biggest bestsellers this year is a novel that seems to have <u>caught everyone's attention</u>.

The novel's plot[1789] and setting[1790] are quite interesting: The story <u>takes place</u> in a town by the sea, but for some strange reason it has no harbors or docks. It's a place where many hawks[1791] fly in the sky and chickens hatch[1792] eggs regularly. Nothing is harmful in this place; everything is natural and healthful, which allows the residents[1793] to have a long lifespan[1794]. The pace of life is slow there, and it is very peaceful. People would never think of harming each other. They are all good at farming and enjoy a great harvest[1795] every season[1796]. Some reviewers[1797] have said that readers love this book because it provides a picture of a life that everyone would like to have. It's like being able to live in the Garden of Eden.

> ⓘ catch one's attention 吸引…的注意
> ⓘ take place 發生

中譯 *Translation*

　　今年度的超級暢銷書之一是一本小說，這本小說似乎吸引了所有人的目光。

　　小說的情節和場景設定十分有趣。故事發生在海邊的小鎮，基於某些奇特的原因，這個小鎮沒有港灣。在這裡，老鷹在空中翱翔，雞則規律地孵蛋。這裡沒有任何的有害的事物，一切東西都是天然且有益健康，所以當地居民普遍都長壽。他們的生活步調很慢，他們的生活寧靜祥和，從不互相傷害鬥爭。每個人都善於農耕，每到收成的季節，他們總是享受豐收的喜悅。一些書評家認為，讀者之所以喜愛這本書，是因為它勾勒出每個人都渴望擁有的生活意象，好似伊甸園裡的生活般美好。

1789 plot

[plɑt] ★★★★
- 名 情節、陰謀、小塊土地
- 動 密謀、策畫、劃分
- 片 plot out 分配

1790 setting

[`sɛtɪŋ] ★★★★★
- 名 背景、設定、布景、沉落
- 片 stage setting 舞台布景

1791 hawk

[hɔk] ★★★
- 名 鷹、鷹派人物
- 動 叫賣、散播、捕捉
- 片 war hawk 好戰份子

1792 hatch

[hætʃ] ★★★
- 動 孵出、策劃
- 名 孵化、(小雞)一窩
- 片 hatch out 孵出

1793 resident

[`rɛzədənt] ★★★★
- 名 居民、住院醫生、留鳥
- 形 定居的、固有的
- 衍 reside 居住、存在於

1794 lifespan

[`laɪf spæn] ★★
- 名 壽命、使用期限
- 同 lifetime 壽命

1795 harvest

[`hɑrvɪst] ★★★★
- 名 收穫、收穫季節、成果
- 動 收穫、獲得
- 片 a poor harvest 歉收

1796 season

[`sizn̩] ★★★★★
- 名 季節、旺季、季票
- 動 給…調味、適應
- 片 in season 時令的

1797 reviewer

[rɪ`vjuɚ] ★★
- 名 評論家、檢閱者
- 同 critic 評論家
- 衍 review 評論、檢閱

1798 exile

[`ɛksaɪl] ★★★
- 動 流放、放逐、離鄉背井
- 名 流放、流亡、離鄉背井
- 片 exile to 流放至

1799 remote

[rɪ`mot] ★★★★
- 形 遙遠的、遙控的、偏僻的、冷淡的
- 片 remote control 遙控器

1800 radiation

[redɪ`eʃən] ★★★★
- 名 輻射、發光、放射線
- 衍 radiative 輻射的、放射的

Fighting!

Give it a shot 小試身手

1. Those who plant in tears will _____ in joy.
2. The _____ poet was exiled[1798] to a remote[1799] place.
3. *Radiation1800* is _____ to humans.
4. My home is the _____ for my heart.
5. What the doctors should do is _____ the sick.

Now

151

🎧 MP3   短文 301   字彙 302

Essay

There was a social worker who loved to help kids <u>overcome their fear</u>. Since she loved kids very much, she thought it was an ideal job for her. She <u>was honored to</u> have this job. One night, a kid ran into her room screaming and told her, "I saw horrible images in my room! I cannot sleep. I can't!" She gave the kid an immediate[1801] hug[1802] and told him, "That was just your imagination[1803]. Maybe you just saw a shadow[1804] of something. From the beginning of time to the present, our holy[1805] God has always been with us to protect[1806] us, especially kids who are innocent[1807] and lovable[1808] like you. That is God's role[1809], to be our protector. If you see horrible images again next time, blow this whistle[1810] to wake up God, and your horror[1811] will be gone."

ⓘ overcome one's fear 克服恐懼

ⓘ be honored to 對做某事感到榮幸

中譯 *Translation*

　　一位社工熱愛幫助孩子克服恐懼。因為她很喜歡小孩子,所以對她來說這是份理想的工作,她也對這份工作感到很驕傲。有一晚,有個小孩尖叫著跑到她房間,跟她說:「我在房間看到好恐怖的東西!我睡不著啦!真的不行!」她馬上抱住他,跟他說:「這只是你的想像,你可能只是看到影子。從古至今,神聖的上帝總是在我們身旁保護著我們,特別像你這樣天真又討人喜愛的小孩。這就是上帝的身分—我們的守護神。如果下次你又看到可怕的東西,你就吹哨子,這可以召喚上帝,你的恐懼就會煙消雲散。」

1801 immediate

[ɪ`midɪət] ★★★
- 形 立即的、當前的、最接近的、直接的
- 反 mediate 間接的

1802 hug

[hʌg] ★★★
- 名 擁抱、緊抱
- 動 擁抱、堅持、緊靠
- 同 embrace 擁抱

1803 imagination

[ɪmædʒə`neʃən] ★★★★
- 名 想像力、幻想
- 片 beyond imagination 無法想像

1804 shadow

[`ʃædo] ★★★★
- 名 幽靈、幻影、影子、陰暗處、陰影
- 動 遮蔽、尾隨、變陰暗

1805 holy

[`holɪ] ★★★
- 形 神聖的、虔誠的、聖潔的
- 反 unholy 邪惡的

1806 protect

[prə`tɛkt] ★★★★
- 動 保護、防護
- 片 protect from 保護免受
- 同 guard 保衛

1807 innocent

[`ɪnəsṇt] ★★★★
- 形 天真的、清白的、幼稚的、無罪的
- 名 涉世未深的人

1808 lovable

[`lʌvəbḷ] ★★
- 形 可愛的、討人喜歡的
- 同 adorable 可愛的
- 反 hateful 討厭的

1809 role

[rol] ★★★★★
- 名 角色、作用、職責
- 片 play a key role 起了關鍵作用

1810 whistle

[`hwɪsḷ] ★★★
- 名 哨子、警笛、汽笛
- 動 吹口哨、鳴笛、呼嘯
- 片 whistle to 對…吹口哨

1811 horror

[`hɔrə] ★★★★
- 名 驚恐、恐怖、毛骨悚然
- 同 terror 恐怖
- 衍 horrify 使恐懼

1812 vivid

[`vɪvɪd] ★★★★
- 形 活潑的、鮮明的、強烈的、生動的
- 衍 vivify 使活躍

Fighting!

Give it a shot 小試身手

❶ The model's vivid[1812] _____ is obsessive.

❷ They celebrated in _____ of Cathy's bravery.

❸ Don't indulge in your _____ but face the reality.

❹ They _____ each other passionately.

❺ My _____ job is which I can fulfill my dream.

Answers: ❶ image ❷ honor ❸ imagination ❹ hugged ❺ ideal

152

Essay

Let me tell you about one of my most memorable[1813] experiences. I used to live at an old inn[1814], which was located in an industrial[1815] area. The companies in the area were mainly involved in manufacturing[1816] and exporting[1817] goods to other countries. Some of the businesses also imported[1818] products and sold them locally. Even though it was a cheap place to live, there were a lot of illegal immigrants[1819] there and there were some crimes, and I even had my wallet stolen from my room at the inn. The day my wallet was stolen, the police coincidentally[1820] showed up and checked everyone's identity, such as driver's licenses, looking for illegal immigrants. The police told me they had found some illegal immigrants living in the basement of the inn and asked to see my ID. But I couldn't show them any because my wallet had just been stolen. They suspected I was in the country illegally and took me to the police station. Luckily, the police finally believed that someone really did steal[1821] my wallet, and I filed a police report over my stolen wallet. I decided to move into a nicer area of town after that incident[1822]. It is not worth it to live in a dangerous place to save money.

中譯 *Translation*

　　跟你講個印象深刻的親身經歷。我以前住在工業區的老舊旅館，那個地方的公司主要是從事製造業以及外銷貿易。有些公司也進口產品在當地銷售。雖然這個區域的生活開銷很便宜，但非法移民很多，也有些治安問題，我的錢包甚至在旅館的房間遭竊。錢包遭竊那天，警察無預警地搜查旅館，並查驗每個人的身分證件，像是駕照，以查緝非法移民。警察表示，他們已查獲藏身在旅館地下室的非法移民，並要求查看我的證件。由於我的錢包失竊，我根本無法向他們證明我的身分，他們懷疑我是非法移民，把我帶到警局。幸運的是，警察最後相信我的錢包真的遭竊，並請我做筆錄。經過這件事之後，我決定搬到治安較好的地方。這個經驗讓我體會到，為了省錢而住在危險的地方，一點都不值得，還可能因小失大。

1813 memorable

[mɛmərəbl] ★★
形 難忘的、顯著的
片 be memorable for 因⋯令人難忘

1814 inn

[ɪn] ★★★
名 小旅館、小酒店
同 tavern 小酒館

1815 industrial

[ɪn`dʌstrɪəl] ★★★
形 工業的、勞資的、從事工業的
名 工業公司

1816 manufacture

[mænjə`fæktʃə] ★★★★
動 製造、加工、捏造
名 製造、製造業、產品
衍 manufacturing 製造業

1817 export

[ɪks`port] ★★★
動 輸出、出口
名 輸出、出口、輸出品
反 import 進口、輸入

1818 import

[`ɪmport] ★★★
動 進口、輸入、意味著
名 進口、輸入、重大
片 import from 從⋯進口

1819 immigrant

[`ɪməgrənt] ★★★
名 移民、僑民
形 移入的、移民的
反 emigrant 移出者

1820 coincidentally

[koɪnsə`dɛntlɪ] ★
副 巧合地、碰巧的是
衍 coincident 巧合的

1821 steal

[stil] ★★★★★
動 偷、竊取、侵占
名 偷竊、贓物、盜壘
片 steal away 偷走

1822 incident

[`ɪnsədnt] ★★★★
名 事件、事變、插曲
片 without incident 平安無事

1823 refusal

[rɪ`fjuzl] ★★★
名 拒絕、優先購買權
同 denial 拒絕
反 acceptance 接受

1824 mechanic

[mə`kænɪk] ★★★
名 技工、機械工、做某事的方法
同 repairman 修理工

Fighting!

Give it a shot 小試身手

1 The words he told me were too _____ to forget.

2 His refusal[1823] really _____ my feelings.

3 The mechanic[1824] _____ all the parts to find what was at fault.

4 The jury pronounced the man _____.

5 We should teach every student based on _____ differences.

Answers: **1** impressive **2** hurt **3** inspected **4** innocent **5** individual

153

MP3 305　短文 305　字彙 306

Essay

I once had a job at a museum. My supervisor was a former[1825] inventor. As part of our training, the supervisor taught us how to distinguish[1826] fakes from genuine[1827] artwork and the methods to conduct[1828] a thorough investigation into the origins[1829] of historical[1830] works of art. For example, the color of a genuine ivory[1831] jar[1832] is totally different from that of a fake one. In fact, the museum had an ivory jar that was the most valuable[1833] piece in the museum's entire collection. The supervisor gave us a very detailed and clear introduction of the ivory jar yesterday. Everyone paid close attention without interrupting[1834] him or <u>making light of</u> his speech. He made a joke, though, saying, "The price of this ivory jar is much more expensive than a jet. Even the jewelry in this museum is jealous of the jar because of its incredible[1835] price. So watch out. If you break the jar, you will have to work here for free until you are 100 years old." Employees were quite surprised and weren't sure if the supervisor was kidding or not.

> ⚠ make light of 輕視

中譯 *Translation*

　　我曾經在博物館工作過，我的主管從前是一名發明家。員工訓練中的一部份就是教導員工如何分辨藝術品的真偽，以及研究歷史文物的起源。比如說，真正的象牙製罈子跟偽造的罈子會有截然不同的顏色。博物館裡最珍貴的收藏就是象牙罈。經理昨天很清楚地介紹了象牙罈，每個人都聚精會神，沒人打斷或忽視他的演講。他開玩笑地說：「象牙罈的價錢比一台噴射機還貴，因為價錢驚人，連珠寶都忌妒。所以小心啊，如果你打破了罈子，就準備當義工當到100歲吧！」員工們吃驚不已，甚至不確定主管是說笑還是來真的。

1825 former

[`fɔrmə] ★★★★

形 從前的、前任的、前者的、一度的

反 present 現在的

1826 distinguish

[dɪˋstɪŋgwɪʃ] ★★★

動 辨別、辨識出、使傑出

片 distinguish from 與…作區別

1827 genuine

[ˋdʒɛnjuɪn] ★★★★

形 真的、非偽造的、真誠的、純血統的

片 genuine breed 純種

1828 conduct

[kənˋdʌkt] ★★★★

動 實施、帶領、管理、指揮、傳導

名 品行、指導、經營

1829 origin

[ˋɔrədʒɪn] ★★★★

名 起源、出身、來歷

反 result 結果

片 have its origin in 源自

1830 historical

[hɪsˋtɔrɪkḷ] ★★★★★

形 歷史的、基於史實的

片 historical data 史料

衍 historicity 確有其事

1831 ivory

[ˋaɪvərɪ] ★★★

形 象牙製的、象牙色的

名 象牙、象牙色

片 an ivory tower 象牙塔

1832 jar

[dʒɑr] ★★★

名 罈、罐、震動、刺激

動 刺激、衝突、震動

片 jar with 與…不一致

1833 valuable

[ˋvæljuəbḷ] ★★★★

形 貴重的、值錢的、有價值的、珍貴的

名 貴重物品、財產

1834 interrupt

[ɪntəˋrʌpt] ★★★★

動 打斷、阻礙

片 interrupt sb. in sth. 打斷某人做某事

1835 incredible

[ɪnˋkrɛdəbḷ] ★★★★

形 驚人的、難以置信的

同 unbelievable 驚人的

反 credible 可靠的

1836 howl

[haʊl] ★★★

名 嚎啕大哭、怒吼、大笑

動 吼叫著說

片 howl off 趕下台

fighting!

Give it a shot 小試身手

❶ The baby _____ their honeyed words by a howl[1836].

❷ Peter concealed that his father had been in _____.

❸ The FBI has been called to _____ the case.

❹ She is _____ of her sister's talent.

❺ We do not use typewriters but use computers _____.

Answers: ❶ interrupted ❷ jail ❸ investigate ❹ jealous ❺ instead

MP3　短文 307　字彙 308

154

Essay

A writer was in the habit of keeping notes about stories on his computer whenever he had an idea. One of his creative ideas was about a joyful journey[1837] in a forest. His notes <u>told of</u> a story about a knight[1838] who was known as a man of justice[1839]. He loved to help people in need. One day, as he passed through the forest, he saw a girl climbing a ladder[1840] to pick fruit from a tree. After a few minutes, the girl climbed down and looked down at her shoes to see her laces had come undone. The gallant[1841] knight knelt down quickly and tied her shoelaces before she could. He also escorted[1842] the girl home. The girl lived in a hut[1843] which was surrounded by a lot of junk. The doors had no knobs[1844]. The girl used a kettle[1845] to boil water for the knight. She said, "Thank you for what you have done for me today. I will knit[1846] you a sweater as a gift." He shook[1847] his head with a smile. He enjoyed helping others <u>rather than</u> getting any kind of payment from them.

⚠ tell of 講述

⚠ rather than 而不是

中譯 *Translation*

　　有位作家習慣用電腦記錄他的故事靈感。其中一個富有創意的點子是關於一趟愉快的森林旅程。這個故事是說一個以行俠仗義的形象為人所知的騎士，他一向熱心助人。某天，他經過森林時，看見一個女孩在梯子上攀爬，採集樹上的水果。幾分鐘之後，女孩爬下梯子，發現她的鞋帶鬆開了。富有騎士風範的他二話不說馬上跪下幫女孩繫鞋帶，然後還護送女孩回家。這女孩住在間簡陋的小屋，小屋四周堆滿了垃圾，門上連個手把都沒有。女孩用水壺煮開水給騎士喝，她說：「謝謝你今天為我所做的一切，我要織件毛衣給你當謝禮。」他搖頭笑了笑。他樂於助人但不求回報。

1837 journey
[`dʒɝnɪ] ★★★★
- 名 旅程、行程
- 動 旅行
- 同 tour 旅行

1838 knight
[`naɪt] ★★★
- 名 騎士、爵士
- 動 授以爵位
- 同 cavalryman 騎兵

1839 justice
[`dʒʌstɪs] ★★★★★
- 名 正義、公平、審判
- 反 injustice 非正義
- 片 do justice to 公平對待

1840 ladder
[`lædɚ] ★★★★
- 名 梯子、階梯、途徑
- 片 kick down the ladder 過河拆橋

1841 gallant
[`gælənt] ★★
- 形 騎士風度的、英勇的、華麗的
- 名 豪俠、時髦男士

1842 escort
[`ɛskɔrt] ★★★
- 動 護送、陪同
- 名 護送、護衛隊、陪同
- 片 escort to 護送至

1843 hut
[hʌt] ★★★
- 名 小屋、茅舍
- 動 住在小屋中、駐紮
- 同 shack 簡陋木屋

1844 knob
[nɑb] ★★★
- 名 球形把手、圓丘
- 同 handle 把手

1845 kettle
[`kɛtl] ★★★
- 名 水壺
- 俚 another kettle of fish 截然不同的人事物

1846 knit
[nɪt] ★★
- 動 編織、接合、皺眉
- 名 編織衣物
- 片 knit into 把…織成

1847 shake
[ʃek] ★★★★
- 動 搖動、發抖、握手
- 名 搖動、發抖、握手
- 片 shake off 擺脫

1848 type
[taɪp] ★★★★★
- 動 打字、把…分類
- 名 類型、榜樣、樣式
- 片 type out 打出

Give it a shot 小試身手

1. The worker climbed up the _____ carefully.
2. Gorillas are living in the _____.
3. My sister keeps a _____ every day.
4. Our family had a wonderful _____ in Japan last month.
5. The _____ of my laptop is broken. I cannot type[1848] right now.

Answers: 1 ladder 2 jungle 3 journal 4 journey 5 keyboard

155

Essay

Everyone has lost face at least once in his or her lifetime. Sometimes stories about people's embarrassment are so funny that you want to <u>burst into laughter</u>. Here are some stories to share with you. There was once a lifeguard[1849] who lost his contact lenses[1850] when he was saving a drowning person. The lifeguard was so upset[1851] that he sailed a boat and kept looking in the water to try to find his contact lenses. Of course, he never found them. There was also a librarian who liked to read and enjoyed sleeping on the lawn[1852] outside the library on sunny days during his break time. However, he once fell down while walking on the sidewalk[1853] towards the lawn and broke his front teeth. Another story was about a woman who sent her leather bag to a laundry[1854]. The cleaner[1855] tore the bag and told her someone else had already come to pick it up for her. Howerer, the woman was very liberal[1856] and told him, "I don't care about the bag, but I don't like liars. Do you want to confess[1857] or remain a liar[1858] forever?" The shopkeeper said, "I prefer being a liar." Now you know how stupid he was.

ⓘ burst into laughter 放聲大笑

中譯 *Translation*

　　每個人一生至少都有一次丟臉的經驗，有時你會因為一些搞笑的故事而突然大笑。這裡有些故事要跟你分享。有個救生員救人時隱形眼鏡掉了，救生員很苦惱，所以他划著船試圖在水中找出他的隱形眼鏡。當然，他什麼都沒找到。還有一位圖書館員，他喜歡在空閒時間看書，也喜歡在晴天時躺在圖書館外的草坪上休息。不過有一次他在往草坪方向的人行道上重重跌了一跤，把門牙都給摔斷了。另一個故事是一個女人將她的皮製包包送洗，但店家把皮包洗壞了，還跟她撒謊說皮包已被領走了。不過這個女人十分寬宏大量，跟他說：「我一點都不在乎這個皮包，但是我很討厭說謊的人。你要從實招來還是要繼續撒謊？」店長說：「我要選擇後者。」現在你知道他有多愚蠢了吧？

1849 lifeguard

[`laɪfgɑrd] ★★
名 救生員、警衛
動 保護、當救生員

1853 sidewalk

[`saɪdwɔk] ★★★
名 (美)人行道
同 pavement (英)人行道

1857 confess

[kən`fɛs] ★★★
動 承認、坦白、懺悔
片 confess to 向…懺悔
衍 confession 坦白

1850 lens

[lɛnz] ★★★★
名 鏡片、鏡頭
動 給…攝影
片 contact lens 隱形眼鏡

1854 laundry

[`lɔndrɪ] ★★★
名 洗衣店、送洗衣物
片 do the laundry 洗衣服

1858 liar

[`laɪɚ] ★★★
名 騙子、説謊的人
同 fibber 慣撒小謊的人

1851 upset

[ʌp`sɛt] ★★★★
形 苦惱的、翻覆的、心煩的、不適的
動 打翻、打亂、心煩意亂

1855 cleaner

[`klinɚ] ★★
名 乾洗工、乾洗店、清潔工、吸塵器
片 dry cleaner 乾洗店

1859 comedy

[`kɑmədɪ] ★★★★
名 喜劇、喜劇成分
同 farce 笑劇
反 tragedy 悲劇

1852 lawn

[lɔn] ★★★★
名 草坪、草地、細棉布
同 grassplot 草地
片 trim a lawn 修剪草坪

1856 liberal

[`lɪbərəl] ★★★★
形 心胸寬闊的、自由的
反 dogmatic 教條的
衍 liberty 自由

1860 barrack

[`bærək] ★★
名 兵營、工房
動 住入營房

fighting!

Give it a shot 小試身手

❶ Ken wore a very cool _____ pants to school today.

❷ The comedy[1859] is so funny that the theater is full of _____.

❸ I like to go shopping in my _____ time.

❹ His parents punished him for being a _____.

❺ The public does not have the _____ to enter the barrack[1860].

MP3　短文 311　字彙 312

156

Essay

There was a maid[1861] who was very sick and needed a liver transplant[1862]. The doctor told her, "You cannot eat lobster[1863] or any seafood before the surgery. Also, you have to wear loose[1864] clothing on the day of your surgery." Since it was an emergency, the doctor launched[1865] a public awareness campaign to encourage people to donate their organs in the event of death. After a month, a healthy liver was finally delivered to the hospital and the girl's surgery <u>went well</u>. Before the surgery, the woman's mother embraced[1866] her daughter excitedly[1867] and gave her a cartoon magnet[1868] and some lipstick as gifts[1869]. After the successful operation, both the maid and her mother described the doctor as as great as an angel who saved people's lives with his great <u>devotion</u>[1870] <u>to</u> his patients.

⚠ go well 順利解決

⚠ devotion to 奉獻、致力於

中譯 *Translation*

　　有個少女病得非常嚴重，必須要進行肝臟移植手術。，醫生跟她說：「手術前妳不能吃龍蝦或是其他海鮮，手術當天必須穿寬鬆的衣服。」由於她的病情危急，醫生發起活動呼籲並鼓勵大家捐贈器官。一個月後，終於有健康的肝臟送抵醫院，而女孩的手術也非常成功。手術之前，女孩的母親激動地擁抱她，還給她卡通磁鐵和口紅作為禮物。手術成功後，女孩和母親形容這位醫生像天使一樣偉大，全心全意為病患奉獻自己、拯救生命。

1861 maid

[med] ★★★
名 少女、女僕、年輕女子
片 maid of honor 伴娘
(= bridesmaid)

1862 transplant

[`trænsplænt] ★★★
名 移植、移植器官
動 移植、移種、移居
片 transplant into 移入

1863 lobster

[`labstɚ] ★★★
名 龍蝦、龍蝦肉

1864 loose

[lus] ★★★★
形 寬鬆的、鬆散的、未控制的、不嚴密的
動 解開、釋放、鬆開

1865 launch

[lɔntʃ] ★★★
動 開辦、發起、發射、投擲、出版
名 發射、下水、發行

1866 embrace

[ɪm`bres] ★★★★
動 擁抱、抓住、信奉
名 擁抱、懷抱
同 hug 擁抱

1867 excitedly

[ɪk`saɪtɪdlɪ] ★★
副 興奮地、激動地
衍 excited 興奮的、激動的

1868 magnet

[`mægnɪt] ★★★
名 磁鐵、磁石、有吸引力的人或物
形 magnetic 有磁性的

1869 gift

[gɪft] ★★★★★
名 禮物、天賦、才能
動 賦予
同 present 禮物

1870 devotion

[dɪ`voʃən] ★★★
名 奉獻、獻身、熱愛
同 dedication 奉獻
衍 devoted 獻身的

1871 allergic

[ə`lɝdʒɪk] ★★★
形 過敏的、對…反感的
片 be allergic to 對…過敏
衍 allergy 過敏症

1872 belt

[bɛlt] ★★★★
名 腰帶、傳送帶、地帶
動 用皮帶抽打、用帶子繫上

Fighting!

Give it a shot 小試身手

1 I cannot eat _____. I am allergic[1871] to it.

2 The Disney Land is like the most _____ place for children.

3 Please help me _____ the belt[1872]. It is too tight.

4 The little girl secretly used her mother's _____ for fun.

5 My father went back from a business trip with a lot of _____.

Answers: 1 lobster 2 magical 3 loosen 4 lipstick 5 luggages

157

Essay

A mayor owned a mall. The majority[1873] of products sold in the mall were made of marble[1874], such as marble statues[1875], tombs[1876], etc. Unfortunately, the mayor was bad at mathematics. Of course, a businessperson must either[1877] be good at math or hire someone who is to do accounting[1878]. Since the mayor would never be good at addition and subtraction, he really needed to hire[1879] someone to help him.

One day, the mayor found a person named Jack who had excellent math skills[1880] and hired him <u>on the spot</u>. The mayor was really happy and thought everything would be great now. As time passed, however, the mayor noticed that he was losing money. It didn't <u>make any sense</u>. Many customers[1881] were buying his marble products, so he should be making a lot of profit. He started to suspect that Jack was stealing money from him. He decided to confront Jack and demand that he repay[1882] the money he stole, but on the day he was going to do that Jack never showed up for work. When the mayor went to Jack's desk he found a note that read: "Goodbye forever, and thanks for all your money! Now you know how good I am at math!"

⚠ on the spot 立即、當場

⚠ make sense 合理

中譯 Translation

　　有位市長擁有一家購物中心，裡頭大多賣大理石製品，像大理石雕像、墓碑等等。市長的數學很差。一個生意人必須精通算數，要不然就是必須雇用會計。既然市長從來都不擅長加減乘除，他勢必需要雇用個擅長算數的人來協助他。

　　某天，市長發現一個名叫傑克的人，他有驚人的數學能力，市長當場就決定雇用他。市長非常開心，心想從此之後就能一帆風順了。然而，隨著時光流逝，市長察覺到他的錢不斷減少。但這並不合理，因為他的大理石製品銷售量很好，有許多客戶購買，照理說他應該從中獲利不少。接著，市長開始懷疑傑克偷錢，他決定當面詢問傑克，並要求傑克償還他所偷的錢。不料，從他要跟傑克當面對峙的那天開始，傑克就再也沒有出現過了。市長在傑克的桌上發現一張紙條，上頭寫著：「永別了！感謝你的錢！現在，你知道我數學有多好了吧！」

1873 majority

[mə`dʒɔrətɪ] ★★★★
名 大多數、多數的票數、多數黨
反 minority 少數

1874 marble

[`mɑrbḷ] ★★★
名 大理石、彈珠、理智
形 大理石的、冷酷無情的

1875 statue

[`stætʃʊ] ★★★
名 雕像、塑像
同 sculpture 雕像
衍 statuary (總稱)雕像

1876 tomb

[tum] ★★★
名 墓碑、葬生之地
同 grave 墓穴
片 ancient tomb 古墓

1877 either

[`iðə] ★★★
連 或者
形 任一的
代 任何一個

1878 accounting

[ə`kauntɪŋ] ★★★★
名 會計、會計學、結帳
片 there's no accounting for taste 人各有所好

1879 hire

[haɪr] ★★★★
動 雇用、租借
名 租用、雇用
同 employ 雇用

1880 skill

[`skɪl] ★★★★
名 技能、技術、熟練性
同 proficiency 熟練
片 skill at …方面的技能

1881 customer

[`kʌstəmə] ★★★★
名 顧客、買主
同 client 顧客

1882 repay

[rɪ`pe] ★★★★
動 償還、報答、報復
片 repay for 為了…而報答

1883 newcomer

[`nju`kʌmə] ★★
名 新來的人、新手
片 newcomer to 對…是新手

1884 psychology

[saɪ`kɑlədʒɪ] ★★★
名 心理學、心理特點、心理、揣測

Fighting!

Give it a shot 小試身手

1 We need to teach the newcomer[1883] some _____.

2 The _____ announced a new policy last week.

3 The little dog ran happily on the _____.

4 I want to do something _____ to help the world.

5 I _____ in psychology[1884] in college.

MP3 315 | 短文 315 | 字彙 316

Essay 158

A merchant[1885] had an electronics store. The store was on Fifth Street, between a medical center and a coffee shop. The medical center was a facility built especially for patients who had mental problems. Last month, the merchant had a big sale on microwaves[1886]. He asked his workers to memorize the operating[1887] instructions[1888] for the microwaves, to promote microwaves with a microphone[1889], and to encourage customers to sign up for a membership[1890] card. He told his staff that the microwaves had received an award for best design. Meanwhile, he also emphasized the benefits of getting a store membership. He said, "Join us, and we will guarantee your microwave for free for two years!" Since he spared no effort[1891] to promote his store during the big microwave sale, he always felt tired and needed to drink several cups of coffee throughout the day. It was all worth it, though, because the microwaves were sold out soon. Business had been so good that he even thought he might open another shop soon. The store was in a mess after the sale, but he cleaned it up in a merry[1892] mood.

> ⚠ in a mess 一團亂、凌亂無序

中譯 *Translation*

　　有個商人在第五大街開了家電器行，兩旁是診所和咖啡廳，那家診所專門為精神病患看診。上個月，商人舉辦了微波爐大拍賣，他要求員工把微波爐的操作方式全背下來，用麥克風做促銷，還要鼓勵客人加入會員。他提到這個微波爐曾經得過最佳產品設計的獎章。同時，他特別強調加入會員能享有的福利。他說：「加入我們，就可獲得兩年免費商品保固。」促銷期間，因為他總是不遺餘力地工作，所以每天早上他總是感到筋疲力盡，一定要來幾杯咖啡才能振作精神。然而，因為微波爐熱賣到銷售一空，所以一切辛勞都是值得的。業績實在太好了，他甚至覺得他很快就可以再開一家分店了。雖然拍賣結束後店裡一團混亂，但是他打掃時的心情是愉快的。

1885 merchant

[`mɝtʃənt] ★★★
名 商人、零售商
形 商人的、商業的
同 trader 商人

1886 microwave

[`maɪkrowev] ★★
名 微波爐、微波
動 用微波爐烹調

1887 operating

[`ɑpəretɪŋ] ★★
形 操作的、營運的、業務上的、手術的
同 operation 操作、手術

1888 instruction

[ɪn`strʌkʃən] ★★★★
名 操作指南、講授、指示
片 instruction in …的講授
衍 instructor 指導者

1889 microphone

[`maɪkrəfon] ★★★
名 麥克風、擴音器
同 loudspeaker 擴音器

1890 membership

[`mɛmbəʃɪp] ★★★
名 會員身分、會員數、全體會員
片 membership of …會員

1891 effort

[`ɛfət] ★★★★★
名 努力、盡力、成就
片 spare no effort 不遺餘力

1892 merry

[`mɛrɪ] ★★★★
形 愉快的、興高采烈的、輕快的
片 make merry 盡情歡樂

1893 plumber

[`plʌmə] ★★★
名 水管工、堵漏人員
片 plumber's helper 裝有把手的吸盤

1894 broken

[`brokən] ★★★★★
形 損壞的、中斷的、破裂的、不流利的
片 get broken 弄壞

1895 dirty

[`dɝtɪ] ★★★★
形 髒的、汙穢的、下流的、惡劣的
動 弄髒、變髒

1896 total

[`totl̩] ★★★★★
形 完全的、總計的
名 總計、合計
動 合計為

Fighting!

Give it a shot 小試身手

1. The plumber[1893] came to help _____ the broken[1894] pipe.
2. He had a minor _____ problem and needed to see the doctor.
3. Look at your dirty[1895] room. It is a total[1896] _____.
4. Helen is good at _____ telephone numbers.
5. Our teacher uses a _____ to make her voice louder.

Answers: 1 mend 2 mental 3 mess 4 memorizing 5 microphone

MP3

短文 317　字彙 318

159

Essay

Peter worked as a miner[1897] at a mine[1898] in the hills[1899] outside a major city. One day, the nearby city was bombed[1900] by a nuclear missile[1901]. People who <u>survived</u> the attack were Peter and his fellow miners who were working underground[1902] in a mine at the time of the huge[1903] nuclear explosion[1904]. The explosion shook the mine so hard that materials from the sides of the mine fell down, <u>exposing</u> a large quantity of very valuable diamonds. The men all looked at each other. They knew no one above[1905] ground could have survived the missile attack[1906]. That meant all of their bosses were dead and they could keep the fortune of diamonds for themselves. However, they also knew that they couldn't leave the mine because of the deadly[1907] radiation. They were rich, but they were also trapped!

> ⓘ survive 倖存、殘留、比…活得長
> ⓘ expose 使暴露於、使接觸到、揭露

中譯 *Translation*

　　彼得是一名在礦坑工作的礦工，礦坑位於大城市外的山丘上。有一天，附近的城市遭到核彈攻擊，正好在地底下工作的彼得和他的礦工同事們是這次攻擊事件的倖存者。核爆強烈撼動整個礦坑，以致礦坑的某一部分塌陷下來，大量的珍貴鑽石暴露在眼前。礦工們不可置信的看了看彼此。他們非常清楚，地面上的人絕對不可能在這次炸彈攻擊中存活，那也意味著，他們的老闆都喪生了，那些鑽石是屬於他們的。但是，他們也知道，由於致命的輻射，他們無法離開礦坑。雖然他們一夕之間致富了，但他們也動彈不得，哪都不能去。

1897　miner

[`maɪnə] ★★

名 礦工
片 a coal miner 煤礦工人
同 minerworker 礦工

1898　mine

[maɪn] ★★★★

名 礦、礦山、寶庫、地雷
動 開礦、埋地雷、破壞
片 mine for 採掘…

1899　hill

[hɪl] ★★★★

名 小山、丘陵、避暑勝地
同 mound 小丘
片 over the hill 正在衰弱

1900　bomb

[bɑm] ★★★★

動 轟炸、投彈、慘敗
名 炸彈、轟動一時的事物
同 ecplosive 炸藥

1901　missile

[`mɪsl] ★★★

名 飛彈、導彈、投射物
形 可發射的、可投擲的
片 a nuclear missle 核彈

1902　underground

[`ʌndəˌɡraʊnd] ★★★

副 在地下、秘密地
形 地下的、秘密的
名 地面下層、地下組織

1903　huge

[hjudʒ] ★★★★★

形 巨大的、龐大的
片 a huge success 大成功

1904　explosion

[ɪk`sploʒən] ★★★

名 爆炸、劇增、爆發
同 blast 爆炸
片 explosion of …的爆發

1905　above

[ə`bʌv] ★★★★★

介 在…上面、超過、高於
副 在上面、更高、更多
名 上文、上述事實

1906　attack

[ə`tæk] ★★★★★

名 攻擊、抨擊、疾病發作
動 進攻、襲擊、抨擊
片 the attack on 對…進攻

1907　deadly

[`dɛdlɪ] ★★★★

名 毒性的、致命的、極度的、非常無聊的
副 死一般地、非常

1908　lottery

[`latərɪ] ★★★

名 獎券、彩票、運氣
同 raffle 彩券

---

fighting!

Give it a shot 小試身手

❶ Jane won the lottery[1908] and soon became a _____.

❷ Everyone in the neighborhood is out to look for the _____ kid.

❸ Water is the _____ of oxygen and hydrogen.

❹ The _____ is not allowed to drink or smoke.

❺ The _____ of his life makes me want to cry.

Answers: ❶ millionaire ❷ missing ❸ mixture ❹ minority ❺ misery

160

 MP3　 短文 319　 字彙 320

Essay

Jimmy was a male nanny[1909] who used to be an officer in the navy. He had big muscles and was therefore quite strong. One day, because it was raining hard and he had forgotten to close the windows of his house, he was in a bad mood since so much water had come in his house and he had to mop[1910] it all up. By the time Jimmy had finished mopping up all the water, he was so tired that he took a nap[1911] on his sofa. Soon afterwards, a monk came to his front door and rang the bell to ask for some food. Jimmy thought it was quite strange for a monk to knock[1912] on his door, but he gave him some food from his cupboard, and the monk left. Then, since the monk had interrupted his nap, Jimmy fell asleep again on the sofa while watching a musical program[1913]. After a while[1914], the police came and asked Jimmy if he had heard or seen anything strange yesterday or today. Jimmy said, "No." He knew a murder[1915] had occurred in his neighborhood yesterday. The police were trying to find any possible clues[1916]. Actually, Jimmy did hear some strange sounds yesterday, and he did think the monk's visit today was quite strange, but he was scared[1917] the police might suspect him and didn't want to admit the truth. He felt so regretful[1918] because he knew he had not done the right thing. By now, you are probably wondering, "Where's the baby Jimmy was supposed[1919] to be taking care of?" Oh, I forgot to mention, it was his day off!

中譯 *Translation*

　　吉米是個男保姆，他曾經是名海軍軍官，他的肌肉發達，身強體壯。某個大雨天，吉米忘記關窗戶，家裡因而進水了，他心情糟透了，因為他必須把水拖乾。好不容易把水拖乾後，他實在累垮了，便在沙發上打起盹來。不久之後，一個和尚按了門鈴，要求施捨一些食物，吉米覺得和尚來敲門有異，但他還是從櫥窗裡拿了些食物給和尚。後來，和尚離開了。然後，因為和尚打斷了他打瞌睡，吉米開始看音樂節目時又睡著了。過了一會，一名警察到吉米家詢問他昨天或今天是否有發現什麼異狀，吉米回答沒有。但他知道，昨天住家附近發生一起謀殺案，警方正在蒐索一切可能線索，事實上，吉米昨天的確聽到了些奇怪的聲音，他也覺得和尚的來訪事有蹊蹺，但他太害怕被警察懷疑而不敢坦白。他因為違背了自己的良心非常後悔。故事進行到現在，或許你該問：「吉米帶的小孩在哪啊？」喔，我忘了說，其實吉米今天休假。

1909 nanny

[`nænɪ] ★★
名 保姆、祖母、母山羊
同 babysitter 保姆

1910 mop

[mɑp] ★★★
動 用拖把拖、擦乾
名 拖把、蓬亂的頭髮
片 mop up 用拖把拖洗

1911 nap

[næp] ★★★
名 打盹兒、午睡
動 打盹、疏忽
片 take a nap 小睡一下

1912 knock

[nɑk] ★★★★
動 敲、碰擊、貶損
名 敲、擊、挫折
片 knock off 擊敗

1913 program

[`progræm] ★★★★★
名 節目、計畫、大綱
動 安排節目、設計程式、制訂計畫

1914 while

[hwaɪl] ★★★★★
名 一段時間、一會兒
連 當…時、然而、雖然
片 for a while 暫時

1915 murder

[`mɝdɚ] ★★★★
名 謀殺、要命的事
動 謀殺、扼殺、破壞
同 assassinate 暗殺

1916 clue

[klu] ★★★
名 線索、跡象、情節
動 提供線索、告知
片 clue in 向…提供情況

1917 scared

[skɛrd] ★★★★
形 恐懼的、不敢的
片 be scared to death 嚇死

1918 regretful

[rɪ`grɛtfəl] ★★
形 懊悔的、遺憾的
同 repentant 後悔的
衍 regrettable 遺憾的

1919 suppose

[sə`poz] ★★★★★
動 認為必須、猜想、假定
片 supposed to 可以、應該

1920 phantom

[`fæntəm] ★★
名 幽靈、幻像
形 幽靈似的、幻覺的
同 illusion 幻覺

Fighting!

Give it a shot 小試身手

1 I am not in the _____ to party today.

2 My mother took a _____ after lunch.

3 My favorite _____ is "The Phantom[1920] of the Opera."

4 The police are investigating a _____ happened last week.

5 I was raised by my _____.

Answers: 1 mood 2 nap 3 musical 4 murder 5 nanny

161

A young woman decided to become a nun because of her feelings of self-doubt and her love for poor[1921] people. She used to work in a nice clothing store, but she always felt nervous and inferior when rich customers come into the store. Their unfriendly[1922] and arrogant[1923] attitude always got on her nerves[1924]. They cared about their images too much. In addition, she knew that many people in the world were so poor they couldn't afford[1925] to eat properly. This made her despise[1926] rich people, who often threw away things poor people would love to have. Finally, she couldn't <u>stand</u> seeing rich people anymore.

Now, the nun has a very simple life in a cloister[1927]. She always observes[1928] people who come to the cloister and sometimes waters[1929] flowers in the garden outside[1930]. She has a lovely nickname[1931], "Cold Beauty." In her new life, she never has to see any rich people and she often helps poor people. <u>As a result</u>, she really enjoys her life in the convent[1932].

> ! stand 忍受(常用於否定或疑問句)
>
> ! as a result 因此、結果

中譯 *Translation*

　　一位年輕的女人因為自我懷疑以及對窮苦人家的關愛，而決定成為一名修女。她曾經在一家不錯的服飾店工作，每當富有的顧客上門，她總是感到緊張又自卑。他們不和善及傲慢的態度常讓她怒火中燒。那些有錢人太在意形象。而且，她很清楚世界上有很多人窮到沒辦法好好吃頓飯，反觀有錢人不懂珍惜，隨手丟棄貧窮人家珍視卻無法擁有的東西，因此，她打從內心鄙視那些有錢人。最後，她再也無法忍受面對有錢人。

　　現在這個修女在修道院過著簡樸的生活，她觀察出入修道院的人，偶爾幫外頭花園裡的花朵澆水。她有個可愛的小名叫「冰山美人」。她展開全新的生活，再也不用看到那些有錢人，她也能經常幫助窮苦人家。因此，她非常享受現在的修道院生活。

1921 poor

[pʊr] ★★★★★
- 形 貧窮的、缺少的、體弱的、不幸的
- 同 needy 貧窮的

1922 unfriendly

[ʌn`frɛndlɪ] ★★
- 形 有敵意的、不利的
- 反 friendly 親切的

1923 arrogant

[`ærəgənt] ★★★
- 形 傲慢的、自大的
- 同 haughty 自大的
- 反 humble 謙卑的

1924 nerve

[nɝv] ★★★★
- 名 神經、憂慮、膽量
- 片 get on one's nerves 激怒某人

1925 afford

[ə`ford] ★★★★
- 動 買得起、提供
- 片 can't afford to 不能冒…之險、無法負擔做…

1926 despise

[dɪ`spaɪz] ★★
- 動 鄙視、看不起
- 同 disdain 鄙視
- 反 respect 尊敬

1927 cloister

[`klɔɪstə] ★★
- 名 修道院、隱居地、迴廊
- 動 幽閉於修道院中、與塵世隔絕

1928 observe

[əb`zɝv] ★★★★
- 動 觀察、注意到、遵守、評論
- 片 observe on 談論
- 衍 observation 觀察

1929 water

[`wɔtə] ★★★★★
- 動 給…澆水、加水稀釋
- 名 水、大片的水、海域
- 片 water down 使緩和

1930 outside

[aʊt`saɪd] ★★★★★
- 副 在外面、在室外
- 形 外面的、外來的
- 名 外面、外側、外觀

1931 nickname

[nɪknem] ★★★
- 名 綽號
- 動 給…起綽號
- 同 pet name 暱稱

1932 convent

[`kɑnvɛnt] ★★★
- 名 女修道院、修女團
- 同 nunnery 女修道院

Fighting!

Give it a shot 小試身手

❶ My sister is very _____ about the coming exam.

❷ She has a lovely _____ called "Cutie."

❸ It is not the right _____ to mention this subject.

❹ The police carefully _____ the man's every movement.

❺ It is _____ that he is falling in love with her.

Answers: ❶ nervous ❷ nickname ❸ occasion ❹ observed ❺ obvious

162

Essay

An organization built a large[1933] house to help orphans who had <u>suffered from</u> domestic[1934] violence[1935]. Although the organization wanted to help many orphans, it found that it didn't have enough[1936] money to assist[1937] as many as it wanted to. This made the people in charge of the organization sad[1938].

One day, there came a great opportunity: a company wanted to cooperate with the organization. Because of this, the organization could have more money to help more orphans. During[1939] the weekends[1940], people who worked for the organization would take kids out to do some outdoor activities. They bought every kid an overcoat[1941] during winter so that they wouldn't get sick while having fun outdoors. They told the orphans not to be sad about their past[1942] but to think of all the good things in their lives and to be optimistic about the future[1943]. The workers also tried to make the orphans be more independent, telling them that everyone can have a good life if they try hard.

ⓘ suffer from 遭受⋯之苦

中譯 *Translation*

　　有個機構為遭受家庭暴力的孤兒建造了一棟大房子，雖然這個機構想幫助更多孤兒，卻沒有足夠資金協助更多孩子。這樣的困境使機構負責人感到難過。

　　有一天，有間公司想和機構合作，這是個大好的機會，如此一來機構便有更多的資金來幫助更多的孤兒。週末時機構員工會帶小孩子從事戶外活動，冬天會幫每個小孩買外套，這樣一來，小孩在戶外玩耍就不會著涼感冒了。員工們告訴孤兒不要為自己的過去感到難過，應該想想生命中的美好，並對未來保持樂觀的態度。員工們也試圖讓孩子學會獨立，並告訴他們，想擁有美好人生就要努力爭取。

1933 large

[lɑrdʒ] ★★★★★
形 大的、多的、廣博的
副 大大地、誇大地
片 extra large 特大號

1934 domestic

[də`mɛstɪk] ★★★★
形 家庭的、國內的
片 domestic violence 家暴

1935 violence

[`vaɪələns] ★★★★
名 暴力、激烈、強力
片 resort to violence 訴諸暴力

1936 enough

[ə`nʌf] ★★★★★
形 足夠的、充足的
名 足夠、充分
副 足夠地、相當地

1937 assist

[ə`sɪst] ★★★★
動 幫助、協助、參加
同 幫助、助攻
片 assist in 在…給予協助

1938 sad

[sæd] ★★★★
形 悲哀的、遭透了的
同 sorrowful 悲傷的
片 sad to say 不幸的是

1939 during

[`dʊrɪŋ] ★★★★★
介 在…期間、在某個時候
同 throughout 在整個期間

1940 weekend

[`wik`ɛnd] ★★★★★
名 週末
形 週末的
片 on the weekends 每週末

1941 overcoat

[`ovəkot] ★★
名 外套、大衣
片 take off one's overcoat 脫下大衣

1942 past

[pæst] ★★★★★
形 過去的、以前的
介 經過、超過
名 過去、昔日、經歷

1943 future

[`fjutʃə] ★★★★
名 未來、前途
形 未來的、將來的
片 in the future 未來

1944 painting

[`pentɪŋ] ★★★★
名 油畫、水彩畫、上油漆、畫法
同 drawing 圖畫

Give it a shot 小試身手

Fighting!

1. Mary is a _____ person. She always looks happy.
2. I like _____ activities such as playing basketball and jogging.
3. This is the _____ painting[1944] mastered by Leonardo da Vinci.
4. The red _____ looks great on you.
5. I do not get the _____ to see my favorite singer.

Answers: 1 optimistic 2 outdoor 3 original 4 overcoat 5 opportunity

163

MP3　短文 325　字彙 326

We heard that Bali was like a paradise[1945], so we saved up some money and took a trip to Bali. It was the first time we had <u>gone abroad</u>. We had to pay for a visa[1946] before we went to Bali. When we arrived at the airport in Bali, a tour guide, who was full of great passion, came to greet us immediately. He took us to the bus stop through a narrow passage[1947]. The hotel we stayed at was like a palace[1948]. We had a maid to make pancakes and other yummy food for us every morning. Besides that, everyone had a safe in the room to keep important and expensive things in. The tour guide also taught us how to set[1949] the password[1950]. The next day, we went to a history museum. We saw the fossils[1951] of prehistoric[1952] animals. The tour guide explained details about the fossils with patience and warned us of the slippery pavement outside the museum. On the third day, we went to watch a parade[1953]. During the event, though, a riot[1954] unexpectedly erupted[1955]. People were all in a panic[1956] and ran to safety. Thus, our trip was disrupted for a few days.

(!) go abroad 出國

中譯 *Translation*

　　我們聽說峇里島就像天堂一樣，所以就存了一些錢去峇里島旅行。那是我們第一次出國，我們出發前花了一些錢辦護照。當我們抵達峇里島的機場時，熱情的導遊立刻過來跟我們打招呼，他帶我們從一條小路走到公車站。我們住的飯店就像皇宮一樣，每天早上女傭都會幫我們做煎餅還有其它好吃的東西，而且每個人的房間都有保險箱可以放貴重物品，導遊也教我們如何設定保險箱密碼。隔天，我們去了歷史博物館，我們看到了史前動物的化石，導遊很有耐心地解釋化石的歷史來源，他也提醒我們注意人行道很滑。第三天，我們去參觀遊行，遊行進行到一半時，無預警地發生暴動。所有人都受到驚嚇，我們的行程因此暫停了幾天。

1945 paradise

[`pærədaɪs] ★★★
名 天堂、極樂、樂園
片 fool's paradise 虛幻的樂境

1946 visa

[`vizə] ★★★
名 護照上的簽證
動 在護照上簽證
片 entry visa 入境簽證

1947 passage

[`pæsɪdʒ] ★★★★
名 通道、出入口、航行、通行許可
動 通過、航行

1948 palace

[`pælɪs] ★★★
名 皇宮、宮殿、豪華住宅
同 castle 巨宅

1949 set

[sɛt] ★★★★★
動 設定、安裝、使處於、著手於、衰弱、下沈
形 固定的、下定決心的

1950 password

[`pæswɜd] ★★★★
名 密碼、口令、暗語
同 watchword 口令

1951 fossil

[`fɑsl̩] ★★
名 化石、頑固不化的人
形 化石的、陳腐的
片 old fossil 老頑固

1952 prehistoric

[prihɪs`tɔrɪk] ★★★
形 史前的、舊式的
片 prehistoric age 史前時代

1953 parade

[pə`red] ★★★★
名 遊行、行進、閱兵典禮、誇耀
動 遊行、列隊行進、誇耀

1954 riot

[`raɪət] ★★★
名 暴亂、喧鬧、盡情發洩
動 參加暴亂、聚眾鬧事
片 run riot 滋事

1955 erupt

[ɪ`rʌpt] ★★
動 爆發、噴出、發疹
片 erupt into 突然發展成
衍 eruption 爆發

1956 panic

[`pænɪk] ★★★★★
名 恐慌、驚慌
形 恐慌的、極度的
動 使恐慌

Fighting!

Give it a shot 小試身手

1 You need to have a _____ to take a plane.

2 Don't park your motorcycle on the _____.

3 I _____ in a science camp on summer vacation.

4 The nurse took care of the old lady with _____.

5 Mary is sick and her face looks very _____.

Answers: 1 passport 2 pavement 3 participated 4 patience 5 pale

164

🎧 MP3

Essay

There was a thief who peeped[1957] through the windows of a pilot's house. The pilot's house was located on a mountain. The thief found that the pilot was not at home, so he <u>broke into</u> his house. The thief immediately stole some pearls, some bottles of expensive pills[1958], and even food on the table. The pilot came home just then after a flight[1959], and he went to his backyard first. He saw pests[1960] on his pine[1961] tree, but he didn't even have a penny[1962] to buy any pesticides to kill them. After he entered[1963] his house, he saw that everything was in a mess. He knew there must be something wrong. He found the thief and confronted him: "You broke into my house. How could you do this?" The thief tried to persuade him not to report him to the police. "I am here to kill the pests on the pine tree!" the clever[1964] thief said. Because of the pilot's naivety[1965], he believed[1966] him. "Why don't you go to bed and I'll work on killing the pests right now?" the thief said to the pilot, and the pilot did just that. But when he awoke, the pests were still on the pine tree and the thief had stolen almost[1967] everything he had!

ⓘ break into 闖入

 Translation

　　有個小偷從窗戶偷窺一名飛行員的家。這名飛行員住在山上。小偷得知飛行員不在家，他便破門而入。偷了他的珍珠和幾瓶昂貴的藥丸，甚至連桌上的食物都不放過。飛行員正好飛行結束回到家，他先到他的後院，發現松樹上有害蟲，但他沒錢買殺蟲劑除蟲。後來他進到屋子裡，看到家裡一團亂，察覺有異。他發現了小偷，質問他：「你沒經過我的允許就闖入我的房子，你怎麼可以這樣做？」小偷說服他不要報警，並靈機一動說：「我是來這兒幫松樹除蟲的！」由於飛行員個性天真，便信以為真。「你何不先去休息一下，我現在馬上就要開始除蟲了。」小偷說道，而飛行員竟不疑有他，跑去休息了。當飛行員一覺醒來，發現害蟲仍然在松樹上，而小偷幾乎偷光了他的東西。

1957 peep

[pip] ★★
動 偷看、隱約顯現
名 窺視、一瞥、隱約顯現
片 peep at 偷看

1958 pill

[pɪl] ★★★
名 藥丸、屈辱的事
動 製成藥丸、服用藥丸
片 sleeping pills 安眠藥

1959 flight

[flaɪt] ★★★
名 飛行、班次、快速移動、逃跑
動 成群飛行、遷徙

1960 pest

[pɛst] ★★★
名 害蟲、害人精
片 pest damage 蟲害
衍 pesticide 殺蟲劑

1961 pine

[paɪn] ★★★★
名 松樹、松木、鳳梨
動 衰弱、痛苦、渴望
片 pine away 憔悴

1962 penny

[`pɛnɪ] ★★★★★
名 (美)一分、(英)便士
片 watch evey penny 精打細算

1963 enter

[`ɛntə] ★★★
動 進入、使參加、輸入
反 exit 出去
片 enter into 加入、開始

1964 clever

[`klɛvə] ★★★
形 聰明的、靈巧的
反 foolish 愚蠢的
片 clever at 擅長

1965 naivety

[nɑ`ivətɪ] ★★
名 天真、輕信
衍 naive 天真的、輕信的

1966 believe

[bɪ`liv] ★★★★★
動 相信、信任、猜想
同 trust 信任
片 believe in 信仰

1967 almost

[`ɔlmost] ★★★★★
副 幾乎、差不多
同 nearly 幾乎

1968 end

[ɛnd] ★★★★★
動 結束、終止
名 結束、結局、盡頭
片 end in 以⋯作結

fighting!

Give it a shot 小試身手

1 She wore a beautiful _____ necklace to attend a party.

2 His piano _____ ended[1968] successfully.

3 Vivian has a great _____. Everyone likes her.

4 You cannot enter my room without my _____.

5 Johnny wants to be a _____ when he grows up.

MP3　短文 329　字彙 330

Essay

165

A plumber wanted to drink a pint[1969] of beer during his day off. He took a beer out from the fridge. The bottle made popping sound when he opened it. He watched the TV, played with his pony, and drank beer at the same time. He saw some political news about a politician near the South Pole. Over there, garbage polluted[1970] the local rivers and lakes, so local residents had tried to dig a pit[1971] to bury the garbage. It was not a good idea because it created more pollution <u>instead of</u> solving the problem. The politician[1972] later <u>won approval for</u> a proposal. The proposal was to encourage everyone to recycle[1973]. The recyclable[1974] materials included plastic[1975], iron, paper, glass, and aluminum[1976].

After he finished watching the news, the plumber heard the phone ringing and picked it up. It turned out to be an urgent[1977] case from a neighbor. A woman's pipe was plugged[1978] by lots of plums[1979]. The plumber pitied the anxious[1980] woman, so he turned off the TV and went out to help her.

> 🔈 instead of 代替
> 🔈 win approval for 贏得認同、許可

中譯 *Translation*

　　有名水管工人想在休假時喝一品脫的啤酒。他從冰箱拿出啤酒，打開瓶子時，瓶口還發出砰的一聲。他看著電視，一邊喝酒一邊和他的小馬玩。他看見了一則關於南極政治家的政治新聞。在那裡，垃圾汙染了當地的河流和湖泊，所以當地居民想挖個坑把垃圾全埋進去。但這個想法並不恰當，不但無法解決問題還製造更多污染。後來，這名政治家的提案獲得認可。這個提案鼓勵每個人動手做回收，回收物包括塑膠、鐵製品、紙類和鋁製品。

　　新聞結束後，這名工人聽見電話響，他接了起來，原來是鄰居的緊急事故，有個女人的水管被一大堆梅子給塞住了，工人同情這名焦急的女人，便把電視關了，出門去幫她。

1969 pint

[paɪnt] ★★★

名 品脫、一品脫的量

片 put a quart into a pint pot 做不可能做到的事

1970 pollute

[pəˋlut] ★★

動 汙染、弄髒、玷污

片 pollute sth. with sth. 汙染

1971 pit

[pɪt] ★★

名 窪坑、凹處、陷阱

動 挖坑於、掉入陷阱

片 pit against 與…較量

1972 politician

[ˌpɑləˋtɪʃən] ★★★

名 政治家、政客

同 statesman 政治家

衍 political 政治上的

1973 recycle

[rɪˋsaɪkḷ] ★★★

動 回收利用、再循環

衍 recycling 回收

1974 recyclable

[rɪˋsaɪkləbḷ] ★★★

形 可回收利用的、可再循環的

1975 plastic

[ˋplæstɪk] ★★★

名 塑膠、塑膠製品

形 塑膠的、可塑的、易受影響的、人造的

1976 aluminum

[əˋlumɪnəm] ★★

名 鋁

1977 urgent

[ˋɝdʒənt] ★★★★

形 緊急的、急迫的

同 pressing 迫切的

衍 urgency 緊急

1978 plug

[plʌg] ★★★★

動 堵塞、接通電源、苦讀

名 塞子、插頭、插播廣告

1979 plum

[plʌm] ★★★

名 梅子、洋李、令人垂涎的東西、深紅色

片 plum tree 李樹

1980 anxious

[ˋæŋkʃəs] ★★★★

形 焦慮的、渴望的

同 concernned 擔心的

片 be anxious for 渴望

---

fighting!

Give it a shot 小試身手

① We have _____ of money to finish this project.

② The _____ bag is harmful to our planet.

③ The polar bear lives in the North _____.

④ The _____ shows that people are not satisfied with the government.

⑤ The waste water _____ our river.

Answers: ① plenty ② plastic ③ Pole ④ poll ⑤ pollutes

MP3

短文
331

字彙
332

Essay

166

Tom received an express delivery from his friend. He paid the postage[1981] and then opened it. It was a poster[1982] with a portrait[1983] on it. The portrait had been painted by his favorite artist[1984], a popular painter. The artist <u>was supposed to</u> have an art exhibition at a museum next week, but it was postponed. Tom didn't know that and planned to visit the museum. He was annoyed, and his blood pressure rose[1985] when he found out.

After he calmed[1986] down, he decided to see the current exhibition of antique pottery[1987] and porcelain[1988] at another museum. Those antiques were precious[1989] because they were extremely old and rare. Furthermore, a portion[1990] of the museum's profits were donated to an orphanage[1991]. After the exhibition, Tom went home. He <u>was impressed by</u> the charitable spirit of the museum. He thought it was a wonderful idea to help people in need. He described that helping people was like pouring[1992] water on flowers. Then he started to pray for all the poor people and orphans in the world. He hoped his prayers would be answered.

(!) be supposed to 應該要

(!) be impressed by 對…感到印象深刻

中譯 *Translation*

湯姆收到了他朋友寄給他的快遞包裹，他付了郵資把包裹打開，裡頭是一幅印有肖像畫的海報，這幅肖像畫出於他最喜歡的一位畫家之手，一位名氣響亮的畫家。這位畫家本來下星期要在博物館辦藝術展覽，但後來延期了。湯姆不知道這件事，還是做足準備去了博物館。當他發現時，氣得血壓升高。

等他冷靜下來後，他決定去看正在展出中的古董陶瓷展，由於年代久遠且稀有，那些古董個個都十分珍貴。另外，博物館也將部分的收入捐贈給孤兒院。參觀完博物館，湯姆回到家。他對博物館的慈善精神印象深刻。他覺得這是一個可以實際幫助到別人的好方法。他說幫助他人就像是替花朵澆水，他開始為窮人和孤兒禱告，並希望他的祈禱能得到回應。

1981 postage

[`postɪdʒ] ★★
名 郵資、郵費
片 postage and packing
包裝加郵寄費

1982 poster

[`postə] ★★★
名 海報、廣告、驛馬
衍 post 張貼、公布

1983 portrait

[`portret] ★★★★
名 肖像、描繪、寫照
同 image 肖像
衍 portray 描繪、描寫

1984 artist

[`ɑrtɪst] ★★★★
名 藝術家、大師、藝人
同 master 大師
衍 artistic 藝術的

1985 rise

[raɪz] ★★★★★
動 上升、增加、起義
名 增加、發跡、加薪
片 rise above 超越、擺脫

1986 calm

[kɑm] ★★★★
動 鎮定下來、平靜
名 鎮定、平靜
形 鎮靜的、沉著的

1987 pottery

[`pɑtərɪ] ★★
名 陶器、陶器廠

1988 porcelain

[`pɔrslɪn] ★★★
名 瓷、(總稱)瓷器

1989 precious

[`prɛʃəs] ★★★★
形 貴重的、珍貴的、寶貝
的、十足的
名 寶貝、心愛的人

1990 portion

[`porʃən] ★★★★
名 一部分、一份、命運
動 分成多份、分配
片 portion out 分配

1991 orphanage

[`ɔrfənɪdʒ] ★
名 孤兒院、孤兒身分
同 orphanhood 孤兒

1992 pour

[por] ★★★★
動 傾瀉、傾注、訴說
名 傾瀉、湧流
片 pour down 傾盆而下

fighting!

Give it a shot 小試身手

❶ Our trip needed to be _____ due to the heavy rain.

❷ Her children are the most _____ thing for her.

❸ Peter _____ some milk in the bowl.

❹ The Korean music is very _____ now.

❺ Do you make enough _____ for the meeting?

MP3　 短文 333　 字彙 334

Essay

167

An old man was worried he might <u>pass away</u> at any time because of his advanced age. He wanted to merge[1993] his two companies. By doing this, his son could inherit[1994] his prosperous[1995] business.

He used to be a factory owner. The factory primarily[1996] processed canned[1997] food. He had earned great profits from that business. Several years later, he bought a computer company. His son was the general[1998] manager in there. He worked hard and was soon promoted. One time, the old man pretended[1999] to be very sick. He wanted to test[2000] his son to see if he was capable[2001] of succeeding[2002] him in his business. He told his son, "You know I am very old now. To ensure[2003] that my efforts do not all <u>go to waste</u>, I need to make sure that I leave my business in good hands. Therefore, I have to <u>put you to the test</u>." His son didn't let him down and showed exceptional competence[2004].

ℹ️ pass away 去世

ℹ️ go to waste 白白浪費

ℹ️ put...to the test 考驗

中譯 *Translation*

　　一位老人擔心自己年事已高，隨時有可能會過世，他計畫要將他的兩間公司合併，這樣他的兒子便可以繼承他蒸蒸日上的事業。

　　他曾是個工廠的老闆，工廠主要生產加工罐頭食品，這個事業獲利可觀。幾年之後，他又買下了一間電腦公司，他兒子是公司裡的總經理，工作非常勤奮，很快就升職了。有一次，他假裝生病，想藉此測試他的兒子是否有能力接手他的事業。他跟兒子說：「你知道我老了，為了確保我的努力不會白白浪費，我必須確認是否把事業交給了可靠的對象。所以我必須考驗你。」他的兒子並沒讓他失望，並展現了卓越的工作能力。

1993 merge

[mɝdʒ] ★★★★
- 動 合併、融合、同化
- 同 combine 結合
- 片 merge into 合併

1994 inherit

[ɪnˋhɛrɪt] ★★★★
- 動 繼承、經遺傳獲得
- 片 inherit from 從…繼承
- 衍 inheritance 繼承

1995 prosperous

[ˋprɑspərəs] ★★★
- 形 興旺的、繁榮的、富足的、有利的
- 同 thriving 欣欣向榮的

1996 primarily

[praɪˋmɛrəlɪ] ★★★★
- 副 主要地、首先、起初
- 同 mainly 主要地
- 衍 primary 主要的

1997 canned

[kænd] ★★
- 形 裝成罐頭的、錄音的
- 片 canned food 罐頭食品
- 衍 can 罐、罐頭

1998 general

[ˋdʒɛnərəl] ★★★★★
- 形 首席的、一般的、大體的、公眾的
- 名 將軍、上將

1999 pretend

[prɪˋtɛnd] ★★★★
- 動 假裝、自稱、裝作
- 形 假裝的、假想的
- 片 pretend to 自稱

2000 test

[tɛst] ★★★★★
- 動 考驗、測驗、分析
- 名 試驗、考察、小考
- 片 test on 針對…檢驗

2001 capable

[ˋkepəbl̩] ★★★★
- 形 有能力的、能幹的
- 片 capable of 有…能力的
- 同 able 有能力的

2002 succeed

[səkˋsid] ★★★★
- 動 成功、接著發生、繼任
- 反 fail 失敗
- 片 succeed in 成功

2003 ensure

[ɪnˋʃʊr] ★★★★
- 動 確保、保證、擔保
- 片 ensure from 保護…免受危險

2004 competence

[ˋkɑmpətəns] ★★★
- 名 能力、稱職、勝任
- 反 incompetence 無能力
- 衍 competent 能幹的

fighting!

Give it a shot 小試身手

① He _____ that he did not see me as I walked by.

② The police needed the _____ to send him in jail.

③ This farm is my grandfather's _____.

④ He set the alarm to _____ himself from sleeping late.

⑤ I like the _____ room I saw rather than the current one.

Answers: ① pretended ② proof ③ property ④ prevent ⑤ previous

168

 MP3 短文 335 字彙 336

Essay

Andy and Lawrence <u>had a quarrel over</u> a girl at a pub, which <u>had a bad reputation as</u> being a place where a lot of fights[2005] occurred. Some people called the police. Andy got punched[2006] in the face by Lawrence and was bleeding, but he soon got up and wiped[2007] the blood away with a rag[2008]. It was pure[2009] luck[2010] that he had been wearing protective[2011] glasses, so his eyes were not injured. The reason the quarrel started was that they were pursuing the same girl. However, the girl didn't really like Lawrence, although she had never told him that. Lawrence saw the girl feeding Andy raisins[2012] and sashimi in the bar. Lawrence was so jealous and fought with him. The queer[2013] thing was that the girl already had a boyfriend. In the end, the police took some witness[2014] statements[2015] and took Andy and Lawrence to the police station.

> ⓘ have a quarrel over 為了…起爭執
>
> ⓘ have a good/ bad reputation 風評很好/聲名狼藉

中譯 *Translation*

　　安迪和勞倫斯為了一個女孩在酒吧起了爭執，這家酒吧因為常有爭執、鬥毆發生而聲名狼藉。有人報了警。安迪被勞倫斯一拳擊中臉部而流血，但他很快站起來用抹布把血擦掉。幸運的是，他當時戴著護目鏡，所以眼睛沒有受傷。他們起爭執的原因是因為他們同時在追求一個女孩子，但是那個女孩不喜歡勞倫斯，雖然他沒告訴勞倫斯實情。勞倫斯在酒吧看到女孩在餵安迪吃葡萄乾和生魚片，醋意大起，便和他大打出手。最奇怪的是這個女生早就有男朋友了。最後，警察採用了目擊者的陳述，把安迪和勞倫斯帶回警局。

2005 fight

[faɪt] ★★★★★
- 名 打架、爭吵、戰鬥力
- 動 打架、奮鬥、反對
- 片 fight back 回擊

2006 punch

[pʌntʃ] ★★★★
- 動 用拳猛擊、猛烈推擠
- 名 拳打、穿孔機
- 片 punch in 用拳擊

2007 wipe

[waɪp] ★★★
- 動 擦去、擦乾、消滅
- 同 erase 擦掉
- 片 wipe away 清除

2008 rag

[ˋræg] ★★★
- 名 抹布、少量、惡作劇
- 動 對⋯惡作劇
- 片 lose one's rag 發脾氣

2009 pure

[pjʊr] ★★★
- 形 純粹的、純淨的、清白的、完全的
- 反 impure 不純淨的

2010 luck

[lʌk] ★★★★
- 名 運氣、命運、僥倖
- 動 走運、湊巧碰上
- 片 out of luck 運氣不佳

2011 protective

[prəˋtɛktɪv] ★★
- 形 保護的、保護貿易的
- 片 protective towards 對⋯關切保護的

2012 raisin

[ˋrezṇ] ★
- 名 葡萄乾、深紫紅色

2013 queer

[kwɪr] ★★★
- 形 奇怪的、不舒服的、神經不太正常的
- 動 破壞、使陷於不利地位

2014 witness

[ˋwɪtnɪs] ★★★★
- 名 目擊者、證人、證詞
- 動 目擊、作證
- 片 witness to 對⋯作證

2015 statement

[ˋstetmənt] ★★★★
- 名 陳述、聲明、結單
- 片 official statement 正式聲明

2016 tourist

[ˋˋturɪst] ★★★
- 名 旅客
- 形 旅遊的、觀光的
- 同 visitor 觀光客

Fighting!

Give it a shot 小試身手

❶ He is very _____ to his younger sister.

❷ They got into a big _____ and stopped talking to each other.

❸ Paris is _____ as the most attractive city for the tourists[2016].

❹ Paul likes to have a beer at the _____ after work.

❺ He has been _____ the girl next door for two years.

Answers: ❶ protective ❷ quarrel ❸ ranked ❹ pub ❺ pursuing

Level

5

新多益藍色證書
必備單字

Essay 169~Essay 210

MP3　短文 337　字彙 338

Essay

169

A man accidentally hurt[2017] himself seriously with a razor[2018]. This made him regret buying the razor. He had bought it because it was known as a reliable brand[2019]. He found the phone number for the store where he had bought the razor and called the store. The person who answered the phone reacted[2020] very coldly[2021] and tried to say that the store was not liable[2022] for him cutting himself. The man got mad because of her rudeness. However, she didn't think what the man said was reasonable.

On the second day, he found the receipt[2023] and went directly to the store. The manager came with a recorder[2024]. He wanted the man to relax first, but the man was too eager to relate[2025] his trouble. Also, the recorder was playing a conversation that happened last night. The man recognized the female voice. He knew she was the one who had talked to him on the phone last night. The manager refunded[2026] the money to the man so that the store wouldn't be sued[2027]. They also promised to cover any medical expenses the man had because of his injury.

中譯 *Translation*

　　有個男人不小心被剃刀重重割傷了，這讓他後悔買了這隻剃刀。他當初是因為這家品牌可靠才買的。他找出這家店的電話，然後撥過去。接線生的反應非常冷淡，還試圖撇清責任，表示店家沒義務為他的傷勢負責。這名男子對這名女接線生的無禮態度感到生氣。然而，她認為這名男子所說的並不合理。

　　第二天，他找到收據後直接拿到店裡。經理帶著錄音機過來，他希望這位客人先冷靜下來，但這名男子急著陳述他的問題。同時錄音機也播著昨晚發生的談話。他認出了錄音機裡女人的聲音，他知道那就是昨晚跟他講電話的接線生。經理退錢給這名男子，以免被告。他們同時也保證會支付男子因為受傷而必須付的醫療費用。

2017 hurt

[hɝt] ★★★★
- 動 使受傷、危害、疼痛
- 名 創傷、傷、痛
- 形 受傷的、受損的

2018 razor

[`rezə] ★★★
- 名 剃刀
- 動 剃、用剃刀刮
- 同 shave 剃刀

2019 brand

[`brænd] ★★★★
- 名 牌子、商標、烙印
- 動 印商標於、銘記
- 片 brand leader 主打品牌

2020 react

[rɪ`ækt] ★★★★
- 動 回應、起作用、反抗
- 同 respond 回應
- 片 react to 對…做出反應

2021 coldly

[`koldlɪ] ★★
- 副 冷淡地、冷漠地、寒冷地、客觀地
- 反 warmly 溫暖地

2022 liable

[`laɪəbl] ★★★★
- 形 有義務的、易…的、可能的、應受罰的
- 同 be liable to 易…的

2023 receipt

[rɪ`sit] ★★★★
- 名 收據、收到、收入
- 動 開收據
- 片 on receipt of 收到…時

2024 recorder

[rɪ`kɔrdə] ★★★
- 名 錄音機、記錄者
- 片 tape recorder 錄音機
- 衍 record 記錄、記載

2025 relate

[rɪ`let] ★★★★★
- 動 敘述、有關、涉及
- 片 relate to 與…有關
- 衍 relation 關係

2026 refund

[rɪ`fʌnd] ★★★
- 動 退還、歸還、償還
- 名 退款
- 同 repay 還錢給

2027 sue

[su] ★★★★
- 動 控告、提起訴訟、要求
- 同 prosecute 起訴
- 片 sue for 請求

2028 hide

[haɪd] ★★★★★
- 動 躲藏、隱藏、隱瞞
- 反 expose 揭露
- 片 hide among 躲在…中

Give it a shot 小試身手

1 My grandmother _____ safely from her illness.

2 Due to bad economy, the company planned to _____ my salary.

3 Please _____ and make yourself at home.

4 I hid[2028] to scare her but she did not have any _____.

5 He is a _____ man so I decided to marry him.

170

 MP3　 短文 339　 字彙 340

I read a journal[2029] yesterday. One of the articles[2030] in the journal reminded me of a report I once read in a newspaper. The article was entitled, "What is the definition[2031] of a democratic republic[2032]?" The article gave the following definition: First, people should be open-minded[2033] about everything. For example, a democracy[2034] is accepting of various religions[2035]. People should accept and respect other religious faiths. Religion is very important. People can often find relief[2036] from religion. Secondly, corrupt officials should be removed from the government. In that way, people can trust and rely[2037] on the government. There are always many things the government needs to do. One representative example is that a country should fairly[2038] support even its remotest areas and upgrade the facilities there whenever necessary.

After reading this journal article, I went back to work. I remained in my office all afternoon. When I was ready to go home, I remembered that I had to pay my rent and asked my landlord[2039] to come over to repair[2040] a broken pipe as soon as possible. What a busy day it was!

中譯 *Translation*

　　昨天我看了一本雜誌。其中有篇文章讓我想起之前曾在報紙上讀過的一篇報導。這篇文章的標題是：「如何定義民主共和國？」文章接著為此下了定義：「首先，人民應該毫無偏見的看待每一件事。舉例來說，民主是要能接受各種宗教信仰的。民主國家的人民應該接受並尊重其它宗教信仰。宗教的地位舉足輕重，人民通常能從宗教信仰得到心靈的慰藉。其次，貪汙的官員應該被政府免職，如此一來人民才可以相信且依賴政府。政府總是有許多事需要處理。其中一個典型的例子就是，即使是偏遠地區，國家也應該隨時公平給予資助並提升當地設施。」

　　讀完這篇雜誌的文章後，我回去繼續工作。我一整個下午都待在辦公室。正當我準備回家的時候，想起今天要付房租，還要請房東儘快過來幫我修理壞掉的水管。真是忙碌的一天啊！

2029 journal

[`dʒɝnḷ] ★★★★★

名 雜誌、期刊、日記、流水帳

同 diary 日記

2030 article

[`ɑrtɪkḷ] ★★★★

名 文章、論文、條款、一件、物品

片 leading article 社論

2031 definition

[dɛfə`nɪʃən] ★★★★

名 定義、釋義、規定、清晰度

衍 define 下定義

2032 republic

[rɪ`pʌblɪk] ★★★★

名 共和政體、共和國

反 monarchy 君主政體

2033 open-minded

[`opən`maɪndɪd] ★★

形 心胸開闊的、無偏見的

反 narrow-minded 心胸狹窄的

2034 democracy

[dɪ`mɑkrəsɪ] ★★★

名 民主、民主制度、民眾

反 autocracy 獨裁政治

衍 democratic 民主的

2035 religion

[rɪ`lɪdʒən] ★★★★

名 宗教信仰、狂熱的愛好

同 faith 宗教信仰

衍 religious 宗教的

2036 relief

[rɪ`lif] ★★★★

名 慰藉、緩和、救濟物品

同 ease 緩和

衍 relieve 緩和

2037 rely

[rɪ`laɪ] ★★★★

動 依賴、依靠、指望

片 rely on 依靠、信賴

衍 reliance 信賴

2038 fairly

[`fɛrlɪ] ★★★

副 公平地、相當地、簡直

反 unjustly 不公平地

片 fairly soon 相當快

2039 landlord

[`lændlɔrd] ★★★

名 房東、老闆、地主

同 proprietor 所有人

2040 repair

[rɪ`pɛr] ★★★★

動 修理、糾正、恢復

名 修理、維修狀況、補償

片 in repair 保養完好的

fighting!

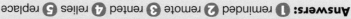

Give it a shot 小試身手

❶ His face _____ me of my dead boyfriend.

❷ I wanted to watch TV but I cannot find the _____ control.

❸ I _____ an apartment near my office.

❹ The baby _____ on his mother very much.

❺ We need someone to _____ Mary's job.

Answers: ❶ reminded ❷ remote ❸ rented ❹ relies ❺ replace

171

MP3 | 短文 341 | 字彙 342

Essay

I once[2041] entered a riddle[2042] contest at school. I tied up my hair with a red ribbon[2043] and had roast duck before I left home. On the way to school, I saw a young man robbing an old woman. The old woman was frail[2044] and feeble[2045] because of her age, so she was unable[2046] to resist[2047] the robber. I thought it was my responsibility[2048] to help her. I ran forward[2049] to hit the man with my bag and screamed at him. People heard my scream and came to help us. The man got rid of the bag and then escaped. The old woman thanked me for helping her at the risk of being seriously[2050] hurt. We then went to the police station to give a statement and describe the robber. After responding[2051] to all questions, the policeman offered to give me a ride to school. Luckily, the riddle contest had just started and the teacher had reserved[2052] a seat for me. I even ended up winning the contest!

中譯 *Translation*

　　我曾經參加過學校的猜謎大賽。我用一條紅色緞帶把頭髮紮起來，並在出門前吃了烤鴨。去學校的路上，我看到一位年輕人在打劫一名老太太。老太太因為年紀大了，既虛弱又無力，所以她對於搶匪毫無還手之力。我認為自己有責任幫她。我衝上前用書包痛打這名男子一頓，還對著他大叫。路人聽到我的尖叫便過來幫我們的忙。年輕人甩掉背包拔腿就跑。老太太感謝我冒著深受重傷的風險捨身相救。後來我們一同去警察局做筆錄並對警察描述搶匪的特徵。在回答完所有問題後，警察先生開車送我去學校。幸好，猜謎大賽才剛開始，老師也幫我留了一個位子。我最後還贏得了勝利呢！

2041 once

[wʌns] ★★★★★
- 副 曾經、一次
- 名 一次、一回
- 連 一旦、一經…便

2042 riddle

[`rɪdl̩] ★★
- 名 謎語、難題、謎一般的人
- 動 解謎、出謎、使困惑

2043 ribbon

[`rɪbən] ★★★
- 名 緞帶、絲帶
- 動 用緞帶裝飾
- 同 lace 帶子

2044 frail

[frel] ★★★
- 動 身體虛弱的、不堅實的、渺茫的
- 反 tough 堅韌的

2045 feeble

[fibl̩] ★★★
- 動 無力的、衰弱的、站不住腳的
- 同 frail 虛弱的

2046 unable

[ʌn`ebl̩] ★★★★
- 動 無能力的、不會的
- 反 able 能夠地
- 片 unable to 不能做…

2047 resist

[rɪ`zɪst] ★★★★
- 動 反抗、抵抗、忍住
- 同 oppose 反抗
- 反 obey 服從

2048 responsibility

[rɪˌspɑnsə`bɪlətɪ] ★★
- 名 責任、職責、義務
- 片 sense of responsibility 責任感

2049 forward

[`fɔrwəd] ★★★★★
- 副 向前、今後、提前
- 形 前面的、提前的
- 動 遞送、轉交、促進

2050 seriously

[`sɪrɪəslɪ] ★★★★
- 副 嚴重地、嚴肅地
- 片 take sth. seriously 認真對待

2051 respond

[rɪ`spɑnd] ★★★★
- 動 回答、做出反應、響應
- 片 respond to 對…回應
- 衍 response 答覆、反應

2052 reserve

[rɪ`zɜv] ★★★★
- 動 保留、儲備、預定
- 名 儲備物、保護區
- 片 in reserve 儲藏

Fighting!

Give it a shot 小試身手

1. Natural _____ such as oil and gas are very precious.
2. He talked back to his boss at the _____ of getting fired.
3. The _____ is too difficult for me to solve.
4. Ken did not know how to _____ to this question.
5. Raising a child is a great _____.

Answers: 1 resources 2 risk 3 riddle 4 respond 5 responsibility

172

 MP3　　

I had a fantastic wedding last week, but I heard a gunshot[2053] when I was walking down the aisle[2054]. A robbery was happening at the bank next to us. The robber wore a robe and a mask, and he showed his gun and put all the money in a big sack[2055]. The locals complained about our rotten[2056] society. The bad economy and terrible welfare[2057] system had rotted[2058] people's minds. Public security was no longer seen as satisfactory.

Due to this situation, I began to feel disappointed that my fighting skill was rusty[2059]. Practicing martial arts used to be my daily routine[2060]. I told my husband I was going to quit my job in order to study martial arts every day and perfect my fighting skills. My husband didn't agree with me at first, but soon he softened[2061]. He said, "Rumor has it that our country will sell rockets[2062] in order to make money." I yelled back, "Don't try to change the topic[2063], OK? How about taking a look my rusty fight skills?" Now you see why he gave in to me.

中譯 *Translation*

　　上禮拜我舉行了一場浪漫的婚禮，不過當我走在紅毯上時聽到了一記槍聲。原來是隔壁的銀行發生了搶案。搶匪穿著長袍並戴著面具，他亮出槍械然後把所有的錢放進一個大麻袋裡。當地居民抱怨世風日下，人心不古。經濟蕭條和差勁的福利制度使人心墮落腐敗，治安滿意度下滑。

　　基於現況，我開始對我的格鬥技巧日漸生疏而感到沮喪。練習武術曾經是我每天的例行公事，我告訴丈夫我要辭去工作，每天專注在武術上，以精進我的格鬥技巧。起先我丈夫並不同意，不過他的態度很快就軟化了。他說：「有謠傳說政府為了賺錢要把火箭賣掉。」我吼著對他說：「拜託，不要想轉移話題好嗎？要不要試試我鈍化的格鬥技啊？」現在你知道他為什麼讓步了吧。

2053　gunshot

[`gʌnʃat] ★★
 槍砲聲、射擊、子彈
形 槍砲射擊所致的
片 gunshot wound 槍傷

2054　aisle

[aɪl] ★★★
 走道、通道、側廊
俚 walk down the aisles 步入教堂、結婚

2055　sack

[sæk] ★★★★
 麻袋、一代的量、解雇
動 裝…入袋、開除、劫掠
俚 get the sack 遭解雇

2056　rotten

[`ratṇ] ★★★
形 腐敗的、腐爛的、發臭的、極差的
同 decayed 腐敗的

2057　welfare

[`wɛlfɛr] ★★★★
 福利、幸福、社會救濟
片 social welfare 社會福利

2058　rot

[rat] ★★★
動 腐壞、破損、墮落
 腐敗、墮落、蠢事
片 rot away 爛掉

2059　rusty

[`rʌstɪ] ★★
形 荒廢的、操作不靈活的、生鏽的
同 eroded 被侵蝕的

2060　routine

[ru`tin] ★★★★
 例行公事、慣例
形 例行的、一般的

2061　soften

[`sɔftṇ] ★★
動 軟化、變輕柔
反 harden 變堅固
片 soften up 削弱、軟化

2062　rocket

[`rakɪt] ★★★★
 火箭、飛彈、信號火箭
動 飛快行進、猛漲、用火箭運載

2063　topic

[`tapɪk] ★★★★
 話題、主題、標題
同 theme 主題
片 topic sentence 主題句

2064　irony

[`aɪrənɪ] ★★★
形 含鐵的、似鐵的
 諷刺、反語
同 satire 諷刺

Fighting!

Give it a shot 小試身手

1 She always dreams of having a _____ wedding one day.

2 The irony[2064] table got _____ because of the rain.

3 The police and I cooperated and got the _____ together.

4 I have heard some _____ about the new neighbor.

5 It is my _____ to go jogging after dinner.

Answers: 1 romantic 2 rusty 3 robber 4 rumors 5 routine

173

 MP3

短文 345　字彙 346

Essay

I am a graduate student who has received scholarships[2065] every year. My dream is to be a well-known scientific scholar after graduation. I think scientific scholars are high on the social ladder. Thus, I have a very busy life with a tight schedule every day.

One day, I had some sausages[2066] and a scoop of ice cream for my breakfast, and I also had some tea in my best cup and saucer[2067]. Then I dressed and went to school. As I passed by a cotton field, I suddenly burst out screaming because I saw a flock[2068] of birds attacking a scarecrow[2069]. The scarecrow looked scary[2070]. The farm owners went out to scatter[2071] the birds and scouted[2072] where their nests were. I told him not to catch[2073] the rare species[2074] of bird but to let them go instead. The farmer replied, "I'm reluctant to kill them. I just want to protect my fields." I sighed[2075] and nodded, and then I went directly to school.

(!) be reluctant to do sth. 不情願、勉強做某事

中譯 *Translation*

　　我是個每年都獲得獎學金的研究生，我的夢想是畢業後成為一名眾所皆知的科學家，我覺得科學家的社會地位很崇高，所以我每天都行程滿檔、生活忙碌。

　　某天我早餐吃了些香腸和一球冰淇淋，用我最高級的茶杯和茶碟喝了杯茶，之後穿好衣服就去上學了。當我經過棉花田時，我突然失聲尖叫，因為我看到一群鳥在攻擊稻草人。稻草人的模樣可怕極了，農場主人出來把這群鳥趕走，然後搜索牠們的巢穴。我告訴他不要抓這些稀有的鳥類，乾脆放了他們。農場主人說：「我也不想傷害他們，我只想保護我的田。」我嘆口氣、點點頭，便直接去學校了。

2065 scholarship

[`skɑləʃɪp] ★★★
名 獎學金、學術成就
片 apply for a scholarship 申請獎學金

2066 sausage

[`sɔsɪdʒ] ★★★
名 香腸、臘腸、極少量
片 not a sausage 一點也沒有

2067 saucer

[`sɔsɚ] ★★★
名 茶碟、淺碟
片 flying saucer 飛碟

2068 flock

[flɑk] ★★★★
名 畜群、鳥群、人群
動 聚集、成群結隊
片 flock to 成群結隊走向

2069 scarecrow

[`skɛrkro] ★
名 稻草人、衣衫襤褸的人

2070 scary

[`skɛrɪ] ★★★
形 可怕的、引起驚慌的、提心吊膽的
同 frightening 令人恐懼的

2071 scatter

[`skætɚ] ★★★
動 使分散、散布、撒播
名 分散、散播、少量
片 scatter over 把…撒在

2072 scout

[skaut] ★★★
動 搜索、偵查、物色人才
名 偵查、童子軍、星探
片 scout about 到處搜尋

2073 catch

[kætʃ] ★★★★★
動 捕捉、逮住、撞見、趕上、吸引
名 捕捉、接球、圈套

2074 species

[`spiʃiz] ★★★★
名 物種、種類、人類
片 endangered species 瀕危物種

2075 sigh

[saɪ] ★★★★
動 嘆氣、婉惜、思念
名 嘆氣、嘆息
片 sigh for sth. 思念

2076 respectful

[rɪ`spɛktfəl] ★★
形 有禮貌的、恭敬的
同 courteous 有禮貌的
反 disrespectful 無禮的

---

fighting!

Give it a shot 小試身手

1 I cannot watch a _____ movie without other people's company.

2 Professor Lee is a very respectful[2076] _____ in school.

3 The little girl _____ and cried for the new Barbie doll.

4 The polar bear is a _____ animal.

5 Dr. Cooper is working on a _____ project now.

Answers: 1 scary 2 scholar 3 screamed 4 scarce 5 scientific

MP3 短文 347 字彙 348

174

Essay

After becoming a mother, I now understand that I am responsible for educating my kids. I always hug my kids to show my love. A hug is the seal[2077] of love.

In my country, sex is a very sensitive issue. Asian parents seldom talk about sex with their kids. However, the correct way is to teach children about sexual[2078] differences[2079] and characteristics. Tell them not to seize every opportunity to chase sexy people; an attractive personality is more important than a beautiful body. That is the first thing I'll teach them. I will also teach my kids about personal security. For example, if you are being stalked[2080] while you are alone, you should seek[2081] help from others right away. The final[2082] thing I will teach them is to <u>help out</u> with the daily housework, such as scrubbing[2083] the kitchen floor, pulling down the shades[2084] on a sunny day, and mending[2085] their own clothes. Every family member should <u>pull[2086] his or her own weight</u>. We should also teach kids to be sensitive to the needs[2087] of others.

> (!) help out 分擔⋯工作、幫⋯一把
> (!) pull one's weight 做好自己份內的工作

中譯 *Translation*

　　當了媽媽以後，我現在了解到教育孩子的責任重大，我總是擁抱我的小孩來表達我的愛意。擁抱是愛的象徵。

　　在我的國家，性是一個非常敏感的話題。亞洲的父母很少會和小孩討論與性有關的事。不過，教導小孩性別差異和性別特徵才是正確的做法。告訴他們不要汲汲營營追求外型性感的人；個性迷人要比肉體迷人來得重要。這是我第一件要教導孩子的事。我也會教導他們關於自身安全。比如當你獨自一人被跟蹤時，你應該有能力立即向旁人尋求協助。最後，我會訓練他們分擔日常家務，像是擦洗廚房地板、艷陽高照時主動拉下簾子遮陽，還有縫補自己的衣服。家庭裡每個成員都應該盡自己的本分。我們也應該教導小孩去察覺他人內心的需求。

2077 seal

[sil] ★★★
名 象徵、印章、封條
動 密封、蓋章、決定
片 seal up 把…封起來

2078 sexual

[ˋsɛkʃuəl] ★★★★
形 性別的、性的
片 sexual relationships 性關係

2079 difference

[ˋdɪfərəns] ★★★★★
名 差別、差距、不合
片 a world of difference 天壤之別

2080 stalk

[stɔk] ★★★★
動 跟蹤、偷偷靠近、猖獗、高視闊步
名 悄悄跟蹤、高視闊步

2081 seek

[sik] ★★★★★
動 尋求、探索、企圖
同 search 尋找
片 seek after 追求

2082 final

[ˋfaɪn̩l] ★★★★★
形 最終的、決定性的
名 決賽、期末考
片 final resort 最後的王牌

2083 scrub

[skrʌb] ★★★
動 用力擦洗、擦亮、中止
名 擦洗、擦淨、灌木叢
片 scrub off 洗掉

2084 shade

[ʃed] ★★★★
名 窗簾、陰涼處、陰影部分、少量
動 遮蔽、逐漸變化

2085 mend

[mɛnd] ★★★★
動 縫補、改正、好轉
名 修繕部位、好轉、痊癒
片 mend with 用…修補

2086 pull

[pʊl] ★★★★★
動 拖、拉開、吸引、行駛
名 拖、拉、門路
片 pull one's weight 盡力

2087 need

[nid] ★★★★★
名 需要、需求、貧窮
動 需要、生活窮困
片 in need of 急需

2088 takeout

[ˋtekaʊt] ★★
形 外賣的
名 外帶、外賣、取出

fighting!

Give it a shot 小試身手

1 Jenny looked very _____ in that miniskirt.

2 My mother _____ cooks. We eat takeout[2088] food a lot.

3 I felt sad about our _____ at the airport.

4 Susan is a _____ girl. She is easily scared over nothing.

5 _____ every chance you can and do your best.

Answers: 1 sexy 2 seldom 3 seperation 4 sensitive 5 seize

175

 MP3   短文 349   字彙 350

Essay

One day, a shepherd[2089] had a date. Before he left the house, he washed his hair with shampoo[2090], shaved[2091], and wore a torn black leather jacket that was more than 15 years old. He met the woman in the park. They chose to sit in a shady[2092] corner. Time went by fast. After spending the entire day with each other, they found that they had a lot in common. Suddenly, a heavy rain spoiled[2093] their date while they sat under a tree. He asked the woman, "Isn't it a shame[2094] that the rain has spoiled our date? I have had such a good time with you anyway." The woman let out a sigh, and looking directly at his old, torn leather jacket. She said, "Truly. I have had a good time with you. I'm not a shallow[2095] woman, but appearance is quite important to me." She signaled that she was going to leave, but the shepherd suddenly stopped her, "What you care about is not my appearance, but my lack of money, right? I love to live with sheep[2096] and the land, even without[2097] a woman!" He left, leaving the woman stunned[2098].

中譯 *Translation*

　　有一天，某個牧羊人要去約會。出門前他用洗髮精洗了頭、刮了鬍子，還穿了一件超過十五年的黑色破舊皮衣。他跟那個女人在公園碰面，一起坐在蔭涼的角落。約會的時間一轉眼就過去了。經過了一整天的相處，他們發現彼此有許多共同之處。當他們坐在樹蔭下時，突然下起大雨，毀了他們的約會。他問那女人說：「讓大雨毀了我們的約會，是不是很遺憾？但不管怎樣，跟妳在一起真的很開心。」女人嘆口氣，看著他又舊又破的皮衣說：「老實說，跟你在一起的確很開心。我不是個膚淺的女人，但外表對我來說還是蠻重要的。」她作勢要離開，牧羊人突然擋住她的去路，對她說：「妳在乎的不是我的外表，是因為我沒錢，對吧？我喜愛與羊群和大地為伍，即使沒有女人的陪伴也無所謂！」他轉身離去，留下這個一臉錯愕的女人。

2089 shepherd

[ˋʃɛpɚd] ★★★
- 名 牧羊人、指導者
- 動 牧羊、帶領、護送
- 片 shepherd dog 牧羊犬

2090 shampoo

[ʃæmˋpu] ★★★
- 名 洗髮精、洗頭
- 動 洗頭髮

2091 shave

[ʃev] ★★★
- 動 刮鬍子、修剪、切成薄片、勉強通過
- 名 剃刀、刮臉

2092 shady

[ˋʃedɪ] ★★
- 形 成蔭的、陰暗的、可疑的、名聲不好的
- 反 sunny 陽光充足的

2093 spoil

[spɔɪl] ★★★
- 動 搞糟、損壞、溺愛
- 名 戰利品、獵物
- 片 spoil with 用…破壞

2094 shame

[ʃem] ★★★★
- 名 倒楣的事、羞恥、恥辱
- 動 感到羞恥、使丟臉
- 同 disgrace 丟臉

2095 shallow

[ˋʃælo] ★★★★
- 形 膚淺的、淺薄的
- 動 變淺
- 名 淺灘

2096 sheep

[ʃip] ★★★★
- 名 羊、羊皮、膽小鬼
- 片 black sheep 害群之馬

2097 without

[wɪˋðaut] ★★★★★
- 介 沒有、在…外面
- 副 在外面、戶外
- 反 with 有…的

2098 stun

[stʌn] ★★★★
- 動 大吃一驚、昏迷
- 名 昏迷、令人震驚的事物
- 同 shock 使震驚

2099 twins

[twɪnz] ★★
- 名 雙胞胎
- 衍 twin 孿生的

2100 within

[wɪˋðɪn] ★★★★★
- 介 在…範圍內、在…裡面
- 副 在裡面、在內部
- 名 裡面、內部

Fighting!

Give it a shot 小試身手

1. The twins[2099] have a lot of _____ besides their appearance.
2. My brother would _____ his hair during summer time.
3. Her new book will _____ be available within[2100] a week.
4. He saw his poor childhood as a _____.
5. My sweater _____ soon after I put it in the water.

Answers: 1 similarities 2 shorten 3 shortly 4 shame 5 shrank

Essay

176

Alice and her friend went skating[2101] last month. They liked skating on the smooth[2102] ice, and they had a great time. Several days later, they planned to go snowboarding in the mountains. That day, they spent a few hours looking for the ski lodge[2103] where they had booked a room. However, a skyscraper blocked[2104] their view[2105] so that they couldn't find the place easily. Finally, they arrived at the lodge. Alice took a sip[2106] of her tea in the lodge's restaurant with her friend and then rolled up her sleeves[2107]. She was ready for the challenge of the ski hill. The hill was so slippery[2108] that she bumped into a tree while she was snowboarding along the slope[2109]. The situation was embarrassing. Her strong snowboard had been snapped in two. A few branches of the tree she hit had been <u>sliced off</u> by the snowboard. She was sent[2110] to the hospital. Her friend accompanied[2111] her to the hospital and bought some nice flowers for her. Although Alice was sad about her accident, she really appreciated her friend <u>more than ever</u>.

ⓘ slice off 切開、割斷
ⓘ more than ever 比起以往更是、尤其

中譯 *Translation*

　　愛麗絲上個月和她的朋友一起去溜冰。她們很喜歡在平滑的冰上滑行，而且玩得非常開心。幾天後，她們計畫要去山上滑雪。那天，她們花了好幾個小時找她們已經定好房間的滑雪小屋，但一棟摩天大樓擋住了她們的視線以至於不太容易找到。後來她們終於到了。愛麗絲和朋友一起在小屋的餐廳裡，她喝了一口茶，然後捲起了袖子。她準備好要挑戰山丘滑雪了。但因為這座山丘太滑了，導致她沿著斜坡滑雪時，一頭撞上了一棵大樹。這真是尷尬的場面，連她堅固的滑雪板都當場斷成兩半，其中幾根樹枝也被滑雪板割斷了。她被送到醫院去，愛麗絲的朋友陪著她到醫院，還帶了幾朵漂亮的鮮花給她。雖然愛麗絲因為這場意外感到難過，但她比起以往更感謝她的朋友。

2101 skating

[ˋsketɪŋ] ★★
- 名 溜冰、滑冰
- 片 skating rink 溜冰場
- 衍 skater 溜冰者

2102 smooth

[smuð] ★★★★★
- 形 光滑的、進行順利的、和藹的
- 動 使光滑、燙平、消除

2103 lodge

[ladʒ] ★★★★
- 名 旅社、山林小屋、集會所、守衛室
- 動 投宿、存放、卡住

2104 block

[blɑk] ★★★★★
- 動 阻擋、妨礙、限制
- 名 障礙物、街區、一批
- 形 成批的、交通堵塞的

2105 view

[vju] ★★★★★
- 名 視野、景色、觀點
- 動 觀看、看待、考慮
- 片 in view of 鑒於

2106 sip

[sɪp] ★★★
- 名 啜飲、一小口
- 動 啜飲
- 片 take a sip 啜一小口

2107 sleeve

[sliv] ★★★
- 名 袖子、袖套
- 片 have sth. up one's sleeve 有錦囊妙計

2108 slippery

[ˋslɪpərɪ] ★★★
- 形 滑的、靠不住的、不明確的
- 同 greasy 油滑的

2109 slope

[slop] ★★★★
- 名 斜坡、傾斜
- 動 傾斜、溜走
- 片 slope off 悄悄溜走

2110 send

[sɛnd] ★★★★★
- 動 送往、寄、派遣、傳遞
- 同 mail 郵寄
- 片 send ahead 預先送出

2111 accompany

[əˋkʌmpənɪ] ★★★
- 動 陪同、伴隨、伴奏
- 反 leave 離棄
- 片 accompany with 伴隨

2112 rink

[rɪŋk] ★★
- 名 溜冰場
- 動 溜冰
- 片 indoor rink 室內溜冰場

fighting!

Give it a shot 小試身手

1. Please accept my _____ apology.
2. I fell down on the _____ floor.
3. Let's go _____ at the skating rink²¹¹².
4. The clothes did not fit me well. The _____ were too long.
5. I would like have a _____ of chocolate cake.

Answers! 1 sincere 2 slippery 3 skating 4 sleeves 5 slice

177

 MP3　短文 353　字彙 354

Susan didn't know that she was dating a married man. One day, they went to a spaghetti[2113] restaurant, which was very famous for its Italian spices[2114]. Unexpectedly[2115], a woman came up to them and <u>slapped her across</u>[2116] <u>the face</u> and spilt water over her skirt. The woman told her, "Don't destroy my family!" and then spat[2117] on Susan's food out of spite[2118]. The woman then left the restaurant. Susan was completely shocked by what had just happened. She didn't mean[2119] to spoil anyone's marriage. She cried all night and felt a deep pang[2120] of sorrow[2121] after she got home. She told herself, "I will take revenge[2122] on that man someday."

On the second day, she got a sore throat and didn't go to work. She spent the whole day working in the garden and later doing housework to distract[2123] herself any way she could. She knew there was no specific remedy for betrayal[2124], but the dark sky would clear sometime.

> ⓘ slap sb. across/in the face 給某人一記耳光、賞了某人一巴掌

中譯 *Translation*

　　蘇珊不知道和她交往的男人是有婦之夫。某天，他們去了一間很有名的義大利麵餐館，這間餐館以其義式香料著名。出乎意料地，有個女人走到他們面前，賞了她一巴掌，並潑水在她的裙子上，對她說：「不要破壞我的家庭！」然後故意在她的食物裡吐口水。這個女人之後離開了餐廳。蘇珊完全不敢相信剛剛所發生的事情。她並不是故意要破壞別人的婚姻。她傷心欲絕，回家徹夜痛哭。她告訴自己：「有一天我一定要這個男人付出代價。」

　　隔天，她因為喉嚨痛而沒辦法去上班，她一整天都在花園裡整理花花草草，晚一點的時候就做家事，她用盡任何方法來分散注意力。她知道沒有治療背叛傷痛的特效藥，但總有一天會雨過天晴的。

2113 spaghetti

[spə`gɛtɪ] ★★
名 義大利麵條
同 pasta 義大利麵食

2114 spice

[spaɪs] ★★
名 香料、風味、少許
動 加香料於、增添趣味
同 season 給…調味

2115 unexpectedly

[ˌʌnɪk`spɛktɪdlɪ] ★★★
副 意外地、未料到地
衍 unexpected 想不到的、意外的

2116 across

[ə`krɔs] ★★★★★
介 穿過、在…那邊、遍及
副 橫過、在對面
片 come across 偶遇

2117 spit

[spɪt] ★★★
動 吐口水、表示唾棄
名 口水、小雨
片 spit on 吐口水在…

2118 spite

[spaɪt] ★★
名 惡意、心術不良、怨恨
動 惡意對待、刁難
片 in spite of 不管

2119 mean

[min] ★★★★★
動 意欲、打算、用意
形 卑鄙的、小氣的
名 平均值、折衷辦法

2120 pang

[pæŋ] ★★
名 一陣傷心、一陣劇痛
動 使劇痛、折磨
同 pain 痛苦

2121 sorrow

[`saro] ★★★
名 悲痛、憂傷、傷心事
動 感到悲傷、遺憾
同 grief 悲痛

2122 revenge

[rɪ`vɛndʒ] ★★★
名 報仇、報復
動 替…報仇、報復
片 revenge on 向…報仇

2123 distract

[dɪ`strækt] ★★★
動 使分心、轉移、困擾
片 distract from 使從…分心

2124 betrayal

[bɪ`treəl] ★★
名 背叛、告密、暴露
同 defection 背叛
衍 betrayer 背叛者

Fighting!

Give it a shot 小試身手

1 I do not like Mexican _____. It is too spicy.

2 My legs were awfully _____ after running.

3 Kevin swore that _____ he will become a rich man.

4 She accidentally _____ the wine and ruined the carpet.

5 The storm really _____ our holiday.

Answers: 1 spice 2 sore 3 someday 4 spilt 5 spoiled

178

MP3　短文 355　字彙 356

Essay

The staff needed to clean the stadium every night. They had to spray cleaner on the seats to clean them thoroughly and pick up litter[2125] from the floor. One day, an unemployed[2126] man squeezed a bottle of orange juice and sprinkled the liquid on the floor[2127] of the stadium because he was angry at life. A cheerleader[2128] was starving and went out to have dinner, but she fell down and sprained[2129] her ankle while walking on the orange juice on the floor. She stared[2130] at the man, who was trying to hide behind[2131] a statue. She knew the man was her aunt's stepson. Since the man didn't have a stable[2132] career, he made money by doing anything he could. She pitied him and climbed[2133] up onto the stage and told her aunt's stepson that she could offer him a steady[2134] job. The man was shocked and felt moved[2135]. He didn't know his new job was to clean the stadium!

中譯 *Translation*

　　體育場工作人員每天晚上必須清理體育場，他們會在座位上噴清潔劑，以便徹底清洗，然後再從地上撿起垃圾。某天，一名失業男子因為對人生感到憤怒，將自己擠好的一瓶柳丁汁撒在體育館的地板上。一名啦啦隊隊員肚子餓要出去吃晚餐，但當她走過滿是柳丁汁的地板時跌了一跤，還扭傷了腳踝。她盯著那名試圖躲在雕像後面的男子，她知道那是她阿姨的繼子。因為沒有穩定的工作，他會做任何他能做的工作來賺錢。她很同情他的遭遇，她走上舞台告訴他阿姨的繼子，她可以提供他一份穩定的工作。這名男子相當震驚也非常感動，但他並不知道新工作是要打掃體育場！

2125 litter

[`lɪtɚ] ★★★

名 垃圾、雜亂
動 亂丟、使充滿
片 litter about 到處亂丟

2126 unemployed

[ˌʌnɪmˋplɔɪd] ★★★

形 失業的、閒著的
名 失業者
同 jobless 失業的

2127 floor

[flor] ★★★★

名 地板、層、發言權、底線、大廳
動 難倒、打倒在地

2128 cheerleader

[`tʃɪrˌlidɚ] ★★

名 啦啦隊隊員

2129 sprain

[spren] ★★

動 扭傷
名 扭傷

2130 stare

[stɛr] ★★★★

動 凝視、注視
名 凝視、注視、瞪眼
片 stare at 盯著看

2131 behind

[bɪˋhaɪnd] ★★★★

介 在…後面、不如、支持
副 在背後、落後
片 behind the scenes 幕後

2132 stable

[`stebl̩] ★★★★

形 穩定的、可信賴的
名 馬廄、一群人
動 拴入馬廄

2133 climb

[klaɪm] ★★★★★

動 爬、登上、上升
名 攀登、攀爬
同 mount 登上

2134 steady

[`stɛdɪ] ★★★★

形 穩定的、平穩的、可靠的、沉著的
動 穩固、使穩定

2135 move

[muv] ★★★★★

動 感動、移動、採取行動
名 移動、遷居、對策
片 move along 往前走

2136 famous

[`feməs] ★★★★

形 出名的、耳熟的
片 be famous for 以…聞名

Fighting!

Give it a shot 小試身手

1 Ann used hair _____ to take care of her hair.

2 I did not eat anything since yesterday and I am _____ now.

3 The patient's condition is getting better and more _____.

4 Roy cannot stop _____ at that pretty lady.

5 The marble _____ located in the park is very famous[2136].

179

 MP3　 短文 357　 字彙 358

I am a stubborn[2137] man who has stuck to his dreams and worked hard for the future. I am confident of my abilities. My strength[2138] is that I am good at planning marketing[2139] strategies. Besides, I know how to quickly structure my proposals to meet the needs of my clients. I just got promoted last month. Using a good strategy, I negotiated[2140] a substantial[2141] pay raise as well.

Once, on a stormy night, as the wind stirred[2142] the leaves, I was listening to the stereo[2143] my stepfather and stepmother had bought me and was eating toast. My fingers were sticky[2144] with jam. I stood on a stool[2145] and tried to find some socks[2146] from the upper closet. I fell down and got stabbed[2147] by a nail. In the hospital, the doctor took the stiff[2148] nail out and gave me some stitches on my injured leg. I was able to go back to work the next day, but I was unable to do any physical exercise with my leg. I decided that I should be more careful in the future, especially when I was on a stool!

中譯 *Translation*

　　我是一個堅持自己夢想而不屈不撓的人，為了未來努力打拼。我對我的能力充滿自信，擅於策劃行銷策略是我的強項。除此之外，我知道如何快速組織提案來滿足客戶的需求。上個月我剛升職。因為用對策略，我也談成了一筆為數可觀的調薪。

　　有一次，在一個風雨交加的夜晚，當強風激烈拍打著樹葉時，我一邊聽著我繼父繼母買給我的立體音響，一邊吃著吐司，手指都被果醬沾得黏黏的。我站在凳子上試著從衣櫃上層找出我的長襪，一不小心摔下來還被釘子插到。到了醫院，醫生幫我把堅硬的釘子拔出來，並在我受傷的腿上縫了幾針。我隔天還有辦法回公司上班，但卻因為我的腿不能做體能鍛鍊。我決定以後應該要更加小心，尤其是站在凳子上的時候！

2137 stubborn

[`stʌbən] ★★★

形 不屈不撓的、頑固的
同 obstinate 頑固的
反 docile 馴服的

2138 strength

[strɛŋθ] ★★★★

名 長處、力量、體力
反 weakness 弱點

2139 marketing

[`mɑrkɪtɪŋ] ★★

名 行銷學、交易、銷售
片 marketing plan 銷售計畫

2140 negotiate

[nɪ`goʃɪˌet] ★★★★

動 談成、協商、洽談
片 negotiate with 與…談判

2141 substantial

[səb`stænʃəl] ★★★★

形 可觀的、實質的、大量的、重要的
名 重要的東西

2142 stir

[stɜ] ★★★★

動 激起、鼓動、攪動
名 騷動、轟動、攪拌
片 stir up 引起、激起

2143 stereo

[`stɛrɪo] ★★★

名 立體音響、立體聲
形 立體聲的
片 in stereo 立體聲效果的

2144 sticky

[`stɪkɪ] ★★

形 黏性的、濕熱的、棘手的、不靈活的
同 adhesive 有黏性的

2145 stool

[stul] ★★★

名 凳子、糞便
片 fall between two stools 兩頭空

2146 sock

[sɑk] ★★★

名 短襪、半統襪、大成功
動 毆打、打擊
反 stocking 長襪

2147 stab

[stæb] ★★

動 刺入、戳、刺傷
名 刺破的傷口、嘗試
片 stab at 刺向

2148 stiff

[stɪf] ★★★★

形 硬的、僵直的、不自然的、費勁的
名 死屍、流浪漢

Fighting!

Give it a shot 小試身手

1 My father is too ____ to negotiate with him.

2 Our marketing ____ is to offer free perfume in the magazine.

3 He cannot dance because his movement is too ____.

4 She did not have enough ____ to pick up the box.

5 The sound quality of my new ____ is perfect.

MP3　短文 359　字彙 360

180

Essay

I work as a supervisor at a studio. One day, after discussing[2149] a project with the staff at the studio, I went to a good viewpoint in the suburbs[2150] to enjoy the beautiful view. Suddenly, I saw a man looking very much depressed[2151], as if he wanted to jump down from the high viewpoint. I supposed that he wanted to commit suicide, so I suggested he calm down. He told me, "I have been suffering from disappointment[2152] in love." I told him, "There must be a girl who is suitable for you somewhere." So he gave up his idea of committing suicide.

After saving[2153] his life, I spent the sum[2154] of $200 to buy some stuff[2155] at the market[2156] and then went back to the studio to work. I had to finish[2157] writing the speech I had to give the next day and decide what clothes I would wear. I thought it was a great idea to suck[2158] a lollipop and give my speech at the same time. I believed that would really impress the audience. However, I had to make sure that the content[2159] of my speech was perfect.

中譯 *Translation*

　　我是一間工作室的主管。有一天，在工作室和員工討論完企劃後，我到了郊區一個視野絕佳的地方欣賞漂亮的風景。突然，我看到一名灰心喪志的男子，一副要從高處跳下去的樣子，我想他應該是要自殺，便勸他先冷靜下來。他跟我說：「我感情路走得不順遂，為情所困。」我對他說：「這世界上一定會有適合你的女孩。」於是他打消了自殺的念頭。

　　在救了他一命之後，我在市場花了兩百元買一些東西，接著便回工作室繼續工作。我必須寫完隔天要發表的演說，並決定穿什麼樣的衣服。我認為在演講的時候邊吸棒棒糖是個很棒的點子，觀眾一定會對此印象深刻。然而，我必須確保我的演說內容夠完美。

2149 discuss

[dɪ`skʌs] ★★★★★
- 動 討論、論述、詳述
- 片 discuss with 與…討論
- 衍 discussion 討論

2150 suburb

[`sʌbɜb] ★★★
- 名 郊區、邊緣、外圍
- 片 the suburbs 市郊
- 衍 suburban 郊區的

2151 depressed

[dɪ`prɛst] ★★★
- 形 沮喪的、蕭條的、低於一般水準的
- 同 dispirited 沮喪的

2152 disappointment

[dɪsə`pɔɪntmənt] ★★
- 名 沮喪、失望、掃興
- 片 to sb's disappointment 使某人失望的是

2153 save

[sev] ★★★★★
- 動 挽救、節省、儲蓄
- 名 救球
- 片 save up 儲存起來

2154 sum

[sʌm] ★★★
- 名 總數、一筆、概要
- 動 總結、共計
- 片 sum up 總結

2155 stuff

[stʌf] ★★★★★
- 名 物品、廢話、材料
- 動 裝滿、塞進、吃過多
- 片 stuff with 用…塞滿

2156 market

[`mɑrkɪt] ★★★★★
- 名 市場、銷路、行情
- 動 銷售
- 片 flood the market 充斥

2157 finish

[`fɪnɪʃ] ★★★★
- 動 完成、結束、用完
- 名 結束、最後階段
- 片 finish + ving 完成某事

2158 suck

[sʌk] ★★★
- 動 吸吮、吸收、吞沒
- 名 吸吮、一口
- 片 suck in 吸入

2159 content

[`kɑntɛnt] ★★★★
- 名 內容、要旨、目錄
- 形 滿足的、滿意的
- 動 使滿足

2160 quiet

[`kwaɪət] ★★★★
- 形 安靜的、溫和的
- 動 撫慰、平息
- 片 quite down 平靜下來

Fighting!

Give it a shot 小試身手

❶ The company _____ from a great loss during the war.

❷ Living in the _____ is very quiet[2160] and comfortable.

❸ This outfit is not _____ for the event.

❹ He was so depressed with his life that he planned to commit _____.

❺ The ingredients are not _____ to make a birthday cake.

Answers: ❶ suffered ❷ suburb ❸ suitable ❹ suicide ❺ sufficient

181

Essay

 MP3 短文 361 字彙 362

While on a holiday in the Middle East, Robert <u>was caught up in</u> an insurrection[2161]. Robert thought he would most certainly[2162] be killed, but he managed to survive the revolt[2163]. Later, Robert was interviewed by the police, and he told them what had happened to him. He was surrounded by reporters and policemen. He sweated a lot and his feet were swollen[2164]. The police took what he said with suspicion; they suspected that he was one of the rebels[2165] who had organized the insurrection. He swore that he was not involved at all in the revolt against the government. As the police were trying to find information from their computer system, Robert suddenly took a sword[2166] from the desk, turned off the light switch[2167] and ran away. He had moved too swiftly[2168] for them to catch him. Subsequently[2169], the police posted[2170] posters with his photo and name on everywhere in order to catch him. However, Robert vanished[2171] <u>for good</u>. No one knew if he had really been involved in the insurrection or not. What do you think?

ⓘ be caught up in 被捲入、涉及

ⓘ for good 永遠

中譯 *Translation*

　　正當羅伯特在中東度假的時候,他被捲入一場暴動。羅伯特以為自己勢必會因此喪命,但他設法在這場叛亂中活了下來。稍晚,羅伯特接受警方面談,他向他們敘述事發經過。他被記者和警察團團圍住,他汗水淋漓且雙腳腫脹。然而,警方對他的供詞抱著懷疑的態度,他們懷疑他就是策劃這場暴動的其中一名叛亂者。他發誓他與這場反政府的叛變一點關係也沒有。正當警察要從電腦系統調閱資料時,他突然從桌上拿了一把刀,關掉電燈後便逃逸無蹤。他的動作太迅速,警察完全抓不住他。隨後,為了逮到他,警方四處張貼印有他的照片和姓名的海報。不過羅伯特從此消失匿跡,沒有人知道他是否與這場暴動有關。你覺得呢?

2161 insurrection

[ɪnsəˋrɛkʃən] ★★
- 名 暴動、叛亂、起義
- 同 rebellion 叛亂
- 衍 insurrectionist 叛亂者

2162 certainly

[ˋsɝtənlɪ] ★★★★
- 副 無疑地、確實、當然
- 反 perhaps 或許、可能
- 衍 certainty 確實

2163 revolt

[rɪˋvolt] ★★★
- 名 造反、起義、厭惡
- 動 反叛、厭惡
- 片 in revolt 嫌惡地

2164 swollen

[ˋswolən] ★★★
- 形 浮腫的、膨脹的、誇大的、自負的
- 同 inflated 誇張的

2165 rebel

[ˋrɛbḷ] ★★★
- 名 造反者、反抗者
- 動 反叛、嫌惡
- 形 反叛的、造反的

2166 sword

[sord] ★★★
- 名 刀、劍、武力、兵權
- 片 fire and sword 大肆燒殺破壞

2167 switch

[swɪtʃ] ★★★
- 名 開關、轉換、調換
- 動 打開開關、轉移、調換
- 片 switch off 關上

2168 swiftly

[ˋswɪftlɪ] ★★
- 副 迅速地、敏捷地
- 反 slowly 緩慢地
- 衍 swift 快速的

2169 subsequently

[ˋsʌbsɪkwɛntlɪ] ★★★
- 副 隨後、接著
- 同 afterwards 隨後
- 衍 subsequent 隨後的

2170 post

[post] ★★★★★
- 動 張貼、設置、調派
- 名 職位、崗位、郵件
- 片 post on 張貼在…上

2171 vanish

[ˋvænɪʃ] ★★★
- 動 消失、突然不見、絕跡
- 同 disappear 消失
- 片 vanish away 消失

2172 twist

[twɪst] ★★★★
- 動 扭傷、曲解、纏繞
- 名 扭傷、歪曲、意外轉折
- 片 twist off 扭斷

fighting!

Give it a shot 小試身手

1 My house is _____ by trees and flowers

2 I twisted[2172] my ankle and now it is _____ like a tennis ball.

3 He was a _____ during that horrible earthquake.

4 The neighbor _____ that he did not steal the bike.

5 The education _____ right now still needs improvements.

Answers: 1 surrounded 2 swollen 3 survivor 4 swore 5 system

182

Essay

A tailor's technique was pretty good, and he was very even-tempered[2173]. If a person tried to tease[2174] him, he would still give him or her a tender smile. However, he knew absolutely[2175] nothing about technology. He was great with a needle and thread[2176], but he knew nothing about 3C products.

One day, he left the tap[2177] open to fill the bathtub with warm water before taking a bath. He found that the temperature of the air conditioner was very low. He called a temporary[2178] worker he had hired to come and fix[2179] the problem with the air conditioner. He was thankful[2180] for what the worker had done, but the worker handed[2181] a letter to him from the government. According to the letter, he needed to pay 10,000 dollars in property[2182] tax[2183]. Although he tended[2184] to handle with things calmly, he <u>went bananas</u> this time.

> ⓘ go bananas 形容焦急煩躁而情緒失控

中譯 *Translation*

　　有名裁縫師的裁縫技術一流，脾氣也很好。如果有人試圖戲弄他，他仍是抱以溫和的一笑。然而，他對科技卻是一竅不通。他的裁縫技術高超，但對 3C 產品卻是一無所知。

　　某天，他在洗澡前把水龍頭開著，在浴缸放滿溫水。他覺得空調的溫度太低了，就打電話請臨時工過來幫他修理冷氣。他很感謝工人幫他修好冷氣，不過工人給了他一封政府的官方信函。信中提到他必須支付一萬元的房地產稅金。雖然他盡量讓自己保持冷靜來處理事情，但他這次還是情緒失控了。

2173 even-tempered

[ˈivənˈtɛmpəd] ★★
形 性情平和的、穩重的、沉著的

2174 tease

[tiz] ★★★
動 戲弄、取笑、挑逗
名 戲弄、取笑
片 tease about 嘲笑

2175 absolutely

[ˈæbsəlutlɪ] ★★★
副 絕對地、完全地
反 relatively 相對地
衍 absolute 完全的

2176 thread

[θrɛd] ★★★★
名 線、頭緒、思路
動 穿線(針)、穿過
片 lose the thread 沒頭緒

2177 tap

[tæp] ★★★
名 龍頭、塞子、輕拍
動 輕拍、接通、開發
片 tap on 輕敲

2178 temporary

[ˈtɛmpərɛrɪ] ★★★★
形 臨時的、暫時的
名 臨時工、臨時房屋
反 permanent 永久的

2179 fix

[fɪks] ★★★★
動 修理、確定、固定、安排、操縱
片 fix up 修補

2180 thankful

[ˈθæŋkfəl] ★★★
形 感謝的、欣慰的
片 thankful to sb. for 為了…感謝某人

2181 hand

[hænd] ★★★★★
動 給、面交、傳遞
名 手、技能、能手、支配
片 at hand 即將來臨

2182 property

[ˈprɑpətɪ] ★★★★
名 房地產、所有權、財產、特性
同 estate 財產

2183 tax

[tæks] ★★★★★
名 稅、稅金、負擔
動 課稅、負重擔、譴責
片 tax with 控告、責備

2184 tend

[tɛnd] ★★★★
動 傾向於、易於、照料、注意、關心
片 tend to 傾向、易於

Fighting!

Give it a shot 小試身手

① Teaching is only my _____ job; I want to become a doctor one day.

② He was sick and the body _____ kept going high.

③ Amanda _____ to get angry when she is hungry.

④ She was _____ for everything she owned.

⑤ This cat looks violent but actually it is very _____.

Answers: ① temporary ② temperature ③ tends ④ thankful ⑤ tame

MP3

 短文 365

 字彙 366

183

Essay

My philosophy[2185] of life is to enjoy life as much as I can because it is too short. I am very tired of being an employee, with tight deadlines[2186] all the time but low pay. I live by the beach. I like to watch tortoises[2187] creeping[2188] on the sand after the high tide[2189]. The tidy[2190] beach provides a healthy and beautiful environment, which helps the animals survive in good health. Sometimes I use wood to make a fire or to make furniture. When I am really thirsty, it's not unusual[2191] for me to drink tons[2192] of beer. My friends and I smoke tobacco and play cards together, as if we had no work or other obligations[2193] in life. We talk about the things we have done in our lives and our hopes and dreams[2194] for the future. My parents urge me to be more diligent and not waste time with my friends. However, I think I have a right[2195] to enjoy my life.

中譯 *Translation*

　　我的人生哲理是人生苦短所以要盡可能地及時行樂。交件時間總是非常緊迫，但薪水卻少得可憐，讓我厭倦了上班族的生活。我住在海邊，我喜歡在漲潮後看著陸龜在沙灘上爬行。整潔乾淨的海灘賦予了一個有益身心且景色優美的自然環境，也有助於動物們活得健康。有時我會用木材生火或是製作家具，當我渴到不行時，一口氣喝下好幾噸啤酒是正常的。我和我的朋友會一起抽菸、玩牌，就好像我的人生中沒有工作和其他責任一樣。我們互相說著自己曾做過的事、希望和未來的夢想。我父母極力勸我要更勤勞，不要浪費時間和朋友廝混。不過，我認為我有享受人生的權利。

你不可不知！

　　還記得羅賓威廉斯的代表作—「春風化雨」(Dead Poets Society)嗎？他在片中飾演一名用反傳統方式教導學生，讓學生得以解放思想、充分發揮想法的文學教授Keating。其中他教大家要 carpe diem(拉丁文)，也就是把握當下、及時行樂的意思(英文為 seize the day)。大家要好好記住Keating 老師的話喔！

2185 philosophy

[fə`lɑsəfɪ] ★★★★

名 人生觀、哲學、哲理、達觀、鎮靜

衍 philosophic 哲學的

2186 deadline

[`dɛdlaɪn] ★★★

名 最後限期、截稿時間

片 tight deadline 時間緊促

2187 tortoise

[`tɔrtəs] ★★

名 烏龜、行動遲緩的人

同 turtle 海龜

2188 creep

[krip] ★★

動 爬行、匍匐而行、蔓延

名 爬、諂媚者、毛骨悚然的感覺

2189 tide

[taɪd] ★★★★

名 潮汐、浪潮、趨勢

動 潮水般地奔流

片 tide over 度過

2190 tidy

[`taɪdɪ] ★★★★

形 井然的、整潔的

動 使整潔、整理

片 tidy up 收拾東西

2191 unusual

[ʌn`juʒʊəl] ★★★★

形 不尋常的、獨特的

同 uncommon 不尋常的

反 usual 通常的

2192 ton

[tʌn] ★★★★

名 噸、大量、許多

同 mass 大量

片 weigh a ton 非常重

2193 obligation

[ɑblə`geʃən] ★★★

名 責任、義務、恩惠、合約

同 duty 責任、義務

2194 dream

[drim] ★★★★★

動 夢想、嚮往、夢見

名 夢、幻想、理想

片 dream on 癡心妄想

2195 right

[raɪt] ★★★★★

名 權利、右邊、正義

形 右邊的、恰當的

副 向右、恰當地、逕直地

2196 breakthrough

[`brekθru] ★★

名 突破性進展、突圍

片 make a breakthrough 取得突破

Fighting!

Give it a shot 小試身手

❶ The bully _____ Adam to give him some money.

❷ I like to sit on the beach and watch the _____ comes and goes.

❸ Einstein's _____ of Relativity was a breakthrough[2196] in the 20th century.

❹ She helped her mother _____ out the garbage.

❺ We are running out of _____ in the toilet.

Answers: ❶ threatened ❷ tide ❸ theory ❹ toss ❺ tissue

Find your level of English.
Level1　Level2　Level3　Level4　**Level5**　Level6

Now

MP3

184

Essay

Since traveling is so popular these days, travel books are also popular. Recently, a very experienced[2197] traveler wrote a book to introduce his travel[2198] experiences all over the world. His book was a bestseller because he talked about some very interesting things he has encountered on his travels. For example, in Guam, he met a trader who imported and exported goods by ship. He told Robert one of his funny experiences. One day, an evil guy trailed[2199] him. He was trembling when he felt something wrong. He went to the police station near the harbor to ask for help. The stalker[2200] was so tricky[2201] that he ran into a restaurant and held a tray[2202] to pretend that he was a waiter. A police officer passed by and saw someone tire[2203] tracks near the trash dump. He thought the vehicle[2204] belonged[2205] to that stalker and then towed[2206] his vehicle away. How could one be so unlucky as he was?

中譯 *Translation*

　　由於現今掀起的旅遊熱潮，讓旅遊書也開始熱賣。近來，有位閱歷豐富旅行家寫了一本書，介紹他在世界各地旅遊的經驗，因為他會分享在旅行中遇到的一些非常有趣的經歷，讓他的書成為了暢銷書。比如說，在關島，他遇到一名靠船運進出口貨物的貿易商。他告訴羅伯特其中一個他遇到的有趣經歷。某天，他被一個壞人跟蹤。當他察覺到事情不對勁時，嚇得全身發抖，於是跑到港口附近的警察局求救。這名跟蹤者非常狡猾，他跑進餐廳，手上拿著托盤佯裝自己是服務生。一名警察經過時發現垃圾場旁的輪胎痕跡。他覺得這輛車應該是那名跟蹤者的，於是他的車子拖走了。這世上大概不會有人比他更倒楣了！

你不可不知！

　　關島是位於西太平洋的島嶼，目前為美國領地，但未正式成為州。關島有半數人口為當地原住民—查莫洛人，而有四分之一的人口來自美洲大陸。關島先後分別為西班牙、日本、美國所佔領，其中以日本佔據時間最短，不過現今島上仍隨處可見日語招牌及公告。

2197 experienced

[ɪkˋspɪrɪənst] ★★
形 有經驗的、熟練的
反 unexperienced 無經驗的

2198 travel

[ˋtrævl] ★★★★★
名 旅行、遊歷、遊記
動 旅行、傳導、掃視
片 travel in 在…旅行

2199 trail

[trel] ★★★★
動 跟蹤、拖曳、蔓生
名 蹤跡、一長串、拖曳物
片 trail along 跟隨

2200 stalker

[ˋstɔkə] ★★
名 跟蹤者、高視闊步者
衍 stalk 偷偷靠近

2201 tricky

[ˋtrɪkɪ] ★★
形 狡猾的、足智多謀的、棘手的、複雜的
同 sly 狡猾的

2202 tray

[tre] ★★★
名 托盤、一盤的量
同 salver 托盤

2203 tire

[taɪr] ★★★★
名 輪胎
動 裝輪胎、使疲倦、厭煩
片 tire of 對…厭煩

2204 vehicle

[ˋviɪkl̩] ★★★★
名 車輛、運載工具、手段
同 conveyance 運輸工具
片 vehicle for …的媒介

2205 belong

[bəˋlɔŋ] ★★★★
動 屬於、適用、處在、合得來
片 belong to 屬於

2206 tow

[to] ★★★★
動 拖、拉、牽引
名 拖、拉、牽引
片 in tow 伴隨、跟隨

2207 represent

[rɛprɪˋzɛnt] ★★★★
動 象徵、意味著、扮演、表現、為…的代表
片 represent to 傳達

2208 luggage

[ˋlʌgɪdʒ] ★★★
名 行李
同 baggage 行李

---

fighting!

Give it a shot 小試身手

❶ _____ behaviors represent[2207] their nation overseas.

❷ The _____ bankrupted for fall in business.

❸ Most of our luggage[2208] was _____ by sea.

❹ She _____ whenever she thinks of the horrible experience.

❺ She always follows the latest _____ in fashion.

Answers: ❶ Tourists ❷ trader ❸ transported ❹ trembles ❺ trends

MP3

185

Essay

I have a twin[2209] sister whom I am very close with. I work as a secretary while my sister works as an English tutor on the weekends. She is a typical undergraduate[2210] student who has a part-time job to make extra[2211] money. She has a lot of common sense and vision. We live together in perfect harmony[2212]. She has great interest in singing. Once she sang out of tune[2213] when she was in the bathtub. I asked her to stop singing because I could not stand the noise[2214] anymore. She pulled the shower curtain angrily and jumped out of the tub[2215], and then she tumbled[2216] over and twisted her ankle. I apologized to her and went to the drugstore to buy some medicine that would help relieve[2217] her pain. I also bought a bouquet[2218] of tulips for her. She was touched by my sincere[2219] apology and said, "Brothers and sisters should live together in harmony. Right?" With those words, I knew that we had come to a complete reconciliation[2220].

中譯 *Translation*

　　我有一個和我關係非常密切的雙胞胎妹妹。我是名秘書，而我妹妹在週末時是名英文家教。她是個典型的大學生，靠打工賺額外的零用錢。她兼具常識與見識，我們住在一起且和睦地相處。她對唱歌有很大的興趣，有一次她在泡澡時唱到走音，我沒有辦法再忍受她難聽的歌聲，就叫她別再唱了。她生氣地拉開浴簾，從浴缸跳出來，結果摔了一跤扭傷腳踝。我向她道歉，然後到藥局買些藥回來，以減輕她的疼痛。我還買了一束鬱金香送給她。她被我真誠的道歉所感動，跟我說：「兄弟姊妹就該一起融洽生活，不是嗎？」因為這些話，我知道我們已經完全和好了。

2209 twin

[twɪn] ★★
- 形 孿生的、成對的
- 名 雙胞胎之一
- 動 使成對、生雙胞胎

2210 undergraduate

[ˌʌndəˋgrædʒuɪt] ★★
- 形 大學生的
- 名 大學生、大學肄業生
- 反 graduate 研究生的

2211 extra

[ˋɛkstrə] ★★★★
- 形 額外的、特大的
- 副 額外地、非常地
- 名 附加費用、臨時演員

2212 harmony

[ˋhɑrmənɪ] ★★★
- 名 和睦、一致、協調
- 片 in harmony with 與⋯協調一致

2213 tune

[tjun] ★★★★
- 名 曲調、旋律、腔調
- 動 調音、使協調
- 片 out of tune 走音

2214 noise

[nɔɪz] ★★★★★
- 名 噪音、喧鬧聲、干擾
- 動 謠傳
- 片 make a noise 吵鬧

2215 tub

[tʌb] ★★★
- 名 浴缸、木桶、一桶的量
- 同 bathtub 浴缸

2216 tumble

[ˋtʌmbḷ] ★★★
- 動 跌倒、墜落、輾轉、倒塌、暴跌
- 名 跌跤、暴跌、翻滾

2217 relieve

[rɪˋliv] ★★★
- 動 減輕、解除、救濟、使寬心
- 片 relieve from 從⋯解脫

2218 bouquet

[buˋke] ★★★
- 名 一束花、花束、香味
- 同 posy 花束

2219 sincere

[sɪnˋsɪr] ★★★★
- 形 真誠的、衷心的
- 同 genuine 真誠的
- 反 fake 偽造的

2220 reconciliation

[rɛkənsɪlɪˋeʃən] ★
- 名 和解、調停、一致
- 衍 reconcile 使和解

fighting!

Give it a shot 小試身手

1. Holland is abundant in _____.
2. I worked as a piano _____ during my leisure time.
3. The little boy _____ the table cloth and everything fell down.
4. The journalist likes to _____ the fact in the newspaper.
5. The European _____ is comprised of twenty-seven countries.

Answers: ❶ tulips ❷ tutor ❸ tugged ❹ twist ❺ Union

MP3　短文 371　字彙 372

Essay 186

The vice-president was a victim of an assassination[2221] attempt last month. Fortunately, he was wearing a bulletproof[2222] vest[2223] while he was in his car when a man driving a van[2224] tried to shoot him dead. Luckily, he was safe and sound. I was upset when I saw this news. I view this crime as the most despicable[2225] one I could imagine. The vice-president is such an important leader who always proposes valuable policies. When the police found the van, it was vacant[2226], and the gun was nowhere to be found. By coincidence[2227], the vice-president had been my university classmate. To buy him a get-well gift, I went to a shop to choose the best vase they had. When I entered his room, he showed me the verses[2228] he was writing. He said, "The styles of verses vary from person to person, just like personality. You know me very well. I cannot put up with political life anymore, but I won't quit until my aspirations[2229] are fulfilled[2230]. There are still many things I have yet to accomplish[2231], right?" I really admire him.

中譯 *Translation*

　　副總統是上個月一場暗殺計畫的受害者。所幸當一名歹徒開著小貨車企圖射殺他時，他穿著防彈背心坐在車裡，幸好他安然無恙。我看到這則新聞時感到相當氣憤，我認為這是世上最邪惡的罪刑。副總統是非常重要的領導者，他總是提出許多有用的政策。當警察發現行凶的車輛時，車內卻空無一人，作案槍枝也消失無蹤。很巧的是，副總統是我的大學同學。為了送他早日康復的禮物，我到店裡挑選最棒的花瓶。我走進他的病房時，他給我看他正著手創作的詩句，他說：「每個人寫出來的詩句風格都不相同，就像每個人都擁有獨特的個性，你很了解我，我無法再繼續忍受這樣的政治生涯，不過除非我的理想抱負實現了，不然我是不會退休的，還有許多事需要我去完成，不是嗎？」我真是打從心底敬佩他啊。

2221 assassination

[əˌsæsəˈneʃən] ★
名 暗殺、行刺

2222 bulletproof

[ˈbʊlɪtpruf] ★★
形 防彈的
片 bulletproof vest 防彈背心

2223 vest

[vɛst] ★★★★
名 背心、馬甲、內衣
動 穿衣服、賦予、歸屬
片 life vest 救生衣

2224 van

[væn] ★★★★
名 有蓋小貨車、箱型車
動 用車搬運
衍 vanguard 先鋒

2225 despicable

[ˈdɛspɪkəbl̩] ★★
形 卑劣的、可鄙的
片 a despicable act 卑鄙的行為

2226 vacant

[ˈvekənt] ★★★
形 空著的、空缺的、空閒的、空虛的
同 unoccupied 空著的

2227 coincidence

[koˈɪnsɪdəns] ★★★
名 巧合、同時發生、一致
片 more than coincidence 蓄意

2228 verse

[vɝs] ★★★★
名 詩作、詩句、韻文
動 作詩、使精通
片 verse in 精通…

2229 aspiration

[æspəˈreʃən] ★★
名 抱負、志向、呼氣
同 ambition 抱負
衍 aspire 熱望、嚮往

2230 fulfill

[fʊlˈfɪl] ★★★
動 實現、滿足、執行
同 perform 執行

2231 accomplish

[əˈkɑmplɪʃ] ★★★
動 完成、實現、達到
同 realize 實現
衍 accomplishment 成就

2232 shape

[ʃep] ★★★★★
名 形狀、形式、狀態
動 塑造、使合身、形成
片 out of shape 變形

Fighting!

Give it a shot 小試身手

❶ The jewelry her grandmother gave her was very _____.

❷ I like _____ kinds of animals.

❸ I will not go _____ you come with me.

❹ The shape[2232] of the clouds _____ everyday.

❺ Do you have any _____ to go to work?

Answers: ❶ valuable ❷ various ❸ unless ❹ varies ❺ vehicle

MP3

短文 373

字彙 374

187

Essay

On a Sunday morning, Peter was wandering[2233] at home. He was thinking about what he needed to buy. After a while, he decided to buy a trailer[2234] for his car as well as a jar of vitamins. He needed a trailer to transport goods to town from his house and vitamins to keep healthy. He also bought some wax[2235] for his trailer and asked the store to deliver the trailer to his home. While walking back towards his home, he also bought a bouquet of violets[2236] for his girlfriend. Visibility[2237] was quite[2238] poor that night because of the darkness[2239] and heavy mist[2240]. Suddenly, a gang stopped him and tried to rob him of his money and the stuff he had just bought. Just then, he realized he had forgotten all about the high rate of violence his mother had warned[2241] him about. Luckily, a young man came along and scared the gang away. Peter was touched by the stranger's assistance[2242]. All of a sudden, he was wakened[2243] by loud sound. He realized it had just been a dream. Shaking his head, he said to himself, "How vivid it was!"

中譯 *Translation*

　　星期天早上彼得在家無所事事，他正在思考有哪些東西是必須要買的。左思右想一陣子後，他決定要幫他的車子買個拖車以及一罐維他命。他需要一輛拖車把貨物運到城裡，而維他命可以讓他保持健康。他也買了蠟要塗在拖車上，並要求店家幫他把拖車運到家裡。在走路回家的途中，他還買了束紫羅蘭要送給女友。因為天色昏暗又起濃霧，路上視線並不好。突然間有一群歹徒擋住他的去路，試圖搶走他身上的財物和剛買的東西。就在那時，他才意識到母親曾警告過他這裡犯罪率很高。幸好，有名年輕人出現把這群惡徒嚇跑。彼得對這名陌生人的熱情相助非常感動，突然間，他被一股巨大的聲響驚醒，才發覺這只是一場夢，他搖搖頭告訴自己：「這個夢好真實啊！」

2233 wander

[`wɑndə] ★★★★

動 閒逛、流浪、徘徊、離題、失神

片 wander over 漫步在…

2234 trailer

[`trelə] ★★

名 拖車、預告片、追蹤者、蔓生植物

動 用拖車運

2235 wax

[wæks] ★★★★

名 蠟、蜂蠟、耳垢、漸圓

動 給…上蠟、變大

片 wax and wane 盈虧

2236 violet

[`vaɪəlɪt] ★★

名 紫羅蘭、羞怯的人、紫羅蘭色

形 紫羅蘭的、紫羅蘭色的

2237 visibility

[ˌvɪzə`bɪlətɪ] ★

名 能見度、清晰度

反 invisibility 看不見

衍 visible 可看見的

2238 quite

[kwaɪt] ★★★★★

副 相當、徹底、很、完全

同 completely 完全地

片 quite a few 相當多

2239 darkness

[`dɑrknɪs] ★★★

名 黑暗、無知、邪惡

片 total darkness 一片漆黑

2240 mist

[mɪst] ★★★

名 薄霧、模糊不清、迷霧

動 蒙上薄霧、變得模糊

片 mist over 蒙上薄霧

2241 warn

[wɔrn] ★★★★★

動 警告、提醒、預先通知

同 caution 警告

片 warn against 當心…

2242 assistance

[ə`sɪstəns] ★★★

名 幫助、援助

片 be of assistance 有幫助

2243 waken

[`wekn̩] ★★

動 喚醒、覺醒、激發

同 awaken 覺醒

片 waken from 從…喚醒

2244 depth

[dɛpθ] ★★★★

名 深度、深奧、深厚

同 profundity 深度

片 in depth 深入地

Fighting!

Give it a shot 小試身手

❶ He takes ＿＿＿ everyday to maintain healthy.

❷ People who use ＿＿＿ to solve problem is not wise.

❸ I used my ＿＿＿ to buy some new shoes.

❹ I should ＿＿＿ you that the depth[2244] of the lake is very deep.

❺ The man was drunk and ＿＿＿ around on the street.

Essay

Isabella was a girl who had been born into a wealthy family. Her family owned an international business that imported and exported wheat[2245] and a grand villa with a backyard filled with willows[2246] along a riverbank. Sometimes, spiders would weave[2247] their webs[2248] on the trees. One day, Isabella went to pick[2249] weeds in the garden. Her friend whistled and invited her to play together in a park near her house. Isabella agreed immediately and then didn't come home until very late. Because she returned so late, she got spanked[2250] by her father. Her father asked her if she had done anything wicked[2251] outside. She denied it firmly. Her father told her, "You belong to a rich family. There are people out there who might kidnap[2252] you to earn a big ransom[2253] from me. You should never again do such a thing!" Isabella could not help but weep[2254] and she dashed to her room. From that moment on, she thought of her background as a great burden, not a privilege[2255], for her.

中譯 *Translation*

伊莎貝拉是個富家女。她的家族是專做小麥進出口生意的國際企業，還有一棟豪華的別墅，別墅後院的河岸上種滿了柳樹，有時可以看到蜘蛛在樹上織網。有一天伊莎貝拉在花園除草，她的朋友吹口哨邀她一起到她家附近的公園玩。伊莎貝拉馬上答應了，之後玩到很晚才回家。因為她太晚回家而被父親打屁股。她爸爸問她在外面有沒有做壞事，她堅決否認，她爸爸告訴她：「你是有錢人家的小孩。外面有許多人可能會為了要從我這裡得到大筆贖金而綁架你。你不應該再做這種事了！」伊莎貝拉哭個不停，一股腦的衝回房間。從那時候起，她就覺得她的家世背景不是個殊榮，而是個沉重的負擔。

新多益藍色證書必備單字

2245 wheat

[hwit] ★★★★
名 小麥、小麥色

2246 willow

[ˋwɪlo] ★★
名 柳樹、打棉機
動 用打棉機清理
片 weeping willow 垂柳

2247 weave

[wiv] ★★★★
動 編織、編入、迂迴前進
名 織法、編織式樣
片 weave into 把…織成

2248 web

[wɛb] ★★★★★
名 網狀物、圈套、網絡
動 結網於、中圈套
片 spin a web 織網

2249 pick

[pɪk] ★★★★★
動 採摘、挑選、獲得
名 選擇、精華、收穫量
片 pick on 挑選

2250 spank

[spæŋk] ★★
動 打屁股、摑、輕快移動
名 一摑、一巴掌
同 slap 摑、拍擊

2251 wicked

[ˋwɪkɪd] ★★★
形 壞的、缺德的、惡劣的、惡作劇的
同 vicious 邪惡的

2252 kidnap

[ˋkɪdnæp] ★★★
動 綁架、誘拐、劫持
同 abduct 誘拐
衍 kidnapper 綁匪

2253 ransom

[ˋrænsəm] ★★
名 贖金、贖回、贖身
動 贖回、勒索贖金
同 redeem 贖回

2254 weep

[wip] ★★★★
動 哭泣、流淚、悲嘆
名 哭泣、眼淚、滴下
片 weep away 不停哭泣

2255 privilege

[ˋprɪvḷɪdʒ] ★★★★
名 特權、殊榮、基本權利
動 給予特權、以特權免除
衍 privileged 享有特權的

2256 setback

[ˋsɛtbæk] ★★
名 挫折、倒退、復發
同 frustration 挫折

Give it a shot 小試身手

1 The backyard is full of _____.

2 The boy _____ to the girl to get her attention.

3 None of these setbacks[2256] could _____ her determination.

4 _____ were symbols of separation in Chinese poetry.

5 The spider was spinning a _____.

189

Essay

John was a young man whom no one in town liked. People described him as a disaster[2257] waiting to happen[2258], and no one dared to approach him. He would yell at passersby[2259], wink at every woman on the street, and yawn[2260] in classes. One day, John had a car accident because he was driving and adjusting[2261] the zipper[2262] on his trousers at the same time. His left wrist[2263] was injured and bled a lot, but he wiped off the blood on his wrist and wrapped it with a bandage. John decided to go to the nearest hospital in town for an X-ray[2264] to see if his wrist was broken. To his surprise, the nurse praised his wisdom[2265] in stopping the bleeding and treated him to a full breakfast that included[2266] sausages, bacon and eggs. He was so touched because she was the only one who had ever treated him so friendly, so he decided to ask her to be his girlfriend, and she accepted[2267].

中譯 *Translation*

在鎮上，約翰是個人見人厭的年輕人，人們都說他是個禍害，根本沒有人敢靠近他。他會對路人大吼大叫，對街上的女孩眨眼放電，在課堂上猛打呵欠。有一天，因為他邊開車邊拉褲子拉鍊，結果發生了車禍。約翰的左腕受傷流了很多血，然而他擦掉手腕上的血，並用繃帶包紮。約翰決定去鎮上最近的醫院照X光片，檢查是否有骨折。令他訝異的是，護士稱讚他的止血知識，還請他吃一頓豐盛的早餐，有香腸、培根，和蛋。他非常感動，因為她唯一一個對他這麼有善的人，所以他決定請她做他的女朋友，而她也答應了。

2257 disaster

[dɪ`zæstə˞] ★★★
名 災難、不幸
同 calamity 災難、大禍
片 disaster area 災區

2258 happen

[`hæpən] ★★★★★
動 發生、碰巧
同 occur 發生
片 happen on 碰巧發現

2259 passerby

[`pæsə˞`baɪ] ★★
名 行人、過路客
複 passersby 行人

2260 yawn

[jɔn] ★★★
動 打呵欠、裂開
名 呵欠、裂口、乏味的人
片 stifle a yawn 忍住呵欠

2261 adjust

[ə`dʒʌst] ★★★★★
動 調整、校準、適應
片 adjust to 使適應
衍 adjusted 已適應的

2262 zipper

[`zɪpə˞] ★★
名 拉鍊
動 拉上拉鍊
同 zip (英)拉鍊

2263 wrist

[rɪst] ★★★
名 手腕、腕關節
片 slap on the wrist 輕微地處罰

2264 X-ray

[`ɛks`re] ★★
名 X光、X光檢查
動 用X光線檢查
形 X光線的

2265 wisdom

[`wɪzdəm] ★★★★
名 知識、智慧、看法
同 sagacity 聰慧
片 wisdom tooth 智齒

2266 include

[ɪn`klud] ★★★★★
動 包含、算入
同 contain 包含
反 exclude 不包括

2267 accept

[ək`sɛpt] ★★★★★
動 答應、接受、認可
衍 acceptable 令人滿意的

2268 caution

[`kɔʃən] ★★★
名 謹慎、小心、告誡
動 警告、使小心
片 caution about 小心…

Fighting!

Give it a shot 小試身手

1. I felt sleepy and started to _____.
2. Sue _____ up the birthday present with caution[2268].
3. The disaster _____ was closed off.
4. Millions of stars are _____ in the sky.
5. Peggy _____ out to scare the exhibitionist away.

Answers: 1 yawn 2 wrapped 3 zone 4 winking 5 yelled

190

 MP3 短文 379 字彙 380

Essay

My mother has been an accountant for twenty years. To me, the field of accounting seems to match her personality perfectly. However, she told me that accounting was not her initial choice. She was actually fascinated[2269] with abstract[2270] philosophy and struggled to acquire[2271] my grandfather's approval regarding this area[2272] of study, but my grandfather was not at all familiar with philosophy and could not accept my mother's choice. He thought it was absolute nonsense[2273] to spend time getting a degree[2274] related to such impractical[2275] knowledge. At that time, my grandfather was a successful real estate[2276] agent and owned several acres[2277] of land. He could not allow my mother to gamble her life on an area of study that would mean she would have to rely on luck in getting a good job. He even threatened to abandon[2278] my mother if she did not get a degree in accounting. No wonder my mother accused[2279] him of being as stubborn as a mule. Finally, out of love, my mother agreed to earn an accounting degree in order to live up to my grandfather's expectations. Although my grandfather could not accompany her forever, his expectations would.

中譯 *Translation*

　　我母親已經當了二十年的會計師。在我看來，會計的職業似乎非常適合她的個性。然而，她告訴我會計並不是她最初的選擇。她告訴我，她其實對抽象哲學很著迷，並且努力想獲得祖父對她朝這個領域研究的認同。但祖父對哲學並不瞭解，無法接受母親的選擇。他認為為了這種不切實際的知識，浪費時間取得學位，根本就毫無意義。在那時，我的祖父是一個成功的房地產經紀人，並且擁有好幾畝的土地。他無法允許母親為了這種必須靠運氣才找的到好工作的科系，而賭上她的人生。他甚至威脅母親如果沒拿到會計學位，就要和她斷絕關係。難怪母親譴責祖父有多麼老頑固。最後，出於親情，我母親還是同意完成會計學位，達成祖父的期望。雖然祖父無法永遠陪著她，但他對她的期許卻會長久相隨。

2269 fascinate

[`fæsṇet] ★★★
動 迷住、神魂顛倒、吸引
同 attract 吸引
衍 fascinating 迷人的

2270 abstract

[`æbstrækt] ★★★★
形 抽象的、深奧的
名 摘要、抽象概念
動 提取、使抽象化、摘要

2271 acquire

[ə`kwaɪr] ★★★★
動 獲得、學到、養成
片 an acquired taste 逐漸培養的愛好

2272 area

[`ɛrɪə] ★★★★★
名 領域、區域、面積
同 field 領域
片 area code 區域號碼

2273 nonsense

[`nɑnsɛns] ★★★
名 無價值物、胡說、廢話
片 talk nonsense 胡說八道

2274 degree

[dɪ`gri] ★★★
名 學位、程度、度數
同 level 程度
片 to a degree 非常、很

2275 impractical

[ɪm`præktɪkḷ] ★★
形 不切實際的、無用的
同 unrealistic 不切實際的
反 practical 實際的

2276 estate

[ɪs`tet] ★★★★
名 地產、資產、社會階級
同 property 地產

2277 acre

[`ekɚ] ★★★
名 英畝、土地、許多
片 acres of 大量

2278 abandon

[ə`bændən] ★★★★
動 遺棄、中止、使放縱
名 放縱、放任
片 abandon to 使陷入

2279 accuse

[ə`kjuz] ★★★★
動 譴責、控告、歸咎於
片 accuse of 指控犯了…
衍 accusation 控告

2280 mission

[`mɪʃən] ★★★★
名 任務、使命、使節團
動 派遣、向…傳教
片 on a mission 執行任務

Fighting!

Give it a shot 小試身手

1. There is no _____ truth in Social Science.
2. Don't write _____ descriptions in your autobiography.
3. I didn't _____ my mission[2280] for the lack of money.
4. _____ is more important than speed in his new job.
5. Bob was _____ of stealing.

Answers: 1 absolute 2 abstract 3 accomplish 4 Accuracy 5 accused

Essay 191

AIDS has been called the Black Death of the 20th century. Until the 1980s, this disease was unknown[2281] to the world. Nowadays, people are alert[2282] to every possible situation involving the infectious[2283] disease and will adjust their lifestyles to protect themselves against[2284] it. Scientists have analyzed various factors[2285] and found out that people who use certain[2286] drugs are high-risk groups. However, analyses also showed that many people do not pay[2287] enough attention to AIDS. Some governments do take action and come up with ambitious[2288] plans to help stop the spread of the disease, but there are still many countries that do not do enough to try and control the problem. We can see many admirable volunteers[2289] and others devoting much of their time to charitable agencies, trying very hard to control[2290] the spread of AIDS. Some of them have lost close family members or friends because of the disease. Admiration is not what they pursue; rather, they proudly declare[2291] that they are "the agents of AIDS's ruin."

中譯 *Translation*

　　愛滋病被稱為二十世紀的黑死病。直到1980年代，愛滋病才逐漸為人所知。現在，人們對於每個可能染病的情況都非常警覺，並且會調整他們的生活方式以保護自己不受感染。科學家分析了許多因素，發現服用特定藥物的人乃是高危險群。然而，分析也顯示許多人對愛滋病並沒有太多的關注。有些政府會採取行動，想出有助於抑制疾病擴張的遠大計劃，但是仍然有許多國家並未努力試著控管問題。我們可以看到許多令人敬佩的志工與更多的人貢獻大多數的時間給慈善機構，非常努力想要抑止愛滋的擴散。當中有許多人都是因為愛滋而失去了自己的至親或朋友。他們追求的並不是他人的讚美；更確切的說，他們驕傲地宣稱自己為「愛滋毀滅特工」。

2281 unknown

[ʌn`non] ★★★★

- 形 陌生的、默默無聞的
- 名 未知的事物
- 同 unfamiliar 陌生的

2282 alert

[ə`lɜt] ★★★★

- 形 警覺的、靈活的
- 名 警戒、警報
- 動 使警覺、通知

2283 infectious

[ɪn`fɛkʃəs] ★★

- 形 有感染力的、傳染的
- 片 infectious disease 傳染病

2284 against

[ə`gɛnst] ★★★★★

- 介 對抗、預防、倚靠、不利於、對照
- 片 go against 違背

2285 factor

[`fæktə] ★★★★

- 名 因素、要素、代理商
- 動 作為因素
- 同 element 要素

2286 certain

[`sɜtən] ★★★★★

- 形 特定的、無疑的、某種程度的
- 代 某些、若干

2287 pay

[pe] ★★★★★

- 動 給予、支付、償還
- 名 報酬、懲罰
- 片 pay off 還清

2288 ambitious

[æm`bɪʃəs] ★★★

- 形 有抱負的、野心勃勃的
- 片 ambitious of 渴望
- 衍 ambition 雄心、抱負

2289 volunteer

[vɑlən`tɪr] ★★★★

- 名 義工、志願兵
- 動 自願做、自願提供
- 片 volunteer as 自願擔任

2290 control

[kən`trol] ★★★★★

- 動 控制、管理、抑制
- 名 支配、操縱裝置、抑制
- 片 out of control 失控

2291 declare

[dɪ`klɛr] ★★★★

- 動 宣稱、宣布、申報
- 片 declare for 聲明贊成
- 衍 declaration 宣告

2292 adorable

[ə`dorəbl] ★★

- 形 可愛的、可敬重的
- 同 lovable 可愛的

Fighting!

Give it a shot 小試身手

❶ He _____ the watch to the right time.

❷ Anyone is not allowed to enter the hall without _____.

❸ We asked the travel _____ to plan our vacation.

❹ Raccoons seem adorable[2292]; however, they are very _____.

❺ Remember to keep fire away from the _____.

Answers: ❶ adjusted ❷ admission ❸ agency ❹ aggressive ❺ alcohol

192

Essay

Our school's annual anniversary is coming up very soon. On that day, a traditional drama[2293] contest will be held on the stage under the arch[2294] of the gymnasium[2295]. Our teacher told the whole class to prepare for it. We got her approval to perform[2296] a comedy about military life. Since I am the leader of the class, I was also responsible for filing an application[2297] to borrow some props[2298] and toy weapons from the student affairs[2299] office. Although we had a month to practice, we were all very anxious because we lack acting experience. To ease our anxiety[2300], our teacher asked her tailor friend to make appropriate[2301] costumes[2302] for us. We deeply appreciate her kindness. As time went by, the contest approached. We practiced every day for many hours. On the day before the contest, a worker at our school came to apologize for accidentally sprinkling red paint on our costumes. We were very shocked at first, but soon we accepted his apology. Now, we have to withdraw[2303] from the contest.

中譯 *Translation*

我們學校一年一度的校慶就快到了。那一天，一場傳統戲劇比賽將在體育館拱門下方的舞台舉行。我們老師要全班都為比賽做準備。她同意我們表演一齣關於軍隊生活的喜劇。因為我是班長，我也有責任向學務處提出申請，借用一些器具和玩具武器。雖然我們有一個月的時間可以排練，我們還是因缺乏演出經驗而非常擔心。為了減輕我們的焦慮，老師請她的裁縫友人為我們製作合適的戲服。我們都非常感謝她的好意。隨著時間過去，比賽慢慢接近了。我們每天都練習好幾個小時。在比賽的前一天，學校工友跑來向我們道歉，因為他不小心把紅色油漆潑到我們的戲服上了。我們一開始非常震驚，但很快地還是接受他的道歉。現在我們勢必得退出比賽了。

2293 drama

[ˋdramə] ★★★★

名 戲劇、戲劇性、劇本

片 make a drama out of sth. 小題大作

2294 arch

[artʃ] ★★★★

名 拱門、牌樓、拱狀物

動 拱起、使呈弧形

形 主要的、淘氣的

2295 gymnasium

[dʒɪmˋnezɪəm] ★★

名 體育館、健身房

同 gym 體育館

2296 perform

[pɚˋfɔrm] ★★★★★

動 演出、履行、完成

同 act 扮演

衍 performance 演出

2297 application

[æpləˋkeʃən] ★★★★

名 申請書、應用、施用

片 file an application 提出申請

2298 prop

[prɑp] ★★★

名 道具、支柱、後盾

動 支持、架起

片 prop up 支持、贊助

2299 affair

[əˋfɛr] ★★★★

名 事務、事件、風流韻事

片 foreign affairs 外交事務

2300 anxiety

[æŋˋzaɪətɪ] ★★★

名 焦慮、掛念、渴望

片 anxiety about 對…的憂慮

2301 appropriate

[əˋprɑprɪet] ★★★★

形 恰當的、相稱的

動 撥出、盜用、挪用

片 suitable 合適的

2302 costume

[ˋkɑstjum] ★★★

名 戲服、裝束

動 提供服裝

2303 withdraw

[wɪðˋdrɔ] ★★★★

動 退出、撤回、取回

片 withdraw from 從…退出

2304 missing

[ˋmɪsɪŋ] ★★★★★

形 失蹤的、缺席的

同 lost 迷途的

 Fighting!

Give it a shot 小試身手

❶ Today is our wedding _____.

❷ She was very _____ about her missing[2304] puppy.

❸ Please accept our _____ for the delay.

❹ There were no _____ for the position for its low salary.

❺ Yoona cancelled the _____ with her dentist.

193

Essay

MP3   短文 385   字彙 386

As a journalist, I find it easy to write articles by using the following four steps. Firstly, make sure that you fully understand the assignment[2305]. No matter what it is, an art exhibition, election or athletic event, etc., you should write about it within the context of current social trends to make your article more relevant and meaningful. Secondly, try to incorporate[2306] into the article as many interesting and insightful[2307] details related to the subject and its background. Remember to arouse[2308] your curiosity[2309] to gather as much information as possible regarding every aspect of the main[2310] theme. Thirdly, avoid artificial[2311] writing by assuming[2312] that your readers are intelligent[2313] and deserve the best from you. You should do your utmost[2314] to ensure your writing includes the most accurate[2315] information available. Finally, and the most importantly, get assistance from your colleagues and supervisors. Don't be ashamed of asking stupid questions. If you can follow the steps mentioned above, I can assure[2316] you that your journalistic career is <u>on the right track to</u> success.

⚠ on the right track to 在通往⋯的正確軌道上

中譯 *Translation*

　　身為一名記者，我發現寫文章只要根據以下四個步驟就容易多了。第一，確定你已充分瞭解你所分配到的任務。不管主題是什麼，藝術展覽、選舉或體育賽事，你應該要把主題和最近的社會趨勢做結合，好讓文章更切題也更具意義。第二，與主題和背景相關的許多有趣和見解深刻的細節，試著讓它們成為你文章的一部分。記得喚起你的好奇心，考量主題的各個面向，盡可能多收集相關資訊。第三，避免假設你的讀者有多聰明且值得你寫出最好的文章，而採用矯揉造作的寫作方式。你必須盡最大努力保證你是根據你得到的最準確的消息而寫出來的文章。最後，也最重要的一點，從同事和上司那裡取得協助。不要因為問蠢問題而感到丟臉。如果你可以遵循以上的步驟，我可以保證你的記者生涯將會一帆風順。

2305 assignment

[ə`saɪnmənt] ★★★
名 任務、作業、指派
片 on an assignment 受委派

2306 incorporate

[ɪn`kɔrpəret] ★★★★
動 使併入、吸收、體現
片 incorporate into 成為…的一部分

2307 insightful

[`ɪnsaɪtfəl] ★★★
形 具洞察力的、有深刻見解的
同 discerning 有鑑賞力的

2308 arouse

[ə`rauz] ★★★★
動 喚起、引起興趣
片 arouse sb. to anger 激怒某人

2309 curiosity

[kjurɪ`asətɪ] ★★★
名 好奇心、珍品、古玩
片 idle curiosity 無謂的好奇心

2310 main

[men] ★★★★★
形 主要的、最重要的
名 要點、總管道、幹線
同 chief 主要的

2311 artificial

[ɑrtə`fɪʃəl] ★★★
形 矯揉造作的、人工的
同 natural 天然的
片 artificial smile 假笑

2312 assume

[ə`sjum] ★★★★
動 假定、取得、假裝
同 suppose 猜想、假定
衍 assumption 假定

2313 intelligent

[ɪn`tɛlədʒənt] ★★★★
形 明智的、有才智的
同 knowing 聰穎的
衍 intelligence 智能

2314 utmost

[`ʌtmost] ★★★
名 最大可能、極限
形 最大的、極度的
片 to the utmost 竭盡

2315 accurate

[`ækjərɪt] ★★★★
形 準確的、精確的
同 exact 精確的
反 inaccurate 不精確的

2316 assure

[ə`ʃur] ★★★★
動 保證、使放心、保障
同 guarantee 保證
片 assure of 對…放心

Fighting!

Give it a shot 小試身手

❶ The drama _____ my memory of the childhood.

❷ I prefer _____ flowers, because they will not fade over time.

❸ We have to consider an issue from different _____.

❹ _____ on the playground with your bags right away.

❺ I _____ that they are a married couple.

MP3

短文 387

字彙 388

Essay 194

I want to briefly tell you about the life of a famous businessman. He was a legend[2317] in his own time since he had gone bankrupt and eventually gained his fortune back when he was old and grey. He always said, "Opportunity awaits[2318] all men." His behavior and attitude gave him the power to get rid of any barrier[2319]. He was born to bargain with people over the price. In his teens, he earned his first fortune by selling backpacks[2320] and luggage. Then he invested[2321] all his money in a friend's battery[2322] factory. It brought him more great wealth while he was just in his twenties. Then the war came. The hardship[2323] brought about by the war led to the loss of his entire fortune. The next year, the authorities[2324] confiscated[2325] his friend's battery factory and he was forced to join the army. After the war, he met a beautiful ballet dancer. There was a special attraction between them, so they got married soon. He started another business by making ATMs and became rich again.

中譯 *Translation*

　　我想簡短地想你們述說一位成功商人的生平。他是當時的傳奇人物，因為他曾經破產，最後在他年老頭髮灰白之際，又把他的財產都贏了回去。他總說：「機會等待著所有人。」他的行為和處事態度使他擁有克服任何障礙的力量。他生來就有和別人討價還價的天份。他十幾歲的時候，靠著賣背包和行李箱賺得了第一桶金。之後他把所有的錢投資在一位朋友的電池工廠。這讓他在年僅二十幾歲時得到了更多財富。後來，戰爭爆發了。戰爭造成的艱辛環境讓他幾乎失去了所有的財富。次年，政府將他朋友的電池工廠充公，並強迫他加入軍隊。戰爭過後，他遇到一位美麗的芭蕾舞者，彼此強烈的吸引力使他們很快就結婚了。他靠著製造自動櫃員機東山再起，並且再度成功致富。

2317 legend

[ˋlɛdʒənd] ★★★★

名 傳奇人物、傳說、圖例

片 living legend 奇才

衍 legendary 傳奇的

2318 await

[əˋwet] ★★★★

動 等候、期待、將降臨於

片 await an opportunity 等待時機

2319 barrier

[ˋbærɪr] ★★★

名 障礙、路障、剪票口

片 trade barriers 貿易壁壘

2320 backpack

[ˋbækpæk] ★

名 登山或遠足用背包

動 背包旅行、野外露營

衍 backpacker 背包客

2321 invest

[ɪnˋvɛst] ★★★★

動 投資、投入、耗費

片 invest in 投資…

衍 investment 投資

2322 battery

[ˋbætərɪ] ★★★★

名 電池、一系列、砲台

片 dead battery 廢電池

2323 hardship

[ˋhardʃɪp] ★★★

名 困苦、艱難

同 difficulty 艱難

片 bar hardship 吃苦

2324 authority

[əˋθɔrɪtɪ] ★★★★

名 當局、權威人士、權力

片 local authority 地方政府

2325 confiscate

[ˋkɑnfɪsket] ★★

動 將…充公、徵收

形 被沒收的

衍 confiscation 充公

2326 lively

[ˋlaɪvlɪ] ★★

形 愉快的、活潑的、栩栩如生的

副 活潑地、生氣勃勃地

2327 refer

[rɪˋfɝ] ★★★★★

動 查閱、論及、涉及、歸屬於

片 refer to 參考

2328 flat

[flæt] ★★★★★

形 電用完的、平坦的、單調的、洩了氣的

動 變平、降半音

Give it a shot 小試身手

1 The _____ became lively[2326] when Elsa came in.

2 Please refer[2327] to the _____ I send you.

3 The _____ man bought a toupee.

4 Do not _____ anymore. It sells at uniform price.

5 Our bus won't start because the _____ is flat[2328].

Answers: **1** atmosphere **2** attachment **3** bald **4** bargain **5** battery

MP3　短文 389　字彙 390

Essay

195

My husband is a biology[2329] professor. He has written some studies on how the crossing[2330] of peach trees with other plants affects[2331] blooming and other qualities. We first met at one of my colleagues' wedding party about ten years ago. He was the bridegroom's best friend. We sat next to each other and started to chat naturally. It was a coincidence that he gave a china cabinet[2332] as a wedding gift and I gave a fine piece of china[2333]. Then he asked me to dance with a blushed[2334] face while a man at our table was boasting[2335] of his brutal[2336] military battles[2337]. Our first dance created a very special bond[2338] between us, and we danced all night. I secretly calculated how many songs we had danced like a human calculator. He praised my gracefulness. One year later, after some planning, we decided to get married with all our family and friends' blessing[2339]. They even put our wedding notice in the local news bulletin[2340]!

中譯 *Translation*

　　我先生是位生物學教授。他寫過一些關於桃樹和其它植物的雜交，如何影響開花狀態與其他特性的論文。我們第一次見面是在十年前某個同事的婚宴上。他是新郎最好的朋友。我們坐在彼此旁邊，開始自然地聊著天。很巧的是，他送了一座擺放瓷器的櫃子作為結婚禮物，而我則是送了一件精美的瓷器。接著，正當我們這桌有個男人吹噓著他以前在軍中殘忍的作戰行動時，他紅著臉邀請我跳舞。我們的第一支舞，讓彼此之間產生了一種特別的默契，我們跳了一整晚。我像計算機般偷偷計算著我們跳了幾首歌。他稱讚我的跳姿很優美。一年之後，經過一番深思熟慮，我們在所有親友的祝福下決定結婚了。他們甚至還把我們的婚禮公告登在本地新聞快報上呢！

2329 biology

[baɪˋɑlədʒɪ] ★★★★
- 名 生物學、生活規律、生物群落
- 衍 biologist 生物學家

2330 crossing

[ˋkrɔsɪŋ] ★★
- 名 雜交、十字路口、橫渡、交叉點
- 衍 cross 使交叉

2331 affect

[əˋfɛkt] ★★★★★
- 動 發生作用、影響、感動、假裝、罹患
- 同 influence 影響

2332 cabinet

[ˋkæbənɪt] ★★★
- 名 櫥櫃、內閣、密室
- 形 內閣的、私下的
- 片 a drinks cabinet 酒櫃

2333 china

[ˋtʃaɪnə] ★★★★★
- 名 瓷器、瓷製品
- 片 bull in a china shop 魯莽闖禍的人

2334 blush

[blʌʃ] ★★★
- 動 臉紅、發窘
- 名 臉紅、羞愧、一瞥
- 片 blush for 因…臉紅

2335 boast

[bost] ★★★★
- 動 自吹自擂、誇耀、以有…而自豪
- 名 大話、引以為榮的事物

2336 brutal

[ˋbrutl] ★★★
- 形 嚴酷的、殘忍的、苛刻的、野蠻的
- 同 barbarian 野蠻的

2337 battle

[ˋbætl] ★★★★
- 名 戰役、戰鬥、爭鬥
- 動 作戰、搏鬥

2338 bond

[bɑnd] ★★★
- 名 連結、聯繫、束縛
- 動 使結合、黏合
- 同 link 聯繫

2339 blessing

[ˋblɛsɪŋ] ★★
- 名 祝福、同意、禱告
- 同 benediction 祝福
- 衍 bless 為…祝福

2340 bulletin

[ˋbulətɪn] ★★★
- 名 公告、新聞快報、會刊
- 動 公告、公布

Give it a shot 小試身手

1 The _____ of the two kinds of wine is popular here.

2 The broadleaf cactus only _____ at night.

3 A _____ on his cheek implied his embarrassment.

4 John _____ that he was the most handsome man in his office.

5 The _____ murder aroused public anger.

Answers: **1** blend **2** blooms **3** blush **4** boasted **5** brutal

MP3　短文 391　字彙 392

196

The campaign season is coming again by the end of this year. All candidates[2341] have already started their propaganda[2342] recently. We can see mobile loudspeakers everywhere playing songs and messages that seem to never cease[2343]. They all want to get a seat in the upper chamber[2344], the Senate[2345]. During the campaign season, each candidate tries very hard to distinguish himself or herself from the others.

One man's image is that of Superman with a red cape[2346]. His chief platform is welfare capitalism[2347]. Another man's championing of women's equality[2348] is well known. He joined several organizations that benefit women. Yet another man's image is that of a laborer with a heavy burden on his back. He began his career as a blue-collar worker, and now he devotes himself to protecting laborers'[2349] rights. He has a great capacity for carving[2350]. It is quite obvious that they have at least one thing in common: they all want to celebrate winning the election.

中譯 *Translation*

今年年底，競選的季節又將來到。近來所有的候選人都已經開始宣傳造勢了。我們可以看到隨處都有播放著歌曲和訊息的宣傳車，好像永遠不會結束似的。他們都希望獲得上議院，也就是參議院的席位。在競選季節期間，每位候選者都努力試著建立一種與眾不同的特質。

其中一名男性候選人以披著紅披肩的超人形象出現。他的主要政見是福利資本主義。另一名男候選人以提倡女權而知名，他加入幾個為女性謀取福利的組織。還有另一個人是以背負重擔的勞工形象出現。他是以身為藍領起家的，現在他則致力於維護勞工權利。他擁有很棒的雕刻才華。很明顯，他們至少有一項共通點：他們都希望可以為勝選慶祝。

2341 candidate

[`kændədet] ★★★★

名 候選人、應試者
片 candidate for …的候選人

2342 propaganda

[prapə`gændə] ★★★

名 宣傳、宣傳活動
衍 propagandize 對…宣傳

2343 cease

[sis] ★★★★

動 停止、終止、結束
名 停息
片 without cease 不停地

2344 chamber

[`tʃæmbə]★★★★

名 議院、寢室、會議廳
形 室內的、私人的
動 關在房間裡、裝彈藥

2345 senate

[`sɛnɪt] ★★★

名 立法機構、(S)美國參議院、大學理事會
同 legislature 立法機關

2346 cape

[kep] ★★★

名 斗篷、披肩、海角、岬

2347 capitalism

[`kæpətḷɪzəm] ★

名 資本主義
反 communism 共產主義
衍 capital 資本、首都

2348 equality

[i`kwalətɪ] ★★★

名 平等、相等、均等
片 be on an equality with 與…平等

2349 laborer

[`lebərə] ★★

名 勞工、勞動者
同 worker 工人
反 capitalist 資本家

2350 carving

[`karvɪŋ] ★★

名 雕刻、雕刻物
衍 carve 雕刻

2351 oppose

[ə`poz] ★★★★

動 反對、對抗
反 agree 同意
片 oppose to 反對…

2352 exploitation

[ɛksplɔɪ`teʃən] ★★

名 剝削、開發、充分利用
衍 exploit 剝削、利用

Give it a shot 小試身手

1 The _____ was accused of bribery.

2 Socialism opposed[2351] the _____ for its exploitation[2352] of the poverty.

3 After the negotiation, the two countries finally _____ fire.

4 Do you remember some _____ of the suspect?

5 He donated a lot of money to the school out of _____.

Answers: 1 candidate 2 capitalism 3 cease 4 characteristics 5 charity

197

 MP3　 短文 393　 字彙 394

Essay

The film industry has become an enormous business. Movies are easily circulated[2353] to other countries around the world. Some movies are seen by millions and millions of people worldwide[2354]. We all enjoy movies with an exciting climax. Thanks to innovative[2355] technology, the excitement and thrills[2356] provided by movies are amazing and wonderful. There are thrilling action movies with cars crashing together or featuring explosions causing buildings to collapse[2357]. We can also learn a lot from movies. For example, we can discover how humans suffered before modern medicine was developed. It's possible that movies may lead to a better, more peaceful world because we have seen too many scenes in movies of people dying in terrible circumstances[2358] during wars. Watching movies gives us time to think about issues like using genetic[2359] engineering to reproduce[2360] life. Of course, there are also many clumsy[2361] and coarse[2362] movies that are made purely for shock value or to make as much money as possible.

中譯 *Translation*

　　電影業現在已經成為一個龐大的產業。全世界的電影都很容易流通到其他國家。有些電影在全世界有一億多的人口觀看。我們都很享受電影中令人激動的高潮橋段。由於科技的創新，電影所製造出來的興奮與激動感，是很驚人且神奇的。緊張刺激的動作片中有的是車子相撞或是以建築物因爆炸而倒塌為主的場景。我們可以從電影中學到很多東西。比如說，我們可以發現在現代藥物發展之前，人類是如何受病痛折磨。因為我們已經看過太多電影場景，是關於人們死於戰爭時的慘況，所以電影是有可能帶領我們進入一個更好更和平的世界。看電影讓我們有時間思考各種議題，像是用基因工程複製生命的可能後果。當然，也有很多製作簡陋且粗糙的電影，純粹是為了譁眾取寵或是盡可能多撈錢。

2353 circulate

[`sɝkjəlet] ★★★

動 流傳、循環、流通
同 broadcast 傳布
衍 circulation 流通

2354 worldwide

[`wɝld`waɪd] ★★★

副 在世界各地
形 遍及全球的
同 global 全世界的

2355 innovative

[`ɪnovetɪv] ★★

形 創新的
同 revolutionary 創新的
衍 innovation 創新

2356 thrill

[θrɪl] ★★★★

名 興奮、顫抖、恐怖
動 感到興奮、毛骨悚然、顫抖

2357 collapse

[kə`læps] ★★★★

動 倒塌、瓦解、垮掉
名 崩潰、突然失敗、衰竭
同 crash 垮台

2358 circumstance

[`sɝkəmstæns] ★★★

名 情況、情勢、環境
同 situation 情況、處境

2359 genetic

[dʒə`nɛtɪk] ★★★

形 基因的、遺傳的、起源的、發生的
衍 gene 基因、遺傳因子

2360 reproduce

[riprə`djus] ★★★

動 複製、繁殖、再現
同 duplicate 複製

2361 clumsy

[`klʌmsɪ] ★★★

形 製作粗陋的、笨拙的、不得體的
同 awkward 笨拙的

2362 coarse

[kors] ★★★

形 粗糙的、粗俗的
同 rough 粗糙的
反 delicate 精緻的

2363 sensational

[sɛn`seʃənəl] ★★

形 轟動社會的、知覺的
同 startling 令人吃驚的
衍 sensation 轟動的事件

2364 spectacle

[`spɛktəkḷ] ★★★

名 景象、奇觀、場面
片 make a spectacle of oneself 出洋相

Fighting! **Give it a shot 小試身手**

① I _____ the moments when you were around me.

② My brother was a conductor of the _____.

③ We went to the _____ to see the sensational[2363] movie.

④ Sam _____ that he didn't steal the money, but nobody trusted him.

⑤ Ching Shui _____ is a famous spectacle[2364] in the eastern Taiwan.

Answers: ① cherished ② chorus ③ cinema ④ clarified ⑤ Cliff

MP3　短文 395　字彙 396

198

Essay

I love the annual festival held on New Year's Eve[2365] in our community[2366]. We started to celebrate every New Year five years ago when we noticed that some residents of our city are professional musicians. We have a composer[2367], a pianist and a conductor[2368] of an orchestra[2369]. To enlarge[2370] the festival this year, the management committee committed most of its budget to it. We plan to perform a musical comedy and hold a charity auction[2371]. The composer is responsible for composing songs for the musical comedy. His compositions[2372] are always touching and can cheer people up. What complicates[2373] matters is that the leader of our committee has invited the community next to us to join the comedy competition. So there are other competitors[2374] in the festival. The combination[2375] of these programs makes it so fascinating, and one of my friends even commented that the festival is world-class. Through the festival, communication between neighboring communities has become easier. It gives us a chance to get to know our neighbors much better.

中譯 *Translation*

　　我喜歡我們社區每年在除夕舉辦的年度慶典。五年前，當我們發現城裡有許多居民都是專業的音樂家時，我們就開始慶祝每個新年。我們有一個作曲家、一個鋼琴家和一個管弦樂隊指揮。為了擴大今年的慶典，管理委員會撥出大部份的預算在活動上。我們計劃要表演一齣音樂喜劇，並舉辦一場慈善競標。作曲家負責為喜劇作曲。他的作品總是很感人，又可以激勵大眾。讓事情變複雜的是，我們社區的負責人，邀請我們的隔壁社區加入喜劇比賽，於是慶典中就有其他競爭者了。這些節目的結合使慶典變得非常吸引人，甚至我有個朋友還評論說這已經達到國際水準了。透過這次慶典，鄰里間的溝通變得更容易了，而且提供我們更多和鄰居相處的機會。

2365 eve

[iv] ★★★★
名 前夕、前一刻
片 Christmas Eve 平安夜

2366 community

[kə`mjunətɪ] ★★★★
名 社區、公眾、群落
片 community spirit 社區精神

2367 composer

[kəm`pozə] ★★
名 作曲家、調停者
衍 compose 作曲

2368 conductor

[kən`dʌktə] ★★
名 指揮、領導者、導體、列車長
同 director 指揮

2369 orchestra

[`ɔrkɪstrə] ★★★
名 管弦樂隊
片 symphony orchestra 交響樂隊

2370 enlarge

[ɪn`lardʒ] ★★★
動 擴大、擴展、詳述
片 enlarge on 詳述、增補
衍 enlargement 擴大

2371 auction

[`ɔkʃən] ★★★
名 拍賣
動 把…拍賣掉
片 auction off 拍賣掉

2372 composition

[kampə`zɪʃən] ★★★
名 作曲、作文、構圖
片 make a composition with 和…妥協

2373 complicate

[`kampləket] ★★
動 使複雜化、併發、惡化
反 simplify 簡化
衍 complicated 複雜的

2374 competitor

[kəm`pɛtətə] ★★
名 競爭者、敵手
同 opponent 對手
衍 competitive 競爭的

2375 combination

[kambə`neʃən] ★★★
名 結合、聯盟、組合
片 in combination with 與…混合

2376 surpass

[sə`pæs] ★★★
動 勝過、優於
片 surpass in 在…方面超越

Fighting!

Give it a shot 小試身手

❶ Please _____ others' essays and correct the misspelling.

❷ He _____ that he would propose to me someday.

❸ We have a weekly assembly in our _____.

❹ Respect and learn from your _____, and then surpass your _____.

❺ The desk is _____ of marble.

Answers: ❶ comment ❷ committed ❸ community ❹ competitor ❺ composed

MP3　 短文 397　 字彙 398

Essay 199

There is an expectation that many things will change after the Party congress[2377]. The Party head confessed that they have confined[2378] themselves to only accepting conservative[2379] ideas for a long time. Thus, they have finally accepted they are to blame[2380] for losing the people's support. People tend to have less confidence in the Party unless it can make obvious changes over time. Many concrete[2381] proposals will be raised at the conference. The most important task for the Party now is to concentrate[2382] on the welfare of the people. To regain[2383] people's trust, conquering[2384] the state of confusion among the three factions[2385] inside the Party is a top priority[2386]. Concerted effort is essential if the Party wants to do a good job. The Party should congratulate[2387] itself on still having time to once again earn the people's trust. On the other hand, the Party might lose everything and a consequential split[2388] would definitely occur. If such a situation happened, the Party would have no chance to reunite again.

中譯 *Translation*

在黨代表大會過後，眾人期盼著會有一番改革。黨領導人坦承，他們長期把自己偏限在保守的觀念之中。因此，他們終於接受承擔失去選民支持的責任。人民傾向於降低對該黨的信任，除非該黨可以隨著時間轉變做出明顯的改變。會議中提出了許多具體的方案。該黨目前最重要的任務是，集中火力在人民的福利上。要重新贏得民眾的信任，第一要務便是要克服黨內三大派系所造成的混亂。如果該黨希望做出一番好成績，共同一致的努力是必要的。該黨應該慶幸自己還有時間再次取得人民的信賴。反之，該黨也有可能失掉一切，隨之而來的分裂也必然會發生。如果真是如此的話，該黨就再也沒有機會重組了。

2377 congress

[`kaŋgrəs] ★★★★

名 會議、(C)美國國會、立法機關、人群

片 congress on …的大會

2378 confine

[kən`faɪn] ★★★★

動 侷限、幽禁、坐月子

名 邊界、區域、範圍

片 confine to 把…限制在

2379 conservative

[kən`sɜvətɪv] ★★★

形 保守的、老式的、有意壓低的、防腐的

名 保守者、防腐劑

2380 blame

[blem] ★★★★

動 責備、歸咎於

名 責備、指責、責任

片 blame for 因…責備

2381 concrete

[`kankrit] ★★★★

形 具體的、有形的

名 具體物、混凝土

動 凝固、結合

2382 concentrate

[`kansɛntret] ★★★★

動 集中、全神貫注、濃縮

名 濃縮物

片 concentrate on 專心於

2383 regain

[rɪ`gen] ★★

動 收復、取回、恢復

片 regain one's nerve 振作起來

2384 conquer

[`kaŋkə] ★★★

動 克服、戰勝、贏得讚譽

同 overcome 克服

反 surrender 投降

2385 faction

[`fækʃən] ★★★

名 派別、派系之爭、內訌

同 party 黨派

衍 factional 派別的

2386 priority

[praɪ`ɔrətɪ] ★★

名 優先考慮的事、優先權

片 give priority to 優先考慮

2387 congratulate

[kən`grætʃəlet] ★★

動 祝賀、恭喜

片 congratulate sb. on 向某人表示祝賀

2388 split

[splɪt] ★★★

名 分裂、裂縫、派系

動 劈開、分擔、斷絕關係

形 分裂的、劈開的

Give it a shot 小試身手

❶ _____ on your study. Don't be absent-minded.

❷ The _____ in Sociology is hard to understand.

❸ Please give me a _____ example instead of a general one.

❹ What's the _____ of your discussion?

❺ My mother is too _____ to accept new ideas.

Answers: ❶ Concentrate ❷ concept ❸ concrete ❹ consequence ❺ conservative

200

 MP3 短文 399 字彙 400

Essay

It is impossible to satisfy all consumers. They are like variously shaped containers that no one can fully fill. Advice from business consultants point²³⁸⁹ out that anyone who wants to own a store should decide the style first and then the types of products to sell. Also, try to build up the store's reputation. Second, avoid being too stubborn to accept new ideas. Creating a business takes a lot of time and effort and it may take several more months or even years to establish²³⁹⁰ a firm customer base. Success consists of keeping on top of the latest trends²³⁹¹. That's why many well-known stores often renovate²³⁹², redecorate²³⁹³ or change stock over a certain period of time. It is a never-ending struggle to retain²³⁹⁴ loyal²³⁹⁵ customers. Excellent stores usually have over sixty percent of their customers walking out with a smile of contentment. If less than sixty percent of their customers are content with the store, it means there is a lot of room for improvement. Listening to constructive²³⁹⁶ suggestions from successful store owners, one can only conclude²³⁹⁷ that it is much better to consult²³⁹⁸ experienced people than learn only through trial and error.

中譯 *Translation*

　　要滿足所有的顧客是不可能的。他們就像許多不同形狀的容器，無法完全滿足所有人的需求。企業顧問的建議指出，任何想要擁有一家店的人，都應該先決定風格，然後才是販售的商品類型。此外，還要試著建立這家店的聲譽。其次，避免過於守舊、一成不變。開一家店需要花費大量的時間和精力，而建立穩固的客源基礎則可能需要好幾個月甚至是好幾年。成功與否在於是否與最新的趨勢接軌。那就是為什麼許多知名商家經常裝修，每過一段時間就會定期裝潢或改變進貨。這是一場為了留住主顧而永無止盡的奮鬥。優良的商家通常都有超過六成的顧客掛著滿足的微笑離開。如果顧客滿意度少於六成，就表示還有很大的進步空間。聽取來自成功經營者具建設性的意見，唯一的結論是請教有經驗的人比花費大半時間反覆試驗來得好多了。

point

[pɔɪnt] ★★★★★
- 動 指明、對準、強調
- 名 要點、分數、意義
- 片 point out 指出、提出

redecorate

[ri`dɛkəret] ★★
- 動 重新裝飾

conclude

[kən`klud] ★★★★
- 動 斷定、結束、作出決定
- 片 conclude with 以…作為結束

establish

[ə`stæblɪʃ] ★★★★
- 動 建立、創辦、制定
- 反 destroy 破壞
- 片 establish in 立足於

retain

[rɪ`ten] ★★★★
- 動 保留、攔住、記住
- 同 maintain 保持
- 反 abandon 遺棄

consult

[kən`sʌlt] ★★★★
- 動 請教、查閱、當顧問
- 片 consult with 與…商議
- 衍 consultation 諮詢

trend

[trɛnd] ★★★★
- 名 趨勢、走向、時尚
- 動 轉向、趨向、傾向
- 同 tendency 趨勢

loyal

[`lɔɪəl] ★★★
- 形 忠誠的、忠心的
- 片 be loyal to 忠於
- 衍 oyalty 衷心

transit

[`trænsɪt] ★★★
- 名 運輸、過境、轉變
- 動 通過、運送至
- 片 in transit 運輸過程中

renovate

[`rɛnəvet] ★★
- 動 裝修、翻新、恢復
- 同 refurbish 刷新
- 衍 renovation 整修

constructive

[kən`strʌktɪv] ★★
- 形 有助益的、建設性的、積極的
- 同 helpful 有益的

bucket

[`bʌkɪt] ★★★
- 名 水桶、一桶、大量
- 動 下傾盆大雨
- 片 kick the bucket 死亡

Fighting!

Give it a shot 小試身手

❶ The Mass Rapid Transit[2399] is still under _____ here.

❷ His viewpoint is _____ with mine.

❸ Your words _____ obvious threat to me.

❹ Use a plastic bucket[2400] as a _____ for the water.

❺ I was totally attracted by the _____ of the book.

Answers: ❶ construction ❷ consistent ❸ constitute ❹ container ❺ content

201

Essay

We conversed[2401] for hours on the phone. He tried hard to convey his point of view and convince[2402] me of his innocence[2403]. He said that he really gave all the money from the charitable organization to a relief fund. Furthermore, he said his cooperation with an advertising[2404] agency was handled in an honest[2405], conventional[2406] manner and that he only acted as a spokesman[2407]. I stressed that charitable contributions donated by the public must be spent all in support of the poor. I know that he thought I was not easy to get along with. On the contrary[2408], though, I am a kind person. Maybe I am not always a diplomatic[2409] person, but I always fight against every injustice[2410]. I carefully compared[2411] his words with his actions, and I concluded that he indeed had been responsible for contributing a lot of money to several charities during the past ten years. However, the amount of money had dramatically declined since he started cooperating with an advertising agency this year. I doubted there was anything dirty going on with him and the agency, but I was suspicious about how much money the ad agency was charging for its services.

中譯 *Translation*

　　我們在電話中談了好幾個小時。他努力試著表達他的觀點,並說服我相信他的清白。他說他真的把慈善團體的錢都捐作賑災基金了。再者,他說他和廣告代理商之間的合作是以誠信、傳統的方式來處理,他只負責當代言人而已。我強調民眾的慈善捐款一定要用在救濟窮人上。我知道他認為我很難相處。但相反的,我是個善良的人。也許我在處事上經常不夠圓滑,但我總是挺身對抗一切非正義的行為。我仔細地觀察他言行是否一致,結果我發現過去十年來,他的確很盡責的將大筆款項捐給數個慈善團體。然而,自從今年他和廣告代理商合作之後,金額就開始戲劇性地大幅下滑。我懷疑他們之間正在進行不可告人的勾當,但我更懷疑廣告商付了多少服務費給他。

2401 converse
[kən`vɝs] ★★★
動 交談、談話
名 相反的事物
形 相反的、顛倒的

2402 convince
[kən`vɪns] ★★★★
動 說服、使信服
片 convince of 使確信
同 persuade 說服

2403 innocence
[`ɪnəsn̩s] ★★
名 清白、純真、無知
反 guilt 有罪
衍 innocent 清白的

2404 advertising
[`ædvɚtaɪzɪŋ] ★
名 廣告、做廣告、廣告業
衍 advertisement 廣告、宣傳

2405 honest
[`ɑnɪst] ★★★★
形 誠實的、坦率的
同 truthful 誠實的
片 to be honest 老實說

2406 conventional
[kən`vɛnʃən̩l] ★★★
形 傳統的、慣例的、過分拘泥的
同 customary 習慣的

2407 spokesman
[`spoksmən] ★★
名 發言人、代言人
同 spokesperson 發言人

2408 contrary
[`kɑntrɛrɪ] ★★★
名 相反、對立面
形 相反的、不利的
副 相反地、反對地

2409 diplomatic
[dɪplə`mætɪk] ★★★
形 圓滑的、有外交手腕的、外交的
同 tactful 圓滑的

2410 injustice
[ɪn`dʒʌstɪs] ★★
名 非正義、不公平
片 do sb. an injustice 冤枉某人

2411 compare
[kəm`pɛr] ★★★★
動 比較、對照
片 compare with 與…相比

2412 pleasure
[`plɛʒɚ] ★★★★
名 愉快、滿足、樂事
動 高興、滿意、尋歡作樂
片 for pleasure 為了消遣

Fighting!

Give it a shot 小試身手

❶ The _____ rain spoiled our pleasure[2412].

❷ Yellow is the _____ of blue.

❸ Everyone should _____ what he or she can afford to the society.

❹ The Global Warming _____ will be held next month.

❺ The suspect tried to _____ me of her innocence.

Answers: ❶ continuous ❷ contrast ❸ contribute ❹ Convention ❺ convince

202

Essay

Last Sunday, we went to an exhibition of modern art that had been praised by the New York critics[2413]. The artist just had returned from abroad, and he has specialized in his craft[2414] for over twenty years. His art reached a peak[2415] of creativity five years ago, and he stands out from other artists because of his incredible versatility[2416]. He has published more than 10 books, including photo collections and ones on modern art criticism. He was even the costume director for a play last year. Lots of his creations have been displayed[2417] around various galleries[2418]. We saw his representation of a cottage bound[2419] by many strong cords[2420]. The work symbolizes[2421] that the middle class is burdened by expensive housing prices and face them with firm silence. The artist thinks it's hard to criticize one's own work, so he is open-minded and welcomes the public's critical analysis. I admire his courageous attitude in coping[2422] with vicious[2423] attacks against some of his pieces. Next month, an art gallery will hold a meeting to discuss the artist's application to become one of the resident artists. I am sure that the art gallery will approve it, for he is undoubtedly one of the great artists of his generation.

中譯 *Translation*

　　上週日我們去了一場備受紐約評論家讚譽的現代藝術展覽。這位藝術家剛從海外歸國，專攻手工藝超過二十年。五年前，他的藝術創造力達到了巔峰，而也因為他驚人的多項才藝，使他能在眾多藝術家中鶴立雞群。他出版超過十本書，包括相片集和現代藝術評論集。他去年甚至為一齣當代戲劇的服裝總監。他的許多創作在很多美術館裡都有展出。我們看到他的一幅畫作是一間被多條細繩牢牢網住的小屋，象徵著中產階級用堅決的沉默反抗高房價的重擔。這名藝術家認為要批評自己的作品很困難，所以他敞開心胸，歡迎社會大眾的批判分析。針對他某些作品所受到的惡意攻擊，我很崇拜他在應對這些事情時的勇敢態度。下個月，美術館將會舉行一場會議，討論該藝術家是否符合駐館藝術家的申請資格。我相信美術館會贊同，因為他無疑是當代最優秀藝術家之一。

2413 critic

[`krɪtɪk] ★★★
名 批評家、評論家
同 reviewer 評論家
衍 criticize 評論

2414 craft

[kræft] ★★★
名 手工藝、手腕、奸計、職業、同業
動 手工製作

2415 peak

[pik] ★★★★
名 高峰、頂端、最高點
形 最高的、高峰的
動 達到高峰、聳起

2416 versatility

[vɜsə`tɪlətɪ] ★★
名 多才多藝、多功能、易變、反覆無常
衍 versatile 多才多藝的

2417 display

[dɪ`sple] ★★★★
動 陳列、展出、顯露
名 展覽、陳列、表現
片 on display 展出

2418 gallery

[`gælərɪ] ★★★
名 畫廊、美術館
片 play to the gallery 譁眾取寵

2419 bind

[baɪnd] ★★★★★
動 綑綁、裝訂、束縛
名 綑綁、困境
片 bind with 用…綑綁

2420 cord

[kɔrd] ★★★★
名 細繩、絕緣電線、羈絆
動 用繩子綑綁
片 cut the cord 變得獨立

2421 symbolize

[`sɪmblˌaɪz] ★★★
動 象徵、標誌
同 represent 象徵
衍 symbolization 象徵

2422 cope

[kop] ★★★★
動 妥善處理、對付
名 斗篷式長袍、籠罩
片 cope with 設法解決

2423 vicious

[`vɪʃəs] ★★★
形 惡意的、墮落的、嚴厲的、有錯誤的
片 vicious circle 惡性循環

2424 stumble

[`stʌmbl̩] ★★★
動 絆倒、跟蹌、躊躇、步入歧途
名 絆倒、失足、錯誤

Give it a shot 小試身手

1 I am clumsy at _____ with love affairs.

2 She was stumbled[2424] by the long _____ on the ground.

3 She lived in a _____ located in the suburbs.

4 He _____ his father for their different values.

5 Do not limit children's _____ by blaming what they want to do.

MP3　 短文 405　 字彙 406

203

Essay

The deadline for making an application for the lantern[2425] exhibition is next Friday. Many decorations have already been put up around Abbot's Park. Many pretty flowers have been planted next to several pathways[2426]. It was announced that the delicate[2427] design of the main lantern was made by clever, talented workmen. However, the main lantern is now surrounded by a protective covering[2428]. People are looking forward to satisfying their curiosity, but the covering is tightly closed so that the exact design will remain[2429] unknown until the last minute[2430]. City Hall even hired guards last week to guard the main lantern. The guards will also be able to control the flow of people who flock to Abbot's Park to see the lanterns. There was a crush of people in the park on the grand opening evening last year. Many people complained that they could not get into the park at all because it was so crowded. This year, the mayor has guaranteed that no one will be disappointed. Besides the guards, several other measures will be taken to decrease[2431] the amount of people rushing into the park at the same time and to prevent another state of chaos[2432]. Every resident is expected to be able to enjoy the delights of the lantern exhibition.

中譯 *Translation*

　　下週五就是申請燈籠展的截止日。Abbot 公園四周已經增加了許多裝飾。許多小徑幾乎都種滿了美麗的花朵。他們說主燈的精緻設計是由靈巧熟練的工匠們所製作而成的。然而，主燈現在用防護簾圍起來。民眾都很期待自己的好奇心能得到滿足，但是他們防護森嚴，所以確切的設計會一直保密到最後一刻。市政廳甚至從上禮拜就聘請警衛來保護主燈。警衛們也將控管湧進 Abbot 公園看燈籠展的人潮。去年晚上在公園舉辦的盛大開幕儀式就因為人潮而擠得水洩不通。許多人抱怨他們無法進入公園，因為實在是太過擁擠了。今年，市長保證沒有任何市民會敗興而歸。除了警衛之外，他們還會採取各種措施來減低同時衝進公園的人潮，以避免另一場混亂產生。他們期望每個市民都能享受參觀燈籠展的喜悅。

新多益藍色證書必備單字

2425 lantern

[ˋlæntɚn] ★★★
名 燈籠
片 Lantern Festival 元宵節

2426 pathway

[ˋpæθwe] ★★
名 小徑、人行道、路線
同 path 小徑、小路

2427 delicate

[ˋdɛləkət] ★★★
形 精美的、易碎的、嬌弱的、敏銳的
衍 delicacy 精美、柔弱

2428 covering

[ˋkʌvərɪŋ] ★★
名 覆蓋物、毯子
形 掩蓋的
同 protection 防護物

2429 remain

[rɪˋmen] ★★★★★
動 保持、餘留、留待、歸屬
片 remain on 繼續

2430 minute

[ˋmɪnɪt] ★★★★★
名 分鐘、片刻、會議記錄
動 記錄下來
形 微小的、精密的

2431 decrease

[ˋdikris] ★★★★
動 減少、減小
名 減少、減少額

2432 chaos

[ˋkeas] ★★★★
名 混亂、無秩序、雜亂
片 in chaos 一片混亂
衍 chaotic 混亂的

2433 casualty

[ˋkæʒjʊəltɪ] ★★★
名 傷亡人員、意外事故、(英)急診室

2434 deceive

[dɪˋsiv] ★★★
動 欺騙、蒙蔽
片 deceive sb. into 騙某人相信

2435 sharp

[ʃɑrp] ★★★★
形 急轉的、鋒利的、機警的、苛刻的、強烈的
副 整(指時刻)、急遽地

2436 inflation

[ɪnˋfleʃən] ★★★
名 通貨膨脹、充氣、自滿
反 deflation 通貨緊縮
衍 inflated 誇張的

Fighting!

Give it a shot 小試身手

1. Luckily, we found no casualties[2433] in the car _____.
2. George was _____ as a fox that he deceived[2434] all his friends.
3. Watch the sharp[2435] _____ of the road when you drive.
4. John failed to meet the _____ of the application.
5. The rate of inflation[2436] _____ to 10% last year.

Answers: 1 crash 2 cunning 3 curve 4 deadline 5 decreased

MP3　短文 407　字彙 408

Essay

204

"Success is dependent on your effort and ability." I was reminded of that motto[2437] when I saw a play last night. The main character in the play really symbolized that saying. It is a story about a desperate[2438] detective who eventually demonstrates[2439] that he is a man of determination[2440]. At the beginning of this play, the death of the main character's lover depresses him. He thinks that fate[2441] continually works against him to deprive[2442] him of everything he deserves. He doesn't think it is fair that an upright[2443] man like himself must suffer so much. Unable to fight his way through the dense[2444] fog of such unlucky outcomes[2445], he decides to depart[2446] for another city. In the city that he moves to, the new environment represents a complete departure[2447] from his previous existence[2448]. Then, in the final act, he takes part in a demonstration to demand the government allow more freedom of speech. In the end, he is able to lead a delightful life, since he finally found his true destiny rather than merely indulging in grief.

中譯 *Translation*

「成功仰賴於你的努力與能力。」我昨晚看戲時想起了這句格言。這齣戲的主角可說確實詮釋了這句俗諺。這是關於一名絕望偵探的故事，最終證明了他是一個有決心的男人。這齣戲的一開始，主角情人的逝去，讓他非常沮喪。他認為命運一直在和他作對，奪走所有他應得的一切。他並不認為像他這樣正直的男人應該受這麼多苦。由於他無法在這種結局不幸的迷霧之中奮鬥出自己的一片天，他決定前往另一個城市。在另一個城市，新環境代表著他完全不同於以往的生活方式。接著，在這齣戲的最後一幕，他參加了一場示威，要求政府開放更多言論自由。最後他得以過著開心的生活，因為他終於找到了自己的目的地，而非只是沉浸於悲傷之中。

2437 motto

[ˋmɑto] ★★★
名 題詞、座右銘、格言
同 saying 格言
片 school motto 校訓

2438 desperate

[ˋdɛspərɪt] ★★★★
形 絕望的、鋌而走險的、孤注一擲的
衍 desperation 絕望

2439 demonstrate

[ˋdɛmənstret] ★★★
動 證明、示範操作、示威
片 demonstrate against 示威抗議

2440 determination

[dɪtɜməˋneʃən] ★★★
名 決心、果斷、確定
同 decision 決心
反 hesitation 猶豫

2441 fate

[fet] ★★★★
名 命運、結局、毀滅
動 命定、注定
片 tempt fate 魯莽、冒險

2442 deprive

[dɪˋpraɪv] ★★★
動 剝奪、使喪失
片 deprive of 剝奪
衍 deprivation 剝奪

2443 upright

[ˋʌpraɪt] ★★★
形 正直的、挺直的、直立的、公平的
動 使豎立

2444 dense

[dɛns] ★★★★
形 濃厚的、密集的
同 thick 濃厚的
衍 density 密度

2445 outcome

[ˋautkʌm] ★★★★
名 結果、結局、後果
同 consequence 結果

2446 depart

[dɪˋpɑrt] ★★★
動 啟程、離開、違反
反 arrive 到達
片 depart for 出發前往

2447 departure

[dɪˋpɑrtʃə] ★★★
名 啟程、出發、違背
片 departure time 出發時間

2448 existence

[ɪgˋzɪstəns] ★★★★
名 生活方式、存在
片 come into existence 成立

Fighting!

Give it a shot 小試身手

1 I cannot help but tell everybody the _____ news!

2 After the teacher's _____, we understood the gravity better.

3 Ivy is reluctant to _____ from her colleagues.

4 Nancy felt greatly _____ when she knew her father's death.

5 The _____ reasoned the suspect's motive.

Answers: 1 delightful 2 demonstration 3 depart 4 desperate 5 detective

MP3   短文 409 字彙 410

205

Essay

My uncle is a diplomat[2449] with two daughters. They have been living abroad for more than ten years. My older cousin just earned a diploma[2450] in music last year. It takes years of discipline[2451] to become a good pianist. She wants to devote herself to music teaching all her life. She once said that she had already mastered most of the important skills in playing piano. However, her first concert ended in disaster. The unhappy memory of it was a great discouragement to her. During that period, she always hid her sadness with the disguise[2452] of a happy smile. She tried to maintain her dignity[2453] in front of the students, but her lack of confidence was a disadvantage[2454] in teaching. Fortunately, she found a way to disconnect[2455] herself from depression and is getting better and better these days. In contrast, my younger cousin is interested in electronic devices[2456]. Her tastes[2457] have differed[2458] from her sister's since childhood. She has a good ability to easily digest[2459] scientific concepts[2460] and the robot she created in college even won the annual science prize. Both of them have enough diligence to fulfill their dreams.

中譯 *Translation*

　　我的叔叔是一個外交官，他有兩個女兒。他們已經在國外生活超過十年了。我的表姊去年拿到音樂學位的證書。要成為一名優秀的鋼琴家需要許多年的訓練。她希望能將畢生奉獻於音樂教學之中。她曾說，她已經把大多數重要的鋼琴彈奏技巧融會貫通了。然而，她的第一場演奏會卻是在一場災難中結束。那令人不快的回憶使得她非常氣餒。在那段期間，她總是用快樂的笑容掩飾她的悲傷。她試著在她的學生面前保持尊嚴，但她缺乏自信的表現是教學上的一大缺失。所幸，她發現一個可以讓自己從低潮中抽離的方法，而他近來的表現也越來越好。相較之下，我的表妹則對電子裝置很有興趣。她的喜好從孩提時代就和姊姊不同。她對科學方面的概念領悟力很高，而且她大學時設計的機器人還曾經得過年度科學獎。他們倆姊妹都非常勤奮，而得以實現自身夢想。

2449 diplomat

[`dɪpləmæt] ★★

名 外交官、有手腕的人
同 envoy 外交使節

2450 diploma

[dɪ`plomə] ★★★

名 學位證書、執照
同 certificate 執照

2451 discipline

[`dɪsəplɪn] ★★★★

名 訓練、紀律、懲戒
動 訓練、使有紀律、懲戒
同 training 訓練

2452 disguise

[dɪs`gaɪz] ★★★★

名 偽裝、掩飾、假扮
動 喬裝、掩飾、隱瞞
片 in disguise 偽裝的

2453 dignity

[`dɪgnətɪ] ★★★

名 尊嚴、尊貴、高尚
片 beneath one's dignity 有失身分

2454 disadvantage

[dɪsəd`væntɪdʒ] ★★★

名 不利條件、損失、損害
動 處於不利地位、損害
反 advantage 有利條件

2455 disconnect

[dɪskə`nɛkt] ★

動 使分離、分開、切斷
同 detach 使分離
反 connect 連結

2456 device

[dɪ`vaɪs] ★★★★

名 裝置、儀器、手段
片 leave sb. to his own devices 不支配某人

2457 taste

[test] ★★★★★

名 興趣、愛好、味道、滋味、體驗
動 嚐起來、體驗

2458 differ

[`dɪfə] ★★★★

動 不同、相異、意見不同
反 agree 意見一致
片 differ from 與…不同

2459 digest

[daɪ`dʒɛst] ★★★

動 領悟、消化、融會貫通
名 摘要、文摘
同 absorb 吸收

2460 concept

[`kɑnsɛpt] ★★★★

名 思想、觀念、概念
同 notion 概念

Fighting!

Give it a shot 小試身手

1 The women were _____ themselves to the charity.

2 Ideas on childcare may _____ from parents' viewpoints.

3 When it comes to physics, she has a weak _____.

4 We study for knowledge instead of _____.

5 His father _____ him from seeing his ex-girlfriend.

Answers: 1 devoted 2 differ 3 digestion 4 diploma 5 discouraged

MP3　

206

Essay

Ted is a distinguished[2461] archaeologist and one of the most prominent[2462] professors in the archaeology[2463] department in this college. He can easily distinguish between genuine antiques and reproductions[2464]. He divorced his wife five years ago and now he lives in the dormitory in campus. His room is often in disorder[2465] for he spends most of his time researching. He studies the makeup and distribution[2466] of past human civilizations[2467]. He says people should take more of an interest in finding out about ancient civilizations. In classes, he always says, "How can you divine[2468] the truth by mere guesswork[2469]?" His ex-wife used to argue over such issues with him because she desired to dominate[2470] over him in everything. He could not bear the fact that she disturbed his research again and again. No wonder their marriage ended in disaster.

> in disorder 亂七八糟、七零八落

中譯 *Translation*

　　泰德是一名出色的考古學家,也是該大學考古系成就最為卓越的教授之一。他可以輕易分辨出真品和複製品間的差別。他五年前和太太離婚,現在住在校園裡的學生宿舍。他把大部分的時間花在研究上,所以他的房間經常是一團亂。他研究過去人類文明的構成和分布。他認為人們應該在了解古代文明上投注更多興趣。在課堂中,他總是說:「你怎能只靠猜想就預知事情的真相呢?」他的前妻曾經和他爭論這類議題,因為她想要掌控所有關於他的一切。他無法忍受她一再地妨礙他的研究。難怪他們的婚姻會以失敗告終。

2461 distinguished

[dɪ`stɪŋgwɪʃt] ★★
形 卓越的、著名的
同 outstanding 傑出的

2462 prominent

[`prɑmənənt] ★★★
形 重要的、突出的
反 common 普通的
衍 prominency 傑出

2463 archaeology

[arkɪ`alədʒɪ] ★★
名 考古學
衍 archaeologist 考古學家

2464 reproduction

[riprə`dʌkʃən] ★★
名 複製品、繁育、再現
同 replica 複製品
衍 reproductive 複製的

2465 disorder

[dɪs`ɔrdə] ★★★
名 混亂、無秩序、失調
動 使混亂、擾亂、使失調
片 in disorder 混亂

2466 distribution

[dɪstrə`bjuʃən] ★★★
名 分布區域、分配、散布
片 the distribution of 分配某物

2467 civilization

[sɪvlə`zeʃən] ★★
名 文明、文化、開化過程
同 culture 文化
反 barbarism 未開化狀態

2468 divine

[də`vaɪn] ★★★
動 預言、占卜、推測
形 神性的、天賜的
片 divine providence 天意

2469 guesswork

[`gɛswɜk] ★★
名 猜測、猜測結果
同 speculation 推測

2470 dominate

[`dɑmənet] ★★★
動 控制、支配、高聳於
片 dominate over sb. 控制某人

2471 complete

[kəm`plit] ★★★★★
形 完全的、完整的、結束的、附帶的
動 使齊全、完成、結束

2472 copyright

[`kɑpɪraɪt] ★★★
名 版權、著作權
形 版權的、版權保護的
動 為…取得版權

fighting!

Give it a shot 小試身手

❶ After being stolen, his house was in complete[2471] _____.

❷ The symptom of color blindness is unable to _____ one color from another.

❸ The map shows the _____ of this species across the world.

❹ The child was abandoned after his parents' _____.

❺ Tommy _____ movies from the website, ignoring the copyrights[2472].

Answers: ❶ disorder ❷ distinguish ❸ distribution ❹ divorce ❺ downloaded

MP3

207

I enjoy watching DVDs at home on the weekends and going to movies, especially[2473] in the summer. When the town becomes very dusty[2474], I turn the electric fan on and <u>make a draft</u>[2475]. I am not the kind of person who spends[2476] several hours dyeing my hair different colors. Instead, I dread[2477] doing anything alone, so I need to spend time with my friends by my side[2478]. I'm not interested in economics[2479], so business[2480] and the economy[2481] are not my main concerns. I care about enjoying my life and doing interesting things so that I won't be bored. One thing I like doing a lot with my friends is going to the movies. My favorite type of movies are comedies. After seeing a movie, we always go out to a pub or restaurant and discuss the movie we just saw. I don't think I could live without movies. I'm not joking[2482]; I say that <u>in all earnestness</u>.

> ⓘ make a draft 在本文中並不是擬草稿的意思，而是指「通風」；draft 在此則指「通風」
> ⓘ in all earnestness 嚴肅地

中譯 *Translation*

　　週末時我喜歡在家看數位光碟，也喜歡到電影院看電影，尤其是在夏天的時候。當整座城滿是灰塵瀰漫的時候，我會打開電扇通風一下。我並不是那種會花好幾個小時把頭髮染成不同顏色的人。相反的，我很害怕單獨做任何事，所以我必須花時間和朋友在一起。我對經濟學不感興趣，所以事業和經濟狀況並不是我會擔心的事。我在意的是如何享受生活，以及做有趣的事情不讓自己感到無聊。我最喜歡的一件事就是和朋友一起去看電影。我最喜歡的是喜劇電影。在看完一部電影後，我們總是會去酒吧或餐廳討論剛剛看的電影。我的人生不能沒有電影，我沒在開玩笑，我可是非常認真的。

2473 especially

[ə`spɛʃəlɪ] ★★★★
- 副 特別、尤其、專門地
- 片 especially for 特地為了
- 同 particularly 特別

2474 dusty

[`dʌstɪ] ★★★
- 形 滿是灰塵的、淺灰色的、枯燥乏味的
- 反 clean 未汙染的

2475 draft

[draft] ★★★★★
- 名 通風、氣流、草稿、匯款單、徵兵
- 動 起草、選派、徵兵

2476 spend

[spɛnd] ★★★★★
- 動 花費、用盡、耗盡
- 名 預算
- 片 spend on 把…花在

2477 dread

[drɛd] ★★★
- 動 懼怕、擔心
- 名 畏懼、恐怖
- 形 令人畏懼的、嚴重的

2478 side

[saɪd] ★★★★★
- 名 旁邊、身邊、方面、側邊、一方
- 動 支持、站在某方

2479 economics

[ikə`nɑmɪks] ★★★
- 名 經濟情況、經濟學

2480 business

[`bɪznɪs] ★★★★★
- 名 生意、職業、交易
- 片 get out of business 停業

2481 economy

[ɪ`kɑnəmɪ] ★★★★
- 名 經濟、節省、經濟艙
- 同 thrift 節約
- 形 廉價的、經濟的

2482 joke

[dʒok] ★★★★★
- 動 開玩笑、戲弄
- 名 玩笑、笑柄、輕鬆的事
- 片 be no joke 非常嚴重

2483 boat

[bot] ★★★★★
- 名 小船、船形容器
- 動 划船、乘船遊玩

2484 eyebrow

[`aɪbrau] ★★
- 名 眉毛
- 片 raise an eyebrow 表示輕蔑

Fighting!

Give it a shot 小試身手

1. He watched the boat[2483] _____ away.
2. I _____ to confess my fault in front of all classmates.
3. The noise was made by the workmen that were _____ the wall.
4. Jessie had her hair and eyebrows[2484] _____ brown.
5. He can not hear your calling because he wears _____.

Answers: 1 drifting 2 dread 3 drilling 4 dyed 5 earphones

208

MP3 短文 415 字彙 416

Essay

The American Electronics Industry Association[2485] hosted a party at the American embassy in Paris last Sunday night. The basic theme of the party was the contradiction[2486] among[2487] the economy, efficiency[2488], and the environment. All the press had received an e-mail about it in advance. Several important leaders of the business empires[2489] in both America and France were present at the party. The atmosphere there was elegant, and pleasant music played in the background. You could not find any occasion like this elsewhere. Suddenly, all the lights were turned off and the ambassador stood in embarrassment and didn't know what to do. The emcee[2490] was a flexible[2491] man and he guided everyone to look through a giant skylight[2492] in the roof up at the night sky. At that moment, the moon emerged[2493] from behind a cloud dramatically. The emcee proceeded[2494] to charm the crowd with his good humor and fascinating stories to the point that the crowd didn't really care that they were enveloped in darkness. About twenty minutes later, all the lights were turned on once again thanks to the help from an electrician who had been sent for.

中譯 *Translation*

　　上週日晚上，美國電子工業協會在美國駐巴黎大使館舉行了一場聚會。這場宴會的基本主題是經濟、效率與環境間的衝突。所有的媒體都事先收到一封關於此聚會的電子郵件。許多美國與法國重要的企業集團領導人皆有出席。那裡的氛圍非常優雅，還播放令人心情愉快的背景音樂。像這樣的場合你在其他地方是找不到的。突然之間燈全滅了，大使站在那裡看起來非常困窘且不知所措。好在這名司儀反應夠快，他引導每個人往屋頂的巨大天窗看去，看著那一片的夜空。就在那時，月亮戲劇性地從雲間露臉。司儀繼續用他的幽默和引人入勝的故事陶醉眾人，讓大家不去在意自己仍身陷黑暗之中。大約二十分鐘後，幸虧有外派的電器技師幫忙修理，所有的燈又恢復了光亮。

2485 association

[ə`sosɪ`eʃən] ★★★

名 協會、社團、聯合
片 in association with
在…幫助下

2486 contradiction

[kɑntrə`dɪkʃən] ★★

名 矛盾、反駁、牴觸
片 in contradiction to
與…相矛盾

2487 among

[ə`mʌŋ] ★★★★★

介 在…之中、在…中間
片 number among 把…算
作

2488 efficiency

[ɪ`fɪʃənsɪ] ★★★

名 效率、效能、功效
衍 efficient 效率高的

2489 empire

[`ɛmpaɪr] ★★★★

名 帝國、大企業、君權
片 huge empire 龐大企業
同 kingdom 王國

2490 emcee

[ɛm`si] ★★

名 司儀、主持人
動 擔任司儀、主持
同 compere (英)主持

2491 flexible

[`flɛksəbl̩] ★★★★

形 靈活的、可變通的、有
彈性的
反 inflexible 剛硬的

2492 skylight

[`skaɪlaɪt] ★★

名 天窗
同 fanlight 天窗、扇形窗

2493 emerge

[ɪ`mɜdʒ] ★★★★

動 出現、顯露、擺脫
片 emerge from 露出、浮
現

2494 proceed

[prə`sid] ★★★★

動 繼續進行、著手、行進
反 recede 後退
片 proceed to 前往

2495 bonus

[`bonəs] ★★★★

名 紅利、額外津貼、獎金
同 premium 額外補貼
片 bonus share 分紅股

2496 affiliate

[ə`fɪlɪet] ★★★★★

名 分會、成員、成員組織
動 附屬於、加盟
片 affiliate to 使隸屬於

Give it a shot 小試身手

Fighting!

1 He got a bonus2495 because of the high _____ on work.

2 My schedule is quite _____, so you can call me anytime.

3 We contact with our colleagues in overseas affilates2496 by _____.

4 The ambassadors lived in the _____.

5 The teacher put _____ on this theory.

Answers: 1 efficiency 2 elastic 3 e-mail 4 embassy 5 emphasis

MP3 短文 417 字彙 418

209

Essay

The shopping mall had been enclosed[2497] by fencing since last month. It was said that they were about to enlarge its size and transform it into an enormous entertainment center. There would also be many new escalators[2498] to carry[2499] customers. Several journalists said the new building would usher[2500] in a new era for the city. The idea was greeted with great enthusiasm[2501] in the beginning. People were envious of the inhabitants[2502] of the neighborhood. However, the construction[2503] encountered some complaints[2504] recently. Schools nearby could not endure[2505] the noise from the engineering equipment[2506] anymore. They asked the City to enforce[2507] the rules concerning noise control so that the teachers and students wouldn't be disturbed too much. Besides that, the construction also endangered some animals around the area. Therefore, the City requested that the mall's owner provide some type of compensation. The spokesman for the mall replied that the owner would give financial support to the schools affected by the noise. Money is always a way for businessmen to solve problems, but is that always the best and fairest method to resolve[2508] problems?

中譯 *Translation*

　　這個購物中心從上個月開始就用柵欄圍住。據說他們要擴大購物中心的規模，並改建成一個巨型的娛樂中心。那裡也將會有許多乘載顧客的新型手扶梯。許多評論家說這座新建築將為這座城市迎來一個新紀元。最初，這個想法受到非常熱情的歡迎。大家都很羨慕住在附近的居民。然而，最近這個建案面臨了一些抗議的聲浪。附近的學校再也無法忍受工程設備的噪音。他們要求市府實施關於控制噪音的規定，這樣老師和學生才不會被過度干擾。除此之外，這個工程也危及一些這個區域四周的動物。因此，市府向購物中心的負責人要求提供幾種賠償。購物中心的發言人回應，負責人將會給予這些受噪音干擾的學校金錢上的資助。金錢總是商人解決問題的方式，但這一直都會是最好又最公平的解決方式嗎？

2497 enclose

[ɪnˋkloz] ★★★★
動 圍住、隨信附上
片 enclose in 把…封入
衍 enclosure 圍住

2501 enthusiasm

[ɪnˋθjuzɪæzəm] ★★★
名 熱情、熱心、熱忱
同 eagerness 熱心
衍 enthusiastic 熱心的

2505 endure

[ɪnˋdjur] ★★★★
動 忍受、忍耐、持續
同 bear 忍受
衍 endurance 耐久力

2498 escalator

[ˋɛskəletə] ★★
名 電扶梯
同 elevator 電梯

2502 inhabitant

[ɪnˋhæbətənt] ★★
名 居民
同 resident 居民
衍 inhabitancy 居住

2506 equipment

[iˋkwɪpmənt] ★★★★
名 設備、裝備、才能
同 apparatus 設備

2499 carry

[ˋkærɪ] ★★★★★
動 運載、攜帶、傳達
同 transport 運送
片 carry on 繼續

2503 construction

[kənˋstrʌkʃən] ★★★★
名 建造、建築物、結構
同 erection 建造
衍 constructive 建設性的

2507 enforce

[ɪnˋfors] ★★★★
動 實施、強制、堅持
同 compel 強迫
衍 enforcement 實施

2500 usher

[ˋʌʃə] ★★★
動 迎接、招待、陪同
名 接待員
片 usher in 領進、引進

2504 complaint

[kəmˋplent] ★★★
名 抱怨、抗議、控訴
片 make a complaint 正式投訴

2508 resolve

[rɪˋzɑlv] ★★★★
動 解決、決心、分解
名 決心、堅決
片 resolve on 決定

Fighting!

Give it a shot 小試身手

1 On _____ the scene, I was astonished and ran away.

2 The decision to run the red light _____ him.

3 The _____ of the law will start on July 1st.

4 Annie sang and danced on the stage to _____ the guests.

5 The most essential of gender _____ is respect.

Answers: 1 encountering 2 endangered 3 enforcement 4 entertain 5 equality

210

Essay

MP3

短文 419　字彙 420

In anticipation[2509] of the job fair to be held two months after Chinese New Year's Eve, job applicants[2510] had been taking various kinds of courses and exams to increase their chances of finding good employment in the tough job market. The key to writing a good resume is not to exaggerate[2511] your abilities or to brilliantly exhibit[2512] your academic[2513] performance, but to demonstrate how your abilities are evident[2514] in the form of certificates such as TOEIC results, recommendation[2515] letters, or those related to computer literacy[2516]. Even the privileged are no exception. It is evident that job interviewers are more interested in how they can determine through reliable evidence that candidates have established bonds with their former colleagues or employers. They do not expect resumes they receive to be good essays, but they should be an accurate evaluation[2517] of a candidate's past education, experience and accomplishments. Therefore, they tend to ask sharp questions that might intimidate[2518] or confuse interviewees. However, the more questions they ask, the more likely they are to be interested in you. I estimate that an interview over half an hour might indicate a successful job hunt.

中譯 *Translation*

　　為了除夕後兩個月即將開始的就業博覽會，求職者都持續參與各項課程與考試，以增加自己在艱困的就業市場中，還能找到好工作的機會。一份優秀履歷的關鍵並不是你如何誇大你的能力，或是你把課業表現呈現得多麼亮眼，而是透過證照證明你的能力，像是多益成績、推薦信、或是與電腦技能相關的證照。即使是特權人士也不例外。很顯然的，面試官更有興趣的是，他們如何透過可靠的跡象來確定應試者和前同事或前主管建立起來的良好關係。他們並不認為他們收到的履歷要是一篇很棒的文章，但他們卻應該要針對求職者過去的教育程度、經歷和成就做一個精確的評估報告。因此，他們傾向於問一些尖銳的問題，受試者可能會覺得受到威脅或感到困惑。然而，他們的問題問得越多，就代表他們可能對你越有興趣。據我估計，一場超過半小時的面試，可能就代表著一場成功的求職。

2509 **anticipation**

[æn͵tɪsəˋpeʃən] ★★

名 預期、期望、先發制人

片 in anticipation of 期待著、預計到

2510 **applicant**

[ˋæpləkənt] ★★★

名 申請人

同 candidate 求職應試者

衍 application 申請

2511 **exaggerate**

[ɪgˋzædʒəret] ★★★

動 誇大、言過其實

同 overstate 誇張

衍 exaggerative 誇張的

2512 **exhibit**

[ɪgˋzɪbɪt] ★★★★

動 顯出、展示、表示

名 陳列品、展示會

衍 exhibition 展覽會

2513 **academic**

[ækəˋdɛmɪk] ★★★★

形 學術的、大學的

名 學者、學究、教授

衍 academy 學院、學會

2514 **evident**

[ˋɛvədənt] ★★★

形 明顯的、明白的

同 apparent 明顯的

衍 evidence 證據

2515 **recommendation**

[rɛkəmɛnˋdeʃən] ★★

名 推薦信、推薦、建議

同 reference 推薦函

衍 recommend 推薦

2516 **literacy**

[ˋlɪtərəsɪ] ★★

名 能力、知識、識字

反 illiteracy 文盲

衍 literate 能讀寫的人

2517 **evaluation**

[ɪvæljuˋeʃən] ★★

名 評價、估價、評估報告

衍 evaluate 對…評價

2518 **intimidate**

[ɪnˋtɪmədet] ★★★

動 威嚇、脅迫

片 intimidate sb. into 威嚇某人做某事

2519 **inadmissible**

[ɪnədˋmɪsəbl̩] ★

形 不可接受的、不允許的

反 admissible 可接受的、有資格進入的

2520 **opponent**

[əˋponənt] ★★★

名 對手、反對者

形 對立的、對抗的

同 enemy 敵人

Give it a shot 小試身手

1. Ken wrote an _____ to contribute to the magazine.
2. I _____ there were more than two thousand fans on the square.
3. The _____ conclusion will be declared next Monday.
4. The judge thought the _____ was inadmissible[2519].
5. The effects of this policy were greatly _____ by its opponents[2520].

Answers: 1 essay 2 estimated 3 eventual 4 evidence 5 exaggerated

Level
6

新多益金色證書
必備單字

Essay 211~Essay 251

211

Essay

It was not experimental for the Niu Chen-Zer to glorify[2521] the gangster[2522] movie in celebration of friendship. As the fame of the movie Monga has grown with catchy[2523] lines such as "Five fingers make up a fist" or "Who gives a damn about meaning? All I know is that you should be faithful to friends," many youngsters adopted[2524] these trendy[2525] phrases and attitudes to an incredible extent[2526] during the winter break. This may be good news for the expansion[2527] of the Taiwanese movie industry since the actors were exposed to the Berlin International Film Festival, expanding Taiwanese movies to a global level. This exposure[2528], fantastic for all the actors, provides a good model for how Taiwanese films should move to the international level. As the handsome male characters explore[2529] male intimacy[2530] and even give aesthetic[2531] qualities to violence, they explode traditional values, making a powerful impact on all members of the audience. However explosive this movie seems to be, the filmmakers were criticized for favoring style over substance and creating a hit not through solid basics such as good acting but through other superficial[2532] means.

中譯 *Translation*

　　鈕承澤美化黑道電影來頌揚友情並不是一個實驗性的嘗試。隨著電影《艋舺》經典台詞的名聲大噪，像是「五根手指頭合起來，才是一個拳頭」或「意義是三小？我只知道義氣！」，許多年輕人學習這些流行用語和處世態度，在寒假期間達到了驚人的程度。這對台灣電影工業的擴展來說可能是一個好消息，因為這些演員都出現在柏林國際影展，把本土台灣電影的格局提升到世界級的水準。這次對所有演員來說的絕佳曝光機會，也給予台灣電影該如何躍上國際舞台一個很好的楷模。隨著這些帥氣的男演員探索著男性親密情誼，甚至還賦予暴力美學的特質，他們引爆了傳統價值觀的變革，並對所有觀眾造成強大的影響。無論這部電影看起來多具爆炸性，製片們還是被批評不重電影本質卻只偏好電影的形式，還被抨擊其賣座原因不是透過紮實的基本功，像是精湛的演技，而是其他膚淺的手段。

2521 glorify

[ˋglorəfaɪ] ★★
- 動 吹捧、頌揚、讚美
- 同 praise 讚美
- 衍 glorification 讚美

2522 gangster

[ˋgæŋstɚ] ★★
- 名 流氓、歹徒、匪盜
- 同 mobster 犯罪集團成員

2523 catchy

[ˋkætʃɪ] ★
- 形 引起注意的、動聽且易記的、易上當的

2524 adopt

[əˋdɑpt] ★★★★
- 動 採用、吸收、領養、接受、正式通過
- 衍 adoption 採納、採用

2525 trendy

[ˋtrɛndɪ] ★★
- 形 流行的、時髦的、受新思潮影響的
- 名 趕時髦的人

2526 extent

[ɪkˋstɛnt] ★★★★
- 名 程度、範圍、廣度
- 片 to the extent of 達到…的程度

2527 expansion

[ɪkˋspænʃən] ★★★
- 名 擴展、膨脹、擴張
- 同 extension 擴大
- 反 contraction 收縮

2528 exposure

[ɪkˋspoʒɚ] ★★★
- 名 曝光、揭露、曝曬
- 同 revelation 暴露

2529 explore

[ɪkˋsplor] ★★★★
- 動 探索、探勘、考察
- 同 search 探究
- 衍 exploration 探索

2530 intimacy

[ˋɪntəməsɪ] ★★
- 名 親密、熟悉、私下
- 衍 intimate 親密的

2531 aesthetic

[ɛsˋθɛtɪk] ★★★
- 形 美學的、有審美能力的
- 名 美學、審美觀
- 同 tasteful 有審美力的

2532 superficial

[ˋsupɚˋfɪʃəl] ★★★
- 形 外表的、表面的、膚淺的、影響不大的
- 同 shallow 膚淺的

Fighting!

Give it a shot 小試身手

1. Elsa _____ her editorial staff by hiring more people.
2. The doctor's _____ relieved me of my fear.
3. He _____ the truth that he had been in prison.
4. It was a _____ experience to be an exchange student in France.
5. The _____ dog will not leave its master in times of trouble.

Answers: 1 expanded 2 explanation 3 exposed 4 fantastic 5 faithful

212

Essay

 MP3　 短文 423　 字彙 424

Have you ever longed[2533] to travel to Disneyland, a theme park where childhood dreams seem to come true? As a dream world filled with cartoon characters such as Donald Duck and Snow White, it is a place even adults may escape to when they suffer from real financial or relationship problems. Fun for people of all ages, Disneyland is a feast for the senses and has a warm atmosphere, making everyone cheerful with a fierce[2534]-looking but kind-hearted Lion King dancing around them. You can see almost anything from Disney cartoons: see how girls flatter[2535] the prince in Cinderella and take a ferry[2536] along the river to visit places that only exist in the world of fantasy[2537].

Don't consider it too childish[2538]; it's terrible to bid[2539] farewell[2540] to your dreams. If you just worry about your finances and curse[2541] the sound of firecrackers outside, you will become a dull person. Why not make your life more colorful?

中譯 *Translation*

　　你是否曾經渴望去迪士尼主題樂園旅行，那個童年時期的夢想似乎成真的地方？因為是一個充滿著像是唐老鴨、白雪公主等卡通人物的夢幻國度，甚至是成年人在現實中因經濟或情感問題受苦時，也會想逃往的地方。因為老少咸宜，迪士尼樂園可說是各種感官的饗宴，也充滿著溫馨的氛圍，讓每個人都因為有著貌似兇猛但卻內心善良的獅子王在身旁跳舞，而感到心情愉悅。你可以看到任何曾經出現在迪士尼卡通裡的事物：看看《灰姑娘》中的女孩們如何諂媚王子，還可以沿河搭著渡輪，拜訪那些只會出現在幻想世界的地方。

　　別認為這些很幼稚，跟夢想告別是非常可怕的一件事。如果你只會整天為財務狀況苦惱，一邊咒罵外面的鞭炮聲，你將會變成一個無趣的人。為什麼不讓你的人生更加多采多姿呢？

2533 long

[lɔŋ] ★★★★★
動 渴望
形 長久的、遠的
片 long for 渴望、羨慕

2534 fierce

[fɪrs] ★★★★
形 兇猛的、好鬥的、激烈的、極糟的
同 ferocious 兇猛的

2535 flatter

[`flætɚ] ★★★★★
動 諂媚、奉承、使高興
片 flatter on 恭維…方面
衍 flatterer 奉承者

2536 ferry

[`fɛrɪ] ★★★
名 渡輪、渡口
動 乘渡輪渡過、運送
同 carry 運載

2537 fantasy

[`fæntəsɪ] ★★
名 幻想、空想、夢想
同 fancy 幻想
衍 fantast 幻想家

2538 childish

[`tʃaɪldɪʃ] ★★
形 幼稚的、孩子般的
同 babyish 孩子氣的
反 adult 成年的

2539 bid

[bɪd] ★★★★
動 向…表示、命令、出價
名 出價、投標、努力
片 bid farewell to 不再有

2540 farewell

[`fɛr`wɛl] ★★★
名 告別、送別會
形 告別的
片 Farewell! 再會！

2541 curse

[kɝs] ★★★★
動 咒罵、詛咒、使遭難
名 詛咒、咒罵、禍根
片 curse with 因…受苦

2542 sake

[sek] ★★★★
名 目的、理由、利益
片 for sb's own sake 為了自己的利益

2543 irrigate

[`ɪrəget] ★★★
動 灌溉、沖洗傷口、滋潤
同 water 灌溉
衍 irrigation 灌溉

2544 desert

[`dɛzɚt] ★★★★
形 荒蕪的、沙漠的
名 沙漠、荒野
動 擅離職守、遺棄

Fighting! **Give it a shot 小試身手**

1 They held a _____ for the friend who was going to resign.

2 He _____ his friends for the sake[2542] of his promotion.

3 We have irrigated[2543] the desert[2544] area to make it _____.

4 The teacher bids the leader to _____ the globe.

5 We set off _____ to celebrate Chinese New Year.

Answers: 1 farewell **2** feasted **3** fertile **4** fetch **5** firecrackers

213

Essay

Three Cups of Tea is a biography about an American mountaineer named Greg Mortenson, the founder of a Pakistani school and the leader of the foundation, the Central Asia Institute[2545] (CAI). As the Taliban forbid girls to receive education, Muslim[2546] girls there do not have any chance to know what a fossil looks like, how weather can be forecasted[2547] with modern technology, and many other pieces of knowledge schoolgirls around the world are quite familiar with. After a promise to the Korphe villagers, Mortenson didn't try to avoid his responsibility. Instead, he has tried to raise money for education in Pakistan. To him, there is no formula[2548] for success. His sincere, flexible and easygoing[2549] attitude has made it possible for him to travel safely to Pakistan. The formation[2550] of the CAI has helped to build a stronger bond between the US and Muslims in Pakistan. Jahan, one of the best female students in Korphe, is fluent in Arabic and English and hopes to be a doctor. With the help of Mortenson's generosity[2551], Korphe won't remain an educational backwater[2552] but will have access[2553] to resources[2554] to assist in removing the veil[2555] of ignorance[2556].

中譯 *Translation*

　　《三杯茶》是一位叫做葛瑞格‧摩頓森的美國登山客的傳記，他是巴基斯坦學校的創辦人和中亞協會的領導人。由於塔利班禁止女孩接受教育，穆斯林女孩毫無機會暸解化石長什麼樣子，如何透過現代科技預測天氣，以及其他許多知識，而這些都是世界各地的女學生相當熟悉的。在對柯爾菲的村民作出承諾後，摩頓森並沒有企圖逃避他的責任。相反地，他努力為巴基斯坦的教育募款。對他來說，成功沒有準則。他真誠、靈敏且隨和的處事態度，使他能夠在巴基斯坦安全旅行。CAI 的組成幫助美國和巴基斯坦的穆斯林建立起強大的連結。科爾菲最優秀的女學生之一賈汗，說起阿拉伯文和英文都非常流利，而且希望能當個醫生。在摩頓森慷慨的幫助下，科菲爾不會是教育落後的地方，而將會有辦法能幫助除去無知的障蔽。

2545 institute

[ˈɪnstətjut] ★★★★
名 協會、學院、規則
動 創立、開始、著手
同 establish 設立

2546 Muslim

[ˈmʌzləm] ★★
形 伊斯蘭教的
名 回教、伊斯蘭教徒
同 Islamic 伊斯蘭的

 2547 forecast

[ˈforkæst] ★★★★
動 預測、預報、預示
名 預報、預測
衍 forecaster 預測者

 2548 formula

[ˈfɔrmjələ] ★★★
名 準則、常規、公式、客套話、配方

 2549 easygoing

[ˈizɪɡoɪŋ] ★
形 脾氣隨和的、不慌不忙的

2550 formation

[fɔrˈmeʃən] ★★★
名 組成、結構、隊形
片 rock formation 岩層結構

 2551 generosity

[dʒɛnəˈrɑsətɪ] ★★
名 慷慨、寬宏大量
同 liberality 慷慨
衍 generous 慷慨的

 2552 backwater

[ˈbækwɔtə] ★
名 與世隔絕的地方、逆流水、落後狀態

 2553 access

[ˈæksɛs] ★★★★★
名 通道、門路、接近
動 使用、接近、電腦存取

 2554 resource

[rɪˈsors] ★★★★
名 辦法、資源、機智
動 向…提供資源
衍 resourceful 有策略的

 2555 veil

[vel] ★★★
名 遮蔽物、面紗、幌子
動 掩飾、遮蓋、戴面紗
片 take the veil 當修女

 2556 ignorance

[ˈɪɡnərəns] ★★★
名 無知、不學無術、愚昧
片 keep sb. in ignorance 不讓某人知道

 Fighting!

Give it a shot 小試身手

1 His _____ English impressed the interviewer.
2 Gary _____ the English test and got punished.
3 You are _____ to enter the mansion without the I.D. card.
4 Betty is such a _____ person who wins the lottery.
5 Mr. Chuang is the _____ of the charity.

Answers: 1 fluent 2 flunked 3 forbidden 4 fortunate 5 founder

214

Essay

As a freshman studying for an art major, my first field trip to the Tate Modern art gallery helped to fulfill my thirst[2557] for modern arts. Furnished with modern sculptures[2558] and stylish sofas, the museum is a good start for avant-garde[2559] artists who enjoy symbolism and impressionism. Instead of displaying traditional framed[2560] paintings, it contains[2561] works of arts that some might frown at, such as paintings of imagery[2562] that might make us feel frustrated like being in icy cold weather and even the portrayal[2563] of people in simple black and white colors at a funeral[2564]. What is revealed by the artwork is a passion for life, brave experimentation of techniques and ideas, and the fundamental[2565] training acquired from good art schools. After the trip, I found myself less eager to show off. Compared to those artists, I was like a turtle on the freeway[2566]. Now, even a boring class in art history might be helpful for my later creation! Furthermore, it might teach me how to distinguish between positive comments and negative ones before I turn furious[2567] if my artwork is criticized.

中譯 *Translation*

　　作為一個主修藝術的新鮮人，我的第一場實習是泰特現代藝術館之旅，滿足了我對現代藝術的渴求。博物館內裝飾著現代雕塑和時髦有型的沙發，這對熱愛象徵主義和印象主義的前衛藝術家而言，是個很棒的起點。博物館裡並不展示傳統的裱框畫，而是包含了可能會讓某些人皺眉的藝術品，例如使人彷彿置身酷寒之中、飽嘗挫敗感的意象畫，甚至還有出席喪禮，只穿著黑色和白色服裝的人物肖像。激發這些藝術品的源頭就是藝術家對生命的熱愛、在想法和創作技巧上的大膽嘗試，以及在優秀的藝術學校中所受的基礎訓練。經過這趟旅程之後，我發現我已經不再急切地想炫耀自我。因為和他們比起來，我就好像在高速公路上爬行的烏龜一樣。現在就算是一堂無聊的藝術史對我接下來的創作也會非常有幫助。此外，這也許教會了我如何在因作品被批評而發怒之前，能分辨出好評論與壞評論。

2557 thirst

[θɜst] ★★★
- 名 渴望、口渴
- 動 渴望、口渴
- 片 thirst for 渴求…

2558 sculpture

[`skʌlptʃə] ★★★
- 名 雕塑品、雕像、雕刻術
- 動 雕刻、做…的雕像
- 同 crave 雕刻

2559 avant-garde

[avɑŋ`gard] ★★
- 形 前衛的
- 名 先鋒、前衛派

2560 frame

[frem] ★★★★★
- 動 裝框、構想出、陷害
- 名 框架、架構、精神狀態
- 片 frame of mind 心境

2561 contain

[kən`ten] ★★★★★
- 動 包含、容納、控制
- 片 contain yourself 克制自己

2562 imagery

[`ɪmɪdʒərɪ] ★★
- 名 (總稱)畫像、意象、形象化描述

2563 portrayal

[por`treəl] ★
- 名 描繪、肖像、扮演
- 同 description 描寫
- 衍 portrayer 肖像畫家

2564 funeral

[`fjunərəl] ★★★
- 名 葬禮、倒楣事
- 形 喪葬的
- 片 at the funeral 出席葬禮

2565 fundamental

[fʌndə`mɛntl̩] ★★★
- 形 基礎的、根本的
- 名 基本原則、綱要
- 同 basic 基礎的

2566 freeway

[`friwe] ★★★
- 名 (美)高速公路
- 同 expressway (美)高速公路

2567 furious

[`fjuərɪəs] ★★★
- 形 狂怒的、猛烈的
- 同 violent 猛烈的
- 反 mild 溫和的

2568 intolerable

[ɪn`tɑlərəbl̩] ★★
- 形 難耐的、不能忍受的
- 同 unbearable 不能忍受的

Fighting!

Give it a shot 小試身手

❶ The _____ covered the window, so I could not see you.

❷ The high _____ of his absence is intolerable[2568].

❸ Those _____ still couldn't adapt to the environment.

❹ I will _____ my dream someday.

❺ We were all in black to attend the _____.

Answers: ❶ frost ❷ frequency ❸ freshmen ❹ fulfill ❺ funeral

215

 MP3 短文 429 字彙 430

Essay

It was shocking to the genuine and pious²⁵⁶⁹ Buddhists in Taiwan that the teenage genius²⁵⁷⁰, son of the host Chen Kai-lun of the DaAi TV program was charged with illegal debt-collection as a gangster. With generosity and love, the Tzu chi Foundation <u>carries on</u> charity work around the globe to those in need, such as cooking ginger soup for disaster victims or killing germs²⁵⁷¹ in their make-shift²⁵⁷² shelters²⁵⁷³ to maintain sanitation²⁵⁷⁴. Such a gigantic²⁵⁷⁵ organization is never shattered²⁵⁷⁶ by scandals like this, but this time many onlookers²⁵⁷⁷ giggled²⁵⁷⁸ behind the members of the organization's backs. Gazing at the unrepentant²⁵⁷⁹ teenager, the police and the judge shed no tears for him. However, Chen, who has been in the entertainment business for nearly 50 years, defended his son. He said his son, Chen Jui, who was 18 at the time, was a good-hearted person who had been led astray²⁵⁸⁰ by his friends.

ⓘ carry on 經營、繼續進行、繼續活動

中譯 *Translation*

　　令台灣虔誠的佛教徒所非常震驚的是，這位十來歲的天才，也就是大愛電視台主持人陳凱倫的兒子，遭控為非法討債的幫派成員。慈濟基金會憑著寬容與愛，肩負起全球的慈善工作，幫助需要被幫助的人，像是煮薑湯給災害的受難者食用、在他們的臨時收容所殺菌以維持衛生等。這樣龐大的機構，從未被這種醜聞打擊過，但這次許多旁觀者都在這些會員的背後竊笑。看著這個毫無悔意的年輕人，警察和法官都沒為他落過一滴淚。然而，在演藝界待了將近五十年的陳凱倫，處處保護兒子。他說當時他的兒子，年僅十八歲的陳瑞是個本性善良的人，是被他的朋友影響才會誤入歧途。

2569 pious

[`paɪəs] ★★★
形 虔誠的、偽善的、不可能實現的
同 devout 虔誠的

2570 genius

[`dʒinjəs] ★★★★
名 天才、天賦、才能
同 talent 天才、天資
片 genius for …的才能

2571 germ

[dʒɝm] ★★★
名 細菌、起源、萌芽
動 萌芽、發生

2572 make-shift

[`mekʃɪft] ★★
形 臨時代用的、權宜的
名 臨時代用品、權宜之計

2573 shelter

[`ʃɛltə] ★★★
名 避難所、遮蔽、庇護
動 躲避、掩蔽、庇護
片 shelter from 保護

2574 sanitation

[sænə`teʃən] ★
名 環境衛生、衛生設備
片 food sanitation 食品衛生

2575 gigantic

[dʒaɪ`gæntɪk] ★★
形 龐大的、巨人似的
同 huge 龐大的

2576 shatter

[`ʃætə] ★★★
動 打擊、動搖、削弱、粉碎、破壞
名 破碎、碎片

2577 onlooker

[`ɑnlukə] ★★
名 旁觀者、觀眾
同 spectator 觀眾
衍 onlooking 旁觀的

2578 giggle

[`gɪgl̩] ★★★
動 咯咯地笑、傻笑
同 chuckle 咯咯地笑
名 咯咯的笑、傻笑、趣事

2579 unrepentant

[ˌʌnrɪ`pɛntənt] ★★
形 不悔悟的、頑固的
同 impenitent 不知悔改的
反 repentant 悔改的

2580 astray

[ə`stre] ★★
副 離開正道、迷路
形 離開正道的、迷路的
片 go astray 誤入歧途

Give it a shot 小試身手

Fighting!

❶ Why does the stranger _____ at me?

❷ Education should be _____ to the society's needs.

❸ There is no _____ gap between my grandma and I.

❹ Thanks to your _____, I will not commit such an error next time.

❺ A _____ diamond costs astronomically.

Answers: ❶ gaze ❷ geared ❸ generation ❹ generosity ❺ genuine

216

🎧 MP3　　

Essay

Do you ever grieve[2581] over your GEPT writing scores? Do you ever feel grateful for passing a writing[2582] test? Most students find it hard to write in English because they seldom study grammar books thoroughly. Although it is tedious[2583] to focus on all the grammatical[2584] points such as greetings[2585] or showing gratitude[2586] or grief, a good quality grammar book is something every ESL learner needs to have. A bad grammar book just reduces your chances of passing tests. However, while grammar is very important, there is much more to good writing than just grammar. You need to choose[2587] your words carefully to properly convey your meaning. Also, what you write should be to the point. You shouldn't give lots of details about your childhood[2588] memories when writing about the topic of "A Bad Day," for example. You will have less[2589] and less time to practice your writing skills after graduation, let alone learn how to write with style. What you should keep in mind is to leave out the faulty[2590] sentences and show the examiners[2591] that you really put effort into your writing.

中譯 *Translation*

　　你是否曾為全民英檢的寫作成績感到難過呢？是否又曾因為通過寫作測驗而感激不已？大多數學生都覺得英文寫作很難，因為他們很少認真仔細讀完文法書。雖然專注在所有文法重點上時，像是問候語或表達感激、悲傷的用法是非常乏味的，但一本品質好的文法書是教導學生英語為第二外語的老師必須要有的。一本內容拙劣的文法書只會降低你通過考試的機會。然而，雖然文法相當重要，但比起文法，撰寫好文章更是不簡單。你必須謹慎選擇用字，以正確傳遞你文章的含意。此外，你的文章應該要切中主題。舉例來說，當你在寫像是「糟糕的一天」這類的主題時，千萬不要寫一堆關於童年時期的枝節瑣事。畢業後你的練習時間將會越來越少，更別說如何寫得優美了。你應該銘記在心的是，省去那些油嘴滑舌的句子，讓主考官知道你確實在寫作方面下過苦功。

2581 **grieve**
[griv] ★★★
使苦惱、悲傷、哀悼
片 grieve over 由於…而傷心

2585 **greeting**
[`gritɪŋ] ★★★
名 問候語、賀詞、招呼
同 salutation 問候
片 greeting card 賀卡

2589 **less**
[lɛs] ★★★★★
形 較少的、較小的
副 較少地、不如
名 更少的數量

2582 **writing**
[`raɪtɪŋ] ★★★★★
名 寫作、著作、書面形式、筆跡
片 in writing 以書面形式

2586 **gratitude**
[`grætətjud] ★★★
名 感激之情、感恩
同 appreciation 感謝
反 ingratitude 忘恩負義

2590 **faulty**
[`fɔltɪ] ★★★
形 有缺點的、不完美的
同 defective 有缺陷的
反 perfect 完美的

2583 **tedious**
[`tidɪəs] ★★★
形 冗長乏味的、厭煩的
同 dull 乏味的
衍 tediousness 乏味

2587 **choose**
[tʃuz] ★★★★★
動 挑選、選擇、決定
片 choose sb./sth. for 把…選作

2591 **examiner**
[ɪg`zæmɪnɚ] ★★
名 主考人、考官、審查員

2584 **grammatical**
[grə`mætɪk!] ★★
形 文法的、合乎文法的
衍 grammar 文法

2588 **childhood**
[`tʃaɪldhʊd] ★★★
名 童年時期
片 in sb's childhood 在某人童年時

2592 **pronunciation**
[prənʌnsɪ`eʃən] ★★★
名 發音、讀法
衍 pronounce 發音、宣稱

Give it a shot 小試身手

1 The _____ they imported were all fakes.

2 The waitresses in the restaurant are very _____ and patient.

3 My classmates and I cried on the _____ ceremony.

4 Not only _____ but also pronunciation[2592] is important in learning English.

5 _____ food is not proper for the patients.

Answers: 1 goods 2 gracious 3 graduation 4 grammar 5 Greasy

217

Essay

Need some refreshment[2593] after a harsh[2594] day? Why not take a sip of brewed[2595] coffee and listen to the sound of relaxing music? If you do, all your stress and tension[2596] might disappear in a minute! Living a busy life, people these days seldom have any time to slow down and take it easy. They rarely write cards to friends because they have no time. They never enjoy the scenery of the places they visit on their business trips. They even feel guilty[2597] when they find piles of work after they come back from their honeymoon. As a result, their body is not in harmony with their mind. Their sense of guilt towards slowing down pushes them to always function at a rapid[2598] pace. Their around-the-clock use of computers tightens[2599] their shoulders and limbs. Their habitual[2600] fast-paced life causes their bodies to age prematurely[2601], creating serious health problems. Such a fast-paced life might seem to guarantee a promising future with a good income, but without health, how can you enjoy it? Try slowing down and not rushing yourself all the time!

中譯 *Translation*

　　辛苦一天後需要來點調劑嗎？何不啜一口研磨咖啡並聽聽令人放鬆的音樂？照著做，你的壓力與緊張將在一秒之內煙消雲散！因為過著忙碌的生活，現代人很少有時間可以放慢腳步、放鬆一下。他們很少會寄送手寫卡片給朋友，因為沒有時間。他們從來沒有在出差時享受過當地的美景。甚至當他們度完蜜月回來，看到成堆的工作時還會有罪惡感。因此，他們的身體無法與心靈達到協調。對於放慢腳步而產生的罪惡感，會促使他們一直快速運轉。他們日以繼夜地使用電腦，也使他們的肩膀和四肢僵硬。習慣性的快節奏生活會導致身體老化，並產生嚴重的健康問題。這種快節奏的生活，或許看起來是光明前途以及高薪的保證，但是沒有了健康，你要如何享受生活呢？試著慢下來，不要總是把自己逼得那麼緊！

2593 refreshment

[rɪ`frɛʃmənt] ★★
名 起提神作用的東西、恢復精力、茶點

2594 harsh

[harʃ] ★★★★
形 艱苦的、嚴酷的
片 be harsh with 對⋯嚴厲

2595 brew

[bru] ★★★
動 釀造、被沖泡、醞釀著
名 釀製飲料、口味、啤酒
片 brew up 沏茶

2596 tension

[`tɛnʃən] ★★★
名 緊張、繃緊、緊張局勢
動 拉緊、繃緊
衍 tensional 緊張的

2597 guilty

[`gɪltɪ] ★★★★
形 內疚的、有罪的
反 innocent 清白的
片 guilty of 有罪

2598 rapid

[`ræpɪd] ★★★★
形 迅速的、陡的、險峻的
名 急流、急湍
同 swift 快速的

2599 tighten

[`taɪtn̩] ★★
動 變緊、繃緊
片 tighten up 使更牢固
衍 tight 緊的

2600 habitual

[hə`bɪtʃuəl] ★★
形 習慣的、習以為常的
同 regular 習慣性的
衍 habituate 使習慣於

2601 prematurely

[pimə`tʃurlɪ] ★
名 過早地、貿然地
衍 prematurity 早熟

2602 bean

[bin] ★★★★
名 豆、毫無價值的東西
片 spill the beans 走漏消息

2603 snore

[snor] ★★★
名 打鼾、鼾聲
動 打鼾

2604 handicraft

[`hændɪkræft] ★
名 手工藝品、手藝
片 handicraft industry 手工業

Fighting! Give it a shot 小試身手

❶ The coffee beans2602 were _____ several times.

❷ I feel _____ of being late; I'm willing to be punished.

❸ His _____ snore2603 disturbed his wife very much.

❹ He performed a melody by his _____.

❺ He _____ his steps and looked at the handicrafts2604 on the vendor.

Answers: ❶ ground ❷ guilty ❸ habitual ❹ harmonica ❺ halted

218

Essay

Tom and his wife went to Italy, his homeland, on their honeymoon. They enjoyed healthful mountain air. They thought it was a peaceful place, but it was not in fact. One day, when Tom was choosing fish hooks, and his wife was buying headphones at a nearby store, many military helicopters[2605] appeared on the horizon[2606], which horrified[2607] many residents, and the noise upset a herd[2608] of cattle. Out of hatred[2609] for the fast-approaching enemy soldiers, local residents picked up their hoses[2610], feeling hopeful that they would somehow magically win an honorable[2611] war against the invaders[2612]. After some hesitation[2613], one of the residents began to speak, "How about playing host to welcome our visitors rather than fighting with them?" Another one said, "You say that just because you know very well that we cannot defeat[2614] the helicopters by using just our hoses." Their quarrel soon turned into a fight, and it made the situation more complicated. Tom decided to escape with his wife, but they were detained[2615] at the airport. Tom and his wife decided that was the worst honeymoon in the world!

中譯 Translation

　　湯姆和他的妻子前往他的故鄉義大利度蜜月。他們享受著有益健康的山間空氣。他們以為這是一個和平的地方，但事實並非如此。有天，當湯姆在挑選魚鉤，他的太太在附近商店購買耳機時，許多軍用直升機出現在地平線上，這嚇壞了許多居民，直升機的噪音也造成一群牛隻騷動。出於對迅速迫近的敵軍的敵意，本地居民拾起他們的水管，懷抱希望地認為他們會贏得這場對抗入侵者的光榮戰役。猶豫了一陣子之後，其中一個居民開口說道：「我們何不做東道主來歡迎我們的訪客，而不要和他們作戰呢？」另一個人說：「你這樣說是因為你很清楚，我們不可能只靠我們的水管贏過直升機。」他們的口角很快就演變成肢體衝突，使得情況變得更加複雜。湯姆決定帶著他的妻子逃離，卻被扣留在機場。那真是史上最糟糕的蜜月了！

2605 helicopter

[`hɛlɪkɑptə] ★★★

名 直升機

動 用直升機載送、坐直升機

2606 horizon

[hə`raɪzn̩] ★★★★

名 地平線、範圍、眼界

片 on the horizon 即將發生的

2607 horrify

[`hɔrəfaɪ] ★★

動 使恐懼、使驚懼

同 terrify 使害怕

衍 horrifying 令人恐懼的

2608 herd

[hɜd] ★★★

名 畜群、牧群

動 放牧、成群

片 herd together 聚在一起

2609 hatred

[`hetrɪd] ★★★

名 敵意、憎恨

同 hate 憎恨、厭惡

片 hatred for 對⋯的仇恨

2610 hose

[hoz] ★★★★

名 水管、軟管、長統襪

同 stockings 長襪

動 用軟管澆水、打敗

2611 honorable

[`ɑnərəbl̩] ★★

名 光榮的、高尚的、表示尊敬的

反 dishonorable 不名譽的

2612 invader

[ɪn`vedə] ★★

名 侵略者

同 aggressor 侵略者

衍 invade 侵入、侵略

2613 hesitation

[hɛzə`teʃən] ★★

名 躊躇、猶豫

片 have no hesitation in 毫不猶豫

2614 defeat

[dɪ`fit] ★★★★

動 擊敗、戰勝、使失敗

名 戰敗、挫折、擊敗

同 overcome 戰勝

2615 detain

[dɪ`ten] ★★★

動 使耽擱、拘留、扣留

反 liberate 使獲自由

衍 detention 滯留、拘留

2616 rescue

[`rɛskju] ★★★★

動 營救、挽救

名 援救、營救

片 come to the rescue 救援

Give it a shot 小試身手

1 He wore the _____ and enjoyed himself in music.

2 They rescued[2616] the victims by a _____.

3 He agreed her invitation without any _____.

4 He missed his _____ but could not come back due to the war.

5 Do not hang your helmet on the _____. It will be broken.

MP3　短文 437　字彙 438

Essay

219

A growing number of housewives have been idle[2617] for the past six months. Some of them have even left their households[2618] to live in a hostel[2619] for they didn't want to cook. Such a phenomenon[2620] may be only the tip of the iceberg[2621]. During the previous generations, women were responsible[2622] for all domestic affairs. For example, Mary was pursued by countless[2623] boys; however, she married an ignorant[2624] man. Since then, she has spent most of the time doing housework. No matter what happened outside her home, she always did the same chores[2625] inside.

"It is inhumane[2626]." Mary said. "A policeman in the community even asked me to show identification[2627] when I went shopping one day because he could not recognize who I was, mainly because I barely go out of the house. However, I have plenty[2628] of time to read the latest novels so at least I can live in a fantasy world. My husband is just a couch potato. I think it's time I woke up to the fact that I am a wife, not a maid!"

中譯 *Translation*

　　過去六個月以來，越來越多家庭主婦變得無所事事。其中有些人甚至會讓家人住在旅舍裡，只因為她們不想煮飯。這種現象也許只是冰山一角。在以前的世代，女人要負擔所有的家庭事務，舉個例子來說，瑪莉曾經是無數男孩追求的對象，不過她卻嫁給了一個無知的男人。從那時起，她就把大部分時間花在家事上。無論她家門外發生了什麼事，她都做著同樣的家庭雜務。

　　「這完全不符人性。」瑪莉說：「有天我去買東西時，社區裡的一名警察甚至還要求我出示身份證，因為他認不出我是誰，主要是因為我幾乎沒出過門。不過，我還有足夠的時間閱讀最新出版的小說，這至少可以讓我活在幻想的世界裡。我先生就只會癱在沙發上看電視，從未離開過。我想該是清醒的時候，事實就是我是一名妻子，不是女傭！」

2617 idle

[`aɪdḷ] ★★★★
形 無所事事的、閒置的、懶惰的
動 虛度、空轉

2618 household

[`haʊshold] ★★★★
名 家庭、家眷、一家人
形 家庭的、為人所熟知的

2619 hostel

[`hastḷ] ★★★
名 青年旅社
片 a youth hostel 青年旅社

2620 phenomenon

[fə`namənan] ★★★★
名 現象、奇蹟、傑出的人才
衍 phenomenal 傑出的

2621 iceberg

[`aɪsbɝg] ★★
名 冰山、冷峻的人
片 the tip of the iceberg 冰山一角

2622 responsible

[rɪ`spansəbḷ] ★★★★
形 承擔責任的
片 be responsible for 對…負責

2623 countless

[`kaʊntlɪs] ★★
形 數不盡的、無數的
同 innumerable 數不清的

2624 ignorant

[`ɪgnərənt] ★★★
形 無知的、不學無術的、不知道的
片 ignorant of 不了解

2625 chore

[tʃor] ★★
名 家庭雜務、例行工作、討厭的工作
同 task 苦差事

2626 inhumane

[ɪnhju`men] ★
形 無人情味的、殘忍的
同 ruthless 殘忍的
反 humane 人道的

2627 identification

[aɪˏdɛntəfə`keʃən] ★
名 身分證明、識別、認同
片 identification card 身分證

2628 plenty

[`plɛntɪ] ★★★★
名 大量、充足、豐富
形 很多的、足夠的
片 plenty of 大量的

Fighting!

Give it a shot 小試身手

❶ I stayed in the _____ last night and it cost me only five hundred dollars.

❷ Everyone in the house is responsible for the _____.

❸ Several years ago, the _____ destroyed New Orleans.

❹ Her new dress is almost _____ to mine.

❺ "Pigs might fly" is a very interesting _____.

Answers: ❶ hostel ❷ housework ❸ hurricane ❹ identical ❺ idiom

MP3　短文 439　字彙 440

Essay

220

The museum is full of the most wonderful and imaginative illustrations[2629] by a man named Lawrence. Lawrence's father and mother came to this country when he was just two. They are illegal immigrants. Lawrence illustrated his childhood life through various paintings, including one in which a child is playing an imaginary[2630] piano on his mother's knees, implying[2631] his love for music. Such paintings have had an obvious impact on modern[2632] art. A lot of painters have tried to imitate[2633] Lawrence's style. As a result, many artists are gradually[2634] losing their imaginative ways of painting, leaving people with the false impression that many works of art are produced by imitation. Although that means Lawrence is a model artist, he doesn't like being copied[2635] because that makes his work seem less unique.

Apart[2636] from his importance to the world of art, Lawrence also has had an essential impact on immigration policy. He stated to the Minister of the Interior[2637] that his case was not an isolated incident, saying that many people like him had to bear the burden of illegality. Thanks to him, the government later loosened[2638] immigration restriction.

中譯 *Translation*

這間博物館充滿了最棒、最富想像力的畫作，皆出自勞倫斯之手。藝術家勞倫斯的父母在他兩歲時移民進這個國家。他們是非法移民。勞倫斯用各種不同的畫描繪他的童年，包括了一幅孩子在母親膝上演奏著假想鋼琴的畫，暗示他對音樂的喜愛。這種繪畫對現代藝術造成了顯著的影響。許多畫家都嘗試模仿勞倫斯的風格。因此，許多藝術家漸漸失去了他們富有想像力的作畫方式，帶給觀眾一種「天下藝術一大抄」的錯誤印象。雖然那表示勞倫斯是名模範藝術家，他還是不喜歡被模仿，希望他自己的作品是獨一無二的。

除了他在藝術界的重要性之外，勞倫斯也對移民政策造成了必要的影響。他曾向內政部長陳情，表示他的情況並不是個案，許多像他一樣背景的人都得背負違法的罪名。多虧有他，政府後來便放寬了移民禁令。

2629 illustration

[ɪlʌs`treʃən] ★★★★

名 插圖、圖案、圖解、實例、圖表

衍 illustrate 用圖例說明

2630 imaginary

[ɪ`mædʒənɛrɪ] ★★

形 想像中的、虛構的

同 fantastic 想像中的

反 actual 實際的

2631 imply

[ɪm`plaɪ] ★★★★

動 暗示、意味著

片 imply by/in 用…暗示

衍 implication 暗示

2632 modern

[`madən] ★★★★★

形 現代的、時髦的

名 現代人

反 ancient 古代的

2633 imitate

[`ɪmətet] ★★★

動 模仿、仿製、偽造

同 copy 模仿

衍 imitation 模仿

2634 gradually

[`grædʒuəlɪ] ★★

副 逐步地、漸漸地

同 bit by bit 漸漸地

衍 gradual 逐漸的

2635 copy

[`kɑpɪ] ★★★★★

動 模仿、臨摹、複製

名 拷貝、複製品、摹本

片 copy from sth. 仿造

2636 apart

[ə`pɑrt] ★★★★

副 分開地、個別地、與眾不同地

片 apart from 除…以外

2637 interior

[ɪn`tɪrɪə] ★★★

形 內政的、內部的、內陸的、內心的

名 內部、內政、內心

2638 loosen

[`lusṇ] ★★★

動 放鬆、鬆開

反 tighten 繃緊

片 loosen up 放鬆

2639 statistics

[stə`tɪstɪks] ★★★

名 統計資料、統計學

2640 picture

[`pɪktʃə] ★★★★★

動 想像、描繪、拍攝

名 照片、寫照、局面

片 the picture of …的體現

Fighting!

Give it a shot 小試身手

❶ The statistics2639 are a clear _____ of the point.

❷ He just pictured2640 his future with _____ ideas.

❸ Children tend to _____ the behaviors of adults.

❹ The news that she got married was a mighty _____ on him.

❺ I have interviewed several celebrities, _____ the President.

MP3

 短文 441

 字彙 442

Essay

221

An infant[2641]'s skin is very sensitive; in other words, it can be easily infected. Parents should read informative[2642] books regarding infections that children are likely to get in order to obtain[2643] more information. From doing that type of reading, parents can know important things, such as what kind of medicine to use to cure diseases during the initial[2644] stages. Although a developed country has a lot of hospitals, regular examinations of children's health is unfortunately uncommon[2645]. Dr. Malvern, who has influential[2646] friends who serve as finance[2647] officials, said that as the annual rate of inflation has risen, it is hard to inspire people to pay extra attention to their children's health, which means they will likely need to spend more money on it. Therefore, as government officials continue to defend the rise in insurance[2648] premiums[2649], Dr. Malvern decided to ask his patients to fill out a survey[2650]. Due to the enthusiastic[2651] contribution of his patients, the survey was able to influence the government to pay more attention to the problem. They believe their efforts will provide inspiration for many government officials to act in good conscience[2652].

中譯 *Translation*

　　嬰兒的皮膚非常敏感，也就是說，很容易受到感染。父母必須閱讀增進知識書籍，像是關於孩童很可能會得到的傳染病，以獲得更多資訊。那類的閱讀可以讓父母得知重要的事情，例如在感染初期可以用哪種藥物來治療疾病。雖然已開發國家有很多的醫院，但不幸的是，對於孩童健康的定期檢查依然不普遍。馬爾文醫生有許多富有影響力的朋友是財政官員，他表示隨著通貨膨脹比率的升高，要激勵民眾多加關注孩童的健康——也就是可能會花更多錢在這上面─就更加困難了。因此，由於政府官員持續抵抗保險費用的增加，馬爾文醫生決定請他的病患填寫一份調查。因為病患的踴躍參與，這項調查才能夠影響政府更加正視這個問題。他們相信他們的努力對許多憑良心做事的官員，會是莫大的鼓舞。

2641 infant

[`ɪnfənt] ★★★
名 嬰兒
形 初創的、嬰兒的
衍 infancy 嬰兒期

2642 informative

[ɪn`fɔrmətɪv] ★★★
形 教育性的、有益的、情報的、見聞廣博的
同 instructive 增進知識的

2643 obtain

[əb`ten] ★★★★
動 獲得、通用、流行
同 acquire 獲得
片 obtain from 從…得到

2644 initial

[ɪ`nɪʃəl] ★★★★
形 最初的、開始的
名 起首字母
同 original 最初的

2645 uncommon

[ʌn`kɑmən] ★★
形 罕見的、不尋常的、傑出的
同 rare 罕見的

2646 influential

[ɪnflu`ɛnʃəl] ★★★★
形 有影響力的、有權勢的
衍 influenza 流行性感冒

2647 finance

[faɪ`næns] ★★★★
名 財政、金融、財務情況
動 融資、為…籌措資金
衍 financial 財政的

2648 insurance

[ɪn`ʃurəns] ★★★★★
名 保險、保險契約、賠償金、預防措施
衍 insurant 被保人

2649 premium

[`primɪəm] ★★★
名 保險費、優質、津貼
形 高價的、優質的

2650 survey

[sə`ve] ★★★★★
名 調查、測量、俯瞰
動 俯視、測量、調查
衍 surveyor 調查員

2651 enthusiastic

[ɪnθjuzɪ`æstɪk] ★★★
形 熱心的、熱烈的
片 enthusiastic about 對…熱心

2652 conscience

[`kɑnʃəns] ★★★
名 良心、善惡觀念
片 have no conscience 沒有良心

fighting!

Give it a shot 小試身手

1 The southern part of the country was slow to _____.

2 Wash your hands frequently to avoid _____.

3 Helen is the most _____ person in the political circle.

4 The _____ of the bread are only three kinds.

5 The children laughed with _____.

Answers: 1 industrialize 2 infection 3 influential 4 ingredients 5 innocence

 MP3　短文 443　字彙 444

222

Essay

John showed high intelligence[2653] from an early age. He interacted well with other intelligent children in computer class. They had installed[2654] a new computer network recently, thanks to their instructor, who gave them a one-week intensive[2655] course in computer science.

"I intend to prevent them from being under intense pressure in my class," said John's computer teacher Andy Chiang. "However, John and several other students are intellectual[2656] children, and they seem to have an aptitude[2657] for absorbing knowledge. Their quick learning ability has intensified[2658] my motivation[2660], so I have decided to instruct[2659] them in more areas. Although I am getting old, I have no intention[2661] of retiring for my students provide me with a nice challenge." Nevertheless, John said, "I hope Mr. Chiang won't feel insulted if I drop[2662] out of his class. I feel somewhat bored in his computer class, and I have decided to register for a physics[2663] class."

中譯 *Translation*

　　約翰在他年紀還小的時候就展現出高超的智能。他和電腦課中其他聰明的兒童都相處得很好。他們最近安裝了新的電腦網絡，多虧有他們的老師，為他們的電腦科目安排了為期一週的加強課程。

　　「我希望能避免讓他們在我的課堂中，承受太大的壓力。」約翰的電腦老師蔣安迪表示：「然而，約翰和其他幾名學生都是非常聰明的孩子，他們似乎有汲取知識的本能。他們快速的學習能力激發了我的幹勁，所以我決定傳授他們更多面向的學問。雖然我已慢慢變老，但我還沒有退休的打算，因為他們成為我職涯中一個很棒的挑戰。」然而，約翰卻說：「我希望蔣老師不會因為我退課而覺得受辱。我覺得他的電腦課有點無聊，所以我已經決定要報名物理學的課程了。」

2653 intelligence

[ɪn`tɛlədʒəns] ★★★★
名 智能、消息、情報機關
片 intelligence agent 情報人員

2654 install

[ɪn`stɔl] ★★★★
動 安裝、設置、使就任
同 inaugurate 使正式就任
片 install in 安置於

2655 intensive

[ɪn`tɛnsɪv] ★★★
形 加強的、密集的、透徹的、精耕細作的
同 detailed 精細的

2656 intellectual

[ɪntḷ`ɛktʃuəl] ★★★
形 聰明的、智力的
名 知識分子
同 intelligent 聰明的

2657 aptitude

[`æptətjud] ★★
名 天資、才能、習性
片 aptitude for …方面的天賦

2658 intensify

[ɪn`tɛnsəfaɪ] ★★
動 增強、強化、變激烈
同 deepen 變強烈
衍 intensity 強度、強烈

2659 instruct

[ɪn`strʌkt] ★★★
動 指導、訓練、吩咐
同 teach 講授、訓練
片 instruct in 講授…

2660 motivation

[motə`veʃən] ★★★
名 幹勁、積極性、刺激
同 impetus 刺激
衍 motivator 動力

2661 intention

[ɪn`tɛnʃən] ★★★★
名 意向、意圖、目的
同 purpose 目的
片 intention to 目標是…

2662 drop

[drɑp] ★★★★★
動 中斷、滴下、落後、下車、遺漏
片 drop out 退出、離開

2663 physics

[`fɪzɪks] ★★★
名 物理學

2664 attribute

[ə`trɪbjut] ★★★★
動 歸因於、歸咎於
名 屬性、特質
片 attribute to 歸因於

Fighting!

Give it a shot 小試身手

1 I will _____ anti-virus software in your computer.

2 I attributed[2664] the honor to my swimming _____.

3 The _____ competition stressed him very much.

4 Be careful. We don't know the stranger's real _____.

5 There is a need for greater _____ between the two departments.

Answers: 1 install 2 instructor 3 intense 4 intention 5 interaction

Essay

The Internet is a wonderful invention[2665]. You can find out practically[2666] anything you want to on the Net. People who have just a basic level of computer literacy can now chat with netizens[2667] around the globe without difficulty. The intimate atmosphere of social networking sites enhances[2668] the quality of interaction among those who are involved in them.

However, my daughter said that I was interfering[2669] whenever I said she was becoming more and more isolated by the virtual[2670] world. Such isolation from face-to-face contact with people, to me, is not a positive development. For one thing, an investigation[2671] into Internet addiction[2672] shows that children should not spend too much time on the Internet before their second language learning acquisition[2673] has improved, or they may suffer greatly in the future. Therefore, I still tried my best to dissuade[2674] my daughter from spending too much time on the Internet and forbade her to frequent Internet cafes. I believe I have made the correct decision regarding[2675] this matter.

中譯 **Translation**

　　網際網路是非常美妙的發明。你可以在網路上找到任何你想要的東西。只具備基本電腦素養的人現在可以毫無障礙地和世界各地的網民聊天。社交網站的親密氛圍，提高了參與者間互動的品質。

　　然而，每當我說女兒把自己孤立在虛擬世界中時，她都會說我在干涉她。這種脫離與他人面對面的接觸，對我來說並不是正向的發展。首先，一個針對網路成癮者的調查表示，在小孩的第二語言學習過程有所進展之前，不應該花太多時間在網路上，否則到了將來他們也許會因此吃很多苦頭。因此，我盡我最大的努力勸我女兒不要花太多時間上網，並禁止讓她太常進出網咖。我認為在這件事情上我做了正確的決定。

2665 invention

[ɪn`vɛnʃən] ★★★
名 發明、創造、虛構
同 creation 創造
衍 inventive 發明的

2666 practically

[`præktɪk]ɪ] ★★
副 幾乎、差不多、實際上
同 almost 幾乎、差不多
衍 practicality 實用性

2667 netizen

[`nɛtɪzən] ★★★
名 網路公民、網民
拆 net 網絡 + citizen 公民

2668 enhance

[ɪn`hæns] ★★★★
動 提高、增加、改進
同 uplift 提高
衍 enhancement 提高

2669 interfere

[ɪntə`fɪr] ★★★
動 干涉、妨礙、牴觸
同 meddle 干涉
片 interfere in 干涉

2670 virtual

[`vɝtʃuəl] ★★★
形 (電腦)虛擬的、實質上的、事實上的
同 actual 事實上的

2671 investigation

[ɪnvɛstə`geʃən] ★★
名 研究、調查
片 under investigation 調查中

2672 addiction

[ə`dɪkʃən] ★★
名 沉溺、上癮、入迷
片 addiction to 對…成癮
衍 addictive 上癮的

2673 acquisition

[ækwə`zɪʃən] ★★★
名 獲得、取得
同 obtainment 獲得
衍 acquire 取得、獲得

2674 dissuade

[dɪ`swed] ★★
動 勸阻
片 dissuade sb. from +ving 勸某人別做某事

2675 regarding

[rɪ`gardɪŋ] ★★
介 關於、就…而論
同 concerning 關於

2676 combat

[`kɑmbæt] ★★★
動 戰鬥、搏鬥、反對
名 戰鬥、格鬥、反對
片 combat with 同…作戰

Give it a shot 小試身手

1 I've passed the _____ level exam of Japanese.

2 Parick _____ the Japanese woman's words into English.

3 They feel _____ with each other and no secrets are between them.

4 The nation will combat[2676]* with those who _____.

5 _____ in real estate needs previous observation.

MP3 短文 447 字彙 448

Essay 224

The beauty and safety of the New England landscape were harmed <u>as a result of</u> tests on laboratory animals carried out by an inexperienced[2677] doctor. Recently, the doctor hired many laborers to dump the animal remains into the river, which is one of New England's most famous landmarks[2678]. It is not lawful[2679] to kill a pet animal, <u>let alone</u> dump them in the river. This incident caused people to feel terribly itchy[2680] around their knuckles[2681] after drinking the river water. Many PETA members were keen[2682] to help. A member said, "The United States is lagging[2683] behind Europe in <u>launching campaigns</u> to protect the environment." However, sometimes it seems that no one cares about the water pollution[2684] or landslide. People simply feel jealousy[2685] when they see other countries having a clean environment. It's time that people respect the environment more and do everything they possibly can to prevent additional[2686] harm being done to it.

> ⚠ as a result of 由於…
> ⚠ let alone 更不用説
> ⚠ launch a campaign 發起活動

中譯 *Translation*

　　新英格蘭美麗的風景與環境因為一位經驗不足的醫生所進行的動物實驗而遭到破壞。近來,這位醫生聘用了許多勞工把動物的殘骸倒進河裡,那條河是新英格蘭最著名的地標之一。殺害寵物已經違法了,更何況把那些動物的殘骸倒進河裡。這個事件導致飲用河水的民眾,關節附近嚴重發癢。許多「善待動物組織」的成員都急切地想要幫忙。有位成員表示:「美國在發起環境保護運動上遠遠落後歐洲國家。」然而,有時候,似乎沒人真的關心水汙染或山崩。人們只不過是因為看到其他國家的環境很好,而心生嫉妒。是時候要開始更尊重環境,並盡力防止環境遭到更多危害。

2677 inexperienced

[ɪnɪkˋspɪrɪənst] ★★★
形 經驗不足的、不熟練的
同 unpracticed 不熟練的
反 experienced 有經驗的

2678 landmark

[ˋlændmɑrk] ★★
名 地標、里程碑
同 milestone 里程碑

2679 lawful

[ˋlɔfəl] ★★
形 合法的、守法的
同 legal 合法的
反 unlawful 犯法的

2680 itchy

[ˋɪtʃɪ] ★★
形 發癢的、渴望的
衍 itch 發癢、渴望

2681 knuckle

[ˋnʌkl] ★★
名 指關節、膝關節
動 開始認真工作、屈服
片 knuckle under 認輸

2682 keen

[kin] ★★★★
形 熱衷的、渴望的、敏銳的、鋒利的
片 knee on 熱衷於

2683 lag

[læg] ★★★★
動 落後、延遲、衰退
名 落後、衰退
片 lag behind 落後

2684 pollution

[pəˋluʃən] ★★★★
名 汙染、汙染地區
片 noise pollution 噪音汙染

2685 jealousy

[ˋdʒɛləsɪ] ★★★
名 妒忌、猜忌、戒備
同 envy 妒忌
反 generosity 寬宏大量

2686 additional

[əˋdɪʃənl] ★★★★★
形 附加的、額外的
同 extra 額外的
衍 addition 附加

2687 ripe

[raɪp] ★★★★
形 成熟的、老成的
片 ripe for 時機成熟的
同 full-grown 成熟的

2688 obvious

[ˋɑbvɪəs] ★★★★
形 明顯的、顯著的
同 clear 清楚的
反 obscure 模糊的

Fighting!

Give it a shot 小試身手

1 The mosquito bite on my arm started to _____.

2 Those new comers went to attend a course for _____ employees.

3 He _____ the apple to see whether it was ripe[2687] or not.

4 The tallest building is an obvious[2688] _____.

5 Long time no see. How have you been _____?

Answers: 1 itch 2 junior 3 knuckled 4 landmark 5 lately

MP3　 短文 449　 字彙 450

Essay

225

Mary is a brilliant lecturer[2689] who won a literary[2690] prize recently. She had to <u>take out a loan</u>[2691] to rent an apartment located near the library so that she could read her favorite ancient Greek myths conveniently[2692]. She had worked at a leisurely[2693] pace, but she became busy after winning the prize. Everybody <u>viewed</u> her <u>as</u> a learned[2694] professor. Moreover, many schools started inviting her to <u>give lectures on</u> Greek literature. Her classes became increasingly crowded with students leaning forward to hear clearly what a woman of great learning would talk about.

"Now I have found my limitations[2695]. I think everybody overestimates[2696] my ability, but I cannot admit that," Mary said when taking out her jacket from her locker. "I forgot to renew[2697] my driver's licence; besides[2698], I have been frequenting[2699] a bar to drink liquor[2700] recently. I'm really under great pressure!"

ⓘ view...as 把⋯視為⋯
ⓘ give a lecture on 演講
ⓘ take out a loan 貸款

中譯 *Translation*

　　瑪莉是個聰慧的講師，最近獲得了文學獎。她以前要貸款來租圖書館附近的公寓，這樣才方便她閱讀最愛的古希臘神話。她以前的工作步調很悠閒，但是得獎之後卻變得忙碌起來了。每個人都認為她是個博學的教授。除此之外，許多學校也邀請她發表關於希臘文學的演講。她的課堂湧進越來越多學生，他們都引頸期盼，想要仔細聆聽這位博學多聞的女士所發表的演講。

　　「現在我已經知道我的極限了。我覺得他們都高估了我的能力，但我卻不能承認。」瑪莉一邊說，一邊把衣服從置物櫃取出：「我忘了重新申請我的駕照，而且，我最近不斷去酒吧喝酒。我的壓力真的好大啊！」

2689 lecturer

[`lɛktʃərə] ★★
名 (大學)講師、演講者
同 speechmaker 演說者
衍 lectureship 講師職位

2690 literary

[`lɪtərɛrɪ] ★★
形 文學的、精通文學的
片 literary works 文學作品

2691 loan

[lon] ★★★
名 貸款、借出
動 借出、貸與

2692 conveniently

[kən`vinjəntlɪ] ★
副 方便地、合宜地
同 expediently 方便地
衍 convenient 方便的

2693 leisurely

[`liʒəlɪ] ★
形 從容不迫的、悠閒的
副 慢慢地
衍 leisure 悠閒的

2694 learned

[`lɜnɪd] ★★★★★
形 博學的、精通的、學術性的
片 be learned in 精通⋯

2695 limitation

[lɪmə`teʃən] ★★
名 極限、限制因素
同 restriction 限制
衍 limit 極限

2696 overestimate

[ovə`ɛstəmet] ★
動 評價過高、估計過高
名 過高的評價
同 overrate 過高估計

2697 renew

[rɪ`nju] ★★★★
動 更新、重新開始、加強
同 resume 重新開始
衍 renewable 可恢復的

2698 besides

[bɪ`saɪdz] ★★★★
副 此外、而且、其他方面
介 在⋯之外、除⋯之外

2699 frequent

[`frikwənt] ★★★★
動 時常出入於、常去
形 頻繁的、慣常的
片 frequent visitor 常客

2700 liquor

[`lɪkə] ★★
名 酒精飲料、烈酒、溶劑
動 使喝醉、灌酒
片 be in liquor 喝醉

fighting!

Give it a shot 小試身手

1 He stood _____ against the sofa.

2 You can gain from book _____ and travel experience.

3 Nearly one hundred students crowded to the hall for the _____.

4 I wonder whether the hero in the old _____ exists.

5 Take your driver's _____ with you when you drive.

Answers: 1 leaning 2 learning 3 lecture 4 legend 5 license

467

MP3　短文 451　字彙 452

Essay

226

　　Elizabeth is the boss of a company that manufactures cosmetics. She leads[2701] a life of luxury in Australia. She lives in a luxurious 30-room villa, which is surrounded by magnificent[2702] scenery. She usually <u>wears</u> heavy <u>makeup</u>, including suntan lotion[2703], even in overcast[2704] weather.

　　She used to work at low-paying[2705] manual[2706] jobs when she was young, which created in her a strong desire to get rich and be called "madam" respectfully. Now, she is planning to create a whole new line of cosmetics made from insects because people enjoy nature so much. Although the logic[2707] behind her statements is often faulty, many customers are still loyal to her brand of cosmetics, which shows her remarkable[2708] achievement[2709]. A logical[2710] reason for this phenomenon might be that the customers' loyalty[2711] <u>results from</u> their good experience with the products.

⚠ wear makeup 化妝

⚠ result from 由於

中譯 *Translation*

　　伊莉莎白是一間化妝品公司的老闆。她在澳洲過著奢華的生活。她住在一間奢華、有著三十間房間的別墅之中，四周圍繞著壯麗的景色。即使是陰天，她也總是畫著大濃妝，並擦上防曬乳。

　　她以前年輕時從事低薪的勞動工作，這使她強烈渴望致富及被尊稱為「夫人」。現在，她打算推出全新系列的化妝品，這系列的產品萃取來自昆蟲的精華，以迎合人們對自然的愛好。雖然她的論述邏輯時常有些缺失，但是許多使用者依然對這個品牌的化妝品十分忠誠，足以顯現她的成就不凡。就這現象而言，一個合理的理由就是，消費者對產品使用經驗非常滿意，因而對這個品牌如此忠誠。

2701 lead

[lid] ★★★★★
- 動 過活、領導、領路、誘使、導致
- 名 領先地位、榜樣、線索

2702 magnificent

[mæg`nɪfəsənt] ★★★
- 形 壯麗的、豪華的、極好的、莊嚴的
- 同 splendid 壯麗的

2703 lotion

[`loʃən] ★★
- 名 乳液、化妝水、塗劑
- 同 cream 乳霜
- 片 suntan lotion 防曬乳

2704 overcast

[`ovəkæst] ★★
- 形 遮蔽的、多雲的、情緒低落的
- 動 變陰、使沮喪

2705 low-paying

[lo`peɪɪŋ] ★★
- 形 低酬的、低工資的
- 同 sweated 廉價勞工的
- 反 well-paying 待遇好

2706 manual

[`mænjʊəl] ★★★★
- 形 手工的、用手操作的
- 名 手冊、簡介
- 反 automatic 自動的

2707 logic

[`lɑdʒɪk] ★★★★
- 名 邏輯、推理、道理
- 衍 logicality 邏輯性

2708 remarkable

[rɪ`mɑrkəbḷ] ★★★
- 形 卓越的、值得注意的
- 同 noteworthy 顯著的
- 衍 remarkably 明顯地

2709 achievement

[ə`tʃivmənt] ★★★
- 名 成就、達成
- 片 a sense of achievement 成就感

2710 logical

[`lɑdʒɪkḷ] ★★★
- 形 合邏輯的、合理的
- 同 reasonable 合理的
- 反 illogical 不合邏輯的

2711 loyalty

[`lɔɪəltɪ] ★★★
- 名 忠誠、忠心
- 片 out of loyalty to 出於對…的忠誠

2712 principle

[`prɪnsəpḷ] ★★★★
- 名 原則、節操、構造
- 片 on principle 出於道德準則

---

fighting!

Give it a shot 小試身手

❶ She has always remained _____ to her political principles[2712].

❷ The lady appeared with a _____ fur coat.

❸ The _____ landscape took my breath away.

❹ It takes her ten minutes to put some _____ on.

❺ The _____ contains the instructions in detail.

Answers: ❶ loyal ❷ luxurious ❸ magnificent ❹ makeup ❺ manual

227

 MP3 短文 453 字彙 454

Essay

Although Garcia was a dwarf[2713], he ran the marathon in under three hours. He indeed performed at a high level but couldn't quite reach his maximum potential, even though he showed no mercy[2714] to other competitors. Garcia's father was a garage mechanic, who always worked in a messy[2715] workspace. His working environment was really terrible, but he enjoyed it just the same. Meanwhile Garcia worked for a microscope[2716] manufacturer.

One day, the microscope manufacturer informed[2717] Garcia that due to mechanical[2718] failures, the company's microscope sales had dropped dramatically. Therefore, measures needed to be taken to improve sales and reduce costs[2719]. Then he said nothing. He just scribbled[2720] a note on the margin of a piece of paper which read, "One day you'll have the maturity[2721] to understand making money is not easy. I hope you understand that I must lay[2722] you off because I don't have enough money to pay you." Then he gave the note to Garcia.

Afterwards, Garcia became much more serious about running and won numerous marathon[2723] competitions and earned a lot of money.

中譯 *Translation*

　　雖然加西亞只是個矮子，他卻能在三個小時內跑完馬拉松。他的確有高水準的表現，但卻未能完全發揮他的最大潛能，即使如此，他對其他的選手仍是毫不留情。加西亞的爸爸是個汽車修理廠的技工，工作的地方一直都亂七八糟的。雖然他的工作環境實在非常糟糕，但他卻甘之如飴。於此同時，加西亞為一名顯微鏡製造商工作。

　　有一天，這名顯微鏡商告訴加西亞因為機械故障的關係，公司的顯微鏡銷售業績大幅下滑。因此，必須採取措施以增加銷售、縮減成本。接著，就不說話了。他只在一張紙的空白處草草寫下：「有一天你會了解賺錢不是件容易的事。我希望你明白，因為我付不出薪水，所以必須解雇你。」

　　之後，加西亞更加認真的練習跑步，贏得許多馬拉松比賽，也賺了很多錢。

2713 dwarf

[dwɔrf] ★★★
名 矮子、侏儒
形 矮小的、發育不全的
動 變矮小、阻礙…生長

2714 mercy

[`mɜsɪ] ★★★★
名 憐憫、幸運、救濟
片 without mercy 毫不留情地

2715 messy

[`mɛsɪ] ★★
形 混亂的、骯髒的、麻煩的、棘手的
同 disordered 混亂的

2716 microscope

[`maɪkrəskop] ★★★
名 顯微鏡

2717 inform

[ɪn`fɔrm] ★★★★
動 通知、告知、告發
片 inform sb. of sth. 把某事通知某人

2718 mechanical

[mə`kænɪkl] ★★★
形 機械的、呆板的、技巧上的
同 automated 機械化的

2719 cost

[kɔst] ★★★★★
名 成本、費用、代價
動 花費、使喪失
片 at cost 按成本

2720 scribble

[`skrɪbl] ★★
動 潦草地書寫、亂畫
名 潦草筆跡、拙劣的作品
同 scrawl 潦草地寫

2721 maturity

[mə`tʃurətɪ] ★★
名 成熟、完善、支票到期
同 ripeness 成熟
反 immaturity 不成熟

2722 lay

[le] ★★★★★
動 使處於、放、擱、準備、產卵
片 lay off 解雇

2723 marathon

[`mærəθɑn] ★★
名 馬拉松賽跑、耐力比賽
形 馬拉松式的、持久的

2724 prime

[praɪm] ★★★★
形 最好的、最初的
名 最初、全盛時期、精華
動 做準備、事先給指導

fighting!

Give it a shot 小試身手

❶ Our company is the prime[2724] _____ of food in Taiwan.

❷ The candidate won by a narrow _____.

❸ The _____ of the capacity is 100 liters.

❹ The _____ problems must be solved instantly.

❺ My friend gave me a _____ gift before graduation.

Answers: ❶ manufacturer ❷ margin ❸ maximum ❹ mechanical ❺ memorial

228

Essay

I lead the Ministry of Agriculture; in other words, I am the Minister of Agriculture. I have felt miserable because I have reached the age for retirement. After my thirty-year effort, I believe I have gained a moderate[2725] degree of success. I have always been modest[2726] about my role in government and in preventing banks from making enormous profits from farmers' misfortunes[2727]. I was quite honored to learn that some of my coworkers in a monthly meeting decided to erect[2728] a monument to pay tribute[2729] to my accomplishments over the years.

However, please don't misunderstand me. I have no intention of misleading[2730] the public into believing that I have never incurred[2731] even mild[2732] criticism. I have. For example, I was criticized once because it was believed that I encouraged parents to feed their children minerals[2733] to keep them out of mischief[2734] for a while. However, that was just an Internet rumor. Someone who hated me made a fake video clip[2735] and posted it on YouTube. I didn't look into who he or she was; I just tried to do my best to make everyone believe me that it wasn't true.

中譯 *Translation*

我是農業部的領導人,也就是說,我是農業部部長。我一直覺得很不幸,因為我已經到了退休的年紀了。經過三十年的努力,我算是小有成就。無論是在政府公務上,或者是在竭力避免銀行藉著農民的苦難獲取暴利的行動上,我都一直扮演著謙虛的角色。一些同事在一次的月會中,決定樹立一座紀念碑,為我的貢獻致上敬意。

然而,絕對不要誤會我。我並不想讓大眾誤以為,我從來沒招致任何批評。事實上,我的確被批評過。像是有一次,我遭到批評的原因是大家誤以為我鼓勵父母餵食小孩礦物質,好讓他們不會調皮搗蛋。然而,那只是一個網路謠言,有個討厭我的人製作了一段扭曲事實的影片,公佈在 Youtube 網站上。我並沒有追究他是誰,我只是試著竭盡所能,讓大家相信我而已。

2725 moderate

[`mɑdərɪt] ★★★★
形 中等的、溫和的
動 減輕、變溫和、主持
同 medium 適中的

2726 modest

[`mɑdɪst] ★★★★
形 謙虛的、穩重的
同 humble 謙恭的
反 arrogant 自大的

2727 misfortune

[mɪs`fɔrtʃən] ★★
名 不幸、災難、惡運
同 distress 不幸
反 blessing 祝福、幸事

2728 erect

[ɪ`rɛkt] ★★★★
動 建立、設立、安裝
形 垂直的、豎起的
衍 erector 建造者

2729 tribute

[`trɪbjut] ★★★
名 敬意、進貢、貢獻
片 pay tribute to 對…表示敬意或讚賞

2730 mislead

[mɪs`lid] ★★★
動 使產生錯誤想法、欺騙
片 mislead sb. into + ving 欺騙某人做某事

2731 incur

[ɪn`kɝ] ★★★★
動 招致、帶來
片 incur sb's anger 惹某人生氣

2732 mild

[maɪld] ★★★★
形 溫和的、不濃烈的
片 mild weather 天氣溫和
衍 milden 使溫和

2733 mineral

[`mɪnərəl] ★★★
名 礦物質、(英)礦泉水
形 礦物的、礦質的
衍 mine 礦、礦坑

2734 mischief

[`mɪstʃɪf] ★★
名 頑皮、惡作劇、禍根
片 make mischief 挑撥離間

2735 clip

[klɪp] ★★★★
名 剪下來的東西、修剪
動 剪短、剪輯、削減
片 clip out of 從…剪下

2736 appoint

[ə`pɔɪnt] ★★★★
動 指派、任命、約定
片 appoint sb. to 任命某人為

---

 fighting!

Give it a shot 小試身手

1 They argued that the _____ wage should be raised.

2 He was appointed[2736] to _____ of Finance.

3 William _____ me to the wrong way.

4 The thief's face was recorded by the _____.

5 I anticipated the _____ assembly with my coworkers very much.

229

MP3

短文 457

字彙 458

Essay

The police were investigating[2737] the mysterious death of several children at the hospital. The prime suspect was a strange man named George who worked as a maintenance[2738] man at the hospital. However, by the time the police had enough evidence to charge George, he had vanished.

"The police will never catch me now," George murmured[2739] to himself. After becoming a suspect in the murders, he hid in a mountainous region[2740] and shaved off his moustache[2741]. He was now motivated[2742] solely[2743] by the thought of living a solitary[2744] life without being arrested. His time was mostly spent mowing[2745] the lawns of people living near his hideout to earn enough money to buy food and other supplies. Because George had changed his appearance and now called himself Norman, none of his neighbors had any idea he was a child killer. Besides, people who lived in that area were very trusting and never even locked their doors at night because the area was so safe. George thought about stealing money from his trusting neighbors, but he knew if he got caught the police would find out where his hideout was, so he never did steal from them. Instead, he lived a boring life and slowly went crazy from his isolated existence.

中譯 *Translation*

　　警方正在調查在醫院裡發生的一樁神秘的兒童死亡案件。主嫌為一名叫做喬治的奇怪男子，他是醫院裡的維修人員。然而，在警方握有足夠證據起訴喬治時，他消失了。

　　「警察現在絕對抓不到我！」喬治自言自語。在成為謀殺案的嫌疑犯後，他藏身於山區，同時也把鬍子刮了。他現在只受「過著逍遙法外的隱居生活」的信念所驅使。他大部分的時間都在替藏身處附近的居民割草，以賺取足夠的生活費購買食物和其他生活用品。由於喬治改變了他的外貌，且自稱是諾曼，因此，他的鄰居都沒認出他就是謀殺案的兇手。除此之外，因為這個地方治安很好，這裡的人們都十分相信彼此，即使到了晚上也不曾鎖門。喬治曾經想過要偷鄰居的錢，但他知道，如果被逮到，警察就會發現他的藏身之處，所以他並沒有真的去偷錢。相反地，他現在過著無趣的生活，孤立、隔絕的生活使他逐漸變得古怪、瘋狂。

2737 investigate

[ɪnˋvɛstəget] ★★★
- 動 調查、研究
- 片 investigate into sth. 調查某事

2738 maintenance

[ˋmentənəns] ★★★★
- 名 維修、保持、生活費
- 同 preservation 保持
- 反 abandonment 放棄

2739 murmur

[ˋmɝmɚ] ★★★
- 動 小聲説話、咕噥
- 名 低聲抱怨、潺潺聲
- 片 murmur to 低聲説

2740 region

[ˋridʒən] ★★★★
- 名 地區、領域、部位
- 片 in the region of 在…部位、大約

2741 moustache

[məsˋtæʃ] ★★
- 名 八字鬍
- 同 beard 山羊鬍

2742 motivate

[ˋmotəvet] ★★★
- 動 為…的動機、激發
- 同 stimulate 刺激
- 衍 motivated 積極的

2743 solely

[ˋsollɪ] ★★★
- 副 唯一地、僅僅、完全
- 同 entirely 完全地
- 衍 sole 專用的

2744 solitary

[ˋsɑlətɛrɪ] ★★★
- 形 隱居的、單獨的
- 名 隱士、單獨監禁
- 衍 solitude 隱居、孤獨

2745 mow

[mo] ★★★
- 動 割草
- 名 乾草堆
- 片 mow down 摧毀

2746 feminine

[ˋfɛmənɪn] ★★★
- 形 女性的、嬌柔的
- 名 女性、陰性
- 反 masculine 男性的

2747 belongings

[bəˋlɔŋɪŋz] ★★
- 名 攜帶物品、財產、家眷
- 同 possession 所有物
- 衍 belong 屬於

2748 unsatisfied

[ʌnˋsætɪsfaɪd] ★★★
- 形 不滿意的、未得到滿足的
- 同 discontented 不滿的

Fighting!

Give it a shot 小試身手

1. Jewelry and lace are _____ feminine[2746] belongings[2747].
2. I wonder the _____ of your cheat.
3. We have to _____ the lawn twice a week.
4. When it rains, the ground becomes very _____.
5. She _____ as if she was unsatisfied[2748].

Answers: 1. mostly 2. motivation 3. mow 4. muddy 5. murmured

230

MP3

Nowadays, numerous parents send their children to nurseries[2749] when at work. In spite of the fact that some people fear that children may feel neglected[2750] or even have nightmares if not taken care of by their parents, working parents have no choice. Nevertheless, some parents might think of that as nonsense, and they have no objections[2751] to leaving their children to someone else while they go to work. They probably don't want to leave their children for so long each day, but they do it in order to earn enough money so the family can all have a good life. If the salary of merely[2752] the husband or wife is not enough, both of them have to earn a living.

A priest who lives in obedience[2753] to the religious teachings said rearing[2754] an obedient child is like running a power plant using nuclear energy. In the beginning, everything works well; however, failing to negotiate with the needy[2755] who cannot afford the fees might result in residents having to sleep in tents made of nylon[2756] under the moonlight. A plant needs continuous[2757] energy, while a child needs continuous care. Parents should not be nearsighted[2758], and should avoid using nouns like "busyness" as an excuse, the priest[2759] believes.

中譯 *Translation*

現今有許多父母都會在工作時把孩子送去托兒所。儘管有些人擔心孩子會覺得被忽略，甚至因此作惡夢，他們也別無選擇。然而，有些父母會覺得那是胡說八道，而且也不反對將孩子托給他人去工作。也許有些父母並不想離開孩子那麼久，但他們還是必須努力賺錢，好讓全家人過上好日子。如果光靠其中一人的薪水無法度日，那夫妻兩人都需要工作。

有個遵從宗教教義的牧師表示，培養一個聽話的孩子，就像管理一座核能發電廠。一開始，一切都很順利，然而，若和無法負擔費用的窮人協商失敗的話，居民都得睡在月光下的尼龍帳蓬裡了。一座工廠需要源源不絕的能量，而孩子則需要不斷的關懷。父母不應該短視近利，而且應該避免用「忙」這樣的字眼作為藉口。

nursery
[`nɝsərɪ] ★★★
名 托兒所、溫床、苗圃、養魚場
衍 nurserymaid 保母

neglected
[nɪg`lɛktɪd] ★★
名 忽視的、疏忽的
同 unheeded 被忽視的
衍 neglect 忽視

objection
[əb`dʒɛkʃən] ★★★
名 反對、缺點、障礙
片 raise an objection 提出反對意見

merely
[`mɪrlɪ] ★★★★
副 只是、僅僅、不過
同 only 僅僅
衍 mere 僅僅

obedience
[ə`bidjəns] ★★
名 順從、服從、管轄
同 compliance 順從
片 in obedience to 服從

rear
[rɪr] ★★★★
動 撫養、培植、豎立
名 後面、背部、臀部
形 後面的、背後的

needy
[`nidɪ] ★★
形 貧窮的
同 poor 貧窮的
片 the needy 窮人

nylon
[`naɪlɑn] ★★★
名 尼龍、尼龍襪

continuous
[kən`tɪnjuəs] ★★★
形 連續的、不斷的
同 constant 持續的
衍 continuity 連貫性

nearsighted
[`nɪr`saɪtɪd] ★★
形 短視的、近視的
同 myopic 近視的
反 farsighted 有遠見的

priest
[prist] ★★★★
名 牧師、神職人員
動 成為神職人員
同 clergyman 神職人員

overuse
[`ovə`juz] ★★
名 過度使用
動 使用過度

Fighting!

Give it a shot 小試身手

1 I got _____ because of overuse[2760] of eyes.

2 The deserted garden was in a state of total _____.

3 Vicky woke up with cold sweat because of _____.

4 Some words have both the _____ and the adjective attribute.

5 _____ to the supervisors is very important in the army.

Answers: 1 nearsighted 2 neglect 3 nightmare 4 noun 5 Obedience

231

Essay

It's hard to give an objective[2761] opinion about the former US president, who likes the Berlin Symphony Orchestra and goes to the opera regularly. His greatest achievement was that he successfully launched a UN rescue operation. However, he seems to have caused the occasional[2762] offense[2763] when he talked in public. For example, his remarks[2764] were a greatly offensive[2765] when it came to the healthcare[2766] budget; therefore, it caused Congress to continuingly oppose his ideas.

Maybe the former president was not good at making remarks, but he really did accomplish something. The most important achievement during his term was the first successful launch of the space[2767] shuttle[2768]. If he could have trained himself not to offend[2769] people, there might have been fewer obstacles when he occupied the Oval[2770] Office. Though serving in the highest occupation in the world, he spent some time under close observation in hospital. Further[2771] information about the controversial president can be obtained from his latest book.

中譯 *Translation*

　　前美國總統很喜歡柏林交響樂團，他也有定期去看歌劇的習慣。要給這位前總統一個客觀的評論有點困難。他最大的成就就是成功地開辦了聯合國救援計劃。然而，他似乎會在公開談話的場合中，發表唐突的言論。例如，他在提及健保預算的時候言論非常不得體，也使得國會一再否決他的意見。

　　雖然總統也許不擅言辭，但是他的確多少有點貢獻。他任期內最重要的成就，是成功地發射第一個太空梭。如果他的嘴上功夫可以訓練到不再冒犯別人，那麼他佔領白宮之路就會遇到少一點障礙。雖然坐在世界最高的職位上，但他也曾被留院觀察。更多關於這位話題總統的資訊，可以在他最近的著作中尋得。

2761 objective

[əb`dʒɛktɪv] ★★★★
- 形 客觀的、無偏見的
- 名 目的、出擊目標
- 反 subjective 主觀的

2762 occasional

[ə`keʒənl] ★★★
- 形 特殊場合的、偶而的、臨時的
- 反 customary 慣常的

2763 offense

[ə`fɛns] ★★★
- 名 冒犯行為、違例、進攻
- 反 defense 防禦
- 衍 offend 冒犯

2764 remark

[rɪ`mɑrk] ★★★★
- 名 言辭、談論、注意
- 動 評論、注意、察覺
- 片 remark on 談論⋯

2765 offensive

[ə`fɛnsɪv] ★★★
- 形 冒犯的、令人作嘔的、進攻的
- 名 進攻、攻勢

2766 healthcare

[`hɛlθkɛr] ★★
- 名 醫療保健、保健事業

2767 space

[spes] ★★★★★
- 名 太空、空間、場所
- 動 留隔間、隔開
- 片 make space 騰出空間

2768 shuttle

[`ʃʌtl̩] ★★★
- 名 太空梭、梭子、短程穿梭運行
- 動 短程穿梭往返

2769 offend

[ə`fɛnd] ★★★
- 動 冒犯、觸怒、違反
- 反 appease 平息
- 片 offend against 違反

2770 oval

[`ovl̩] ★★★
- 形 卵形的、橢圓形的
- 片 Oval Office (美國白宮的)總統辦公室

2771 further

[`fɝðɚ] ★★★★★
- 形 進一步的、更遠的
- 副 進一步地、再者
- 動 促進、推動

2772 grind

[graɪnd] ★★★★★
- 動 磨碎、壓榨、苦學
- 名 研磨、摩擦聲、苦學
- 片 grind away 輾成粉末

fighting!

Give it a shot 小試身手

1 We should be more _____ about this issue.

2 The _____ did not prevent her from keeping on.

3 His and his wife's _____ are both public servants.

4 The boy's rude words _____ his mother.

5 The _____ of the machine is to grind[2772] the coffee beans.

MP3　短文 463　字彙 464

Essay

232

I had been in partnership[2773] with Kathy for five years. She took a very passive[2774] role in the business relationship. My father expected[2775] perfection from our business and sometimes was quite <u>critical of</u> me. Recently, some peculiar[2776] things were going on. The first was that a board member[2777] with a forty percent stake[2778] gave up his permanent[2779] position on the board of directors. It took a great deal of persuasion[2780] from him to get us to accept his resignation. The second was that Kathy started to wear the perfume I gave her as a birthday present, and she invited me to a pasta restaurant near a beach. The beach was covered with pebbles[2781]. After the dinner, she invited me for a ride in her car. As soon as she put her foot on the accelerator[2782], she said, "Please read this letter, and then you will understand why I invited you out for dinner tonight." So I started to read carefully, and I found that she no longer wanted to be my business partner because she said that she couldn't stop thinking about me. Now, she is my domestic partner - my wife.

ⓘ critical of 對…吹毛求疵

中譯 *Translation*

　　我已經和凱西合夥五年了。她在這段關係中一直處於非常被動的角色。我爸爸對我們的事業非常要求完美，有時候還會對我吹毛求疵。近來，有些奇怪的事發生了。首先是一位持有百分之四十股份的董事會成員，放棄了他在董事會的永久職位。他花了很大的功夫才說服我們接受他離職的事實。第二件事就是凱西開始擦我之前買給她的香水，並邀請我去海灘附近的一間義大利麵餐廳用餐。海灘覆滿了礫石。飯後，她提議要載我回家。她一把腳放上油門踏板時便說：「看了這封信你就會明白為什麼今晚會邀你出來吃飯。」所以我開始仔細讀信。我明白她不想再當我的事業夥伴了，因為她的心有一大部分都被我佔據。現在，她成了我的「家庭夥伴」——我的妻子。

2773 partnership

[`pɑrtnəʃɪp] ★★
名 合夥關係、合資公司
片 enter into partnership with 與…合夥

2774 passive

[`pæsɪv] ★★★
形 被動的、消極的、順從的
同 submissive 順從的

2775 expect

[ɪk`spɛkt] ★★★★★
動 要求、期待、認為
片 expect sth. of sb. 期待某人會做某事

2776 peculiar

[pɪ`kjuljə] ★★★
形 奇怪的、獨特的
名 特權
片 peculiar to 為…特有的

2777 member

[`mɛmbə] ★★★★★
名 會員、成員、一部分
片 full member 正式成員
衍 nonmember 非會員

2778 stake

[stek] ★★★★
名 股份、樁、風險
動 拿…冒險、以樁支撐
片 stake out 監視

2779 permanent

[`pɜmənənt] ★★★★
形 永久的、固定性的
同 eternal 永久的
反 temporary 暫時的

2780 persuasion

[pə`sweʒən] ★★
名 說服、勸說、信念
片 powers of persuasion 說服的技巧

2781 pebble

[`pɛbḷ] ★★★
名 小卵石、礫石
動 用卵石鋪走道

2782 accelerator

[æk`sɛlə͵retə] ★★
名 加速裝置、油門
衍 accelerate 使加速

2783 scheme

[skim] ★★★★
名 計畫、結構、陰謀
動 策畫、擬訂計畫、密謀
片 scheme for 陰謀奪取

2784 pave

[pev] ★★★★
動 鋪設、密布、使容易
片 pave the way for 為…做好準備

fighting!

Give it a shot 小試身手

1 I'd like to be excused from further _____ in this scheme[2783].

2 The "healthy road" was paved[2784] with _____.

3 The fish has a _____ taste. You really think it is all right?

4 Eighty _____ of the students pass the exam.

5 The _____ was made in France and exported to other countries.

Answers: 1 participation 2 pebbles 3 peculiar 4 percent 5 perfume

MP3   短文 465   字彙 466

233

Essay

Trevor, who is a pianist and who does fashion photography[2785] for Vogue Magazine, is very passionate[2786] about music. However, he has a pessimistic[2787] view of life. This is partly[2788] because he studied philosophy at university, and his thinking was deeply influenced by Greek philosophers. The other reason is that he always has odd thoughts.

He often argues philosophical questions with others. He thinks that since homelessness[2789] is a common phenomenon, there is nothing really wrong for a homeless person to become a pickpocket[2790] in order to survive, as long as he only steals from rich people. After all, he reasons, if a man has difficulty surviving, he must try everything he can to keep on living. Moreover, he has even suggested that adults who cannot satisfy their physical and emotional[2791] needs become pirates. He said, "Instead of being a physician or a pioneer[2792] in the field of research, I encourage people to explore the world. Nowadays, many people who have special training in physics, physicists, fail to appreciate nature. We need to go back to being naive[2793] and explore the world by ourselves."

中譯 *Translation*

特雷弗是一個鋼琴家，也為 Vogue 雜誌拍時尚照片，他他非常熱愛音樂。然而，他的人生態度非常悲觀。一部分的原因是他大學的時候修習哲學，他的思想深受希臘哲學家的影響。另一個原因則是因為他總是存有奇怪的想法。

他總是和其他人辯論哲學問題。他認為無家可歸是個非常普及的現象，因此，他覺得無家可歸的人為了生存而去當扒手並沒有什麼不對，前提是他們只偷有錢人的東西。他又分析道，畢竟，一個人若有生存上的困難，那麼他(她)一定得想盡辦法活下去。此外，他甚至建議無法滿足生理和情感需求的人去當海盜。他說：「與其當醫生或是研究先驅，我更鼓勵人們去探索這個世界。現今，有許多受過物理學專門訓練的人，也就是物理學家們，不懂得欣賞自然之美。我們應該回到純真的狀態，主動去探索這個世界。」

2785 photography
[fə`tɑgrəfɪ] ★★
名 照相術、攝影術
衍 photographer 攝影師

2786 passionate
[`pæʃənɪt] ★★★
形 熱情的、易怒的
同 ardent 熱切的

2787 pessimistic
[pɛsə`mɪstɪk] ★★★
形 悲觀的、悲觀主義的
片 be pessimistic about 對…感到悲觀

2788 partly
[`pɑrtlɪ] ★★★
副 在一定程度上、部分地
反 wholly 完全地

2789 homelessness
[`homlɪsnɪs] ★★
名 無家可歸
衍 homeless 無家的

2790 pickpocket
[`pɪkpɑkɪt] ★★
名 扒手
同 thief 小偷

2791 emotional
[ɪ`moʃənl] ★★★
形 感情的、激起情感的
同 emotive 表現感情的
反 cold 冷酷的

2792 pioneer
[paɪə`nɪr] ★★★★
名 先驅者、拓荒者
動 當先驅、開闢、倡導
片 pioneer in …的先鋒

2793 naive
[nɑ`iv] ★★★
形 天真的、輕信的
反 sophisticated 世故的
衍 naivety 天真

2794 insistence
[ɪn`sɪstəns] ★★★
名 堅持、竭力主張
片 at sb's insistence 由於某人的堅持

2795 recent
[`risṇt] ★★★★★
形 最近的、近代的
同 up-to-date 最新的
衍 recently 最近

2796 meditate
[`mɛdətet] ★★
動 深思熟慮、打算、計畫
片 meditate on 沉思
衍 meditation 沉思、冥想

Fighting! Give it a shot 小試身手

1 The reasons she proposed were _____, so I was convinced.
2 Insistence2794 of keeping single is not just a recent2795 _____.
3 He always meditates2796 on _____ questions.
4 The _____ told me not to stay up.
5 The _____ hid in the crowd and stole women's purses.

Answers: 1 persuasive 2 phenomenon 3 philosophical 4 physician 5 pickpocket

234

MP3   短文 467 字彙 468

Essay

The house has been in the family's possession[2797] since the 1500s. People living here always have a plentiful[2798] supply of food and a porter[2799] ready to carry things for the family members all the time. The family has also hired various workers who possess useful skills. Take me as an example; my job is polishing the silver accessories and the furniture.

Recently, the popularity of the Internet has soared[2800], and our community was portrayed in a negative way on some web forums. <u>Rumor has it that</u> we are plotting to bomb the UN headquarters at 5 p.m. tomorrow night, plant poisonous[2801] mushrooms, and create air pollution. I do not respond to these accusations[2802], since I know people <u>tend to</u> have a negative attitude towards the rich. Reading newspapers is preferable[2803] to surfing[2704] the Internet because newspapers contain accurate information and fair comment. The accuracy[2805] of the Internet is lower than I originally believed it was, as proven by the unfounded[2806] rumors against our community.

(!) rumor has it that 謠傳
(!) tend to 往往、趨向

中譯 *Translation*

　　這間房子從16世紀起就屬於這個家族。住在這裡的人總是有著非常豐富的食物來源，還有一個搬運工人隨時待命。他們還雇用不同技能的工人。舉我自己為例，我的工作是把銀製飾品和家具擦亮。

　　近來，網際網路的普及性驟升，我們的社區在網路論壇上收到負面評價。謠言指出我們密謀在明天下午五點炸掉聯合國總部，種植有毒的菇類，並且製造空氣汙染。我並沒有回應他們的指控，因為我知道社會大眾易有仇富情結。閱讀報紙是比上網更好的選擇，因為報紙內容有更精確的資訊和公正的評論。網路資訊的準確性比我原先預期的低，沒有事實根據地造謠詆毀我們的社區便是最明顯的例證。

2797 **possession**

[pə`zɛʃən] ★★★★

名 擁有、財產、領地、自制、著魔

衍 possess 擁有、掌握

 2798 **plentiful**

[`plɛntɪfəl] ★★

形 豐富的、充足的

同 ample 豐富的

反 scarce 缺乏的

 2799 **porter**

[`portɚ] ★★★

名 搬運工人、雜物工

同 redcap 行李搬運工

2800 **soar**

[sor] ★★★★

動 猛增、高飛、升騰

名 高飛、高漲、

片 sour up 高飛

 2801 **poisonous**

[`pɔɪznəs] ★★

形 有害的、有毒的、惡毒的、不愉快的

同 toxic 有毒的

 2802 **accusation**

[͵ækjə`zeʃən] ★★

名 指控、指責、控告

片 be under an accusation 被控告

 2803 **preferable**

[`prɛfərəbl] ★★★

形 更合意的、更好的

片 be preferable to +ving 比…更好

2804 **surf**

[sɝf] ★★★

動 上網瀏覽、衝浪運動

名 碎浪、浪花

片 go surfing 衝浪

 2805 **accuracy**

[`ækjərəsɪ] ★★★

名 正確性、準確性

同 exactitude 正確性

反 inaccuracy 不正確

 2806 **unfounded**

[ʌn`faundɪd] ★

形 沒有事實根據的、未建立的、虛幻的

同 groundless 無根據的

 2807 **scorpion**

[`skɔrpɪən] ★

名 蠍子、天蠍座的人

衍 Scorpio 天蠍座

2808 **jointed**

[`dʒɔɪntɪd] ★★

形 有節的、有接縫的、有關節的

衍 joint 關節、接縫

 Fighting!

Give it a shot 小試身手

① The book is well organized in _____ of plots.

② Media is the _____ form of medium.

③ A scorpion[2807] has a _____ sting in its long jointed[2808] tail.

④ The _____ of the river became severe this year.

⑤ The police _____ that the bandit would hide himself in the woods.

Answers: ① terms ② plural ③ poisonous ④ pollution ⑤ predicted

235

Essay

MP3 | 短文 469 | 字彙 470

Dr. Evans thanked Mary for coming to make the presentations[2809] during her pregnancy[2810]. For a pregnant woman to make an excellent presentation is not easy. However, Mary has been working for the preservation[2811] of the environment for a long time, and it has become her job to encourage people to preserve[2812] our existing[2813] woodlands[2814]. Mary said," We must teach people that prevention[2815] is better than cure." "Human beings are the prime cause of pollution. We no longer live in a primitive society, and nobody has the privilege to harm our environment."

However, how can we save our earth? First, one needs to reduce the production of his or her daily carbon[2816] emissions[2817]. It takes determination to lead a sustainable[2818] life. One can argue over the best way to reduce carbon emissions, but the main thing is to take positive, concrete action[2819] now in order to protect the environment.

中譯 *Translation*

　　埃文斯博士很感謝瑪麗在懷孕期間還願意過來發表演說。對一個懷孕婦女來說，完成精彩的演說不是一件容易的事。不過，瑪麗從事環境保護的工作已經有很長一段時間了，所以，呼籲民眾保護現存林地對她來說，不過是一件例行公事罷了。瑪麗說：「我們必須教導民眾預防勝於治療的觀念。」「人類是環境污染的根本禍源，我們已經不是生活在原始社會了，沒有人有權力去傷害我們的環境。」

　　然而，我們要如何拯救地球呢？首先，我們需要降低每日的碳排放量。展開永續發展生活所需要決心。減少碳排放量的最佳方式因人而異，最重要的是，採取積極、明確的行動來保護環境。

2809 presentation

[prɪzɛn`teʃən] ★★★★
名 報告、遞交、演出、介紹、授予
衍 present 提出、介紹

2810 pregnancy

[`prɛgnənsɪ] ★★
名 懷孕、豐富、意義深長
片 take pregnancy tests 驗孕

2811 preservation

[prɛzəˇveʃən] ★★
名 保護、維持、防腐
同 conservation 保存
衍 preservative 防腐劑

2812 preserve

[prɪ`zɝv] ★★★★
動 保護、保存、防腐
名 蜜餞、保護區、禁獵區
片 preserve from 防止

2813 existing

[ɪg`zɪstɪŋ] ★★
形 現存的、現行的
衍 existence 存在、生存

2814 woodland

[`wʊdlænd] ★
名 森林地帶、林地

2815 prevention

[prɪ`vɛnʃən] ★★★
名 預防、防止、妨礙
俚 Prevention is better than cure. 防患未然

2816 carbon

[`kɑrbən] ★★★★
名 碳、複寫紙
衍 carbohydrate 碳水化合物

2817 emission

[ɪ`mɪʃən] ★★★
名 排放物、散發、發行
衍 emissive 放射性的

2818 sustainable

[sə`stenəbl] ★★
形 能維持的、能承受的、支撐得住的
同 maintainable 可維持的

2819 action

[`ækʃən] ★★★★★
名 行為、作用、功能
反 inaction 無為
片 take action 採取行動

2820 series

[`sɪriz] ★★★★★
名 系列、連續、叢書
同 succession 連續
片 a series of 一連串的

Fighting!

Give it a shot 小試身手

❶ Could you leave me alone and give me some _____?

❷ The police regarded him as the _____ suspect.

❸ Work is _____ slowly.

❹ We will do everything to _____ peace.

❺ It needs a series[2820] of _____ to apply for a visa.

Answers: ❶ privacy ❷ prime ❸ proceeding ❹ preserve ❺ procedures

236

Essay

 MP3 短文 471 字彙 472

"It is essential[2821] to get good professional advice when <u>suffering from</u> psychological problems," said a prominent Russian psychologist[2822], Victor Chekhov. As a renowned professor of psychology, Chekhov also claimed that opening up a highly[2823] profitable[2824] business is a promising[2825] start to one's life. However, the proverb[2826], "When poverty comes in the door, love flies out of the window," is not necessarily[2827] true. The prosperity[2828] of a business does not automatically guarantee that its owner will be happy. Then when can you announce your success[2829]? Chekhow answered, "An excellent income from sales is not the correct determination of success, neither is being able to afford expensive food or the finest wine. True success <u>lies in</u> the fact that not a single employee[2830] wants to <u>stage a strike</u> outside your company." In other words, true success means being a good businessman and that workers in your company respect you from the bottom of their hearts.

⚠ suffer from 遭受…之苦

⚠ lie in 在於

⚠ stage a strike 發起罷工

中譯 *Translation*

　　一位著名的俄國心理學家,維克多契科夫說:「當受精神問題所苦時,尋求專業的建議非常重要的。」身為一個著名的心理學教授,契科夫也主張開創一個高獲利的事業是前途光明的開始。然而,「貧窮進門來,愛情飛窗外」這句諺語也不盡然是對的。事業成功並不保證生活快樂。那麼,何時才能發表成功宣言呢?契科夫回答:「真正的成功不是生意好、獲利高,也不是負擔得起昂貴的食物或上好的酒。真正的成功,在於沒有任何一個員工想在公司門外發起罷工。」換句話說,真正的成功代表的是成為一個好的企業家,公司裡的每一位員工都發自內心的尊敬你。

2821 essential
[ɪˋsɛnʃəl] ★★★★
形 必要的、不可或缺的、實質的、精華的
同 vital 不可少的

2822 psychologist
[saɪˋkɑlədʒɪst] ★★
名 心理學家
衍 psychology 心理學

2823 highly
[ˋhaɪlɪ] ★★★★★
副 非常、很、高額地
同 very 非常
片 think highly of 評價高

2824 profitable
[ˋprɑfɪtəbļ] ★★★
形 有利的、有益的、有利可圖的
反 unprofitable 無益的

2825 promising
[ˋprɑmɪsɪŋ] ★★
形 有前途的、有希望的、大有可為的
反 unpromising 沒出息的

2826 proverb
[ˋprɑvəb] ★★★
名 諺語、格言、眾所周知的人或事
同 saying 諺語、格言

2827 necessarily
[ˋnɛsəsɛrɪlɪ] ★★★
副 必定、必要地
同 certainly 必定
衍 necessary 必要的

2828 prosperity
[prɑsˋpɛrətɪ] ★★★
名 興盛、繁榮、成功
衍 prosperous 繁榮的

2829 success
[səkˋsɛs] ★★★★★
名 成功、成就
片 success in 在…方面取得成功

2830 employee
[ɛmplɔɪˋi] ★★★★
名 雇員、雇工
同 worker 工作者
反 employer 雇主

2831 source
[sors] ★★★★★
名 來源、源頭、提供消息、出處
動 從…購得

2832 deal
[dil] ★★★★★
名 交易、大量、發牌
動 交易、處理、分配
片 fair deal 公平交易

Give it a shot 小試身手

1. Nancy is a _____ dancer who has danced for ten years.
2. Fish is one of the major source[2831] of _____.
3. He accepted the deal[2832] without any _____.
4. Your English _____ is excellent.
5. My mother _____ me to hurry up.

Answers: 1 professional 2 protein 3 protest 4 pronunciation 5 prompted

489

237

Essay

John is a clinical[2833] psychologist whose first book was published in 1965. Since then, he has become an <u>expert in</u> the field of developmental[2834] psychology, and he has received much publicity[2835] over the last few years. Now he is in England as part of an international book tour, following the recent publication[2836] of his new book. The book publishers[2837] in the UK all gave him a warm reception[2838].

One night, as he slept on a bed with a quilt[2839], he had a strange dream. He dreamed of a rebel leader <u>in a rage</u>, quaking[2840] with fury[2841]. The rebel's life was spent in the pursuit[2842] of pleasure, and he'd never done anything serious. The following day, in an interview with a British newspaper, John was quoted as saying, "Although I know not everybody believes that dreams foretell[2843] the future, I really think my dream last night means I will become a rebel someday."

ⓘ expert in …領域的專家

ⓘ in a rage 怒氣沖沖

中譯 *Translation*

約翰是一位臨床心理學家，他的第一本著作於1965年出版，從此之後，他便成為發展心理學領域的專家，並在幾年間引起大眾廣泛的關注。他現在人在英國為他的新書發表進行國際巡迴宣傳，英國的出版商都熱烈地接待他。

夜裡，他蓋著被子躺在床上，做了一個奇怪的夢。他夢見一位怒氣沖沖的反叛份子的領袖，十分憤怒地抖動著。那個反叛份子一生都在尋歡作樂、不務正業。隔天，英國報章媒體訪談約翰時，約翰說：「我知道不是每個人都相信夢能預知未來，但我認為我昨晚的夢是在預示我將成為一名反叛分子。」

2833 clinical

[`klɪnɪkl] ★★
- 形 臨床的、診所的、科學的、客觀的
- 衍 clinician 臨床醫生

2834 developmental

[dɪvɛləp`mɛntl] ★★
- 形 發展的、開發的、啟發的
- 衍 developing 開發中的

2835 publicity

[pʌb`lɪsətɪ] ★★
- 名 名聲、宣傳、公開場合
- 片 seek publicity 一心想出風頭

2836 publication

[pʌblɪ`keʃən] ★★★
- 名 出版、發行、刊物
- 片 date of publication 出版日期

2837 publisher

[`pʌblɪʃə] ★★
- 名 出版者、出版商、發行公司、發行人
- 衍 publish 出版、發行

2838 reception

[rɪ`sɛpʃən] ★★★
- 名 歡迎會、接待、接收
- 片 reception desk 接待處
- 衍 receive 接到、接待

2839 quilt

[kwɪlt] ★★★
- 名 被子、被褥
- 動 縫被子、拼湊
- 片 coverlet 床罩

2840 quake

[kwek] ★★
- 動 顫抖、哆嗦、搖晃
- 名 顫抖、地震、搖晃
- 同 shake 震動

2841 fury

[`fjʊrɪ] ★★★★
- 名 暴怒、猛烈
- 片 like fury 飛快、猛烈
- 衍 furious 狂怒的

2842 pursuit

[pɚ`sut] ★★★
- 名 追求、追蹤、繼續進行、消遣
- 片 in pursuit of 追求

2843 foretell

[for`tɛl] ★★
- 動 預言、預示
- 同 predict 預言

2844 goal

[gol] ★★★★★
- 名 目標、球門、得分數
- 動 射門得分
- 片 keep goal 當守門員

 Fighting!

Give it a shot 小試身手

1. I cannot _____ the dream I had last night.
2. The first edition of his book was _____ in 1999.
3. We must set _____ goals[2844].
4. I majored in _____ when I was in college.
5. He stared at me with _____.

Answers: 1 recall 2 published 3 realistic 4 Psychology 5 rage

238

 MP3 短文 475 字彙 476

Essay

Annie's only recreation[2845] is cooking. She makes the best tomato[2846] soup that anyone has ever tasted. She has never taken any cooking lessons, yet[2847] she knows that <u>practice</u>[2848] <u>makes perfect</u>. She experiments all the time with different ingredients to find the best flavors for her soups and other creations[2849]. She makes other types of soup, but she <u>prefers to</u> make tomato soup. There is a general belief that a tomato soup will make people healthy[2850] and feel refreshed. Therefore, many mothers have a recipe for tomato soup, which some people think can also <u>relieve pain</u>[2851]. These days, most mothers remember that empty[2852] tomato cans[2853] can be recycled. However, Annie's refusal to recycle is a reflection of the older generation. I hope that one day Annie and people like her will realize[2854] the true value of recycling.

> ⓘ practice makes perfect 熟能生巧
> ⓘ prefer to 較喜歡、寧願
> ⓘ relieve pain 減緩疼痛

中譯 *Translation*

　　安妮唯一的娛樂就是烹飪。她做的番茄湯無人能及。她從沒上過正規的烹飪課程，但她相信熟能生巧。她總是發揮實驗精神並多方嘗試不同食材，試圖為她製作的湯品及其他餐點找出最佳風味。她會做各式各樣的湯品，但番茄湯還是她的最愛。我們都知道，番茄湯不但有益健康，還能讓人感到神清氣爽。因此，媽媽們大都有番茄湯的食譜。有些人甚至認為番茄湯能減緩疼痛。近來，大部分的媽媽都記得回收用完的番茄罐頭。然而，安妮拒絕做回收的行為正好反映出傳統一代的觀念。我希望，安妮和那些不做回收的人將來能了解資源回收的價值與重要性。

2845 **recreation**
[rɛkrɪ`eʃən] ★★★
名 娛樂、消遣
同 amusement 消遣
衍 recreative 供娛樂的

2846 **tomato**
[tə`meto] ★★★★★
名 番茄、(俚)漂亮的女人

2847 **yet**
[jɛt] ★★★★★
連 卻、可是、然而
副 還沒、已經、更
片 yet again 再一次

2848 **practice**
[`præktɪs] ★★★★★
名 練習、實踐、常規
動 練習、實行、開業
片 in practice 開業中

2849 **creation**
[krɪ`eʃən] ★★
名 創造、創作品、世界
片 all creation 全世界
衍 create 創

2850 **healthy**
[`hɛlθɪ] ★★★
形 有益健康的、健全的
片 a healthy appetite 旺盛的食慾

2851 **pain**
[pen] ★★★★★
名 疼痛、痛苦、努力
動 使痛苦、煩惱、使疼痛
片 be in pain 疼痛

2852 **empty**
[`ɛmptɪ] ★★★★
形 空的、未占用的、徒勞的
動 成為空的、倒空

2853 **can**
[kæn] ★★★★★
名 罐頭、金屬容器、一罐
動 把食品罐裝、解雇
助 能、可以、必須

2854 **realize**
[`rɪəlaɪz] ★★★★
動 實現、領悟、認識到
同 understand 了解
片 realize on 變賣

2855 **educational**
[ɛdʒʊ`keʃənl̩] ★★
形 教育的、有教育意義的
衍 education 教育

2856 **system**
[`sɪstəm] ★★★★★
名 體系、制度、規律、方法、全身
片 solar system 太陽系

Give it a shot 小試身手

❶ My father's _____ include golf, jogging and baseball.

❷ Our educational[2855] system[2856] needs to be _____.

❸ His favorite music style _____ his personality.

❹ Our company used _____ paper for printing.

❺ I have no further question _____ your request.

Answers: ❶ recreations ❷ reformed ❸ reflects ❹ recycled ❺ regarding

493

239

Student registration[2857] starts in the first week of September. Many students have registered for English classes to improve their English ability. During their four years of studying, many students have <u>made</u> remarkable <u>progress in</u> their chosen[2858] fields of study. I have many friends at university, and we do a lot of fun things together. Recently, however, one of my classmates <u>was involved in</u> a major[2859] car accident, and because his injuries[2860] were life-threatening he was flown[2861] by helicopter to hospital. His friends and relatives asked the doctor about his condition. The doctor said, "Because he was seriously injured, we cannot find a simple remedy. We have given him some medicine to relieve the pain first." We were devastated[2862] by the news. Later, we found out that it would be a long time before my injured classmate could walk on his own again. I was saddened[2863] to know that someone who had been such a good athlete now needed to learn how to walk again through tedious repetition[2864]. I think stricter driving regulations[2865] to help protect people more are needed.

⚠ make progress 進步
⚠ be involved in 涉入、陷入

中譯 *Translation*

　　學校註冊開始於九月的第一個禮拜，許多學生為了增進英文能力，都選修了英文課。經過四年的學習，學生們在選修研讀的領域都有卓越的進步。我在大學裡有很多朋友，我們一起做了許多有趣的事。最近，班上的一位同學出了重大車禍，因為他的傷勢太嚴重了，因此他是被直升機送至醫院。他的朋友和親戚紛紛向醫生詢問他的狀況。醫生說：「由於他傷勢嚴重，治療起來不容易，我們已經給他一些能減緩疼痛的藥了。」得知這個消息，我們都很震驚。我們後來知道，這個同學可能需要花很長一段時間的治療，才能恢復正常行走。我為他感到難過，他曾經是如此傑出的運動員，而現在卻必須熬過漫長的復健才能再次行走。我認為，有需要建立更嚴謹的行車規範來保護自身安全。

2857 registration

[ˌrɛdʒɪˈstreʃən] ★★★
- 名 註冊、掛號、登記
- 同 enrollment 登記
- 衍 register 登記、註冊

2858 chosen

[ˈtʃozn̩] ★★
- 形 挑選出來的、精選的
- 衍 choose 選擇、挑選

2859 major

[ˈmedʒɚ] ★★★★★
- 形 較大的、主要的、一流的、主修的
- 動 主修

2860 injury

[ˈɪndʒərɪ] ★★★★
- 名 傷害、損害
- 片 add insult to injury 雪上加霜

2861 fly

[flaɪ] ★★★★★
- 動 空運、飛行、逃離
- 名 門簾、高飛球
- 片 fly by 飛越

2862 devastate

[ˈdɛvəstet] ★★★
- 動 極度震驚、破壞、蹂躪、使垮掉
- 衍 devastating 毀滅性的

2863 sadden

[ˈsædn̩] ★★
- 動 悲哀、悲痛、使黯淡
- 片 sadden at 因…悲傷

2864 repetition

[ˌrɛpɪˈtɪʃən] ★★★
- 名 反覆、副本、背誦
- 同 recitation 背誦
- 衍 repeated 反覆的

2865 regulation

[ˌrɛgjəˈleʃən] ★★★
- 名 規則、規定、調整
- 形 標準的、正規的
- 衍 regulate 管理

2866 burning

[ˈbɝnɪŋ] ★★
- 形 著火的、發熱的、強烈的、緊急的
- 名 燃燒

2867 building

[ˈbɪldɪŋ] ★★★★★
- 名 建築物、房屋
- 片 office building 辦公大樓

2868 cancer

[ˈkænsɚ] ★★★★
- 名 癌症、弊端、(C)巨蟹座
  breast cancer 乳癌

Fighting!

Give it a shot 小試身手

1. He has built up a great _____ as a singer.
2. His joke helped _____ the tension among the passengers.
3. That little boy is _____ to go to school.
4. The fireman _____ an old lady from a burning[2866] building[2867].
5. The doctors are hoping to find a _____ for cancer[2868].

Answers: ① reputation ② ease ③ reluctant ④ rescued ⑤ remedy

Essay

Mary <u>resigned from</u> the government last week, partly because a resolution[2869] was rejected[2870] by a two-thirds majority of Congress. The resolution concerned research on the causes of cancer. Since then, funding for this research has come under greater scrutiny[2871] and control. Only a limited[2872] number of researchers who earned a respectable[2873] income could afford to spend the time and effort needed to do proper research. Therefore, Mary decided to retire and retreated to the mountains until the issue was resolved through negotiations[2874]. Nevertheless, the government wanted to retain control over this issue, thus inciting[2875] people's resistance[2876] to accept the bill[2877]. As a result, more scientists and researchers filed letters of resignation. To solve the crisis, the government promised to pass the resolution and be respectful of people's will[2878]. The incident proved[2879] the power of democracy and how people can work to make positive change happen. Now, cancer patients can <u>rest</u>[2880] <u>assured</u> that everything is being done to try to improve the treatment they receive.

⚠ resign from 離職
⚠ rest assured 放心

中譯 *Translation*

　　瑪麗從政府機關離職了，部分的原因是因為某項決議被國會三分之二多數否決了。此決議是關於癌症成因的研究。從那之後，這項研究受到越來越嚴格的監督與管制。只有少數賺得高薪的研究人員負擔起這項研究的開支。因此瑪莉決定退休，退隱山林間，直到這個問題能夠協商解決。然而，政府想要維持掌控權，於是他們煽動人民，讓人民抗拒這項法案。結果，越來越多的科學家和研究員提出辭呈。為了解決危機，政府只好答應通過決議案，並聲明會尊重人民的意願。這次的事件印證了民主的力量，也證明了人們可以藉由自身的力量為社會帶來更好的改變。 現在，癌症病患也能對日益改善的治療環境與技術感到放心。

2869 resolution

[rɛzə`luʃən] ★★★★

名 決議、決心、分解、解答、果斷力

片 resolution on …的決議

2870 reject

[rɪ`dʒɛkt] ★★★★

動 否決、抵制、丟棄

名 被拋棄的東西、廢品

反 accept 同意

2871 scrutiny

[`skrutnɪ] ★★★

名 監督、詳細檢查、監視

同 examination 檢查

片 under scrutiny 受監視

2872 limited

[`lɪmɪtɪd] ★★★★★

形 有限的、特快的

名 特快車

反 limitless 無限的

2873 respectable

[rɪ`spɛktəbḷ] ★★

形 可觀的、名聲好的、體面的

衍 respect 尊敬、尊重

2874 negotiation

[nɪgoʃɪ`eʃən] ★★

名 談判、協商、通過

片 enter into negotiation 開始談判

2875 incite

[ɪn`saɪt] ★★

動 煽動、激起、激勵

同 stir 煽動

衍 incitation 刺激、鼓勵

2876 resistance

[rɪ`zɪstəns] ★★★★

名 反抗、抵抗力、抵制

反 obedience 服從

片 put up resistance 抵抗

2877 bill

[bɪl] ★★★★★

名 法案、帳單、目錄、單據、鈔票

動 開帳單、貼海報宣布

2878 will

[wɪl] ★★★★★

名 意志、意願、決心

動 決心要、願意

助 將要、經常、可能

2879 prove

[pruv] ★★★★★

動 證明、顯示、原來是

同 verify 證實

片 prove to 向…證實

2880 rest

[rɛst] ★★★★★

動 放心、休息、依賴

名 休息、停止、安靜

片 rest on 依賴

Give it a shot 小試身手

1 The problem is not yet fully _____.

2 My mother _____ from her position as a teacher last month.

3 She _____ her sister not only in face but also in personality.

4 Dr. Lee spent two years in Africa _____ fossils.

5 We should always be _____ to the elders.

Answers: 1 resolved 2 retired 3 resembles 4 researching 5 respectful

MP3 短文 481 字彙 482

241

There are roughly[2881] ten rural[2882] bus routes[2883] near my home. Therefore, I hear the rumbling[2884] of old buses every morning. I hope the authorities will revise[2885] the bus routes because the noise has ruined my life. I used to have a family get-together[2886] every weekend, but since they are also building a new metro[2887] line near my home, plus the noise of the buses, it is always too noisy[2888] to have a get-together. I have even had to sacrifice my wine-tasting parties. If there isn't a revision[2889] in bus routes or <u>an improvement in</u> the metro system construction soon, I think I will organize[2890] a petition[2891]. I will ask everyone in the area to sign the petition to demand that something be done to reduce the amount of noise being made. If the petition gets enough signatures[2892], the politicians will have to do something to <u>fix the problem</u>. Life is too short to live with such a problem!

> ⓘ an improvement in 在⋯上有所改善
>
> ⓘ fix the problem 解決某個問題，定冠詞 the 可依語意換成 a。

中譯 *Translation*

　　我家附近大約有十班鄉村公車的路線會經過，所以每天早上，我都可以聽見公車的各種聲響，我希望政府當局能修改這些公車路線，因為我的生活已經被這些噪音給毀了。我以前本來每個週末都有一次家族聚會，但是自從我家附近開始蓋新的捷運路線後，再加上公車的噪音，我家變得太過吵鬧，不再適合任何的聚會，我甚至要犧牲掉我的品酒派對。如果我近期內看不到公車路線有所修正，或是捷運工程有任何改進的話，我想我會組織一次請願，我會請附近的住戶在請願書上簽名，要求改善這些大量的噪音，如果請願書上有足夠的簽名，政客們就必須做些事情來解決這個問題，人生實在太短暫，不應該活在這樣的問題當中！

2881 roughly

[`rʌflɪ] ★★
- 副 大約、大體上、粗糙地、粗暴地
- 同 approximately 大概

 2882 rural

[`rurəl] ★★★★
- 形 農村的、有鄉村風味的、農業的
- 同 rustic 農村的

 2883 route

[rut] ★★★★
- 名 路線、路程、途徑
- 動 按特定路線發送
- 同 course 路線

 2884 rumbling

[`rʌmblɪŋ] ★★
- 名 隆隆聲、打鬧
- 形 隆隆聲的、打鬧的
- 衍 rumble 隆隆響

 2885 revise

[rɪ`vaɪz] ★★★★
- 動 修改、校訂
- 名 修訂、校訂
- 片 revised edition 修訂版

 2886 get-together

[`gɛttəgɛðə] ★★
- 名 聚會、聯歡會
- 片 a family get-together 家庭聚會

 2887 metro

[`mɛtro] ★★
- 名 地鐵
- 同 subway (美)地鐵
- 片 Taipei Metro 台北捷運

2888 noisy

[`nɔɪzɪ] ★★★★
- 形 嘈雜的、吵吵鬧鬧的、過份渲染的
- 反 quiet 安靜的

 2889 revision

[rɪ`vɪʒən] ★★★
- 名 修訂、校訂、修訂本
- 同 alteration 修改
- 衍 revisor 校訂者

2890 organize

[`ɔrgə,naɪz] ★★★★
- 動 組織、安排、使有條理
- 同 arrange 安排
- 片 organize into 組成

2891 petition

[pə`tɪʃən] ★★★
- 名 請願、請願書、申請
- 動 請願、請求
- 片 petition for 請求給予

 2892 signature

[`sɪgnətʃə] ★★★
- 名 簽署、簽名、特徵
- 片 put your signature on 在…上簽字

Fighting!

 Give it a shot 小試身手

1 The country was _____ by the flood.

2 He received a _____ for being helpful.

3 I just attended my annual class _____.

4 We have to _____ our plan because of the bad weather.

5 The air is fresher in the _____ areas.

Answers: 1 ruined 2 reward 3 reunion 4 revise 5 rural

499

MP3　短文 483　字彙 484

242

Essay

Paul is a senior[2893] salesperson in a big company and his ancestors[2894] were early settlers in Australia. He gets a lot of satisfaction[2895] from encouraging people to buy screwdrivers[2896] and satellite[2897] TV dishes. He spends a lot of time at work every day. However, recently he decided to take a trip to enjoy the scenery and go on a whale-watching tour[2898]. When he got back from his marvelous[2899] trip, his stern father <u>scolded him for</u> upsetting his mother by making the decision to <u>go on a holiday</u> without his parents, and he thought of him as a shameful[2900] family member. The criticism from his father was quite severe[2901], and that is why Paul decided to move out of the house and get his own apartment[2902] so that he could be independent from his family. As he was leaving, he used one of his screwdrivers to scratch his father's car, an act that he later deeply regretted.

- ⓘ scold sb. for 為了…而責罵某人
- ⓘ go on a holiday 去度假

中譯 *Translation*

　　保羅是一家大公司的資深銷售員，他祖先是澳洲早期的移民者。當他說服顧客購買螺絲起子或是衛星電視的天線時，他能從中獲得很大的滿足感，他每天花在工作的時間很多，然而，最近他決定去旅遊享受風景，參加賞鯨的行程。當他享受完一趟絕妙的旅程回到家時，他那嚴厲的父親斥責他，說他沒有帶父母一起去旅遊的這件事，讓他母親感到不滿，還說他是丟臉的家人。他父親的批評相當嚴厲，所以保羅決定搬出家裡，找間自己的公寓，離開家人獨立過生活。臨走之前，他用他其中一把螺絲起子把他父親的車刮花，這一時的行為讓他在不久之後後悔不已。

2893 senior

[`sinjə] ★★★★
形 資深的、年長的、高級的、前輩的
名 前輩、上司、大四生

2894 ancestor

[`ænsɛstə] ★★★
名 祖先、先驅、原型
反 descendant 子孫
片 noble ancestors 名門

2895 satisfaction

[ˌsætɪs`fækʃən] ★★
名 滿足、稱心、樂事
片 with satisfaction 滿意地

2896 screwdriver

[`skruˌdraɪvə] ★
名 螺絲起子
衍 screw (用螺釘等)固定或擰緊

2897 satellite

[`sætlˌaɪt] ★★★★
名 衛星、追隨者
片 launch a satellite 發射衛星

2898 tour

[tur] ★★★★
名 遊覽、旅行、巡迴演出
動 旅遊、巡視、巡迴演出
片 on tour 正在巡迴演出

2899 marvelous

[`marvələs] ★★
形 令人驚嘆的、妙極的
同 miraculous 驚人的
衍 marvel 感到驚訝

2900 shameful

[`ʃemfəl] ★★
形 丟臉的、可恥的
同 disgraceful 可恥的
衍 shame 羞愧

2901 severe

[sə`vɪr] ★★★★
形 嚴厲的、劇烈的、艱難的、嚴肅的
同 strict 嚴厲的

2902 apartment

[ə`partmənt] ★★★★
名 公寓大樓、房間
同 penthouse (尤指頂層的)豪華公寓

2903 gently

[`dʒɛntʃɪ] ★★
副 溫和地、輕輕地、和緩地、有教養地
同 lightly 輕輕地

2904 rough

[rʌf] ★★★★
形 粗糙的、未加工的、劇烈的、簡陋的
名 梗概、草圖、艱難

---

fighting!

Give it a shot 小試身手

❶ Annie _____ her child gently²⁹⁰³ for the bad behavior.

❷ We eat meat every night, but _____ have any vegetables.

❸ Our teacher is very _____. He cannot allow any mistakes.

❹ They built a rough²⁹⁰⁴ _____ to hide from the war.

❺ If you cannot get any _____, you should complain to the landlord.

Answers: ❶ scolded ❷ scarcely ❸ severe ❹ shelter ❺ satisfaction

243

The prime minister recently announced an important shift[2905] in a shortsighted[2906] policy. Though it may have seemed like a slight[2907] change to some people, it was of major significance[2908] and would cost a great deal of extra money to implement[2909] the change. Another policy change was to work to reduce smog[2910] near the huge city park which was mainly the result of shuttle bus emissions. Now, the prime minister is on vacation[2911] doing some sightseeing[2912] in Europe. While some have criticized the country's leader[2913] for taking too many vacations, no one can really doubt his sincere devotion to the country. However, the prime minister must have been in a hurry to leave on his vacation because he forgot to sign an important document[2914] to allow for the change in policies. That means people who visit the city park will have to put up with the pollution for a little while longer.

Essay

---

the result of …的結果

put up with 容忍、忍受

中譯 *Translation*

　　首相對一項目光短淺的政策，公布了重大的變動，對某些人來說，這或許只是一個小改變，但這項改變其實有很大的重要性，為了實行這項政策，將會增加一筆額外的經費支出。另一項政策目的在於降低大型都市公園的煙霧，煙霧大多是區間車所排放出來的廢氣。首相目前正在度假，遊覽歐洲，雖然有些人會批評一個國家的領導者不該這麼常度假，但沒有人能質疑首相對國家的認真與奉獻。然而，首相必須盡早結束他的旅程，因為他忘了簽讓政策改變的重要文件。這意味著都市公園必須再多忍受一會兒汙染問題。

2905 shift

[ʃɪft] ★★★★
名 轉變、輪班、手段
動 轉移、變動、推卸
片 shift about 四處飄蕩

2906 shortsighted

[`ʃɔrt`saɪtɪd] ★★
形 目光短淺的、近視的
同 nearsighted 目光短淺的

2907 slight

[slaɪt] ★★★★
形 輕微的、不足道的
動 輕視、怠慢
名 輕視、怠慢

2908 significance

[sɪg`nɪfəkəns] ★★★
名 重要性、含意
同 meaning 重要性
衍 significant 重要的

2909 implement

[`ɪmpləmənt] ★★★★
動 履行、實施、提供工具
名 工具、器具、手段
同 carry out 實行

2910 smog

[smɑg] ★★★
名 煙霧(=smoke and fog)
同 fog 煙霧、霧氣

2911 vacation

[ve`keʃən] ★★★★
名 假期、休假、騰出
動 度假
片 on vacation 度假

2912 sightseeing

[`saɪtsiɪŋ] ★★
名 觀光、遊覽
形 觀光的、遊覽的
片 go sightseeing 遊覽

2913 leader

[`lidə] ★★★★
名 領袖、領導者、指揮者
同 chief 領袖
反 follower 追隨者

2914 document

[`dɑkjəmənt] ★★★★
名 公文、文件、證件
動 用文件證明、提供文件、記載

2915 agreement

[ə`grimənt] ★★★★
名 協議、同意、一致
片 agreement with 與…達成的協議

2916 headache

[`hɛdek] ★★★
名 頭痛、麻煩
片 splitting headache 頭痛欲裂

---

fighting!

Give it a shot 小試身手

❶ We both refused to put our _____ to the agreement[2915].

❷ I woke up with a _____ headache[2916].

❸ _____ has polluted the air.

❹ He quickly drew a _____ of the beautiful scenery.

❺ I never doubt her _____.

Answers: ❶ signatures ❷ slight ❸ Smog ❹ sketch ❺ sincerity

244

🎧 MP3　　短文 487　　字彙 488

John's mother started sobbing[2917] uncontrollably[2918] after she heard that her son had <u>dropped out of college</u> in his sophomore[2919] year to open a souvenir shop. "This is like a solar[2920] eclipse[2921] happening suddenly on a bright[2922] sunny day," said John's mother sorrowfully. Several months later, John was reported hurling[2923] a rock at a former professors' office window after drinking spicy vodka. <u>What's more</u>, John's discarded[2924] cigarette sparked[2925] a small brush fire, which burned down a software company. John's mother thought John should seek spiritual[2926] guidance. "He is like a curious sparrow[2927]," said John's mother, who sells headphones. She also volunteers at an organization dedicated[2928] to the protection of endangered species. "He should bring a towel with him and some spare clothes, and then try to enjoy the sea sparkling in the sun," she said of her son.

ⓘ drop out of college (大學)退學，休學則用 suspend。

ⓘ What's more 除此之外，同義用法還有 Furthermore、In addition 等。

中譯 *Translation*

　　在約翰的媽媽得知約翰在大二這年退學，並且決定開一家紀念品店時，她忍不住開始啜泣，她悲傷的說：「這就像在艷陽天發生了日蝕一樣的突然。」幾個月後，有人通報約翰喝完辛辣的伏特加之後，跑去他以前一位大學教授的辦公室，朝他辦公室的窗戶丟了一塊石頭。除此之外，約翰隨手扔掉的菸蒂，竟燃起了一小叢火苗，把一家軟體公司燒毀了。約翰的媽媽認為他應該要去尋求心靈指引，「他就像一隻好奇的小麻雀。」他媽媽這麼說，她是一位賣耳機的女士，並致力於保護瀕臨絕種的物種，「他應該要帶條毛巾和一些換洗衣物，然後試著享受一下在陽光下閃閃發亮的大海。」他媽媽這樣建議。

2917 sob

[sab] ★★★
 嗚咽、啜泣、哭訴
名 嗚咽、啜泣
片 sob sth. out 哭訴

2918 uncontrollably

[ʌnkənˋtroləblɪ] ★
副 控制不住地
同 irrepressibly 抑制不住地

2919 sophomore

[ˋsafmor] ★★
名 (大學、高中的)二年級學生、具兩年經驗者
形 二年級的、二年級生的

2920 solar

[ˋsolə] ★★★★
形 太陽的、利用太陽光的
反 lunar 月亮的
衍 solar system 太陽系

2921 eclipse

[iˋklɪps] ★★★
名 蝕、黯然失色
動 遮蔽、使失色
片 in eclipse 被埋沒

2922 bright

[braɪt] ★★★★★
形 晴朗的、鮮明的、聰穎的、前途光明的
反 gloomy 陰暗的

2923 hurl

[hɝl] ★★★
動 猛力投擲、發射、投球
名 猛力投擲
片 hurl into 使落入

2924 discard

[dɪsˋkard] ★★★
動 丟棄、摒棄、擲出
名 丟棄、拋棄
同 reject 丟棄

2925 spark

[spark] ★★★★
動 發出火花、點燃、激勵
名 火花、閃耀、活力
片 spark off 引爆

2926 spiritual

[ˋspɪrɪtʃuəl] ★★
形 心靈的、神聖的、超自然的、理智的
反 material 物質的

2927 sparrow

[ˋspæro] ★★
名 麻雀
片 eat like a sparrow/bird 胃口小

2928 dedicate

[ˋdɛdəˏket] ★★★
動 致力於、以…奉獻
同 devote 奉獻給
片 dedicate to 奉獻給

Fighting!

Give it a shot 小試身手

❶ _____ power is from the sun's heat and light.

❷ My friend went on a trip and bought me some _____.

❸ You look _____. What's in your mind that makes you sad?

❹ I left a _____ key at my friend's house for any emergency.

❺ The sky _____ with shinny stars.

Answers: ❶ Solar ❷ souvenirs ❸ sorrowful ❹ spare ❺ sparkled

505

245

Essay

"John Marks has masterfully²⁹²⁹ kicked the ball and scored once again in the final minute to win the game for his team," said the sports reporter excitedly. John is a talented all-round²⁹³⁰ sportsman, whose sportsmanship²⁹³¹ and style of play are refreshing. He likes spending his leisure time <u>surfing the Internet</u> and collecting submarine²⁹³² models. John's father is a famous brain surgeon²⁹³³ who has conducted countless successful operations and is involved in stem²⁹³⁴ cell research. He doesn't like athletic activities, so he disapproves²⁹³⁵ of John's decision to choose a sporting career. On the other hand, John's mother, who <u>is known as</u> a stingy²⁹³⁶ woman, tends to offer objective suggestions and sometimes even splendid²⁹³⁷ ideas in order to strengthen²⁹³⁸ John's confidence and to motivate him to keep striving to be successful in his career. An author summarized²⁹³⁹ John's parents' views in the introduction of John's biography²⁹⁴⁰, which was released last month. It said, "John's parents appeared deeply split on the issue of John's success."

ⓘ surf the Internet 上網瀏覽，surf 也有衝浪的意思。

ⓘ be known as 以…出名，若要強調出名的程度，可用 be well-known as。

中譯 *Translation*

　　「約翰‧馬克斯在最後一分鐘替球隊踢出了關鍵的致勝球！」體育播報員興奮地說。約翰是一位天才型的全能運動員，他的運動精神和打球風格都令人煥然一新。閒暇的時候，他喜歡上網或搜集潛水艇模型。

　　約翰的父親是一位知名的腦科醫師，他執行了無數次成功的外科手術，並參與幹細胞研究，他並不喜歡體育活動，所以他不贊成約翰投身運動界的決定；另一方面，約翰那位以小氣出名的母親，則常常提供一些客觀的建議，甚至是一些很棒的想法給約翰，來強化他的自信心，讓他在自己的志業中，努力朝成功邁進。一名作家在約翰上個月出版的傳記序文中，概述了他父母的意見，上面寫道：「約翰成功與否，他雙親的意見似乎相當分歧。」

2929 masterfully

[`mæstəfulɪ] ★★
- 副 技巧熟練地、專橫地、能幹地
- 衍 masterly 熟練的

2930 all-round

[`ɔl`raund] ★★
- 形 全面的、萬能的、綜合性的
- 衍 all-rounder 全能選手

2931 sportsmanship

[`sportsmən͵ʃɪp] ★
- 名 運動員精神、光明正大
- 反 dishonesty 不正直
- 衍 sportsman 運動員

2932 submarine

[`sʌbmə͵rin] ★★★
- 形 潛艇的、海底的
- 名 潛艇、水下裝置
- 同 undersea 海底的

2933 surgeon

[`sɝdʒən] ★★★
- 名 外科醫生
- 反 physician 內科醫生
- 衍 surgery 外科手術

2934 stem

[stɛm] ★★★★
- 名 幹、莖、血統
- 動 起源於、給…裝柄
- 片 stem from 起源於

2935 disapprove

[͵dɪsə`pruv] ★★
- 動 不贊成、不喜歡
- 片 disapprove of 不同意
- 衍 disapproval 不贊成

2936 stingy

[`stɪndʒɪ] ★★
- 形 吝嗇的、小氣的、不足的、有刺的
- 反 generous 慷慨的

2937 splendid

[`splɛndɪd] ★★
- 形 壯麗的、燦爛的、顯著的、極好的
- 反 dull 不鮮明的

2938 strengthen

[`strɛŋθən] ★★★
- 動 加強、鞏固、變強大
- 同 fortify 加強、增強
- 反 weaken 削弱

2939 summarize

[`sʌmə͵raɪz] ★★★
- 動 概述、總結
- 同 outline 概述
- 衍 summary 總結

2940 biography

[baɪ`ɑgrəfɪ] ★★★
- 名 傳記、興衰史
- 同 life history 傳記、個人經歷

Fighting!

Give it a shot 小試身手

1. Mary agreed with my _____ that we should get together sometime.
2. I had a ten-hour _____ on my broken leg last week.
3. Basically, my speech can be _____ in three sentences.
4. The teaching profession has a high _____ in Taiwan.
5. He _____ very hard to achieve his goal.

246

🎧 MP3　短文 491　字彙 492

Essay

Thomas was a laboratory technician[2941] who made a telescope[2942] that was considered the greatest technological advance of the 19th century. One night, after he just finished enjoying a symphony performance and was preparing to go to the telegraph[2943] office, he saw a suspicious man hitting a girl on the street, and the abusive[2944] man told her to shut up and stop resisting. Out of sympathy, Thomas decided to do something. He examined his surroundings[2945] and hid behind a tree at first. Strangely[2946], none of the other people on the street seemed to show any sympathetic[2947] attitude toward the girl. Therefore, Thomas decided to come up with a systematic[2948] approach to save the girl. Since the girl was too afraid to scream, Thomas decided to scream in a loud, high-pitched[2949] voice like a girl. All of a sudden, he remembered that his beloved[2950] wife was about to go into labor. In the end, he abandoned that girl and rushed to the hospital. Fortunately, the police had heard his screaming and rushed to save the girl and arrest the man.

中譯 *Translation*

　　湯瑪士是一名實驗室的技術員，他做出來的望遠鏡被視為當時十九世紀最先進的技術。有一晚，當他欣賞完交響樂的表演，正準備動身前往電信所時，途中看見了一個可疑的男子在街上攻擊一名女孩，這名口出惡言的男子要女孩閉嘴然後停止反抗。出於同情，湯瑪士決定要做些什麼。他勘查了一下周遭的情況，然後就先躲在一棵的大樹後面。奇怪的是，街上似乎沒有其他人對女孩感到同情。所以，湯瑪士決定想出一個有系統的方法來拯救那名女孩。女孩因為太害怕而不敢叫出聲，湯瑪士決定用大高分貝和高音頻，像女孩一樣尖叫。突然間，他想起他親愛的老婆即將要分娩了。最後，他拋棄了那名女孩，然後衝到醫院。所幸，警察聽到湯瑪士的尖叫趕來救了女孩，並逮捕了這名男子。

2941 technician

[tɛk`nɪʃən] ★★★
名 技術人員、技師、技巧純熟的人
同 mechanic 技工

2942 telescope

[`tɛləskop] ★★★
名 單筒望遠鏡
反 binoculars 雙筒望遠鏡
動 縮短、套疊

2943 telegraph

[`tɛləgræf] ★★★
名 電信、電報
動 打電報、電匯、流露出

2944 abusive

[ə`bjusɪv] ★★
形 罵人的、濫用的
同 insulting 侮辱的
衍 abuse 濫用、辱罵

2945 surroundings

[sə`raundɪŋz] ★★
名 環境、周遭情況
同 circumstance 環境

2946 strangely

[`strendʒlɪ] ★
副 奇妙地、不可思議地
片 strangely enough 說來也奇怪

2947 sympathetic

[ˏsɪmpə`θɛtɪk] ★★★
形 有同情心的、贊同的、和諧的
名 交感神經

2948 systematic

[ˏsɪstə`mætɪk] ★★★
形 有系統的、有條理的、徹底的
同 methodical 有條理的

2949 high-pitched

[`haɪ`pɪtʃt] ★
形 尖聲的、聲調高的、激烈的、陡的
同 shrill 尖聲的

2950 beloved

[bɪ`lʌvɪd] ★★★
形 心愛的、受鍾愛的
名 心愛的人

2951 hijacker

[`haɪdʒækə] ★
名 強盜、劫盜
衍 hijacking 攔路搶劫

2952 motive

[`motɪv] ★★★
名 動機、目的、主旨
形 成為原動力的
動 產生動機、激起

Fighting!

Give it a shot 小試身手

1. I have no _____ for John. He deserved it.

2. Vivian likes her pancake with _____ and cream.

3. The hijackers[2951] finally _____ themselves to the police.

4. His motives[2952] are very _____ to me.

5. That _____ is highly skilled.

Answers: 1 sympathy 2 syrup 3 surrendered 4 suspicious 5 technician

247

 MP3   短文 493   字彙 494

Essay

We lived in terror[2953] of our father when he was drinking. His violent behavior terrified[2954] us. The doctor said he was in need of thorough mental help. In addition, the doctor suggested we show no tolerance[2955] towards his behavior. My mother had had a tough life, and I was a timid[2956] child. My father's behavior was not tolerable despite the fact that he had been raised in a tolerant household. It was tiresome[2957] to live with a family member who had a tendency[2958] to resort[2959] to violent behavior. Now, in order to escape from the stressful environment, I decided to move out and live with Paul, who is a very thoughtful[2960] friend. When I am with him, I feel no tension. He recommended[2961] that I read a book, in which the theme was the conflict[2962] between love and duty[2963]. Of all my friends, Paul helps me the most. Most importantly, I don't have to tolerate my father anymore. I don't think I will ever visit him again until he is on his deathbed[2964].

中譯 *Translation*

　　以往，每當父親一喝酒，我們就活在恐懼當中。他的暴力惡行令我們很害怕。醫生說他需要一個完善的心理治療。除此之外，醫生還告訴我們不要容忍父親的惡行。我母親一直過著很艱苦的生活，我從小就是個害羞的孩子。儘管我父親是在一個開放的家庭中長大的，但他的行為實在是令人無法容忍。家裡出現一個有著暴力傾向的家人真的很討厭。所以現在，為了逃離這個充滿壓力的環境，我決定搬出去和保羅一起住。保羅是一個非常體貼的朋友，每次和他在一起時，我都覺得很輕鬆。他介紹我讀一本書，主題是關於愛與責任的衝突。我所有的朋友當中，就屬保羅最幫我的了。最重要的是，我再也不必忍受我的父親了，我想只有在他進了祖墳之後我才會再見到他吧。

2953　terror

[`tɛrə] ★★

名 恐懼、恐怖活動、極討厭的人

片 in terror 驚恐地

2954　terrify

[`tɛrəfaɪ] ★★★

動 使害怕、使恐怖

片 be terrified at 被…嚇一跳

2955　tolerance

[`tɑlərəns] ★★★

名 容忍、寬容、忍受程度

片 tolerance for 對…容忍

反 intolerance 無法忍受

2956　timid

[`tɪmɪd] ★★★

形 怕羞的、膽小的的

同 bashful 羞怯的

反 bold 大膽的

2957　tiresome

[`taɪrsəm] ★★

形 討厭的、煩人的

同 wearisome 令人厭煩的

2958　tendency

[`tɛndənsɪ] ★★★

名 傾向、天分、趨勢

片 have a tendency to 傾向於做某事

2959　resort

[rɪ`zɔrt] ★★★★

動 訴諸、憑藉

名 名勝、訴諸、常去

片 resort to 訴諸於

2960　thoughtful

[`θɔtfəl] ★★★

形 體貼的、深思的、細心的、考慮周到的

同 considerate 體貼的

2961　recommend

[rɛkə`mɛnd] ★★★★

動 介紹、推薦、建議、使受歡迎、託付

片 recommend to 託付給

2962　conflict

[kən`flɪkt] ★★★★

名 矛盾、衝突、鬥爭

動 矛盾、衝突、戰鬥

片 conflict with 與…衝突

2963　duty

[`djutɪ] ★★★★★

名 責任、本分、職責、稅、功率

片 on duty 上班

2964　deathbed

[`dɛθbɛd] ★★

名 臨終的一段時間

形 臨終時做的

片 on sb's deathbed 臨終

Fighting!

Give it a shot 小試身手

❶ A _____ person is usually more open-minded.

❷ She has a _____ to blush whenever a guy talks to her.

❸ After a _____ discussion with others, I finally made my mind.

❹ This task is _____ than I thought. I probably won't finish it on time.

❺ The main _____ of this book is about friendship.

Answers: ❶ tolerant ❷ tendency ❸ thorough ❹ tougher ❺ theme

248

 MP3　 短文 495　 字彙 496

Essay

A tragedy[2965] struck a family when their two-year-old son was killed in an accident. Mike, a translator[2966], was to blame for the tragic hit-and-run[2967] accident. He was making a tremendous[2968] effort to appear calm afterward. However, he still got caught and his life was transformed from that moment on. In jail, he was asked to finish a new translation[2969] of the Bible into Chinese. It could have been a great triumph[2970] for him. Yet due to the fact that Mike was a slow typist[2971], he failed to finish it on time for publication.

One day, the judge said, "You'll be transferred[2972] to a facility on the mountain under our watch. We need someone to translate tribal[2973] texts into English." At night, stars twinkled[2974] beautifully in the sky, and Mike was happy to get away from the depressing environment of the jail, but he started to fall into an emotional tug-of-war[2975]. He wondered whether he should face his guilt or try to keep hiding from it. In the end, Mike said, "I have decided that instead of taking public transportation in the future, I want to avoid any chance of anyone seeing me." Clearly, he chose to hide from his guilt[2976].

中譯 *Translation*

　　一場悲劇襲擊了一個小家庭，他們僅僅兩歲大的兒子在一場意外中死亡，麥克是這場令人遺憾的肇事逃逸當事人。他是一位翻譯員，雖然他在事發後盡可能保持鎮定，但還是被抓了，他的一生也因此改變。在獄中，他被要求完成聖經中文版的新譯本，這對他來說，本來應該會成為一項成功的事蹟，但麥克打字太慢，沒有及時趕上出版日期。

　　有一天，法官說：「你要在我們的監視下，轉調去山上的另一機構，我們需要有人將以部落方言寫成的文件翻譯成英文。」當晚，星星在天空中美麗地閃爍，麥克很開心可以脫離惱人的監獄，但是心中也開始產生了拉鋸戰，他心想，他是該勇敢面對自己的罪行還是試著逃避。最後，約翰說：「我決定了，將來的日子裡，與其搭乘大眾交通工具，我寧願盡我所能地避開其他人的視線。」很顯然，他選擇了逃避。

2965 tragedy

[`trædʒədɪ] ★★★

名 悲劇、慘案、災難

同 adversity 災難

反 comedy 喜劇

2966 translator

[træns`letə] ★★

名 翻譯員、翻譯機、翻譯家

反 interpreter 口譯員

2967 hit-and-run

[`hɪtŋ`rʌn] ★★

形 逃走的、擊球跑壘的

片 hit and run driver 肇事後逃跑的司機

2968 tremendous

[trɪ`mɛndəs] ★★★

形 巨大的、驚人的

同 enormous 巨大的

反 normal 正常的

2969 translation

[træns`leʃən] ★★★

名 翻譯、譯本、調任

反 interpretation 口譯

片 in translation 翻譯的

2970 triumph

[`traɪəmf] ★★★

名 勝利、成功、業績

動 獲得勝利、得意洋洋

片 triumph over 擊敗

2971 typist

[`taɪpɪst] ★★

名 打字員

　 type in 輸入

衍 type 打字

2972 transfer

[træns`fɝ] ★★★★

動 調動、轉變、轉讓

名 轉移、讓渡

片 transfer to 轉調到

2973 tribal

[`traɪbl] ★★

形 部落的、種族的

片 tribal warfare 部落戰爭

衍 tribe 部落

2974 twinkle

[`twɪŋkl] ★★★

動 閃爍、閃亮、輕快移動

名 閃爍、閃亮、瞬間

同 sparkle 閃耀

2975 tug-of-war

[`tʌɡ ɑv wɔr] ★★

名 拉鋸戰、拔河比賽

衍 tugboat 拖船

2976 guilt

[ɡɪlt] ★★★

名 過失、內疚、有罪

同 guiltiness 愧疚

片 sense of guilt 罪惡感

Fighting!

Give it a shot 小試身手

❶ I go to work by public _____.

❷ I am sorry for causing you in such a _____ situation.

❸ The soldier is about to be _____ to another post in China.

❹ Could you help me _____ this article from English to Chinese?

❺ After studying abroad, she has _____ into a new person.

MP3　 短文 497　 字彙 498

Essay 249

The unemployment rate in urban areas has risen sharply[2977] recently; therefore, Wendy urged that an emergency public vote be held by December. "Regimes[2978] that <u>fail</u>[2979] <u>to</u> protect workers' rights indirectly[2980] violate[2981] human rights," said Wendy. "There's a word that describes how the government is dealing with human rights: hypocrisy[2982]!"

Wendy studied physics at university, and she is truly[2983] a unique politician. For example, she published a book on modern language usage[2984] among government officials, and uploaded[2985] embarrassing videos of other politicians. She often said, "For the benefit of all, politicians should donate vast amounts of money to <u>prevent</u> our efforts in green energy <u>from</u> being <u>in vain</u>. Besides that, we should encourage our youngsters[2986] to become vegetarians[2987] and encourage them to drink vinegar. Also, fishing vessels[2988] should stop illegal fishing."

> ⓘ fail to 未能、無法
> ⓘ prevent...from 防止…做…
> ⓘ in vain 徒勞

中譯 *Translation*

　　都市的失業率近來急遽升高，因此，溫蒂強烈主張，十二月以前要趕緊舉行緊急公投。「無法保護勞工權益的制度就是間接地危害人權。」溫蒂說，「政府處理人權問題的方式只有這兩個字足以形容：偽善。」

　　溫蒂在大學時代主修物理學，她是一個很特別的政治家。例如，她曾出版一本政府官員現代用語書，也把一些政治家的難堪影片上傳到網路上。她常說：「為了全體利益著想，政治家應該要捐出大筆的金錢，避免我們在環境保護上的努力成為一場空。除此之外，我們也要鼓勵年輕人吃素和多喝醋。另外，也要禁止漁船非法捕撈。」

2977 **sharply**

[`ʃɑrplɪ] ★★
- 副 猛烈地、突然、激烈地、清楚地
- 衍 sharp 鋒利的

2978 **regime**

[rɪ`ʒim] ★★★★
- 名 社會制度、政權、統治
- 同 rule 統治

2979 **fail**

[fel] ★★★★★
- 動 失去作用、不及格
- 名 不及格
- 片 fail in 在…失敗了

2980 **indirectly**

[ɪndə`rɛktlɪ] ★★
- 副 間接地、迂迴地
- 反 directly 直接地
- 衍 indirection 間接

2981 **violate**

[`vaɪəlet] ★★★
- 動 違反、侵犯、褻瀆
- 同 break 違反
- 衍 violation 違反

2982 **hypocrisy**

[hɪ`pɑkrəsɪ] ★★
- 名 偽善、虛偽
- 同 insincerity 偽善
- 衍 hypocritical 偽善的

2983 **truly**

[`trulɪ] ★★★★
- 副 真實地、確切地、非常、真誠地
- 片 well and truly 完全地

2984 **usage**

[`jusɪdʒ] ★★★★
- 名 用法、習慣、習俗、使用方法

2985 **upload**

[ʌp`lod] ★★
- 動 上載
- 反 download 下載

2986 **youngster**

[`jʌŋstɚ] ★★
- 名 年輕人、小孩
- 反 oldster 老人

2987 **vegetarian**

[vɛdʒə`tɛrɪən] ★★
- 名 素食者、食草動物
- 形 吃素的、素菜的

2988 **vessel**

[`vɛsl] ★★★★
- 名 船、艦、容器、血管
- 同 container 容器
- 片 fishing vessel 漁船

Fighting!

Give it a shot 小試身手

❶ Everyone's look is _____. Even twins are not exactly the same.

❷ This case is not _____, so you don't need to rush.

❸ English is called the _____ language.

❹ I am a _____. I cannot even stand the smell of meat.

❺ Those who _____ the law should be punished.

MP3　短文 499　字彙 500

Essay 250

　　A virgin²⁹⁸⁹ has often been used as a symbol of virtue²⁹⁹⁰. Such an ideal²⁹⁹¹ is vital²⁹⁹² to Chinese culture, while it sometimes seems to be a degradation²⁹⁹³ of female dignity. However, the idea has been like a virus²⁹⁹⁴ that spreads very quickly. <u>As a result</u>, volunteers from a charitable organization providing help for women have started a campaign to <u>dissuade</u> people <u>from</u> overemphasizing²⁹⁹⁵ visual²⁹⁹⁶ images of women.

　　As for me, after going on a voyage²⁹⁹⁷ from England to India and witnessing a volcanic²⁹⁹⁸ eruption²⁹⁹⁹ in Iceland, I decided not to waste my leisure time on idle pursuits such as games but to explore more life experiences instead.

> (!) as a result 因此
> (!) dissuade...from 勸阻

中譯 *Translation*

　　「處女」常用來作為美德的象徵。這種理想典範在中國文化裡非常重要，但似乎也是對女性尊嚴的詆毀。然而，這種觀念還是像病毒一樣快速擴散。因此，一個專為婦女提供協助的慈善組織已經發起運動，呼籲民眾不要過分重視女性的外在形象。

　　而我，結束英國到印度的航行及親眼見證冰島的火山爆發之後，我決定不再將閒暇時間虛擲在打發時間的遊戲上，我要開始探索更多不一樣的人生體驗。

你不可不知！

　　相信大家對英國維京集團(Virgin Group)並不陌生，最知名的莫過於維珍航空 Virgin Atlantic Airways。不過鮮少人知道，創辦人Richard Branson 在為公司取名時，居然是因為「Since we're complete virgins at business, let's call it just that: Virgins.」，敢如此昭告世人自己是企業界的生手，應該也只有他而已了！

virgin

[ˋvɝdʒɪn] ★★★

名 處女

形 初次的、純潔的

同 pure 純潔的

 virtue

[ˋvɝtʃu] ★★★★

名 美德、優點、憑藉

片 by virtue of 由於、憑藉

 ideal

[aɪˋdiəl] ★★★★

名 理想、典範

形 理想的、非常合適的、不切實際的

 vital

[ˋvaɪtl̩] ★★★★

形 生命的、重要的、充滿活力的

名 要害、重要器官

degradation

[dɛgrəˋdeʃən] ★★

名 降低、墮落、丟臉、退化、惡化

衍 degrade 使降級

virus

[ˋvaɪrəs] ★★★

名 病毒

片 virus infections 病毒感染

overemphasize

[ovɚˋɛmfəsaɪz] ★

動 過分強調、過份著重

衍 overemphasis 過份的強調

visual

[ˋvɪʒuəl] ★★★★

形 視力的、視覺的

衍 vision 視力、視覺、幻想

 voyage

[ˋvɔɪɪdʒ] ★★★★★

名 航海、航行

動 航行

同 navigation 航行

volcanic

[vɑlˋkænɪk] ★

形 火山的、猛烈的

衍 volcano 火山

eruption

[ɪˋrʌpʃən] ★★

名 爆發、噴出、發疹

同 outburst 爆發

衍 eruptive 爆發的

 punish

[ˋpʌnɪʃ] ★★★★

動 懲罰、處罰、大量消耗

片 punish for 為⋯懲罰

衍 punishment 處罰

 fighting!

Give it a shot 小試身手

1 Modesty is regarded as a _____ in Chinese society.

2 The Titanic sank on its first _____.

3 This is the _____ voyage of the ship.

4 Her paintings have a very strong _____ appeal.

5 Any _____ of regulations should be punished[3000].

Answers: 1 virtue 2 voyage 3 virgin 4 visual 5 violation

 MP3　 短文 501　 字彙 502

Essay

"It is alcohol that has wrecked[3001] her life," said a witness to the car accident. "The driver appeared[3002] to be very drunk." Not only did the driver break her leg, but she also needed to undergo[3003] major surgery. It also <u>forced</u> the driver <u>to withdraw from</u> a yogurt-eating competition and to be examined on a yearly[3004] basis[3005].

A website[3006] that was updated[3007] weekly[3008] showed the driver's once youthful[3009] appearance. She was very pretty, but now she has a mass[3010] of wrinkles[3011] on her face <u>due to</u> alcohol. "Everybody now <u>thinks of</u> me <u>as</u> a witch," said the driver, who used to volunteer regularly at an orphanage. As well, because of her <u>sharp wit</u> the orphans all liked her. However, all of that has been taken away from her because of her drinking problem.

(!) force...to 迫使⋯做⋯

(!) withdraw from 撤離、退出

(!) due to 由於

(!) sharp wit 機敏

中譯 *Translation*

「酒精誤了她的一生，」車禍現場的一位目擊者這麼說，「那個駕駛看起來醉得不省人事。」那位駕駛不但摔斷了腿，還必須進行重大手術。這也使她必須退出優格大胃王的比賽，每年還得接受定期的追蹤檢查。

一個每週更新的網站把那位駕駛以前年輕的模樣秀出來，她曾經非常漂亮，現在卻因為酗酒的關係，滿臉都是皺紋。「每個人都覺得我像巫婆。」那位駕駛說道。她以前會定期去孤兒院當志工，孤兒院的孩子們也都對她的機智崇拜不已。然而，一切都因為她的酗酒問題而毀了。

3001 wreck
[rɛk] ★★★★
- 動 破壞、失事、遇難
- 名 失事、殘骸、破壞
- 同 ruin 毀壞

3002 appear
[əˋpɪr] ★★★★★
- 動 似乎、出現、露面
- 反 disappear 消失
- 片 appear in 在某處出現

3003 undergo
[ʌndəˋgo] ★★★
- 動 經歷、忍受、接受治療
- 同 experience 經歷

3004 yearly
[ˋjɪrlɪ] ★★★
- 形 每年的、一年一次的
- 副 每年、一年一度
- 同 annual 每年的

3005 basis
[ˋbesɪs] ★★★★★
- 名 基礎、準則、基本成分
- 片 on the basis of 以…為基礎

3006 website
[ˋwɛbsaɪt] ★★★★
- 名 網站
- 衍 web 網際網路

3007 update
[ʌpˋdet] ★★★★
- 動 更新、使現代化
- 名 最新報導、更新
- 同 renew 使更新

3008 weekly
[ˋwiklɪ] ★★★★
- 形 每週的、一週一次的
- 副 每週、每週一次
- 名 週刊、週報

3009 youthful
[ˋjuθfəl] ★★
- 形 年輕的、朝氣蓬勃的、初期的
- 同 young 年輕的

3010 mass
[mæs] ★★★★★
- 名 大量、大眾、團、塊
- 形 大規模的、民眾的
- 動 聚集起來、集中

3011 wrinkle
[ˋrɪŋkḷ] ★★★
- 名 皺紋、困難、難題
- 動 起皺紋、皺起來
- 片 wrinkle up 使起皺紋

3012 visit
[ˋvɪzɪt] ★★★★★
- 動 參觀、拜訪、視察
- 名 參觀、訪問、視察
- 片 pay a visit to 參觀

Fighting!

Give it a shot 小試身手

❶ The local residents have _____ from the dangerous area.

❷ Two passengers were injuired in the _____.

❸ Tax is reviewed on a _____ basis.

❹ Please visit³⁰¹² our official _____ for more information.

❺ There were fine _____ around her eyes.

Answers: ❶ withdrawn ❷ wreck ❸ yearly ❹ website ❺ wrinkles

附錄篇

收錄Level1-Level6
的單字以及分布於
各篇短文中的基本單字，
共4000個單字。

單字 從A-Z排列共4000個單字

頻率 為美國人使用該單字的頻率

詞性 該單字最常使用到的詞性

中譯 該單字最常使用到的中文釋義

頁碼 該單字在本書中出現的頁碼,提供更豐富
的單字訊息

★（星形符號）因為其對應單字普遍都會出現在本書
收錄的短文中,其頁數不一,所以並未特別標註頁碼

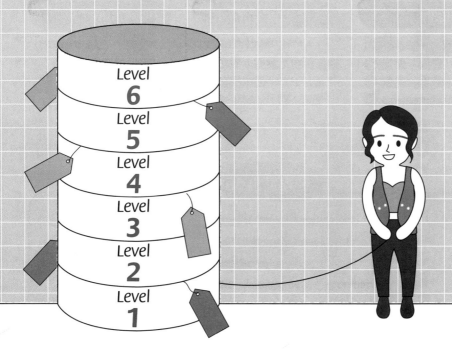

Level
6

Level
5

Level
4

Level
3

Level
2

Level
1

單字	頻率	詞性	中譯	頁碼
abandon	4	動	遺棄、中止、使放縱	395
abase	2	動	貶低、使謙卑	139
ability	4	名	能力、能耐、才能	223
able	5	形	能夠、有能力的	9
aboard	3	副	在(船、飛機、火車)上	11
aboriginal	3	形	土著居民的、原始的	257
about	5	介	關於、對於	★
above	5	介	在⋯上面、超過	331
abroad	4	副	到(在)國外、傳開	137
absence	4	名	缺乏、缺席	137
absolute	4	形	絕對的、專制的	255
absolutely	3	副	絕對地、完全地	379
absorb	3	動	吸收、理解、承受	65
absorbing	3	形	引人入勝的	★
abstain	2	動	戒、避開、棄權	257
abstract	4	形	抽象的、深奧的	395
abusive	2	形	罵人的、濫用的	509
academic	4	形	學術的、大學的	435
accelerator	2	名	加速裝置、油門	481
accent	4	名	腔調、重音、著重	111
accept	5	動	答應、接受、認可	393
acceptable	3	形	合意的、可接受的	103
access	5	名	通道、門路、接近	443
accessory	2	名	配件、房間陳設	103
accident	4	名	意外、事故、災禍	267
accidentally	2	副	意外地、偶然地	83
acclaim	2	名	讚賞、歡呼	297
accompany	3	動	陪同、伴隨、伴奏	367
accomplish	3	動	完成、實現、達到	387
accomplishment	3	名	成就、造詣	★
according	4	形	相符的、相應的	★

單字	頻率	詞性	中譯	頁碼
account	5	名	帳戶、描述、理由	161
accountant	3	名	會計師、會計人員	★
accounting	4	名	會計、會計學、結帳	327
accuracy	3	名	正確性、準確性	485
accurate	4	形	準確的、精確的	401
accusation	2	名	指控、指責、控告	485
accuse	4	動	譴責、控告、歸咎於	395
ache	4	動	疼痛、渴望	123
achieve	4	動	實現、贏得	27
achievement	3	名	成就、達成	469
acquire	4	動	獲得、學到、養成	395
acquisition	3	名	獲得、取得	463
acre	3	名	英畝、土地、許多	395
acrobatics	2	名	雜技表演、巧妙手法	267
across	5	介	穿過、在⋯那邊	369
act	5	動	演戲、行動、見效	281
action	5	名	行為、作用、功能	487
active	4	形	活潑的、積極的	137
activity	3	名	活動、活躍、消遣	139
actress	5	名	女演員	★
actually	4	副	實際上、真的	★
add	5	動	增加、加起來	29
addict	3	動	沉溺、成癮	33
addiction	2	名	沉溺、上癮、入迷	463
addition	3	名	附加、加法	137
additional	5	形	附加的、額外的	465
address	5	名	住址、地址	★
adept	3	形	熟練的、內行的	247
adjust	5	動	調整、校準、適應	393
admirable	2	形	令人欽佩的	★
admiration	2	名	欽佩、讚美	★
admire	4	動	欽佩、欣賞、稱讚	267
admirer	2	名	讚賞者、欽佩者	119

單字	頻率	詞性	中譯	頁碼
admit	4	動	承認、准許進入	11
adopt	4	動	採用、吸收、領養	439
adorable	2	形	可愛的、可敬重的	397
adult	4	名	成年人	191
advance	4	名	前進、發展、預付	111
advancement	3	名	促進、晉升	★
advantage	3	名	優勢、利益	21
adventure	4	名	冒險、奇遇	267
advertise	3	動	做宣傳、廣告、通知	193
advertising	1	名	廣告、做廣告	417
advise	4	動	當顧問、勸告、通知	269
advisor	4	名	顧問、勸告者	★
aesthetic	3	形	美學的	439
affair	4	名	事務、事件	399
affect	5	動	發生作用、影響	405
affection	3	名	鍾愛、感情、影響	33
affiliate	5	名	分會、成員組織	431
afford	4	動	買得起、提供	335
affordable	3	形	負擔得起的	45
afraid	5	形	害怕的、擔心的	9
after	5	介	在…以後	★
afterwards	3	副	隨後、後來	113
again	5	副	再、再一次	★
against	5	介	對抗、預防、倚靠	397
age	5	名	年齡、年代	★
aged	4	形	年老的、舊的	★
agency	4	名	仲介、代辦處、作用	269
agent	5	名	(化)劑、仲介	27
agree	5	動	意見一致、贊同	269
agreement	4	名	協議、同意、一致	503
agriculture	3	名	農業、農耕、農學	269
ahead	4	副	在前、向前	★
aid	5	動	幫助、支援、有助於	137

單字	頻率	詞性	中譯	頁碼
air	5	名	空氣、大氣	★
aircraft	4	名	飛機、飛行器	205
airplane	4	名	(美)飛機	★
airport	4	名	機場、航空站	289
aisle	3	名	走道、通道、側廊	359
album	3	名	唱片集、相簿	73
alcohol	4	名	酒精、含酒精飲料	61
alcoholic	3	形	酒精的、含酒精的	★
alert	4	形	警覺的、靈活的	397
alive	5	形	活著的、現存的	★
allergic	3	形	過敏的、對…反感的	325
alley	2	名	小巷、胡同	269
allow	5	動	允許、給與、認可	117
all-round	2	形	全面的、萬能的	507
almost	5	副	幾乎、差不多	341
alone	5	形	單獨的、獨自的	★
along	4	副	向前、一起、來到	215
aloud	3	副	大聲地、出聲地	139
alphabet	3	名	字母表、初步、入門	139
already	5	副	已經、先前	★
also	5	副	也、還	★
although	5	連	雖然、儘管	★
altogether	3	副	總之、完全、合計	139
aluminum	2	名	鋁	343
always	5	副	總是、經常	★
amaze	5	動	使大為驚奇	★
amazing	5	形	驚人的	★
ambassador	3	名	大使、使節	269
ambition	3	名	雄心、抱負	211
ambitious	3	形	有抱負的	397
ambulance	2	名	救護車、傷患運輸機	9
among	5	介	在…之中、在…中間	431
amount	5	名	總額、數量	51

單字	頻率	詞性	中譯	頁碼
ample	3	形	豐富的、寬敞的	261
amusement	2	名	娛樂、消遣、樂趣	135
analyze	3	動	分析、分解	175
ancestor	3	名	祖先、先驅、原型	501
ancient	3	形	古代的、舊的	299
anesthesia	2	名	麻醉、麻木	9
angel	5	名	天使、天使般的人	★
anger	5	名	生氣、怒火	259
angle	4	名	角度、立場、觀點	269
angry	5	形	發怒的、狂暴的	★
animal	5	名	動物	★
animation	3	名	動畫片、活潑、熱烈	95
ankle	3	名	腳踝、踝關節	63
anniversary	3	名	週年紀念日	281
announce	4	動	宣布、聲稱、播報	221
annoying	2	形	惱人的、討厭的	109
annual	5	形	每年的、全年的	171
anonymous	3	形	匿名的、來源不明的	165
another	5	形	另外的	★
answer	5	動	回答、答覆	★
ant	3	名	螞蟻	★
anthem	3	名	國歌、頌歌、讚美詩	91
anticipation	2	名	預期、期望	435
antique	3	形	古董的、古老的	139
anxiety	3	名	焦慮、掛念、渴望	399
anxious	4	形	焦慮的、渴望的	343
anymore	5	副	再也(不)	★
anything	5	代	任何東西、任何事情	★
anytime	5	副	在任何時候	★
apart	4	副	分開地、個別地	457
apartment	4	名	公寓大樓、房間	501
ape	2	名	黑猩猩	★
apologize	3	動	道歉、認錯	★

單字	頻率	詞性	中譯	頁碼
apology	3	名	道歉、賠罪、辯解	259
appeal	4	動	有吸引力、訴諸	81
appear	5	動	似乎、出現、露面	519
appearance	3	名	外貌、出現	27
appetite	3	名	食慾、胃口、愛好	139
applaud	3	動	鼓掌、喝采、稱讚	237
appliance	3	名	家用電器、裝置	183
applicant	3	名	申請人	435
application	4	名	申請書、應用、施用	399
apply	4	動	申請、塗、應用	141
appoint	4	動	指派、任命、約定	473
appointment	3	名	約會、委派、職位	149
appreciate	4	動	感激、欣賞、領會	99
apprentice	3	名	學徒、初學者	31
approach	5	動	靠近、接近	229
appropriate	4	形	恰當的、相稱的	399
approval	4	名	認可、贊同、批准	101
April	5	名	四月	★
apron	3	名	工作裙、圍裙	141
aptitude	2	名	天資、才能、習性	461
arch	4	名	拱門、牌樓、拱狀物	399
archaeologist	2	名	考古學家	★
archaeology	2	名	考古學	427
architectural	1	形	建築學的	147
area	5	名	領域、區域、面積	395
argue	4	動	爭論、主張、說服	163
arithmetic	3	名	算數、算術知識	271
arm	5	名	臂、衣袖	★
armchair	4	名	扶手椅	★
army	4	名	陸軍、大批、團體	75
around	5	副	到處、周圍	★
arouse	4	動	喚起、引起興趣	401
arrange	4	動	整理、布置、安排	45

單字	頻率	詞性	中譯	頁碼
arrest	4	動	逮捕、阻止、吸引	141
arrive	5	動	到達、成功、達成	259
arrogant	3	形	傲慢的、自大的	335
arson	2	名	縱火罪	309
art	5	名	藝術、美術	★
article	4	名	文章、論文、條款	355
artificial	3	形	矯揉造作的、人工的	401
artist	4	名	藝術家、大師、藝人	345
artistic	3	形	藝術的、精美的	★
artwork	2	名	美術品、藝術品	213
ashamed	3	形	羞愧的	★
Asia	5	名	亞洲	★
ask	5	名	詢問、要求	★
asleep	3	副	進入睡眠狀態	113
aspect	4	名	方面、觀點、外觀	191
aspiration	2	名	抱負、志向、呼氣	387
aspire	3	動	嚮往、懷有大志	35
assassination	1	名	暗殺、行刺	387
assembly	4	名	集會、立法機關	241
assignment	3	名	任務、作業、指派	401
assist	4	動	幫助、協助、參加	337
assistance	3	名	幫助、援助	389
assistant	4	名	助理、助手	141
association	3	名	協會、社團、聯合	431
assume	4	動	假定、取得、假裝	401
assure	4	動	保證、使放心、保障	401
astonish	3	動	使吃驚、使驚訝	113
astray	2	副	離開正道、迷路	447
athlete	4	名	運動員	91
athletic	3	形	運動員的、體育家的	★
atmosphere	4	名	氣氛、大氣、魅力	49
attach	5	動	固定、裝上、繫上	305
attack	5	名	攻擊、抨擊	331

單字	頻率	詞性	中譯	頁碼
attempt	4	動	企圖、試圖做	271
attend	4	動	出席、照料、注意	61
attention	5	名	注意、專心、照顧	213
attitude	4	名	態度、意見、看法	209
attract	5	動	吸、吸引	★
attraction	3	名	吸引力	★
attractive	3	形	吸引人的、有魅力的	83
attribute	4	動	歸因於、歸咎於	461
auction	3	名	拍賣	411
audience	4	名	觀眾、聽眾、謁見	111
audition	2	名	試鏡、試聽、聽力	71
August	5	名	八月	★
aunt	5	名	阿姨、伯母	★
Australian	3	形	澳大利亞(人)的	65
author	4	名	作家、創辦者	273
authority	4	名	當局、權威人士	403
automatically	3	副	自動地、無意識地	39
autumn	5	名	秋天、凋落期	15
available	3	形	有空的、可利用的	261
avant-garde	2	形	前衛的	445
avenue	3	名	大街、大道、方法	273
average	5	形	平均的、普通的	15
avoid	5	動	避免、防止、撤銷	57
await	4	動	等候、期待	403
awake	3	形	醒著的、意識到的	249
award	4	名	獎、獎狀、獎學金	261
aware	4	形	知道的、察覺的	267
away	5	副	離開	★
awful	4	形	可怕的、極糟的	145

B

單字	頻率	詞性	中譯	頁碼
bachelor	3	名	單身漢、(B)學士	11
back	5	名	背部、後面	★

單字	頻率	詞性	中譯	頁碼
background	4	名	背景、經歷、幕後	163
backpack	1	名	登山或遠足用背包	403
backwards	3	副	向後、逆、往回	143
backwater	1	名	與世隔絕的地方	443
backyard	2	名	後院、後花園	85
bacon	3	名	培根、鹹豬肉	273
bacteria	4	名	細菌	153
bait	3	名	誘餌、圈套	275
bake	5	動	烘烤	★
bakery	5	名	烘焙坊、麵包店	★
balance	4	名	平衡、協調、鎮定	243
balcony	3	名	陽台、劇場包廂	143
bald	3	形	禿頭的、赤裸裸的	53
ballet	3	名	芭蕾舞	★
balloon	3	名	氣球、球狀物	15
bamboo	4	名	竹子	★
banana	5	名	香蕉	★
band	4	名	細繩、樂團	★
bandage	3	名	繃帶	275
bank	5	名	銀行、堤	★
bankrupt	3	形	破產的、喪失…的	25
bar	5	名	酒吧、橫槓	★
barbecue	2	名	烤肉架、烤肉野餐	217
barber	3	名	理髮師	17
barely	3	副	僅僅、幾乎沒	21
bargain	3	動	討價還價、達成協議	253
bark	3	動	吠叫、咆哮	143
barn	4	名	穀倉、糧倉、大車庫	275
barrack	2	名	兵營、工房	323
barren	3	形	貧瘠的、不生育的	51
barrier	3	名	障礙、路障、剪票口	403
base	5	名	基地、總部、基礎	125
baseball	5	名	棒球	★

單字	頻率	詞性	中譯	頁碼
basement	4	名	地下室、地窖	143
basic	5	形	基本的	★
basis	5	名	基礎、準則	519
basket	4	名	一籃的量、籃網	143
basketball	5	名	籃球	★
bass	3	名	貝斯、男低音	★
bathroom	5	名	浴室	★
bathtub	5	名	浴缸	★
battery	4	名	電池、一系列、砲台	403
battle	4	名	戰役、戰鬥、爭鬥	405
battlefield	2	名	戰場、戰地	143
beach	5	名	海灘、湖濱	★
beam	4	動	發送、對準、照射	213
bean	4	名	豆、毫無價值的東西	451
bear	5	動	忍受、承擔、運送	143
beard	3	名	鬍鬚、山羊鬍	143
beat	5	動	跳動、擊、打敗	55
beautician	2	名	美容師	183
beautiful	5	形	美麗的、出色的	★
beauty	4	名	美人、美麗、優點	227
because	5	連	因為	★
become	5	動	變得、成為	★
bedroom	5	名	臥室、寢室	★
beer	5	名	啤酒	★
before	5	副	以前、向前	★
beg	3	動	乞討、乞求	★
beggar	2	名	乞丐、窮光蛋	95
begin	5	動	開始、著手	★
beginning	4	名	開始、最初	★
behavior	4	名	行為、(事物的)反應	55
behind	4	介	在…後面、不如	371
belief	4	名	看法、相信、信仰	145
believe	5	動	相信、信任、猜想	341

單字	頻率	詞性	中譯	頁碼
belong	4	動	屬於、適用、處在	383
belongings	2	名	攜帶物品、財產	475
beloved	3	形	心愛的、受鍾愛的	509
below	4	副	在下面	★
belt	4	名	腰帶、傳送帶、地帶	325
bench	4	名	長凳、法官	105
bend	4	動	彎曲、屈從、致力於	145
beneath	4	介	在…下面、低於	275
beneficial	3	形	有利的、有幫助的	227
benefit	4	名	津貼、利益、優勢	81
beside	4	介	在旁邊、和…無關	19
besides	4	副	此外、而且	467
bestseller	4	名	暢銷書	★
betrayal	2	名	背叛、告密、暴露	369
between	5	介	在…之間	★
beverage	2	名	飲料	117
beyond	3	介	超出…之外	★
bicycle	5	名	腳踏車	★
bid	4	動	向…表示、命令	441
big	5	形	大的、巨大的	★
bikini	3	名	比基尼泳裝	★
bill	5	名	法案、帳單、目錄	497
billboard	3	名	廣告牌	★
billion	4	名	十億	★
billionaire	2	名	億萬富翁	25
bind	5	動	綑綁、裝訂、束縛	419
biography	3	名	傳記、興衰史	507
biology	4	名	生物學、生活規律	405
birth	3	名	出生、血統、誕生	281
birthday	5	名	生日	★
bite	5	動	咬、啃、上當、纏住	207
bitter	4	形	苦的、尖刻的	145
bizarre	3	形	奇異的、古怪的	169
blackboard	3	名	黑板	145
blackout	2	名	停電、燈火管制	299
blame	4	動	責備、歸咎於	413
blank	4	形	空白的、茫然的	145
bleaching	2	形	漂白的	27
bleed	4	動	流血、犧牲、榨取	277
blessing	2	名	祝福、同意、禱告	405
blind	4	形	盲的、未加思考的	145
blink	3	名	一瞬間、眨眼睛	273
block	5	動	阻擋、妨礙、限制	367
blog	5	名	部落格、網路日誌	★
bloody	4	形	流血的、血淋淋的	★
blooming	3	形	開著花的、繁盛的	85
blossom	3	名	花、開花、生長期	261
blow	5	動	吹、隨風飄動	21
blush	3	動	臉紅、發窘	405
board	5	名	板、委員會、布告牌	47
boast	4	動	自吹自擂、誇耀	405
boat	5	名	小船、船形容器	429
body	5	名	身體、肉體	★
boil	4	動	沸騰、激動、起泡	225
bomb	4	動	轟炸、投彈、慘敗	331
bombing	4	名	轟炸、砲轟	147
bond	3	名	連結、聯繫、束縛	405
bonus	4	名	紅利、額外津貼	431
book	5	動	預訂、登記	51
boot	4	名	靴子、解雇	155
booth	3	名	公共電話亭、貨攤	141
border	4	名	邊境、國界、邊緣	277
bore	3	動	使厭煩、煩擾、鑽孔	277
boring	3	形	令人生厭的、乏味的	119
born	5	形	出生的、天生的	★
borrow	3	動	借入、採用、抄襲	197

單字	頻率	詞性	中譯	頁碼
boss	4	名	老闆、有權勢者	259
both	5	代	兩個…(都)	★
bother	4	動	打擾、使惱怒、費心	311
bottle	4	名	瓶子、酒、一瓶的量	117
bottom	4	名	臀部、底層、盡頭	61
bottomless	2	形	深不可測的、無限的	55
boundary	3	名	限度、範圍、邊界	229
bouquet	3	名	一束花、花束、香味	385
boutique	3	名	精品店	103
bowed	3	形	彎成弓形的	★
bowl	5	名	碗、草地滾木球戲	★
bowling	4	名	保齡球、滾木球	★
boyfriend	5	名	男朋友	★
bracelet	2	名	手鐲	273
brain	5	名	頭腦	★
brake	3	動	煞車、抑制、約束	143
branch	4	名	樹枝、分公司、分支	61
brand	4	名	牌子、商標、烙印	353
brand-new	4	形	嶄新的、新製的	
brass	3	名	黃銅、黃銅色、銅器	277
brave	4	形	英勇的、壯觀的	277
bravery	3	名	勇敢、勇氣	★
bread	5	名	麵包、生計	★
break	5	動	打破、毀壞、闖入	129
breakfast	5	名	早餐	★
breakthrough	2	名	突破性進展、突圍	381
breast	4	名	胸部、乳房、心情	71
breath	4	名	呼吸、微風	37
breed	3	動	飼養、培育、引起	305
brew	3	動	釀造、被沖泡	451
bribe	2	名	賄賂、誘餌	165
brick	4	名	磚塊、積木	147
bride	3	名	新娘	279

單字	頻率	詞性	中譯	頁碼
bridegroom	1	名	新郎	★
bridge	5	名	橋、鼻梁、橋梁	243
brief	5	形	簡略的、短暫的	203
briefly	4	副	簡潔地、短暫地	★
bright	5	形	晴朗的、鮮明的	505
brightly	4	副	明亮地、鮮明地	★
brilliant	4	形	優秀的、技藝高超的	279
bring	5	動	帶來、拿來	★
broad	4	形	廣泛的、遼闊的	147
broadcast	4	動	廣播、播放	77
broken	5	形	損壞的、折斷的	329
broker	3	名	經紀人、掮客	87
brook	3	名	小溪、小河	279
brother	5	名	兄弟	★
brown	5	形	棕色的、褐色的	★
brownish	2	形	呈褐色的	135
bruise	3	名	傷痕、青腫、擦傷	293
brush	4	動	刷牙、掠過、拂去	251
brutal	3	形	嚴酷的、殘忍的	405
bubble	4	名	氣泡、泡影	279
bucket	3	名	水桶、一桶、大量	415
Buddhist	3	名	佛教徒	★
budget	4	名	預算、生活費、經費	227
buffet	3	名	自助餐、快餐	279
build	5	動	建造、發展、擴大	209
building	5	名	建築物、房屋	495
bulletin	3	名	公告、新聞快報	405
bulletproof	2	形	防彈的	387
bully	3	動	威嚇、欺侮人	13
bump	3	動	碰撞、猛擊	55
bundle	4	名	捆、包裹、大量	149
burden	4	名	重擔、負擔	131
bureaucracy	3	名	官僚政治、繁文縟節	81

單字	頻率	詞性	中譯	頁碼
bureaucratic	1	形	官僚政治的	★
burn	4	動	燃燒、發熱	★
burning	2	形	著火的、發熱的	495
burst	3	動	爆發、破裂、塞滿	143
bury	4	動	埋葬、掩藏、使沉浸	281
bus	5	名	巴士、公車	★
business	5	名	生意、職業、交易	429
busy	5	形	忙碌的	★
butter	5	名	奶油、黃油	★
butterfly	5	名	蝴蝶	★

C

單字	頻率	詞性	中譯	頁碼
cabbage	4	名	甘藍菜、卷心菜	★
cabin	3	名	小屋、客艙、駕駛艙	199
cabinet	3	名	櫥櫃、內閣、密室	405
cable	4	名	有線電視、電纜	149
cafeteria	2	名	自助餐館	★
cage	3	名	獸籠、座廂	★
calculate	3	動	計算、估計、打算	129
calculator	1	名	計算機	★
calendar	3	名	行事曆、日曆、曆法	149
call	5	動	打電話給、稱…為	★
calligraphy	2	名	書法、筆跡	245
calm	4	動	鎮定下來、平靜	345
calorie	2	名	卡路里、大卡	53
camel	2	名	駱駝	★
camp	4	名	兵營、營地	239
campaign	4	動	參加競選、從事運動	101
campus	4	名	大學、校園	311
can	5	名	罐頭、金屬容器	493
cancel	4	動	取消、刪去	149
cancer	4	名	癌症、弊端	495
candidate	4	名	候選人、應試者	407

單字	頻率	詞性	中譯	頁碼
candle	4	名	蠟燭	★
candlelight	4	名	燭光	★
cannabis	1	名	印度大麻、大麻煙	41
canned	2	形	裝成罐頭的、錄音的	347
canyon	2	名	峽谷	281
cap	4	名	無邊便帽、制服帽	★
capable	4	形	有能力的、能幹的	347
capacity	4	名	容量、生產力、能力	167
cape	3	名	斗篷、披肩、海角	407
capitalism	1	名	資本主義	407
capture	4	動	獲得、俘虜	241
carbon	4	名	碳、複寫紙	487
card	5	名	紙牌、卡片、名片	★
cardboard	2	名	硬紙板、卡紙板	159
care	5	動	關心、擔心、想要	131
career	5	名	職業、生涯、歷程	271
careful	5	形	仔細的、小心的	★
carnivore	2	名	肉食動物	79
carpet	3	名	地毯	151
carriage	3	名	四輪馬車、火車車廂	281
carrot	4	名	紅蘿蔔	★
carry	5	動	運載、攜帶、傳達	433
cart	3	名	手推車	★
cartoon	4	名	卡通、諷刺畫	151
carving	2	名	雕刻、雕刻物	407
case	5	名	箱、盒	★
cash	5	名	現金	★
Cashmere	2	名	喀什米爾羊絨	★
cassette	3	名	錄音帶、膠捲盒	151
cast	4	動	投擲、投射、丟棄	279
castle	4	名	城堡、堡壘	195
casual	4	形	便裝的、漫不經心的	281
casualty	3	名	傷亡人員、意外事故	421

單字	頻率	詞性	中譯	頁碼
catch	5	動	捕捉、逮住、撞見	361
catchy	1	形	引起注意的	439
cattle	3	名	牛	★
cause	5	名	原因、動機	★
caution	3	名	謹慎、小心、告誡	393
cave	4	名	洞穴、洞窟	★
cease	4	動	停止、終止、結束	407
ceaseless	2	形	不停的、不間斷的	239
ceiling	4	名	天花板、頂篷	★
celebrate	4	動	慶祝、頌揚、舉行	145
celebration	4	名	慶祝、慶祝活動	★
celebrity	4	名	名人、名聲	67
cell	5	名	小囚房、細胞、電池	151
cement	3	動	鞏固、水泥接合	177
center	5	名	中心、中樞	271
central	4	形	中心的、中央的	★
century	3	名	世紀、一百年	★
cereal	5	名	麥片、穀類植物	★
ceremony	3	名	典禮、禮儀、客套	279
certain	5	形	特定的、無疑的	397
certainly	4	副	無疑地、確實、當然	377
certificate	3	名	證明書、執照、憑證	159
chalk	3	名	粉筆、白堊岩	151
challenge	4	名	挑戰、艱鉅的事	271
chamber	4	名	議院、寢室、會議廳	407
champion	4	名	冠軍、鬥士	57
chance	5	名	機會、可能性、運氣	211
change	5	動	改變、使變化	★
changeable	2	形	易變的、不定的	127
chaos	4	名	混亂、無秩序、雜亂	421
chapter	4	名	重要時期、章、回	283
character	4	名	性格、特性、名聲	127
characteristic	3	名	特徵、特性、特色	191

單字	頻率	詞性	中譯	頁碼
charge	4	名	指控、索價、責任	101
charitable	2	形	慈善的、寬厚的	307
charity	3	名	慈善團體、善舉	223
charm	4	動	使陶醉、吸引	283
charming	4	形	迷人的、有魅力的	★
chart	4	名	進排行榜、圖表	27
chase	4	動	追逐、追求、追捕	11
chat	5	動	聊天、閒談	283
cheap	5	形	便宜的、廉價的	★
cheat	3	動	作弊、欺騙、不忠	67
check	5	動	核對、檢查、開支票	127
cheek	4	名	臉頰、腮幫子	283
cheer	3	動	歡呼、喝采	283
cheerful	3	形	興高采烈的	283
cheerleader	2	名	啦啦隊員	371
cheese	5	名	乳酪、乾酪	★
chemical	4	形	化學的、化學用的	153
chess	5	名	西洋棋	★
chest	4	名	箱子、胸膛、金庫	49
chick	3	名	(俚)小妞、小雞	27
chicken	5	名	雞、雞肉	★
chief	4	名	酋長、首領、長官	257
child	5	名	兒童	★
childhood	3	名	童年時期	449
childish	2	形	幼稚的、孩子般的	441
chili	4	名	辣椒	★
chilly	2	形	冷颼颼的、冷淡的	261
chimney	3	名	煙囪、岩石裂縫	47
chin	4	名	下巴、頦、聊天	153
china	5	名	瓷器、瓷製品	405
Chinese	5	名	中國人、中文	★
chip	4	名	炸馬鈴薯片、碎片	285
chocolate	5	名	巧克力	★

單字	頻率	詞性	中譯	頁碼
choice	5	名	選擇、供選擇範圍	153
choke	3	動	窒息、堵塞、抑制	285
choose	5	動	挑選、選擇、決定	449
chop	4	動	砍、劈成、剁碎	285
chopstick	3	名	筷子	★
chore	2	名	家庭雜務、例行工作	455
chosen	2	形	挑選出來的、精選的	495
Christmas	5	名	聖誕節	★
chubby	2	形	圓胖的、豐滿的	215
church	5	名	教堂	★
cigar	3	名	雪茄煙	85
cigarette	3	名	香菸、紙菸	★
cinema	3	名	電影院	★
circulate	3	動	流傳、循環、流通	409
circumstance	3	名	情況、情勢、環境	409
citizen	3	名	公民、老百姓	29
city	5	名	城市、市	★
civilian	3	名	平民百姓	147
civilization	2	名	文明、文化	427
claim	4	動	聲稱、索取、要求	153
class	5	名	班級、社會階級	★
classic	3	形	經典的、古典的	285
classmate	5	名	同班同學	★
classroom	5	名	教室	★
clay	4	名	泥土、黏土、肉體	155
clean	5	形	清潔的、純潔的	★
cleaner	2	名	乾洗工、乾洗店	323
clerk	5	名	職員、店員	★
clever	3	形	聰明的、靈巧的	341
client	4	名	客戶、委託人	285
climate	3	名	氣候	★
climax	3	名	頂點、高潮	15
climb	5	動	爬、登上、上升	371

單字	頻率	詞性	中譯	頁碼
clinic	3	名	診所、會診	123
clinical	2	形	臨床的、診所的	491
clip	4	名	剪下來的東西、修剪	473
clock	5	名	時鐘	★
cloister	2	名	修道院、隱居地	335
close	5	形	接近的、密切的	★
closet	3	名	衣櫥、碗櫥、小房間	155
cloth	4	名	布、衣料、桌巾	155
clothes	5	名	服裝、衣服	★
clothing	4	名	(總稱)衣服、覆蓋物	209
cloudy	3	形	多雲的、不愉快的	155
clown	4	名	小丑、丑角	285
club	5	名	俱樂部、社團、會所	119
clue	3	名	線索、跡象、情節	333
clumsy	3	形	製作粗陋的、笨拙的	409
coach	4	名	教練、普通車廂	157
coarse	3	形	粗糙的、粗俗的	409
coast	4	名	海岸、沿海地區	★
coaster	2	名	沿岸貿易船、杯墊	135
coat	4	名	大衣、皮毛、塗層	187
cockroach	4	名	蟑螂	★
cocktail	3	名	雞尾酒、(西餐)開胃品	77
coffee	5	名	咖啡	★
coincidence	3	名	巧合、同時發生	387
coincidentally	1	副	巧合地、碰巧的是	317
coke	4	名	焦炭、可樂	★
coldly	2	副	冷淡地、冷漠地	353
coldness	2	名	寒冷、冷酷、冷靜	11
collapse	4	動	倒塌、瓦解、垮掉	409
collar	4	名	衣領、項圈	285
colleague	3	名	同事、同僚	197
collect	4	動	使鎮定、收集、聚積	69
collection	4	名	收藏品、募捐、大量	85

單字	頻率	詞性	中譯	頁碼
college	4	名	大學、學院、學會	117
cologne	2	名	古龍香水	131
colonel	4	名	陸軍上校	125
colony	4	名	殖民地、僑居地	75
colorful	3	形	鮮豔的、多采多姿的	157
column	4	名	圓柱、專欄、柱狀物	287
comb	5	名	梳子、毛刷	★
combat	3	動	戰鬥、搏鬥、反對	463
combination	3	名	結合、聯盟、組合	411
comedy	4	名	喜劇、喜劇成分	323
comfort	4	動	安慰、慰問	107
comfortable	5	形	舒適的	★
comic	3	形	連環漫畫的、喜劇的	113
coming	4	形	即將到來的、接著的	71
command	4	名	命令、指揮、掌握	287
commander	4	名	指揮官、領導人	13
comment	4	名	評論、意見、閒話	89
commercial	4	形	商務的、商業的	291
commit	4	動	犯罪、做承諾	161
committee	4	名	委員會、監護人	287
common	5	形	共有的、常見的	195
commonplace	4	名	司空見慣、老生常談	9
communicate	4	動	溝通、表達	287
community	4	名	社區、公眾、群落	411
company	5	名	公司、商號	★
compare	4	動	比較、對照	417
compensate	3	動	補償、酬報、抵銷	67
compensation	3	名	補償、賠償金	★
compete	4	動	比賽、對抗、比得上	287
competence	3	名	能力、稱職、勝任	347
competition	3	名	競爭、比賽、競爭者	111
competitive	3	形	競爭的、好勝的	245
competitor	2	名	競爭者、敵手	411

單字	頻率	詞性	中譯	頁碼
complain	4	動	抱怨、發牢騷、控訴	157
complaint	3	名	抱怨、抗議、控訴	433
complementary	1	形	互補的、相配的	135
complete	5	形	完全的、完整的	427
complicate	2	動	使複雜化、併發	411
complicated	3	形	複雜的、難懂的	131
comply	4	動	依從、遵守	13
compose	3	動	作曲、構圖、使鎮靜	15
composer	2	名	作曲家、調停者	411
composition	3	名	作曲、作文、構圖	411
composure	2	名	鎮靜、沉著、平靜	237
comprehensively	2	副	廣泛地、全面地	65
computer	5	名	電腦、電子計算機	★
comrade	2	名	同事、共患難的夥伴	13
conceivable	3	形	想得到的	287
concentrate	4	動	集中、全神貫注	413
concept	4	名	思想、觀念、概念	425
concern	5	名	擔心、關係	287
concert	4	名	音樂會、一致、和諧	119
concerted	1	形	商定的、一致的	★
conclude	4	動	斷定、結束	415
conclusion	4	名	結論、結局、締結	289
concrete	4	形	具體的、有形的	413
condition	3	名	情況、環境、條件	59
conditioner	4	名	調節器、調節員	★
conduct	4	動	實施、帶領、管理	319
conductor	2	名	指揮、領導者、導體	411
conference	3	名	會議、協商會、會談	121
confess	3	動	承認、坦白、懺悔	323
confidence	3	名	自信、信賴	27
confidently	3	副	確信地	★
confine	4	動	侷限、幽禁、坐月子	413
confirm	3	動	確定、證實、鞏固	157

單字	頻率	詞性	中譯	頁碼
confiscate	2	動	將…充公、徵收	403
conflict	4	名	矛盾、衝突、鬥爭	511
confront	3	動	正視、面臨、使對質	67
confused	4	形	困惑的、混亂的	181
confusion	3	名	騷動、困惑	★
congratulate	2	動	祝賀、恭喜	413
congratulations	2	名	祝賀、恭喜	157
congress	4	名	會議、(C)美國國會	413
conquer	3	動	克服、戰勝	413
conscience	3	名	良心、善惡觀念	459
consequential	2	形	隨之發生的	★
conservation	3	名	保存、保護、守恆	79
conservative	3	形	保守的、老式的	413
consider	5	動	考慮、細想、認為	9
considerable	3	形	相當多的、重要的	193
consideration	5	名	考慮	★
consist	3	動	組成、存在於、符合	95
constantly	3	副	不斷地、時常地	41
constellation	1	名	星座、薈萃、群集	219
construction	4	名	建造、建築物、結構	433
constructive	2	形	有助益的、建設性的	415
consult	4	動	請教、查閱、當顧問	415
consultant	4	名	顧問、諮詢者	175
consulting	2	形	諮詢的	175
consume	4	動	花費、吃光、耗盡	53
consumer	3	名	消費者、消耗者	245
contact	5	動	聯繫、接觸	159
contain	5	動	包含、容納、控制	445
container	3	名	容器、集裝箱、貨櫃	159
content	4	名	內容、要旨、目錄	375
contentment	1	名	知足、滿意	★
contest	4	名	競賽、爭奪、爭論	275
contestant	2	名	參加競賽者、角逐者	275

單字	頻率	詞性	中譯	頁碼
continue	5	動	繼續、延伸	★
continuous	3	形	連續的、不斷的	477
contract	4	名	契約、合同、婚約	105
contradiction	2	名	矛盾、反駁、牴觸	431
contrary	3	名	相反、對立面	417
contrast	4	名	對比、對照、反差	81
contribute	3	動	貢獻、捐助、投稿	75
contribution	3	名	捐獻、貢獻、投稿	223
control	5	動	控制、管理、抑制	397
controversial	3	形	有爭議的	33
conveniently	1	副	方便地、合宜地	467
convent	3	名	女修道院、修女團	335
conventional	3	形	傳統的、慣例的	417
conversation	5	名	會話、談話	★
converse	3	動	交談、談話	417
convey	4	動	傳達、運送、傳播	195
convince	4	動	說服、使信服	417
cook	5	動	烹調、煮	★
cooker	2	名	炊具、烹調器具	159
cookery	1	名	烹調、烹飪術	31
cookie	5	名	餅乾	★
cool	5	形	涼快的、冷靜的	★
cooperate	3	動	配合、合作	287
cooperation	2	名	合作、協力	★
cope	4	動	妥善處理、對付	419
copy	5	動	模仿、臨摹、複製	457
copyright	3	名	版權、著作權	427
cord	4	名	細繩、絕緣電線	419
corn	5	名	玉米、穀物	★
corner	5	名	街角、困境、壟斷	173
corporation	3	名	股份公司、社團法人	213
correct	4	形	正確的、恰當的	127
corrupt	3	形	腐敗的、貪汙的	185

單字	頻率	詞性	中譯	頁碼	單字	頻率	詞性	中譯	頁碼
corruption	2	名	貪汙、賄賂、墮落	223	craze	2	名	一時狂熱、風尚	177
cosmetics	2	名	化妝品	27	crazy	5	形	瘋狂的、愚蠢的	★
cost	5	名	成本、費用、代價	471	cream	5	名	奶油、乳脂	★
costly	3	形	貴重的、代價高的	31	create	5	動	產生、創造、創作	301
costume	3	名	戲服、裝束	399	creation	2	名	創造、創作品、世界	493
cottage	3	名	農舍、小屋、別墅	63	creative	4	形	創造的	151
cotton	4	名	棉花、棉布	159	creativity	4	名	創造力	33
couch	4	名	長沙發、睡椅	★	credit	3	名	信譽、賒欠	★
cough	4	動	咳嗽、咳出	159	creep	2	動	爬行、匍匐而行	381
council	4	名	地方議會、會議	141	cricket	3	名	蟋蟀、板球	291
count	5	動	計算、數	★	crime	4	名	罪行、罪過	161
countless	2	形	數不盡的、無數的	455	criminal	4	形	犯罪的、刑事上的	161
country	5	名	國家、故鄉、鄉下	★	crisis	4	名	危機、緊急關頭	161
countryside	2	名	農村、鄉間	159	critic	3	名	批評家、評論家	419
couple	3	名	(未婚)夫妻、一對	19	critical	4	形	批判的、愛挑剔的	111
coupon	2	名	優惠券、贈貨券	297	criticism	4	名	批評、評論、指責	35
courage	3	名	膽量、勇氣	11	criticize	3	動	批評、評論、苛求	109
courageous	1	形	英勇的、勇敢的	★	crop	4	名	作物、莊稼	★
course	5	名	課程、路線、方針	117	crossing	2	名	雜交、十字路口	405
court	5	動	向…獻殷勤、追求	61	crowded	3	形	擁擠的、閱歷豐富的	59
cousin	4	名	堂(表)兄弟姊妹	129	cruel	4	形	殘忍的、慘痛的	11
cover	3	動	覆蓋、適用於、報導	75	cruise	4	動	航行、航遊、漫遊	103
covering	2	名	覆蓋物、毯子	421	crush	3	名	迷戀、極度擁擠	311
cow	4	名	母牛、乳牛	★	cry	5	動	哭、叫喊	★
cowardice	2	名	膽小、懦弱	55	cub	2	名	幼獸、毛頭小子	79
cowardly	1	形	膽小的、懦弱的	289	cultural	3	形	文化的、修養的	291
cowboy	1	名	牛仔、莽撞的人	★	culture	4	名	文化	★
coworker	2	名	同事、幫手	291	cup	5	名	杯子、一杯的容量	★
craft	3	名	手工藝、手腕、奸計	419	cupboard	3	名	櫥櫃、碗櫥	291
cram	3	動	把…塞進、把…塞滿	★	cure	4	動	治癒、消除、糾正	161
crash	4	動	撞擊、墜毀、垮台	255	curio	1	名	古董、珍品	285
crawl	2	動	爬行、徐徐行進	289	curiosity	3	名	好奇心、珍品、古玩	401
crayon	5	名	顏色粉筆、蠟筆	★	curious	3	形	好奇的、愛探究的	★

534

單字	頻率	詞性	中譯	頁碼
current	5	形	當前的、通用的	173
curse	4	動	咒罵、詛咒、使遭難	441
curtain	4	名	窗簾、帷幔	163
custom	4	名	習俗、慣例	47
customer	4	名	顧客、買主	327
cute	5	形	可愛的、漂亮的	★
cuteness	5	名	可愛、漂亮	★

D

單字	頻率	詞性	中譯	頁碼
daily	4	形	每日的、日常的	41
damage	4	動	損害、毀壞	161
dancer	5	名	跳舞者、舞蹈演員	★
danger	5	名	危險	★
dangerous	5	形	危險的、不安全的	★
dare	4	動	膽敢、敢於面對	263
dark	5	形	黑暗的、邪惡的	★
darkness	3	名	黑暗、無知、邪惡	389
dart	3	名	飛鏢、標槍、飛奔	279
dash	4	動	急奔、擊碎、潑灑	11
dastardly	1	形	殘酷的、懦弱的	287
data	5	名	數據、資料	77
date	5	動	過時、約會	33
daughter	5	名	女兒、媳婦	★
daytime	3	名	白天、白晝	★
dead	5	形	死的、枯的	★
deadline	3	名	最後限期、截稿時間	381
deadly	4	形	毒性的、致命的	331
deaf	3	形	聾的、不願聽的	163
deal	5	名	交易、大量、發牌	489
dear	5	形	親愛的、珍視的	★
death	5	名	死、死亡	★
deathbed	2	名	臨終的一段時間	511
debate	3	動	辯論、討論、思考	65

單字	頻率	詞性	中譯	頁碼
debt	4	名	債務、人情債	29
decade	1	名	十、十年	43
decayed	2	形	爛了的、腐敗的	89
deceit	3	名	欺騙、騙局	17
deceive	3	動	欺騙、蒙蔽	421
deceiver	3	名	騙子、詐欺者	17
December	5	名	十二月	★
decide	5	動	決定	★
decision	4	名	決定、判斷	★
deck	4	名	露天平台、甲板	115
declare	4	動	宣稱、宣布、申報	397
decline	4	動	下降、衰退、婉拒	79
decorate	3	動	裝飾、修飾、布置	89
decoration	4	名	裝飾、裝潢、獎章	233
decrease	4	動	減少、減小	421
dedicate	3	動	致力於、以…奉獻	505
deed	3	名	功業、功績、行為	293
deep	5	形	深的、濃的	★
deer	5	名	鹿	★
defeat	4	動	擊敗、戰勝、使失敗	453
defend	4	動	保衛、防禦	231
define	3	動	給…下定義、限定	39
definition	4	名	定義、釋義、規定	355
degradation	2	名	降低、墮落、丟臉	517
degree	3	名	學位、程度、度數	395
delay	4	名	延遲、耽擱	91
delicate	3	形	精美的、易碎的	421
delicious	5	形	美味的	★
delight	4	動	高興、喜愛	211
delightful	2	形	令人愉快的	★
deliver	4	動	傳遞、投遞、宣布	163
delivery	3	名	傳送、交貨、分娩	91
demand	4	動	要求、需要、查問	259

單字	頻率	詞性	中譯	頁碼
democracy	3	名	民主、民主制度	355
democratic	4	形	民主的、民眾的	231
demonstrate	3	動	證明、示範操作	423
demonstration	2	名	證明、示範、示威	★
dense	4	形	濃厚的、密集的	423
dentist	3	名	牙醫	165
deny	4	動	否認、拒絕給予	165
depart	3	動	啟程、離開	423
department	4	名	部門、系、局	153
departure	3	名	啟程、出發	423
depend	5	動	依賴、取決於	★
dependent	4	形	依靠的、從屬的	★
depressed	3	形	沮喪的、蕭條的	375
depressing	3	形	令人沮喪的、憂愁的	47
deprive	3	動	剝奪、使喪失	423
depth	4	名	深度、深奧、深厚	389
describe	4	動	形容、描述、描繪	269
desert	4	形	荒蕪的、沙漠的	441
deserve	4	動	應受、值得	243
design	5	動	設計、計畫	301
designer	4	名	設計師、策畫者	293
desire	4	動	渴望、要求	165
desk	5	名	書桌、寫字台	★
despair	4	名	令人絕望的事物	★
desperate	4	形	絕望的、鋌而走險的	423
desperately	2	副	拼命地、絕望地	259
despicable	2	形	卑劣的、可鄙的	387
despise	2	動	鄙視、看不起	335
despite	5	介	儘管、任憑	31
dessert	5	名	餐後甜點	★
destiny	3	名	命運、天命	★
destroy	4	動	毀壞、消滅、打破	293
detail	4	名	細節、詳述、局部	175

單字	頻率	詞性	中譯	頁碼
detain	3	動	使耽擱、拘留、扣留	453
detect	4	動	察覺、看穿	79
detective	3	形	偵查用的	★
determination	3	名	決心、果斷、確定	423
determine	4	動	決定、確定	★
devastate	3	動	極度震驚、破壞	495
development	4	名	生長、發展	★
developmental	2	形	發展的、開發的	491
device	4	名	裝置、儀器、手段	425
devote	3	動	獻身、投入、專用於	171
devotion	3	名	奉獻、獻身、熱愛	325
dial	4	動	撥號、打電話、收聽	165
dialogue	3	名	交談、對白	251
diamond	3	名	鑽石、菱形、內野	233
diarrhea	2	名	腹瀉	123
diary	4	名	日記、日誌	165
dictionary	3	名	字典	297
diet	4	動	按規定進食、節食	235
differ	4	動	不同、相異	425
difference	5	名	差別、差距、不合	363
different	5	形	不同的、各種的	★
difficulty	5	名	困難	★
digest	3	動	領悟、消化	425
digger	2	名	挖掘者、挖掘機	23
digital	4	形	數字的、指狀的	167
dignity	3	名	尊嚴、尊貴、高尚	425
diligence	2	名	勤勉、勤奮	★
diligent	3	形	勤勉的、勤奮的	193
dim	3	形	暗淡的、模糊的	293
diminish	3	動	減少、縮減、失勢	79
dine	4	動	用餐、宴請	295
dining	4	名	進餐	183
dinner	5	名	晚餐、正餐	★

單字	頻率	詞性	中譯	頁碼
dinosaur	4	名	恐龍	★
diploma	3	名	學位證書、執照	425
diplomat	2	名	外交官、有手腕的人	425
diplomatic	3	形	圓滑的	417
direct	4	動	指揮、命令、針對	191
direction	5	名	方向、方位	★
directly	5	副	筆直地、坦率地	★
director	4	名	導演、主管、指揮	231
dirt	4	名	泥、爛泥、灰塵	253
dirty	4	形	髒的、汙穢的	329
disadvantage	3	名	不利條件、損失	425
disappear	4	動	消失、滅絕	★
disappointed	3	形	失望的、沮喪的	295
disappointment	2	名	沮喪、失望、掃興	375
disapprove	2	動	不贊成、不喜歡	507
disaster	3	名	災難、不幸	393
discard	3	動	丟棄、摒棄、擲出	505
discipline	4	名	訓練、紀律、懲戒	425
disconnect	1	動	使分離、分開、切斷	425
discount	3	名	折扣、打折扣	295
discouragement	2	名	沮喪、勸阻	★
discover	4	動	發現、找到、發覺	271
discuss	5	動	討論、論述、詳述	375
disease	5	名	疾病、不健全、弊病	107
disguise	4	名	偽裝、掩飾、假扮	425
disgusting	3	形	令人作嘔的	61
dish	4	名	菜餚、盤子、美女	203
dishonest	3	名	不誠實的、欺詐的	★
dislike	3	動	不喜歡、厭惡	295
disorder	3	名	混亂、無秩序、失調	427
display	4	動	陳列、展出、顯露	419
displease	2	動	使不高興、得罪	163
dissatisfied	2	形	不滿的、流露不滿的	259

單字	頻率	詞性	中譯	頁碼
dissuade	2	動	勸阻	463
distance	5	名	距離、路程	★
distinct	4	形	不同的、有區別的	241
distinguish	3	動	辨別、辨識出	319
distinguished	2	形	卓越的、著名的	427
distract	3	動	使分心、轉移、困擾	369
distribution	3	名	分布區域、分配	427
district	4	名	區域、行政區	★
disturb	4	動	擾亂、妨礙	215
ditch	3	名	水溝、渠道	295
diverse	4	形	不同的、多變化的	273
divide	3	動	分開、劃分	★
divine	3	動	預言、占卜、推測	427
divorce	4	動	離婚、使分離	19
dizzy	3	形	頭暈目眩的	167
dock	4	動	進港	291
doctor	5	名	醫生、博士	★
document	4	名	公文、文件、證件	503
documentary	1	形	記錄的、記實的	281
doll	5	名	玩偶、洋娃娃	★
dollar	5	名	(美、加等國)元	★
dolphin	4	名	海豚	★
domestic	4	形	家庭的、國內的	337
dominate	3	動	控制、支配、高聳於	427
donate	3	動	捐贈、捐獻	223
doorbell	5	名	門鈴	★
dorm	3	名	宿舍、寢室	61
double	5	形	兩倍的、加倍的	★
doubt	4	動	懷疑、不能肯定	169
doughnut	5	名	甜甜圈	★
down	5	副	向下、在下面	★
download	3	動	(電腦)下載	167
downstairs	3	副	往樓下	37

單字	頻率	詞性	中譯	頁碼
downtown	3	名	城市商業區	29
downturn	2	名	衰退、下降、低迷	81
dozen	3	名	一打、許多	37
draft	5	名	通風、氣流、草稿	429
drag	4	動	拖著前進、拉	169
dragon	4	名	龍	★
drain	3	動	排掉、使流出、耗盡	297
drama	4	名	戲劇、戲劇性、劇本	399
dramatically	2	副	戲劇性地	53
drastically	1	副	徹底地、激烈地	289
draw	5	動	吸引、拉長、描寫	37
dread	3	動	懼怕、擔心	429
dream	5	動	夢想、嚮往、夢見	381
dress	5	動	使穿著、打扮	★
drift	4	動	漂流、漂泊	37
drip	2	名	點滴、滴下、滴水聲	105
drive	5	動	駕駛、用車載	★
drop	5	動	中斷、滴下、落後	461
drought	3	名	乾旱、(長期)缺乏	51
drown	3	動	溺死、淹沒、蓋過	99
drowsy	3	形	昏昏欲睡的、沉寂的	297
drug	4	名	藥品、毒品	★
drugstore	4	名	藥房、雜貨店	★
drum	5	名	鼓	★
dry	5	形	乾的、乾燥的	★
duck	4	名	鴨子	★
due	5	形	應支付的、欠的	★
dull	4	形	乏味的、晦暗的	169
dumbfounded	2	形	驚得目瞪口呆的	113
dump	4	名	垃圾場、沮喪	119
dumpling	2	名	餃子	★
during	5	介	在…期間	337
dust	4	動	打掃、灑農藥	297

單字	頻率	詞性	中譯	頁碼
dusty	3	形	滿是灰塵的	429
duty	5	名	責任、本分、職責	511
dwarf	3	名	矮子、侏儒	471
dye	3	動	染上顏色	175
dynamite	2	名	炸藥、具爆炸性的事	303

E

單字	頻率	詞性	中譯	頁碼
each	4	形	各自、每	★
eager	4	形	渴望的、熱切的	297
eagle	4	名	鷹	★
early	5	形	提早的、早期的	★
earn	4	動	賺得、贏得、博得	133
earnestness	2	名	誠摯、認真	171
earth	5	名	地球	★
earthquake	3	名	地震、社會大動盪	113
ease	4	動	減輕、緩和	37
east	5	名	東方	★
easy	5	形	容易的、不費力的	★
easygoing	1	形	脾氣隨和的	443
eclipse	3	名	蝕、黯然失色	505
economical	2	形	節約的、精打細算的	19
economics	3	名	經濟情況、經濟學	429
economy	4	名	經濟、節省、經濟艙	429
edge	5	名	優勢、邊緣、激烈	39
edition	4	名	版本、發行數、翻版	297
editor	5	名	編輯、主筆、校訂者	103
educate	3	動	教育、培養、訓練	43
educational	2	形	教育的	493
effect	5	名	效果、作用	★
efficiency	3	名	效率、效能、功效	431
efficient	4	形	效率高的、能勝任的	299
effort	5	名	努力、盡力、成就	329
egg	5	名	蛋、雞蛋	★

單字	頻率	詞性	中譯	頁碼
either	3	連	或者	327
elderly	3	形	年長的、老式的	137
elect	3	動	選舉、推選、決定	171
election	3	名	選舉、當選	★
electric	4	形	發電的、電動的	63
electrician	2	名	電工、技師	★
electronic	4	形	電子的、電子操作的	299
elegant	3	形	優美的、講究的	103
element	4	名	元素、要素	61
elementary	3	形	初級的、基本的	99
elevator	3	名	電梯、升降機	171
elsewhere	4	副	在(往)別處	45
email	5	名	電子郵件	★
embarrassing	3	形	尷尬的、令人為難的	83
embarrassment	1	名	難堪	★
embassy	3	名	大使館、全體外交官	269
embrace	4	動	擁抱、抓住、信奉	325
emcee	2	名	司儀、主持人	431
emerge	4	動	出現、顯露、擺脫	431
emergency	4	名	緊急情況、非常時刻	299
emission	3	名	排放物、散發、發行	487
emit	3	動	散發、發表、發行	47
emotion	4	名	情緒、情感、激動	171
emotional	3	形	感情的、激起情感的	483
emperor	3	名	皇帝	299
emphasis	3	名	強調、重點	★
emphasize	4	動	強調、著重	269
empire	4	名	帝國、大企業、君權	431
employee	4	名	雇員、雇工	489
employment	4	名	雇用、工作	★
emporium	1	名	商場、商業中心	199
empty	4	形	空的、未占用的	493
enable	4	動	使能夠、賦予…能力	299

單字	頻率	詞性	中譯	頁碼
enclose	4	動	圍住、隨信附上	433
encore	2	名	要求加演、加演曲目	15
encounter	3	動	遭遇(敵人)、偶然相遇	149
encourage	4	動	鼓勵、激發、支持	65
end	5	動	結束、終止	341
end	5	名	末端、盡頭、結局	★
endangered	3	形	瀕臨絕種的	309
endorsement	2	名	背書、支持、簽署	121
endorser	2	名	背書人、轉讓人	175
endure	4	動	忍受、忍耐、持續	433
enemy	4	名	敵人、敵軍、危害物	263
energy	5	名	能量、活力、精力	261
enforce	4	動	實施、強制、堅持	433
engage	2	動	從事、訂婚、占用	301
engine	4	名	引擎、發動機	195
engineer	5	名	工程師、技師、專家	23
engineering	3	名	工程、工程學	★
English	5	名	英國人、英語	★
enhance	4	動	提高、增加、改進	463
enjoy	5	動	欣賞、享受	★
enjoyable	3	形	快樂的、有樂趣的	63
enlarge	3	動	擴大、擴展、詳述	411
enlighten	3	動	啟發、開導	303
enormous	3	形	巨大的、龐大的	95
enormously	3	副	巨大地、龐大地	★
enough	5	形	足夠的、充足的	337
ensure	4	動	確保、保證、擔保	347
enter	3	動	進入、使參加、輸入	341
entertain	4	動	使娛樂、使歡樂	★
entertainment	3	名	娛樂、演藝、款待	35
enthusiasm	3	名	熱情、熱心、熱忱	433
enthusiastic	3	形	熱心的、熱烈的	459
entire	4	形	整個的、完全的	139

單字	頻率	詞性	中譯	頁碼
entitle	2	動	給…命名、給予權利	251
entrance	4	名	入口、登場	83
entrepreneur	3	名	企業家、事業創辦者	245
entry	4	名	入場、參加、通道	119
envelope	3	名	信封、封套、外殼	51
envious	2	形	嫉妒的	★
environment	3	名	環境、四周狀況	125
envy	4	動	妒忌、羨慕	85
equality	3	名	平等、相等、均等	407
equipment	4	名	設備、裝備、才能	433
era	4	名	時代、歷史時期	167
erase	3	動	擦掉、抹去、消除	173
eraser	5	名	橡皮擦、板擦	★
erect	4	動	建立、設立、安裝	473
err	3	動	犯錯、犯罪	67
error	4	名	錯誤、過失、誤差	173
erudite	2	形	博學的、學問精深的	185
erupt	4	動	爆發、噴出、發疹	339
eruption	2	名	爆發、噴出、發疹	517
escalator	2	名	電扶梯	433
escape	4	動	逃脫、逃跑、漏出	301
escort	3	動	護送、陪同	321
especially	4	副	特別、尤其、專門地	429
essay	3	名	散文、論說文	★
essence	4	名	精髓、本質、要素	241
essential	4	形	必要的、不可或缺的	489
essentially	2	副	實質上、本來	185
establish	4	動	建立、創辦、制定	415
estate	4	名	地產、資產	395
estimate	4	動	估計、判斷、估價	177
Europe	4	名	歐洲	★
evaluation	2	名	評價、估價	435
eve	4	名	前夕、前一刻	411

單字	頻率	詞性	中譯	頁碼
even	5	形	平坦的、整齊的	★
evening	5	名	傍晚、晚上	★
event	4	名	事件、大事、項目	173
even-tempered	2	形	性情平和的、穩重的	379
eventually	3	副	最後、終於	229
ever	5	副	從來、至今	★
everyone	5	代	每個人	★
everything	5	代	每件事、一切事物	★
everywhere	5	副	到處、每個地方	★
evidence	4	名	證據、跡象、清楚	61
evident	3	形	明顯的、明白的	435
evil	4	形	討厭的、邪惡的	301
exact	4	形	確切的、精確無誤的	173
exaggerate	3	動	誇大、言過其實	435
examination	5	名	檢查、調查	★
examine	5	動	檢查、測驗	★
examiner	2	名	主考人、考官	449
example	5	名	例子、樣本	★
excel	4	動	勝過、優於、擅長	71
excellent	4	形	出色的、傑出的	137
except	5	介	除…之外	★
exception	3	名	例外、除去	★
excessive	3	形	過度的、過分的	293
exchange	4	動	交換、兌換	227
excited	5	形	興奮的、激動的	★
excitedly	2	副	興奮地、激動地	325
excitement	5	名	刺激、興奮	★
exciting	5	形	令人興奮的	★
exclusive	4	形	獨有的、排外的	241
excursion	3	名	遠足、短途旅行	219
excuse	4	名	藉口、辯解、道歉	173
exercise	5	名	運動、鍛鍊、行使	249
exhausted	3	形	精疲力竭的、耗盡的	129

單字	頻率	詞性	中譯	頁碼
exhibit	4	動	顯出、展示、表示	435
exhibition	3	名	展覽、顯示、陳列品	139
exhibitionism	2	名	裸露癖、表現狂	17
exile	3	動	流放、放逐	313
existence	4	名	生活方式、存在	423
existing	2	形	現存的、現行的	487
exit	4	名	出口、退場	301
expand	3	動	展開、擴大	★
expansion	3	名	擴展、膨脹、擴張	439
expect	5	動	要求、期待、認為	481
expectation	3	名	期待、預期、前程	57
expense	4	名	開支、費用、損失	159
expensive	5	形	高價的、昂貴的	★
experienced	2	形	有經驗的、熟練的	383
experiment	3	動	進行實驗、試驗	233
experimental	3	形	實驗性的、實驗用的	★
experimentation	1	名	實驗(法)	★
expert	4	名	專家、能手、熟練者	175
expertise	4	名	專門知識、專門技術	71
explain	4	動	解釋、說明、闡明	115
explode	3	動	爆炸、推翻、戳穿	303
exploitation	2	名	剝削、開發	407
explore	4	動	探索、探勘、考察	439
explosion	3	名	爆炸、劇增、爆發	331
explosive	3	名	炸藥、爆炸物	303
export	3	動	輸出、出口	317
exporter	3	名	出口商、輸出國	★
expose	4	動	使暴露於、揭發	67
exposition	3	名	博覽會、闡述、說明	239
exposure	3	名	曝光、揭露、曝曬	439
express	4	動	表達、快遞、擠壓出	133
expression	3	名	臉色、表達、措辭	49
expressive	2	形	意味深長的、表現的	303

單字	頻率	詞性	中譯	頁碼
extent	4	名	程度、範圍、廣度	439
extra	4	形	額外的、特大的	385
extraordinary	4	形	異常的、非凡的	31
extremely	3	副	極端地、非常	33
eye	5	名	眼睛	★
eyebrow	2	名	眉毛	429
eyelid	1	名	眼皮、眼瞼	★

F

單字	頻率	詞性	中譯	頁碼
fable	3	名	寓言、無稽之談	303
fabulous	3	形	驚人的、極好的	39
face	5	名	臉、表面	★
facility	4	名	設施、工具、能力	309
fact	5	名	事實、真相	★
faction	3	名	派別、派系之爭	413
factor	4	名	因素、要素、代理商	397
factory	4	名	工廠、製造處	159
fade	3	動	凋謝、枯萎、褪色	303
fail	5	動	失去作用、不及格	515
failure	4	名	失敗、不足、故障	111
faint	4	動	昏厥、變得微弱	13
faint	4	動	暈倒、昏厥	303
fair	5	形	白皙的、公正的	27
fairly	3	副	公平地、相當地	355
faith	4	名	信仰、信念、約定	221
faithful	3	形	忠實的、忠誠的	★
fake	4	形	假的、冒充的	47
fall	5	動	落下、跌倒	★
false	3	形	不正確的、謬誤的	★
fame	4	名	聲譽、名望	★
familiar	4	形	熟悉的、親近的	51
family	5	名	家庭、家人	★
famous	4	形	出名的、耳熟的	371

單字	頻率	詞性	中譯	頁碼
fan	4	名	迷、風扇、螺旋槳	271
fancy	4	形	別緻的、昂貴的	23
fantastic	3	形	極好的、驚人的	279
fantasy	2	名	幻想、空想、夢想	441
far	5	形	遠的、久遠的	★
fare	3	名	票價、車費、伙食	305
farewell	3	名	告別、送別會	441
farm	4	名	農場、畜牧場、農家	263
farmer	5	名	農夫、農場主	★
farming	2	名	農業、農場經營	43
fascinate	3	動	迷住、神魂顛倒	395
fascinating	3	形	迷人的、極好的	115
fashion	5	名	時尚、風氣	★
fast	5	形	快的、迅速的	★
fasten	2	動	扣緊、釘牢	305
fatal	3	形	致命的、生死攸關的	231
fate	4	名	命運、結局、毀滅	423
father	5	名	父親	★
fatigue	3	名	疲勞、勞累	95
fault	4	名	缺點、錯誤、故障	53
faulty	3	形	有缺點的、不完美的	449
favor	3	名	贊成、偏愛	★
favorable	3	形	有利的、贊同的	267
favorite	4	名	特別喜歡的人或物	★
fax	4	名	傳真機	★
fear	5	動	害怕、擔憂	★
feasible	3	形	可行的、合適的	13
feast	3	名	盛宴、宗教節日	231
feather	3	名	羽毛、羽飾、種類	217
feature	5	動	特載、以…為特色	31
February	5	名	二月	★
fee	4	名	服務費、入場費	31
feeble	3	形	無力的、衰弱的	357

單字	頻率	詞性	中譯	頁碼
feed	4	動	餵養、撫養、滿足	43
feel	5	動	觸摸、感覺	★
feeling	5	名	感覺、觸覺	★
fellow	4	名	夥伴、同事、傢伙	291
female	4	名	女人、雌性動物	119
feminine	3	形	女性的、嬌柔的	475
fence	4	名	柵欄、籬笆、擊劍術	177
ferry	3	名	渡輪、渡口	441
festival	4	名	節日、慶祝活動	163
few	5	形	很少數的、一些	★
field	5	名	田地、原野、領域	161
fierce	4	形	兇猛的、好鬥的	441
fight	5	名	打架、爭吵、戰鬥力	349
figure	5	名	體態、人物、數字	23
file	4	名	檔案、文件夾、存檔	305
fill	5	動	使充滿、滿足、填滿	43
film	5	名	軟片、電影	★
filmmaker	4	名	影片製作人及導演等	★
fin	3	名	鰭、鰭狀物、散熱片	103
final	5	形	最終的、決定性的	363
finally	5	副	最後、決定性地	★
finance	4	名	財政、金融	459
financial	4	形	金融的、財政的	21
find	5	動	找到、發現	★
fine	5	形	美好的、優秀的	★
fingernail	5	名	手指甲	★
finish	4	動	完成、結束、用完	375
fire	5	動	開除、激起、開槍	45
firecracker	2	名	爆竹、鞭炮	★
firefighter	2	名	消防隊員	117
firm	4	形	堅定的、穩固的	271
first	5	形	第一的、最高的	★
fisherman	4	名	漁人、漁夫	★

單字	頻率	詞性	中譯	頁碼
fist	4	名	拳頭、掌握	305
fit	5	動	適合、合身	107
fitness	4	名	健康、恰當	13
fix	4	動	修理、確定、固定	379
flag	5	名	旗	★
flamboyant	2	形	艷麗的、炫耀的	25
flash	3	名	閃光、新聞快報	23
flashy	2	形	俗艷的、閃爍的	25
flat	5	形	電用完的、平坦的	403
flatter	5	動	諂媚、奉承、使高興	441
flavor	4	動	給…調味、增添風趣	305
flesh	4	名	肉、果肉、肉體	305
flexible	4	形	靈活的、可變通的	431
flight	3	名	飛行、班次	341
floating	2	形	漂浮的、流動的	69
flock	4	名	畜群、鳥群、人群	361
flood	4	動	湧進、淹沒、充斥	177
floor	4	名	地板、層、發言權	371
flour	4	名	麵粉	★
flow	5	動	泛濫、流動、源自	181
flower	5	名	花	★
flu	4	名	(口)流行性感冒	★
fluctuate	3	動	動搖、波動、變動	87
fluent	3	形	流利的、流暢的	201
flute	3	名	長笛、橫笛	181
fly	5	動	空運、飛行、逃離	495
focus	4	名	焦點、焦距	★
fog	4	名	霧氣、困惑	45
fold	3	動	關閉、垮台、對摺	307
folk	3	名	廣大成員、雙親	307
follow	5	動	跟隨、密切注意	45
fond	4	形	喜歡的、溺愛的	49
fondness	2	名	喜愛、鍾愛	117

單字	頻率	詞性	中譯	頁碼
food	5	名	食物	★
foolish	3	形	愚蠢的、荒謬的	181
forbid	3	動	禁止、妨礙	97
force	5	動	強迫、強行攻佔	295
forecast	4	動	預測、預報、預示	443
forehead	3	名	額頭、前額	307
foreign	5	形	外國的、陌生的	259
foreigner	3	名	外國人	181
forest	4	名	森林、林區	47
foretell	2	動	預言、預示	491
forever	4	副	永遠	★
forget	5	動	忘記、忽略	★
forgive	4	動	原諒、寬恕	★
fork	5	名	叉、耙	★
form	5	動	形成、組織、養成	15
form	5	名	形式、類型	★
formal	4	形	正式的、拘泥形式的	155
formation	3	名	組成、結構、隊形	443
former	4	形	從前的、前任的	319
formula	3	名	準則、常規、公式	443
forth	4	副	向前、向外	307
fortune	4	名	財產、巨款、好運	253
forum	4	名	論壇、討論會	193
forward	5	副	向前、今後、提前	357
fossil	2	名	化石、頑固不化的人	339
found	5	動	創立、基於、鑄造	307
foundation	4	名	基金會、創辦、根據	307
founder	3	名	創立者、奠基者	★
fox	4	名	狐狸、狡猾的人	★
frail	3	形	身體虛弱的	357
frame	5	動	裝框、構想出	445
frank	4	形	坦白的、真誠的	181
freak	3	名	狂熱愛好者	211

單字	頻率	詞性	中譯	頁碼
free	5	形	自由的、免費的	★
freedom	5	名	自由、解脫、大膽	65
freeway	3	名	(美)高速公路	445
freezer	2	名	冰箱、冷藏室、冰櫃	183
frequent	4	動	時常出入於、常去	467
frequently	3	副	頻繁地、屢次地	153
fresh	5	形	新鮮的、清新的	47
freshman	3	名	大一生、新生	★
Friday	5	名	星期五	★
friend	5	名	朋友	★
friendly	4	形	友好的、贊成的	75
friendship	4	名	友誼、友好	★
frighten	4	動	使驚恐、使害怕	183
frog	5	名	青蛙	★
front	5	名	前面、正面	★
frown	3	名	皺眉、不悅之色	235
frozen	2	形	嚇呆的、冰凍的	113
fruit	5	名	水果、成果	★
frustrate	2	動	感到灰心、挫敗	297
frustrated	3	形	挫敗的、失意的	★
fulfill	3	動	實現、滿足、執行	387
full	5	形	滿的、充滿的	★
fully	3	副	完全地、徹底地	★
fume	3	名	煙、憤怒、煩惱	159
function	5	動	工作、運行、起作用	183
fund	5	動	積累、提供資金	309
fundamental	3	形	基礎的、根本的	445
funeral	3	名	葬禮、倒楣事	445
funny	5	形	有趣的、滑稽的	★
furious	3	形	狂怒的、猛烈的	445
furnish	3	動	配置傢俱、裝備	★
furniture	4	名	家具、設備	103
further	5	形	進一步的、更遠的	479

單字	頻率	詞性	中譯	頁碼
furthermore	3	副	而且、此外、再者	183
fury	4	名	暴怒、猛烈	491
fuse	2	名	保險絲、導火線	299
future	4	名	未來、前途	337

G

單字	頻率	詞性	中譯	頁碼
gain	4	動	得到、增添、獲利	73
gallant	2	形	騎士風度的、英勇的	321
gallery	3	名	畫廊、美術館	419
gamble	4	動	賭博、打賭	★
gambling	2	名	賭博	277
game	5	名	運動、遊戲	★
gang	4	名	一幫、一幫年輕人	309
gangster	2	名	流氓、歹徒、匪盜	439
garage	4	名	車庫、汽車修理廠	183
garbage	3	名	垃圾、剩菜、廢話	73
garden	5	名	花園、菜園、庭院	★
gardener	1	名	園丁、花匠	★
gardening	3	名	園藝	85
gas	5	名	快樂的事、氣體	49
gate	4	名	大門、登機門、途徑	183
gather	4	動	收集、積聚、漸增	183
gaze	4	動	凝視、注視、盯	207
gel	3	名	凝膠、膠體	169
general	5	形	首席的、一般的	347
generation	4	名	世代、產生	65
generosity	2	名	慷慨、寬宏大量	443
generous	4	形	慷慨的、豐富的	51
genetic	3	形	基因的、遺傳的	409
genius	4	名	天才、天賦、才能	447
gentle	4	形	溫和的、文靜的	★
gentlemanly	2	形	紳士的、有禮貌的	25
gently	2	副	溫和地、輕輕地	501

單字	頻率	詞性	中譯	頁碼
genuine	4	形	真的、非偽造的	319
geography	3	名	地理學、地形、佈局	185
germ	3	名	細菌、起源、萌芽	447
gesture	4	名	手勢、表示、姿態	309
get-together	2	名	聚會、聯歡會	499
ghost	5	名	鬼、幽靈	★
giant	4	形	巨大的、巨人般的	205
gift	5	名	禮物、天賦、才能	325
gigantic	2	形	龐大的、巨人似的	447
giggle	3	動	咯咯地笑、傻笑	447
ginger	4	名	薑、生薑	★
giraffe	2	名	長頸鹿	★
girlfriend	5	名	女朋友	★
glance	4	動	一瞥、掃視	305
glass	5	名	玻璃	★
global	5	形	全世界的、球狀的	307
glorify	2	動	吹捧、頌揚、讚美	439
glove	4	名	手套	★
goal	5	名	目標、球門、得分數	491
goat	4	名	山羊	★
gold	5	名	金	★
golfer	3	名	打高爾夫球的人	★
good	5	形	好的、令人滿意的	★
goodbye	5	嘆	再見	★
goofy	2	形	愚笨的、傻的	255
gossip	4	動	說長道短、說閒話	283
Gothic	3	形	哥德式的	151
government	4	名	政府、內閣	★
governor	3	名	州長、總督、調節器	309
grace	3	名	優美、優雅	★
graceful	3	形	優美的、典雅的	245
gracefulness	1	名	優雅	★
gracious	3	形	親切的、慈祥的	75

單字	頻率	詞性	中譯	頁碼
gradually	2	副	逐步地、漸漸地	457
graduate	5	動	畢業	★
graduation	2	名	畢業、畢業典禮	223
graffiti	2	名	塗鴉、亂塗亂抹	141
grammar	4	名	文法	★
grammatical	2	形	文法的、合乎文法的	449
grand	4	形	重要的、雄偉的	51
grandfather	5	名	祖父、外祖父	★
grandmother	5	名	祖母、外祖母	★
grasshopper	1	名	蚱蜢、蝗蟲	311
grassland	4	名	牧草地、草原	★
grateful	4	形	感激的、表示感謝的	117
gratitude	3	名	感激之情、感恩	449
gray	5	形	灰色的、偏灰的	★
greatly	4	副	極其、非常	★
greedy	3	形	貪婪的、渴望的	185
green	5	形	綠色的	★
greenhouse	3	名	溫室	311
greet	3	動	問候、迎接、接受	187
greeting	3	名	問候語、賀詞、招呼	449
grey	4	形	灰色的、陰暗的	★
grief	4	名	悲痛、不幸、失敗	247
grieve	3	動	使苦惱、悲傷、哀悼	449
grilled	2	形	烤的、炙過的	217
grind	5	動	磨碎、壓榨、苦學	479
grocery	4	名	食品雜貨店	311
ground	5	名	地面、海底	★
group	5	名	群、組、集團	★
grow	5	動	成長、發育	★
growth	5	名	生長、發育	★
guarantee	4	名	保證、擔保品	39
guard	4	名	守衛、衛兵、防守	187
guess	5	動	猜測、推測	★

單字	頻率	詞性	中譯	頁碼
guesswork	2	名	猜測、猜測結果	427
guest	4	名	賓客、顧客	311
guidance	3	名	引導、領導	★
guide	5	名	嚮導、指導、簡介	53
guilt	3	名	過失、內疚、有罪	513
guilty	4	形	內疚的、有罪的	451
guitarist	3	名	吉他手	★
gunshot	2	名	槍砲聲、射擊、子彈	359
gymnasium	2	名	體育館、健身房	399

H

單字	頻率	詞性	中譯	頁碼
habit	5	名	習慣、習性、氣質	59
habitual	2	形	習慣的、習以為常的	451
haircut	5	名	理髮、髮型	★
hairdo	4	名	髮型	★
hairdresser	1	名	美髮師	311
hairstyle	5	名	髮型	★
half	5	名	一半、二分之一	★
hall	5	名	會堂、大廳、走廊	181
hallway	4	名	走廊、玄關	311
ham	5	名	火腿	★
hamburger	3	名	漢堡	★
hand	5	動	給、面交、傳遞	379
handbag	4	名	(女用)手提包	★
handicraft	1	名	手工藝品、手藝	451
handkerchief	3	名	手帕、紙巾	187
handle	4	動	處理、操作、經營	133
handsome	5	形	英俊的、健美的	★
hang	5	動	把…掛起、吊著	187
hanger	2	名	衣架、掛鉤、懸掛物	187
hangover	3	名	宿醉、殘留物、遺物	117
happen		動	發生、碰巧	393
happy	5	形	高興的、幸福的	★

單字	頻率	詞性	中譯	頁碼
harbor	4	名	海港、港灣、避風港	291
hard	5	形	堅硬的、困難的	★
hardly	4	副	幾乎不、簡直不	187
hardship	3	名	困苦、艱難	403
harm	4	動	危害、傷害	107
harmful	3	形	有害的	41
harmony	3	名	和睦、一致、協調	385
harsh	4	形	艱苦的、嚴酷的	451
harvest	4	名	收穫、收穫季節	313
hatch	3	動	孵出、策劃	313
hate	4	動	嫌惡、不喜歡、憎恨	271
hatred	3	名	敵意、憎恨	453
hawk	3	名	鷹、鷹派人物	313
head	5	名	頭、頭腦	★
headache	3	名	頭痛、麻煩	503
headline	3	名	頭條新聞、章節標題	149
headphone	3	名	頭戴式耳機	★
headquarters	2	名	總公司、司令部	307
health	5	名	健康	★
healthcare	2	名	醫療保健、保健事業	479
healthily	2	副	健康地	153
healthy	3	形	有益健康的、健全的	493
hear	5	動	聽、聽見	★
heart	5	名	心臟、內心	★
heater	2	名	暖氣機、加熱器	187
heavily	3	副	猛烈地、沉重地	243
heavy	5	形	大量的、重的	75
height	4	名	身高、高度、海拔	189
helicopter	3	名	直升機	453
helpful	4	形	有幫助的、有益的	189
herd	3	名	畜群、牧群	453
heroine	4	名	女主角	★
hesitation	2	名	躊躇、猶豫	453

單字	頻率	詞性	中譯	頁碼
hibernation	2	名	冬眠、過冬	261
hidden	2	形	隱藏的、隱秘的	189
hide	5	動	躲藏、隱藏、隱瞞	353
hideout	3	名	隱匿處	★
high	5	形	高的	★
highlighter	2	名	螢光筆	151
highly	5	副	非常、很、高額地	489
high pitched	1	形	尖聲的、聲調高的	
hijacker	1	名	強盜、劫盜	509
hill	4	名	小山、丘陵	331
hillbilly	1	名	(帶侮辱性字眼)鄉巴佬	127
hint	3	名	暗示、微量、建議	293
hip	4	名	臀部、屁股	189
hip hop	2	名	說唱的嘻哈文化	
hire	4	動	雇用、租借	327
historical	5	形	歷史的、基於史實的	319
history	5	名	歷史、歷史學	★
hit	5	動	擊中、碰撞、達到	277
hit-and-run	2	形	逃走的	513
hobby	5	名	業餘愛好、嗜好	★
hold	5	動	舉行、抓住、支撐	281
hole	5	名	洞、孔眼	★
holiday	5	名	節日、假日	★
hollow	3	形	空洞的、凹陷的	41
holy	3	形	神聖的、虔誠的	315
homeland	3	名	祖國、家鄉	★
homelessness	2	名	無家可歸	483
homely	2	形	不好看的、家常的	115
homesick	2	形	想家的、思鄉的	189
homestay	2	名	客居外國家庭	189
homework	4	名	家庭作業、副業	249
honest	4	形	誠實的、坦率的	417
honesty	4	名	正直、誠實、坦率	★

單字	頻率	詞性	中譯	頁碼
honey	4	名	蜂蜜、寶貝	★
honeymoon	3	名	蜜月期、蜜月旅行	173
honor	3	動	尊敬、使增光、實踐	277
honorable	2	形	光榮的、高尚的	453
hook	4	動	被鉤住、引人上鉤	285
hope	5	動	希望、期盼	★
hopeful	4	形	有希望的、有前途的	★
horizon	4	名	地平線、範圍、眼界	453
horn	3	名	角、喇叭、警笛	33
horrible	3	形	糟透的、可怕的	123
horrify	3	動	使恐懼、使驚懼	453
horror	4	名	驚恐、恐怖	315
horse	5	名	馬	★
hose	4	名	水管、軟管、長統襪	453
hospital	5	名	醫院	★
host	4	名	節目主持人、主人	175
hostel	3	名	青年旅社	455
hot	5	形	熱的、熱情的	★
hotel	5	名	旅館、飯店	★
hour	5	名	小時	★
house	5	名	房子、住宅	★
household	4	名	家庭、家眷、一家人	455
housewife	3	名	針線盒、家庭主婦	★
hover	2	動	盤旋、徬徨、停留	37
however	5	副	無論如何、不管怎樣	★
howl	3	名	嚎啕大哭、怒吼	319
huddle	2	動	聚在一起、縮成一團	283
hug	3	名	擁抱、緊抱	315
huge	5	形	巨大的、龐大的	331
human	4	形	人的、人類的	★
humble	4	形	謙遜的、卑微的	189
humid	3	形	潮濕的	189
humor	2	名	幽默	★

單字	頻率	詞性	中譯	頁碼
income	4	名	收入、收益、所得	169
incomparable	2	形	無比的、舉世無雙的	177
incorporate	4	動	使併入、吸收、體現	401
increase	5	動	增加、增大	★
increasingly	4	副	漸增地	★
incredible	4	形	驚人的、難以置信的	319
incur	4	動	招致、帶來	473
indeed	5	副	確實、當然、甚至	15
independent	3	形	獨立的、自主的	19
indicate	4	動	表明、象徵、指出	89
indignation	2	名	憤怒、憤慨	125
indirectly	2	副	間接地、迂迴地	515
indispensable	3	形	不可或缺的	69
indulge	3	動	沉迷、放縱、遷就	157
industrial	3	形	工業的、勞資的	317
industry	5	名	企業、工業、勤勉	191
inevitably	2	副	必然地、不可避免地	291
inexperienced	3	形	經驗不足的	465
infant	3	名	嬰兒	459
infect	3	動	傳染、感染、汙染	105
infection	3	名	感染、傳染、影響	273
infectious	2	形	有感染力的、傳染的	397
inferior	3	形	較差的、次於…的	253
infidelity	1	名	不信神、不貞行為	121
infinite	3	形	無限的、極大的	77
inflation	3	名	通貨膨脹、充氣	421
influence	4	名	影響力、權勢	35
influential	4	形	有影響力的	459
information	5	名	消息、報導、資訊	115
informative	3	形	教育性的、有益的	459
inform	4	動	通知、告知、告發	471
ingredient	3	名	原料、構成要素	31
inhabitant	2	名	居民	433

單字	頻率	詞性	中譯	頁碼
inherit	4	動	繼承、經遺傳獲得	347
inhumane	1	形	無人情味的、殘忍的	455
initial	4	形	最初的、開始的	459
initially	3	副	最初、開頭	33
injured	3	形	受傷的	9
injury	4	名	傷害、損害	495
injustice	2	名	非正義、不公平	417
ink	4	名	墨水、油墨	★
inn	3	名	小旅館、小酒店	317
innocence	2	名	清白、純真、無知	417
innocent	4	形	天真的、清白的	315
innovative	2	形	創新的	409
insect	3	名	昆蟲	311
insert	3	動	插入、添寫、刊登	249
inside	4	名	內部、裡面	★
insightful	3	形	具洞察力的	401
insist	3	動	堅持、堅決主張	225
insistence	3	名	堅持、竭力主張	483
inspiration	3	名	靈感、鼓舞、啟示	15
inspire	4	動	鼓舞、激勵、喚起	193
install	4	動	安裝、設置、使就任	461
installation	3	名	裝置、設置、就職	141
instance	3	名	實例、情況、請求	193
instant	3	名	頃刻、一剎那	99
instead	5	副	作為替代	★
institute	4	名	協會、學院、規則	443
instruct	3	動	指導、訓練、吩咐	461
instruction	4	名	操作指南、講授	329
instructor	4	名	指導者、教練	303
instrument	4	名	儀器、樂器	★
instrumental	2	形	有幫助的	121
insult	3	名	辱罵、侮辱性言行	245
insurance	5	名	保險、保險契約	459

單字	頻率	詞性	中譯	頁碼
insurrection	2	名	暴動、叛亂、起義	377
intellectual	3	形	聰明的、智力的	461
intelligence	4	名	智能、消息	461
intelligent	4	形	明智的、有才智的	401
intend	3	動	想要、打算	181
intense	4	形	劇烈的、熱切的	185
intensify	2	動	增強、強化、變激烈	461
intensive	3	形	加強的、密集的	461
intention	4	名	意向、意圖、目的	461
interact	3	動	互動、互相影響	99
interaction	4	名	互相影響、互動	★
interest	5	名	興趣、愛好	★
interested	5	形	感興趣的、關心的	★
interesting	5	形	有趣的、令人關注的	★
interfere	3	動	干涉、妨礙、牴觸	463
interior	3	形	內政的、內部的	457
international	4	形	國際性的	181
Internet	5	名	網際網路	★
interpret	3	動	理解為、說明、口譯	293
interrupt	4	動	打斷、阻礙	319
interview	4	名	面試、接見、採訪	59
interviewee	4	名	受訪者、面試者	★
interviewer	4	名	採訪者、面試官	★
intimacy	2	名	親密、熟悉	439
intimate	3	形	親密的、熟悉的	★
intimidate	3	動	威嚇、脅迫	435
intolerable	2	形	難耐的、不能忍受的	445
intravenous	1	形	靜脈內的	105
introduce	4	動	介紹、引進、提出	193
introduction	3	名	介紹、引進	★
invader	2	名	侵略者	453
invent	4	動	發明、創造、虛構	193
invention	3	名	發明、創造、虛構	463

單字	頻率	詞性	中譯	頁碼
invest	4	動	投資、投入、耗費	403
investigate	3	動	調查、研究	475
investigation	2	名	研究、調查	463
investigative	2	形	調查的、研究性的	101
investment	4	名	投資、投入、花費	87
invitation	3	名	邀請、引誘、鼓勵	137
invite	4	動	邀請、招待、徵求	85
involve	4	動	連累、包含	★
iron	4	名	鐵、熨斗	★
irony	3	形	含鐵的、似鐵的	359
irreplaceable	2	形	不能調換的	167
irresistible	2	形	無法抗拒的	23
irrigate	3	動	灌溉、沖洗傷口	441
irritated	3	形	惱火的、急躁的	163
isolated	3	形	孤立的、隔離的	55
isolation	3	名	隔離、孤立	★
issue	5	名	問題、爭議、發行物	65
Italian	5	名	義大利人、義大利語	★
Italy	5	名	義大利	★
itchy	2	形	發癢的、渴望的	465
item	4	名	品目、細目、條款	127
ivory	3	形	象牙製的、象牙色的	319

J

單字	頻率	詞性	中譯	頁碼
jacket	5	名	夾克、上衣	★
jail	4	名	監獄、監禁、拘留所	295
jam	3	名	擁擠、堵塞、窘境	59
Japanese	5	名	日本人、日語	★
jar	3	名	罈、罐、震動、刺激	319
jazz	4	名	爵士樂(舞)	★
jealous	4	形	妒忌的、小心守護的	9
jealousy	3	名	妒忌、猜忌、戒備	465
jeans	4	名	牛仔褲、工裝褲	83

單字	頻率	詞性	中譯	頁碼
jeep	3	名	吉普車	★
jewelry	5	名	珠寶、首飾	★
job	5	名	工作、職業	★
jobless	2	形	失業的	191
jog	4	動	慢跑、輕搖、顛簸	195
join	5	動	加入、連接、會合	187
jointed	2	形	有節的、有接縫的	485
joke	5	動	開玩笑、戲弄	429
journal	5	名	雜誌、期刊、日記	355
journalist	4	名	新聞記者	201
journalistic	2	形	新聞工作(者)的	★
journey	4	名	旅程、行程	321
joyfully	2	副	喜悅地、高興地	73
judge	4	名	裁判員、鑑定人	105
juice	5	名	果汁	★
July	5	名	七月	★
jump	5	動	跳、躍躍	★
June	5	名	六月	★
junior	4	形	資淺的、年紀較輕的	57
junk	5	名	廢棄的舊物	★
just	5	副	正好、僅僅	★
justice	5	名	正義、公平、審判	321

K

單字	頻率	詞性	中譯	頁碼
keen	4	形	熱衷的、渴望的	465
keep	5	動	保存、保持	★
ketchup	1	名	番茄醬	★
kettle	3	名	水壺	321
keyboard	4	名	鍵盤	★
kick	4	動	踢、踢進得分	61
kid	5	名	小孩	★
kidnap	3	動	綁架、誘拐、劫持	391
kill	5	動	殺死	★

單字	頻率	詞性	中譯	頁碼
killer	4	名	殺人者	★
kilogram	2	名	公斤	129
kind	5	名	種類	★
kindergarten	3	名	幼稚園、學前班	195
kindness	4	名	仁慈、和藹、好意	★
kitchen	5	名	廚房	★
kite	4	名	風箏、空頭支票	63
knee	4	名	膝蓋	63
knight	3	名	騎士、爵士	321
knit	2	動	編織、接合、皺眉	321
knob	3	名	球形把手、圓丘	321
knock	4	動	敲、碰擊、貶損	333
know	5	動	知道、了解	★
knowledge	5	名	知識、學問、了解	19
knowledgeable	2	形	博學的、有見識的	★
known	5	形	知名的	★
knuckle	2	名	指關節、膝關節	465
koala	2	名	無尾熊	195

L

單字	頻率	詞性	中譯	頁碼
labor	3	名	工作、勞工、陣痛	21
laboratory	3	名	實驗室、研究室	193
laborer	2	名	勞工、勞動者	407
lack	4	動	缺少、不足	99
ladder	4	名	梯子、階梯、途徑	321
lag	3	動	落後於、衰退	43
lag	4	動	落後、延遲、衰退	465
lake	5	名	湖	★
lamb	4	名	小羊	63
land	4	動	登陸、卸貨、使陷於	137
landlord	3	名	房東、老闆、地主	355
landmark	2	名	地標、里程碑	465
landscape	4	名	風景、風景畫	63

單字	頻率	詞性	中譯	頁碼
landslide	2	名	山崩、壓倒性大勝利	175
lane	4	名	巷弄、車道、泳道	59
language	5	名	語言、語言文字	★
lantern	3	名	燈籠	421
lap	4	名	膝部、重疊部分	197
large	5	形	大的、多的、廣博的	337
latest	4	形	最新的、最遲的	45
Latin	2	名	拉丁人、拉丁語	★
laugh	5	動	笑、嘲笑	★
launch	3	動	開辦、發起、發射	325
laundry	3	名	洗衣店、送洗衣物	323
lavish	3	形	過分鋪張的、大量的	85
law	5	名	法律	★
lawful	2	形	合法的、守法的	465
lawn	4	名	草坪、草地、細棉布	323
lawyer	4	名	律師、法學家	★
lay	5	動	使處於、放、擱	471
lazy	3	形	懶散的、怠惰的	271
lead	5	動	過活、領導、領路	469
leader	4	名	領袖、領導者	503
leadership	5	名	領導地位、領導才能	197
leaf	4	名	葉子	★
learned	5	形	博學的、精通的	467
least	5	形	最小的、最少的	★
leather	4	形	皮的、皮革製的	155
leave	5	動	離開(某處)、遺留	★
lecture	4	名	授課、演講、責備	65
lecturer	2	名	(大學)講師、演講者	467
left	5	形	左方的、左側的	★
leg	5	名	腿、小腿	★
legal	4	形	法定的、合法的	197
legend	4	名	傳奇人物、傳說	403
legendary	2	形	傳奇的、著名的	177

單字	頻率	詞性	中譯	頁碼
leisure	4	形	空閒的、業餘的	43
leisurely	1	形	從容不迫的、悠閒的	467
lemon	3	名	檸檬、瑕疵品	★
lemonade	2	名	檸檬汁	★
lens	4	名	鏡片、鏡頭	323
leopard	2	名	豹、美洲豹、獅像	197
lesbian	2	名	女同性戀者	229
less	5	形	較少的、較小的	449
lesson	5	名	一課	★
lest	3	連	唯恐、擔心、免得	267
letter	5	名	信件、字母	★
leukemia	1	名	白血病	41
level	5	名	程度、級別	★
liable	4	形	有義務的、易…的	353
liar	3	名	騙子、說謊的人	323
liberal	4	形	心胸寬闊的、自由的	323
library	4	名	圖書館、藏書、書庫	197
licence	5	名	許可、證照	★
license	4	名	執照、許可、放縱	105
lick	4	動	舔、輕拍、克服	197
lie	4	動	躺臥、置於、撒謊	37
lifeguard	2	名	救生員、警衛	323
lifespan	2	名	壽命、使用期限	313
lifestyle	2	名	生活方式	★
lift	4	動	舉起、振作、抄襲	67
light	5	動	點燃、照亮	219
light	5	名	光、光線、燈火	★
lighter	2	名	打火機、點火器	285
lightning	3	名	閃電、意外的幸運	197
lightweight	2	形	較輕的、思想膚淺的	155
likely	4	副	很可能地	★
lily-livered	1	形	膽怯的	
limb	3	名	肢、臂、腳、翼	★

單字	頻率	詞性	中譯	頁碼
limit	4	動	限制、限定	77
limitation	2	名	極限、限制因素	467
limited	5	形	有限的、特快的	497
line	5	名	線條、行列	★
link	4	名	連繫、關係、環節	199
lion	5	名	獅子	★
lip	3	名	嘴唇	★
liquid	3	名	液體	291
liquor	2	名	酒精飲料、烈酒	467
listed	2	形	登記上市的	197
listener	3	名	傾聽者、收聽者	199
literacy	2	名	能力、知識、識字	435
literary	2	形	文學的、精通文學的	467
literature	2	名	文學、文獻資料	131
litter	3	名	垃圾、雜亂	371
little	5	形	小的、少的	★
live	5	動	活著、生活、居住	★
lively	2	形	愉快的、活潑的	403
livestock	3	名	(總稱)家畜、牲畜	263
loaf	5	名	一塊麵包	199
loan	3	名	貸款、借出	467
lobby	3	名	大廳、門廊、會客室	171
lobster	3	名	龍蝦、龍蝦肉	325
local	5	形	當地的、局部的	199
locate	3	動	座落於、設置在	153
location	4	名	場所、位置	119
lock	5	動	把…鎖起來、卡住	193
locker	3	名	寄物櫃、冷藏室	17
lodge	4	名	旅社、山林小屋	367
log	4	名	原木	199
logic	4	名	邏輯、推理、合理	469
logical	3	形	合邏輯的、合理的	469
lollipop	4	名	棒棒糖	★

單字	頻率	詞性	中譯	頁碼
lonely	5	形	孤獨的、寂寞的	★
long	5	動	渴望	441
loose	4	形	寬鬆的、鬆散的	325
loosen	3	動	放鬆、鬆開	457
lose	5	動	丟失、輸去	★
loss	4	名	損失、失敗、減少	199
lot	5	名	一塊地、很多	39
lotion	2	名	乳液、化妝水、塗劑	469
lottery	3	名	獎券、彩票、運氣	331
loudly	5	副	高聲地、吵鬧地	★
loudspeaker	1	名	喇叭、擴聲器	★
lounge	4	名	休息室、候機室	119
lovable	2	形	可愛的、討人喜歡的	315
lovely	4	形	可愛的、令人愉快的	135
lover	5	名	戀人、(一對)情侶	★
low paying	2	形	低酬的、低工資的	
loyal	3	形	忠誠的、忠心的	415
loyalty	3	名	忠誠、忠心	469
luck	4	名	運氣、命運、僥倖	349
luckily	5	副	幸運地、幸好	★
luggage	3	名	行李	383
lunar	3	形	陰曆的、月球上的	51
lunch	5	名	午餐、便當	★
lung	3	名	肺	★
lure	3	動	引誘、誘惑	275
lush	3	形	蒼翠繁茂的、豐富的	51
luxurious	2	形	奢侈的、豪華的	223
luxury	3	名	奢華、奢侈、享受	39

M

單字	頻率	詞性	中譯	頁碼
machine	4	名	機器、機械	301
mad	4	形	惱火的、發瘋的	163
magazine	5	名	雜誌、期刊	★

單字	頻率	詞性	中譯	頁碼
magically	4	副	不可思議地	★
magician	2	名	魔術師、巫師	★
magnet	3	名	磁鐵、磁石	325
magnificent	3	形	壯麗的、豪華的	469
maid	3	名	少女、女僕	325
main	5	形	主要的、最重要的	401
mainly	4	副	主要地、大部分地	223
maintain	4	動	維持、保養、堅持	201
maintenance	4	名	維修、保持、生活費	475
major	5	形	較大的、主要的	495
majority	4	名	大多數、多數的票數	327
make-shift	2	形	臨時代用的、權宜的	447
makeup	4	名	化妝品	★
make up	2	名	化妝、構造、性格	
maltreat	2	動	虐待、濫用	225
manage	5	動	經營、控制	175
management	4	名	經營、管理部門	★
manager	5	名	主任、經理	★
mango	2	名	芒果	★
manicure	2	動	修指甲、修剪	53
manner	4	名	手法、方法、態度	201
mansion	3	名	大廈、宅第、公館	87
manual	4	形	手工的、用手操作的	469
manufacture	4	動	製造、加工、捏造	317
manufacturer	3	名	製造商、製造廠	★
many	5	形	許多的、大量的	★
map	5	名	地圖	69
marathon	2	名	馬拉松賽跑	471
marble	3	名	大理石、彈珠、理智	327
March	5	名	三月	★
margin	3	名	差數、邊緣	101
marijuana	1	名	大麻、大麻煙	41
marital	2	形	婚姻的、夫妻的	19

單字	頻率	詞性	中譯	頁碼
mark	2	名	符號、目標	★
market	5	名	市場、銷路、行情	375
marketing	2	名	行銷學、交易、銷售	373
marriage	5	名	婚姻、結婚儀式	229
married	5	形	已婚的、婚姻的	★
martial	2	形	尚武的、戰爭的	177
marvelous	2	形	令人驚嘆的、妙極的	501
mash	2	動	搗成糊狀、壓碎	221
mask	5	名	面具、口罩、遮蔽物	★
mass	5	名	大量、大眾、團、塊	519
massage	5	名	按摩、推拿	★
massive	3	形	大規模的、厚實的	95
master	5	名	主人、能手、決定	301
masterfully	2	副	技巧熟練地、專橫地	507
masterpiece	3	名	傑作、名作、代表作	273
mat	4	名	墊子、草蓆	201
match	4	動	和…相稱、比得上	71
mate	4	名	同伴、配偶、助手	203
material	4	名	材料、資料、工具	157
matter	5	動	要緊、有關係	69
maturity	2	名	成熟、完善	471
maximum	3	名	最大限度、最大量	91
mayor	3	名	市長、鎮長	299
meal	5	名	膳食、一餐	★
mean	5	動	意欲、打算、用意	369
meaning	4	名	意義、重要性、含義	203
meaningful	2	形	有意義的	★
meaningless	2	形	無意義的、不重要的	261
meanwhile	4	副	同時	297
measure	5	動	測量、估量、權衡	203
meat	5	名	(食用的)肉	★
mechanic	3	名	技工、機械工	317
mechanical	3	形	機械的、呆板的	471

單字	頻率	詞性	中譯	頁碼
media	4	名	媒體	★
median	3	名	中央分隔島	9
medical	5	形	醫學的、醫療的	41
medicine	4	名	內服藥、醫學、良藥	203
meditate	2	動	深思熟慮、打算	483
meet	5	動	遇見、碰上	★
meeting	5	名	會議、會面、匯合點	203
melody	3	名	歌曲、旋律	73
melon	3	名	甜瓜	★
member	5	名	會員、成員、一部分	481
membership	3	名	會員身分、會員數	329
memorabilia	2	名	重要記事、紀念品	95
memorable	2	形	難忘的、顯著的	317
memorize	2	動	記住、背熟	65
memory	5	名	記憶、紀念、記憶體	283
mend	4	動	縫補、改正、好轉	363
mental	4	形	精神的、智力的	161
mention	4	動	提到、說起	35
menu	5	名	菜單、選擇單	★
merchandise	3	名	商品、貨物	295
merchant	3	名	商人、零售商	329
mercy	4	名	憐憫、幸運、救濟	471
mere	4	形	僅僅的、極小的	97
merely	4	副	只是、僅僅、不過	477
merge	4	動	合併、融合、同化	347
merry	4	形	愉快的、興高采烈的	329
mess	4	名	混亂、一團糟、食堂	185
message	5	名	口信、訊息、消息	★
messy	2	形	混亂的、骯髒的	471
metal	5	名	金屬、金屬製品	205
meteoric	2	形	疾速的、流星的	35
method	5	名	方法、條理、秩序	205
metro	2	名	地鐵	499
microphone	3	名	麥克風、擴音器	329
microscope	3	名	顯微鏡	471
microwave	2	名	微波爐、微波	329
middle	5	形	中部的、中間的	★
mighty	3	形	強大的、偉大的	257
mild	4	形	溫和的、不濃烈的	473
mile	5	名	英里、哩	★
military	3	名	軍隊、軍方、陸軍	125
milk	5	名	乳、牛奶	★
million	4	名	百萬、無數、大眾	205
mind	5	動	注意、介意	★
mindlessly	2	副	不用腦子地	225
mine	4	名	礦、礦山、寶庫	331
miner	2	名	礦工	331
mineral	3	名	礦物質、(英)礦泉水	473
minister	4	名	部長、大臣、執行者	165
minor	4	名	未成年人、副修科目	97
minus	3	介	失去、減去	205
minute	5	名	分鐘、片刻	421
miracle	4	名	奇蹟、驚人的事例	261
mirror	4	名	鏡子	★
mischief	2	名	頑皮、惡作劇、禍根	473
miserable	3	形	不幸的、痛苦的	169
miserably	1	副	糟糕地、悲慘地	303
misfortune	2	名	不幸、災難、惡運	473
mislead	3	動	使產生錯誤想法	473
miss	5	動	未達到、錯過	★
missile	3	名	飛彈、導彈、投射物	331
missing	5	形	失蹤的、缺席的	399
mission	4	名	任務、使命、使節團	395
mist	3	名	薄霧、模糊不清	389
mistake	4	名	弄錯、誤解	★
misunderstand	3	動	誤會、曲解	★

單字	頻率	詞性	中譯	頁碼
mix	4	動	使混和、發生牽連	61
mixture	3	名	混合、混雜、合劑	205
mobile	3	形	移動式的、流動的	151
mobility	3	名	流動性、機動性	59
model	5	動	當模特兒、做模型	237
moderate	4	形	中等的、溫和的	473
modern	5	形	現代的、時髦的	457
modest	4	形	謙虛的、穩重的	473
modification	2	名	修改、緩和、修飾	39
modify	3	動	修改、緩和、修飾	59
moldy	2	形	發霉的、乏味的	29
moment	5	名	片刻、時機	235
money	5	名	貨幣、財產	★
monkey	5	名	猴子	★
monster	3	名	怪物、(口)巨人	★
month	5	名	月	★
monthly	5	形	每月的、每月一次的	★
monument	3	名	紀念碑、遺跡	281
mood	4	名	心情、生氣	149
moonlight	4	名	月光	★
mop	3	動	用拖把拖、擦乾	333
moral	3	形	道德的、品行端正的	249
moreover	4	副	並且、此外	★
morning	5	名	早晨、上午	★
mortgage	3	名	抵押	29
mosquito	3	名	蚊子	★
moth	3	名	蛾、蠹、蛀蟲	205
mother	5	名	母親	★
motivate	3	動	為…的動機、激發	475
motivation	3	名	幹勁、積極性、刺激	461
motive	3	名	動機、目的、主旨	509
motorcycle	2	名	摩托車	★
motto	3	名	題詞、座右銘、格言	423

單字	頻率	詞性	中譯	頁碼
mountaineer	2	名	爬山能手、登山家	★
mountainous	2	形	多山的、巨大的	63
mouse	5	名	鼠	★
moustache	2	名	八字鬍	475
movable	3	形	可移動的、動產的	207
move	5	動	感動、移動	371
movement	4	名	動作、傾向、行動	71
movie	5	名	電影	★
mow	3	動	刈草	475
much	5	形	許多的、大量的	★
mud	4	名	泥、泥漿	★
mudslide	2	名	山崩、泥流、坍方	239
mug	4	名	一杯的量、惡棍	75
mule	3	名	騾、固執的人	207
multiply	4	動	增加、使相乘、繁殖	207
municipal	3	形	市立的、市政的	161
murder	4	名	謀殺、要命的事	333
murderer	2	名	謀殺犯、兇手	277
murmur	3	動	小聲說話、咕噥	475
museum	4	名	博物館、展覽館	207
mushroom	3	名	迅速增長的事物	241
music	5	名	音樂	★
musical	3	形	音樂的、配樂的	★
musician	3	名	音樂家	★
Muslim	2	形	伊斯蘭教的	443
mutual	4	形	相互的、共同的	131
mysterious	4	形	神秘的、不可思議的	201
myth	3	名	神話、虛構的人事物	★

N

單字	頻率	詞性	中譯	頁碼
nag	3	動	不斷嘮叨、使煩惱	229
nail	4	名	指甲、釘子、爪	207
naive	3	形	天真的、輕信的	153

單字	頻率	詞性	中譯	頁碼
naive	3	形	天真的、輕信的	483
naivety	2	名	天真、輕信	341
naked	4	形	裸體的、無覆蓋的	17
name	5	動	命名、提名、列舉	241
nanny	2	名	保姆、祖母、母山羊	333
nap	3	名	打盹兒、午睡	333
napkin	3	名	餐巾、小毛巾	207
narrow	4	形	狹窄的、心胸狹窄的	269
narrowly	3	副	狹窄地、勉強地	★
nasal	2	形	鼻子的、鼻音的	113
nasty	4	形	惡意的、卑鄙的	253
nation	3	名	國民	★
nationwide	3	副	在全國	269
natural	4	形	自然的、天然的	153
naturally	4	副	天生地、自然地	★
nature	5	名	大自然、簡樸、天性	75
naughty	3	形	頑皮的、不守規矩的	109
navy	4	名	海軍、海軍艦隊	231
near	5	介	在…附近	★
nearby	4	形	附近的	279
nearly	4	副	幾乎、差不多	★
nearsighted	2	形	短視的、近視的	477
necessarily	3	副	必定、必要地	489
necessary	4	形	必要的、必然的	53
necessity	3	名	必需品、必要性	275
neck	4	名	脖子	★
necklace	2	名	項鍊	173
need	5	名	需要、需求、貧窮	363
needle	5	名	針、唱針、注射針	★
needy	2	形	貧窮的	477
negative	4	形	反面的、消極的	209
neglected	2	形	忽視的、疏忽的	477
negotiate	4	動	談成、協商、洽談	373

單字	頻率	詞性	中譯	頁碼
negotiation	2	名	談判、協商、通過	497
neighbor	2	名	鄰居、鄰國、同胞	209
neighborhood	2	名	鄰近地區、整個街坊	233
neither	4	連	既不…也不	209
nephew	3	名	姪兒、外甥	★
nerve	4	名	神經、憂慮、膽量	335
nervously	3	副	焦急地、提心吊膽地	★
nest	4	名	巢、窩、溫床	209
net	5	名	網、陷阱、網狀系統	209
netizen	3	名	網路公民、網民	463
network	5	名	網絡、網狀物	289
networking	4	名	電腦連線	★
never	5	副	從未、永不	★
nevertheless	3	副	儘管如此、不過	39
newcomer	2	名	新來的人、新手	327
newly	3	副	以新的方式、重新	17
newlywed	3	名	新婚的夫或婦	173
news	5	名	新聞、報導	★
newspaper	5	名	報紙	★
next	5	形	下一個、緊鄰的	★
nice	5	形	好的、可愛的	★
nickname	3	名	綽號	335
niece	3	名	姪女、外甥女	★
nightclub	3	名	夜總會	★
nightfall	2	名	黃昏、傍晚、日暮	91
nightmare	3	名	惡夢、夢魘	297
noble	3	形	崇高的、高尚的	293
nod	4	動	點頭表示、搖曳	55
noise	5	名	噪音、喧鬧聲、干擾	385
noisy	4	形	嘈雜的、吵吵鬧鬧的	499
none	5	代	一個也沒、無一人	209
nonsense	3	名	無價值物、胡說	395
noodle	2	名	麵條、傻瓜	95

單字	頻率	詞性	中譯	頁碼
normally	5	副	通常、正常地	49
north	5	名	北、北方	★
northern	4	形	向北方的	★
nose	5	名	鼻、嗅覺	★
notables	3	名	著名人士、顯耀人士	17
note	4	動	提到、注意到、記下	79
notebook	3	名	筆記本、筆電	★
notice	4	動	注意到、通知、提到	113
noticeboard	3	名	布告欄、布告牌	217
notorious	3	形	惡名昭彰的	59
noun	2	名	名詞	★
novel	4	名	(長篇)小說	251
November	5	名	十一月	★
nowadays	3	副	現今、時下	★
nowhere	3	副	任何地方都不	★
nuclear	5	形	原子核的、核心的	221
number	5	名	數、數字	★
numerous	4	形	許多的、為數眾多的	77
nurse	5	名	護士、護理	★
nursery	3	名	托兒所、溫床	477
nylon	3	名	尼龍、尼龍襪	477

O

單字	頻率	詞性	中譯	頁碼
oatmeal	3	名	燕麥片、燕麥粉	21
obedience	2	名	順從、服從、管轄	477
obedient	2	形	服從的、順從的	13
obey	4	動	聽從、遵守、執行	47
object	5	名	物體、對象、目標	209
objection	3	名	反對、缺點、障礙	477
objective	4	形	客觀的、無偏見的	479
obligation	3	名	責任、義務、恩惠	381
observation	3	名	觀察、注意、言論	25
observe	4	動	觀察、注意到、遵守	335

單字	頻率	詞性	中譯	頁碼
obsess	2	動	使著迷、纏住	23
obstacle	3	名	妨礙、障礙物	21
obtain	4	動	獲得、通用、流行	459
obvious	4	形	明顯的、顯著的	465
obviously	4	副	明顯地、顯然地	83
occasion	4	名	場合、時機、理由	25
occasional	3	形	特殊場合的、偶而的	479
occasionally	2	副	偶而、間或	73
occupation	3	名	職業、佔領時期	285
occupy	4	動	佔據、使忙碌、擔任	275
occur	5	動	發生、出現、浮現	211
ocean	5	名	海洋	★
October	5	名	十月	★
odd	4	形	奇特的、奇數的	49
odds	3	名	機會、區別、不和	27
offence	3	名	冒犯行為、違例	479
offend	4	動	冒犯、觸怒、違反	479
offensive	3	形	冒犯的、令人作嘔的	479
offer	5	動	提供、給予、出價	211
offering	2	名	祭品、提供、貢獻	281
office	5	名	辦公室	★
officer	4	名	警官、官員	273
official	4	形	官方的、正式的	211
off road	2	形	越野的	
often	5	副	時常	★
omit	2	動	省略、刪去、忘記	283
once	5	副	曾經、一次	357
online	5	形	網路上的	★
onlooker	2	名	旁觀者、觀眾	447
only	5	副	只、僅僅	★
open	5	形	打開的、開放的	★
open minded	2	形	心胸開闊的	
opera	4	名	歌劇、歌劇院	109

單字	頻率	詞性	中譯	頁碼
paralyze	2	動	癱瘓、麻痺、使驚呆	171
paraphernalia	2	名	隨身用具、設備	141
pardon	4	動	原諒、饒恕、赦免	215
parent	5	名	雙親	★
park	5	名	公園、停車場	★
parrot	3	名	鸚鵡、應聲蟲	215
part	5	名	一部分、部分	★
participate	3	動	參加、分擔、帶有	139
particular	4	形	獨特的、特定的	201
particularly	4	副	特別、詳細地	49
partly	3	副	在一定程度上	483
partner	4	名	搭檔、合夥人、配偶	131
partnership	2	名	合夥關係、合資公司	481
part-time	4	形	兼職的	
party	5	名	聚會、派對	★
pass	5	動	傳遞、通過、消失	83
passage	4	名	通道、出入口、航行	339
passenger	4	名	乘客、旅客	59
passerby	2	名	行人、過路客	393
passion	3	名	熱情、情慾、盛怒	23
passionate	3	形	熱情的、易怒的	483
passionately	2	副	熱情地、激昂地	311
passive	3	形	被動的、消極的	481
password	4	名	密碼、口令、暗語	339
past	5	形	過去的、以前的	337
pasta	3	名	麵糰	★
paste	4	動	用漿糊黏貼	215
pat	4	名	輕拍、小塊	215
patent	4	名	專利權、特權	★
path	5	名	小徑、途徑、軌道	215
pathway	2	名	小徑、人行道、路線	421
patience	4	名	耐心、毅力	★
patient	4	名	病人	127

單字	頻率	詞性	中譯	頁碼
patrol	3	動	巡邏、偵查	13
pave	4	動	鋪設、密布、使容易	481
pawn	3	動	典當、抵押	127
pay	5	動	給予、支付、償還	397
payment	2	名	支付、付款、報價	121
peaceful	4	形	愛好和平的、平靜的	215
peach	3	名	桃子、桃紅色	215
peak	4	名	高峰、頂端、最高點	419
pearl	3	名	珍珠、珠狀物、珍品	97
pebble	3	名	小卵石、礫石	481
peculiar	3	形	奇怪的、獨特的	481
peep	2	動	偷看、隱約顯現	341
peer	3	名	同儕、同輩	125
pencil	5	名	鉛筆	★
penitentiary	2	名	監獄、宗教裁判所	101
penny	5	名	(美)一分、(英)便士	341
pension	3	名	退休金、撫恤金	81
people	5	名	人們	★
pepper	4	名	胡椒粉、胡椒	★
per	5	介	每、按照、經	273
percent	5	名	百分之一、百分比	★
perfect	5	形	完美的、理想的	★
perfectionism	2	名	完滿主義、圓滿論	267
perform	5	動	演出、履行、完成	399
performance	4	名	演出、履行	33
perfume	3	動	使充滿香氣	★
period	5	名	時期、週期、月經	21
permanent	4	形	永久的、固定性的	481
permission	3	名	許可、同意	31
permit	4	動	許可、准許、容許	167
perseverance	2	名	堅持不懈、毅力	129
Persian	2	形	波斯的、波斯人的	★
person	5	名	人、(貶)傢伙	★

單字	頻率	詞性	中譯	頁碼
personal	5	形	個人的、私人的	★
personality	4	名	個性、品格、名人	227
persuade	3	動	說服、使某人相信	239
persuasion	2	名	說服、勸說、信念	481
pessimistic	3	形	悲觀的、悲觀主義的	483
pest	3	名	害蟲、害人精	341
pesticide	3	名	殺蟲劑、農藥	133
pet	5	名	寵物	★
petition	3	名	請願、請願書、申請	499
phantom	2	名	幽靈、幻像	333
phenomenon	4	名	現象、奇蹟	455
philosophically	2	副	冷靜地、哲學上	131
philosophy	4	名	人生觀、哲學、哲理	381
phone	5	動	打電話	261
photo	5	名	照片	★
photography	2	名	照相術、攝影術	483
phrase	4	名	詞組、說法、片語	257
physical	5	形	身體的、物質的	13
physically	2	副	身體上、實際上	163
physician	8	名	醫師	★
physics	3	名	物理學	461
piano	5	名	鋼琴	★
pick	5	動	採摘、挑選、獲得	391
pickpocket	2	名	扒手	483
picky	2	形	吹毛求疵的、挑剔的	207
picnic	5	名	郊遊、野餐	217
picture	5	動	想像、描繪、拍攝	457
pie	5	名	派、餡餅	★
piece	5	名	作品、一片	141
piercing	3	形	刺耳的、有洞察力的	37
pigeon	3	名	鴿子、易受騙的人	217
pile	4	動	堆積、疊、累積	143
pill	3	名	藥丸、屈辱的事	341

單字	頻率	詞性	中譯	頁碼
pillow	3	名	枕頭、枕狀物、靠墊	217
pilot	4	名	飛行員、舵手、嚮導	205
pin	4	動	釘住、壓住、歸咎於	217
pine	4	名	松樹、松木、鳳梨	341
pink	5	形	粉紅色、粉紅色的	★
pint	3	名	品脫、一品脫的量	343
pioneer	4	名	先驅者、拓荒者	483
pious	3	形	虔誠的、偽善的	447
pipe	4	名	煙斗、導管、管樂器	219
pirate	3	名	海盜、剽竊者	49
pit	2	名	窪坑、凹處、陷阱	343
pitch	4	動	搭帳篷、紮營	219
pity	4	名	憾事、憐憫、同情	137
place	5	動	放置、安置、想起	85
plan	5	動	計畫、打算	123
planet	3	名	行星	255
plant	4	動	栽種、設置、插入	99
plaque	2	名	匾牌、徽章、牙斑	277
plastic	3	名	塑膠、塑膠製品	343
plate	4	名	盤子、碟、薄板	109
platform	3	名	平台、月台、講台	123
playboy	1	名	尋歡作樂的有錢男子	25
player	5	名	運動員、演奏者	★
playful	2	形	愛玩耍的、開玩笑的	219
playground	3	名	操場、運動場	87
pleasant	4	形	令人愉快的、舒適的	219
please	5	動	討好、使滿意、請	23
pleased	3	形	高興的、滿意的	★
pleasure	4	名	愉快、滿足、樂事	417
plentiful	2	形	豐富的、充足的	485
plenty	4	名	大量、充足、豐富	455
plot	4	名	情節、陰謀	313
pluck	3	動	摘、拔、拉、扯	69

單字	頻率	詞性	中譯	頁碼
plug	4	動	堵塞、接通電源	343
plum	3	名	梅子、洋李	343
plumber	3	名	水管工、堵漏人員	329
plus	4	介	加上、另有	219
pocket	5	名	口袋	★
poetry	4	名	詩、作詩技巧、詩意	87
point	5	動	指明、對準、強調	415
pointless	3	形	無意義的	87
poison	3	動	毒害、破壞、汙染	107
poisonous	2	形	有害的、有毒的	485
poke	3	動	把…戳向、伸出	201
polar	3	形	極地的、電極的	131
pole	4	名	極地、柱、竿	131
police	5	名	警察	★
policy	5	名	政策、方針、保單	219
polish	4	動	磨光、擦亮、潤飾	205
political	4	形	政治上的、政黨的	185
politician	3	名	政治家、政客	343
politics	4	名	政治、政見	★
pollute	2	動	汙染、弄髒、玷污	343
pollution	4	名	汙染、汙染地區	465
pond	4	名	池塘、大西洋別稱	87
pool	5	名	水塘、水池	★
poor	5	形	貧窮的、缺少的	335
popcorn	5	名	爆玉米花	★
popular	5	形	流行的、大眾的	★
popularity	3	名	聲望、流行、受歡迎	89
population	5	名	人口、全部居民	221
porcelain	3	名	瓷、(總稱)瓷器	345
port	4	名	港口、避風港、接口	221
porter	3	名	搬運工人、雜物工	485
portion	4	名	一部分、一份、命運	345
portrait	4	名	肖像、描繪、寫照	345

單字	頻率	詞性	中譯	頁碼
portray	3	動	描寫	★
portrayal	1	名	描繪、肖像、扮演	445
pose	3	動	造成、擺姿勢、假裝	221
position	4	名	位置、身分、立場	73
positive	4	形	積極的、真實的	221
possess	4	動	擁有、支配、迷住	199
possession	4	名	擁有、財產、領地	485
possibility	3	名	可能性、潛在價值	221
possible	5	形	可能的	★
post	5	動	張貼、設置、調派	377
postage	2	名	郵資、郵費	345
postcard	3	名	明信片	69
poster	3	名	海報、廣告、驛馬	345
postpone	4	動	使延期、延緩	105
pot	5	名	罐、壺、鍋	★
potato	4	名	馬鈴薯、洋芋	109
potential	5	名	可能性、潛力	77
pottery	2	名	陶器、陶器廠	345
pour	4	動	傾瀉、傾注、訴說	345
poverty	4	名	貧困、貧乏、不毛	289
powerful	5	形	強大的、有力的	★
practically	2	副	幾乎、差不多	463
practice	5	名	練習、實踐、常規	493
praise	4	動	讚美、表揚、歌頌	221
pray	4	動	祈禱、懇求	221
precious	4	形	貴重的、珍貴的	345
prefer	5	動	更喜歡、寧可、控告	223
preferable	3	形	更合意的、更好的	485
pregnancy	2	名	懷孕、豐富	487
pregnant	3	形	懷孕的、多產的	41
prehistoric	3	形	史前的、舊式的	339
prematurely	1	副	過早地、貿然地	451
premium	3	名	保險費、優質、津貼	459

單字	頻率	詞性	中譯	頁碼
prepare	5	動	準備、籌劃、編纂	57
presence	4	名	存在、出席、風度	79
present	4	名	禮物、贈品、目前	123
presentation	4	名	報告、遞交、演出	487
preservation	2	名	保護、維持、防腐	487
preserve	4	動	保護、保存、防腐	487
president	5	名	總統、校長、主席	223
presidential	3	形	總統的、總統制的	★
press	5	名	新聞界、報刊、壓平	121
pressure	4	名	壓力、困援、催促	37
prestigious	3	形	有名的	31
pretend	4	動	假裝、自稱、裝作	347
pretty	5	副	相當、頗、非常	263
prevent	5	動	防止、阻擋、預防	305
prevention	3	名	預防、防止、妨礙	487
previous	4	形	以前的、先的	135
prey	3	名	獵物、犧牲者、捕食	79
price	5	名	價格	★
priceless	2	形	貴重的、無價的	41
priest	4	名	牧師、神職人員	477
primarily	4	副	主要地、首先、起初	347
prime	4	形	最好的、最初的	471
primitive	3	形	原始的、早期的	207
prince	4	名	王子、親王	★
principal	4	名	校長、首長、資本	223
principle	4	名	原則、節操、構造	469
print	4	動	出版、印刷、銘記	89
priority	2	名	優先考慮的事	413
prison	4	名	監獄、監禁、拘留所	195
prisoner	3	名	犯人、失去自由的人	161
privacy	3	名	隱私、私下、隱退	229
private	5	形	私人的、喜歡獨處的	21
privilege	4	名	特權、殊榮	391

單字	頻率	詞性	中譯	頁碼
privileged	3	形	享有特權的	★
prize	4	名	獎品、獎金	49
probably	4	副	大概、或許	★
problem	5	名	問題、疑難問題	★
proceed	4	動	繼續進行、著手	431
process	4	名	過程、程序	★
proclaim	3	動	聲明、宣告、顯示	225
produce	5	動	生產、製造、創作	263
producer	4	名	製作人、製造者	225
product	4	名	產品、出產	★
production	3	名	生產、產量、製作	187
professional	4	形	職業性的、內行的	71
professor	4	名	教授、老師、專家	117
profit	4	名	利潤、收益	43
profitable	3	形	有利的、有益的	489
program	5	名	節目、計畫、大綱	333
progress	4	動	前進、提高、進步	67
project	5	名	企劃、方案、工程	225
prominent	3	形	重要的、突出的	427
promise	4	動	允諾、答應、有指望	225
promising	2	形	有前途的、有希望的	489
promote	4	動	晉升、促進、宣傳	125
promotion	3	名	促銷、宣傳	★
promptly	2	副	立即地、敏捷地	267
pronounce	4	動	發音、宣稱、表示	111
pronunciation	3	名	發音、讀法	449
prop	3	名	道具、支柱、後盾	399
propaganda	3	名	宣傳、宣傳活動	407
proper	5	形	循規蹈矩的、適合的	155
properly	4	副	適當地、正確地	★
property	4	名	房地產、所有權	379
proposal	3	名	提案、計畫、求婚	303
propose	3	動	提議、計畫、求婚	225

單字	頻率	詞性	中譯	頁碼
prosecutor	2	名	檢察官、公訴人	101
prosperity	3	名	興盛、繁榮、成功	489
prosperous	3	形	興旺的、繁榮的	347
protect	4	動	保護、防護	315
protection	3	名	防護、警戒	★
protective	2	形	保護的、保護貿易的	349
protest	3	動	抗議、反對、聲明	133
proud	4	形	驕傲的、輝煌的	57
proudly	4	副	得意洋洋地	★
prove	5	動	證明、顯示、原來是	497
proverb	3	名	諺語、格言	489
provide	5	動	提供、供給、規定	249
prowl	3	動	四處覓食、徘徊	25
psychological	3	形	心理學的	★
psychologist	2	名	心理學家	489
psychology	3	名	心理學、心理特點	327
public	4	形	公務的、公眾的	235
publication	3	名	出版、發行、刊物	491
publicity	2	名	名聲、宣傳	491
publish	4	動	出版、發行、刊登	89
publisher	2	名	出版者、出版商	491
pull	5	動	拖、拉開、吸引	363
pump	4	名	淺口包頭高跟鞋	165
pumpkin	2	名	南瓜、稱呼所愛之人	109
punch	4	動	用拳猛擊、猛烈推擠	349
punish	4	動	懲罰、處罰	517
punk	2	形	龐克的、無用的	169
pupil	4	名	小學生、弟子、瞳孔	225
purchase	4	動	購買、努力取得	183
pure	3	形	純粹的、純淨的	349
purely	3	副	純粹地、完全	★
purple	5	形	紫的、紫紅的	★
purpose	5	名	意圖、用途、決心	89

單字	頻率	詞性	中譯	頁碼
pursue	4	動	追求、追捕、進行	73
pursuit	3	名	追求、追蹤	491
push	5	動	推、推動、催促	★
put	5	動	放、擺	★
puzzle	4	動	使困惑、苦思而得出	227

Q

單字	頻率	詞性	中譯	頁碼
quake	2	動	顫抖、哆嗦、搖晃	491
qualification	2	名	取得資格、能力	87
quality	5	名	品質、特性、地位	175
quantity	4	名	數量、大宗	227
quarrel	4	名	爭吵、不和	9
quarter	5	名	四分之一、一刻鐘	227
queer	3	形	奇怪的、不舒服的	349
question	5	名	問題、詢問	★
questionnaire	2	名	問卷、調查表	145
quickly	5	副	快、馬上	★
quiet	4	形	安靜的、溫和的	375
quilt	3	名	被子、被褥	491
quit	5	動	放棄、退出、辭職	107
quite	5	副	相當、徹底、很	389
quiz	4	動	對…測驗、考問	227
quote	4	動	引述、引用、報價	121

R

單字	頻率	詞性	中譯	頁碼
race	5	名	種族、血統、競賽	189
racer	2	名	賽跑者、比賽用汽車	195
radiation	4	名	輻射、發光、放射線	313
radio	5	名	無線電、無線電廣播	★
rag	3	名	抹布、少量、惡作劇	349
rage	4	動	肆虐、發怒、流行	243
railway	3	名	鐵路、鐵道	91
rainbow	5	名	彩虹	★

單字	頻率	詞性	中譯	頁碼
rainy	4	形	下雨的、多雨的	227
raise	5	動	提出、舉起、增加	131
raisin	1	名	葡萄乾、深紫紅色	349
ram	4	動	猛撞、硬塞	277
range	5	名	一系列、範圍、類別	245
ransom	2	名	贖金、贖回、贖身	391
rapid	4	形	迅速的、陡的	451
rapidly	2	副	迅速地、很快地	187
rapper	2	名	饒舌歌手、敲門者	35
rare	4	形	罕見的、珍貴的	227
rarely	4	副	很少、難得	★
rat	5	名	鼠	★
rate	5	動	對…評價、列為	233
rather	4	副	相當、寧願、倒不如	115
razor	3	名	剃刀	353
reach	5	動	抵達、達到	★
react	4	動	回應、起作用、反抗	353
read	5	動	閱讀、察覺	★
readable	1	形	易讀的、可讀的	★
reader	5	名	讀者、愛好閱讀者	★
ready	5	形	準備好的	★
realize	4	動	實現、領悟、認識到	493
really	5	副	真正地、實際上	★
rear	4	動	撫養、培植、豎立	477
reason	5	名	理由、動機	★
reasonable	4	形	合理的、有理智的	89
rebel	3	名	造反者、反抗者	377
rebuild	2	動	重建、改建	121
recall	4	動	回想、召回、取消	283
receipt	4	名	收據、收到、收入	353
receive	5	動	接收、容納	21
recent	5	形	最近的、近代的	483
recently	4	副	最近	★

單字	頻率	詞性	中譯	頁碼
reception	3	名	歡迎會、接待、接收	491
recipe	3	名	食譜、處方、訣竅	217
recognize	5	動	辨認、認可、認清	203
recommend	4	動	介紹、推薦、建議	511
recommendation	2	名	推薦信、推薦、建議	435
reconcile	3	動	和解、調停、使一致	157
reconciliation	1	名	和解、調停、一致	385
record	4	動	錄音、記錄	95
recorder	3	名	錄音機、記錄者	353
recover	3	動	重新獲得、恢復	★
recreation	3	名	娛樂、消遣	493
recruit	3	動	聘用、徵募	299
recruitment	2	名	徵募新兵、補充	239
rectangular	2	形	矩形的、長方形的	229
recyclable	3	形	可回收利用的	343
recycle	3	動	回收利用、再循環	343
redecorate	2	動	重新裝飾	415
reduce	4	動	減少、把…歸納	53
refer	5	動	查閱、論及、涉及	403
refill	4	動	再裝滿、再灌滿	★
reflection	4	名	深思、反省、反射	293
refresh	4	動	恢復精神、重新振作	45
refreshment	2	名	起提神作用的東西	451
refrigerator	2	名	冰箱、冷凍庫	215
refund	3	動	退還、歸還、償還	353
refusal	3	名	拒絕、優先購買權	317
refuse	4	動	拒絕、不准、不願	229
regain	2	動	收復、取回、恢復	413
regard	5	動	把…看做、注重	229
regarding	2	介	關於、就…而論	463
regime	4	名	社會制度、政權	515
region	4	名	地區、領域、部位	475
register	4	名	收銀機、註冊	151

565

單字	頻率	詞性	中譯	頁碼
registration	3	名	註冊、掛號、登記	495
regret	4	動	懊悔、痛惜、遺憾	55
regretful	2	形	懊悔的、遺憾的	333
regular	4	形	經常的、有規律的	163
regularly	5	副	有規律地、定期地	★
regulation	3	名	規則、規定、調整	495
rehearsal	3	名	排練、彩排、詳述	71
reject	4	動	否決、抵制、丟棄	497
rejection	3	名	拒絕、退回、廢棄	53
relate	5	動	敘述、有關、涉及	353
relationship	3	名	關係、關聯	107
relative	4	名	親戚、親屬	51
relax	5	動	使鬆弛、放鬆	★
release	4	動	釋放、豁免、發行	71
relevant	4	形	有關的、有意義的	★
reliable	4	形	可信賴的、可靠的	239
relief	4	名	慰藉、緩和	355
relieve	3	動	減輕、解除、救濟	385
religion	4	名	宗教信仰	355
religious	4	形	篤信宗教的、虔誠的	221
reluctant	4	形	勉強的、不情願的	247
rely	4	動	依賴、依靠、指望	355
remain	5	動	保持、餘留、留待	421
remark	4	名	言辭、評論、注意	479
remarkable	3	形	卓越的、值得注意的	469
remedy	3	名	補救法、治療、補償	219
remember	5	動	記得、想起	★
remind	3	動	使想起、提醒	137
remit	3	動	匯款、免除、移交	267
remote	4	形	遙遠的、遙控的	313
remove	4	動	消除、移動	97
renew	4	動	更新、重新開始	467
renovate	2	動	裝修、翻新、恢復	415

單字	頻率	詞性	中譯	頁碼
renowned	3	形	著名的、有名望的	173
rent	4	動	租用、出租	29
repair	4	動	修理、糾正、恢復	355
repay	4	動	償還、報答、報復	327
repeat	5	動	重複、背誦、重播	229
repetition	3	名	反覆、副本、背誦	495
replace	4	動	取代、把…放回	167
reply	5	動	回答、回應	105
report	4	名	報告、報導、成績單	91
reportedly	2	副	據傳聞、據報導	101
reporter	4	名	記者、通訊員	★
represent	4	動	象徵、意味著、扮演	383
representative	3	名	代表、代理人、典型	197
reprocessed	2	形	經過再加工的	217
reproduce	3	動	複製、繁殖、再現	409
reproduction	2	名	複製品、繁育、再現	427
republic	4	名	共和政體、共和國	355
reputation	3	名	名聲、信譽	17
request	4	動	要求、請求給予	111
require	4	動	需要、要求、命令	89
rescue	4	動	營救、挽救	453
research	5	名	研究、調查	★
researcher	5	名	研究員、調查員	★
resemble	3	動	像、類似	205
reserve	4	動	保留、儲備、預定	357
resident	4	名	居民、住院醫生	313
resign	3	動	辭去、放棄、順從	289
resignation	2	名	辭職、放棄、順從	167
resist	4	動	反抗、抵抗、忍住	357
resistance	4	名	反抗、抵抗力、抵制	497
resolutely	1	副	堅決地、毅然地	165
resolution	4	名	決議、決心、分解	497
resolve	4	動	解決、決定、分解	433

單字	頻率	詞性	中譯	頁碼
resort	4	動	訴諸、憑藉	511
resource	4	名	資源、物力	443
resourceful	1	形	機智的、資源豐富的	289
respect	5	動	尊重、重視、顧及	65
respectable	2	形	可觀的、名聲好的	497
respectful	2	形	有禮貌的、恭敬的	361
respectfully	3	副	恭敬地	★
respond	4	動	回答、做出反應	357
responsibility	5	名	責任、職責、義務	357
responsible	4	形	承擔責任的	455
rest	5	動	放心、休息、依賴	497
restaurant	5	名	餐館	★
restrict	3	動	限制、約束	77
restriction	3	名	限制、約束	★
restroom	2	名	公共廁所、洗手間	83
result	5	動	導致、發生	255
resume	4	名	(美)履歷、摘要	73
retain	4	動	保留、攔住、記住	415
retired	4	形	退休的	75
retirement	3	名	退休、退役	★
retreat	3	動	撤退、退縮、躲避	289
return	4	動	返回、歸還	★
reunite	1	動	使重聚	★
reveal	4	動	揭露、展現、洩漏	121
revenge	3	名	報仇、報復	369
review	5	動	檢閱、複習、回顧	231
reviewer	2	名	評論家、檢閱者	313
revise	4	動	修改、校訂	499
revision	3	名	修訂、校訂、修訂本	499
revolt	3	名	造反、起義、厭惡	377
revolution	4	名	革命	★
revolutionize	2	動	徹底改革	77
ribbon	3	名	緞帶、絲帶	357

單字	頻率	詞性	中譯	頁碼
rice	5	名	稻米、米飯	★
rich	5	形	富有的	★
rid	3	動	使免除、使擺脫	★
riddle	2	名	謎語、難題	357
ride	5	動	騎乘、搭乘	★
ridiculous	3	形	可笑的、荒謬的	287
right	5	名	權利、右邊、正義	381
rightly	2	副	理所當然地、公正地	175
ring	5	名	鈴聲、鐘聲	★
rink	2	名	溜冰場	367
riot	3	名	暴亂、喧鬧	339
rip	4	動	裂開、劃破、拆	185
ripe	4	形	成熟的、老成的	465
rise	5	動	上升、增加、起義	345
risk	5	名	危險、風險	169
rival	4	名	競爭者、對手	157
river	5	名	江、河	★
riverbank	3	名	河岸、河堤	★
road	5	名	路、公路	★
roast	3	形	烘烤的	307
rob	4	動	搶劫、盜取、使喪失	309
robber	2	名	強盜、搶劫者	27
robbery	3	名	搶劫、盜取	149
robe	3	名	長袍、浴衣、睡袍	★
robot	3	名	機器人	95
rock	5	名	岩石、基石	★
rocket	4	名	火箭、飛彈	359
rocky	2	形	多岩石的、搖晃的	231
rod	4	名	桿、棍棒、懲罰	243
role	5	名	角色、作用、職責	315
roll	5	名	名單、滾動	219
roller	3	名	滾動物、滾筒、捲軸	135
romantic	3	形	浪漫的、幻想的	63

單字	頻率	詞性	中譯	頁碼
roof	5	名	屋頂、車頂	★
rooster	2	名	公雞、狂妄自負的人	95
root	4	名	根源、根部、本質	97
rose	5	名	薔薇、玫瑰	★
rot	3	動	腐壞、破損、墮落	359
rotten	3	形	腐敗的、腐爛的	359
rough	4	形	粗糙的、未加工的	501
roughly	2	副	大約、大體上	499
round	4	名	一回合、巡迴	251
route	4	名	路線、路程、途徑	499
routine	4	名	例行公事、慣例	359
row	4	名	一列、一排座位	235
royal	4	形	盛大的、王室的	231
rubber	3	名	橡膠、橡膠鞋	97
rude	4	形	粗魯的、無禮的	99
rudeness	4	名	無禮貌、粗野	★
ruin	3	動	毀壞、使成廢墟	19
rule	4	名	常規、規定、支配	129
rumbling	2	名	隆隆聲、打鬧	499
rumor	3	名	謠言、傳聞、咕噥	201
run	5	動	跑、奔	★
runway	2	名	伸展台、跑道、車道	237
rural	4	形	農村的	499
rush	4	動	衝、匆忙地做、湧現	149
rusty	2	形	荒廢的	359

S

單字	頻率	詞性	中譯	頁碼
sack	4	名	麻袋、一袋的量	359
sacrifice	3	名	犧牲的行為	89
sacrificial	2	形	獻祭的、犧牲的	281
sad	4	形	悲哀的、遭透了的	337
sadden	2	動	悲哀、悲痛、使黯淡	495
sadness	3	名	悲傷、哀傷	★

單字	頻率	詞性	中譯	頁碼
safety	5	名	安全	★
sail	5	動	航行、駕駛、飄過	97
sailor	3	名	水手、船員	231
sake	4	名	目的、理由、利益	441
salad	5	名	沙拉	★
salary	3	名	薪資	81
sale	5	名	出售、賣出	★
salesperson	4	名	店員、售貨員	★
salon	3	名	客廳、交誼廳	★
salty	3	形	鹹的、含鹽的	251
same	5	形	相同的、同樣的	★
sample	4	名	試用品、樣本、實例	233
sanatorium	2	名	療養院、靜養地	225
sand	5	名	沙	★
sandwich	3	名	三明治	233
sanitation	1	名	環境衛生、衛生設備	447
satellite	4	名	衛星、追隨者	501
satisfaction	2	名	滿足、稱心、樂事	501
satisfactory	4	形	令人滿意的	★
satisfy	4	動	使滿意、符合、履行	157
Saturday	5	名	星期六	★
sauce	4	名	醬汁、樂趣、莽撞	203
saucer	3	名	茶碟、淺碟	361
sauna	2	名	蒸汽浴、桑拿浴	57
sausage	3	名	香腸、臘腸、極少量	361
save	5	動	挽救、節省、儲蓄	375
savings	4	名	存款、積蓄	29
saw	5	動	鋸開	99
saying	4	名	格言、常言道、言論	121
scale	4	名	磅秤、規模、刻度	129
scandal	2	名	醜聞、恥辱	121
scar	4	名	疤、傷痕、創傷	255
scare	5	動	驚嚇、使恐懼	★

單字	頻率	詞性	中譯	頁碼
scarecrow	1	名	稻草人	361
scared	4	形	恐懼的、不敢的	333
scarf	3	名	圍巾、披巾、頭巾	★
scary	3	形	可怕的、引起驚慌的	361
scatter	3	動	使分散、散布、撒播	361
scene	5	名	景色、場面	★
scenery	3	名	景色、舞台布景	63
scenic	3	形	景色秀麗的	291
scent	3	名	氣味、香味、線索	279
schedule	4	名	計畫表、清單	45
scheme	4	名	計畫、結構、陰謀	481
scholar	3	名	學者、人文學者	★
scholarship	3	名	獎學金、學術成就	361
school	5	名	學校	★
science	5	名	科學、學科、技術	233
scientific	4	形	科學的、科學上的	★
scientist	3	名	科學家	233
scissors	3	名	剪刀	233
scold	2	動	責罵、訓斥	109
scoop	3	名	一勺、獨家新聞	35
score	4	名	得分、成績、宿怨	247
scorpion	1	名	蠍子、(S)天蠍座的人	485
scout	3	動	搜索、偵查	361
scrap	4	名	碎片、片段、資料	183
scratch	3	名	抓痕、亂塗	293
scream	3	動	尖叫、放聲大哭	113
screen	4	名	螢幕、掩護、隔板	233
screwdriver	1	名	螺絲起子	501
scribble	2	動	潦草地書寫、亂畫	471
scrub	3	動	用力擦洗、擦亮	363
scrutiny	3	名	監督、詳細檢查	497
sculpture	3	名	雕塑品、雕像	445
sea	5	名	海、海洋	★

單字	頻率	詞性	中譯	頁碼
seal	3	名	象徵、印章、封條	363
search	5	動	搜尋、調查、穿過	233
season	5	名	季節、旺季、季票	313
seat	5	名	座位、席位、所在地	99
second	5	形	第二的、第二次的	★
second-hand	3	形	二手的、中古的	★
secret	5	形	祕密的、機密的	★
secretary	4	名	秘書、書記官、部長	103
secretly	5	副	祕密地、背地裡	★
section	4	名	部分、區域、片、塊	167
sector	4	名	部門、部分、扇形	81
security	4	名	保障、安全、債券	81
seed	4	名	種子	★
seek	5	動	尋求、探索、企圖	363
seem	5	動	似乎、感覺好像	★
seesaw	2	名	蹺蹺板、上下動	99
seize	4	動	抓住、掌握、利用	111
seldom	5	副	很少、難得	255
select	4	動	挑選、選拔	171
seller	5	名	銷售者、賣方	★
semester	3	名	(美)一學期、半學年	43
senate	3	名	立法機構	407
send	5	動	送往、寄、派遣	367
senior	4	形	資深的、年長的	501
sensational	2	形	轟動社會的、知覺的	409
sense	5	名	感覺、知覺、效用	191
sensitive	4	形	靈敏的、敏感的	79
sentence	3	名	判決、宣判、句子	101
separate	4	動	分開、區分、分居	235
September	5	名	九月	★
series	5	名	系列、連續、叢書	487
serious	5	形	嚴重的、嚴肅的	★
seriously	4	副	嚴重地、嚴肅地	357

單字	頻率	詞性	中譯	頁碼
servant	3	名	公僕、僕人、事務員	235
serve	5	動	為…服務、供應	125
service	5	名	服役、服務	239
set	5	動	設定、安裝、使處於	339
setback	2	名	挫折、倒退、復發	391
setting	5	名	背景、設定、布景	313
settle	4	動	鎮定下來、安頓	235
settler	2	名	開拓者、移居者	307
several	4	形	幾個的、數個的	135
severe	4	形	嚴厲的、劇烈的	501
severely	4	副	嚴重地、嚴格地	9
sew	2	動	做針線活、縫補	209
sexual	4	形	性別的、性的	363
shade	4	名	窗簾、陰涼處	363
shadow	4	名	幽靈、幻影、影子	315
shady	2	形	成蔭的、陰暗的	365
shake	4	動	搖動、發抖、握手	321
shallow	4	形	膚淺的、淺薄的	365
shame	4	名	倒楣的事、羞恥	365
shameful	2	形	丟臉的、可恥的	501
shampoo	3	名	洗髮精、洗頭	365
shape	5	名	形狀、形式、狀態	387
share	5	動	分享、分擔、共有	235
shark	5	名	鯊魚	★
sharp	4	形	急轉的、鋒利的	421
sharply	2	副	猛烈地、突然	515
shatter	3	動	打擊、動搖、削弱	447
shave	3	動	刮鬍子、修剪	365
shed	3	動	流下、散發、擺脫	247
sheep	4	名	羊、羊皮、膽小鬼	365
sheet	4	名	床單、一張(紙)	★
shelf	4	名	架子、擱板	235
shell	4	名	貝殼、果殼	235

單字	頻率	詞性	中譯	頁碼
shelter	3	名	避難所、遮蔽、庇護	447
shepherd	3	名	牧羊人、指導者	365
shift	4	名	轉變、輪班、手段	503
shine	4	動	出眾、照耀、顯露	103
ship	5	名	船、艦	★
shipment	3	名	裝載的貨物	★
shirt	5	名	襯衫、男式襯衫	★
shock	5	動	使震動、使休克	★
shocked	4	形	震動的、震驚的	★
shocking	3	形	令人震驚的	149
shoe	5	名	鞋	★
shoot	4	動	發射、拍攝、投射	53
shop	5	名	商店、零售店	★
shore	4	名	岸、濱	★
short	5	形	短的、矮的	★
shortage	3	名	缺少、匱乏、不足額	205
shortcut	2	名	捷徑	35
shortly	5	副	簡短地、立刻	★
shortsighted	2	形	目光短淺的、近視的	503
short tempered	2	形	脾氣暴躁的、易怒的	
shot	5	名	嘗試、射擊、注射	71
shoulder	5	名	肩膀	★
shout	4	動	喊叫、大聲說出	135
show	5	動	露出、展示	★
shower	5	名	淋浴、一陣(陣雨)	★
shrub	3	名	灌木、果汁甜酒	47
shut	4	動	關上、停止營業	105
shuttle	3	名	太空梭、梭子	479
shy	5	形	害羞的、靦腆的	★
side	5	名	旁邊、身邊、方面	429
sidewalk	3	名	(美)人行道	323
sigh	4	動	嘆氣、婉惜、思念	361
sight	4	名	視力、見解、目睹	105

單字	頻率	詞性	中譯	頁碼
sightseeing	2	名	觀光、遊覽	503
sign	5	動	簽約雇用、簽名	105
signal	4	動	以動作向…示意	235
signature	3	名	簽署、簽名、特徵	499
significance	3	名	重要性、含意	503
significantly	4	副	意味深長地	★
silence	4	名	寂靜、沉默	★
silent	4	形	沉默的、靜止的	55
silk	4	名	絲綢、蠶絲	155
silly	4	形	愚蠢的、糊塗的	★
silver	4	名	銀、銀色	★
similar	5	形	相仿的、類似的	163
simple	5	形	簡單的、樸實的	75
simply	5	副	簡單地、簡易地	★
simultaneous	3	形	同步的、一齊的	147
since	4	連	自…以來、由於	★
sincere	4	形	真誠的、衷心的	385
sincerely	3	副	由衷地、真誠地	247
singer	5	名	歌唱家、歌手	★
single	5	形	單身的、唯一的	237
sip	3	名	啜飲、一小口	367
site	5	名	地點、場所	★
situate	3	動	使位於、使處於	91
situation	4	名	處境、情況、位置	133
size	5	名	尺寸、大小	★
skating	2	名	溜冰、滑冰	367
ski	5	動	滑雪	★
skill	4	名	技能、技術、熟練性	327
skillful	2	形	熟練的、有技術的	237
skinny	2	形	皮包骨的、極瘦的	237
skirt	5	名	裙子、襯裙	★
sky	5	名	天空、太空	★
skylight	2	名	天窗	431

單字	頻率	詞性	中譯	頁碼
skyscraper	2	名	摩天大樓	55
slack	3	動	懈怠、放鬆、懶散	299
slam	3	動	猛撞、猛地關上	273
slap	3	動	打…耳光、用手掌打	★
slave	3	名	苦工、奴隸	29
sleep	5	動	睡覺	★
sleepy	3	形	想睡的、呆滯的	237
sleeve	3	名	袖子、袖套	367
slender	3	形	修長的、纖細的	237
slice	4	名	切片、部分、曲球	125
slide	3	動	滑落、滑行	285
slight	4	形	輕微的、不足道的	503
slightly	5	副	稍微地、嬌弱地	297
slim	3	形	苗條的、微薄的	23
slip	3	動	滑一跤、滑落、下降	237
slipper	3	名	拖鞋	237
slippery	3	形	滑的、靠不住的	367
slope	4	名	斜坡、傾斜	367
slow	4	形	遲緩的、慢的	239
slump	3	動	下跌、衰弱、陷落	291
small	5	形	小的、少的、瘦小的	★
smart	5	形	聰明的、漂亮的	★
smartphone	5	名	智慧型手機	★
smell	4	動	發出…氣味、嗅到	73
smile	5	動	微笑	★
smog	3	名	煙霧	503
smoke	5	動	抽菸、燻製、冒煙	85
smoker	5	名	吸菸者	★
smoking	5	名	抽菸	★
smooth	5	形	光滑的、進行順利的	367
smuggle	2	動	走私、偷運	309
snack	5	名	快餐、小吃、點心	★
snake	5	名	蛇	★

單字	頻率	詞性	中譯	頁碼
snap	5	動	快照拍攝、猛咬	177
sneak	3	動	偷溜、偷偷地做	83
snore	3	名	打鼾、鼾聲	451
snow	5	名	雪	★
snowboarding	3	名	單板滑雪	★
soak	3	動	濕透、浸漬、吸收	83
soap	5	名	肥皂	★
soar	4	動	猛增、高飛、升騰	485
sob	3	動	嗚咽、啜泣、哭訴	505
social	4	形	社交的	107
society	5	名	社會	★
sock	3	名	短襪、半統襪	373
soda	3	名	蘇打、碳酸氫鈉	109
sofa	5	名	沙發、長椅	★
soft	5	形	柔軟的	★
soften	2	動	軟化、變輕柔	359
software	4	名	(電腦)軟體	★
solar	4	形	太陽的	505
soldier	4	名	軍人、陸軍	★
solely	3	副	唯一地、僅僅、完全	475
solid	3	形	固體的、結實的	★
solidify	2	動	凝固、變堅固、團結	199
solitary	3	形	隱居的、單獨的	475
solitude	3	名	孤獨、隱居	★
solo	3	形	獨奏的、單獨表演的	181
solution	4	名	解答、溶液	★
solve	4	動	解決、解答、清償	239
somebody	5	代	某人、有人	★
somehow	3	副	不知怎地	★
someone	4	代	某人、有人	★
sometimes	5	副	有時候	★
somewhat	3	副	有點、稍微	39
somewhere	3	副	在某處、到某處	★

單字	頻率	詞性	中譯	頁碼
song	5	名	歌、歌曲	★
songwriter	4	名	流行歌的作曲者	★
soon	5	副	不久、很快地	★
sophomore	2	名	大二生	505
sore	4	形	痛的、痠痛的	75
sorrow	3	名	悲痛、憂傷、傷心事	369
sorrowful	2	形	悲傷的、令人傷心的	121
sorry	5	形	感到抱歉的	★
soulful	2	形	深情的、充滿感情的	109
sound	4	動	聽起來、發聲、響起	109
soundly	2	副	酣然地、穩健地	293
soup	5	名	湯	★
source	5	名	來源、源頭	489
souvenir	3	名	紀念品	51
space	5	名	太空、空間、場所	479
spaghetti	2	名	義大利麵條	369
spam	2	名	垃圾郵件	207
spank	2	動	打屁股、摑	391
spare	4	動	騰出、免去、剩下	57
spark	4	動	發出火花、點燃	505
sparkling	3	形	閃閃發光的	★
sparrow	2	名	麻雀	505
speak	5	動	說話、講話	★
speaker	4	名	說話者、演講者	★
special	5	形	特別的、特殊的	★
specialize	3	動	專攻、詳細說明	185
species	4	名	物種、種類	361
specific	5	形	特定的、明確的	11
spectacle	3	名	景象、奇觀、場面	409
speech	4	名	演說、言論	111
speed	5	動	加速、快行	301
speedily	2	副	迅速地、立即	189
spell	3	動	拼字、招致	111

單字	頻率	詞性	中譯	頁碼
spelling	3	名	拼字、拼寫、拼法	241
spend	5	動	花費、用盡、耗盡	429
spice	2	名	香料、風味、少許	369
spicy	3	形	辛辣的、有香料味的	69
spider	5	名	蜘蛛	★
spill	3	動	濺出、溢出、洩密	83
spirit	4	名	精神、心靈、氣魄	65
spiritual	2	形	心靈的、神聖的	505
spit	3	動	吐口水、表示唾棄	369
spite	2	名	惡意、心術不良	369
splendid	2	形	壯麗的、燦爛的	507
split	3	名	分裂、裂縫、派系	413
spoil	3	動	搞糟、損壞、溺愛	365
spokesman	2	名	發言人、代言人	417
sponsor	3	動	發起、主辦、贊助	307
spoon	4	名	匙、湯匙	★
sport	5	名	遊戲、運動	★
sportsmanship	1	名	運動員精神	507
spot	4	動	發現、認出、弄髒	275
sprain	2	動	扭傷	371
spray	3	動	噴灑、濺散	133
spread	4	動	蔓延、普及、伸展	241
spring	5	名	春季、春天	★
sprinkle	3	動	撒、點綴	177
squeeze	3	動	榨出、擠出、強取	197
stab	2	動	刺入、戳、刺傷	373
stable	4	形	穩定的、可信賴的	371
stadium	4	名	體育場、球場	271
staff	4	名	(全體)工作人員、幕僚	45
stage	5	動	上演、籌劃、發動	101
stain	3	名	汙點、瑕疵、色斑	97
stair	5	名	樓梯、梯級	★
stake	4	名	股份、椿、風險	481

單字	頻率	詞性	中譯	頁碼
stalk	4	動	跟蹤、偷偷靠近	363
stalker	2	名	跟蹤者、高視闊步者	383
stamp	3	名	郵票、印花、特徵	241
stand	5	動	忍受、站立、抵抗	229
standard	4	名	標準、規格、水準	241
staple	3	名	訂書針、主要產品	169
star	5	名	星、恆星、天體	★
stare	4	動	凝視、注視	371
start	5	動	出發、開始	★
starve	4	動	挨餓、餓死、渴望	263
state	5	動	說明、聲明	35
statement	4	名	陳述、聲明、結單	349
station	5	名	站、車站	★
statistics	3	名	統計資料、統計學	457
statue	3	名	雕像、塑像	327
status	5	名	身分、地位、狀態	87
stay	5	動	停留、暫住	★
steady	4	形	穩定的、平穩的	371
steak	5	名	牛排、肉排、魚排	★
steal	5	動	偷、竊取、侵占	317
stealthy	2	形	鬼鬼祟祟的、悄悄的	79
steam	4	動	蒸、冒熱氣、行駛	209
steel	4	形	鋼鐵的	243
steep	4	形	陡峭的、大起大落的	231
stem	4	名	幹、莖、血統	507
step	5	名	步伐、足跡、步驟	55
stepson	2	名	繼子	★
stereo	3	名	立體音響、立體聲	373
stern	3	形	嚴厲的、堅定的	243
stick	5	名	枝條、棍、棒	★
sticker	3	名	標籤、貼紙	201
sticky	2	形	黏性的、濕熱的	373
stiff	4	形	硬的、僵直的	373

單字	頻率	詞性	中譯	頁碼
still	5	副	還、仍舊	★
stingy	2	形	吝嗇的、小氣的	507
stink	3	動	發惡臭、名聲臭	73
stir	4	動	激起、鼓動、攪動	373
stitch	3	動	縫合、固定、連結	185
stock	5	名	股票、存貨、蓄積	87
stomachache	2	名	胃痛、腹痛	135
stone	5	名	石頭	★
stool	3	名	凳子、糞便	373
stop	5	動	停止、止住	★
storage	4	名	存儲器、貯藏、保管	167
store	5	名	店鋪	★
storey	2	名	樓層	39
stormy	4	形	暴風雨的、多風暴的	★
story	5	名	故事、情況	★
stove	3	名	火爐、爐灶	159
straight	5	形	筆直的、純粹的	★
strange	4	形	奇怪的、不熟悉的	273
strangely	1	副	奇妙地、不可思議地	509
stranger	5	名	陌生人、外地人	★
strap	4	名	帶子、金屬帶、皮條	305
strategy	4	名	對策、戰略、計謀	81
straw	3	名	吸管、稻草、麥桿	243
stray	3	動	流浪、走散、分心	213
street	5	名	街、街道	★
strength	4	名	長處、力量、體力	373
strengthen	3	動	加強、鞏固、變強大	507
stress	5	名	壓力、緊張、著重	43
stressful	3	形	充滿壓力的、緊張的	81
stretch	4	動	舒展肢體、拉直	243
strict	4	形	嚴格的、嚴謹的	299
strike	4	動	攻擊、簽訂	243
string	4	名	一串、細繩、弦	243

單字	頻率	詞性	中譯	頁碼
strip	4	名	條、細長片	263
strive	4	動	努力、奮鬥、反抗	67
strong	5	形	強壯的、有力的	★
structure	4	名	結構、組織、建築物	211
struggle	4	動	奮鬥、掙扎、對抗	29
stub	2	名	票根、殘肢、殘根	301
stubborn	3	形	不屈不撓的、頑固的	373
stuck	3	形	困住的、無法擺脫的	59
student	5	名	(大中學校的)學生	★
studio	4	名	錄音室、畫室	85
study	5	動	學習、研究	★
stuff	5	名	物品、廢話、材料	375
stumble	3	動	絆倒、跟蹌、躊躇	419
stun	4	動	大吃一驚、昏迷	365
stupid	5	形	愚蠢的、笨的	★
style	5	名	風格、時髦	★
stylish	2	形	時髦的、流行的	25
subject	5	名	主題、科目	89
submarine	3	形	潛艇的、海底的	507
subordinate	3	名	部屬、部下	45
subsequently	3	副	隨後、接著	377
substance	3	名	物質、主旨、要義	153
substantial	4	形	實質的、大量的	373
substitute	3	名	代替品、代用品	77
subtle	4	形	隱約的、微妙的	199
subtract	3	動	減、去掉	245
subtropical	2	形	亞熱帶的	213
suburb	3	名	郊區、邊緣、外圍	375
subway	3	名	(美)地下鐵、(英)地道	23
succeed	4	動	成功、接著發生	347
success	5	名	成功、成就	489
successfully	2	副	順利地、成功地	139
such	5	形	這樣的、此類的	★

單字	頻率	詞性	中譯	頁碼
suck	3	動	吸吮、吸收、吞沒	375
sudden	4	形	迅速的、突然的	149
suddenly	4	副	意外地、忽然	★
sue	4	動	控告、提起訴訟	353
suffer	4	動	患病、遭受、經歷	123
suggest	5	動	顯示、建議	191
suggestion	4	名	建議、聯想、暗示	267
suicide	3	名	自殺、自毀	147
suit	5	名	套裝、訴訟、懇求	181
suitable	4	形	適宜的、合適的	155
sum	3	名	總數、一筆、概要	375
summarize	3	動	概述、總結	507
summer	5	名	夏天	★
sunbathe	2	動	做日光浴	115
Sunday	5	名	星期天	★
sunglasses	5	名	太陽眼鏡	★
sunny	5	形	陽光充足的	★
sunscreen	4	名	遮光劑	★
sunshine	5	名	陽光	★
suntan	2	名	曬黑、棕色	★
superficial	3	形	外表的、表面的	439
supermarket	5	名	超級市場	★
supermodel	4	名	超級名模	★
superstar	4	名	超級明星	★
supervise	3	動	管理、指導、監督	311
supervisor	3	名	監督人、指導者	61
supper	4	名	晚飯、晚餐時間	115
supply	3	動	供應、補充、滿足	245
support	5	動	支持、擁護、扶養	73
supporter	3	名	支持者、擁護者	★
suppose	5	動	認為必須、猜想	333
supreme	3	形	最高的、最大的	101
sure	5	形	確信的、必定的	★

單字	頻率	詞性	中譯	頁碼
surf	3	動	上網瀏覽、衝浪運動	485
surface	5	名	表面、水面、外觀	37
surfboard	2	名	衝浪板	37
surge	3	動	激增、洶湧、澎湃	77
surgeon	3	名	外科醫生	507
surgery	4	名	手術、外科、開刀房	203
surgical	2	形	外科的、手術用的	193
surpass	3	動	勝過、優於	411
surprise	5	名	驚奇、令人驚訝的事	★
surprising	4	形	驚人的	★
surround	3	動	圍住、包圍、圍繞	187
surroundings	2	名	環境、周遭情況	509
survey	5	名	調查、測量、俯瞰	459
survive	4	動	倖存、比⋯活得長	245
suspect	3	名	嫌疑犯	309
suspicion	3	名	猜疑、嫌疑	★
suspicious	3	形	懷疑的、有蹊蹺的	19
sustainable	2	形	能維持的、能承受的	487
swallow	3	動	吞下、吞併、耗盡	245
swear	4	動	發誓、詛咒、宣示	123
sweat	4	動	出汗、焦慮、剝削	57
sweater	3	名	毛線衣、針織衫	283
sweep	3	動	打掃、颳起、環視	247
sweet	5	形	甜的、可愛的	★
sweetheart	2	名	心上人、甜心	35
swiftly	2	副	迅速地、敏捷地	377
swimming	5	名	游泳	★
swing	4	名	盪鞦韆、擺動、音律	247
switch	3	名	開關、轉換、調換	377
swollen	3	形	浮腫的、膨脹的	377
sword	3	名	刀、劍、武力	377
symbol	4	名	象徵、記號	35
symbolism	2	名	象徵之使用、象徵性	★

單字	頻率	詞性	中譯	頁碼
symbolize	3	動	象徵、標誌	419
sympathetic	3	形	有同情心的、贊同的	509
sympathy	4	名	同情、贊同、慰問	295
symphony	3	名	交響樂、和聲、和諧	207
symptom	3	名	症狀、徵兆	41
system	5	名	體系、制度、規律	493
systematic	3	形	有系統的、有條理的	509

T

單字	頻率	詞性	中譯	頁碼
table	5	名	桌子、餐桌、檯	★
tactic	2	名	戰術、策略、手法	147
tail	4	動	變少、尾隨、跟蹤	115
tailor	3	名	裁縫師、(男裝)服裝店	21
Taiwanese	5	形	台灣的、台灣人的	★
take	5	動	拿走、取得	★
takeout	2	形	外賣的	363
tale	4	名	故事、敘述、閒話	115
talent	4	名	才能、天資、藝人	247
talented	4	形	有才能的、有天賦的	★
talk	5	動	講話、談話	★
talkative	2	形	健談的、多嘴的	247
tall	5	形	身材高的、高大的	★
tame	2	形	溫順的、易駕馭的	13
tank	4	名	坦克車、大容器、槽	247
tanned	3	形	被曬成棕褐色的	27
tap	3	名	龍頭、塞子、輕拍	379
tar	3	名	焦油、柏油、瀝青	107
target	4	動	把…作為目標	17
task	5	名	任務、苦差事	★
taste	5	名	興趣、愛好、味道	425
tasteful	2	形	有鑑賞力的、高雅的	103
tasting	2	名	品酒集會、嚐味	117
tasty	2	形	美味的、高雅的	247

單字	頻率	詞性	中譯	頁碼
tattoo	2	名	紋身	143
tax	5	名	稅、稅金、負擔	379
taxi	4	名	計程車	★
teacher	5	名	老師、教師	★
team	5	名	隊、組、班	★
teammate	2	名	隊友、同隊隊員	157
teapot	2	名	茶壺	115
tear	4	動	撕開、扯破	★
tease	3	動	戲弄、取笑、挑逗	379
technician	3	名	技術人員、技師	509
technique	4	名	技巧、技術、手段	141
technology	4	名	工藝、技術	★
tedious	3	形	冗長乏味的、厭煩的	449
teenager	3	名	十幾歲青少年	11
teeth	5	名	牙齒(複數形)	★
telegraph	3	名	電信、電報	509
telescope	3	名	單筒望遠鏡	509
television	4	名	電視	★
temperature	4	名	溫度、氣溫、氣氛	295
temple	3	名	寺廟、聖殿、太陽穴	249
temporarily	3	副	暫時地、臨時地	47
temporary	4	形	臨時的、暫時的	379
tend	4	動	傾向於、易於	379
tendency	3	名	傾向、天分、趨勢	511
tender	4	形	嫩的、溫柔的	217
tension	3	名	緊張、繃緊	451
tent	4	名	帳篷、寓所、帷幕	219
term	5	名	任期、條款、術語	101
terrible	4	形	極差的、可怕的	249
terrify	3	動	使害怕、使恐怖	511
terror	2	名	恐懼、恐怖活動	511
terrorist	4	名	恐怖分子	147
terrorize	2	動	使恐怖、恐嚇、脅迫	147

單字	頻率	詞性	中譯	頁碼
test	5	動	考驗、測驗、分析	347
text	5	名	文字、正文、文本	203
textbook	2	名	教科書、課本	57
thank	5	動	感謝	★
thankful	3	形	感謝的、欣慰的	379
theme	4	名	主題、話題、文章	49
then	4	副	那時、然後	★
theory	4	名	理論、學說、意見	125
therefore	5	副	因此、所以	★
thick	3	形	厚的、濃厚的	249
thief	3	名	小偷、賊	249
thing	5	名	物、東西	★
thirst	3	名	渴望、口渴	445
thirsty	3	形	渴的、缺水的	251
thorough	4	形	完善的、徹底的	231
though	5	連	雖然、儘管	★
thoughtful	3	形	體貼的、深思的	511
thousand	5	名	一千、一千個	★
thread	4	名	線、頭緒、思路	379
threat	4	名	威脅、恐嚇、凶兆	19
threaten	3	動	威脅、恐嚇	★
threatening	3	形	脅迫的、險惡的	★
thrill	4	名	興奮、顫抖、恐怖	409
thrilling	2	形	毛骨悚然的	★
throat	4	名	喉嚨、窄路、嗓門	251
through	5	介	穿過、通過	★
throughout	4	介	遍及、從頭到尾	177
throw	5	動	舉行(宴會)、投擲	119
thumb	4	動	請求搭便車	251
thunder	4	名	雷聲、恐嚇	★
Thursday	5	名	星期四	★
thus	5	副	因此、以此方式	119
ticket	5	名	票、券	★

單字	頻率	詞性	中譯	頁碼
tide	4	名	潮汐、浪潮、趨勢	381
tidy	4	形	井然的、整潔的	381
tie	4	動	繫上、打結、約束	97
tiger	5	名	虎、公虎	★
tight	4	形	繃緊的、牢固的	145
tighten	2	動	變緊、繃緊	451
time	5	名	時間、次數	★
timid	3	形	怕羞的、膽小的	511
timing	2	名	時間的安排	217
tip	4	動	給小費、泄露、暗示	251
tire	4	名	輪胎	383
tiresome	2	形	討厭的、煩人的	511
toast	3	動	舉杯祝酒、烤麵包	251
tobacco	4	名	菸草、煙葉	★
today	5	名	今天	★
toe	4	名	腳趾、足尖	295
together	5	副	一起、共同	★
toilet	4	名	廁所、盥洗室	83
tolerance	3	名	容忍、寬容	511
tolerant	2	形	容忍的、有耐性的	137
tomato	5	名	番茄、(俚)漂亮的女人	493
tomb	3	名	墓碑、葬生之地	327
tomorrow	5	名	明天	★
ton	4	名	噸、大量、許多	381
tone	4	名	音色、音調	★
tongue	4	名	舌頭、口才、語言	251
tonight	5	名	今晚	★
tool	5	名	工具、器具、手段	213
topic	4	名	話題、主題、標題	359
tortoise	2	名	烏龜、行動遲緩的人	381
torture	3	動	拷打、折磨、扭曲	147
total	5	形	完全的、總計的	329
totally	4	副	完全、整個地	201

單字	頻率	詞性	中譯	頁碼
touch	5	動	接觸、碰到	★
tough	5	形	棘手的、堅韌的	129
tour	4	名	遊覽、旅行	501
tourist	3	名	旅客	349
tow	4	動	拖、拉、牽引	383
toward	3	介	朝、接近、關於	113
towards	4	介	朝向、面對	★
towel	4	名	毛巾、紙巾	253
tower	4	名	高樓、塔、堡壘	253
town	5	名	市鎮	★
toy	5	名	玩具、玩物	★
track	4	動	跟蹤、留下足跡	19
trader	4	名	商人	★
trading	2	名	貿易、交易	253
tradition	4	名	傳統、慣例、常規	253
traditional	5	形	傳統的、慣例的	★
traffic	4	名	交通、買賣、交流	59
tragedy	3	名	悲劇、慘案、災難	513
tragically	2	副	悲慘地、不幸地	277
trail	4	動	跟蹤、拖曳、蔓生	383
trailer	2	名	拖車、預告片	389
train	4	動	訓練、培養、瞄準	157
training	5	名	訓練	★
tranquilizer	1	名	鎮定劑	279
transfer	4	動	調動、轉變、轉讓	513
transform	3	動	改變、改觀、變換	139
transit	3	名	運輸、過境、轉變	415
translate	3	動	翻譯、解釋、調動	165
translation	3	名	翻譯、譯本、調任	513
translator	2	名	翻譯員、翻譯機	513
transplant	3	名	移植、移植器官	325
transport	3	動	運送、使激動、流放	99
transportation	3	名	運輸工具、交通費	23
trap	3	名	陷阱、陰謀、困境	253
trash	5	名	廢物、垃圾	★
travel	5	名	旅行、遊歷、遊記	383
tray	3	名	托盤、一盤的量	383
tread	3	動	踩、步行、踐踏	147
treasure	4	名	珍寶、財富	69
treat	4	動	請客、對待、處理	19
treatment	3	名	對待、待遇、治療	125
tree	5	名	樹、喬木	★
tremble	2	動	發抖、擔憂、搖晃	67
tremendous	3	形	巨大的、驚人的	513
trend	4	名	趨勢、走向、時尚	415
trendy	2	形	流行的、時髦的	439
trial	3	名	審判、試驗、嘗試	253
tribal	2	形	部落的、種族的	513
tribe	3	名	部落、種族、一夥	257
tribute	3	名	敬意、進貢、貢獻	473
trick	4	名	詭計、癖好、竅門	17
tricky	2	形	狡猾的、足智多謀的	383
trifle	2	名	瑣事、小玩意兒	97
trim	4	動	修剪、削減、使平穩	113
trip	5	名	旅行、行程、失誤	289
triumph	3	名	勝利、成功、業績	513
troop	4	名	軍隊、一群、許多	151
trot	3	名	拉肚子、慢跑、急行	135
trouble	4	動	使憂慮、費心、折磨	123
trouser	2	名	褲子、長褲	253
truly	4	副	真實地、確切地	515
trumpet	3	動	大力宣傳、吹喇叭	255
trust	5	動	信任、信賴	★
truth	5	名	實話、事實	★
tub	3	名	浴缸、木桶	385
tube	4	名	軟管、管子、(英)地鐵	255

單字	頻率	詞性	中譯	頁碼
Tuesday	5	名	星期二	★
tug of war	2	名	拉鋸戰、拔河比賽	513
tuition	3	名	學費、講授	31
tulip	2	名	鬱金香	★
tumble	3	動	跌倒、墜落、輾轉	385
tummy	2	名	肚子、胃	123
tune	4	名	曲調、旋律、腔調	385
tunnel	2	名	隧道、地道、洞穴	255
turkey	4	名	火雞	★
turn	5	動	轉動、轉彎	★
turntable	2	名	轉盤、轉車台	189
tutor	4	名	家教、輔導教師	181
twice	4	副	兩次、兩倍	129
twin	2	形	孿生的、成對的	385
twinkle	3	動	閃爍、閃亮	513
twins	2	名	雙胞胎	365
twist	4	動	扭傷、曲解、纏繞	377
type	5	動	打字、把…分類	321
typical	4	形	典型的、獨特的	43
typist	2	名	打字員	513

U

單字	頻率	詞性	中譯	頁碼
ugly	5	形	醜的、難看的	★
umbrella	4	名	雨傘、保護傘、庇護	119
unable	4	形	無能力的、不會的	357
unaware	4	形	不知道的	★
uncle	5	名	伯父、叔父、舅父等	★
uncommon	2	形	罕見的、不尋常的	459
uncontrollably	1	副	控制不住地	505
under	5	介	在…下面、在…之下	★
undergo	3	動	經歷、忍受	519
undergraduate	2	形	大學生的	385
underground	3	副	在地下、秘密地	331

單字	頻率	詞性	中譯	頁碼
understand	5	動	理解、懂	★
underway	2	形	進行中的	79
underwear	3	名	(總稱)內衣、襯衣	239
undoubtedly	2	副	毫無疑問地	★
unemployed	3	形	失業的、閒著的	371
unemployment	3	名	失業、失業人數	15
unexpectedly	3	副	意外地、未料到地	369
unforgettable	2	形	難以忘懷的	63
unfortunately	5	副	不幸地	★
unfounded	1	形	沒有事實根據的	485
unfriendly	2	形	有敵意的、不利的	335
unhealthy	2	形	不健康的、有病的	107
uniform	4	名	制服、軍服	255
union	4	名	工會、聯盟、結合	171
unique	4	形	獨特的、無可匹敵的	31
unit	4	名	單位、一員、組件	125
university	5	名	大學、綜合性大學	★
unknown	4	形	陌生的、默默無聞的	397
unless	4	連	除非	★
unlike	4	形	不同的、相異的	★
unlucky	4	名	不幸的、倒楣的	★
unpredictable	1	形	出乎意料的	169
unquestionably	3	副	毫無疑問地	★
unrepentant	2	形	不悔悟的、頑固的	447
unsatisfied	3	形	不滿意的	475
until	4	連	直到…時	★
unusual	4	形	不尋常的、獨特的	381
update	4	動	更新、使現代化	519
upgrade	3	動	使升級、提高	81
upload	2	動	上載	515
upon	5	介	在…後立即、在…上	289
upper	3	形	上面的、較高的	255
upright	3	形	正直的、挺直的	423

單字	頻率	詞性	中譯	頁碼
upset	4	形	苦惱的、翻覆的	323
upstairs	4	副	在樓上、往樓上	★
urban	4	形	城市的、住在都市的	43
urge	3	動	慫恿、催促、驅策	245
urgent	4	形	緊急的、急迫的	343
usage	4	名	用法、習慣、習俗	515
useful	5	形	有用的、有幫助的	★
user	5	名	使用者、用戶	★
usher	3	動	迎接、招待、陪同	433
usually	5	副	通常地	★
utmost	3	名	最大可能、極限	401

V

單字	頻率	詞性	中譯	頁碼
vacant	3	形	空著的、空缺的	387
vacation	4	名	假期、休假、騰出	503
vain	3	形	徒勞的、愛虛榮的	55
valentine	2	名	情人	173
valley	4	名	山谷、流域、低凹處	257
valuable	4	形	貴重的、值錢的	319
value	5	名	價值、重要性、價值觀	257
van	4	名	有蓋小貨車、箱型車	387
vandalize	2	動	任意破壞	309
vanish	3	動	消失、突然不見	377
variety	4	名	種類、多樣化	275
various	5	形	形形色色的、許多的	15
vary	4	動	使不同、變更	★
vase	5	名	花瓶	★
vast	4	形	遼闊的、龐大的	123
vegetable	5	名	蔬菜	★
vegetarian	2	名	素食者、食草動物	515
vehicle	4	名	車輛、運載工具	383
veil	3	名	遮蔽物、面紗、幌子	443
vend	1	動	出售、販賣	69

單字	頻率	詞性	中譯	頁碼
vendor	3	名	小販、自動售貨機	49
versatility	2	名	多才多藝、多功能	419
verse	4	名	詩作、詩句、韻文	387
versus	3	介	對、對抗	★
vessel	4	名	船、艦、容器、血管	515
vest	4	名	背心、馬甲、內衣	387
via	3	介	經由、透過	★
vice	3	名	老虎鉗	★
vicious	3	形	惡意的、墮落的	419
victim	4	名	犧牲者、受害者	17
victory	4	名	勝利、成功	171
video	5	名	錄影、錄影節目	★
view	5	名	視野、景色、觀點	367
viewpoint	2	名	觀點、視角、見解	133
villa	2	名	別墅、莊園	85
village	4	名	村莊、村民、聚居處	257
villager	4	名	村民、鄉村居民	★
vinegar	3	名	醋	305
vinyl	2	名	黑膠唱片、乙烯基	167
violate	3	動	違反、侵犯、褻瀆	515
violence	4	名	暴力、激烈、強力	337
violent	3	形	暴力的、激烈的	97
violet	2	名	紫羅蘭、羞怯的人	389
virgin	3	名	處女	517
Virgo	3	名	處女座、處女宮	★
virtual	3	形	(電腦)虛擬的	463
virtue	4	名	美德、優點、功效	517
virus	4	名	病毒	517
visa	3	名	護照上的簽證	339
visibility	1	名	能見度、清晰度	389
vision	4	名	視力、所見事物	145
visit	5	動	參觀、拜訪、視察	519
visitor	5	名	觀光客、訪問者	257

單字	頻率	詞性	中譯	頁碼
visual	4	形	視力的、視覺的	517
vital	4	形	生命的、重要的	517
vitality	3	名	活力、生命力	33
vitamin	3	名	維他命、維生素	★
vivacious	1	形	活潑的、快活的	301
vivid	4	形	活潑的、鮮明的	315
vocalist	2	名	歌手、聲樂家	15
vodka	3	名	伏特加酒	★
voice	5	名	聲音、嗓子	★
volcanic	1	形	火山的、猛烈的	517
volume	3	名	音量、卷冊、容積	91
volunteer	4	名	義工、志願兵	397
vomit	3	動	嘔吐、噴出、吐出	145
vote	5	動	投票決定、選舉	133
vow	2	動	發誓、鄭重宣告	165
voyage	5	動	航行	517

W

單字	頻率	詞性	中譯	頁碼
wage	4	名	薪水、報酬、代價	171
waist	4	名	腰、腰部	259
wait	5	動	等待、服侍	★
waiter	4	名	(男)侍者、服務生	★
waive	3	動	放棄、撤回、推遲	211
wake	5	動	醒來、覺悟	★
waken	2	動	喚醒、覺醒、激發	389
walk	5	動	走路、散步	★
wall	5	名	牆、壁	★
wallet	3	名	錢包、皮夾	127
wander	4	動	閒逛、流浪、徘徊	389
want	5	動	要、想要	★
war	5	名	戰爭	★
warm	5	形	溫暖的、保暖的	★
warmth	3	名	溫暖、親切、熱情	127

單字	頻率	詞性	中譯	頁碼
warn	5	動	警告、提醒	389
wash	5	動	洗、洗滌	★
waste	4	動	浪費、濫用、使荒廢	127
watch	5	名	表	★
water	5	動	給…澆水、加水稀釋	335
wave	4	名	(情緒)高漲、波浪	259
wax	4	名	蠟、蜂蠟、耳垢	389
way	5	名	路、道路、方法	★
weak	5	形	虛弱的、懦弱的	★
weaken	3	動	削弱、減少、動搖	41
weakness	5	名	虛弱、軟弱、薄弱	★
wealthy	4	形	富裕的、豐富的	21
weapon	4	名	武器、兵器、手段	189
wear	5	動	穿著、佩戴	★
weather	5	名	天氣	★
weave	4	動	編織、編入	391
web	5	名	網狀物、圈套、網絡	391
webcam	1	名	網路攝影機	77
website	4	名	網站	519
wed	4	動	與…結婚、使結合	259
wedding	4	名	婚禮、結婚紀念日	127
Wednesday	5	名	星期三	★
weed	3	名	雜草、廢物	263
weekday	3	名	平日、工作日	195
weekend	5	名	週末	337
weekly	4	形	每週的、一週一次的	519
weep	4	動	哭泣、流淚、悲嘆	391
weigh	4	動	有…重量、權衡	129
weight	5	名	體重、負擔	53
welcome	4	動	歡迎、欣然接受	257
welfare	4	名	福利、幸福	359
Western	4	名	歐美國家的人	★
wet	4	形	濕的、潮濕的	259

單字	頻率	詞性	中譯	頁碼
whale	3	名	鯨	★
whatever	5	代	任何⋯的事物	★
wheat	4	名	小麥、小麥色	391
whenever	3	連	無論什麼時候、每當	★
wherever	3	連	無論在哪裡	★
whether	5	連	是否	★
while	5	名	一段時間、一會兒	333
whiskey	2	名	威士忌酒	★
whisky	2	名	威士忌酒	★
whisper	2	動	颯颯地響、低語	261
whistle	3	名	哨子、警笛、汽笛	315
whiter	5	形	較白的	★
whole	5	形	全體的、完整的	★
wicked	3	形	壞的、缺德的	391
wild	5	形	瘋狂的、野生的	169
wildlife	3	名	野生動物	195
will	5	名	意志、意願、決心	497
willow	2	名	柳樹、打棉機	391
wimp	2	名	軟弱無能者	67
win	5	動	在⋯獲勝、贏得	★
wind	5	名	風	★
window	5	名	窗戶、櫥窗	★
windy	3	形	風大的、颱風的	261
wine	5	名	葡萄酒、水果酒、酒	★
wing	5	名	翅膀、機翼、派系	★
wink	3	名	眨眼、閃爍、瞬間	271
winter	5	名	冬天、冬季	★
wipe	3	動	擦去、擦乾、消滅	349
wisdom	4	名	知識、智慧、看法	393
wise	4	形	有智慧的、有見識的	185
wish	4	動	希望、但願、渴望	131
wit	3	名	機智、風趣	★
witch	4	名	女巫、巫婆	★

單字	頻率	詞性	中譯	頁碼
withdraw	4	動	退出、撤回、取回	399
within	5	介	在⋯範圍內	365
without	5	介	沒有、在⋯外面	365
witness	4	名	目擊者、證人、證詞	349
woman	5	名	女性	★
wonder	4	動	想知道、感到疑惑	239
wonderful	5	形	極好的、非比尋常的	★
wooden	3	形	木製的、呆板的	263
woodland	1	名	森林地帶、林地	487
woods	4	名	森林	★
wool	3	名	羊毛	★
work	5	名	工作、勞動、事	★
worker	5	名	工人、勞動者	★
workload	2	名	工作量、工作負荷	103
workspace	4	名	工作空間	★
world	5	名	世界、地球	★
world-class	2	形	世界級的	★
worldwide	3	副	在世界各地	409
worm	2	名	蟲、蠕蟲	★
worry	5	動	憂慮、擔心	★
worse	5	形	更差的、更惡化的	227
worsen	2	動	使惡化、使變差	107
worship	3	動	信奉、做禮拜、崇拜	249
worst	5	形	最壞的、最差的	133
worth	5	形	值⋯、有⋯價值的	117
wound	4	名	傷口、傷疤、創傷	263
wrap	4	動	包起來、覆蓋、纏繞	275
wreck	4	動	破壞、失事、遇難	519
wrinkle	3	名	皺紋、困難、難題	519
wrist	3	名	手腕、腕關節	393
writer	5	名	作家、撰稿人	★
writing	5	名	寫作、著作	449
wrong	5	形	錯誤的、不正常的	★

單字	頻率	詞性	中譯	頁碼
X				
X-ray	2	名	X光、X光檢查	393
Y				
yam	2	名	蕃薯、山藥、馬鈴薯	133
yard	4	名	庭院、天井、碼	263
yawn	3	動	打呵欠、裂開	393
yearly	3	形	每年的、一年一次的	519
yell	3	動	叫喊著說、大聲嚷道	215
yellow	5	形	黃色的	★
yesterday	5	名	昨天	★
yet	5	連	卻、可是、然而	493
yoga	3	名	瑜伽	★
yogurt	4	名	酸奶、酸乳酪	★
young	5	形	年輕的、初期的	★
youngster	2	名	年輕人、小孩	515
youthful	2	形	年輕的、朝氣蓬勃的	519
yucky	2	形	討人厭的、噁心的	45
yummy	2	形	美味的、令人喜愛的	135
Z				
zipper	2	名	拉鍊	393
zone	4	動	劃分為區、環繞	287
zoo	5	名	動物園	★
zoology	2	名	動物學	★

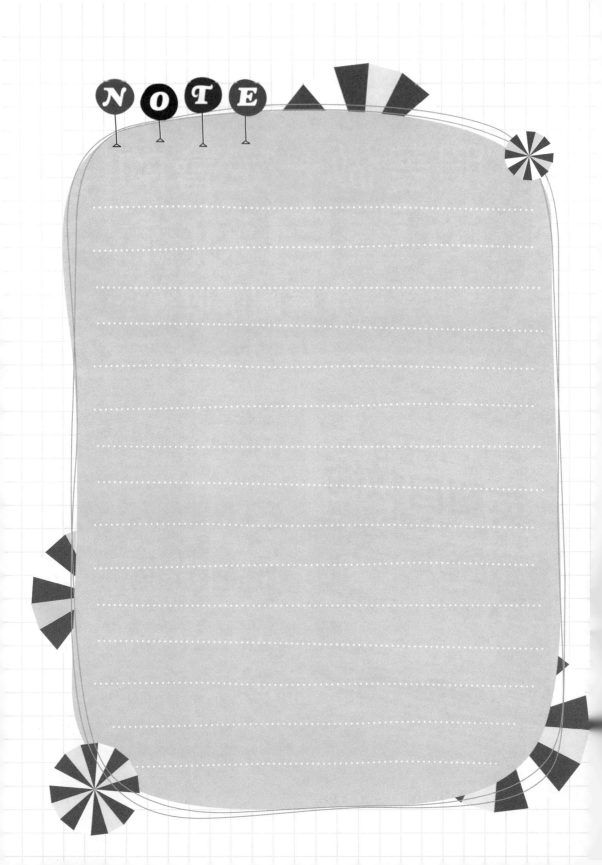

NOTE

NOTE

NOTE

國家圖書館出版品預行編目資料

別瞎忙，看過就記住！4000英單早該這樣背 / 張翔 編著.
-- 初版. -- 新北市：華文網, 2014.06
　面；　公分. -- (Excellent；69)
ISBN 978-986-271-489-8(平裝)

1.英語　　　　2.詞彙

805.12　　　　　　　　　　　　　　　103004593

別瞎忙，看過就記住！

4000 英單 早該這樣背

拋開繁複冗長的學習枷鎖，重拾你對背單字的熱忱！

知識工場・Excellent 69

別瞎忙，看過就記住！
4000英單早該這樣背

出 版 者／全球華文聯合出版平台・知識工場　　印 行 者／知識工場

作　　者／張　翔　　　　　　　　　　　　　英文編輯／何牧蓉

出版總監／王寶玲　　　　　　　　　　　　　美術設計／蔡瑪麗

總 編 輯／歐綾纖

. . . .

台灣出版中心／新北市中和區中山路2段366巷10號10樓

電　　話／（02）2248-7896

傳　　真／（02）2248-7758

ISBN-13／978-986-271-489-8

出版日期／2021年8月七版十五刷

. . . .

全球華文市場總代理／采舍國際

地　　址／新北市中和區中山路2段366巷10號3樓

電　　話／（02）8245-8786

傳　　真／（02）8245-8718

. . . .

港澳地區總經銷／和平圖書

地　　址／香港柴灣嘉業街12號百樂門大廈17樓

電　　話／（852）2804-6687

傳　　真／（852）2804-6409

. . . .

全系列書系特約展示

新絲路網路書店

地　　址／新北市中和區中山路2段366巷10號10樓

電　　話／（02）8245-9896

傳　　真／（02）8245-8819

網　　址／www.silkbook.com

知識工場
Knowledge is everything！

Knowledge is everything！